BOOK TWO

JOURNEY T

ANGELS of FIRE

JOHN PONTIUS

Latter-day Legends
Salt Lake City

ISBN 13: 978-1-944200-83-1

Published by Latter-day Legends, a division of Digital Legend Press & Publishing Inc.
Salt Lake City, UT 84121
www.digitalegend.com

Inquiries or Permissions: info@digitalegend.com

Cover design by David Christenson
Interior design by Jacob F. Frandsen

Printed in the United States of America

In Gratitude to:

The Author of all truth, for all thin
Terri, for loving me without rese
and for great editorial labors.
My parents, for a birthright of righ
Daughters-in-law and grandb

Thank You

INTRODUCTION

Angels of Fire is the final book of the "Journey to Zion" series [originally called "Millennial Quest" series] which were all initially written in the summer of 1995.

This final book takes Sam through the purifying fires of his journey and on to the dramatic and glorious conclusion of his mortal life, and the beginning of the millennial age with Christ's return.

The stories and characters in this book are fictional. Although some of the experiences described within are based upon the author's own life, most are a faith-filled product of my hopes and imagination. The spiritual occurrences, visions, visitations, conversations and events in this novel are fictitious, and should be considered as such. As well, references to world events and possible end-time scenarios are merely this author's attempt to contrast the tragedy of wickedness with the transcendent joy and deliverance available to those walking in obedience to the Lord's voice.

No attempt is being made to define Church doctrine or to describe events as they should, or even might occur in someone's life. Having so said, may I also note that many of the events of spiritual impact in this book are based upon scriptural accounts of similar events in the lives of the ancient faithful, as well as upon prophecies regarding the challenging and exciting pre-Millennial future ahead.

I have great faith in the idea that Father did not cause these great epiphanies to be recorded in scripture simply for our entertainment. I believe that these magnificent events were included in holy writ to show us that we, too, can walk the path of holiness, drink freely from the waters of the Atonement, and receive equally glorious blessings as the ancient faithful did. I believe these blessings are at our fingertips, as achievable today as in any period of antiquity.

I invite you to read *Angels of Fire* with a light and hopeful heart, with an eye focused upon Jesus Christ, and ponder, as I have, the incredible power of what lies just beyond the veil, and your place in it all.

John Pontius
1997

EDITOR'S NOTE

I am pleased to release this never-before published conclusion of the "Journey to Zion" series by my late husband, John Pontius. This is a compilation of John's last three fictional novels all written in the summer of 1995, now entitled "Angels of Fire." I have edited this text somewhat liberally, and some events described herein have been resequenced and refined to capture what I know were John's intent and core beliefs.

The reader should be aware that while this book features glorious scenarios involving rich relationships and spiritual joys, it also includes some graphic and potentially disturbing situations. As he states in his introduction, John was attempting to portray the consequences of evil, along with the peace and deliverance that the Lord promises to the faithful.

Readers of "Journey to the Veil" may also notice that there are some similar stories told in that book as in this series. John felt free to embellish these events for his fictional novels, but recounted them accurately in his personal blog "UnBlog My Soul" and as published in the subsequent book "Journey to the Veil."

Another note of interest is that fifteen years after he had written these novels, John met "Spencer" and eventually interviewed him in preparation for compiling the book "Visions of Glory." John was struck by similarities of some of Spencer's true experiences and what John had penned in this fictional series years before. This was surprising to him, and something that we concluded was the obvious workings of the Spirit.

I wish to clearly state that John was completely faithful to The Church of Jesus Christ of Latter-day Saints, and a member in good standing all of his life. He wholeheartedly supported the Church's positions, doctrine, and those in authority. In "Journey to the Veil" John wrote, "I am now and always will be a warrior in defense of the Latter-day Church. Not only is it 'true' but it works. It brings to our lives the very blessings we are seeking . . . I think one of the missions of the UnBlog has been to say over and over that The Church of Jesus Christ of Latter-day Saints is not broken. It is not somehow true-but-not-functioning, or a kindergarten class one must enroll in and then graduate from to go beyond. The voice of the UnBlog is that this Church is profoundly true, that it is operating as Jesus Christ directs it, and that it will be the organization through which He finally authorizes and orchestrates the building of the latter-day Zion."

This novel is not an attempt to establish Church doctrine or to imply that anything would, or even should, happen as described. That said, I pray that "Angels of Fire" may ignite your spiritual imagination and draw you closer to Jesus Christ, our Savior and the Rock of our Salvation.

Terri Pontius
February 2020

PROLOGUE

We return to the story of Sam Mahoy after he has come home to Alaska from his mission in South Africa. While in South Africa he has met a young musician, Melody, whose life he saves during a train brawl. Now returning home he brings Dawn, another faith-filled young woman he taught on his mission, whom he has fondly nicknamed "Princess." Sam and Princess marry, and their twin daughters, Bonnie and Lisa, are now just one year old.

Following a long illness and an entangled relationship struggle which nearly cost their marriage, Princess has gone through a period of estrangement from the Church. In an effort to repent and find herself, she asks Sam to again call her by her given name, "Dawn."

RHODESIA, AFRICA

Just then, another rifle fired, and someone started fighting in the hall. The train jolted as bodies grappled not far from their door. Men cursed, and the sound of blows echoed in the train.

On impulse, Sam stood and quickly strode to the violins. "May I?" he asked. Melody nodded, and Sam retrieved one of the violin cases. He opened it to find an expensive instrument neatly packed in velvet. He picked it up and strummed the strings. The instrument was in perfect tune. It smelled of wax as he tucked it under his chin. He pulled the bow across the strings and made a long, solemn tone. Then he slowly began to play the only tune that came to mind, "Abide with Me; 'Tis Eventide." He played slowly, carefully, his fingers unsure what to do next. He was grateful to find that even though his fingers may be unsure, his soul was not, and the music swelled within him, flowing out of the little violin. He played with feeling, and peace settled over him.

Somewhere in the middle of the song, the brawl in the hallway stopped abruptly. Sam switched to another hymn and played with deep feeling. After two or three hymns, he stopped. The silence in the train was almost as if everything outside their door had ceased to exist. Even the crying in the adjacent cabin had stopped. From far away, a small, frightened voice called, "Sing Amazing Grace."

Sam loved that song. He played it with a sense of joy, and was vaguely aware of voices singing in the distance. Marcia stood and retrieved the other case as he played. She lovingly lifted the instrument and tuned it quietly. Afterward, she handed it to Melody, who tucked it under her chin.

Sam began the second verse as Melody played a quiet harmony. It was the most beautiful thing he had ever heard. He watched her eyes close and felt the power of her love for the instrument she held. She played with great skill, her touch sure and masterful. She allowed the harmony to flow unrestrained. The complexity and unabashed beauty of her music made Sam's contribution seem rather amateurish; yet her powerful music was like a full orchestration, the perfect accompaniment to Sam's simple melody.

Another request came from outside the train. The name of the song was French, and unfamiliar to Sam. Melody smiled and pulled the bow across the strings in quick, sure strokes. A joyful melody danced through the train, lifting hearts and causing toes to tap everywhere.

After the tune capered to its conclusion, someone requested "I Am a Child of God." Sam knew the person must be a Latter-day Saint, and it warmed his heart. He lifted the bow and played with a joyful heart. Melody listened carefully and joined him on the second verse, again quietly playing harmony. It was breathtakingly beautiful. The person who had made the request began to sing in a powerful tenor voice. The words of the precious hymn rolled through the train like a summer breeze. Peace settled upon them. Few even noticed the next few rifle shots. Sam and Melody certainly did not. All they heard was the music in their souls as it spilled from the strings.

SALT LAKE CITY, UTAH

Sam waited nervously in the long hall below the Salt Lake Temple, his clothing entirely white. His heart raced like a chariot of fire, and his eyes continually pooled with tears. He had tried all his life to imagine this moment—this frightening, celestial moment. He had rehearsed and replayed this image in his mind a thousand times, and each had been less in every respect than what he felt now. He had imagined less fear, less nervousness, less love, less sheer joy.

A rustle of skirts to him was like the parting of the veil, and he turned to see the heavenliest of all God's creations coming toward him in a wedding dress. Oh, how he strained to imprint that image in his mind, to remember every detail, every nuance of her beauty, the glow of her righteousness, the halo of love that surrounded her face! He wanted to be able to replay this moment every day of his life and remember the intensity of the love that was now filling his soul to overflowing.

Surrounded by his mother, family, and friends, Princess walked toward him like a glorious preview of the Second Coming. Her dress was rich and full, entirely made of lace with thousands of lace rosebuds in an intricate pattern. He marveled, wondered, and felt his heart race. She was lovelier than any dream mortal man could devise—awake or asleep—and she came to him, of all people.

He reached out to her and felt her silken hands slide into both of his. He pulled her to him and was immediately hindered by billowing lace. He laughed to himself for joy, happiness, and love and leaned forward to kiss her lightly. Her face was radiant. Her lips moved without making a sound.

"I love you," she whispered. It was the most perfect thing she could have said.

WALES

Melody consulted the best solicitor she could find in their little town. The old barrister listened to her plight with interest as she explained through tears what had brought her to Wales, and then England, and of her struggle to obtain papers, then of her decision to "purchase" legality.

"I understand your decision, and the plight that motivated it," he concluded after listening carefully. "However, I am sorry to inform you that under English law, the truth of what has occurred is the controlling factor. That a law was broken, not why it was broken, is the rule of law. The magistrate will attempt to determine whether the charges are true, and if they are—since they are—there can be no defense. You *will* be found guilty of those charges and punished accordingly."

He leaned back in his chair and pondered for a moment.

"Even though your motivation for doing what you did has no bearing upon your guilt, it may soften the ultimate punishment. I suspect in the least you will be fined and deported."

Melody fell back in her chair, crushed and terrified. Her voice was frightened. "How much fine?"

"More than you possess, I'm sure. The purpose of the fine is to strip you of all your assets plus enough to prohibit your return to England."

"That's the best case? What's the worst case?"

"In the extreme the court could find you guilty of all charges, including espionage, and sentence you to a very large fine, and as much as twenty-five years in prison."

"Twenty-five years! But I haven't committed espionage!"

"Then all you have to do is prove you are innocent."

"How can I prove I am innocent? Is there no presumption of innocence?"

He raised his chin as if the idea were repugnant to his thinking. "The assumption is that you are guilty or you would not be accused. You yourself told me you are guilty of the lesser crimes."

"God help me," Melody whispered to nobody present.

"Indeed. God may be your best hope," the old gentleman replied pensively.

WASILLA, ALASKA

Princess began to sob, her entire body shaking. She looked up at him, her eyes swollen but determined. "I want to find my real self again—the woman that I know I am, the woman I can be. So, there is a favor I must ask of you."

She drew a ragged breath before continuing. "Sam, I have let you and everyone in Alaska call me 'Princess.' It was a sweet nickname, and I have been flattered by it. But really, I am not 'Princess.' I need to find the real me! I want to be true to myself once again."

She looked beseechingly into his eyes. "Sam, I would like you to call me by my real name. I want you to call me 'Dawn.' Please, would you do that—for me?"

Sam was stunned to silence. It was all more than he could assimilate and understand. His heart felt like someone had been playing crack-the-whip with his emotions, and he had lost grip and been flung off into a thicket of thorns. But he could tell she was serious in her introspection and resolve.

He answered slowly. "I guess I can try," he said, looking at his hands. "After all, you were 'Dawn' when I first fell in love with you." His eyes fell on their family picture in the hallway. "But it will take me a while. All of this will take some time—probably a long time."

"I know. Thank you," she whispered. Then she slowly took him by the arm and escorted him to their room. They spent the whole night in one another's arms. They were together, apart, in love, hurting, so close, so far away. Neither of them slept.

"I'm going to go look in on the twins," Dawn said as she slipped a light robe over her nightgown.

Sam had just opened his mouth to say he was sure they were fine when they distinctly heard a door bang downstairs. Sam looked at Dawn and bolted from the room out onto the landing. The door to their room was directly at the top of the long spiral staircase. Below them the massive front door was wide open, still moving ominously.

Dawn stifled a scream. Sam ran down the hallway barely ahead of her. The twins' door was open. Sam flipped on the light, his heart paralyzed by fear.

Both beds were empty! On Bonnie's bed a dozen stuffed animals had been arranged into a large '22'. Dawn screamed and ran from the room.

Sam spun to follow and was slammed by a sound that seemed to shake the organs within his body. It took his mind a few seconds to realize it was the report of a gun from inside his home.

1

THE GRACE OF GOD

Sam found himself nearly tripping over Dawn as he ran down the stairs toward the front door that was still swinging open. He bolted past her, taking the broad steps three at a time. The very instant his feet touched the floor another gunshot rang out.

The open door was just steps away when Sam heard a different sound. It was so quiet, so unobtrusive compared to a gunshot that he nearly missed it. Dawn flew past him as he slid to a stop in his slippered feet and tore frantically toward the back of the house.

A hundred paces separated him from the back of the house; functionless rooms that once seemed opulent now blurred past in agonizing slow motion. What he had heard was the throaty whine of a powerful snow machine.

As he ran, shouts came to his hearing from the open front door behind him. Logic screamed to reverse his course, yet an impression kept his legs pumping with all the fury he possessed. He heard the gravelly voice of his hired bodyguard shouting, then Dawn's panicked voice, and others coming from behind. An engine raced just as he dashed through the laundry room, across the boot room, and out onto the back porch.

Two black snow machines sat idling at the base of the porch. As Sam emerged from the house at a hard run, two sinister-looking black helmeted faces turned toward him. Still running, he realized that each rider had one of his daughters in his lap. The babies were still in their nightgowns, seemingly asleep, leaning back against the riders.

A steely sword of panic pierced Sam's soul. They were too far away, and Sam knew he could not stop either machine no matter what he did. Still running as fast as he ever had in his life, he took the last step on the porch and leaped, his arms wide, toward the machines.

The world went into slow motion. Sam saw the shiny black, full-face helmets turning slowly to watch him flying through the air. He saw their thumbs tighten on the throttles as the machines moved forward with a throaty roar. The distance between them seemed to close with agonizing slowness. The machines were moving away. Sam reached toward the nearest helmet. His fingers slapped the side of the black surface, then raked across the back of the second rider. He watched their heads turn toward him as he flew past them into the snow. Sam knew he had missed. He cried out just as time returned to normal speed and he plowed hard into the deep, crusted snow face first. A searing sense of failure tore through him even as the sub-zero snow and ice lacerated his face and arms.

Dawn had run out the front door where she found Bart, their hired bodyguard standing on the porch, his gun drawn. A large black Suburban was backing down their lane at high speed, its headlights off. Bart fired once, then again.

Dawn screamed, clapping her hands to her ears. At that moment a startling thought came to her.

"Where's Sam?" she cried as she slapped Bart on the shoulder. Bart's eyes rounded on her with fury. His mind was fully occupied upon stopping the truck, and her words entered his consciousness as an annoying distraction. His large, athletic body tensed, and his eyes narrowed.

"What!?" he bellowed without looking at her.

"Listen!" Dawn cried, pointing toward their right. Bart's head reluctantly turned the direction she was pointing. The sound of a small, powerful engine screamed into the night like the cry of a banshee. "They're not in the car!" she cried, and began running through the deep snow with an ungraceful, long-legged lope.

Bart immediately understood and passed Dawn on her third step. He rounded the end of the building to find himself standing directly in front of two black snow machines that were roaring toward him. A part of his mind registered that Sam was flailing through the air, as he hit one driver with a blunt groan and flew off into the snow.

The second machine was a few feet ahead, blasting toward Bart at high speed. Without hesitation Bart took two running steps toward him and jumped into the air, his feet coiled under him. Dawn rounded the building just in time to see Bart seemingly hovering in the air, both feet flashing forward, to slam the chest of the second rider a crushing blow. The rider flipped several times from the impact. Bart landed on his feet bellowing an incomprehensible war cry, both fists balled and coiled against his chest, quickly standing and reaching for his weapon. Dawn screamed. Sam rose to his knees with a cry on his lips, his face and arms raw and bloodied.

Dawn ran after the now-riderless machines as they coasted to a stop. She found her daughters sleeping against the cowling of the machines, a small harness holding them safely in place. This was no random kidnapping. The kidnappers had been prepared, even to the point of having a diversion in the black truck, and child-sized safety harnesses.

Her cold fingers fumbled with the buckles. She glanced up just as Sam joined her and began working on the other harness.

"They're still asleep!" Sam said in amazement as he lifted Bonnie into his arms. He glanced behind him to see Bart holding a gun on the two kidnappers. "Bart, I'll call 911 as soon as we get inside!"

"We better hurry; those guys won't be out for long," Bart replied. Both men were stunned, just barely beginning to move. Bart's face was an odd mixture of hatred and icy calm. Sam's fears relaxed in that moment, as Bart ran to the front of the house.

Dawn gently lifted Lisa and laid her against her body. "They must be drugged."

"They must be," Sam seethed. "It makes me furious!"

"It makes me grateful," Dawn replied soberly. "They'll have no memory of this."

Sam stared at her. "I hadn't looked at it that way," he replied, and they all hurried toward the house.

They had just reached the front door when two gunshots pierced the night. Both he and Dawn ran the remaining few steps to the open door and slammed it behind them. Seconds later a snow machine roared into the night, followed shortly by two others.

Sam picked up the phone and found no dial tone just as Bart banged on the front door, his gait weary, his face sober. His face and chest were caked with powdery snow.

"What happened?!" Dawn demanded as she pulled open the door for him. He beat the snow from his body and stepped inside.

"There was a third rider in the woods," Bart answered, his face ashen. "The third guy fired at me. Fortunately, I hit the deck and he missed! But, they got away. I'm lucky they didn't kill me. I just hadn't considered . . ."

Sam shook his head. "They were obviously prepared for anything. I tried to remove the keys from the snow machines so they couldn't escape, but there were no keys."

"I'm so sorry I let you down," the big man said gruffly. He sounded as if he was on the verge of tears.

"Bart." Dawn turned to face him. "Do you see this precious bundle in my arms? Your cursing aside," she inserted in a slightly scolding voice, "you didn't let us down! You saved our babies!" Dawn's face softened into a weary smile. "Besides, I'll never forget the image of you flying through the air just before you hit that man in the ugly black helmet. That image is seared into my brain forever!" she exclaimed, then added ironically, "Martial Arts have never interested me, but you may have just made a convert of me. That was the most beautiful thing I've ever seen!"

Bart looked up sheepishly. "You wouldn't say that if you had seen your husband flying through the air like a greenhorn cowboy doing a screaming swan dive off the backside of a bull hitting that guy. Now, that was *truly* impressive!"

Sam blushed awkwardly, then bent down to kiss the sleeping angel in his arms, over and over again.

The police were unable to discover anything about the kidnappers. They concluded their "investigation" by suggesting that Sam install a burglar alarm in his home. Sam thanked them for the advice and suppressed the urge to strangle them as they left. The next day he quickly installed an elaborate security system which included burglar bars on the lower-story windows and steel-reinforced doors.

Melody returned to the park after two days of tearful sulking. The words of the barrister echoed in her mind like a sentence passed, "Guilty, guilty, guilty." It was the cadence of doom, and it haunted her day and night.

But the thought of playing her violin once again brought peace into her soul, and eventually drew her back into its welcoming embrace. The love and acceptance of her adoring fans brought Melody a small feeling of success that no global failure elsewhere in her life could erase. She arrived at the small white pavilion near noon to find a gathering of about fifty people awaiting her arrival. When she walked through the crowd they parted. A small murmur of happiness broke into spontaneous applause.

Fresh and beautiful in a lacy white dress, long cascades of her glossy auburn hair were pulled back softly. A fountain of soft curls fell down her neck. Had she gossamer wings upon her back, she would not have looked more angelic.

She turned to face them, her violin cradled in her arm. "Thank you. Thank you so much." Her voice broke, and she bowed her head. "You will notice that I have left my violin case closed. I don't want your kind gifts today. I just want to play for the joy of music, to thank you for your kindness, and for the opportunity I've had to play for you these past months."

Soft applause and many smiles answered these words.

"There is reason to believe that today will be my last public appearance before you."

"No! Why?" people called up at her. It was at that moment that Theodore stepped through the crowd to the front of the gathering. Her eyes fell upon him.

"I can't explain. Forgive me," she said softly, and raised her precious instrument to her cheek. A tear slid down her face and across the polished wood. The bow hovered above the strings as if unsure, then struck downward like a cobra. The air exploded with music, fierce and volatile. It was not music anyone had heard, nor would they ever hear again. It was music of the soul, and Melody's soul was twisted in agony. Her music pounded angry fists against the fates that seemed to dominate her. In a minute, the rage evaporated into a cascade of runs like honey falling from a silver spoon, the waterfall of tears tumbling in her heart. They rolled into a sweet melody that danced and wove magic into every soul who heard.

Melody's eyes were closed, her chin raised, her body laboring as it coaxed the magic from the strings. Perspiration and tears dripped from her chin. Again and again fire erupted, then was extinguished with love and faith, hope and sweet escape. Finally a single note hovered in the afternoon air—steady, absolutely desolate, alone, yet unafraid. Then in a heartbeat it skipped joyfully to a conclusion, full of childlike happiness, hope and peace. Before anyone was prepared, the masterpiece had evaporated in the wind.

Cries of "Maestra, maestra, encore, brava!" ripped through the air. Tearful faces gazed up at her with questioning eyes, wondering how such music had been unleashed.

Melody opened her eyes as if aware for the first time that anyone but she had seen her heart dancing naked and unadorned in the music of her soul. She blushed slightly and lowered her instrument. A part of her mind searched for what she should play next. There was nothing that could follow such music. She returned her instrument to the case, closed it slowly, and stepped from the pavilion. The applause finally died as her crowd reluctantly dispersed. Many kind words and sad smiles bid her farewell. At last only one admirer remained.

"Melody, that was . . . breathtaking!" he spoke after a stunned pause.

Melody looked up, startled. "Theodore!"

His face was deeply concerned. "What dark tragedy has pulled such beauty from you and left you so exhausted?" he asked earnestly. "And, why will this be your last concert in the park?"

She looked down at her still-trembling hands. "I can't really say. Thank you, but there's nothing anyone can do about it," she said. Then she sidestepped him and continued her escape from the park.

"How do you know what I can't do? At the very least I can listen," he persisted kindly after her.

Melody stopped to look back at him. "I'm just not sure. My solicitor has told me to not speak of this to anyone."

"Solicitor? Is it that serious?" They were by a park bench. Theodore took her elbow insistently, and motioned for her to sit. Melody hesitated, then gave up and sat down dejectedly. Tears began to slip silently down her face once again. She snubbed them away angrily with the back of her gloved hand. She refused to look up.

Theodore sat beside her with his whole body turned toward her. He placed a hand on hers. "Tell me what is happening," he asked softly. "Please."

"There's nothing you can do about it. It would only drag you into something you're not involved with."

"Please. I have powerful friends. Perhaps . . ."

Melody looked up at him, her eyes pooled with tears. Suddenly she found herself telling him much more than she had intended. She told him everything...everything.

When she finally finished, he stood, a look of determination on his face. "Let me check into this. When do you meet again with your solicitor?"

"Next Tuesday. The hearing is still several weeks away."

"How can I reach you? Do you have a phone?"

Melody hesitated for a moment, then opened her case and tore a small corner from a concerto score. Theodore fished a pen from his pocket, which she took to write something on the paper. She handed him the paper with questioning eyes.

"I'll talk to you in a day or two," he told her, slipping the paper into his overcoat. "In the meantime, have faith."

Melody looked at him hopelessly. "In you? I'm grateful for your concern, but I hardly know you."

"Then, have faith in God. He won't let you down. As for me, I'll just make a few inquiries and let you know what I find."

"Thank you," she said weakly, failing to find comfort in his words.

Theodore stood resolutely, smiled oddly, and left in a hurry. Melody watched him depart with detached amazement, as if he were living in a world very different from hers. What was that which she saw in his eyes—anger, betrayal, fury? She had expected none of those, except perhaps a vague concern or forced sorrow. This new revelation of strange behavior simply added to her confusion, and also to her fear: fear that he would somehow impale himself upon her trials, and fear that in so doing he might actually make her fate far worse. As her solicitor had strongly suggested, her guilt would only be amplified if she attempted by some circuitous route to escape justice.

Theodore's heart was swelling with rage as he stomped away from her. It had taken all his self-control to keep from screaming in rage at her revelation. As she had related the long tale of her sad life, fragments of conversations came to him with great force. The first time her lips had formed the word "Rhodesia," he had made the fateful connection.

He slipped into his car near the park and made an illegal U-turn. He left town a few miles later and sped into the countryside. Seventeen miles from town he slowed and pulled onto a new-looking cobblestone lane. An elegant brick fence stretched as far as he could see in both directions. The lane lead past a manicured hill and around a small lake. Across the lake an elaborate English Tudor mansion sprawled amid lush formal gardens. Fountains and reflecting pools dotted the landscape.

He pulled up to the front door and stepped out. He trotted to the door, which opened for his arrival.

"Good afternoon, Master Theodore," a butler in formal attire greeted him pleasantly. "What an unexpected pleasure. May I inform your uncle you have arrived?"

"Yes please, Alvin, and ask if I may speak to him immediately."

"Certainly, sir. Please make yourself at home. You know the way around."

"Thank you," Theodore said as he stepped into the sumptuous foyer. A massive stair began before him, with gilded lions sitting upon the lintels, their heads resting upon paws with watchful eyes. The staircase rose halfway and split at a landing, each side gliding in opposite directions to a balcony high above. A massive crystal chandelier hung in the cavity between the stairs. It was a sight he had seen many times, one that he loved and planned on calling his own someday. He was, after all, the eldest and most favored heir, and destined to his family's wealth and title.

Theodore's devotion to the seminary and the Church was real and fervent, but also a large part of his uncle's devotion to him. It was Uncle Tennison's oft-stated desire that his heir should be an ordained minister, which was what had initially interested Theodore in priestly pursuits. Theodore's imminent ordination to the priesthood had elevated him above a host of cousins as their uncle's heir apparent. It was a happy coincidence for Theodore that the yoke of the Church suited him at least as well as the idea of wealth and privilege.

"How is my favorite nephew?" a voice boomed from his left.

Theodore looked up. "I am well, uncle. I am very well. And you?"

"The same, the same. I still haven't found a way to live forever, so unfortunately, my boy, the same."

Theodore laughed; though the subject was near and dear to his Uncle's heart, it was a family joke of sorts.

Uncle Tennison descended the stairs dressed in a silk smoking jacket with a wide black collar and gold-embroidered body. He was in his late seventies, and still hale, though somewhat stooped. He commanded a sprawling empire that stretched across most of Europe, his name universally honored and feared. He wore his full head of white hair to his shoulders, and stubbornly resisted anyone's suggestion that he cut it. His entire demeanor manifested an air of arrogance, and his obsession with doing exactly as he pleased, no matter the consequence. Let the whole world step aside if it must!

His uncle slipped a manicured hand through Theodore's arm and turned him back in the direction he had come. A look of affection softened his otherwise angular and age-cratered face. "Come into my study. What brings you out to the country? It must be urgent."

Theodore followed his uncle into the study, a room of dark woods and deep green carpet. Bookshelves a full two stories tall towered over them, filled with ancient tomes. "Uncle, you know I love you," Theodore began in a warning voice.

His uncle waved him off with an impatient gesture and shake of his head. He rolled his eyes as he sat in a plush red chair before the massive fireplace. "I can see I had better sit down for this one," he quipped in mock gravity, a patronizing smile upon his face.

Theodore sat opposite his uncle on the edge of an identical chair, leaning forward. He forced his voice to be calm. "I just pieced together several statements I remembered you making last weekend."

His uncle smiled. "About the spy from Rhodesia?"

It always amazed Theodore how perceptive his uncle was. It was no wonder that he ruled a far-flung private empire with nothing but his brilliant analytical mind and his flawless memory.

But Theodore would not be deterred, even by admiration. "Uncle, I met the person in question, and she's no spy."

Tennison waved his hand in dismissal. "Of course not! But, she is a person of unsavory background, and hardly fit company for one of your noble birth," he said forcefully, though still amiably.

Theodore wagged his finger at his uncle. "Are you playing matchmaker again? I thought you were going to stay out of my love life."

"I do stay out of it!" he cried. Then his voice grew conspiratorial. "Unless you start gravitating toward gutter tripe and street musicians."

"This particular street musician happens to be from a very old family from Devonshire. They were easily as wealthy as you until their father took his family to Rhodesia to colonize."

"They were—about the time I was born. I'm aware of all that, of course. He was later stripped of his lands and titles for treason against the Crown."

"His treason was nothing more than loving his new land, and being willing to give everything to possess it. He was a nobleman, and his family still is. Melody is a marvelous woman of great talent and depth."

"Melody. What an appropriate name for a street musician." Tennison's voice was rich with sarcasm.

"Uncle, you're being haughty. She plays in the park for the love of music."

His uncle's eyes narrowed. "And to make money!"

"She makes money because she is a world-class musician, and because our government denied her a visa and passport, and with that any possibility of making a living. A lesser woman would have turned to something menial, or prostitution. I tell you she is a noble woman."

"Posh! She's a street musician."

"Uncle, if you met her, you'd be charmed and probably ask her to marry you yourself."

His uncle laughed heartily. "You know I can never deny you. You hypnotize me even when you defy me. What do you want me to do?"

Theodore's mind relaxed, sensing the possibility of a win. "I want you to stop her prosecution. It was you who started it. Don't deny it."

"I do what I must to protect the kingdom," Tennison said airily, then drew his face into an expression that was more of a wolfish grin than a smile. "What's in it for me?"

"There's nothing you don't have, including my undying fealty," Theodore avowed with a regal wave of his hand from chin to knee.

Tennison grew serious. "Theodore, I want you to marry in your class. I want you to possess all this," he said with an expansive wave of both arms, "after I am gone, or even before. I don't want you to sully my name by marrying beneath yourself."

"I haven't decided to marry Melody, nor have we even remotely discussed it. But, I must marry who I love, Uncle."

"Nonsense! You marry who you must for title and power, then go wherever else you have to for love. It is what must be."

Theodore did not want to engage his uncle in a debate about love and lust. He knew Tennison to be well endowed with the latter, and agnostic about the former. Theodore thought it wise to not succumb to his uncle's clever bait. "Then, I will give you a challenge," he said upon a sudden inspiration.

"You? Challenging me? You grow bold in your cleric's collar," Tennison said jovially, but with an obvious nip of warning.

Theodore leaned back in his chair, feigning an air of confidence he did not feel. "Yes. A challenge even you can't resist."

"Intriguing, go on."

"Take the woman I choose to accompany me on life's journey and elevate her to whatever status you feel is appropriate." Cold silence filled the room. Theodore promptly added, "Or, perhaps you haven't the power to raise, dear Uncle, only to tear down," he said, his words tonal with jest, his eyes flashing with earnest.

"I can turn a potato into a princess if I desire!" Tennison asserted hotly.

Theodore's voice remained impassive. "Then, I challenge you to do whatever you must to satisfy your lusts, and leave my happiness to my discretion. I'm afraid if you destroy this fragile flower I have found I shall be forever moody and sullen when I'm around you," he pouted, only partly in jest.

His uncle blustered uncharacteristically. "Happiness has nothing to do with women, love or discretion. It has only to do with power!"

Theodore stood slowly. "Then, I offer you the happiness of using your power to restore my street musician and elevate her to the station you feel she must possess to remain in my circle. She needn't know anything of our involvement in her life, and I prefer that she does not."

His uncle took his chin in both fingers. Only the crackling of the fire in the grate interrupted the silence that lingered for a long moment. "It is an intriguing challenge," he said at last.

"You will do it then?"

"You know I cannot say no to you," Uncle affirmed, once again amiable. Still, there was a steely look in his eyes that conveyed strict warning.

Theodore knew he had walked very close to the edge—in fact, beyond the edge, and only Uncle's very real desire for his nephew's happiness, along with a consuming desire for an appropriate heir, had yanked Theodore back from a fatal fall.

Theodore grinned. "A fact I was counting on." He reached out a hand to touch his uncle's shoulder. "Uncle, I do thank you with all my heart."

"Posh. You just want my money."

"That too," Theodore laughed.

"Get out of my house!"

"Yes, Uncle," Theodore, smiling broadly as he hurried to the door.

Uncle Tennison watched him until the butler was pulling open the door. "Theodore," he called across the large foyer, his voice echoing in the vast emptiness.

"Yes, Uncle?"

"Well played," he said softly.

Theodore bowed formally, and left without a word. His heart sang as he sped back to town. Well played indeed! Had not the stakes been so high he might have actually enjoyed it. Wielding power was indeed intoxicating.

Fred and Connie Miller, Sam and Dawn's nearest neighbors, continued to grow in their love of the gospel, and in their love of the Mahoys. Their interest in the gospel had begun in earnest many months before when their neighbors had wrapped their arms around Connie's wayward sister Angelica, and offered their home for Angelica's missionary discussions.

During the fifth discussion the missionaries asked Angelica if she would like to be baptized after she had gotten her life in order. Angelica answered that she was already a member. An awkward moment of silence followed while the missionary who had asked the question turned red. His companion poked him in the ribs with an elbow, and the room erupted into laughter. When solemnity returned, Sam realized that Fred had not laughed.

"Fred," Sam asked. "Is something troubling you?"

"Yes," he answered frankly. "I'm grateful that Angelica is taking the missionary lessons and finding truth for herself. But I'm evidently the real non-member here, and nobody has bothered to ask me a single question."

There was a moment of stunned silence while everyone, including Fred, pondered the meaning of his complaint. One of the missionaries started to apologize, and promised to include Fred in their gospel discussion. But Sam politely interrupted him.

"Fred, would you like to be baptized?"

"Well, yes!" he almost shouted. Connie turned to him with an expression of total amazement.

"Fred!" she exclaimed. "I had no idea you knew it was true!"

Fred fumbled with his hands, then looked directly at his wife. "I watched a miracle take place in your life because of the gospel, and now with Angelica. I'm stubborn, Connie, but I'm not stupid. I know something good when I see it, and I want to be a part of it. I want to have these miracles a part of my life from now on. Yes, I know it's true." He smiled happily at her, and patted her good-naturedly. "Don't look so amazed!"

"I'm sorry, Honey. It's just that I, well you, I mean, we never . . ."

"When would you like to be baptized?" Sam asked, interrupting Connie's stammering.

"As soon as it can be arranged," Fred replied forcefully.

"That would be tomorrow night," the senior of the two missionaries replied. Fred merely nodded, and smiled broadly.

True to his word, Fred was baptized that following evening.

For Sam and Dawn, the year following Fred's baptism passed in a whirl of family and business. These months were exciting and challenging. The business was expanding nicely into Washington State, requiring that Sam travel frequently to the "Lower Forty-Eight," as it was commonly called by Alaskans. He had made some specific goals regarding the business and was ahead of schedule in achieving them.

To make his stays in Washington more comfortable, Sam leased a condo in Seattle, hired a housekeeper and a cook, and bought a car. No more rental cars, hotel rooms, and lonely meals in smoky restaurants! He felt quite pleased with himself.

It was late September, and it had already snowed in Wasilla. In Seattle, the weather was cool and rainy, with brief periods of sunshine. Sam found himself reluctant to return to the land of ice and snow. Somewhere on one of the back burners of his mind, he was brewing a plan to move his family to Seattle. He was just waiting for the opportune moment to spring the idea on Dawn.

It was more a matter of incorrectly reading his calendar when booking flights than anything else, but Sam's flight did not return to Anchorage until Sunday morning. It was only Friday afternoon and he was finished with business. His mind was pondering what to do when the phone rang in his condo.

"Did I remember correctly that you are not going back to Alaska until Sunday?" Winston's familiar voice asked without saying hello.

Winston Allen was Sam's biggest client in Seattle, and about his age. Sam enjoyed his company, as well as doing business with him. "That's right."

"Then come out to dinner with Lucy and me." In typical form for his new friend, it was not a request.

"I'd be pleased to," Sam responded.

"Good! I'll have the car pick you up at 4:00 o'clock then," Winston replied.

"Why so early?"

"We're taking my jet," Winston answered cryptically.

Sam was somewhat startled, although he shouldn't have been. "I didn't know you had a jet. Where are we going?"

"Why not just let us surprise you," Winston replied with a laugh.

"You're on!" Sam agreed happily.

A limo arrived exactly at 4:00 o'clock, and whisked Sam to a small airport. Winston and his wife Lucy met him beside a sleek business jet.

"This is impressive," Sam said enthusiastically.

Winston shook Sam's hand and smiled. "I know," he replied. "I'm surprised you don't have one."

Winston was a little older than Sam. His money was old, inherited from his great-grandfather who was the first seafood retailer in Seattle in the 1890's. Winston was a little over six feet tall, and dashingly handsome. He had an easy charm that disarmed admirers of both sexes. He wore his dark brown hair long, his mustache neatly trimmed, and his cowboy hat tilted back on his head. He even wore a cowboy hat with his tux. When one has as much money as Winston, people don't criticize; they wonder how they might look in a cowboy hat and tux.

Besides all this, Winston was a wizard with money, and had quadrupled the family's already sizeable fortune. His most ingratiating quality was that there was not even the smallest drop of arrogance in him. When he was involved in a conversation, the topic at hand was never Winston Allen. If it turned his way, he frankly answered whatever question had arisen, and then turned the topic back to something or someone else.

If Winston had a glaring flaw, it was his brutal honesty. If one didn't really want to know the answer, they had best not ask him. Sam had been surprised more than once by Winston telling him he was acting unwisely. Every time it had occurred, it had cost Winston money, but it had won him a friend in Sam Mahoy.

"Actually, owning a jet has never crossed my mind," Sam replied as he boarded. But, this was definitely on his radar now. He was shown to a plush, white leather seat and buckled in by an attractive stewardess. Winston disappeared into the cabin. For a moment Sam thought Winston was going to pilot the plane, but Winston returned and took a seat beside his wife Lucy and facing Sam. In just a few minutes the engines whined to life, and they were on their way.

Sam didn't know where they were going until they began their descent about two hours later. He looked out the window at the unmistakable glitz of the Las Vegas strip.

"Why didn't you tell me we were heading for Las Vegas?" Sam asked, a little irked at his friend.

"Because, you wouldn't have come," Winston answered with his typical candor.

"You're probably right. I'm out of place here. I don't drink. I don't gamble. I don't go to burlesque shows. I don't ..."

"You do eat, don't you?" Lucy interrupted him with a charming smile.

"Of course. But ..."

"Las Vegas has the most incredible dining in the world," Lucy continued. "Believe me, I know. We're not going to corrupt you. We only blow a few quarters in the machines, and if it offends you, we won't even do that. We just love the lights, the glamour, and the food. We hoped you would too," she said patiently.

Lucy was a slender, long-legged woman in her thirties, with almost black hair. She wore a short black silk dress, high heels, and a beaming smile. Lucy was a drop-dead beauty. Not cute, not pretty—beautiful. Part of her beauty was the fact that she *felt* beautiful, and even something as minute as a tiny smile, or blink of her eyes, was part of her one-woman pageantry. The only thing that made her performance perfectly acceptable was that she was doing it all for her husband, whom she clearly, openly adored.

"I'm sorry. I didn't mean to be a prude," Sam said.

"You can't help it," Winston declared brusquely, then laughed at his own words. He was right, as usual. Sam forced himself to lighten up. He was determined to not spoil the evening.

Another limo took them to Le Village Buffet, inside the Paris Casino on the Strip. It wasn't the biggest casino in town, but the buffet was world-famous, and to Sam, quite mind-boggling. Every form of fine food from prime rib to exotic delicacies was laid out in seemingly endless array. Five separate stations presented cuisine from different French provinces. Lobster, shrimp, steak, and a mind-numbing display of rich desserts stretched before them. They spent over an hour relishing delicacies from all over the world. Even though Sam had dined in fine restaurants all over Europe, Africa and throughout the States, he was fully impressed. It was an exquisite culinary experience.

As they ate, Sam looked around at the casino and restaurant. Everywhere he gazed the visage of fantastic wealth was evident. The architecture was styled in French Renaissance. Massive crystal chandeliers hung from vaulted ceilings, held aloft by gilded columns. All around him were fantastic works of art, stained glass windows of world-class beauty, and incredible displays of exotic plants and flowers. He wondered at the amount of money that had gone into all of this glitz, and realized grimly that it had no doubt come from gambling.

"We're going to go dunk a few quarters," Winston said as he plopped his napkin on his plate. "Wanna come and watch?"

"I suppose," Sam replied. He had never really understood gambling, either the method nor the motivation to do it. And although he had no desire to learn, he thought he would be polite and tag along as sit alone.

Winston began pumping quarters into a machine whose display was a computer monitor. It made Sam wonder if they had programmed the computer inside honestly. After a few minutes the machine lit up, played loud music, and then belched a bunch of quarters into a tray.

"Yahoo!" Winston cried. "I just won twenty bucks!"

His elation surprised Sam, since Winston was a millionaire many times over. Sam had seen Winston drop a hundred dollars on a tip to an attentive, or even just a pretty waitress. It wasn't the money, Sam decided; it was the thrill of beating the odds.

"Here," Winston said enthusiastically as he shoved a small bucket full of quarters into Sam's hand. "Take that machine and pump quarters into it for me, would you? We're going to win *big* tonight. I can feel it!"

"Winston, I told you, I don't gamble."

"I know. You're not. It's my money, so it's my gamble. See? You're just helping me. Just take that machine there and put the silly quarters into it. If it pays off, I get the money, since it's my quarters. So make yourself useful," Winston said, and turned his attention back to his own machine.

Sam studied the big machine before him, and decided it was harmless. He brushed aside an urging to walk away, pushed a quarter into the slot and pulled the handle. He watched the four wheels spin and clank to a stop one by one. He wasn't sure why, but two of the four matched, and his machine clanked out a couple dollars in a noisy display of lights and coins.

"Hey! You're hot!" Winston proclaimed enthusiastically.

Sam hardly heard him. He scooped up the quarters and fed them back into the machine. Soon his bucket was empty, and he bought some quarters of his own. Every now and then he won a few dollars. Ignoring the overwhelming evidence of mounting losses, Sam felt like a world-class winner. When he finally hit the machine's limit and won a hundred dollars, he was addicted. Sam felt heady, almost spiritual, watching the machine pump out so many quarters. It took what seemed like minutes for the machine to pay off as it whistled, flashed and rang bells congratulating him. As it pumped quarters at him, Sam had an odd feeling toward the machine strangely akin to adoration. He scooped the quarters into buckets and immediately started pumping them all back in.

By the time Winston and Lucy were ready to leave, Sam had graduated to the dollar machines, and was still buying tokens. They had to pry him away from his slot machine and force him to come home. It didn't even occur to Sam as he walked reluctantly away that even though he still had three buckets of quarters and one of dollar tokens, he had lost over five hundred dollars. The other thing that was obscure to him was that he was solidly hooked.

Sam returned to Alaska thinking about gambling. Somewhere in his mind he realized it was wrong, but also considered it a harmless, one-time event. However, the next time he returned to Washington State, Sam waited anxiously for Winston to invite him to Las Vegas. When it didn't occur, Sam called him. Winston happily agreed. This second trip, Sam spent the whole time learning blackjack. He lost thousands. In some odd way it didn't seem to matter. The real thrill for him was in the act of gambling, not just the elusive hope of winning. Though winning money was the stated object, and brought a fiery justification to his actions, in a way, winning was almost undesirable because it brought the rush and risk of gambling to an immediate end. It took time to build it back up for another win.

By the time he returned to Alaska a week later, Sam had not felt the Spirit in two weeks, and hadn't even noticed its absence. He felt a new spirit that seemed to replace the sweetness of the Holy Spirit with a glittering emotional high he found intoxicating and demanding. Even though he was still in the bishopric, it was beginning to feel almost time-consuming to go to church. The whisperings of the Holy Spirit tried to remind him that he was getting caught up in the allure, but his mind was good at making up excuses, and he ignored the invitation to listen.

Months passed, and Sam covertly made many trips from Seattle to Las Vegas. Each succeeding experience served to strengthen the chains of addiction that had quickly wrapped themselves around his soul.

Dawn noticed her husband's new demeanor and was concerned for him. When she asked about it, Sam waved his hands dismissively, and gave her a generic excuse. He could tell she didn't believe him, but he tried his best to pacify or ignore her queries.

"Sam, I have no idea why you're different, but I would be willing to bet a hundred dollars it's coming from something you are doing in Seattle. You've changed, and you're dragging me and the girls into it. We have been married eight years, and I know you better than you think I do. You don't read the scriptures now, or pray like you used to, or speak of spiritual things, or play beautiful music."

Sam hadn't realized he had stopped playing the piano that he (used to) love so well. He listened to his wife's firm denunciation of his behavior with annoyance at first, then with anger, then with increasing chagrin. He knew she was right; so did she.

Dawn finished getting ready for bed, and started turning down the covers. "I married you as much for your spiritual greatness as for anything else. I don't mean to threaten you, darling, but if you don't figure out what's going on, and end it immediately, I will pack up the girls and go live with your parents until you do," she warned him.

"Dawn, there's nothing going on," Sam lied. He just wanted her to not be angry with him. "I'm just tired, and need a change of pace."

"Don't you lie to me!" Dawn warned him. "You listen to me, Sam Mahoy! If you were systematically cutting off pieces of your body do you think I wouldn't notice, or that I wouldn't care? Do you think I would believe you even if you repeatedly told me nothing was wrong with your bleeding fingers and toes? Do you think I love you so little that I wouldn't do whatever it took to get you to stop destroying yourself?"

Sam kept his eyes averted. Dawn continued.

"Well, you are slowly hacking off something much more precious than body parts. I will not stand by and watch you. I love you too much to become a party to your self-destruction either through my silence, or through joining you in whatever it is you're doing. Either you get a grip on your life, or I'm going to leave until you do. I love you too much to not use any tool at my disposal to wake you up, and that includes walking out that door!" She turned the light off, and that was the end of the conversation.

Sam sat by himself on the big sofa most of the night. He alternately fought a terrifying fear of losing the person he loved most in this world, and losing the most psychologically stimulating thing he had ever found. For a few moments he would hate her for attempting to manipulate him, then he would love her for her courage, then hate himself for stooping so low. Then, he'd start all over again. It was a maddening treadmill of vile emotions.

Loud voices argued persuasively in his head that gambling was not breaking a commandment, and it was harmless. He certainly had the money to lose. It was not a hardship on his family, so what difference did it make? He knew deep-down it was wrong; but for Sam this form of being wrong was so completely stimulating, that he had difficulty even considering abandoning it.

After the emotional turmoil they had been through, Sam could only hope that Dawn wouldn't actually leave him forever. She might make good on her threat to spend a few days with his parents, he reasoned, but she would not abandon him—would she?

Sam reasoned he had offended himself far more than he probably had his wife. He had betrayed no covenants, no moral laws or sacred trust. Although he still felt vaguely unsure of her love, he told himself that this was just her way of opening his eyes. But Sam could not doubt that she did not respect him in his current state of spiritual decay, and that stung deeply.

Sometime during that painful night, Sam found the remorse he had previously lacked. Finally, Dawn's rebuttal became irrelevant, and even his addiction became irrelevant. Only his relationship with the heavens mattered.

Sam fell down on his knees and prayed earnestly. The heavens above him were stone, and silent. He arose, feeling himself being buffeted. His heart was a confused garble of emotions: waves of rebellion, then contrition. He fell again to his knees, each time begging his God more earnestly for forgiveness. This process repeated many times during the night. By the first morning light, he had arrived at the inglorious point in true repentance of feeling completely filthy.

At seven a.m. Sam called his landlord in Seattle and canceled his condo lease. He would never return there. He called his business contacts and informed them they would be doing business by long distance telephone from now on. When Dawn arose, he sat her down and told her everything.

Dawn listened quietly, nodded sadly and occasionally sniffed back some tears. When he had finished laying out the pathway to his pollution, she stood and came to sit beside him.

"Sam," Dawn began somewhat contritely, "I've been thinking about last night, and want to apologize for what I said. I was wrong to threaten you. Will you forgive me? It wasn't my place to judge you."

"Forgive *you*?" Sam asked, incredulously. He was in fact, grateful, notwithstanding the fact that she had pressured him.

"I truly am sorry I said what I did. I was wrong." She paused and added gently, "No wife has that prerogative."

Sam nodded but said nothing.

“Sam, after all we’ve been through, I would never leave you because you were fighting some internal battle, or because I was disappointed with the direction of your life,” she continued earnestly.

Sam nodded again. “Thanks for saying so.”

Dawn’s mood lightened, and she laid her head on his shoulder. “Is there anything I can do?”

Sam kissed the top of her head. “Keep reminding me how much I love you.”

“Even better, I’m going to keep reminding you of how much you love the Lord,” she replied, lifting her head to look at him. “I have no illusions about who you love better. I have always known I was number two on your list, Sam Mahoy.”

Sam shook his head in confusion, not entirely sure he wasn’t getting into more trouble even as she spoke.

Dawn’s voice became teasing. “There was a time when I was a tiny bit jealous. Now that I see what a scumbag you are when I move up to the number one slot, I find I miss being number two. As a matter of fact, I don’t think I could love you as much as I do if you actually dropped the Lord from the number one position.”

Sam gave her a wry smile.

“Just so there’s no misunderstanding,” she continued, “you’re number two on my list, too.” She stood to leave, and kissed him on the forehead.

That evening Sam felt the heavens open a tiny crack as he urgently sought spiritual healing. The power once again washed over him, and he heard these words. “Prepare quickly, lest the trials come upon you and find you unprepared.” It startled Sam so completely that he started a fast then and there.

Nearly six months after his chance immersion into the seductive world of gambling, Sam finally emerged victorious. In the weeks and months that followed, his prayers slowly became a joy once again, and the gift of the Holy Spirit returned to his life.

Sam had learned something about himself through all this. He learned that he could fall. Somehow since childhood, Sam had always assumed he was rather invincible, almost spiritually indestructible. Sure, he knew he made errors, and occasionally made prideful blunders which took the Holy Spirit away for a day or two. But this was the first time that he had seen how easily he could be completely enticed away from righteousness. It frightened him to realize how vulnerable he really was.

He printed this statement on several pieces of paper and hung them around his office:

ONLY THE GRACE OF GOD
SEPARATES ME FROM TEMPTATIONS
I AM POWERLESS TO RESIST

Another time he penned this thought and pinned it up beside his desk:

I HAVE DISCOVERED I *AM* FOR SALE
I JUST KEEP THE PRICE SO HIGH
NO ONE BUT GOD CAN PAY IT.

These little reminders helped him remember that he apparently did have a price, and that only Christ could ensure that he did not sell out. He had seen that given the right set of circumstances, he could be duped. He truly did believe his only salvation was in remembering his absolute vulnerability, and he pleaded with his Savior to give him the strength and grace to stay so far away from the edge that he would not be tempted beyond his ability to resist.

Now that Sam had finally embraced his weakness and utter dependence upon his Savior, it seemed to him as if spiritual sunshine had burst into his life in such glorious brightness that he almost needed celestial sunglasses. Yet, had he owned such a thing, he would never have considered using them. He basked in the thrill of spiritual oneness, in the perfect brightness of hope that he now felt.

How he rejoiced in the days and weeks that followed! He had never experienced such an outpouring of the Spirit. Suddenly, not because of any element of self-discipline or self-mastery, but simply because he was for the first time in his life completely humbled to the dust, Sam was infused with the Holy Ghost, and his soul shucked off every untoward attribute. He knew all this to be a gift from God, a divine upgrading of his soul, a sweet endowment of a small measure of the stature of the fullness of the Master.

Suddenly, Sam's faith in the Savior was far more absolute, his humility rekindled, his desires truly pure, his joy immense and utterly perfect. His mind was continuously pointed heavenward, and his every thought was a prayer. The desire for sin utterly departed, and his love of fellow man became heartrendingly real. To his surprise, the world with all its enticement and reward was losing its appeal. His soul yearned for righteousness and rejoiced in glorious prayer. The scriptures spoke peace to his soul, and all the world was colored with a celestial hue.

He often awoke at night, having dreamed of praying. He wrote long passages in his journal that would take him years to fully understand. He lived as one whose life had been purified in the furnace of extreme trial, and who had emerged triumphant. His joy was so profound that every moment his bosom burned with the Holy Ghost, and every spiritual thought brought the distinct impression that the veil was about to part and allow him into the presence of his Savior.

2

PURIFICATION BY FIRE

Sam was still rejoicing as he took Dawn's arm and escorted her to the Jeep. She was dressed in a flowing blue gown, and he had on a tuxedo. It was New Year's Eve, and they were attending the formal dance at the church. Deep snow had fallen, and Sam considered it wise to take the faithful four-wheel-drive Jeep, rather than the much nicer Cadillac.

The cultural hall was decorated with sparkling streamers, balloons, and colored lights. A multifaceted mirrored ball turned slowly overhead, casting a thousand glitters of light throughout the hall. The band was live and quite good. Sam and Dawn danced happily until a few minutes before midnight.

Sam's version of dancing was standing in one place and alternately shuffling one foot and then the other. Dawn was an exquisite dancer and accomplished in ways Sam could never hope to be. They seldom went to dances because Sam felt so awkward. Yet he loved standing there, slowly moving in harmony with his precious wife, and gazing into her eyes. He rejoiced to watch her watch him, loving him and cherishing their time together. Sam had just gathered her closer to him as the music shifted to the familiar tune always played just before the stroke of midnight. It was magical, sweet and perfect.

"Should auld acquaintance be forgot . . ."

From not far away Sam heard the unexpected sound of a muffled cry, and the unmistakable thud of a body hitting the floor. He turned around simultaneously with a hundred others to see Bishop Dowling slumping to the floor. He ran to assist and found himself kneeling with many others beside their bishop. Bishop Dowling was not breathing and was rapidly turning blue. He was obviously having a massive heart attack. The alarmed crowd quickly gathered around him, and a sister ran to call 911.

One of the church members was a doctor and a few others there were paramedics who pushed through the crowd to render immediate care. As they worked to stabilize the bishop, Sam found himself kneeling with his hands on the bishop's head, along with many others. Hands rested upon his shoulders. As the highest church authority present, Sam opened his mouth to call upon the Lord through His holy priesthood to restore this good man to his proper place in this world. With complete faith in Christ and knowledge born of righteous experience, Sam opened his mouth ready to pronounce a blessing with great faith that the bishop would be called back, even from beyond the very gates of death. It was a marvelous experience to feel such faith, and he spoke with power.

"Bishop David Dowling, in the name of Jesus Christ, and by the power of the holy Melchizedek Priesthood, I lay my hands upon your head and give you this blessing. In this your time of greatest need, I bless you with continued life…"

Sam paused, for the words on his lips startled him. He felt hands move on his shoulders in discomfort, and seconds stretched as slowly as hours. He tried to say other words, to find another blessing, but there was no other. Being filled with the power of the Holy Ghost, and flooded with that sweet warmth of heaven-born peace, he completed the sentence his fears had caused him to delay.

". . . however, not life as you have known it in this world. I release you. Your labors in this world are completed. Further work only you can perform awaits you in another sphere, and great glory in the resurrection to come. In that day when all is made known, you and all those who love you will rejoice in this departure, which to us now seems so untimely, and so unfair. Until then, we who love you bid you farewell. In the name of Jesus Christ, Amen."

Sister Dowling fell on her husband's body and wept; others burst into tears as well. Loving hands comforted and finally lifted Sister Dowling. Those working on his body continued, but with a different spirit. Their actions were seen by no one as defiant to the blessing given, but as a physical necessity to complete their obligation to their training and profession.

When Sam finally thought to look at the clock again, it was past 1:00 AM. The new year had come in tragically. Sam and Dawn returned home slowly through heavily falling snow. Somehow, the dense white blanket of silence seemed appropriate to the heaviness in their hearts.

Two days later Sam was called and set apart as Bishop of the Wasilla 2nd Ward. The suddenness of the change was startling. One minute he had been perfectly content as Bishop Dowling's first counselor. Now the faithful bishop was dead, Sam was the bishop, and he had a funeral to arrange and conduct. His heart pounded in apprehension every time his thoughts turned to the funeral. He often swallowed the lump in his throat as he attempted to deal with the affairs and tragedy of the Dowling family's loss.

Bishop Dowling had been 48, his wife was one year older, and the mother of four sons. She was educationally untrained and unable to make a living for her family. Her loss was profound, and she crumbled under the weight of grief and despair.

The funeral was scheduled for Saturday, a mere three days away. Dawn was out of the house on business relative to the funeral when Sam entered his study and closed the door. He sat at the big desk and lowered his head into his hands. His prayer was nearly always the same these last few days.

"Father, help!" he pled, his heart heavy with the burden of his new office. He felt broken and sick at heart.

"Brother Mahoy," a voice distinctly spoke to him. Sam was certain no one was in the house and looked up in shock. He was completely alone. He checked the house, and found himself alone. Returning to his study, he locked the door and resumed his prayer. Then he heard the same voice..

"Brother Mahoy," the voice said. This time he recognized the voice, and it sent a thrill of happiness and confusion through him.

"Bishop Dowling?" Sam asked aloud. As he watched, a light formed in front of his desk and a form took shape. He instantly recognized his former Bishop and friend. He was dressed in a familiar business suit, although his young countenance was very bright, almost colorless. He was standing nearly a foot above the floor.

"Brother Mahoy," the image before him repeated, and smiled. "I have come to give you instructions concerning my family," he said. "I was called away from my earthly family because of a pressing need here," he continued, making a sweeping motion with his right hand. "I am the first of my genealogical line to hold the priesthood. I did not know then that all missionaries in this world of spirits go to their own kin. Most of my family here have accepted the Gospel, but could not receive their full blessings until a priesthood holder returned home to complete the process.

"Though untimely by earthly measures, my arrival has been anticipated here for a thousand years. I literally have more work to do than I can possibly accomplish." With this, the bishop seemed to shift his stance to the other foot as he made a motion with his right hand that Sam had seen a thousand times, which seemed to signify a change of subject.

"I have been granted this great gift of returning to instruct you, and comforting my wife and children. Otherwise, my wife will be overwhelmed, and my sons lost. I asked this blessing of our dear Savior in answer to the apparent untimeliness of my passing. As you can see, it was granted," his former bishop informed him.

"I will do whatever I can, Bishop," Sam replied. He had never seen an angel before and was amazed that he beheld it with his natural eyes, and heard with his normal hearing. He wondered if he had had a tape recorder at hand, if he could have recorded the conversation. He thought it likely.

"Thank you, Sam. Tell my family I am serving the Lord in this most important calling. Tell them I love them, and have prepared a place for them. Tell them to be faithful, and to endure without fear. All is well, all is well."

Sam was jotting notes on a pad. He looked up to see Bishop Dowling watching him, waiting for him to finish writing. Sam smiled and nodded.

"Tell my sweet wife to carry on. Tell her to prepare herself to remarry in due time. Tell her I desire it for her welfare and happiness. She will always be my eternal companion. Tell her to never doubt that."

"I will," Sam assured him.

"I have little time left. I want you to speak at my funeral. Tell my family what I have said."

"I will," Sam repeated.

"And Sam, please tell Evelyn I did have life insurance. Thank you, Sam. God bless you, and farewell," he added in obvious haste.

Sam scribbled this final note and looked up in time to see the light gathering around his former friend. In the blink of an eye, he was gone. Except for a few scribbled notes before him, a racing heart, and a profound burning in the bosom, there was no evidence that a heavenly messenger had just been in the room.

Not many minutes elapsed before the phone on his desk rang, startling him back to reality.

"Hello?"

"Bishop. This is Sister Dowling," a sad voice informed him.

"Hello, how are you doing?" he replied, suppressing the urge to literally blurt out what had just occurred.

"As well as can be expected, I suppose."

"Is there anything I can do for you, Sister Dowling?"

"I just called to ask a favor."

"Anything I can," Sam replied softly.

"I would like you to speak at the funeral. Would you be willing to do that?" Sam was not surprised, yet it struck him with great force.

"I would be most honored," he replied.

Sister Dowling seemed to relax. "Thank you, Bishop. I won't trouble you further."

Samuel stopped her from hanging up. "Sister Dowling?"

"Yes?"

"Did you find any insurance papers?" As Sister Dowling's bishop, Sam had already had discussions with her regarding her needs and her future. He had previously been assured there was no insurance.

"We didn't have any life insurance, Bishop," she reminded him. She was too polite to add that she had already discussed this with him.

"I have reason to believe there is an insurance policy," Sam insisted politely.

"If he bought insurance he never told me about it," Sister Dowling replied evenly.

"Perhaps he acquired it recently. Did you look in his briefcase, his personal files, places like that?"

"No. That thought hadn't occurred to me. I'll look though. I have to put his things away anyway. I'll check." Her voice was small, and without hope.

A thought occurred to him. "Also look in the glove box of the car or any place he might have stuffed it on a quick, temporary basis. Perhaps he hid it to make a gift of it to you later. Perhaps he had a special place he liked to hide things like that. Please make it a matter of prayer."

"I will. Thank you again," she replied weakly, and the phone went dead.

The day before the funeral the phone rang again. It was Sister Dowling.

"Bishop," she nearly shouted. "Bishop, you were right. I found it! He did buy an insurance policy!"

"Where was it?" Sam asked, understanding perfectly her immense relief.

"He had put it in the sidecar on his old motorcycle. Can you imagine that?"

"I didn't even know he had a motorcycle."

"It was our only transportation when we were first married," she explained, a note of tenderness in her voice. "He's kept that silly thing all these years. It was his baby. Last Christmas he hid my Christmas presents in the sidecar. I have no idea why he put the insurance policy there."

"Maybe he was going to surprise you with it later."

"You know, my birthday's in January. I'll bet he was going to surprise me with it then. He just didn't …"

"Nobody expects to need insurance when they buy it," Sam interjected into the brittle silence.

"I'm sure," she agreed unhappily.

"Will it be enough for your needs?" Sam wondered.

"I don't know how to read these things. I've never seen one before. But, it looks as if he took it out on the 17th of December. Just a few weeks prior to his..." She couldn't bring herself to complete the sentence.

"If you flip to the last page, you may find a column of numbers. One of those will be the amount."

Sam could hear pages rustling over the phone. "Here it is. Let's see... Oh my gosh. It's for $500,000 dollars!" she cried. "We can't afford that!"

Sam had to chuckle in spite of himself. "Sister Dowling, it's already paid for. It's not a bill. It's an insurance policy."

"Oh! Right! I'm sorry. Like I said, I'm not great at financial things. I've been going over our bills, and I'm used to thinking that every piece of paper is a bill." She paused to take a deep breath. "You mean I *get* that much money? Someone actually owes *me* money?"

"It appears to be the case," Sam replied happily.

There was a long silence. Finally, she said, "It's not enough."

Sam was surprised by her statement. "Don't you think you can get by on that much money for a while?"

"Oh, goodness yes," she responded emphatically.

"Then, what did you mean, it's not enough?"

"This is what the world thinks his value is. But his life is worth more than that to me. Much more," she responded in a small voice.

Sam smiled, touched by her words. Then he simply said, "He was indeed a blessed man to have a wife like you."

Sam had only attended one other funeral in his life, that of his little brother, Jimmy, who had tragically died at age two. Now, on the day of Bishop Dowling's funeral, the minutes ticked away until the time he would not only attend the funeral of a dear friend but would conduct and speak. He both dreaded, and anticipated what was ahead. His dread emanated from his former unhappy experience with his little brother, and his anticipation came from a hope that his words might bring comfort and truth to those who attended.

The funeral was not intended to be long, but the chapel was filled to capacity with grieving loved ones and ward members. Catherine Fowler, the deformed young woman who a year ago had captured the hearts of all their ward with her angelic voice, slowly arose from the congregation to sing Bishop Dowling's favorite hymn, "O My Father." As she concluded her beautiful song, she stumbled awkwardly as she stepped onto the stairs. Sam jumped up and caught her curled hand, escorting her down to her family. With tears in her eyes, Catherine gave him a look of profound gratitude and heartfelt love.

Sam soon found himself standing before the pulpit, a few notes before him, his heart racing. He waited until peace rested upon him before beginning. He surveyed the sea of faces and those of Sister Dowling and her children. Their faces were strained and sorrowful.

"Brothers and sisters, friends and family, it is with considerable hesitation that I stand before you today. David Dowling was my bishop, my spiritual brother, and my dear friend. I think few things could be more difficult than to preside at the memorial service of a dear friend. I'm not sure I can offer the comfort and peace his family needs when I, myself, am grieving his loss."

The congregation nodded in understanding, and he continued.

"I was standing close to him when he passed away. It was I who laid my hands on his head and filled with faith and the power of the Priesthood, proceeded to give him a blessing to restore him to life and health. I felt the fire of faith to do it. We, all of us there, had the faith to do it. But, faith can only exist in things that are true. And, the truth of Bishop Dowling's life is that Heavenly Father has a greater need for him there than we have for him here. As I now look into the tear-streaked faces of his wife and children, I can scarcely imagine how anyone could need him more than they do. He loved each of them with a love that is eternal, and which eclipses the bands of death, and will bridge the expanses of eternity."

The family looked at each other, and new tears welled up in their eyes. "As I knelt there on the dance floor, my hands on his head, I was not allowed to say the words to bring him back. I struggled, wished, even silently begged Heavenly Father to let me do it. But, when the words came they were the words our loving Father wanted me to say, and those words released him from this life to complete his journey into the next."

He paused to draw a labored breath. "We know so little about life after this world. What we do know fills us with comfort and peace, and tells us of a continuation of love between the departed and those left behind. In that blessing to Bishop Dowling as he bridged that great separation between this world and that which follows, I was prompted to use words to the effect that he had a great work to perform beyond the grave which only he could perform. For this reason, I believe, he was taken from us in the prime of his life, to go do a greater good elsewhere."

Sam's voice grew stronger. "Anyone who knew Bishop Dowling knows that he would have responded to such a call. He would have gone with pleasure to any part of the Lord's vineyard to do His will, even to a field of labor from which he could not return, even to say goodbye."

Sam paused to ponder his next words. His heart was full of sweetness, and he wanted to impart that comfort to Bishop Dowling's family. He wanted to deliver the message he had been given, but suddenly he didn't quite know how. A feeling of uncertainty as to when and how to deliver this extraordinary message assailed him. He sensed a gentle urging to wait, to deliver this specific message to the Dowlings in another way, in another setting.

I am only carrying out Bishop Dowling's wishes! he thought. He pushed aside the warning and plunged ahead.

"I wish to share with Sister Dowling and her children a very special and unique blessing I received a short three days ago. It is difficult for me to relate it without becoming emotional, so I hope you will bear with me."

Sister Dowling shifted in her seat, and looked at him expectantly.

"I had been set apart as bishop in Bishop Dowling's stead. It was an awful thing, and a wonderful thing, to feel the mantle settle upon me that had rested so correctly on our beloved bishop's able shoulders. I had gone home early that afternoon to ponder and to pray. I entered my study and closed the door. Having laid my head on my desk in heaviness, I proceeded to pray earnestly to know the will of the Lord, for the calling of my office felt heavy and unwieldy to my soul.

"No sooner had I done this than I heard my name spoken. This startled me, and I arose from my desk to see who was in the house. Having determined I was alone, I returned to my study, this time locking the door.

"Immediately upon seating myself and returning to my former meditations, I heard my name distinctly spoken. This time, however, I recognized the voice addressing me. It was the voice of my friend, and Bishop.

"I looked up and found the center of my room filling with light, when in an instant I found myself in the presence of Bishop Dowling. He looked exactly as I remember him, dressed in his dark blue suit. His face was youthful and luminescent, and seemed to radiate light. He smiled at me as he spoke."

There was an audible gasp from Sister Dowling, and several others.

"Brothers and sisters, I still don't know why he came to me instead of to someone else. All I can tell you is that he came. He asked me to deliver a specific message to his family. I am trying to discharge that obligation as best I can."

The room was deathly quiet.

"He addressed me by name, and informed me that he had instructions for me to give to his family. I reached for a pad of paper and made notes while he spoke. As he spoke he paused periodically to give me time to write down what he was saying.

"He first informed me that he had been called away because of a pressing need in the world he now occupies. He then told me that he had been given the great gift of returning to this world with a message for his family because of the untimely nature of his departure. He said if he did not return his family would be overwhelmed, and maybe lost. But the justice of God would not allow this to happen."

Sam leaned earnestly toward the stunned congregation in open honesty. "I must tell you that this whole conversation occurred as naturally as one friend speaks to another. I heard his words with my natural ears, and beheld his presence with my natural eyes. I suspect that had I turned on a tape recorder, I could have captured his voice for you to hear. However, I did not, and do not feel it would have been appropriate even had the opportunity presented itself.

"I told him I would do whatever I could, to which he smiled and said, "It is well.'" I have heard him say those very words many times, as have all of you. He next told me to deliver this message. I will read it from the notes I took at the time." Sam shuffled a few papers.

"He said, 'Tell my wife to carry on. Tell her to prepare herself to remarry in due time. Tell her I desire it for her welfare and happiness. She will always be my eternal companion. Tell her to never doubt that.'"

Sister Dowling gave a little cry, and hid her face in her hands, but she did not take her eyes from Sam. He suddenly hoped he had not made a mistake by telling her these sacred things in public. But having gone this far, he finished his story.

"I assured him I would do as he asked. He then informed me that I was to speak at his funeral and deliver this message to his family. He then mentioned that he had an insurance policy. He asked God to bless me, and bid me farewell.

"I had barely written down those words when the light closed around him and he vanished from my sight. The image of his presence is etched in my mind. I shall never forget what it was like to speak with him. In every way, word and mannerism, he seemed to be the same man I had served with in the Bishopric."

The congregation stared at him in stunned silence. Sam was oblivious to that, and went on with his story.

"Not many minutes later Sister Dowling called to ask me to speak at this funeral, he said. "I agreed, and then asked her to search for an insurance policy. She was sure there was none to find, but agreed to try. She called me back yesterday to tell me she had found it in a most unlikely place. Bishop had purchased the policy a few weeks prior to his passing without her knowledge.

Sam paused to feel the warmth of the Spirit, which had suddenly departed. But he finished quickly, knowing that what he had experienced was true. "All of this has had the effect of strengthening my testimony of the reality and truth of the gospel of Jesus Christ. It has filled me with a simple, yet sweet perspective about the nearness of our loved ones, and the labors they perform. It is my testimony that they continue to love us, and are concerned for our welfare. It is also my testimony that the love of God occasionally allows the veil to thin, that we might take direct comfort from their love.

"I bear you this testimony in the name of Jesus Christ, Amen."

Several days passed in serenity before the phone rang at work. It was the Stake Executive Secretary. Sam agreed to meet with the Stake President that evening.

Being a newly-called bishop, and being in great need of training and support, Sam thought little of this sudden interview. He traveled to the meeting making mental notes of things he wished to ask concerning his new duties.

President Apsek was an Alaska Native, and a man of faith and extensive leadership experience. Sam considered it a privilege to serve with him. He entered the President's office to find both counselors to the Stake President also in the office. Sam shook their hands and took a seat.

"Thanks for coming, Bishop Mahoy. Sorry for the short notice, but something important has come to our attention that we desired to discuss with you."

"I'm glad to come. How can I be of service?"

President Apsek smiled. "Good," he said. "This won't take long. We have received several reports regarding the funeral of Bishop Dowling. It has been reported to us that you had some sort of vision of Bishop Dowling, and that he delivered a message for you to give to Sister Dowling. Did I get that right?"

Sam flushed, then nodded. "Essentially, yes that's correct. He appeared to me in my study, and asked me to speak at his funeral, and gave me a specific message to deliver to his family."

"I see. Has anyone else ever appeared to you?" The President's voice held a taint of accusation.

Sam was taken back by the question, and suddenly realized his truthfulness was being questioned. "No, I have never had a similar experience to this," he replied carefully.

"Good, good. Your remarks have caused quite a stir. Quite a few people were disturbed by your remarks. Someone even said you had spoken directly to Joseph Smith. Needless to say, this has caused considerable unrest."

"No, sir," Sam interjected. "I have received no revelations for the Church, or even for my ward. I was only asked to deliver a message to Bishop Dowling's family. I did as I was asked, nothing more."

"So, you actually believe that he appeared to you?"

"Yes. He actually did appear. It isn't a matter of belief, but of reality."

President Apsek sat in silence for a moment before speaking again. "Bishop, I'll allow it is possible that Bishop Dowling did appear to you. I don't see any contradiction with Church doctrine in this possibility. What disturbs me is that you chose the forum of a public funeral, when feelings are already tender, to deliver a message that smacked of sensationalism. Perhaps you should have thought about this more deeply before you spoke. I have often counseled new bishops to bring any questions you have to me. Perhaps I failed to communicate that to you."

Sam bowed his head with a sense of deep failure and embarrassment. "No, President, I do remember you saying that. It was just that I thought it would be appropriate, even healing."

"I'm sure you had noble intentions in your heart. Let me ask you something. Did you at any time feel a warning from the Spirit that you should not say what you did?"

Sam nodded. "I did have a twinge of doubt just as I was about to tell the story of his message. Standing at the pulpit, and wanting so badly to comfort Sister Dowling and her family, I ignored it. I'm really sorry. I just didn't realize . . ." He could think of nothing else to say.

"Bishop Mahoy, I certainly understand that you are new to this calling, and I wholeheartedly accept that you meant no harm. All of us here appreciate the strained circumstances into which you have been thrust with very little warning or preparation. I would just like to admonish you to fly a very straight course from here on."

"Absolutely, President. Of course," Sam assured him with great earnest.

"Very good. Well, I guess there is nothing further we can accomplish tonight. I'll of course consult with those in authority, and we will be in touch. I am hoping there are no further issues regarding this matter. Except for a few ruffled feathers, it doesn't seem that any lasting harm was done."

"Yes, President," Sam replied meekly.

"Please attend to your duties as bishop without embellishment. Consult your Handbook of Instructions in everything you do. If it isn't specifically in that book, just call me and we can iron it out beforehand."

"Yes, President."

"Very good. Thank you for coming." President stood, signaling the end of this most uncomfortable experience. As Sam was shaking his hand he looked intensely into Sam's face, and Sam knew it wasn't over.

He returned home with a sinking heart.

Stake Priesthood meeting was scheduled for Saturday two weeks away. Sam was called back into the President's office a few hours before that meeting.

President Apsek seemed oppressed as he shook Sam's hand. Sam took a seat with a feeling of dread in his heart.

"Thank you for coming again, Brother Mahoy." Sam made note that he did not address him as Bishop.

"Certainly," he replied. He felt like shouting "Let's get this over with!" but did not.

The President sighed as he began. "I have to tell you these past two weeks have been a tremendous struggle for me. I have wrestled with this decision more than with any other I have made. I have fasted and prayed and feel as if I have fought a battle with the devil. At this point I'm not sure if I have lost or won."

"I'm sorry this has been difficult for you," Sam said sincerely. President looked at him sharply to see if he was being sarcastic. He was not, and President perceived that.

President continued. "Your indiscretion has caused great contention in the stake. Many voices are crying both for and against you. I have never seen anything like it. The matter has been thrust into my lap to decide. There are no general guidelines concerning these things. I have been at a complete loss as to how to handle this situation."

Sam struggled with this, because in his own life, battling with indecision had always meant he had yet to arrive at the right decision. But, Sam was restrained by the Spirit from speaking at all.

President Apsek continued. "I strongly believe that you had no malicious intent in what you did and were in no way trying to perpetuate a deception. In fact, I have no trouble with the idea that you saw Bishop Dowling, but question only with how and when you chose to report it."

"Thank you," Sam said softly. It was at least something.

President nodded, then continued carefully. "What I am concerned about is that this unfortunate event has damaged your stature among your ward members, and has now rendered you ineffective in your office. I am reluctantly persuaded that no matter your diligence and faithfulness in discharging the office of a bishop, that you would not be able to reach the people who need you most. Those who have taken offense are those who need you most. I fear a great falling away would occur should you be left in office."

Sam brushed tears away with the back of his hand. "I think I understand."

President Apsek's voice grew softer, almost sad. "In keeping with all this, I have determined that it is the Lord's will that you be released as bishop immediately. This action is not meant to punish you, but to preserve the efficacy of the office you are vacating."

Sam had to think about this a moment. "You mean, this action is to satisfy my critics, so they will not take further offense, even though I meant no harm?"

President pushed back in his chair. "Please don't feel defiant. As I said, I have pondered this long and hard, and this is the right solution. Besides being appropriate to the error involved, I believe it will keep dozens of people from storming away from the Church. I'm sorry that it publicly humiliates you, but it was your lack of discretion that caused the embarrassment," President Apsek replied a little more forcefully.

Sam shook his head. "I'm not feeling defiant, President. I'm disappointed. I don't feel that this response is appropriate, because I didn't do anything with the intent to harm, and I don't consider myself a threat to the Church."

President did not respond, and Sam shook with emotion as he continued. "I love the Lord, and I love the Church. I have ordered my whole life to be of service and a blessing to my fellow saints. I can accept that my action has created a stir within the stake, but I don't believe it has made it impossible for me to continue as bishop. I truly loved being of service, and my soul anguishes at the idea of being released. I'm sorry, but it just strikes me as unjust."

President Apsek shook his head sadly. "These measures are necessary as damage control. Brother Mahoy, your words convince me even further that I have made the right decision. Your best option is to simply submit. In time all will be well."

Sam thought carefully before replying. "President Apsek, I guess the thing that troubles me is the public ridicule and innuendo this will heap upon my head, and upon my family. I may be guilty of some form of misjudgment, but certainly of no gross sin worthy of public ridicule."

The President's face hardened. "Because you are a bishop, and a public figure, it is impossible to release you under any circumstances without several thousand people knowing it. This simply is necessary to keep harmony within the members who were offended by your words. Not only is it the best way, but it is the right way."

"I don't agree," Sam muttered.

"I can see that, and I'm sorry," President replied as he stood. The matter was closed.

"But why?" Dawn shouted at him in distress. "It's so unfair, and so unjust, and so unnecessary. I can't believe President Apsek released you!"

"Calm down, Sweetheart. It is honestly my own fault. I'm the one who didn't heed the prompting I had to be more discreet. President Apsek is just doing what he thinks is right. We have to forgive, and get on with our lives."

"If he were your boss at work or someone like that, I could forgive him as an ignorant fool. But he's supposed to be a man of God, a man who relies upon inspiration, and who doesn't destroy people's lives on a foolish whim. This isn't how the true church is supposed to operate!"

Dawn was furious, and nothing Sam could say would satiate her. He was actually amazed at how deeply this had struck at her. He suddenly feared for her more than for himself.

"Really, I should have been more circumspect in what I said. I should have just spoken to Sister Dowling privately. It was my own mistake."

But Dawn would not be cajoled. "Maybe all that is true. It changes nothing really. You were doing what Bishop Dowling asked you to do. Who are you to resist an angel's instructions? I can't believe this! It's insane! I feel like marching into that man's office and demanding he take my name off the records of the Church. I don't want to be associated with this Church if that's the way it treats those who serve within it with all their hearts! I've never known anyone who loves the Church more than you do. You talk about the Lord in your sleep, for crying out loud. How could they do this to you?"

"Dawn, now you're scaring me. Don't talk like that, and please don't feel like that. The Church is true no matter what its members do. You know that. Come on, it's late, and we're tired. In time this will all go away."

"Oh, I know. I'm sorry, but it strikes me so wrong. Maybe I'll calm down in a few days, I suppose."

She did calm down, but not in the way Sam wished. In the coming weeks, she slowly simmered until it began to affect her testimony.

The hardest thing Sam ever did in his life was to get out of bed the next morning and go to church. He had to force himself to take every footstep toward church. He turned back a thousand times, and waged a running battle inside his soul. By the time he was walking out to the car holding Lisa and Bonnie's hands, he was sick to his stomach from stress. Dawn had refused to go. Yet, Sam was determined to do what was right and attend the meeting, no matter the cost. But this cost was far more agonizing than he could have imagined, and the pain tore open his heart, which he had thought previously would be immune to such damage.

Sam walked into the chapel with every eye upon him, or so it seemed to him. He took his former place on the fourth row, and struggled to keep from hiding beneath the pews.

President Apsek was on the stand, and took charge of the meeting. Sam fully expected him to stand and deliver a scathing denunciation. He steeled himself, which took all his courage and faith to endure. As President walked to the stand Sam felt sickness rising in his throat, and wished he could simply vanish, rather than endure this humiliation.

"Brothers and Sisters, we have some Stake business to conduct. Brother Samuel Mahoy has been released as bishop of this ward. We have called Brother Ethan McDougall to be your new bishop. All those who can support the Stake and Bishop McDougall in this calling, please signify." Sam heard a few low gasps, and then gentle muttering throughout the room. After the voting was noted as unanimous, President Apsek simply sat back down. Sam realized that he was sweating profusely, and wiped his brow with the back of his sleeve. He glanced at President Apsek, who he found to be looking directly at him, a look of confusion on his face.

Sam could not have known that the confusion stemmed from the fact that President Apsek's planned explanation of the release of their former Bishop had just been rendered mute by the Lord. It was a miracle about which Sam would never know, yet one sweet and merciful. Had he not attended church that day the rebuke would have occurred as planned, and damage would have been done that even time could not have healed.

Sam returned home and went to bed, where he remained until the following morning. He felt himself buffeted by doubts and anger such that he could scarcely sleep, and he awoke more exhausted than before.

In the coming weeks and months, Sam found it easier to forgive and forget than Dawn did, who continued to fume. She began missing meetings, and asked to be released from her Relief Society teaching position. Less than two months after her husband's disgrace, she quit attending church completely. Nothing Sam could say seemed to have any effect on her, and she grew more passionate about her objections to the Church with each conversation they had.

For Sam, his wife's spiritual alienation was far more devastating than his own rebuke had been. She was his love, his wife and friend, and her self-imposed exile terrified him. What was even more frightening was that her decision was not hot—it was cold, and grimly sincere. He had seen her make decisions in a cold, calculated way before, and no earthly thing could dissuade her.

While everything spiritual in Sam's world seemed to crumble around him, the one element of his life which actually grew sweeter was prayer. How healing it was to kneel before the Lord hour after hour and worship Him. On every subject, the Lord answered his needs with instruction, or simply with peace. But, on the subject of his struggles within the Church, he received no guidance, no peace, and no idea of how to deal with it.

Sam's only glimmer of divine instruction came the first night after he had been released. He had fallen on his face in anguish and humiliation, and the Holy Spirit had whispered. "Be faithful, be fearless, be patient." Sam was so struck by the appropriateness of this divine communiqué that he printed it on sheets of paper and taped it up in several places throughout the house. It was the only direction he received in this regard, and ultimately, it was the only instruction he would need.

However, this succinct counsel often seemed initially inadequate. Sam struggled, thought, wrestled, reasoned, and anguished over this tragedy. His whole life had been geared toward service in the very church which now seemed to spurn him. It caused his soul to mourn, and his heart to break.

The twins turned four that July. It was a beautiful hot summer day for Alaska, pushing into the upper seventies. The hot days made their world nearly devoid of the mosquitoes so common that time of year. Sam and Dawn had completed the screened pavilion near the lake, and they held a wonderful birthday party for the girls there. The lawns and gardens surrounding the pavilion were serene and stately. They had a full-time gardener whose only job was to maintain and beautify their yard.

A cobblestone path curved softly through lush beds of flowers toward the new pavilion and beyond to the lake. Sam's floatplane was tethered on the sparkling water at the end of a floating pier. An expanse of sandy beach had been created with sand shipped from California at considerable expense. Sam truly loved sitting near the lake and watching the big trout jump in the evenings.

A dozen little friends from school and church came to the twins' party. The girls were thoroughly charming in their pink party dresses, and they laughed with glee as they opened each package. Dawn was very careful to purchase small, inexpensive gifts. She seldom lavished things upon them, even though they could have emptied several toy stores without scratching their considerable wealth.

Sam retired to bed that evening with a burdened heart. Watching his girls laugh and play with the carefreeness of youth had unexpectedly depressed him. Dawn seldom mentioned the Church anymore, and seemed fully intent upon abandoning it altogether. Just yesterday she had told him she was going to attend church with a Catholic friend of hers. She asked Sam to take the twins to church with him. He had agreed, but it was intensely sorrowful for him to hear. He wondered how long it would be before she insisted on taking the twins with her to some other church. He wondered what he would say when it occurred, and if it would divide them, and ultimately cause them to cease loving one another.

Over eight months had passed since his brief tenure as bishop. It seemed as if each month brought a greater deterioration of his world. Every day brought Dawn nearer to that awful cliff that is nearly impossible to cross again in the opposite direction. No amount of prayer, no amount of fasting, no amount of anguish seemed to have any effect on the downward spiral of his life. He slowly, fatalistically, came to the conclusion that forces beyond his control had thwarted the purpose of his life. He did not fear condemnation, since he could not identify any sin other than stupidity, perhaps, that was responsible for this grand failure. He considered the highest Celestial reward now beyond his reach.

For Sam, this was not merely a setback, not just a lost battle, but a total loss of the war. His great anguish was that he was now in a position wherein he could not complete his life's work. This felt like a death sentence to him, and one pronounced for a crime of which he felt he was innocent.

What was most inexplicable about this spiritual decline was that it did not altogether rob him of the incredible joy he had discovered in his life. Before this astonishing experience, joy had been upon Sam almost constantly. Now he had to seek it, to yearn for it, and to request it in mighty strivings; but joy still continued to be no farther away than earnest prayer. So in his lowest moments he often sought the transport of delight the Spirit mercifully brought him.

Still, Sam felt cheated, and he told the Lord so. Most nights his prayers carried the burden of his loss unto the heavens. It was late at night when his prayers finally changed from quiet complaining to downright murmuring. Had he been a small child his actions would have been to lie face down on the floor and throw a tantrum. For reasons he did not understand, this untoward, spoiled approach seemed to awaken a quick response from the Lord. It was simple and direct. The rebuke was unmistakable, as was the deep love in the message he heard. The Lord simply said, "It is the way of growth." The hidden message was that these trials were simply the only way he could continue to grow.

Sam pondered this for most of the night. "Be it unto me according to Thy word," he finally muttered in utter sincerity. At that moment, as if his heartfelt words had snuffed out the only candle in the world, he was suddenly plunged into utter darkness. Months passed wherein he strived against a mountain mass of opposition. Voices rang day and night in his mind, urging him to rebel. His flesh suddenly flared in importance, and begged him to indulge his senses. His mind reeled with dark ideas, and sin once again became enticing. To one whose mind was so recently spotlessly pure, it was like drinking sewage.

Calling upon his greatest courage, Sam fought back with every ounce of willpower he possessed. He stayed on his knees hour after hour despite raging opposition. He cast aside every temptation, and turned his face away from sin. Months ground by in a dark tournament of desperate struggle. In spite of all his efforts, his world continued to spin out of control. And as the months of darkness continued, Dawn systematically dismantled her testimony.

Through it all, the one thing that did not desert Sam was prayer. No matter how vast his sense of failure grew, if he sought the Lord with all his heart, he could sense a flicker of hope, a brief gift of peace, and a moment of sweet joy. Prayer became his lifeboat in a tempest-tossed world of spiritual survival. He developed a diamond-hard resolve to obey what he knew to be right and yearned for every whisper of the Spirit he could possibly discern.

Melody wept as she packed her few meager belongings. Marcia cried with her as they carefully stacked her boxes in a closet. Together they sobbed as they drove to the magistrate's office.

The hallway was oppressive with dark woods, a light green ceiling high above, and dim lamps hanging on ancient chains. The door through which the secretary directed them was tall and narrow, and bore the ominous inscription "Immigration Inquiries" in faded gold letters.

"It looks like an executioner's door," Melody remarked quietly as she turned the ancient knob and pushed it open. Marcia grimaced and followed her sister into the room. The room was small, hardly large enough for a dozen people to sit before the raised platform upon which resided an officious pulpit with a high-backed chair behind it. Hanging on either side behind the chair were large flags that neither women recognized.

Marcia stiffened just inside the room. "This seems like an unlikely place to seek justice," she mumbled.

Shortly after they arrived, a man entered wearing a robe of flowing black with a white wig haphazardly perched upon his gray, balding head. He walked straight toward them. His gait was sure, his posture erect and formal, his eyes a penetrating black. He was short, and slight of build. His face was as smooth as a baby's, although his age reached well into his sixth decade.

"May I inquire which of you is Miss Melody McUlvany?" he asked icily.

Melody flinched. "I am." Her voice came out very small, she thought.

The man smiled and offered a small, effeminate hand. "I am Wellford Wooding, Solicitor at Large. I have been appointed by the court to represent you in the matter of your immigration into England."

Melody stepped back. "I can't afford a solicitor," she said carefully.

"I am court-appointed, and as such, there will be no charge for my services," he assured her politely.

It was Marcia who asked. "Aren't you a famous attorney? I mean, I've read about you in some high-profile cases over the years, haven't I?"

"If you will forgive me the burden of my history," he said with a formal, though shallow bow, "I shall do the same for you. I assure you I will do everything possible to represent your interests in this matter."

Melody sighed in relief she could express no other way, but remained unsure, or in the least, curious. "Who sent you?"

"As I said, my dear, I am court-appointed."

Melody shook her head in disbelief. "I was unaware that well-established solicitors, like yourself, ever accepted such lowly cases as mine, and never for free."

The honorable Wellford Wooding turned and placed his ancient leather satchel upon the dull surface of a worn table. He turned to face them. His eyes glittered with deep intelligence, and a certain hardness she found both frightening and comforting. Though not devoid of kindness, his voice nevertheless was colored by an unspoken warning. "May I suggest that we discuss my reasons for representing you at another time, and proceed to discuss your case? I have asked the court to delay this hearing thirty minutes for this very purpose. We had best use the time wisely, should we not?"

"I shall place my future into your hands, then," Melody said meekly.

"You are wise," the solicitor replied as he snapped his head forward slightly in another bow. "Very good, then. You are charged with entering this country without a visa, falsely obtaining a visa, living under a false name, applying for work permits on that visa, and several other related charges. Is any of this true?"

"I am ashamed to say, all of it—well, except the false name. This is my true name."

He nodded blandly. "I see. Are these documents correct in that you were born in Rhodesia?"

"I was born in Devonshire England. We both were. My father . . ."

Mr. Wooding interrupted impatiently. "Just answer the questions asked. Never volunteer information, especially to the court."

"Yes, sir. I'm . . ."

"So, you traveled with your family from England to Africa in your youth."

"Yes, sir."

"Good. And, did your more recent journey to this country originate in Rhodesia?"

"Yes."

"I see. But, your father was an English land baron, was he not?"

Melody's face was flushed. "Yes, he was of the McUlvany clan of historical note in and around Devonshire. But, I believe he was stripped of his land and titles when Rhodesia rebelled."

"That is what my research indicated as well," Mr. Wooding said curtly. " I believe that is all I need to know. I must go and prepare a few documents. I will return by the time the Magistrate arrives. Please relax and rest assured that all will be well."

"Can you . . ."

"Leave everything to me." His stiff smile reminded her of a dog baring its teeth just before it bites. He turned and left in a flutter of robes.

Presently, Mr. Wooding walked back through the door just as a clerk entered the chamber and seated himself on a lower portion of the stage. The judge entered moments later in long, black robes and a huge, white wig. He sat pompously, bidding all to be seated without looking across the small room below him. Another man similarly attired, but with a smaller wig, entered and sat to the judge's right on a lower portion of the stage before them.

The clerk read the charges and placed everyone under oath, while the judge studied documents on his desk high above them. Melody thought he appeared bored and a little malevolent, as if his mind were already decided on the case.

When the magistrate finally looked up his eyes wandered across the three of them, then flicked back to Mr. Wooding. "It is an unexpected honor to have you in my court, Sir Wooding," he said evenly. "Nowhere in my documents did it mention Miss McUlvany had acquired a solicitor, especially one of your caliber. I have here the name of a junior defender," he said, his voice registering a slight complaint.

"The junior defender you mention was most gracious in allowing me to step into his place. I therefore ask to be recognized as counsel to Miss McUlvany."

"Granted, and so ordered."

"Thank you, your Honor."

The judge sat up straighter, and his eyes flickered momentarily to Melody, and then back to the barrister. "May I ask what your employer's interest is in this case?"

"My employer in this case, is the Empire, your Honor."

Melody's mind spun at light speed for a moment. His employer? She turned suspicious eyes upon him, but the old bewigged barrister did not look at her, keeping his attention squarely upon the magistrate before him.

"As you wish," the magistrate replied somewhat ironically. "Let us get onto the matter before us, then. Melody McUlvany, did you hear and understand the charges against you?"

"I . . ."

Her solicitor had placed a hand upon her arm. She looked at him with frightened eyes. His eyes were so steady they appeared to bore into hers. "Answer no question without first looking at me for direction," he whispered.

"I'm sorry, I . . ."

"Reply, that you do," he commanded tersely.

She looked up. "I do," she whispered back.

The magistrate repeated the question. "How do you plead, Madam?"

She looked at Mr. Wooding. He whispered, "Not guilty, your Honor."

Melody flinched, her eyes large, but after a moment she replied as steadily as she could. "Not guilty, your Honor."

"The prosecution may begin its case for the Empire," the judge said, nodding toward the man sitting in the table to their right, who was even then rising from his chair.

The prosecutor cleared his throat, but before he spoke Mr. Wooding was standing. "Your honor. If it please the court, I have information which may save the court time and expense. May I present some background information which bears directly upon Miss McUlvany's past and future?"

"You may proceed," the judge ordered. The prosecutor lowered himself back into his chair with a scowl on his face.

"Miss McUlvany was born in England of Donavan McUlvany, who was born and raised an English gentleman. He served with honor in Her Majesty's navy, and fought with distinction in various campaigns around the globe. His family was titled, and bore the distinction and title of a Baronage until he chose to leave England some forty years prior."

"I am aware of all this," the judge said with impatience. "You should also be aware that he was stripped of his land and titles for treason after siding with the rebels in Rhodesia."

"Forgive me, your Honor. That was true up until two days ago. May I approach?"

The judge frowned, but nodded. Wooding approached solemnly while the prosecutor leaned toward the magistrate with an almost-bored expression. Wooding handed a copy of a formal-looking document to the court, then a copy to the prosecutor, and returned to his seat beside Melody. He slid a copy of the document in front of Melody to read, and leaned back in his chair.

"This is an order of Her Majesty, Queen Elizabeth, restoring Donavan McUlvany's title, and removing all taint from his family name. It is an—shall we say, extraordinary document—and extraordinarily good fortune for your client," the judge informed the room.

"I thought it would bear upon your deliberations," Mr. Wooding replied humbly.

"You were well-informed. Miss McUlvany, would you rise?"

Melody stood, but only after Mr. Wooding nodded at her reassuringly and stood with her.

"Melody McUlvany, daughter of Sir Donovan McUlvany, I adjudge you to be an honored citizen of the Empire, and grant you full membership, title and citizenship. I further dismiss all charges." At this point he stood. "And, I ask your indulgence for the inconvenience of these unfortunate proceedings. On behalf of the Crown, I offer my humblest apologies."

Melody looked with astonishment at the judge, and then at her solicitor, who was at that moment beaming at her. He raised his eyebrows, as if urging her to say something.

"Oh, uhm, I mean, thank you, your Honor, and I accept your apology."

"Very gracious of you indeed," the magistrate replied earnestly, and bowed deeply.

Mr. Wooding took her arm and hurried her from the courtroom. Melody walked as if in a trance, her mind reeling at what had just occurred.

"Well, that is all I can do for you," he informed her as if in a hurry to depart.

"I am so grateful. You saved my life!" she proclaimed.

"Hardly. But, you are welcome. It was a pleasure meeting you."

"Thank you so much," Melody answered, tears spilling down her cheeks.

Mr. Wooding seemed to pause at the sight of her tears. His face softened. "It was indeed a pleasure," he assured her, and quickly turned and walked away.

He was a dozen paces away when Melody remembered Theodore's proffered assistance, and the suggestion that he had powerful friends. "Mr. Wooding?"

He turned back toward them, a pleasant smile upon his face. "How may I be of further service, my dear?"

"Please extend my deepest gratitude to Mr. Tennison. Would you please?"

"My pleasure," he said happily. Then his face blanched as if he had just foreseen his own death. "My dear, I do not know a Mr. Tennison," he recanted, and forcing a smile back onto his face, he turned and hurried away.

As was his habit of late, Sam retired to bed after Dawn was already sleeping. He knelt beside his bed in prayer, his heart heavy with failure. Yet even as he knelt, he knew he was blameless before God, because he had again fallen on his face and repented mightily of his sins and weaknesses. He had solemnly committed again to obey the voice of the Spirit, no matter the cost. Sam's gratitude intensified as he vividly remembered the Lord's kind bestowal of grace and charity to him, unworthy as he knew he was.

Sam's prayers tonight flowed in particularly wonderful strivings of praise and worship. He was delighted to sense a greater power move within him, and to feel the heavens open as the Holy Spirit descended upon him. How sweet it was, how filling, how precious and peaceful it was to sing His praises again! Sam released his fears, abandoned his pain, and soared. His guilt melted into a bright hope in the Son, His merits, perfections, righteousness, and His precious blood of atonement—for Sam.

At long last, this prayer was like others he had rejoiced in, and Sam delighted in the gift once again. For it truly was a gift, coming upon the timetable of the Lord, and there were few gifts sweeter. But on this night there was more, and after hours of mighty prayer he felt a powerful change. It was as if a new and greater power now flowed through him. For the first time in his life words failed—or rather they ceased to be necessary. Now the words came in a language that was greater than speech, more beautiful than a chorus of angels, and more powerful than anything previously known to him. It was as if he had entered a higher realm of glory where those who worship God do so in greater power, unfettered by language.

Sam's soul seemed to transport out of him, to flow into a glorious oneness with all things eternal. His praise seemed to him to rhyme in a way too complex and beautiful to duplicate in any spoken tongue. It seemed to have meter, rhythm, tone, melody, and a beauty distinctly divine.

This divine state seemed to last a long time until it came to a sudden crescendo, and then was silent. Without warning the music stopped, the flow of worship ceased, and though he was still on the same celestial plane, Sam was given to know that he might of his own voice speak. No sooner did this come to him than dark sadness flooded his mind again; he suddenly felt deep anguish in the knowledge that he could progress no further. He remembered acutely his absolute failure as a mortal, and the satanic thought came, "The Celestial Kingdom is beyond your reach."

"Oh, Father!" Sam cried out in anguish. "Oh Father, I'm so sorry! How I wanted to accomplish more, to do so much good, to be a blessing to Dawn and my children, and to be a worker of righteousness. I am ashamed unto death. I count myself among the lost ones, having failed Thee in this life."

He wept bitterly in darkness and new shame. Then a sweet urging unexpectedly came to him, uplifting and encouraging him. In spite of the fact that he knew he would never enter into God's rest, it occurred to Sam that he still had a few things left. Perhaps there was some way, some insignificant task, some small service known only to God that he could yet perform. Without any hope that such a thing might substitute for the actual tasks of righteousness he could never perform, he still felt such delight in this thought that his heart cried out from the depths of his soul.

"Father, I know I am nothing, even less than the dust of the earth, and I have so very little left to give! But, in all things, and by every means I possess, I wish to do some good. Such as I have, such as I am, such as I have left, I give it all to Thee; freely, completely, without reservation, or expectation of reward, I give it to Thee. From this day, unto all eternity, all that I possess is Thine, whether it be my life, my possessions, my home, my sweet children, my beloved wife: all I have, all that I am, I consecrate unto Thee, now and forever!"

No sooner had he uttered these words than a sudden power washed over him so profoundly that it brought from him a spiritual gasp of delight; how gloriously perfect it was, how sweet, how infinitely loving! He felt himself reaching outward, opening his heart in much the same way that one spreads his arms to the sun to absorb all its warmth.

"My son," a voice spoke with great authority and perfect love. Sam heard it, felt it, knew it and rejoiced in it. His soul sang in exquisite joy. Suddenly, Sam was of no consequence anymore. His entire universe was the Son.

For a long time, he was instructed, loved and taught. Sam marveled as he listened and pondered, laboring to impress every word and detail into his soul. Still unsure of what it all meant he listened raptly, savoring every promise, every pronouncement, and every precious word. Flows of healing love and divine acceptance permeated his mind and body with indescribable warmth and comfort. He was a beloved babe in his Father's arms.

There was a slight pause, and then Sam heard unthinkably glorious words. "Thy sins are forgiven thee, and thou shalt be exalted."

It was not until he heard these words that he barely understood the wonder of what had just occurred. It was truly more than he could fathom. And then, no sooner had these words echoed in his soul, and had been recorded in the Book of Life, than the divine Presence withdrew and he was left to himself.

Sometime during this whole event, Sam had climbed into bed. He had no memory of having done so. He had the absolute sensation that he was hovering a foot above the bed. So powerful was this impression that he reached down to touch the mattress, and was surprised to find it exactly at his back. He was lying beside his wife, who was still fast asleep. Still overcome with joy, he glanced at the clock. It was 3:00 AM. Five hours had elapsed.

No sooner had he made this observation than the power returned quite unexpectedly. Sam found himself again caught up in the power of heaven, and heard exactly the same message, in exactly the same way, repeated a second time.

By the time this second iteration ended, he was physically exhausted. As soon as he was again alone, he heard the familiar voice of the Spirit. "Arise," it said. "Write it down."

Sam got out of bed and pulled a robe around himself. He quickly went to his study and turned on the computer. He did not have his contacts in, and was barely able to activate the word processor; he actually did so more from memory than from sight. He opened the file containing his journal and realized with a sinking feeling that he was not able to remember all that had occurred. Certainly, he could not recall the exact words, nor the exact promises and pronouncements in which he had twice rejoiced. He was about to despair when again the sweet voice commanded, "Just write."

Sam placed his hands upon the keys, and without even being able to read the screen wrote: "I have just had the most beautiful experience of my life." Following these words, the same message burst upon him a third time. He listened and wrote as fast as he could. Having spent so many years playing the piano, and having done a considerable amount of writing, he was a uniquely fast typist. Even throwing all caution away and typing as hard as he could, he struggled to record the glorious details fast enough. They came at lightning speed, and he forced himself to type faster. He found himself missing things, then jumping ahead and catching the essence, but not every word. He labored as if running for his life—or perhaps running *to* his life. When the vision closed for the final time, he collapsed on the keys, overcome with joyous exhaustion.

He would later come to realize that he had typed twenty-two pages detailing the events of that night. In the final analysis he had been caught up for over seven hours in the most gloriously transcendent experience of his life.

In response to a final urging, Sam password-protected the precious document, and switched off the computer. It was a day of days, and one he would never forget.

Walking from the study early that morning was for Sam like entering a new life. All was fresh and beautiful to him. It was as if he had never noticed the glorious details of his world, like the intricate designs in the carpet, or the mosaic of random texture on the walls. Several times he looked down to assure that his feet were actually touching the floor.

A magnet of love drew him to the room where his wife still slept peacefully. He wanted to awaken her, to excitedly share all that had happened. He stood by her bed and watched her sleep for a while, rejoicing in the glorious tale he had to tell her.

Yet, he knew it was not her time to know, and he slipped quietly away. He was overflowing with happiness, so much so that it felt as if he might explode, or that the very walls and floors might burst into song if he did not. He sat at the piano, clicked on the recorder he now kept in the piano bench, and played as he had never played before.

His fingers leaped on the keys, straining to express his inexpressible joy. His heart soared as the sweet tones tried to give voice to his indescribable feelings. He closed his eyes and with tears of joy on his face, pouring his whole soul into this single expression of love. How perfectly it came from him, how powerfully it thundered in the silence, how sweetly it chimed in the quiet of the morning. He realized that he was also speaking as he played—words of joy and worship, words of wonder and hope. Far too soon, much too suddenly, the music found its own echoing conclusion. It was done. It was perfect. It was on the tape.

"What has come over you this morning?" Dawn asked from her favored position on the couch. He turned, startled, to look at her. "Oh, you've been crying," she added sweetly, and stood to come to him. She gently wiped his face with the corner of her blue robe.

He slipped an arm around her waist. It was sweet that she had come down and quietly listened to him play. "Something beautiful happened last night," he said quietly. "I was so filled with love and joy, that I could scarcely help myself from playing. I felt as if I might burst if I couldn't express it somehow. I hope I didn't wake you."

"Oh you did wake me—and I'm not sure you didn't burst," Dawn laughed. "I have never heard you play so powerfully, and with so much joy. Did you know that you were also speaking while you played?"

"I was hardly aware of it until the end."

"You were. And, Sam, I have to tell you, what you said was stunning. Toward the end, when the music grew worshipful. I kept hearing *I Need Thee Every Hour.*"

Sam nodded. "I've always loved *I Need Thee Every Hour*," he said. "I believe I will write that small part of the song as a duet to that wonderful hymn, meant to be sung as a solo in the first verse, and as a descant in the third verse. When I heard it in my heart, it was in four glorious female voices. It sounded like four angels singing."

"So, that's why I kept hearing parts of *I Need Thee Every Hour*," Dawn replied, suddenly understanding. "Oh, I can see that they would be breath-taking together. You were singing the parts, and hearing a quartet. That's amazing. Do you really hear the music in voices?"

"Sometimes I hear complete orchestrations with full choirs; sometimes just a single voice, or a piano. But, most of the time the melody just comes to me, almost as if I were remembering a song I had loved long ago, and just remembered; kind of like unexpectedly meeting a beloved friend you haven't seen in far too long."

"Well, that song is truly beautiful," Dawn said sincerely.

"Thanks," he replied almost shyly.

"What will you call it? Does it have a name?"

"I believe I may call it *Sweet, Sweet The Joy*."

"That's a lovely title. What does it mean?"

Sam closed the piano lid and turned to her, his face alight with joy. "It was how I was feeling inside. I had been pondering the joy that has come into my soul recently, and thinking on the great hope of seeking the Lord's face with faith like the ancient ones. The title and the music all say the same thing. It is the sweetest joy I have ever known." He paused for just a heartbeat, his eyes focused deeply upon hers. "Speaking of things which bring me joy, have I told you lately that I love you?"

"As a matter of fact, just yesterday."

"That long ago? What's wrong with me?"

"You're slipping," she said happily. She lifted a leg over his lap and sat between him and the keys. He kissed her affectionately.

"Dawn, something wonderful has occurred in my life. I'm exceedingly anxious to share it with you."

"Please do," she encouraged him.

"It's the type of thing that must wait until the time is exactly right. I'm sorry, but when I do explain, you'll understand."

Dawn grew pouty. "You're right, I don't understand. And, I really don't want to hear it if it's something preachy, or intended to soften me toward the Church. You know how I feel."

Sam decided to redirect the conversation to safer ground. "Um-hum," he whispered, "Well, you already feel very, very soft."

She smiled in spite of herself, then leaned forward to kiss him.

Three months later "*Sweet, Sweet the Joy*," was published. Unlike its successor, this song did not sweep the records and radio stations. It quietly rolled through the worshipful meetings of the Church. To Sam's great delight, the Tabernacle Choir performed it a year later at the opening session of General Conference. Even better yet, no one suspected he was *that* S. Mahoy.

Oh, sweet, sweet the joy
Dear Savior, Lord from Thee.
The blessings Thou Imparts
Thy mercy kind and free.
My heart an open book,
Thy face I long to see.
Dear Lord, please thin the veil,
Oh, let me come to Thee.

For Sam, it felt as if a new world had been born all around him. Every labor he performed was an expression of his new-found joy. Every moment of every day was a prayer. Even while sleeping, he often found his soul in communion with the Divine. He would wake up in the middle of the night to find he had been praying in his sleep.

What was most startling above all else, however, was the absolute fearlessness this experience had brought to him. Suddenly, he was immune to any and all that might harm him. This was not due to the idea that something bad could not occur, but that when it did, all would be well. God would provide, and all would be well.

There was one great puzzle which seemed to be unanswered though: Why? Why had this glorious experience happened to him? Of all the people on earth, Sam knew most keenly that he was imperfect. He had always assumed that such glorious blessings were reserved until one approached perfection. Certainly, he was mortal still, and painfully aware of every untoward thought and temptation which still catapulted into his awareness with regularity.

He discovered that the main difference now was that these things repelled him, rather than tempted. What a glorious blessing it was to have all the previous gifts of the Spirit back upon him once again! This time, he did not expect them to be permanent. The fact that he knew the gifts were temporary made them that much sweeter, and that much more to be rejoiced in while they remained. Still, the question of *why* troubled Sam.

He felt unqualified for the supernal blessing of knowing his exaltation was unalterably decreed.

He made it a matter of prayer. As he pleaded to understand, in a sweet and now-familiar voice the Holy Spirit replied, "Yes, you are not perfect, but you are obedient. It is not required of man that he become perfect in this life. What is required is obedience."

It suddenly made such sense—such simple, divine sense. The glorious plan of exaltation suddenly unveiled itself before his eyes. Never before had he seen or contemplated such stark, perfect beauty. The plan was incredibly straightforward. "We will prove them herewith," the Lord had said as he announced the creation of their world, "to see if they will do all things whatsoever the Lord their God shall command them."

Sam suddenly understood that the great battle of life is not toward perfection, which is in fact an impossible goal for a mortal, but toward obedience, which through the grace of Christ is incredibly achievable. Once obedience is the maxim of one's life, the Lord pours out the Holy Ghost, which purifies, sanctifies, empowers, and works such perfection as is attainable for mortal man. Such perfection as man may acquire in life all comes as a gift of grace, not as a byproduct of self-discipline and personal housekeeping. Certainly, discipline plays into the initial act of obedience, as does repentance; but when salvation is ultimately attained, it comes as a precious gift from a loving God, with grace given all along the journey in response to humble obedience.

For the first time, Sam understood Moroni's admonition that men and women become perfect in Christ. Man cannot be perfect in his own right; it is simply not possible. It is Christ's righteousness that saves each soul, as they strive to rely upon their Savior, His merits and mercy, and then willingly obey His voice.

Suddenly, Sam wanted to shout, to stand upon the rooftops and street corners. Fire burned within his soul so brightly that he thought he might be consumed by it. He yearned to bear his testimony to the world concerning these wonderfully exalting truths! It was so simple—not easy, but so simple! Yet in every arena his voice was not welcomed, and dense silence overlaid the beauty of his unspoken words. Even with his bride, he was able to say very little.

From that morning Sam felt an overflowing sense of love. It was not love originating within him, but was charity from Jesus Christ flowing over, into and through him. His heart yearned with such singleness of purpose to be a blessing to all his brothers and sisters, that he could conceive of little else worth doing.

On the way to the office the next day Sam stopped at a stoplight. Facing him from the opposite lane was a battered little Toyota belching blue smoke and sputtering as it went. When the light turned green, it shuddered and barely managed to move again. Sam's heart was torn because of this person's plight. He immediately began to make a U-turn, to go offer help, or offer to trade cars. His eyes filled with tears of sorrow as the Spirit said "No," and led him away. It was painful to depart without doing something more immediately beneficial than just praying.

As he passed the grocery store, Sam saw the big parking lot filled with cars. He suddenly wanted to turn in, to stand near the door and ask everyone who passed if they had everything they needed, if they were happy, and did they know about the joy of the gospel? He stepped on the brake to do exactly that, but was constrained by the Spirit to continue on. Again, disappointment settled upon him, and his eyes filled with tears.

At the office Sam struggled to complete financial transactions with clients, to limit his conversations to matters of business, and to not give away everything he possessed. It was such a struggle that he finally asked his assistant to handle all incoming calls, and he closed the door to his office. His mind jumped from person to person he knew, and he deeply pondered their needs and prayed for their happiness. This love was so consuming and intense it seemed to be incapacitating to his life.

After an afternoon of struggling in the Spirit and yearning to do things that would have eventually culminated in his being arrested for insanity, Sam gathered himself together and slowly drove home. His heart burned, his eyes were aching and red from so many tears, and his soul cried out for some way to bless these people. He knew he had the means. He was wealthy, but the Spirit would not give him a direction to go, and his mind spun its wheels on the loose sands of desire. But although the pain was piercing, he was obedient and did not act on his impulse.

Finally, Sam locked himself in his study and wept. He wept for joy, for incomprehensible love, and for deep frustration. More than he had ever considered possible, more than he thought a mortal could, he wished to serve and bless, to witness and praise, to shout truths from the rooftops—yet he could not.

As he wept, he felt a new flow of the Holy Spirit, and a gentle understanding distilled in his soul. "This is what it means to know Christ," the Spirit whispered. Immediately thereafter, the overwhelming feeling of incomprehensible love began to dissipate, and in a few minutes was largely gone. He was left as he was before.

Sam pondered how gloriously wrenching it had been to experience in part what the Savior feels for us. He knew better than he could find words to express why Christ was willing to die for us, His wayward and rebellious children. For part of a day Sam had felt but a small portion of the love which had motivated Christ to allow Himself to be nailed to a cross. Yet, what Sam felt was a gift, and was temporary—mercifully temporary. With Christ, this love was the very essence of His existence. Sam knew then that no mortal could survive for long with that powerful love upon them as Christ had experienced it in His mortal life.

Sam was startled to realize that to have this all-consuming love would literally compel him to live as Christ had lived—as a wanderer, healer, and teacher. He could not own a business, for it would be too painful to profit from any transaction. More than that, any telestial pursuit would squander the time needed to otherwise bless people. There were too many brothers and sisters to help, too many blessings to give, too many lame, blind and hurting souls to heal. Such a person endowed with this love could not own things, for possessions would obligate him or her to maintain and protect them, which would also keep them from doing what this love demanded. One could not be as other men, for that perfect love would be like a white-hot fire of perfect desire, and any person possessed of it in full measure would eventually end up on a cross somewhere, dying for the love of those driving the nails.

Sam savored all this in his heart, recorded it in his journal, and spoke of it to no one. He could not have known how important this experience would be in the future.

THE CRUCIBLE

The twins were best friends with Fred and Connie's young son, Freddie. When Lisa and Bonnie played with Freddie, there was often another playmate with them. All three of the youngsters called this invisible companion "our friend." Whenever something needed to be divided, such as a lump of clay, invariably four mounds of clay were made, the last one set before an empty seat.

Dawn thought it was cute that all three of them acknowledged this imaginary friend. Whether they were playing at their house or at Freddie's, the girls' "friend" was always included. Occasionally their friend joined Dawn and Sam for dinner. When they were so blessed, the twins carefully set another place, provided a chair, and made sure no one disturbed their guest. If someone tried to sit in that seemingly unoccupied chair, there arose such a fuss that the invisible guest invariably kept his seat.

When their friend blessed the whole family with his presence, the twins acted as interpreters. "Our friend says he would like to have some more ice cream," Bonnie would announce. Or, "Our friend says he loves you, Grandma," Lisa would whisper solemnly to Sam's mother. The messages were always sweet, and occasionally somewhat startling. Such was the case when one day their "friend" called their grandmother "Mama Laura." It was a name Laura had not heard since her baby Jimmy had died, nearly twenty years before. Sam could not recall whether or not he had ever mentioned this name to his two precocious daughters. He finally concluded they had heard him use the term at some odd moment, and it had somehow stuck in their minds. He had frequently told them stories of his childhood, and he chalked it up to that.

With regard to his diminished church status, Sam endured the time with patience, remained faithful in every respect, and refused to allow himself to wallow in fear. He was never officially informed of any change in his membership by the Stake. Either time had dimmed the memory of his error, or the Spirit had instructed a quiet change, or perhaps both. Whatever the reason, Sam's first chance to teach again came quietly when he was asked to give the lesson in High Priests group. The group leadership was going to be gone hunting for two Sundays, and Sam was asked to conduct and teach during their absence. Sam calmly nodded his acceptance of the assignment—a simple response much too benign for the giddy happiness he felt inside.

All during the week Sam read the lesson many times and contemplated what he might say. When Sunday finally arrived, he was over-prepared and had sufficient material to teach for hours. However, when the actual moment came, the Holy Spirit settled upon him; he set aside most of his preparations and taught from his heart and the workings of truth within him.

Because of the influx of tourists, the population of the Matanuska Valley had, as usual, increased dramatically that summer. It was not uncommon at times to have a dozen visitors at church. For this reason, Sam thought little of the two older gentlemen who visited his class that day.

The taller, and apparently younger, of the two, introduced themselves as visitors from "the old country." He described themselves as brothers, but did not give a family name. When asked for a surname, he replied with a smile, "You probably couldn't pronounce it," and then chuckled. That seemed to satisfy all present.

The two visitors attend the High Priests group meeting. Since Sam was conducting, he asked them what had brought them to Alaska. The younger of them replied, "We travel all over the world for our employer, doing whatever he needs done." It was an odd answer, but again seemed to satisfy the question.

These discussions took place solely with the younger man. The only comment the elder man made was, "Don't pay any attention to me. I just like to listen." While his English was flawless, his accent was decidedly foreign, probably European, Sam thought.

The older gentleman walked with a cane and a slight limp, had a full head of gray hair, and seemed more interested in who was talking than what was actually being said. Sam knew this was an odd concept to lay to someone's credit. Yet, while the younger man made several worthwhile comments during the course of Sam's lesson, the older man looked intently at whoever was speaking at the moment, but said nothing. It was impossible to tell from the expression on his face if he agreed with, or even cared about what was being said. Since Sam was doing most of the speaking, it was Sam who he watched most intently.

When the lesson was over, the two enigmatic gentlemen stood and left the room without comment.

The following Sunday they returned. It was somewhat uncommon for tourists to remain in the area that long, so during group meeting, Sam made a special point of welcoming them back. They acknowledged his kindness graciously.

"Are you actually here on business, or vacation?" Sam asked.

It was now the older man who replied. "Mostly business, but we are also making this a pleasure trip of sorts."

"Will you be with us long?" Sam wondered aloud.

"Just a little longer, I think," he replied. "Our business is nearly completed."

The lesson in the Priesthood manual was entitled "The Holy Spirit," a subject dear to Sam's heart. His own experiences, his own vast blessings, had begun the moment he had learned to hear and obey the Spirit. The lesson was sweet, uplifting, and punctuated with testimony. The Holy Spirit was there in abundance, and Sam felt his heart soar as he freely bore testimony of this glorious principle for the first time in far too long. When it was over, many of the brethren shook his hand and thanked him for the lesson. He was very pleased to bear his testimony once again, and that it blessed their lives.

The older of the two visitors lingered, and was obviously waiting to say something to Sam. They were the only two left in the room as Sam placed his books in his briefcase, and snapped it closed. As if this were his cue, the older brother stood in a graceful move, looped his cane over his arm, and walked toward Sam without the hint of a limp. Sam observed all this somewhere outside his conscious mind.

"Brother Mahoy," the man said as he stepped up to Sam. Sam could not help but notice that the man drew much closer than is ordinarily comfortable. Yet, Sam did not feel an urge to step back.

"Yes?" Sam replied. The older man reached out his hand, which Sam accepted. The visitor placed his other hand atop Sam's, his grip firm and sure, as he spoke.

"I just want to tell you that the Lord is pleased with what you have been teaching these brethren. I urge you to continue at every opportunity. Yours is a great mission to be a blessing to your brethren. You have great gifts in this regard. Be fearless in your service." This he stated with authority, as if actually delivering a message from the Lord.

Sam thought this odd, but did not have time to say more than "Thank you."

The visitor continued, still holding Sam's hand. "In my work, I travel all over the world representing my employer. I have been in nearly every country, city, town and village on the map," he said. "My work often precludes my meeting with the Saints as much as I would like. It is always a joy to meet with the Saints and to find the Holy Spirit there in rich abundance. For this, I thank you. I can tell you with some authority that this is not the case everywhere I go. It is largely true, but not a rule."

"Thank you," Sam said again, unsure of what all this meant.

Still holding Sam's hand, the man looked him squarely in the eye and stated. "I just want to know if you will be as good a man thirty years from now as you are this day."

Sam thought about this for a moment, and then answered with boldness. "If I have my desires, and if my prayers are answered as I hope, I will be a much better man."

The gentleman leaned forward slightly, gazing intently into Sam's eyes. "It will be as you say," he replied with absoluteness. With this, he released Sam's hand and took a small step back.

"Endure faithfully," he admonished. "Perhaps we shall meet again."

"I would like that," Sam said sincerely, his heart burning with the Spirit. A dozen questions popped into his head, but he could ask none of them.

"Farewell," the gentleman said, lifting his hand in a type of salute. Then he turned, took three quick steps toward the door, lowered his cane and limped out into the hall.

Sam wanted to run after this strange visitor and ask him who he was, for the burning within his bosom made him suspect he was no ordinary tourist. Sam could see his gray head moving slowly down the hall amid the press of people. Sam took one step to the table, picked up his briefcase, and took two more quick steps to the door to follow the man. He surveyed the hall and was surprised to see that the old gentleman had vanished from sight. There were no exit doors anywhere near.

Two Sundays later, Sam entered the chapel with Dawn on his arm. It was Mother's Day, and she had come to church of her own volition. Sam was so pleased to have her with him, and so anxious for it to be a spiritually edifying meeting, that he paid little attention to who else was there.

One of his favorite people in the ward was Sister Wadsworth. He was pleased to see her name was in the program. Sister Wadsworth was the mother of six grown children, and a stalwart in the ward. She had served in practically every church position except Bishop. Sam had no doubt she would have made a great one. She was one of those magnificent people whose quiet strength feeds the faith of others in lasting ways.

Sister Wadsworth spoke of her mother in loving terms and told of her childhood. The message was touching, emotional, and profound. Tears flowed freely as she remembered time after time when her mother had taught her life's great lessons, often at tremendous expense to herself.

When the sister concluded her talk Sam felt as if he had attended a temple session, and he silently rejoiced that Dawn had heard it. He glanced at his wife, and to his great delight found a look of sweetness on her face. Even more meaningful to Sam was the glow of the Holy Spirit in her eyes.

Sister Wadsworth came directly from the stand to where they stood. She took Dawn's hand in both of hers, and in a way only one filled with the Holy Spirit can, told her how wonderful it was to see her again. Had anyone else said the same thing it might have offended her. As it was, Dawn was pleased, and told Sister Wadsworth how much she had enjoyed her talk. They started speaking of Dawn's mother, whom she had barely known, when they were interrupted.

"Excuse me, Sister Wadsworth," a man's voice interjected. Sister Wadsworth was standing in the row directly behind Sam and Dawn and turned to see who had spoken to her. Sam was amazed to see the older gentleman from his quorum meeting two weeks ago. The brother extended his hand with a warm smile.

"Sister Wadsworth, I just wanted to tell you how sweet your testimony was to my soul today. You made me remember my own mother, and I can tell you, at my age, that is no small affair." He chuckled to himself. "It was a long, long time ago." He smiled meaningfully. "You bore a powerful testimony; I shall remember your words for a long time."

Sister Wadsworth smiled. "Well, thank you. I don't believe I've met you before. You already know who I am. May I ask your name?"

"Oh," he said as he leaned forward slightly, "I'm just one of the three Nephites going around visiting the Saints!" With this, he smiled, then released her hand, glanced pointedly at Sam, and turned.

"What do you suppose he meant by that?" Sister Wadsworth asked Sam with a puzzled expression.

As she spoke, Sam was watching the gentleman's old gray head move slowly down the crowded row, greeting people as he went. Reluctantly, Sam turned his attention to Sister Wadsworth.

"I think he's telling the truth," he replied emphatically. "I want to talk to him some more." Sister Wadsworth looked at him with startled eyes, and they both turned to where the old gentleman had been but seconds before. He was gone.

"Where did he go?" Sister Wadsworth asked, bewildered. "He was just there! Now I don't see him, and it's too crowded for him to have gotten to any door. He should be right there!" she insisted, pointing not ten feet from where she stood.

"He seems to have a way of doing that," Sam said soberly.

As Sam recorded these things in his journal, he pondered them over and over. He had read of the Three Nephites visiting people before, but certainly had never anticipated one might visit him. And, for what purpose? To what end had he come?

What surprised him was Dawn's reaction to the whole thing. Having stood right there and having heard the whole exchange, she could not recall the old gentleman actually talking to them. Sam had to admit the possibility that the old man's words were just his poor humor; but remembered the way the Spirit had burned within him.

Still, his soul hungered to know the truth of such things, and he pondered them in his heart.

Angelica continued to live with Fred and Connie all that year. As time went by she grew, matured, repented, overcame her drug dependency, and returned to school. She first finished high school with honors, then enrolled in the community college studying psychology with an emphasis in addiction counseling. Her thirst for knowledge was nearly compulsive, and she studied hard to find the answers not only to her own problems, but to become a source of strength to others she knew still languished in the dungeons of addiction, ignorance and despair.

Prior to Bishop Dowling's untimely death, he had met with Angelica. She was disfellowshipped almost immediately, and the good Bishop began meeting with her weekly to buoy her up and strengthen her.

Bishop McDoogle was likewise loving and diligent in servicing Angelica's special needs. In time a light shimmered within, and was gently nurtured as she grew and blossomed. Sam learned she was just 23 years old; he would have guessed her to be 43. Her face had been haggard, her skin taut and sallow, her complexion blotched and unhealthy. Yet, as the Holy Spirit took up residence within her, her body rejuvenated, and she slowly became a young woman once again.

Connie worked with her tirelessly, teaching her everything from common courtesy and manners to personal hygiene. Connie slowly helped her niece restructure her speech to eliminate the crude and crass, and taught her to cook, clean, and even to dance. She retrained her niece's attempts to be beautiful by first throwing away every item of garish makeup she owned. Angelica learned the principles of internal beauty, cleanliness, and natural loveliness. In time she emerged a lovely young woman, full of hope, happiness, and testimony. Only her dismal self-image kept her from becoming the perfect bride for some lucky man.

Sam was pleased at how completely their small ward had welcomed Angelica. Her sad story was well known, but that seemed to matter very little. If anything, it seemed to unite the ward in a common cause of reclaiming this fragile daughter of Heavenly Father. The sisters gathered her into their midst, and loved her without critiquing her. It was an act of pure Christian fellowship, and it warmed Sam to see it.

Personally, Sam had little to do with her recovery; but as it turned out, Angelica had much to do with his.

It was a Monday afternoon, and Sam was at work. The twins were asleep upstairs, and Dawn was sitting at the piano plunking out a Christmas melody with one finger while she sang softly in her rich voice. She never played when Sam was home, yet she found a simple solitude in her private reveries at the piano. Had Sam understood her interest he would have welcomed the chance to teach her. As it stood, he hadn't the slightest clue that she even looked at the piano except to identify some particle of dust needing banishment.

The doorbell startled her, and she stood in haste, hoping whoever had come had not heard her juvenile plinking on the keys. She pulled open the heavy oak door with a smile on her face. Being a naturally friendly soul, she liked visitors.

"Angelica!" she said with a little too much surprise in her voice. Her shy neighbor had never ventured over to their home on her own before, and it surprised Dawn to see her there, cowering on the porch.

"Sister Mahoy, I hope I'm not intruding on you. I could come back later," she offered unsteadily, turning away in haste.

"Of course you're not intruding. Come in. And please call me Dawn!" Dawn told her, taking her elbow and almost dragging her inside.

Angelica entered slowly, her eyes traveling quickly from object to object. Even though the Mahoys had tried to keep their wealth from being obvious, it was still apparent that they were not struggling. The unexpected guest stopped in her tracks before the grand piano and ran a hand gently along the edge of its glossy black cabinet.

"Do you play?" Dawn asked gently. Angelica jumped as if a gun had gone off near her. She was dressed in a plain cotton dress that was utterly featureless except for a faux pearl necklace around her neck. Her coat was an unremarkable gray, exactly the wrong color on her in every way. Her clothing seemed to have been selected with the intent of shouting to everyone who saw her, 'I'm a nobody." But, her face was shining, and her bronzed blond hair brushed to the texture of fine gold. She looked more well and wholesome than Dawn had ever seen her.

Angelica laughed at the notion. "Who me? No, I don't have any notable talents," she said in her self-effacing way.

"You're too hard on yourself Angelica. One of your most obvious talents is humility. Another is your amazing ability to overcome incredible odds."

"You're far too generous with your compliments," Angelica returned earnestly, her voice somewhat breathy and childlike. "But, I'm thankful you think good things of me. Even I don't share your perspective, so don't be surprised if you are alone in your opinion of me."

Dawn frowned. "Oh, Angelica, cut that out. Let's make a rule here and now. When people come to visit I don't allow them to gossip or talk badly of my friends. That includes you. So, since you're my friend, you can't talk disparagingly about yourself. Do we have a deal?"

Angelica smiled broadly, and almost said something else defamatory, but swallowed it with effort. "OK," she said instead. Her tension was released, and she genuinely smiled.

Dawn steered her to a seat on the big sofa and sat near her. "To what do I owe the honor of your visit?" she asked kindly.

"Well, I'm not sure. I was just doing homework and this urging came over me to come visit you. I have to admit that it does frighten me to come here. But, you were the one who taught Connie to be obedient to the Holy Spirit, and she taught me, so here I am," she said with childlike simplicity, arching her shoulders as if she were helpless to do anything else.

Dawn was surprised by these words. She no longer felt as she once had about the Holy Spirit, or about obedience and faith, or actually anything else spiritual for that matter. Instead of commenting on that, she focused on something else. "Why would you feel frightened to come here? Am I such a terrifying person?"

"Oh, no, not at all!" Angelica said hurriedly, her words heavy-laden with apology. She swallowed hard, and her eyes darted from her hands to Dawn's face. "I'm afraid I've given you the wrong impression. You're not at all bad. It's not you, it's me."

Dawn gave her a meaningful look, and Angelica changed the thrust of her next statement. "What I mean is, I admire you so much, and so totally look up to you, that it's kind of like making an uninvited visit to the prophet or something. I just can hardly believe that you even let me in, let alone that you are sitting here talking to me like—like I was normal or something."

"I thought we discussed you talking down about my friends," Dawn reminded her in a kindly, but insistent voice.

"Sorry," Angelica muttered with her head lowered. "But it's true. You're everything I'm not. You're beautiful, you're good, you're happy, you're married to a wonderful man, you have beautiful children..."

"You have many blessings yourself," Dawn interjected forcefully.

"Oh yes, I do, I know I do." Angelica glanced up at her with longing eyes. "But you know what I mean. There *is* so much to admire about you that I feel out of place coming over."

"Well, put yourself at ease. I'm mortal. Perhaps more mortal than you are."

"I can't believe that!"

"It's true. I'll bet if you think about it, you can think of something wonderful you have that I don't," Dawn ventured.

"Oh, that's easy," Angelica proclaimed, then immediately bit her lip, pained that she had spoken so quickly.

Dawn smiled broadly, happy that Angelica had this wonderful possession. "Tell me. What wonderful thing do you have that I don't?" Dawn asked teasingly. She wanted to hear what this dear girl possessed she considered of such worth. With all her negative attitude toward herself, a self-generated compliment would be refreshing and therapeutic for her. "Come on, tell."

"I don't want to offend you."

"Why would it offend me? 'Fess up. Come on," Dawn coaxed.

"It isn't polite to flaunt your prized possessions under people's noses. Especially when those people have made it plain they don't think your prize is valuable. Please don't make me tell you," Angelica begged in complete seriousness.

Dawn pondered this for a moment. She did not want to make her guest uncomfortable but was quite certain that Angelica's well-being depended upon her being willing to give herself a compliment, no matter how minute it might be. Dawn decided to gently press the issue. "Angelica, now you've got me curious. Either you tell me, or I'm going to put salt in your Red Bush tea, instead of sugar!"

Angelica laughed at this, and then grew sober.

"I have a testimony," she said simply.

Dawn felt the smile fall from her face. Angelica's simple answer was so powerfully true that it cut to her heart, again and again. It was as if that simple sentence continued to echo back and forth across the room, striking her with each return.

"I think I'll get that tea now," Dawn said, rising.

Angelica was stricken with remorse. “Oh, Dawn, I’m so sorry. I didn’t want to tell you. I really didn’t. Now I’ve offended you, and I didn’t mean to. I really didn’t. I’ll leave now. I’m sooo sorry,” she insisted as she stood hurriedly, fumbling with her coat.

Dawn stopped mid-stride, nearly on the other side of the piano. This was all so unexpected, so innocent and truthful, that she suddenly yearned to put her young friend at ease.

“Angelica you spoke from your heart. Anyone who takes offense at another’s deepest feelings isn’t really their friend. Please allow me to be your friend, and never ever withhold from me the treasures of your heart. Come. Help me fix the tea. I would like you to tell me more about your treasure.” Three seconds earlier she could not have honestly said what she just did. But now, somehow, it was the truth.

Angelica almost ran to her side. Dawn put her arm through hers and started for the big porcelain monument she called her kitchen.

“I know you remember what I was like not long ago,” Angelica began. “I had nothing, less than nothing, not even hope or self-respect. The very first thing I ever had, ever felt that was good, ever possessed that was special, was a testimony. It was the beginning of my resurrection. And, Dawn, I got it mostly from you. You are my hero, my inspiration in all those dark days.”

“Why from me?” she asked, genuinely perplexed. “Why not from Connie, or Fred?”

“Connie and Fred are awesome! They had a lot to do with my recovery, but they had their own road to travel. In my eyes, you were a saint. I wanted to be like you so badly that I was willing to risk everything to achieve it.”

“I didn’t know you had observed that Connie and Fred were on their own journey.”

“Give me a little credit,” Angelica laughed. “No, you were my ideal, my rock-solid example. No matter what else ever happens, I will always love you for that.”

Dawn was silent for a long moment. “Angelica, would you do me a favor?” she asked with a lump in her throat.

“I will if I can, but I’m not very . . .” she said, then added, “Sorry.”

Dawn ignored that. “I would like you to come over here every day and remind me of what you just said. Would you do that for me?”

Angelica spun to face her. “Do you mean it? Can I really do that? Oh, Dawn, it would mean so much to me! You just can’t imagine how much it would bless my life to come over here every day and talk about my testimony. I would so love to do that!"

"I was thinking more of it blessing my life. You're the one with the testimony, remember?" Dawn said, almost under her breath.

"Oh, fiddlesticks," Angelica said dismissively. "You have a testimony. You've just buried it beneath your pain. Believe me, I'm an expert on pain. It has a way of burying almost everything worthwhile. I can tell you *all* about it."

"I'm looking forward to that," Dawn admitted.

"Me too. Oh, me too, Dawn. I can't wait! You are so beautiful, and good, and even regal—you have always seemed like royalty to me."

Dawn laughed. "Sam still calls me 'Princess' sometimes! But my real name is 'Dawn,' as in the rising of the sun."

Angelica tried to say "Dawn" with the same elongated vowels of Dawn's accent. She wasn't particularly successful. "I love your accent, too! Someone told me you grew up in a castle. Is that true?"

"It was a replica of a castle."

"Wow..." Angelica exclaimed with childlike wonder. "And you grew up a princess in a castle..."

The afternoon following Angelica's visit passed slowly for Dawn. Her new friend had gone home shortly after their conversation, and she had pondered on that special visit for hours thereafter. What startled her most wasn't what Angelica had said to her, so much as what she had said to Angelica. When faced with wounding so delicate a soul as Angelica, Dawn could not allow it to happen; and the most potent remedy had been the truth. The truth was that Dawn was starved, nearly spiritually emaciated for want of spiritual food. Once her pride had taken second seat to her love of Angelica, it took third seat to her need for spiritual sustenance, and then forth, and fifth, until that once-stubborn pride now hardly existed within her.

Good to her word, Angelica came over nearly every day thereafter. In time she and Dawn became special friends, connected by a great spiritual unity. Small miracles began to occur—that is, if any miracle can really be called small. Not only did Dawn's pain soften so that her testimony found its way to the surface and once again grew in splendor, but Angelica herself achieved the full bloom of spiritual and emotional maturity. Dawn's affection and admiration were like water on a desert flower. Angelica's soul devoured these new feelings of worth, and where once stood barren sands of self-loathing, now grew a lush garden of rich personal worth.

Had you asked Angelica, she would have told you she gave very little to Dawn, and had gained a million dollars in return. But Dawn, Sam knew from long conversations with her, thought exactly the same of Angelica. She viewed Angelica almost as her salvation. In her heart, Angelica held a place right next to the courageous young missionary who had found her in the castle of her childhood and taught her the gospel. The parallels were intriguing to Dawn, for in both cases, her teachers had had to scale both figurative and actual castle walls, behind both of which she had foolishly run to hide.

Several weeks later, Sam came home tired and emotionally drained. Now that he no longer traveled to Washington, the growing business was proving to be more involved than he had anticipated. Sam asked himself a hundred times a day why he had expanded. It couldn't have been for the money; they already had more than they needed, or could consume in their lifetime.

Dawn had a nice dinner waiting, which they ate while engaging with the twins in small talk. It always struck Sam how the intellectual level of the dinner conversation fell to the age of the youngest at the table. With the girls always present, their dinner topics evolved around their latest adventures with their stuffed animals or some new toy that they had their eyes on. It always made him smile; it was the perfect cure for a long day.

After dinner Sam helped clean up the kitchen and then wandered aimlessly to his spot on the big couch near the piano. He picked up the newspaper, read a few lines, and laid it back down. He seldom enjoyed reading the news and felt unusually repelled by it tonight. It was one of those nights when he honestly would have just snapped on the TV and vegetated.

However, they didn't own a television. Dawn had grown up in a world without television, and she simply saw no need for it. They had owned one for a while, and when she saw how much time was wasted, and how much family interaction was foolishly sucked into the black hole of TV, she simply took the matter into her own hands.

Sam had come home one day to find they no longer owned one. It had taken him about six weeks to learn to survive happily without it. Now, instead of sitting in a trance before the tube, he played with the girls, studied the gospel, wrote music, kept his journal up-to-date, and teased his wife until she had to kiss him long and hard to shut him up. He was a hard-won convert, but now solidly behind their (actually her) decision to eliminate the one-eyed monster from their home.

The twins were in bed, or more accurately on their beds jumping, when Dawn joined him on the sofa. She often sought him out, and his heart grew a little fonder of her every time she sat beside him. He looked at her and smiled. She smiled back, cocking her head to one side. It was her unconscious signal that she was either going to tease him or ask some earth-shattering question.

"Explain something to me, would you?"

"Something is a noun. It's used to specify anything not clearly defined, an indefinite quantity, or… ooof!"

She had punched him in the side. "I'm serious now."

"How was I supposed to know?" Sam protested innocently. "You give me the same look when you are about to tease me."

"I do?" she asked, genuinely surprised he had her looks mapped well enough to identify what she was planning.

Sam grinned at her. "Well, usually. Anyway, what is it you want me to explain? I probably don't know any more about it than you do."

"On this subject you do."

"OK then, what is it?"

Dawn grew earnest. "Why is it that you have let almost a year go by without us studying the scriptures together?"

Sam stared at her, shocked. "What?" he asked in total surprise.

"Don't you realize that the Prophet has instructed married couples to study the scriptures together every night?"

"I…I…" he stammered.

"As the highest priesthood authority in this home, I think you should repent and do your duty."

"But…"

"Here are your scriptures," Dawn said as she laid his books in his lap. "And, here are mine. If it's not too much trouble, I would really like to hear you read. I think I'm a little starved for spiritual food, and hearing your voice reminds me of the days when you taught me. OK?"

"Well… sure. I—"

"Start at the first verse in First Nephi," she urged gently. "I'll tell you when to stop."

During that evening read Sam had frequent difficulty reading the words because of a pesky water problem in his eyes. Every time he blinked, it seemed more tears showed up. He read to her for a long time. During the entire reading she sat with her head resting gently on his shoulder. It seemed she was having water problems, too.

Before going to bed Sam sat down at the piano and wrote a happy love song. It was warm sunshine after a summer shower and sparkles of sunlight on the lake in the early morning. It was sweet and gentle, and it warmed his heart to write it. The song was only a tiny part of the great love he was feeling, but even that small part was sufficient to put to music. "A Little Love Song" was published a short time later.

It had now been almost two years since Sam had been summarily released as bishop. Since Dawn's miraculous return from her self-imposed exile, Sam had scarcely given his sudden release a thought. Considering how great an outpouring of blessings had come to him since that day, he hardly felt as if the trials had been for naught. In some ways, he was even grateful. Deep reflection had revealed that he surely would not have achieved the greatest of these—his beautiful experience beyond the veil—had he not been tried in the fires of awful adversity.

At some future date he hoped to fully understand the process whereby great blessings are bestowed, and the price required to receive them. For now, he only knew that those great trials were an important part of his blessings. He knew his response to those trials, however unjust they may have seemed at the time, was what had been important. In some way completely unplanned, unrehearsed and unanticipated, he had chosen faithfulness, and sweet had been the resultant blessings.

Almost like a mother delivered of her first child, Sam was inclined to say, "I don't ever want to go through that again! But, look how beautiful a child it has brought us."

Dawn awoke nauseated early one morning, and after throwing up, returned to bed, shaken.

"I think I'm pregnant," she said mournfully.

"Really? Oh wow sweetheart, that's wonderful!" Sam proclaimed. He gathered her into his arms and kissed her gently. She lay back down and snuggled against him.

"I'm afraid," she said quietly.

"Afraid? Oh, I know you had problems last time, but this time we'll be better prepared. We'll have the best doctors, and we'll…"

"Not about that," she interrupted him.

"What then?"

"About what I told you earlier, my feeling I would not have more than two babies."

"I remember now. You were afraid you would die, or something?"

"I have always known I would only have two children, and after that I wouldn't live to have a third. I don't know why, but I just believe it." Her voice was small and pensive.

"Dawn, this is just your imagination," Sam assured her forcefully.

"Perhaps, but it's been part of my imagination since I was a small girl."

"Well, that only shows you how silly it is. You're still laboring under some dark childhood fear. Probably it comes from losing your own mother so young."

"It could be," she allowed quietly.

"Let's change the subject," Sam urged. He didn't like this one at all. "When are you going to go see the doctor?"

"I have an appointment tomorrow. I've been suspecting this for about three weeks now."

Sam was elated. "I am so happy about this, Dawn! Everything will be wonderful. You'll see!"

"I love you," she told him quietly. It was music to his soul.

The doctor appointment went well. Doctor Green said her health was good, and this birth should be a normal delivery. Both Sam and Dawn were encouraged. Still, in spite of all the hopeful words they spoke to one another, Dawn never forgot her fear. For that matter, neither did Sam.

Even though Sam did not believe his wife's fears to be based in reality, yet the fact that she believed them so strongly worried him. He had heard of people actually making their own fears come to pass simply by fixating upon them. He discussed this with her at length, and urged her to keep her eyes on the happy birth of this child.

Sam came home one day to find her writing in her journal. Dawn was not comfortable using the computer, so she kept her journal in a bound book by her bed. He could tell by where the ribbon was placed that she had written quite a bit that day.

Summer that year was unusually rainy and bleak. Late in August, the sun broke through for three glorious weeks and temperatures soared into the upper 70's—hot for that time of year in Alaska. Everywhere one looked people stampeded toward the mountains and lakes. For a civilization tucked inside a perpetual forest, the call of their mountains was heard and obeyed. For days a non-stop caravan of motor homes, boats, and trailers loaded with three-wheelers and canoes streamed toward the hills.

Dawn was about seven months along, and feeling awkward. She was healthy and in good spirits, but it was hard for her to drive, and she dreaded the trip to the doctor. Sam came home from work around noon to drive her. They swung by his parents' home and dropped off the twins, now ridiculously mature for their seven years.

Sam drove down the crowded Parks highway to its intersection with the Glenn Highway. The Parks highway wound slowly north to Fairbanks, and was popular with tourists who were anxious to see the beautiful lakes, campgrounds, rivers rich with fish, and Denali Park. Both Sam and Dawn felt relieved to get past the bumper-to-bumper traffic and turn on to the Glenn Highway toward Palmer.

Sam sped up in the lighter traffic and relaxed. They had just reached the speed limit of 55 when a pickup pulled out behind them to pass. Sam was surprised the truck wanted by, but the road was straight and nearly empty. He held his speed as the truck quickly pulled by them. The truck was a new Ford pickup with a matching camper shell, and an aluminum canoe tied to the top. Just as it pulled in front of them Sam glanced at the thick dust on the tailgate of the pickup. What he saw caused his heart to lurch in terror.

"That canoe doesn't look like it's tied down very well," Dawn commented.

"I think you're right. I'm going to slow…"

At that moment the leading rope on the canoe broke and the canoe launched almost straight upward, flipped completely over, and for a moment seemed to hover in the air like a kite, still secured to the truck by the last rope. Sam applied his brakes severely just as the last rope broke. The end of the canoe hit the pavement and began cart wheeling through the air. Sam locked the wheels of the Thunderbird and skidded out of control. They had almost come to a stop when the bow of the flying canoe hit the hood of their car and sliced toward Sam. Instinctively he swerved to the left at the last second, which caused the canoe to strike the windshield right in front of Dawn.

The canoe broke through the windshield in a spray of glass.

"Princess!" Sam yelled toward his wife, in this moment of panic addressing her by the nickname she had used years before.

Dawn screamed and Sam turned just in time to see the canoe stop a few inches short of her. She turned toward him. Sam had expected to see fear, panic, anything but what he saw. She was smiling, a look of peace on her face.

Sam looked back to the road but could only see the canoe on the hood. They were still skidding forward. He looked out the side window to see that they were in the oncoming lane of traffic. He pumped the brakes to regain control, and brought the heavy car back into their lane. At that exact moment, a car whizzed by them in the opposite lane with its horn blaring.

"That was close!" Sam cried, feeling a moment of relief. But then a sudden impact stopped their car with finality. Even wearing a seat belt Sam was thrown forward, his face hitting something unyielding. Blackness overcame him, and then there was nothing.

Sam awoke three days later in the hospital in which the twins had been born. He slowly gained consciousness to find himself looking into his mother Laura's face. She was stroking his arms, saying his name, urging him to wake up. His mouth felt like it was stuffed with cotton. He tried to speak, and found it impossible.

He watched in a blur of pain as a nurse carefully opened his mouth and removed something from inside. It seemed to be a block of plastic like a football mouth guard. He had used one many times playing football. He tried to move his arms and found them pinned to the bed by straps.

"What happened?" Sam mumbled hoarsely as soon as he could speak. His tongue explored his mouth to find nothing where it belonged. His mouth tasted bloody, and his breath was foul, even to him. He began to panic.

"Keep your tongue still," the nurse instructed, "or I'll have to put the mouthpiece back in. You have extensive injuries to your face. Your upper and lower jaws are broken, and you have many loose teeth. You're going to heal completely, so don't worry. Your injuries are not life-threatening. Our only concern was that you may not wake from your coma. Now that you're awake, you are out of danger." She gave him a faint smile. "You can talk if you speak slowly. But don't push with your tongue against your teeth. Do you understand?"

Sam tried to nod and found his head restrained by a stiff brace on his neck.

"Where'th Dawn?" he demanded, trying to not move his tongue. It was very hard to do, yet easy to remember as the slightest movements by his tongue against his teeth shot sharp pains inside his head.

"You were hit by a canoe. Do you remember?" his mother asked earnestly.

"Yeth. I rememberrr the canoe flyink thhhrough the air. It almotht hit Dawn in the chetht. It wath very clowth," he said laboriously, suppressing a sigh.

"The canoe did hit Dawn," his mother said softly.

"No! I thaw it. It stopped jutht thort of her. It didn't hit her. I wath there!" Sam insisted.

"When you changed lanes, the pickup truck had stopped in the road. You ran into the back of it…"

"I did?" he asked quietly. This was all unknown to him. Then he remembered the sudden impact after he had changed lanes.

"Ith my wife OK? I want to talk to her," he insisted.

There was a long silence. Sam tried to look into his mother's face, but without contacts could not see her clearly. Even in the blur, he could see grief etched on her face.

Laura placed a hand on his chest. "Dawn was killed in the accident," she said softly. "I'm sorry. I'm so, so sorry," she barely managed to say through her tears.

"Oh no! Dawn…." he cried. "Dawn, my Printheth….pleathe don't be dead! Pleathe! I need you… Oh no! Printheth….." Sam sobbed uncontrollably until the nurse did something to his IV, and sleep took him away. The last image he remembered before oblivion rescued him was a large "22" drawn in the dust on the tailgate of the pickup.

Her funeral was delayed for two weeks so Sam could attend. He came in a wheelchair, his face bandaged from his eyes down. Sam had insisted on seeing her. The funeral director had flatly refused, locked the casket, and walked away. Sam was inconsolable, and tears soaked his bandages until they were sliding down his face, stinging his wounds. He did not care. He simply did not care.

The twins were still with Grandma Laura, and just barely able to understand what had happened. Sam had not seen them in the hospital. Everyone, including his mother, thought they would be too frightened by his swollen eyes and halting speech. They saw him for the first time in two weeks there at the funeral and ran to him crying. For the first time his own grief relented, and he saw the deep wounds inside his girls. He knew at that moment as surely as he had ever known anything, that he had to rise above his own grief, and stand firmly for his young daughters, or their loss would be too great.

He gathered his daughters lovingly onto his lap and wrapped his arms around them. They snuggled carefully against his bandaged chest and whimpered softly. He remembered the grief he had felt when his little brother Jimmy had died, and could only imagine that their loss was exponentially greater. His sorrow turned from self-pity to empathy, and the healing quietly began.

Sam's legs and arms were undamaged, and he was able to hold the girls all through the service. He had had nothing to do with arranging the program and was surprised how many people came. Sam did not recognize the somber-faced older man who offered his hand.

"I'm very sorry," he said, and choked back a sob. "Dawn really loved you." It wasn't until Sam heard his distinct British accent that Sam realized whose hand he was shaking.

"Brother Pawley!" Sam exclaimed, both happy and sad. Besides he and the twins, this man, Dawn's father, was undoubtedly the most shaken by her passing.

"Yes, it's me. And for the record, I haven't joined your church yet," he replied in a halfhearted attempt at humor.

"I didn't…"

"I know. You have always called me 'Brother.' I would have been disappointed had you called me anything else. We were the two men who loved her most in this whole world. At least in that respect, we are brothers," he said quietly.

"She often spoke of you in loving words," Sam said honestly.

"Every letter she wrote me," her father said, "she mentioned how much she loved you. If only you hadn't taken her . . ." his voice trailed off in sadness tinged with deep regret at having said something to further Sam's pain. Sam's befuddled mind clearly registered the sadness, but missed the regret. He simply heaped further blame and self-loathing upon himself for his wife's death.

The service was healing and uplifting. Beth and Angela, Sam's sisters, sang a beautiful duet of Sam's song "I Have Always Loved You." It was a powerful tribute to both Dawn and to Sam. Few people there had previously known that Sam had written that haunting melody. For Sam this song struck a huge tone of irony in his soul. He had certainly never intended, or even suspected, it might someday be part of his wife's funeral farewell.

Sam's father, James Mahoy, delivered the main address and eulogy. Sam had never heard his father speak more eloquently, nor with greater conviction. There was such power in his words, such healing, that Sam began to feel his burden lifting. There was no lifting of his sense of loss, but the grief of untimely parting was at least temporarily eased. Much more importantly, the searing burden of guilt lost some of its steely grip upon his soul.

"I have often pondered," his father was saying, "the timing of life, how it is that a young mother, loved and needed, would be called home to

Heavenly Father in the prime of her life. I don't know the answer to that question. As pressing as it may seem at this moment, I don't need to know the answer. In fact, it is largely irrelevant.

"But I can say with absolute finality that her passing is not untimely, nor is it the effect of dark fate, or the random workings of chance. It is not hateful, evil, or forever. And, though her passing may have been the result of some evil scheme of unseen enemies, she left this life because it was her time to leave. She left this life because she was called home. She left this world because, in some way unknown to us, it meshes with that plan being played out under the divine guidance of a loving and all-knowing God.

"In a day yet distant, glorious and holy, Dawn shall rise from the earth into which we will shortly place her. She will hear the trumpeted call of the Savior as He comes to reclaim His own, and she will arise, restored to youth and beauty, to her perfect and proper form, and will rise to join Him who she loved and served in the days of her probation on earth. In that great day, we will join her there, and our love and joyous association will resume as if it had never paused.

"May God bless us that we so live that we rise to her station, and there dwell eternally in love, where the tears we shed today only empower the joy we shall then enjoy, is my prayer in Jesus's holy name, Amen."

Dawn's father returned to the Hilton Hotel immediately after the service. He did not go to the grave dedication but simply vanished without explanation.

He paced back and forth in deep agitation before grabbing the phone from the hook and dialing a long series of numbers. When the answer came he hissed into the phone, barely able to force rational words past his hatred.

"I want you to find the two hell-spawned demons who killed my daughter by their incredible stupidity and make sure it was their last act in mortality. Make sure they clearly understand my displeasure as they are leaving this world. Then, I want you to find everyone who had any knowledge of this insane "22" campaign and banish them from my employ. Tell them only silence will keep them alive. Inform them that if I hear one word of this floating on the wind, *all* their lives will be worth nothing! Then, I want you to contact my lawyer and find out what legal means are open to me to bring my granddaughters back to South Africa *where they belong*. Do I make myself clear? I'll be there in a few days, and I want results!" He slammed the receiver home.

Only a few miles away, special agent Chris Holt punched the recorder off and pulled the headphones from his head. Before speaking he carefully placed a large black cowboy hat upon his black hair. He looked at his partner, Alan Reed, and frowned.

"Now, all we gotta do is figure out what to do with this. In reality, he has committed no crime on US soil that we can prove. Conspiracy in a foreign country to harass someone in the States, even if it goes sour and turns to murder, is hardly the kind of thing one could hope to successfully prosecute. Besides being insane, the man is obviously insanely rich. His attorneys would have him back on a plane before the ink was dry on an arrest warrant." He shook his head regretfully. "I'm afraid there's nothing we can do, even though he's as guilty as hell itself," he muttered.

Sam moved back into his parent's home until he was able to care for himself again. His mouth had to be wired shut, and he was unable to speak or eat for six full weeks. His only food came through a straw, and consisted entirely of liquids. In those weeks following his accident he lost forty pounds. During this whole time he was listless, and only brightened when his daughters came into the room.

Though they occasionally asked about their mother, and wanted to know details about what it was like where she now lived, the twins accepted their loss with greater resilience than Sam ever could. In time, they became his comfort, his joy, and his emotional road map.

Even after his jaw was healed and the wires holding it shut were removed, swelling prevented Sam from opening his mouth wide enough to push anything between his teeth. His doctors urged him to patience, and to gently working his jaw. It finally began to move without pain on the morning of November 23rd, Thanksgiving Day. He awoke late in the morning with the realization that his jaw was no longer completely immobile. He arose quickly, ran to the bathroom and gratefully brushed his teeth. He carefully brushed everything, savoring the sweet cleanliness. He finally stopped only because his gums began to bleed from the scrubbing.

He went downstairs to find preparations fully underway for Thanksgiving. The smells in the house were a tapestry of fine spices. His mouth watered, and his jaws ached for something to chew. He found a dinner roll newly removed from the oven, and slowly ate it one tiny piece at a time. Oddly, his tongue seemed to have lost its natural ability to coordinate with his teeth, and he bit it regularly. But the rhythm returned easily, and he savored the sweet bread as if it were manna.

By the time dinner was served Sam's stomach was rumbling, and he truly felt grateful for the bounty before him. He cut tiny pieces of food, and inserted them between his teeth, still not fully separated. He chewed each bite, savoring the texture of solid food once again. Perhaps from nerve damage, his lips lacked strength, and would not close firmly enough to clean his fork. He didn't mind, and periodically cleaned his fork on a napkin. By the time he had sampled the food on his plate, he was full. He had eaten a small fraction of his normal fare. His stomach had shrunken on a completely liquid diet.

It required two major surgeries and several minor ones to restore Sam's face to its previous condition. When these were all completed his only remaining deficiency was a slightly lopsided smile. Several muscles on the left side of his face were no longer able to pull his left side into a complete smile. Since he hardly felt like smiling anymore anyway, he decided it was a disability he could live with.

Sam and the twins moved back into the big house a little before Christmas. They all dreaded the move. They felt comfortable and loved at Grandma and Grandpa's. Yet, they all knew, especially Sam, they could not exist as a family unless they lived in their own home. Sam didn't want the twins to feel their mother's loss even more keenly by returning to the one place that would constantly remind them of her. Yet, he did want them to finish their mourning and get on with their lives in a healthy way. That meant not prolonging the inevitable sorrow of moving back into the house whose every feature reminded them of their mother. It was something they could not escape, but delaying the inevitable would only made it more difficult.

Christmastime without Dawn was hollow, but Sam kept every holiday tradition. They put up the tree, decorated the house inside and out, bought and wrapped special gifts, played Christmas music, and spent long, quiet evenings together remembering what it used to be like, and trying to recapture the old happy feelings.

It was New Year's Eve when Sam found her diary. For reasons not clear to him, Dawn had placed it in the night stand on his side of the bed. For as many years as they had been together, the thick book with the red leather binding stayed inside her night stand. He had hardly thought of it until he stumbled across it that night.

He sat for a long time on the edge of the bed and held the book in his lap. He had always considered her privacy a sacred trust, and he felt a little guilty opening it now. Yet, he felt certain she had placed it there so he would find and read it. His heart leapt up into his throat when he saw her flowery script covering the many pages. She had written far more than he had suspected. The book was nearly full of her careful handwriting.

He started at the beginning and read her innermost hopes, dreams and expectations. He learned things, things he had never known about her. He read about her love of lilacs. He read about her aching love for him prior to their marriage, and of her fear he would never love her in return.

He read page after page of her complete astonishment when he had asked her to marry him. He suddenly realized that moment had been the highlight of her life, and those words had banished hopelessness from her soul.

He laughed at the things she thought funny, felt sick inside at her descriptions of her loss of faith, and rejoiced with her in her return to hope. He learned to see Angelica through her eyes, and to love her for the gentle urgings that had brought Dawn back into faith and testimony again. There was a little poem about being pregnant. She had written words to a song about the twins with a note that it was to be sung to the tune of "I Wonder When He Comes Again."

He was surprised to find that Dawn considered their big home to be an extension of him. She saw in the big building an echo of Sam's strength, a reflection of his hopes for a larger-than-life marriage and family. She wrote of her love for him, and spoke candidly of his failings and weakness. He was astounded to find that in many respects, she knew him even better than he knew himself.

It was nearly morning before he came to the pages written just prior to her death. He was surprised to find the last entry addressed to him.

> My Beloved Sam,
>
> That you are reading this means that your heart must be broken. For the last few weeks I have known with increasing surety that I have but a few days left in this life. How I have wanted to hold you during the time we have remaining to us, to merge with you, if such a thing were possible, and to become an indistinguishable part of you.
>
> Yet, it was not possible, and every time I tried to tell you of my growing sense of imminent departure, you didn't want to believe. I don't blame you, and I understand why you turned your mind aside from what I alone felt to be true. I hope you remember these last few weeks with joy, as I know I will. They were sweet and special, and they held our finest love.
>
> Sam, I love you. I know I hurt you many times, and for this I am more sorry than you can know. I want you to know that even when

I couldn't feel it because of my own pain and poor choices, I never stopped loving you.

I don't think you grasp the grandeur of my love for you. I see you almost like a savior. You found me in a lost and worldly condition and saw through that. I have occasionally found myself blushing as I think of myself standing there in that tiny bikini, answering the door to two Mormon missionaries. I was so confident, so sure of my beauty, so willing to display my body. I realize now that all I expected of you then was to lust after me. At that time in my life it seemed enough.

I still don't know how you did it, but you saw past my skin and glimpsed something eternal, and far more beautiful than flesh. You brought me faith and joy in my Savior. Besides all that, you saved my life in England, brought me to America, provided for my needs, cared about me, gave me two beautiful daughters, taught me faith and obedience, and even best, grew to love me as much as I love you. I shall eternally be grateful for all you have given me.

Sam, I suppose nobody knows for sure when they will die. But this feeling is very strong, so I am writing what may well be the last entry in my journal to thank you for our life together. The baby inside me is happy and active. Every time he moves, I think of you. I know he would be proud to come to your family, and to be raised by his father. But, I do not believe he will ever have this privilege. I'm not sure how these things work, but I believe this is his mortal experience. When I go back home I will take him with me. Don't grieve for us, it is the way it should be.

Sam had to stop here to wait for his eyes to again focus through his tears. He had not known she felt this way about the baby she carried, nor that she was certain it was a boy. After the accident, the doctor had told him their unborn child had been male. She had been buried with her baby's body still inside her. It is the way she would have wanted it.

I have a request of you. Please speak my name often to our daughters. When you speak of me be happy, laugh at the silly things I did, and teach them from my mistakes. Always tell them how much I love them, and how I always will. I know you will teach them that they will see me again, and this is a great comfort to me. Even though my faith has faltered at times, I do believe these things with all my heart.

This is especially important to me because of my next request. It is my deepest desire that you find another companion. I know the idea of it may seem like betrayal to you now. But, in time, when the hurt has healed, you will come to understand why. There is a purpose in all of this.

Sam, I know that you love me too much to fault me even in the things where I am very weak. You know I am not as spiritually alive as you are. I am quite certain that most, if not all, of my spirituality came from you. I can't even guess what the eternities will hold. I only know that in this world, after I am gone, you need to love again.

You will come to feel, as I do, that all the purposes for our meeting, loving and marrying have been fulfilled. I accept that it is my time to leave this world because of some grand premortal plan for this life, which has now reached an end.

I want you to know that my preparations are complete. I am at peace, and ready to move on. I shall miss you and my sweet daughters deeply, but shall not be far away either. I know I have accomplished everything in this life I was sent here to do. It is my time to depart.

Farewell until we meet again,
Dawn

P.S. I almost forgot. The answer to a little secret lies here.
Banque de Zurich 8521553-35 Zurich, Switzerland.

When Lisa and Bonnie arose the next day they found their father sitting on his bed, a leather-bound book in his lap, his face streaked with tears. Even as young as they were, they could tell that these were sweet tears of tender farewell.

4

FIRE IN THE HOLE

Perhaps it was the promise she had made to Theodore. Perhaps it was her own curiosity that brought Melody to the church that Sunday evening. Whatever these motivations were, they were secondary to the profound gratitude she felt that the charges against her had been dropped, and the fact that she knew somehow Theodore had been involved, though he loudly denied it. The news had come simply and suddenly. Everyone she knew claimed complete, though joyful, ignorance of why it had occurred. In any case, she was truly grateful. She found that she wanted to play in a church—any church, as a token of her gratitude to God for his miraculous intervention in her affairs.

She had prepared several pieces, hoping to make an appropriate selection when she saw the nature and tone of the gathering.

She and her sister Marcia, who accompanied her, had never been to Saint Michael's Anglican Church before, and were quite pleased to find a fine old cathedral built in the late 1800's. It wasn't at all large, barely seating 300 parishioners on hand-carved pews under a precipitous balcony that clung to three sides of the very tall hall. It was stunningly beautiful inside with exquisite craftsmanship and stained glass windows that stretched gracefully from floor to ceiling.

Melody and Marcia were greeted at the door by an elderly cleric who smiled warmly upon seeing her.

"Miss Melody MacUlvaney, I presume?" Melody nodded slowly, a Mona Lisa smile on her face. "I'm Father Alan Culkins. It is so nice of you to come. Theodore asked me to greet you and escort you to your seat. Will you be playing this evening?"

"Yes," she replied simply.

"Wonderful." He turned to Marcia, and motioning to a younger priest near the door to the chapel, said, "Father Winston will help you find a seat as near the front as you like. Melody, if you would please follow me?" he asked with deep obeisance, pointing to his right.

The old priest led the way through an arched door and turned down a poorly lit hallway of polished stone. They walked a long distance passing doors on her right. Several were opened slightly to reveal classrooms and offices. They came to a short flight of stairs. He ascended these, turned left and opened a narrow door. Melody stepped out to find herself directly beside the console of a big pipe organ. He helped her to a seat on the very first row of what appeared to be several dozen choir seats between the organ and pulpit. He suggested she get out her violin now, and indicated that she could go into the hallway and tune it if she wished.

Melody did as suggested and returned to her seat. She was sitting a few steps below the pulpit, which presided over the congregation from behind an ornate railing. Everywhere she looked she saw an opulence that both enthralled and troubled her. Her seat was narrow and straight-backed, and richly though uncomfortably upholstered with a deep maroon brocade fabric which seemed to Melody to be more for appearance than to add to the comfort of the chair. It felt more like a witness box than a choir seat. The railing was nearly six feet from her knees, and high enough that she could not see the first dozen rows of the congregation some ten feet below her. Had she slouched in her seat at all, she would have been invisible to people in the congregation. She noted that quite a few parishioners were now entering the hall. Theodore was nowhere to be seen.

At exactly eight p.m. Father Culkins entered, accompanied by four elderly men in priestly attire. His fellow clerics sat directly behind the pulpit while Father Culkins walked to the pulpit and pulled the microphone to his height.

"My friends, thank you for coming this evening. Let us pray," he said, and lowered his head.

After a brief prayer he continued, "We will be pleased to hear two doctoral dissertations this evening. But first we are delighted to have Miss Melody McUlvany with us this evening to perform on the violin. Following her selection we will be pleased to hear from Doctor Theodore Tennison. Following his offering, we will hear from Doctor Eric Spry. Miss MacUlvaney," he said, turning and motioning toward her with an outstretched palm.

Melody stood and walked near the railing. She raised her violin and played Bach's "Jesu Joy of Man's Desiring." As she played, she felt as if this music had been written for that very moment in time, and had been waiting several hundred years just to be played then and there. The melodic harmonies swelled to fill the old cathedral with astonishing beauty. The music seemed to continue on even after she lowered her bow. She returned to her seat in the reverent hush that followed. She hadn't considered that no one might clap following the performance. The sustained silence was greater praise for the rare beauty she had just created than any amount of applause could have been.

She sat and bowed her head, waiting for Theodore to take the pulpit. She raised her head to the swish of silken robes and looked up to see Theodore walking past, his eyes turned toward her. Though he did not turn his head, he winked surreptitiously at her. It made her smile, but ever so soberly. Her eyes slid from his nearly expressionless face to the collar above his robes. It was the collar of a priest. The term Doctor of Philosophy suddenly meshed with all else he had told her. He was indeed employed by the Church as a "caretaker of sorts."

She understood very little of what he said, though she listened closely, except that he spoke with passion and conviction. It was almost as if the message emanated from his soul, rather than the tidy bundle of papers before him. When he was done, she felt rejuvenated, though she had not comprehended his message. In a way quite rare, she found herself in love with someone she had but moments before barely known, someone she was quite sure had somehow wrought an impossible miracle in delivering her from the clutches of the law. In her young heart, hero worship felt like love, and love felt to her like a home, and safety she had never known.

Almost as if on a great downbeat by some demented conductor, the symphony of Sam's life came to a crashing, disharmonic conclusion. Dawn's death seemed to trigger a mechanism in the great, mindless grinder of the Federal Government. It was a mere six weeks following her funeral that two men climbed the stairs to the Princess Gems offices above the bank. The secretary showed them to Sam's door. They identified themselves as agents with the IRS.

"You haven't responded to our letters," they accused, after terse introductions.

"I was in the hospital for nearly a month, and convalescing for six weeks beyond that," Sam explained.

"Don't you have employees to handle such things?"

"I do, but we just closed our doors during that time. I haven't had the heart to dig through the pile of mail. So much of it is addressed to her…" his voice trailed off.

"We sympathize with your loss, Mr. Mahoy." The steely cutting edge of threat fatally lacerated whatever sympathy his voice held. "However, we now need to inquire into the details of your wife's foreign business activities. Do you want to do that now? Or, should we make another appointment with your attorney or accountant?"

“I suppose now is just as well,” Sam said wearily. He didn’t have any reason to delay. He had faithfully filed every report and tax return required by every governmental agency of which he was aware. He hoped to put this issue to rest in short order.

Both men set their briefcases on their laps, took out big pads, and moved their chairs toward his desk. The older man seemed to be about fifty, while the other was in his early thirties. The elder of the two smiled in a way that somehow missed his eyes, and began.

“Dawn Pawley Mahoy was your wife?”

“Yes, she was,” Sam responded unhappily. The “was” part of that sentence still stung him

deeply.

“Was she a citizen of the United States?”

“No,” Sam replied. “She was a citizen of South Africa, although she had permanent residency in the United States. We applied for US citizenship, but it had not been granted before her death.”

“Did she file US taxes?”

Sam nodded. “Of course. You should have all that in your records. We filed every year.”

“Did she have any overseas bank accounts or signature authority for any foreign bank accounts?” he asked, ignoring Sam’s previous answer.

“She did bank some money overseas,” Sam replied evenly. “Our company maintains foreign bank accounts to support our international business activities.”

“Do you have records of your foreign business transactions and bank activity that we could examine, and take copies of?”

Sam thought about this for a moment. He was suddenly aware that to his knowledge Dawn had not kept records of those transactions, and had in fact been somewhat cryptic about both how much she banked, and with whom. Until seconds ago he had merely thought of her actions as mysterious in a cute and harmless sort of way. He knew she had some grand plan that she would unveil at some point, and none of it worried him—until now.

“I would have to discuss that question with my accountant, and with a tax attorney,” Sam replied, knowing even as he spoke the words that his accountants knew even less than he did about her overseas transactions. Suddenly, he had a very bad feeling about where this was all headed.

The younger man leaned forward. “Are you aware that all income earned by a person residing in the United States must be reported and taxed inside this country? To transfer money to an off-shore account without paying taxes due is a crime."

Sam could not have known that this last statement was not entirely true. All of the monies in those accounts had, in fact, been earned through transactions outside of the States, through businesses residing entirely within other countries, and not in Dawn's name. His unfortunate answer would cost him literally millions. "I understand that. I have no idea what Dawn did with those accounts. But, I can show you records for every dime we earned. We paid taxes on it all," Sam protested.

The young man's eyes narrowed.

"Mr. Mahoy, we have international bank records showing significant amounts of money being moved through overseas accounts. We have no record of US or foreign taxes being paid on those transactions, and we believe some of that activity relates to income that would be subject to tax in the United States. Your wife, your former wife, made all of those transfers. Although some international transactions may not be subject to U.S. tax, adequate business records have to be maintained to support both your US tax returns and the US Treasury reports that have been filed. Without adequate support, all of the bank transactions could get pulled into your business and personal tax liabilities."

Sam stared at him, his mind reeling. The young man coughed slightly and continued, "While you may not even have been aware of those transactions, and have no criminal culpability in the matter, your wife may have actually placed you in a situation where you may now be liable for federal taxes on the international transactions since you filed joint tax returns and owned the business together. Her estate consists of her interest in this business, your home and other assets, and any bank accounts bearing hers, or both your names. Do you see where this is headed?"

"Clearly," Sam replied sarcastically.

The younger agent looked at him coldly. "We don't wish to make your wife's passing any more difficult than it is, but she appears to have done some things which were, in fact, illegal. We will need to see all records regarding her business dealings. Will you cooperate with us, or do we need to issue a summons?"

Sam nodded. "I will do whatever I can to cooperate. If you don't mind though, I will be working through someone specializing in this type of thing. I'm not equipped to answer your questions."

"We understand," he said as he stood.

The older man tossed his pad back into his briefcase and snapped it closed loudly before standing as if he were perturbed, though his face remained impassive. “We will contact you in a week,” he said pointedly. “We will expect the names of your lawyer and accountant at that time.” He stuck out his hand and Sam shook it reluctantly. He felt like he was shaking hands with the devil. It made his skin crawl.

Sick at heart, Sam immediately contacted his attorney, who referred him to a tax attorney. They arranged a meeting, and began sorting through the relevant papers. After nearly a week of long days pouring over documents, the tax attorney summed it up this way.

“Sam, I’m afraid you don’t have a prayer. Large amounts of money have been transferred between foreign accounts that cannot be properly tracked. The way it was done is probably perfectly legal, since the money originated overseas, and was banked overseas. Our position is that the funds never in fact entered this country. In a case like this, it becomes a fine line to prove money you are controlling isn’t actually taxable income.”

The attorney looked sympathetically at his client, who was growing paler by the minute. He continued, “If Dawn were still alive to reconstruct those transfers and acquire receipts from all her foreign sources, which I’m sure she could, we could put this to rest in a heartbeat. Without that knowledge she took to the grave with her, I’m sorry, we don’t have a clue who to contact.”

Sam stared at the man in distress. “The bright side is she did it all in her name, or the business name,” the attorney comforted him. “None of the transfers bear your name, so they will not attack you personally. You don’t have to worry about being prosecuted for tax fraud. The bad side is they are going to attack the business, and any joint property you two owned. I can keep them from taking what is absolutely necessary for you to live, but I would start looking for another place to live.”

“What about the business?” Sam asked, his heart sinking rapidly into sickness.

“Unfortunately, they can use the assets of the business to pay off the tax debts. Furthermore, since the business is structured as a partnership, with you and Dawn as owners, you’ll also be personally liable.”

Sam shook his head. “You mean, they can take all of the business, and come after me when they’re done?”

The attorney’s face went deadly sober. “They can clean out every account you have, and take every asset the business owns, including inventories. If your suppliers will work with you, maybe you can stay in business. If not, then you will be looking for another line of work. Oh, and by the way, did I mention that I will need payment before I can do anything more on your case?”

Sam gave him a hard look and wrote him a check, which he was sure got cashed that very afternoon.

Less than a month later Sam and his daughters moved from their estate to live with his parents. Sam and Dawn's home was immediately sold at auction for a quarter of its value. The remaining inventory of gems was appraised and sold far below cost to customers formerly buying from Princess Gems. In the final wash, Sam ended up with the Jeep, their personal clothing, the kid's toys, photo albums, and a small part of his library. He was also able to keep a few things Dawn had loved. Everything else was sold at auction. Their home was purchased by a church and promptly turned into a chapel. It was a windfall for the little congregation, a tragedy for Sam.

The IRS also tried to take Fred and Connie's home. However, the documents dividing it from their former property held firm, and they escaped—then almost immediately sold it for a tidy sum to the pastor of the new church. Sam was happy that his friends were so fortunate.

For Sam, by far the hardest possession to part with was his grand piano. He arranged to be far away when the new owners came to carry away their prize purchased for a pittance.

The business was methodically dismantled until every bank account was empty, and every asset sold. They finally identified all Dawn's overseas accounts, even some Sam had no knowledge of, and emptied them. In the long run, the assets of the business approximately covered the cost of imposed taxes, penalties and interest. Sam and the girls went from being vastly wealthy, to homeless in a few short weeks. The whole thing left him stunned.

Sam had no reason to believe the IRS had acted contrary to their own omnibus of rules and pseudo-law. It was just that their rules seemed crafted specifically to eviscerate his life, and he could muster no saving defense. His small army of attorneys ensured that no laws were actually broken as they impotently presided over the dismantling of his world, and the acquisition of their own fees. Sam was stunned that they had no way of substantiating the fact that the money never entered the US. As it was, they could prove nothing in their favor, but Sam's inability to disprove wrong-doing was sufficient to trigger the decimation of his world. Sam often thought wryly that it was a good thing he lived in a country where children could not be sold to satisfy a debt, or they too would have vanished.

Sam began to get threatening letters from their former suppliers. He eventually took out bankruptcy in the name of the business. After they persisted, he took out bankruptcy in his own name. He was astounded to learn that the total debt absolved in the bankruptcy was literally millions of dollars owed to people and companies all over the world.

The letter he found most disturbing though, came from his former father-in-law.

Dear Sam,

You know I suffered considerable losses when moneys owed me were not paid and contracts were not fulfilled as promised. I understand these things were beyond your control. I'm willing to make good on your debts myself under certain conditions. It is my wish that my daughter's memory not be tainted by your inability to pay your bills.

Since Dawn's death, and the demise of your business, I have come to the conclusion that you need a boost to get going again. I'm sure all these things have been a tremendous drain on you. I am also informed you have moved back in with your parents, and can no longer provide for my granddaughters. You have no skills and no trade, other than those my daughter taught you, and have no bright prospects of recovering soon.

I know you will bounce back in time, and things will return to normal soon enough. Until then I have a proposal for you. Why not let the girls come live with grandpa for a while. I will put them in the finest schools, and see to their needs and upbringing, just as I did their mother. They will have the best of everything. I will even consent to have them taken to the Mormon church each Sunday to keep them in the faith their mother chose, at least until they are old enough to make up their own minds on such things.

In consideration of this I will happily satisfy all of your outstanding obligations to suppliers here in Africa, as well as provide you with a line of credit to enable you to quickly reestablish yourself in the diamond trade.

I think this would be best for everyone involved. I have already begun to make arrangements to receive the girls. I have had an entire wing of the castle outfitted for them. The will have playrooms, a movie theatre, fitness facilities, a pool, and anything else their hearts desire. Their rooms have been beautifully remodeled, and I have hired maids, nannies and tutors for them.

Your daughters, my granddaughters, will grow up in luxury much the same as their mother did, with the additional advantages of their mother's religion to guide them if they choose to remain associated with it.

Sam, you know this is for their best good. Please let me know what you think, and if you agree, when they will be coming. They will become citizens of the world with all the honor and accolades the world can bestow. They will become my heirs.

I miss them terribly already, and I've only been home a few months. Of course you will always be welcome to come visit them any time, and as often as you like. I would even welcome it if you chose to move to Africa yourself and become my business partner if you like. Of course, when you are back on your feet, in a few years perhaps, the girls can choose to return to the US if they prefer. That door will always remain open.

I have thought about this a long time. I know this is what Dawn would have wanted for all of us. She will be smiling in heaven at you for doing this for her babies. She will be smiling from heaven at me for helping you get back on your feet.

Sincerely, Grandpa Pawley

When Sam didn't reply to the first letter, a second came, and then a third. Each letter became a little more insistent, then threatening. Sam began to fear the girls would be kidnapped and taken to South Africa. He knew that should this happen, he would not ever be able to recover them. Mr. Pawley seemed fixated on having the twins grow up with him, and he had sufficient wealth to make it happen by means legal or otherwise.

Still, Sam realized that what Dawn's father said was true. Sam did not have a trade or skill. He had never gone back to college as he had originally hoped. The only thing he knew was diamonds, and without investment money, there seemed to be few opportunities to make a living in that field. Sam wondered at times if he were being completely selfish in keeping his daughters from an easier life in Africa; but he couldn't imagine his daughters growing up without the gospel.

He looked for work in the diamond trade of course, and impressed every prospective employer with his knowledge of diamonds. However, when they connected his name with the now defunct Princess Gems, he invariably did not get the job. Apparently Dawn's words about the diamond world being very tightly controlled were truer than he had allowed. Even now, whoever made such decisions had apparently done so to keep him completely away from diamonds. This dark mandate seemed iron-clad.

In Alaska at that time there was one place almost anyone could get a job. The Trans-Alaska pipeline had been completed a mere five years earlier. It was still in the process of being brought up to full speed. There seemed to be an endless demand for workers, and Sam was almost immediately hired by Alyeska Pipeline Service Co., the operators of the pipeline.

On his application Sam had listed his long-standing interest in computers, and his typing skills. His new employer decided he was to become an instrumentation technician, and assigned him appropriately. Sam was not sure what an instrument tech even did. He didn't really care; it was a job. They paid well, nearly fifty thousand dollars a year. It was a fraction of his former income, but it was more than what was needed for a comfortable, middle-class life.

The main drawback was that Sam would have to travel to the far north of Alaska for a week at a time. He would then come home for a week off. Except for the obvious limitation it placed on attending church and holding church jobs, it didn't seem so bad. The twins would be safe and happy at Grandma's while he was away.

It was late January when he climbed onto the plane for his first trip to the "North Slope" of Alaska. He was soon to find out why it bore that enigmatic name. The plane flew to Deadhorse, a jarring four-hour flight in a twin engine Convair 580 turboprop, a slow, but rugged plane well-suited to the brutal weather and icy runways.

As a city, Deadhorse was a major failure. As a purely industrial town whose only public accommodation was an airport, it was an amazing success. It was built near the ocean on the vast flatlands between the Brooks Range and the Bearing Sea. The "North Slope" was so named because there was nothing to see in any direction but flat tundra which sloped gradually from the mountains to the sea.

The only notable thing about that icy wasteland was its incredible collection of wildlife in the spring and fall. In years to come Sam would see herds of caribou so dense it would take hours to slowly drive through them; simply because there were so many animals, there was no place for them to run.

Spring would bring an army of geese, ducks, swans, and other winged creatures so numerous that every bare spot of ground, every inch of open water was packed. Since ice still covered 90 percent of the ground in early spring, if every bird landed at once, the available space would have been three birds deep. After the ice melted to reveal the vast expanse of tundra, the birds dissipated quickly to be replaced by an explosion of tiny wild flowers of every color imaginable which burst out as if in a grandiose sigh of colorful relief.

For now, in January, Deadhorse seemed aptly named. There were no homes, no stores, no gas stations, no public buildings, no accommodations of any type but for one dingy motel made of a string of conjoined ATCO trailers. There wasn't even a public road leading to this unimaginably desolate land. A single road led from the airport to a vast parking area for huge equipment waiting its turn out on the rich oil fields of Prudhoe Bay. To protect the fragile tundra, almost all work that required driving across the ground was postponed until hard winter. It was just as well; winter lasted 10 months of the year.

The air temperature outside was sixty below zero, with dead-calm winds. Sam stepped from the plane and took a deep breath. It instantly froze his nose hairs. He felt a pricking sensation and rubbed his nose. The frozen hairs punctured him, and his nose began to trickle red. A stewardess handed him a tissue and smiled knowingly.

By the time he walked the fifty feet or so from the plane to the small terminal his pants were as stiff as plywood, and walking was difficult and chafing. He wondered how anything could survive in such a harsh environment.

The journey to his assigned station took a little over an hour. The landscape was as flat as a frozen pond, and as vast as an ocean. Only a hint of a mountain range far to the south gave any indication that the frozen wasteland did not go on forever.

Sam thrived at his new job. It was sufficiently demanding to be emotionally distracting, and sufficiently laid-back to be comfortable. As the weeks slid slowly into years, the stinging memory of his great loss grew to a dull ache, and then to silence. In the clang and clatter of Babylon, he forgot. Part of what he forgot was the joy that had once swelled his breast.

Working for Alyeska Pipeline Service Company, the consortium steward of the arterial supply of black gold flowing from Alaska's far-north heartbeat, was like working for a rich heiress whose only desire was to pump oil, and to pay her favorite employees insane amounts of money for helping her doing so. She was a seductive, though demanding mistress. She gave richly in return, but her price, extracted ever so slowly, was his soul. Even those who could care less about the cost in spiritual terms, referred to their employer as "the golden handcuffs."

By the time he was made acting supervisor at his station three years later, Sam had finally glimpsed the enormous cost of his growing spiritual apathy, and had begun to fight back. Though he had carefully avoided any act that could be considered truly sinful, his was a carefully orchestrated symphony of a million omissions.

Winter on the North Slope begins about August, and reaches full fury in October. This winter was unique in that it brought an almost continual blanket of ice fog. Ice fog is hard to imagine, even when one is standing in it. It's like a snow fall that doesn't actually fall, made of microscopic particles of ice that glisten and shine in permanently suspended glitter. The most memorable week of Sam's pipeline career came during that winter.

The ice fog had been thick for days before it began to blow. In less than fifteen minutes the winds topped 90 miles an hour, and the wind chill reached the maximum low their instruments could display of minus 98 degrees Fahrenheit. With the weather this ferocious, it was forbidden to go outside except in extreme emergencies. In less than a minute of outdoor exposure, cold could penetrate every layer of clothing and turn them stiff as thick leather. No matter how many pairs of gloves one wore, fingers turned stiff and immobile in two minutes. Even with full arctic clothing, a man's feet were numb in just a few minutes. Frostbite on the nose and cheeks could set in in as little as ten minutes, with hypothermia in fifteen, and on and on until a human body simply ceased to live in about thirty minutes.

Yet the mandate was to pump oil at any cost, so when the inlet screens to the mighty jets began to cake with ice, Sam gave the order to clear them. Not being of a mind to send others where he himself refused to go, Sam elected to go out first. He and a fellow technician put on every piece of arctic gear they could find, and stepped out into the howling wind a few feet from the access ladder to the screens. They climbed two stories above the ground to a narrow catwalk that led across the roof to the turbine inlet housing. A door about four feet tall was locked shut with a big padlock. A red and white sign on the door read "Danger, do not enter. Extreme Hazard."

Sam's partner unlocked the door. It took both of them to pry it open against the enormous vacuum of the jet. A light switch turned on twin lights inside the enclosure. Sam knelt down to peer inside. The vacuum threatened to suck his hardhat right off his head. A few feet inside the door a row of horizontal bars held a screen mesh in place. The mesh was about ten feet across, and the height of a man. The screen was nearly plugged closed with ice.

Sam gave his partner a grim look, and with a short-handled tool clutched in his gloved hand, he crawled through the opening. He got to his feet and was immediately sucked against the screen. For a terrifying instant, he feared the screen may give way and he would be sucked into the screaming mouth of the big jet a dozen feet away. When it held, he pried himself from the screen enough to use his tool. With all his adrenaline-enhanced fury he chipped at the ice. Everything he chipped off disappeared down the throat of the jet. As feeling left his face, fingers, hands, arms and legs, he fought to clear about a three-foot square area. Opening that portion of the screen caused the blast of air to release him. He fell to his knees, and crawled out the little door. His partner grabbed the tool, and crawled inside. In a few minutes he climbed back out, chilled to the bone. Sam took his place for less than a full minute, and returned when he feared for his life from the cold.

Trading off every few minutes, they somehow managed to clear most of the screen. The vacuum slammed the little door shut with the sound of a gunshot. They were too cold to even remember the padlock, but scrambled down the ladder and into the building. They both slumped onto the floor just inside the door. Two more technicians took their place and returned in less than ten minutes, themselves nearly perishing from the cold. Sam and his partner had to go out three times during the night. But, the oil continued to flow. Their only thanks was their usual, very sizable, paycheck.

Legends of strange visions in the arctic sky were voluminous, and considered fantasy by modern skeptics—tales by those whose brains had been frozen one too many times in the arctic chill. Though not commonplace, strange visual phenomenon did occur in the bitter cold.

It was early afternoon, and they were just leaving the station to drive to the airport for crew change. The winds had died down, and the ice fog had disappeared as if by magic. It was bitter cold and dead calm. The sun had already set, but it was still twilight, just barely dark enough to force them to turn on the headlights of the truck.

"What is that?" the driver of the truck asked, pointing out the windshield.

Sam looked up to see an airplane sitting on the tundra directly ahead of them. It appeared to be about two miles away. They could plainly see people walking down the steps, around the nose of the plane, and into the terminal building.

"That's Deadhorse airport," someone in the back seat said in wonder. "And that's our incoming crew getting off the plane. You can read the numbers on the tail of the plane!" he cried. Sam watched in amazement as the plane seemed to move toward, then away from them. It would grow so tiny that it disappeared from sight, then surge forward as if it were less than a mile away. The airport was in reality over 50 miles away. Somehow the cold, dense air had formed a lens in the sky, allowing them to watch their crew mates that far away. Sam mentally punched himself for not having his camera with him. The odd phenomenon persisted during most of their trip to Deadhorse.

This startling visual phenomenon was apropos to Sam's struggle to regain his spirituality. One of his many prayerful requests for reprieve from his spiritual stagnation was met by the whispered injunction, 'When you learn to thrive spiritually in this setting, I will release you. You must walk through the fire, not around it.'"

To Sam, this was a startling revelation, and it focused his mind upon the need to be valiant at work, as well as during his week at home. Sam began to study his scriptures during the evening instead of watching TV or entertaining himself with coworkers. Rather than maintaining an almost embarrassed silence concerning his beliefs, Sam began to allow people to see that he was unique, faith-filled, and faithful.

His spirituality would sometimes surge into focus, then vanish from sight. There were dramatic ups and downs, but the general trend was finally upward again, and Sam's soul felt as if it had just been released from prison. His prayers became sweet, the scriptures spoke peace to his soul, and the writings of the prophets thrilled him as before.

One Sunday afternoon a few years later, while at his parents' home for dinner, Sam sat down at the piano for the first time in years. It was the very piano on which he had learned to play as a child, and music gratefully poured from his soul in a velvet ribbon of happiness. It was on that day that Sam decided they had lived too long in a rented apartment. His family needed the solidarity of being alone, of being permanent, of being at peace.

Accordingly, that same week Sam took the twins house hunting. Bonnie and Lisa were fourteen now, and bubbling with the joy of living. Sam knew he was prejudiced as every father who loves his daughters must be, but to his eyes they were more sparkling and beautiful than any of the gems he had ever handled. They both had their mother's beauty and long-legged grace. Their hair was somewhere between Dawn's blond and his dark brown. They wore it long and softly curled. They preferred clothing that was feminine, and often dazzling on them. They had begun the many complex changes from adolescence to womanhood, and their feminine antics were a continual joy to him.

The girls shopped houses with an energy that left him in their wake. Their passion reminded him of their mother, and he followed them from house to house until both he and their real estate agent were exhausted. By the end of the week, they had found the perfect one. It was a sunny, three-bedroom 'A' frame home with large cathedral windows, bright colors and a two-car garage. They proclaimed that he got the large bedroom, they the next largest, and the third would be his study. They wouldn't even think of having separate rooms. "We belong together," they stated in unison. Anyone looking at their identical beauty and eternal friendship could not have made a convincing argument otherwise.

Sam and his little family moved into their new home several weeks later. They had very little furniture, certainly not enough for a large home. They went shopping for beds and bedding, a sofa and kitchen utensils. They came home with a piano, and little else. He considered their shopping unwise, yet the twins had insisted to the point of physically dragging him into the piano store. Sam found an upright console by Baldwin in American walnut, with a rich tone. Its feel was quite good, and its action quick enough to respond to his most aggressive playing. He sat and played an hour until the store was ready to close. When he finally stood, he was wiping tears from his cheeks. The owner of the store sighed and offered him a considerable discount.

Sam initially refused, although they needed many other things, and he hated buying on credit. The twins aggressively asserted their opinion of purchasing the piano, no matter the obvious economics. The salesman agreed.

"I am going to sell you that piano even if I have to lower the price to fifty cents," the owner said. "You play with such incredible love, I would not feel good about myself if you didn't take it home." Sam looked into his eyes and saw that he was serious—it wasn't a sales gimmick.

They bought it on credit, $500 dollars down, and brought it home in Grandpa's new pickup. They still didn't have much furniture, but they were happy. Sam often found himself playing until the wee hours of the morning. It was a time of sweet healing. For the first time since his Dawn had departed this world, he was at peace. The twins sensed this in a way their mother would have, and any price they might have paid to have that piano in their own little house was worth it to them. They often lay silently in their dark room, and listened to their father's soul as it gently laid a warm blanket of love over their tender hearts.

Six years had passed since he lost her; six long, soul-stripping, desolate, debilitating years. He felt as if it had been sixty, yet now once again, he felt whole. Dawn's absence from his life had left a definitely empty spot, but it was a spot filled with precious memories now, not searing pain. When he remembered her, he felt warm, happy, and at peace. For the first time in many years he knew he would survive, and his survival would be rich and rewarding, not as a refugee shivering in the cold blizzards of reality. With equal intensity, he realized that his torment these last six years had been from another untimely farewell. His soul had languished dreadfully from the constancy of the Holy Spirit. Now that healing had begun, he felt as if an unjust sentence of death had been commuted.

Sam's spiritual journey resumed in earnest the day he clearly heard the Holy Spirit prompt him to make an in-depth study of Isaiah. "You must prepare for your future role in the pre-millennial Zion," he heard clearly. "Study the words of Isaiah as you have never done before." As he obeyed, windows of light and truth illuminated his soul, and he marveled at the messages he received night after night during his studies, and even in his dreams. His soul was stretched to the heavens, and his heart reborn on a deeper level. He came to understand that no matter the circumstance, the Lord would hear his cries and succor him. This truth became an anchor to his soul.

Then Sam was prompted to fast one day at work. He struggled with the obvious: the loss of energy while being paid for working, the necessity of explaining why he was not eating, and the backlash of his possibly appearing to be too goody-goody. As soon as he laid his fears aside and simply obeyed, the Spirit washed through him, and he was catapulted out of his spiritual malaise. And, oddly enough, none of his fears were actually realized.

It was a small price to pay for what would come.

5

GET THEE INTO THE MOUNTAIN

Six weeks later, in the same historic church where she had played for Theodore, Melody MacUlvaney became Mrs. Theodore Lyman Tennison, Jr.

Theodore Lyman Tennison III was born exactly ten months later. Shortly thereafter they were transferred to a little village just outside London, where her new husband was appointed their shepherd. Life for Melody seemed to begin the day she married Theodore. He was kind, devoted, passionately solicitous of her well-being, and completely devoted to his work. He spent long hours performing his duties and often returned home exhausted, but animated.

Their new parish was smaller than Saint Michael's and considerably older. It was constructed of native stone gathered from farmer's fields long since buried beneath generations of housing. Directly above and behind the pulpit, the little church had an awe-inspiring stained glass window of John the Baptist baptizing Christ. The glass had been so long in that position that the bottoms of each pane of glass had settled, and were noticeably thicker.

Theodore's parishioners were generally lower-middle-class—either older persons on small pensions or young couples struggling with too little pay and too many children. Yet, they were more than friendly toward their new priest and his bride, and treated Melody like the Queen Mother herself. They deferred to her in everything, whether it be a suggestion on how the Christmas pageant might be, or where to place a vase of flowers. Her authority seemed to be second only to her husband's, and in some cases, even superior. She was frequently sought after to dispense soothing words, much-needed advice, or gentle doses of well-deserved chastisement. Melody was amazed that they instinctively considered her second in command, and not infrequently used her as a conduit for messages to her husband which they feared, or at least were reluctant to approach themselves.

Just as amazing to Melody was that Theodore also respected her notable skills with his parishioners, and used her that way, too. In situations too ticklish for him to intervene directly, he simply told Melody, who instinctively knew a way to tactfully deliver the message. Sometimes she worked miracles not possible in any other way.

Their new home was a cottage attached to the side of the church. It was small, but recently remodeled and quite comfortable. She loved to fantasize about how many hundreds of pastor's wives had dwelt in that very stone home, washed dishes at that same little copper sink, and rubbed their husband's tight shoulders as they sat before that very stove.

They heated their little cottage with a small coal stove. It was one of the old features that had survived many renovations. The church and cottage had been constructed in 1847, and still had stone floors. Most everything else had been updated to modern standards. Melody stoked the stove with coal two to four times a day, depending on the weather, and carried out the clinkers once each day. It was a job she both hated and loved. She hated it for the oily smell, the powdery dust and constant demands on her time, but loved it for its rustic charm and satisfying heat. It was around this little stove that they gathered when he or she needed their shoulders rubbed, or when waiting for the last few moments of day to surrender to night.

George Alexander Tennison was born nearly three years after his older brother's entry into the family. It was both a happy and sad day for Melody. While she gave birth in the large hospital just inside London, her husband was attending to the bereaved family of a man killed in a mining accident. He sadly arrived several hours after she had delivered his second son.

As time progressed, though, something seemed to change in Theodore. He grew more passionate in his religion and more vocal about politics. While still professing devotion to his family, he spent less time with them and dedicated large blocks of time to study. Sometimes he didn't come home until early morning. When he finally slid into bed he was often angry. He insisted he was not angry with Melody of course, but with what he saw as the invasion of cult religion into England, and the insanity of the current political decline of his homeland. In his thinking, the two were inseparably connected, although he never fully explained how.

Theodore's main ire seemed focused on two cults in particular: Jehovah's Witnesses and Mormons. Of the former Melody knew nothing. Of the Mormons, she only knew that she had seen nothing but good of those she knew to be members of that sect. When she tried to explain her feelings to her husband, he admitted that all their members were probably not inherently evil, but they had all surely been deceived—which deception would ultimately cost them their eternal souls. His divinely-ordained mission slowly changed from saving his flock from sin to saving them from the heresy of false religions and false politics in its multitudinous forms.

Theodore's sermons began to include warnings, then denunciations, then thunderous damnations of the "cults." He sought out and joined well-established sources of "anti" publications. He distributed pamphlets to anyone willing to take them and held classes and seminars in the evenings on how to successfully debate with any representative of those sects. He published articles and editorials in the local papers, and openly challenged any representative of a non-Catholic religion to debate him in public. To his immense disappointment, none came forth to do him battle.

His focus on what he saw as a grave threat to true religion fell on increasingly troubled ears. Being the heart and conscience of the congregation, Melody heard many express concerns and misgivings about their spiritual shepherd's fiery denunciations from the pulpit. Even if they partly, or even largely, agreed with him, they still longed for the former peaceful days of preaching Christ, stories from the Bible, and tales of the miracles of love. When Melody tried to communicate these concerns to her husband, his ire turned upon her, and he raged until she dared not mention it again.

With all this, Theodore's heart slowly turned away from the sweetness she once cherished. He seemed more critical of everyone, including Melody and his boys. He had little or no time for the small problems he once devoted himself to healing. He stopped visiting his flock in their homes, and slowly lost touch with their needs. He became a speaker of some popular demand and often traveled away from his little flock for days at a time.

Because she loved him and the memory of the sweet days of their lives, Melody clung to her husband, supported him, and even defended him to those who felt alienated from the church.

The bursting of the dam came when a young family in his congregation actually began taking lessons from the Mormon missionaries. Theodore's fury was stoked to such conflagration that he literally slept on their doorstep to keep the hated "messengers of damnation" from teaching the family. Rather than endearing him to his parishioners, it had the opposite effect; they insisted that he leave. He left shouting the horrors of hell, which only served to alienate them further.

Perhaps to spite him, perhaps as a manifestation of new faith, or perhaps a little of both, they were eventually baptized Mormons. The next Sunday, Theodore preached such damnations against all such heinous sinners that spittle flew from his lips quite unseen by himself. From that day, attendance at church steadily declined. Theodore saw it as a further manifestation of the awful influence of the cults. It never occurred to him that he had driven his once-loving parishioners away with his rabid anger. In the following two years, four other families were "lost" to the hated American cult.

When Theodore finally came to Melody in tears of frustration, she tried to tell him how he was alienating his flock, but he would not hear it. All that was in his eyes was the threat of an enemy much larger than himself, and he steeled himself to tilt the windmill monsters of darkness.

For Melody, her husband's obsession evolved into something personally loathsome to her. Following her failed attempt to open his eyes to his own failures, he stood before the congregation and insisted that anyone with family belonging to any cult or demonic sect must sever all ties with them, or be sanctioned by the Church. He even threatened excommunication in cases where the unrepentant were prominent members of the congregation. Melody felt his attack was specifically aimed at her and her sister, and justifiably so. She had been sitting on the stand waiting to direct the choir when Theodore's scathing injunction was delivered. The humiliation of his public denunciation put a strangle-hold of resentment on her heart.

It had been nearly three years since Theodore had visited his uncle in his palatial home in the country. The old man's health was failing, as was his patience with his heir apparent. Uncle Tennison wanted an heir, one upon whom he could count to continue his political goals and to safeguard his vast fortune. While Uncle Tennison soundly approved of Theodore's pursuit of cleric robes, he did not approve of the devotion which Theodore had shifted from his uncle to his flock.

Melody had only been to the mansion once before, during their whirlwind engagement. At that time she had found her fiancé's uncle to be intriguing, albeit lofty, condescending, and unapproachable. She had left with the distinct impression that the old gentleman did not like her, or at the least considered her beneath himself—even perhaps beneath his nephew's status.

That she sensed this was not in error and would have remained forever true had she not brought her violin and, at the quiet urging from her then-future husband, played for Tennison. From that moment on his assessment of her seemed to change. He was clearly charmed by her talent and beauty, although just as clearly convinced of her inferior breeding.

So, it was with reluctance that Melody now saw the big mansion across the picturesque grounds and lake. The boys, eight and five years old, were beside themselves with excitement. They had never seen such a mansion, nor had they ever guessed someone so wealthy could be a near relative of their seemingly-impoverished parents.

The spacious entryway smelled faintly of cigar smoke and wood polish. The same aged butler greeted them warmly and escorted them to their

 Uncle's living room. Melody felt tiny and insecure in that massive room, trying to restrain her sons, fumbling to keep from dropping her violin, and trying in vain to read her husband's mood. She felt nothing but trepidation and a twinge of nervous anticipation.

"So! The prodigal son returns!" a voice boomed.

They all spun to see a white-haired man moving slowly toward them, supporting himself with a golden cane.

"Uncle!" Theodore cried, and rushed to him. His uncle received him with happy slaps on his back.

"And, you've brought me heirs! Why haven't you brought these beautiful young boys sooner?" he demanded loudly, hobbling toward the boys who stood their ground beside their mother, their faces smiling but unsure.

The uncle stood next to the boys, using his cane as a measuring stick. "OK, let's see. You're the tallest, so you are named after my favorite nephew—you must be Theodore Lyman the third."

"Yes, sir. I like to be called Teddy," the boy said bravely.

"Whoa ho! You are a brash lad. I shall call you Teddy then, as long as it pleases you."

"Thank you, Uncle Tennison," Teddy said formally.

"Spank me, but I'm your great uncle, lad. Well, call me anything you like."

"Yes, sir."

"And, this must be my namesake. George Alexander Tennison!" Uncle boomed as he leaned toward five-year-old Alex."

Alex looked up with frightened eyes, but he did not step back. "I'm not your namesake," he said, his lip quivering. "I'm my daddy's namesake," he stated with surety.

To his credit, Uncle Tennison straightened and laughed softly. "Of course you are. What I meant was, you and I have the same name. Did you know that?"

"No sir," Alex replied softly while looking at the ground.

"Well, we do. And it is a grand thing. Would you boys like a dish of ice cream?"

"Yes!" they chorused. At that moment a young, unusually attractive maid dressed in white appeared as if her entrance had been scripted.

She held out both hands. "If you wan' to tyke my 'ands, I'll tyke you boys to the biggest collection of ice cream in England. Wha' do ya you say, mates?" The boys literally flew to her.

"Please," Melody urged the maid as she took their hands, "No more than one bowl."

"Yes, misses. A large one then?"

"I suppose," Melody acquiesced.

She watched the boys depart, then realized Uncle Tennison was watching her intently.

"You didn't know your youngest bore my name, did you?" he asked once the boys were beyond earshot.

Melody flinched. "Are you clairvoyant, Uncle?"

"No, I'm a keen observer of people. You flinched when I mentioned it."

"I see. Did I seem to disapprove?" she asked kindly, but with an obvious challenge in her words.

"As a matter of fact, you seemed pleased. I believe you smiled," he replied.

"Then you are not as good an observer as you profess," Melody suggested calmly.

Uncle Tennison laughed heartily. "I love it that you stand up to me. Did you know that?"

"Actually, yes," Melody replied with a smile. She walked to him and looped an arm through his. "How have you been, Uncle? You look a little worse for wear, I'm afraid."

"Stupid doctors," he grunted. "I have offered them billions for a key to living forever, and they give me plastic surgery and aspirin. So, my face looks like the million pounds I've spent on it, and my viscera all feel the hundred years old they actually are. I'm considering hiring witch doctors."

Melody laughed lightly. "Theodore tells me John the Beloved received a promise from Our Lord that he would not die. So, perhaps there is a way."

"Ha! Out of the mouth of babes, that is beautiful babes, comes the truth. All I have to do is figure out a way to become a holy apostle!"

"May it be so simple," Melody grinned at him.

"Simple for you or saint Theodore here, perhaps. But for a reprobate like me, I had best find those witch doctors."

"Rubbish," she asserted. "you're as much of a saint as Theodore is."

At that moment Uncle stopped walking and turned to her with an aghast look on his face. Surprised, she glanced at Theodore who also wore a stricken look on his face.

"Well," Melody said, her voice apparently amazed, "It appears I have insulted both of you with a single compliment."

Uncle Tennison's face spread into a smile. "Jolly well done."

"I didn't really mean . . ." she began.

"Tripe!" Uncle interjected. "You're bloody delightful. Theodore doesn't deserve you. Have you considered divorcing that sanctimonious sot and marrying a real man?"

"Only one with lots of money," Melody said with mock seriousness.

Uncle turned toward his nephew. "You were right," he said. "I did just ask her to marry me. Too bad for you, I guess."

Theodore did not seem pleased at this, and took his Uncle's arm opposite Melody, as if in a tug of war with the old man as the prize. "Uncle, you know, anything I have is yours. All you need do is ask."

At this it was Melody's turn to look stricken.

At this, the old man laughed so hard he went into a wheezing coughing fit. It took most of a minute for him to calm down. By this time a nurse had produced a wheelchair and oxygen bottle.

They were sitting by the fire in his grand study when he finally pulled the plastic oxygen mask from his face.

"That was the most fun I've had since Theodore came to beg me to elevate you from a street musician to a Baroness."

Theodore stiffened, his face a mask of fear and anger.

"*You* did that?" Melody asked, turning to her husband. She had never known for sure.

"Of course! Who else do you think could get the Queen Mother herself to write a document restoring your family title and name. Certainly, you didn't suspect my nephew. He has pathetic little power but what falls from my table to his floor. His appeal would have been to God, who in all likelihood would have also begged me to do what I did."

Melody bridled at this insult, yet considered her words. "I suppose that makes you more like John the Beloved than you suspected. Perhaps living forever is not so far fetched for you after all."

"Now you disappoint me," the old man said with chastisement in his voice. "I insult your husband, and you elevate me to holiness? Where is the honesty I so recently admired in you?"

"But, Uncle, you didn't insult my husband. You insulted yourself by suggesting he had power with God, who had power over you. It is an odd order of power, is it not? Perhaps the crumbs fall from Theodore's floor to your table."

"I see," he replied jovially. "While Theodore remains silent, probably praying for all he's worth, and I joust with his wife, I think it best to warn you that I fear nobody, neither man nor God. And, no real man would ignore his dying uncle, then bring his gutter-born wife to insult him and remain silent. Have you no loyalties here, my nephew?"

Theodore stammered. "What? I mean, Uncle, this is no contest of wills. Melody has deported herself well and honorably, and I meant to allow her time to get to know you, is all. I saw no need to defend either one of you. Forgive me if . . ."

"Oh, shut up, Theodore. I just called your darling wife gutter-born, and you did not spring to her defense. When you've a spine, then you can join the conversation."

Melody's eyes went from closed with fury to wide open with amazement. "You are a vile man, aren't you," she said quite slowly.

The aged Tennison smiled broadly. "Now we understand one another, my dear. I suggest neither you nor my nephew forgets it. I fear no one. I have offended God often enough that fear of deity is meaningless in any case. I have only my interests to entertain me, and to bring me solace. So, bear in mind, if either of you tries to stop in my path, I will destroy you, and will sleep easily for having done so."

Melody placed a graceful hand upon his gnarled claw. "You bark very loud for a toothless old hound. Say you're sorry to my husband so he'll quit brooding, then we'll go get some ice cream with the boys."

Uncle's eyes narrowed to near-slits, then a smile spread across his face. "I like you, woman. You have pluck and spine. Very well, Theodore, I am sorry. I was merely baiting you, not suggesting you are spineless, even though you were just then. So, do you forgive me?"

Theodore opened his mouth, then closed it. "Not yet, he said moodily, "but I do love you just the same."

"Tripe! You just want my money!"

It was Melody who spoke next. "I'm afraid you are mistaken, Uncle. My husband has spoken from his heart. If he eventually acquires your fortune he would undoubtedly squander it on little churches all across England. His love for you is disconnected from your money."

"Then he's a fool!" Uncle spat, then sat for a moment in thought. "Oh, well. Perhaps then my money would serve to curry some favor with God, whom I've often enough denied. Very well, Theodore, your charming wife has saved you. You are once again my heir. So, be nice to her. If you lose her, or my grandnephews, you are out on your sanctimonious ear."

Theodore leaned forward, glanced at Melody with palpable gratitude, then back at his cantankerous uncle. "Yes, Uncle," was all he could think to say. It was an answer that originated in his early childhood, and it boiled his soul in smoldering resentment.

"Good. Then let's go get some ice cream before my strapping young heirs eat it all."

In the months that followed, Melody and the boys visited Uncle Tennison with increasing regularity, and oftentimes of necessity going without Theodore. In time it became apparent to both Melody and Theodore that Uncle's true affections were upon their sons. The old miser lusted for heirs and had chosen their sons as his own.

Melody was afraid of what vast wealth might do to her boys, yet she couldn't help but be pleased for their good fortune. It soothed her fears that they still remained very close to her as well as to the religious teachings of their father; she reasoned that the boys could be molded to do vast good with their impending wealth.

For her husband, this development was only troubling. Theodore was both frightened at what might happen to himself should this new succession of heirs cut him personally off from the flow of wealth, and also resentful that Melody was becoming so close with his uncle. More than merely wanting Uncle's empire, Theodore simply refused to countenance the idea that anyone *except* him might inherit it.

Somewhere in the back of Theodore's mind was the idea that the time might come, should Melody ever leave, that he would have to make sure his sons' affections and home remained with him.

From that moment on, whether intentional or subconscious, Theodore carefully began driving tiny splinters of discord between himself and his wife, and her relationship with his sons. A feeling of hyper-criticality entered his soul, and most everything Melody did became food for criticism, most often spoken only to the boys. And he continued to deliver volley after volley from the pulpit in fiery denunciations of apostasy in its varied forms.

Theodore's diminishing congregation grew more and more disenchanted with their shepherd and began to ferry complaints to his superiors As their disaffection with Theodore grew, they more openly loved Melody, who continued to embrace them with all her soul. As allegations from his superiors flowed back into Theodore's face, he became more and more convinced that everyone adored his wife and detested him. This only served to add distrust to the sins he had already heaped upon her head.

Tension mounted between Melody and her husband until she found herself alienated as well, although her love for him would not let her abandon him. She pleaded with him, wept before him, and begged his God to soften his heart. She had no intention of joining any silly sect, as he often accused her of doing; yet his campaign had become a blinding obsession, and she could find no place left within him where he still harbored love for her. Even her sons, now twelve and nine, feared him and hid in the back of their cottage when he was home. He scarcely seemed to observe their absence except when the mood hit him to secure their affections, at which time he suddenly lavished attention and gifts upon them, which the boys neither understood nor received as tokens of real affection.

The most startling event in this long line of sadness occurred when Melody's sister Marcia and her husband brought their children to visit them in their quaint cottage beside the church. Marcia, unaware of the complicated twists and turns of Theodore's passion, and innocent of any ill will, simply marched into their home with "Mormon" practically labeled across her chest. Theodore tolerated her cheerful words and loving gestures toward Melody and the boys most of the way through dinner, but after dinner he suddenly ordered them from his home in a loud voice of righteous indignation. Shocked beyond words, Marcia fled their home in tears. Melody was equally as horrified, grabbed her sons and fled with her sister. She spent the next six weeks at Marcia's home.

The contrast was so stark between Melody's little stone cottage where anger and vitriol spilled like water on the stone floors, and this small home where love, respect, and gentleness graced their lives, that Melody was compelled to wonder why. Every evening they knelt in family prayer. She listened carefully as Marcia's four-year-old daughter prayed in a way more meaningful than she herself could pray. For the first time in many years, Marcia felt warmth in her bosom, and then a memory surfaced of a train ride in Africa, where once before she had known peace, hope, and the joy of faith.

Melody could never have violated her husband's trust so far as to actually study Marcia's religion, but her sons felt no such inhibition. They pumped their cousins for information, which was freely dispensed. The very thing that made Melody decide to return to her husband was her oldest son's request to be baptized a Mormon. She knew she had stayed too long, and to her sister's dismay, almost ran from the house.

Melody's hopes that this brief separation would mellow her husband's attitude had not been in vain. He welcomed them with great relief, and held her so gently and forlornly that she repented of ever having left him, and accepted him willingly back into her heart. She found herself pregnant three weeks later, a fact she carefully kept to herself.

Everything seemed as if it might mend until young Teddy mentioned that he had read part of the Book of Mormon at his cousin's house. His father calmly asked what he thought of it. When the young man honestly answered that he didn't understand it, but that he liked the feeling he had when he read it, Theodore detonated. The explosion that resulted was atomic in scope, and send waves of destruction in every direction.

For the first time in their marriage, Theodore struck Melody, giving her a bloody nose. He screamed at her in the presence of her sons as they cowered on the opposite side of the room. When he moved toward her as if he might strike her again, young Teddy attacked his father with flailing arms. A single well-struck blow sent the boy tumbling onto the stone floor, which broke the boy's arm. Even the wailing of his son's pain could not placate him, and he stormed from the house, cursing vilely.

Melody took advantage of his absence to rush her son to the hospital. As Theodore had never trusted her with the keys to their car, Melody and the boys had to walk part-way, and then take a cab the remainder of the distance. From the hospital, she called Marcia, who made the two-hour drive to fetch them.

Melody was baptized into the Mormon church that spring, three months from the day Theodore had bloodied her nose. She applied for divorce that same month, and for the first time in years felt the darkness lifting from her soul. What a thrill it was to see a world of sweet faith and hope. How peace-filled it was to clearly understand truth rather than the empty "feeling" engendered by rehearsed catechisms. How wonderful it seemed to live without fear, intimidation, or the threat of eternal damnation.

For all these reasons she was not expecting what next occurred. One afternoon after school, a police car arrived at Marcia's home. Two armed men served Melody with a legal document decreeing her sons into the custody of their father. When calm explanation failed she turned to pleading, then tears, then anger, and finally violence. She attacked the men with ferocity as they threatened her with criminal arrest, and then physically forced the screaming boys out the door. With Marcia restraining her, Melody cried openly as she watched her terrified sons being dragged away from her. Faster than she could utter a prayer, her precious sons were gone from her life. Except for one time during a heated court battle, she was never allowed to see or speak to them again.

"Hello again," a voice said behind him in the grocery line. Sam looked up from the check he had been writing to see a gray-haired gentleman smiling at him. He instantly recognized him and almost dropped his pen. "Please, don't stop on my account," the old man said with a smile, wiggling a finger at Sam's checkbook. Sam tore his eyes away to glance at his check. He looked back up and actually felt surprised that his visitor was still standing there. The last two times they had spoken, the gentleman had suddenly vanished the second Sam had looked away.

"Uh, excuse me. I'll just finish…you won't leave, or anything—will you?" Sam asked haltingly.

"I have a few things to get myself," the gentleman said with a laugh, holding up a bag with a shiny green apple, and another with a few red grapes.

"Oh, sure." Sam quickly wrote the check and stepped away from the check stand. He was watching the man so intently that he didn't immediately hear the clerk asking if he wanted help carrying his groceries out.

"Oh! Sorry. I can get it," he told the lady, who looked at him as if he were nuts. Sam had a lot of groceries for one individual to carry, but he was determined he would not take his eyes off the stranger for any reason. It had been eight long years since he had first seen his aged friend, and he didn't want any potentially wonderful exchange hampered by the presence of the grocery store clerk. "Thanks, I'll manage," Sam assured her again without turning his eyes from the older man.

Sam pushed the cart slowly as the gentleman walked beside him, who seemed genuinely fascinated with the apple in his small plastic bag. Sam nearly ran into shoppers as he was watching the old man instead of where he was going. The gentleman put a hand on the cart to keep Sam from colliding with a young pedestrian.

"You're not limping," Sam observed. It was the only thing that came to mind.

"No, I'm not limping, am I?" the gentleman replied, then chuckled. He retrieved the apple from the bag and took a big, crunching bite.

"You should probably wash it first," Sam suggested, still at a loss for words.

The visitor gave him an ironic smile. "Yes, usually that's a good idea," he admitted with a smile.

"But, not really necessary in your case?" Sam asked.

"Not really. Not really," the gentleman replied as he chewed the apple with pleasure.

"Do you really even get hungry?" Sam asked suddenly.

The old man looked at him with a sparkle in his eyes, and then back at his apple. "The older I get, the less appetite I have," he replied.

"That's not quite what I was asking," Sam said with some poignancy.

"I know what you're asking," the old gentleman said, and took another bite of the apple without answering the question at hand.

The silence was deafening. "I am really glad to see you again," Sam said a little nervously, trying to start over.

"Can you tell me why you're here? I'm very confused about who you are, and what you are doing here. Since those couple of times you came to church I have often wondered about you. Because you—like—disappeared."

The older man put the apple core in his mouth and bit it in two as he locked his eyes on Sam. For an instant Sam felt uncomfortable, but it was only an instant. "When we met for the first time a few years ago, I asked you a question," the gentleman said between bites. "You said you were going to be an even better man than you were then. Have you managed to live up to that lofty ideal?"

"No," Sam admitted with his head lowered. "I've had a lot of trials, and it has taken me a few years to recover. But, I'm back on track again, and it feels really good."

"I see. Do you still hold the promises sacred?"

Sam knew exactly which promises he was referring to. Seldom a day went by that he didn't think of the great promises he had received on that visionary night many years ago.

"Oh, yes!" he declared emphatically.

"And, when you had the opportunity to trade them for a return to worldly grandeur, how did you respond?"

"You know about that?" Sam asked in surprise. He had told no one about it. This had come to him during prayer one evening in a very startling way. It still sent chills up Sam's spine to remember it. He had been presented with a frightening opportunity to trade his eternal welfare for a return to wealth, or anything else he desired. Sam shuddered. "I did not accept. It terrified me. But, surely you already know that."

The man smiled. "You have much to learn."

"I'm anxious to learn," Sam asserted.

"And I am here to teach you. I must go now, but I'll see you again."

Sam felt panicked. "When? Must you leave so soon? I have a thousand questions!"

Sam's visitor chuckled in his rich way and placed a hand on Sam's shoulder. It felt kindly and almost fatherly there. "That all depends upon you. I will return when you are ready. Until then, you must press forward with all diligence. Do all you know to be faithful. Be flawlessly obedient, and be patient."

"I will. I will. I'll try," Sam replied, answering each instruction in order.

"Very good," he said, patting Sam's shoulder gently, and turned to walk away. Sam stopped him.

"Could you at least tell me your name?"

The old gentleman halted, then moved back toward Sam, speaking in a low voice. "Helaman. My name is Helaman," he whispered.

Sam felt a thrill of recognition throughout his body. He wanted to follow after the old man, but somehow knew he should not. He glanced at his groceries still in the cart beside his Jeep. When he looked back up he could not spot the old gentleman. It didn't surprise him at all.

Throughout his life, Sam had had one overriding question. It never seemed to get answered to his satisfaction, and it never went away. Now, more than ever before, that question cried out. "What's next?" it demanded, over and over. When Sam was a little child, the question haunted him. His vision of his life then scarcely reached beyond cub scouts and interminably long school years. On his mission, he pondered what was expected of him, and yearned for a concise direction in his life. After his marriage, it seemed as if everything known to him had been done. He had lived a good life, married a wonderful woman in the temple, and was serving in every way he knew. But something inside his soul knew this was not all to his life, and the nagging question, "What's next?" called to him constantly.

After the glorious night that Sam had had his calling and election made sure, the question only grew louder. He could not imagine any blessing greater, yet he felt a powerful tugging at his soul as if a celestial tide were sweeping him out to sea, or perhaps sweeping him home from sea. Yet, where it was taking him was unknown, and the question grew louder.

One of the startling changes that had swept through him after that night was the almost total loss of interest in the material world. His mind had become fully centered upon things celestial, and even the act of going to work strained him. Had he been given the choice, he would have walked away from it all to live in poverty, and to serve with joy every hour of every day. Yet, it seemed as if the greater his focus on eternal things, the greater the opposition arose to attempt to make it impossible to actually be spiritual, until the dichotomy was fire and ice.

After he had lost the business and was forced to go to work on the slope, Sam's face had been jammed into the slimy underbelly of Babylon once again. At first, it was extremely distasteful, then tolerable, then almost enjoyable. Now, with this joyful return to righteous desire, his soul once again disdained the material world, and he felt a yearning of irresistible force to enter into some life situation where he could do a great work of lasting worth for Heavenly Father and the Savior.

Seeing and speaking with the unexpected visitor again only heightened Sam's desire to progress with rapid strides toward that visionary future. Finally once again, he felt no desire to pursue anything worldly, and it racked his soul with conflict to think of getting onto that plane and heading north to the oil slopes once again.

The night after speaking with Helaman, Sam's prayer shifted, refocused and aligned as if without his conscious thought. Suddenly, he knew what was next, and it filled his soul with desire more terrific than anything ever had. His heart yearned for a single thing—a blessing so profound, so bold, so unthinkably wonderful, that he could scarcely bring himself to speak the words. Yet, the desire was a flaming fire, and it threatened to consume him.

More than anything he had ever known, he wanted the marvelous gift of entering into the presence of the Lord. For the first time in his entire life, he knew what was next, but it seemed impossible. Yet, he knew his desire was righteous, and that it was prompted by the Spirit. He also knew the scriptures contained numerous promises that one might with certainty seek the Lord's face in this life. He realized that such a marvelous, eternity-altering experience was not reserved for a select few, but had been promised to all, according to their faith and the Lord's timetable.

He thought on the precious temple ceremony, and the sublime promises of the final moments that brought him great joy. Yes, he knew what was next! He also knew that he was not sure exactly how to get there.

Sam read the passages in Ether of the Brother of Jared's visitation of the Lord. He read each phrase and dissected it. He deeply pondered the words, each nuance of meaning, and prayed diligently concerning them. He purchased every book written by Elder McConkie and scoured them for references to this great blessing. He struck gold in an entire chapter on that subject, and read it again and again. Slowly, as if the gradual dawning of a new day, a simple understanding began to form. It was so startling that he was not sure if it thrilled, or terrified him. Perhaps a little of both.

Every instance Sam could find of a mortal having this glorious visitation resulted in the Lord asking if that blessed person had a request of him. John the Beloved had asked to remain upon the earth, as had the three Nephite apostles. The other apostles, both in Jerusalem and Zarahemla, had asked for a swift passage into His rest. Nephi, Enos, Mosiah, Alma, and many others had asked for blessings upon their posterity. Perhaps there were many more occurrences of this blessing not recorded in scripture. Sam could not even guess, but faith told him it was a pattern followed since the beginning of time.

"What will I ask for?" he found himself pondering one day. It thrilled him that the question in his heart had formed around the word "will," not "would." As if there were two of him, Sam heard the other reply. "I will ask for that which I have always wanted, and always secretly hoped for. I will ask for that same gift given to John the Beloved and the Three Nephites. I will ask to be translated, stay on this earth and work righteousness to prepare His children for the return of the Savior Jesus Christ."

This thought distilled upon his soul with great force. It was to Sam as if it had always been there, always waiting for him to simply observe it. It was as if no other object in life had ever, or could ever exist.

Another thought occurred to him, and he hurried into his bedroom. Somewhere in a box of precious things was his patriarchal blessing. He hunted until he found the yellowed envelope, removed the pages and opened them with care. He had read the inspired words many times, but for the first time in over twenty years, he finally understood them. The phrase he had just remembered fell beneath his eyes, and he read with a thrill of understanding never available to him before.

> A great blessing awaits those who dedicate their all to the service of the Lord. Such a blessing was given to John, the Beloved disciple, and the three Nephite disciples, who were promised by the Lord that they would remain upon this earth, free from the aches and pains of mortality, to help prepare His children for His glorious return. And you will have the privilege of associating with those so blessed by the Lord.

Sam read the passage over and over until they were seared into his soul. He had never understood those words, never fully considered their impact, nor pondered their immense meaning. With great clarity he now understood. He would attain this great promise by asking the Lord himself for it! Now, more than ever, Sam knew the answer to "What's next?"

But now, more than ever, he had no idea of how to actually do it.

That same day two letters arrived from South Africa. The larger letter looked official, with a return address from the chief prosecuting attorney of the criminal justice system. The smaller one held the familiar address of his former father-in-law. Sam opened the larger one, and was delighted to find it was from Brother and Sister Van Der Kerk, a wonderful couple whom Sam had taught and baptized many years ago in South Africa. A lawyer at the time of their meeting, Brother Van Der Kerk was apparently now a chief prosecutor.

My Dear Elder Sam Mahoy,

You can well imagine my amazement when this case involving your wife crossed my desk. I studied it with growing dismay as I learned the details of Mr. Pawley's, your former father-in-law's, inimical actions in this regard.

It occurs to me that you may know but few details in this matter. I think it best to not belabor you with details unless you request it of me in a letter. Suffice it to say that your former father-in-law took it upon himself to intimidate and frighten you and your dear wife into returning to Africa. He attempted to use the figure of 22 and memories of your past to cause your wife to leave you and flee to Africa. He even tried kidnapping your daughters. His plan apparently was that you would call him in your grief, and he would sweep into your lives and rescue them. Of course his plan was that they would have ended up in South Africa, and Dawn would have had to return to Africa to retrieve them. One can only surmise that there would have been no place for you, Sam, in their new lives. It was a heinous plot, and one which ultimately brought about his daughter's death.

After she died, he apparently blamed you even more for his sorrows and determined to kidnap your daughters, which he nearly accomplished on several occasions.

Though the wheels of justice do grind along slowly in this country, rest assured they have caught Mr. Pawley in their grist and he has been justly dealt with.

You can rest assured that he has been convicted and imprisoned for a very long time, probably for the rest of his life. All his assets have been determined to be ill-gotten and have been confiscated by the court. I have petitioned the court in his daughter's name and succeeded in having all his wealth revert to her heirs, who would be yourself and your daughters. I have asked and been granted guardianship of this considerable estate, and await your instructions on its disposal.

I will not discuss here the exact sums involved as they are yet to be fully determined. You may be assured they are vast. His holdings in diamonds alone are phenomenal. You and your daughters need never want for anything again.

As you may know, the present laws of the country prohibit the export of any moneys or assets from this country. Accordingly, the only way your daughters could benefit from this action is if you brought them to Africa to live—a thing I think unlikely, and unwise, in light of current events. Perhaps after a few years it will become safe for you to return to this wonderful land. Sister Van Der Kerk and I, as well as many others, would rejoice should you decide to return.

In the meantime, I request that you forward whatever instructions for the maintenance or disposal of your estate that you feel appropriate.

One final note I hope will bring joy to your soul in this day of trial. I was recently set apart as Bishop of the Germiston Second Ward. Emma, my dear wife is with child, due to deliver in May. We have determined to name him Samuel, in your honor. We had never expected to have children for medical reasons, and find ourselves unexpectedly rejoicing because of the Lord's blessings to us.

We are forever yours in Christ,
Brother Van Der Kerk

Sam took the second letter and ripped it to shreds without opening it. After much prayer, he penned the following letter to the Van Der Kerks.

My Dear Brother and Sister Van Der Kerk,

It is with joy that I received your latest letter and the news of your wife's pregnancy. I feel deeply honored, and truly flattered, but hardly worthy that you should name him after me. I pray to Father that we may one day live nearer.

I also am relieved to hear of Dawn's father's conviction. I thank you for your faith and good efforts in her and my behalf. It is a fitting closure to this awful chapter of my life, and I thank you with all my heart.

I will write later with more details regarding my life and hopes for the future.

Regarding Dawn's inheritance, I have prayed earnestly, and after consulting with my daughters, we wish you to make the following arrangements:

Please take all liquid assets and invest them in wise investments able to produce safe but steady growth. The principal amount shall be increased by 10 percent of earnings each year, and remain in trust forever, or until I, or my legal heirs, instruct otherwise.

I wish 50 percent of the investment income to be given to the Church of Jesus Christ of Latter-day Saints to whatever funds you feel appropriate. The other 25 percent I wish to be used to convert Dawn's castle home into a women's retreat. I wish part of it to be set aside as a shelter for young women in whatever needy circumstances you determine are worthy. The shelter should focus on teaching the principles of the gospel, life skills and education. The goal is to provide temporary assistance that works as a permanent solution in their lives.

I further instruct you to make a portion of this facility available to the Church as a girl's camp, and women's retreat at their request.

Whatever funds remain beyond the needs of the castle-retreat please use as a missionary fund for young men and women who wish to serve full-time missions.

I leave sole management of these affairs to you, and grant you complete discretion within the parameters I have specified, to do as you see fit, to hire whatever staff you think appropriate, and to pay yourself whatever reasonable fees or salary you deem appropriate.

I further instruct that you send me no reports or records of the dealings and financial affairs of the estate, nor to seek my opinion in any matter regarding it, but to keep an accurate record of all your transactions on my behalf in perpetuity.

With warmest love and thankful heart, I am
Your friend forever, and Brother in Christ,
Samuel Mahoy

That October the stock market crashed nearly 2000 points. The economy crumbled under foolish fiscal policy, both nationally and internationally. The oil companies announced huge losses because of falling oil prices. The output from the vast oil fields at Prudhoe Bay began to decline, and for the first time in fifteen years, the pipeline was throttled back from its maximum output of 2 million barrels a day. Alyeska announced severe personnel cutbacks and layoffs at management levels. People moved out of Alaska in droves.

By January of that year, forty percent of all single-family homes in the Matanuska Valley were unoccupied and in the process of foreclosure. Eighty percent of all multi-family homes were likewise abandoned. Banks began to fail and close their doors. Unemployment in the Valley officially rose to 23 percent; in actuality, it was closer to 50 percent. The appraised value of homes dropped by half in a month's time. This month would live in the memory of millions of Americans as "Black October."

Sam escaped the layoffs simply because he was neither management nor a regular worker. He was suspended in some neverland in-between. Having acted as the supervisor of Pump Station Two for three years now, yet never having been actually called to that position, left him in a unique position. Alyeska didn't mind because they paid him less than a regular supervisor. Sam didn't mind because he didn't have to put up with endless meetings and company politicking. He knew it was a situation that couldn't last, but he was content to ride the soap bubble. At any rate, Sam felt his time at Alyeska was growing short. He had no idea what he was going to do afterward, but he also didn't care. The Lord would provide, and it would be wonderful.

Marcia's husband Tim, a gifted linguist, applied for and accepted a job translating English into Russian for The Church of Jesus Christ of Latter-day Saints in Salt Lake City. They sold their small home and all their furniture, packed up their most cherished possessions and left their beloved England. For Melody, her decision to leave with them was not arrived at in a moment, but took every ounce of faith she could muster. After much fasting and prayer, she knew she must go to America. She was torn, but could find no peace at the prospect of leaving her two young sons, although she had no contact with them. With nothing to live for in England, and afraid that her unborn baby would be taken from her as soon as it was delivered, she allowed herself to be caught up in the move, and eventually made her way to America.

It was a season of deep despair for Melody. Her heart could not be consoled for the loss of her precious children. During the entire trip to America she sat despondently, unable to think of anything else. The only reason she forced herself to eat was to sustain the life of her unborn child. Only the fact that one of her children had escaped with her gave her reason to live. Had she not feared for this child, she would have remained in England and waged a hopeless battle for the future of her sons. She would not have won—this both she and Theodore knew. He and his uncle had too much power, too much influence, and too much money for her to successfully challenge them.

Once in America, Melody easily obtained a visa and work permit. As a respected musician of some note, she was welcomed without reservation to her new country. When she applied for citizenship a year later, she dropped her married name.

She delivered a healthy baby boy in America, and affectionately named him Samuel Donavon McUlvany after a cherished memory of a missionary in Africa, her beloved father, and her ancestral name.

Alaska's greatest attraction is its limitless outdoors. Thousands come to the "Great Land" to bask in what was known nationwide as "The Last Frontier." Alaska is so large that dividing it into two states would have made Texas the third-largest state. Over 90 percent of the land in Alaska is reserved as National Parks, or some other designation not open for public development. There are more lakes in Alaska than all of the other states combined; more miles of river, more glaciers, more forest land, more herds of caribou, moose … the list could go on.

As an Alaskan, Sam was unique in the fact that he did not hunt, did not especially enjoy fishing, and did little in the vast outdoors except fly over it in his floatplane. Even that was no longer possible since his plane had evaporated in the feeding frenzy of his economic demise.

For this reason, he was somewhat surprised when the Spirit quite specifically whispered, "Get thee into the mountains." It was during his workweek when this occurred, and he quickly made arrangements to swap shifts so he could have two weeks off. He called a friend and made arrangements to rent a floatplane for a few days. By the time he arrived home all he did was kiss the twins, grab a few personal items, and drive to the lake.

It was the first week of July, and the sky was clear and sunny. He charted a course north and lifted off from Lake Lucille with a giddy sense of happiness and a deafening roar of unleashed power. He banked to his right and climbed steadily to the drone of the sturdy little plane.

Sam loved to fly, and was actually very good at it. He had earned his pilot's license almost fifteen years before, and had logged many hours flying in every circumstance that Alaska's varied terrain and weather could provide.

Far to his left he could see the great mountain Denali reaching some 20,000 feet above sea level, rising nearly 17,000 of those feet in a mere twelve miles. He would keep Denali to his left the entire flight. He flew over Wasilla, then Willow, and beyond that over land never inhabited by mankind. He was not sure to which lake he would fly but knew he would recognize it when he saw it.

Not more than forty minutes into the trip he spotted his lake. It was long and narrow, nestled between a low hill and a tall sloping mountain. After radioing in his modified flight plan, he circled, found the wind direction and glided to a smooth landing on the glassy waters.

Sam tethered the plane to some dead wood, hitched his pack over one arm, and hopped carefully from the float onto a large log conveniently fallen into the lake. The woods began immediately at the water's edge; the tangle of brush was impassable. But the log on which he stood cut a narrow path through the willows as if it were divinely inspired to fall there. A little log-hopping found a route beyond the marshy shore. In twenty steps Sam found himself among tall spruce, facing a verdant, sunlit meadow crossed by a cheerful little stream. The setting was stunning, and immediately inspired a sense of reverence within him.

Sam could just barely see the plane through the thick woods. He made several trips back to the plane to unload supplies and set up camp near the stream. For a few minutes he had a feeling as if he had been here before, then realized it reminded him of that clearing high in the Swiss forests where he and Dawn had met after their abduction in England. He built a small fire, and pondered the events that had brought him this far.

The long summer day was just yawning sleepily with long shadows and azure skies as Sam returned to the plane and retrieved his fly rod. The lake was as calm as a sheet of glass, the sky reflecting its golden fire in the waters, as Sam quickly landed a large lake trout. This he cleaned and soon had cooking over the fire. The smell was tantalizing, and his mouth watered as he waited for it to cook.

He pulled two plates from his pack, divided the fish in half, and placed part on each plate. He had barely finished when a twig snapped not far away. He was not at all surprised to see that Helaman had walked into the clearing.

His visitor stepped spryly toward Sam, a pleasant, though solemn look on his face. He came forward and squatted by the fire, held out his hands to the warmth and rubbed them together.

"I am so glad you came," Sam said, needing no introduction. "I have a thousand questions, but you seem pensive tonight," he observed. He wondered at Helaman's mood, because Sam had somehow thought a translated being would be somehow immune to any emotion but joy.

Helaman glanced up from the flames and smiled apologetically. "It was in forests like this that we camped, knowing that in a few days the

Lamanites would be upon us to destroy us. Since that time, whenever I come to the forest, I have a sense of dreaded finality."

Sam listened to this with wonder. Here he was sitting but a few feet away from a man who was nearly two thousand years old. He realized that he was communicating with Helaman spirit-to-spirit more than just with spoken words. Even so, Sam restrained himself from peppering his distinguished visitor with too many questions.

"That must have been very hard," Sam observed instead. His visitor nodded toward the flames, his eyes soft as if remembering long-gone beloved faces.

"It was for my people, at least. We righteous few knew they were past repentance by then, and we had actually been called out from among them. They had become hard, cruel, and without conscience. We could not bear to witness their barbarism and horror any longer. But, even with the power of God at our fingertips, we were often forbidden to interfere. It was extremely painful to us. The worst things always happened at night, after the day's fighting was done, and prisoners were the only entertainment they had, or that they wanted."

He paused and made a sound that was as much a groan, as a sigh.

"We were only among them to preserve a few whose work was not yet finished. We knew all the others would perish in the next few days. It was hard sitting among people who were friends, even our posterity, and not have them recognize us. But it also felt good to know that we had the power to protect those few, no matter the forces that came against us." This he said with a note of wonder and pride. Sam could tell it was not pride in himself, but in the Master whom he served.

"The few you were there to preserve were Mormon and Moroni?" Sam asked.

"That is correct; and some others. The Book of Mormon doesn't record everything that occurred, nor everyone who had assignments to fulfill during the destruction of our people."

"I hadn't really thought about that. I just assumed Moroni was the only survivor."

Helaman prodded the fire with his toe before continuing. "Moroni was the last to survive with his faith and salvation intact. He was the sole survivor of that great, last battle. He was the last righteous man, but he was not the only survivor."

Sam looked at him curiously, which caused his visitor to pause. "I've often wondered what Moroni was like. He must have been an incredible man."

"I knew Moroni personally, but he did not know who I was until near the end. I worked alongside him for many years. The Book of Mormon fails to describe him adequately. Have you ever wondered why the Nephites made him the captain of their armies like his father when he was just a teenager?"

"I sure have."

"It is because he was a giant of a man."

"A spiritual giant?" Sam wondered.

"That too, but he was more than seven feet tall. He was stronger than five normal men. He was so large that he could not ride a horse, but had to ride in a chariot drawn by at least three horses. His arms were massive. Besides being born a giant, he worked hard on his body to keep it in top condition. Even though he was huge, he could outdistance a horse, and often did. I once saw him without his armor, and thought I was looking at the body of an angel. No man ever lived who had a finer form."

Helaman paused as the memories flooded his mind. Then he continued.

"The sword he carried in battle could hardly be lifted by most men. His voice was low, like the rumbling of thunder. His eyes were stark blue, and bore the spark of both deep intelligence and kindness. But there was also a fierceness about him that was unmistakable. He had no patience for disobedience, liars, or politicians."

Sam shook his head. "I'll bet just seeing him at the head of an army caused the Lamanites to run the opposite direction."

"That is largely true, at least in the beginning. His cunning as a general was highly feared—so much so that the Lamanites soon decided that Moroni had to die if they were to win the war. Hence, no man has ever lived whose life was in greater danger. Every day there were threats on his life. Vast sums of money were laid on his head, and many a cunning man died in the attempt to claim it."

Sam was fascinated. "I have always wondered how he could be a man of war, and also a man of God. The two seem incongruent," Sam asked.

"They are, unless you were raised up to that end, unless your mission in life was to stand at the head of nations and in the name of God, defend them. Moroni was unique. He was everything the scriptures say about him, and much more."

"You said Moroni was not the last Nephite alive. I thought he was."

Helaman shook his head. "Many Nephites survived by defecting to the Lamanites. Some escaped into the Canadian mountains both before, and after the final battles."

Sam had never considered such a thing. "What happened to those people, the ones who went into Canada?"

Helaman looked up from the flames with a faint smile. "One of those I protected in that final battle was my great, great grandson. It's far too complicated a tale for me to relate tonight, but I had one branch of my family that did not apostatize. I asked the Lord for permission to preserve that line from destruction. In His mercy, He granted my plea."

Sam was stunned. "That's wonderful! Were your grandchildren Nephites?"

"My people were by then a mixture of both races, but mostly Lamanite. For many years prior to the final battles, many of the righteous were led away so that they escaped destruction. The Book of Mormon mentions those who went to the South Sea Islands. It doesn't mention a whole family who actually returned to Europe. There were many Nephites who left the land of Zarahemla before that war. Thousands moved far into the north, some going as far as Northern Canada and eventually into Greenland to escape the wars they knew were coming."

Helaman's eyes seemed far away as they stared into the fire. "My great-grandson was a righteous man, but stayed to fight for his beloved people in the last terrible battles. He was a powerful warrior, and a true patriot. He sent his family away into the North, and then he and his two eldest sons remained to defend their people."

Helaman looked at Sam with tears in his eyes. "I was there to see that they survived. They had no idea who I was, or why I was there. They survived of course, and years later I accompanied him to Canada where he rejoined his wife and children, and lived out his days in relative peace."

"My father's family is from Canada," Sam observed off-handedly.

Helaman looked up slowly with a one-sided smile on his face. "I know."

"I wonder if there could be any connection…" Sam stopped, the words frozen in his throat, a warm flush of the Spirit upon him. "Do you mean to tell me that you and I are . . .?"

"I can't answer that question," Helaman interrupted softly. "But, in general terms I can tell you this: Most all of the work of the Lord is done within the family structure. When family matters are in order, or in the hands of capable others, we are at times sent on other assignments pertinent to the Lord's work. But generally, we labor with people who are, or will become, a member of our family."

Sam looked at Helaman with new eyes, and Helaman smiled. "When the prophet said that families are the fundamental organization of the Church, he was speaking not only of this world, but the previous one, and the next. As the human family draws nearer and nearer to the perfect day, they draw into more perfectly-organized families. In the eternities when all is finally exactly as it should be, the Lord's work will be conducted only within the family structure."

Sam just had to ask. "So—are you a resurrected being, or are you translated?"

Helaman reached out to touch Sam's arm. "I am not resurrected yet, Sam. I have much work to do within my family as a translated servant of the Lord."

Sam stared at him in amazement. "So, as a translated being, is everyone you work with a relative of yours?" he asked incredulously, not from doubt, but from the sheer enormity of the concept and the obvious implications.

"Yes, most everyone—or they will become such," Helaman affirmed with a slight nod.

Sam thought for a long moment, trying to take it all in. Finally he spoke. "How could you, a Nephite, be an ancestor of mine?" he asked, not to question what his heart told him was the truth, but to understand how it could be.

"My great-great-grandson wasn't a full Nephite," Helaman responded quietly. "He was more than half Lamanite."

"I seem to recall that my father's great-grandfather was part American Indian."

Helaman smiled. "All that doesn't matter really. What does matter, and before long you will come to understand this truth, is that you and I have had a long and colorful history together. I can't remember the premortal world that well, but I do remember my mortal life, and you were heavily involved with my life."

"Me?!" Samuel gasped.

"Yes."

"How could that be? You're much older than I am, by thousands of years." Sam insisted, his mind whirling.

"Your perspective is very limited," Helaman said with a chuckle. "How do you know you're not older than I am? Remember, we were in the premortal world a very long time. We knew each other there. Isn't it most probable that when I went to the earth ahead of you, that you, being my righteous lineage, would have assisted me in my mortal life as a ministering spirit? We know that righteous, unborn spirit men and women minister to their living ancestors upon the earth."

"We do? We actually know that?"

"I know this to be a fact. I just assumed you did too," Helaman attested.

"I guess I sort of knew it, but had never thought of the ramifications of it. How can you be so certain I was there? You said you can't remember the premortal world, and neither can I."

Once again Helaman paused, as if waiting for direction, or perhaps permission to say more. "I know it for two reasons. First of all I am here with you. That tells me we are connected. Our connection did not begin in that priesthood meeting a couple years ago. It began in that great pre-earth life."

Helaman paused before continuing. "Secondly, I know it because I saw you once."

"You saw me? When? How?"

Helaman interrupted Sam with a chuckle and upraised hands. When Samuel calmed down, he explained.

"I was a young man, and was trying to escape from the Lamanites. There was a young woman with me I was desperately trying to save. We were hunted down and captured. The Lamanites beat me until I died." He paused here, his eyes a glassy stare as if focused upon events long past.

"Please don't stop there!" Samuel urged him. There had to be much more to it, because he knew this man had not died; he was now a translated being.

"I remember standing above my body, looking down at it and feeling so glad to be out of it. It looked horribly battered, and I literally rejoiced to be free. The process of dying had been very, very painful, and I was much relieved to finally be finished. Besides that, I had lived since my childhood as a slave among the Lamanites. My life hadn't been easy, and I rejoiced that it was over."

He shuddered as the raw memories flowed relentlessly from his mind.

"After the Lamanites perceived I was dead, they turned their violence from my body to the young woman with me. I remember a feeling of complete calm for her, because I knew the peace that leaving your body is. I was anxious for her to get past her pain, and come join me. I was actually happy for her.

"At that moment I became aware of a man standing beside me. He called me by name, and I turned my attention away from the Lamanites. I instantly recognized the person who had joined me as a dear and beloved friend whom I had known and trusted all of my life"

"Who was it?" Samuel asked breathlessly.

"It was you."

Samuel had no need to ask for confirmation, for he suddenly knew, as if his own memory of the event had momentarily returned and then was shrouded again by the veil, leaving him only misty memories and the conviction that it was so.

"I told you that your life was not finished, and that you had to go back into your body," Samuel stated with quiet confidence.

"That is correct. I did not want to return, and argued against it. You convinced me that great things awaited me, but I must go back and finish my life," Helaman explained.

"You went back, was healed after they left you both for dead, and became my forefather," Samuel concluded very softly.

"Yes, and much more!" Helaman corrected. "A distant relative is the lesser part of what I became. I became what you see before you now. I am here to continue the eternal cycle of righteousness that exists between us."

Helaman regarded Sam with love flowing from his soul.

"I am able to be here now because you were there then," he continued. "You were able to be there for me, because at some prior time, I was there to assist you. While you fulfill your labors for the Lord in this life, I will be here for your family, to aid and assist them in your absence. I can do this because you—they—are my family. I have a just and righteous interest in their salvation. At some time, you did the same for my family, and on and on and on. This is the pattern, one that has been repeating itself for millennia."

Sam felt the Spirit positively affirm to him that what Helaman was saying was pure truth. He nodded for him to continue.

"At some point we will enter the Celestial Kingdom because of the atonement and salvation of He who is worthy, our Savior Jesus Christ. And we will be there together because you and I are eternally, inseparably joined in a familial chain that has existed for a very, very long time. It is beautiful, is it not?" Helaman concluded with a slow, sweeping movement of his arm, which seemed to include all of eternity.

"It's the most beautiful thing I've ever contemplated," Samuel avowed. "It sure does cast bright light upon temple work, and genealogical research, and families, and the mercy of Christ!"

The visitor smiled at him. As if it were now time to change the subject, he nodded toward the plate of fish with a questioning look.

"Oh yes, please excuse me. I cooked you some," Sam said as he handed him a plate. The old gentleman bowed his head and whispered a short prayer of thanksgiving. Then he opened his eyes and with a smile, pulled off a few small bits of white meat with his fingers. He ate very little, but seemed to enjoy it immensely.

Sam ate hungrily, and finished his portion quickly. He opened a can of beans and propped it by the coals. In a few minutes it was bubbling, and Sam had difficulty lifting it from the fire. He was fishing at it with two sticks when his friend reached into the fire and picked up the can. Sam watched in amazement as he dumped some onto Sam's plate, and a little onto his own. He set the can back into the fire.

"I guess normal things can't harm you," Sam commented as he picked up his plastic fork.

"Hum? You know, I hardly think much about it anymore. I didn't mean to show off. I normally don't interfere. But, it is such a pleasure to be able to be myself without so many limitations." Helaman smiled, and leaned toward the fire with a small sigh of contentment. He looked back at Sam somewhat pointedly. "Do you want to know what the difference now is?"

"I'm your relative?" Sam guessed.

Helaman chuckled. "Much more importantly, you have faith—great faith actually, and your eternal progression is neither hindered, nor helped by what you see. I did not affect your agency by allowing you to see me pick up a hot can of beans. It is really as simple as that. So, your faith is what makes all this possible," he concluded with a grandiose tone to his voice. Silence followed as the sky waned from orange to red to maroons and purples.

Samuel studied him for a long time before daring to break the gentle silence between them. "What is it you actually do? You said you travel all over the world. What is your assignment, if you can tell me?"

"I work with my family, people like yourself."

"Is your, *our* family large enough to keep you busy?" Samuel asked.

"There are thousands in our family all over the globe. It keeps me and many others, very busy."

"Doing what, exactly?"

"I will explain as much as I can to you, but there's much you're not ready to learn. I will say this. After someone has received the promised blessings as you have, they have the opportunity to go through a testing period. It is always harsh, and tests their resolve to remain true and faithful in all things in the face of great conflict. It always includes a powerful opportunity, and even the apparent justification, to apostatize."

"Is that how you knew I had gone through severe trials?"

"Yes. I knew you had gone through them, or I wouldn't have received instructions to meet with you again."

"But, you didn't seem to know if I had been faithful."

"I did know you had triumphed, or I would not have been sent back. I asked you if you had been faithful only so you had the honor of answering in the affirmative. It is done that way to signal the end of the trial."

"I see," Sam replied.

The stranger chuckled. "What you see is very limited. However, that is about to change."

"Can we begin now?" Sam asked, excitement in his voice.

"Yes. Let us begin," Helaman said, and sat back on the grass with crossed legs. Two thousand years younger, Sam was not nearly limber enough to emulate his posture.

Helaman looked at him intently. "Let us first discuss where this is all headed, and what will be required of you if you choose to accept the opportunities before you."

"Yes, tell me everything!" Sam exclaimed, his eyes shining.

"You have, through your obedience, walked a steep path to this moment in time. You did not realize it as you were walking it; actually, no one does. The Holy Ghost clearly illuminates the path for each soul who has ears to hear, and eyes to see. This path is walked by many, but completed by very few in this life. It was the Lord's plan from the beginning that every man and woman should walk this path blind, by faith and obedience, following the promptings of the Holy Spirit—the Iron Rod if you will—until they arrived at the gateway to blessings more powerful than the mind of man can conceive."

Helaman stopped to make sure Sam was looking at him. "Through your faithfulness in Christ, Sam, and by His grace, you have arrived at that gate," he pronounced.

Sam dropped his head in humble gratitude.

"Beyond this point the path is not defined, with little more than hints in scripture concerning what lies ahead. When such a one as yourself arrives at this point, then he or she must be taught personally, face to face, in order to continue. Such things have a type in the temples. This instruction is my assignment. This pattern has existed since Adam and Eve first received heavenly messengers hundreds of years after being expelled from the garden."

"That's wonderful!" Sam exclaimed. His heart was pounding in his chest, and he felt as if he might jump up and start singing for joy.

"Yes, it truly is. However, there is also a sacred obligation which you must agree to if you are to continue."

"Anything! I will do anything you ask."

"It isn't I who asks it." Helaman admonished.

Sam grew sober. "I understand."

"You must remain silent about everything that happens to you—what you hear, what you see, learn, and do, from the moment of your Election onward. In time, you may write about these things, but until directed to do so, even writing them is not permissible. This is a sacred requirement, and you must take an oath thereto."

Sam nodded solemnly. "I agree, and I do covenant even as you say."

"Very good," Helaman said, and smiled. "Very good."

"Will this eventually bring me to the time when I can actually enter the presence of the Lord?" Sam asked softly.

Helaman nodded. "It will. But, that is a long way off. There are many things you must learn, many personal attributes you lack, and many perfections you must acquire from the Lord before you could ever be comfortable in His *glorious* presence." He spoke the word "glorious" with prolonged emphasis. Sam had no need to ask him if he knew of this glory first-hand.

"I'm curious. Is it required for all men and women to have a personal visitation with Christ in this life?"

Helaman smiled and shook his head. "That's a good question, because it is a "yes" and a "no" answer. Yes, in order to inherit all that God has, each of His children must become worthy to return to the presence of Christ, who then brings them to the Father. This sacred event must happen if a person desires to dwell in the Celestial Kingdom, and be in God's family. There is no option, and no other way."

"But," Helaman continued with a voice of warning, "it is not required that all accomplish it in this life. Few righteous do, actually, and yet can still attain celestial glory. The Second Comforter is a glorious possibility in this life, a grand and triumphant accomplishment, but it is not required."

Sam was puzzled. "Then, why do the scriptures, and even the temple, seem to point to it as the greatest achievement of life?"

"It *is* the greatest achievement of life! It just isn't necessary to do it in mortality."

"Then, why even try, I'm wondering?" Sam said a little dejectedly. "I've discovered that road is paved with tears."

"It is, but not more so in mortality than it will be after this life," Helaman assured him. "The task is actually of equal difficulty in either sphere. But, there are special blessings that flow to the individual who achieves it in this life, which can be attained in no other way. An example of such a blessing is right here, with me being allowed to minister to you, and other unique blessings that will flow to your posterity."

Sam brightened. "I do have faith that these blessings far outweigh any price. So, how was it possible that so many of your people were worthy to be in the presence of the Lord when He came to Bountiful?" he pondered out loud.

Helaman thought about this. "I think it's because we went through much of what you will face before the Lord comes again. We were faithful to our testimonies of Jesus and followed the Holy Spirit and our Prophet, in spite of the subtle and severe trials leading up to His coming to us. Many dear friends and family deserted to our enemies after facing execution for believing Samuel the Lamanite's prophesies. There were years of worldly abundance in our corrupt society, with our leaders steeped in secret combinations, not unlike today."

He got up to place more wood on the fire and sat again. "Actually, there were several Anti-Christs in the history of my people who were a type and shadow of a great tyrant yet to come. This new Anti-Christ will have the combined attributes of the cunning of Amalickiah, the flattery of Nehor, the subtlety of Gadianton, and King Jacob's desire for absolute power when he overthrew the entire Nephite government."

"Really? That's pretty frightening."

Helaman nodded. "When our entire society finally fell into chaos, we had to rely upon the Holy Spirit to know friend from foe, and where to go to keep our families safe. The wicked were finally destroyed with the sign of the Lord's death, but those who could hear His voice were told what to do and were miraculously saved. Many angels intervened on our behalf, just as your people will experience."

"How long after the destructions ended did the Lord come to you?" Sam asked in wonder.

"It was less than a year. The Prophet urged us to serve each other and purify our hearts and minds with all diligence to receive Christ. The day the Savior came, many of us had felt strongly to go to the temple, and found many others there who had also followed that prompting. As we heard the voice of the Father and Christ descended, we were drenched in His glorious presence and inexpressible love. We knew in that moment that all that we had endured was worth any price."

Helaman stood up and paced excitedly around the campfire. "Now after all this time, you and I have been called to prepare the world for His Second Coming! The coming days of tribulation are near! I remember Jesus telling us that when 'the words of Isaiah should be fulfilled—behold they are written, ye have them before you, therefore search them… then is the fulfilling of the covenant which the Father hath made unto his people, O house of Israel.' We are assisting in that fulfillment."

Sam paused before asking, "Then, do you think Isaiah is the key to understanding the events leading up to Christ's return?"

"Yes," Helaman said, and smiled. "That is why the Spirit told you to carefully study the words of Isaiah."

Sam nodded. "I can see why now," he said with new understanding.

"The events from the history of my people you know as the Book of Mormon, have been carefully chosen to help prepare your people for just this time ahead," Helaman said soberly.

"Wow," Sam said with wonder. "I feel I've always known that, but it's certainly more real to me now."

Sam then paused before asking his next question. "Are you what the scriptures call an angel?"

His visitor chuckled as he poked at the fire.

"The term is used loosely in this generation, I'm afraid. In my day the term specifically meant one without a body, who had either lived on this earth, or was destined to, who labored in unseen ways to guide the children of men toward righteousness. Persons such as myself were never called 'angels' back then. We were workers, laborers, ministers, men and women not unlike yourself, who had earned the great blessing of prolonging our lives in mortality to continue our ministry."

Helaman thought for another moment and continued, "Because we are not able to appear in glory, as a resurrected being might, we rarely think of ourselves as angels. However, by modern-day definition, I suppose I am indeed an angel," he said matter-of-factly.

"Do you get to be around resurrected beings?" Sam asked impulsively.

Helaman waved his hand. "In time you will understand all these things. For now, it's not important."

"Oh," Sam replied, a little embarrassed for having asked.

Helaman just grinned at him good-naturedly.

Sam had so many questions, yet he wanted to be inoffensive in asking them. He didn't want this wonderful moment to evaporate because he probed foolishly. "I suppose it's possible there are a lot of beings like yourself working among the people, isn't it?"

"More than anyone suspects," Helaman replied with a wink.

"Do you appear to, and help guide the living prophets of this dispensation?" Sam asked more cautiously..

"That's a good question. We only appear to conduct the same preparatory work with them that I am now doing with you. We have nothing to do with the administration of the kingdom in this dispensation. Our work is always with individuals. The Prophet takes his direction from Jesus Christ; then we respond to the living prophet's direction in all things relative to the latter-day work."

"So, you take orders from the Prophet?" Sam asked with wonder in his voice. His estimation of what the prophet could do was taking a mighty leap upward.

"It would be more accurate to say I sometimes assist him as the Lord directs. This is Christ's kingdom, after all," he added.

"I should have known that already," Sam responded soberly, and grew silent.

Helaman placed his hand on Sam's shoulder. "Please, ask your questions without so much self-effacement. I'm here to answer them. If you ask something I can't answer, I'll just tell you. You needn't worry that I'll stand up and leave if you err. You have passed the tests, and this is your time to learn."

Sam visibly relaxed. "So, are most general authorities translated?

Again Helaman laughed. "I get asked that quite often. No. In fact, very few are. Ours is a great work that is parallel to the earthly church. They have their mission, and we have ours. They cannot possibly minister directly to every living soul. So we labor where they cannot. Our assignments are in complete harmony, but separate. In fact, if we stopped what we do, their work would become frustrated, unfinished and incomplete. If their work stopped, ours would become impossible.

"It is actually quite naïve to think that mortals are the only ones performing a great work in this dispensation. Simple logic will tell you there are nearly infinite numbers of righteous non-mortals, and but a few righteous mortals presently on this earth. There are significantly more of us non-mortals engaged in what we do than there are of you."

Sam nodded with understanding.

"Of course, mortals become aware of the rest of Father's works only gradually," Helaman continued. "Even as you sit here talking with me, you cannot begin to comprehend the vastness of the labors of Jesus Christ for the Father. I, myself, am not able to comprehend it all." He said this a bit ironically as he poked at the glowing embers with his stick. Sam suddenly realized it was twilight, and the fire was nearly extinguished. Sam tossed more wood on the fire and it came back to life.

"Where will I labor? What will my assignment be?" Sam asked after he sat back down.

"That will depend upon you. What you are able to accomplish will depend entirely on how diligent you are, and how much you actually want to do. When you reach your full potential, then you will receive an assignment commensurate with your abilities. Even among people like yourself, there is a wide range of abilities and desires. Until then, what you will eventually do is not known to me."

"Do some people come this far, and then decide to just sit back and relax?" Sam wondered. It was something that had occurred to him several times, but which did not appeal to his soul.

"As far as I know, that hasn't happened yet," Helaman replied evenly.

"I'm glad to hear that," Sam allowed.

His visitor stood in an effortless motion and looked around the woods, now only visible in the flickering light of the fire. Sam knew it was late, since in the summer, darkness only descends in Alaska in the wee hours of morning.

"It's beautiful isn't it?" his visitor commented, not really expecting a reply. "I've never been here before. You picked a beautiful spot."

"When will I see you again?" Sam asked, sensing the interview was over.

"When you are ready." Helaman smiled at Sam, turned toward the lake. He took several steps, stopped and pointed at the plane floating peacefully nearby. "Never got used to one of those things," he said, and began walking again. After a few steps he turned back toward Sam.

"Man *was* meant to fly, contrary to contemporary wisdom, but not in one of those insane things. Even as a translated being, they scare me to death!" Nearly out of sight, Sam heard him chuckle. He vanished from sight somewhere between the edge of the woods and the lake. Sam gazed into the woods for a long time. He finally picked up his journal and made notes about the weather, his flight, the fish he caught, and nothing more.

Sam stayed in the woods for three days, fasting and praying. It was a wonderful time, and his spirit grew in precious ways. He had never before sensed the temple-like sacredness of an unsullied portion of nature. It was silent, innocent, spiritual, and in many ways, a temple. He understood why God had often used a mountaintop as an appropriate place to appear to His servants. Every day thereafter, the Nephite visitor returned for a lengthy discussion.

The pristine Alaskan mountain was now holy ground.

SONG OF THE HEART

Sam returned to his home with a diamond-hard resolve to press forward in his quest for the greater blessings. He had never felt such inner power before, and it thrilled him. Those who knew and loved Sam commented on the obvious change. Besides the light in his face, they often described this new aspect to his being as serenity, or peace. It was a good description of how Sam felt, yet a wholly inadequate descriptor of its cause.

To express his inner joy, Sam wrote a beautiful, nearly operatic duet for tenor and soprano. "Here Am I, Send Me" was published a short time later, and almost immediately found wide acceptance among the Saints. He began to get strange calls as people connected his name with that of the composer. He quietly got an unlisted number.

Upon balancing his checkbook that week, he was startled to see a sizable balance remaining. In prior years he had had so much money that knowing the balance available actually made little difference in how much he could spend. Not that long ago, there had been no balance to worry about. But, since going to work on the North Slope, he had sufficient for his needs. Now for the first time in his life, Sam actually analyzed his finances, and realized with a start that he was making nearly as much money from music royalties as from his job. Warmth swept through him, and he picked up the phone to give two-week's notice to his employers.

He was actually sad to leave Alyeska in many ways. They had been very good to him, and had been there in his hour of desperate need. They had trained him, promoted him, given him opportunities, taught him leadership, patience, and obedience in the trenches of Babylon. They had opened his eyes to a world filled with good people, few of whom even acknowledged the existence of God, let alone actually sought after Him. He had worked for them a little short of ten years, and left with a sizable retirement and savings. In worldly terms, it had been a good thing, and he felt grateful. In spiritual realities it had been both devastating, and exalting. The cost of making a living had thus far been enormous.

Alyeska did not accept his resignation gracefully, but called him in to numerous interviews. They offered him promotions, raises, new opportunities, even a normal schedule, all of which he turned down. When it became apparent he was truly leaving, they threw him a party, and reluctantly bid him farewell. At his going-away party he played "I Have Always

 Loved You," while the twins sang the beautiful words. When the music came to an end, they all understood why he was leaving, and wished him well with a little amazement in their voices. Many had heard this song, and none had suspected it was he who had written it. They never even suspected he wrote music, let alone music of such renown.

Now that he was unemployed, and officially a starving artist, Sam had a need to promote his work. He contacted his long-time friend and musical associate, Mike, and made arrangements to travel to meet him in Utah. It was early August, and the LDS Booksellers Convention was in a few days.

The LDS Booksellers Association was the largest organization of its type, and promoted the creation and distribution of all types of LDS art, music, literature, and merchandise. The convention was closed to the public. Guards stood at every entrance, and only those with passes could enter.

Those invited fell into three general classes, each with a different colored name badge. Green badges were for publishers, wholesalers, manufacturers, and sellers of LDS wares. Red badges were buyers from all over the world. To qualify as a buyer they had to own or represent some retail outlet. Blue badges were for artists, authors, musicians and other LDS artisans.

Sam was not prepared for the hugeness of the affair. It involved three floors of the Salt Palace Convention Center. Sam found a nice booth set up promoting his, and other artist's music. When he was not autographing his work he walked slowly from booth to booth. Almost every notable author or musician was there. He shook hands with General Authorities, as well as many other well-known figures. He found that, with few exceptions, they at least knew about his music, and were pleased to meet him. Happily, he met no one who was critical. In fact, the spirit of love and brotherly kindness was so strong during the convention that such feelings simply did not exist.

Sam remained at the convention for three days signing sheet music and CD's as souvenirs. At the table next to him a line ten times in length waited patiently to meet his friend Mike. Almost all the people who asked him for autographs came from Mike, who introduced him as "the one" who had written "I Have Always Loved You." Thanks in large part to Mike's kind referrals, hundreds walked away having decided to stock and promote Sam's work in their stores.

Though not as well-known as other LDS artists there, Sam nevertheless found himself much better known, and his music more loved than he could have hoped. In ways more wonderful than he could have anticipated, his visit to the convention was a great blessing, and a needed boost to his career.

Lisa and Bonnie had come to Utah with their father. This was the twin's first trip out of Alaska in ten years. They were now eighteen, tall, blond, and in the full bloom of womanhood. Besides their obvious beauty in duplicate, what added to their attraction was that they were innocent, vivacious, and sweetly naïve.

They accompanied Sam to the convention each day, and created a small stir as they walked around the convention hall arm in arm. People stopped to watch them go by, which was all very novel to the girls. They were amused and flattered by the attention they got, and were asked more than once if they would pose for photographs, or model wares. One studio at the convention offered a sizable model's fee. They politely refused. However, when the director of the convention asked if they would pose for the cover of next year's convention brochure, they agreed if the brochure also plainly introduced them as songwriter Samuel Mahoy's daughters. The convention agreed, and they became poster girls quite unexpectedly. Their desire to help their father took higher priority than their native modesty. Samuel was touched to tears.

When the convention ended they still had three days left in Utah, and wandered among the historic sites surrounding Temple Square. Sam was so proud and pleased to have the twins along, that he found himself watching them as much as the sites. They often took an arm on either side of him, and he felt escorted by royalty.

There was one other string they pulled in his heart: they were the spitting image of their mother. Every time he looked at them he thought how nearly they looked like Dawn that first hot sunny day in South Africa. His heart felt both happy, and a little sad each time he thought of it. As far as he knew, they had never worn a bright pink bikini in their lives. He was quite sure that if they did, they would be mirror images of their mother that day.

They were slowly walking down the beautiful main avenue in Temple Square, the Temple to their right, with the glorious white Christus in the glassed rotunda visible on their left, when a man skidded to a stop directly in front of the twins. His face was such a mask of surprise that he looked silly standing there with his mouth open.

"Dawn?" he finally stammered. Sam and the girls stopped short, looking at each other with wide eyes.

"Excuse me?" Sam asked the man, who was still gaping at his daughters.

"No, you couldn't be," the man finally said, and in apology took a step back. He turned toward Sam. "I was mistaken. I once knew someone in Africa who looked very much like…"

Sam stared at him with sudden recognition. "You were in South Africa? You knew Dawn Pawley?"

"I did!" he replied. "I helped teach her the gospel. Are you…"

"Sam Mahoy!" Sam cried and stuck out his hand.

"Elder Mahoy? I'm your former companion, Elder Kim Hall!"

Sam threw his arms around Kim and gave him a bear hug. They were pounding each other on the back so hard that the twins winced. It had to hurt. But, the two men didn't seem to notice.

"What are you doing in Salt Lake City? I thought you lived in California?" Sam asked once they were separated.

"I do. I'm here for the South African Mission reunion. Didn't you know about it? It's tonight."

"No kidding!" Sam cried. "We've got to go. Do you want to go, girls?"

"Sure, Daddy! Let's do!" they replied happily.

"Why do they look so much like Dawn?" Kim asked suspiciously.

"I married Dawn after we returned to America together," Sam explained, feeling a little sheepish.

"No!" he cried. "I didn't know that. You two weren't in love when you left Africa," he proclaimed.

"No, but a year later we fell in love and were married."

"Twin Dawns!" Kim proclaimed, looking them up and down. "So, where is Dawn herself?" he asked suddenly.

"She passed away almost ten years ago," Sam said evenly.

A look of surprise, then sadness, crossed his former companion's face. "I am so sorry," he said. Then he said exactly the right thing to honor Dawn's memory, and keep the conversation from turning sad.

"You two young women certainly radiate your mother's inner, and outer beauty," he said with a smile.

"Thank you," they replied, both deeply touched.

Sam talked with his friend for several more minutes, and they parted with a vow to meet again that evening at the reunion.

There were about a hundred people at the South Africa Mission reunion. Sam was sad to learn that President Carlson had died of a heart attack two years previously in the recently completed South African temple. He was quite certain he would have wanted to go that way.

Most of the people there recognized Sam, and it was a pleasant evening. It was surprisingly well-known that he was *the* Samuel Mahoy—the musician. He was pretty flattered. He actually forgot about the girls in his haste to meet everyone possible. As the evening began to wind down, he looked around and found his daughters talking with a woman at the other end of the hall.

Bonnie introduced them. "Daddy, this is Marcia. She's from England. We have been talking about modeling there. She used to be a model."

"She's really nice. She's been entertaining us while you ignored us," Lisa added in a teasing voice.

"Pleased to meet you," Sam said as he shook her hand even while thinking she looked very familiar, though no memory surfaced to identify her.

Marcia was a woman about his age, perhaps younger. Her hair was soft brown, and quite long. Her face was beautiful, though somewhat rounded by time. Her smile seemed natural, as if smiling were something she was used to doing.

"What brings you to America?" Sam asked her conversationally.

"I've actually been here several years. My husband is a linguist for the LDS translation department. We live in Logan. I'm here at the reunion with my sister, who is about to be married." Her accent was definitely English, though leaning somewhat toward a lilt he thought perhaps Australian.

"Oh, how wonderful. I hope you've enjoyed the reunion," he said happily.

She smiled even more brightly at this and nodded. "So where are you from, Elder Mahoy?"

"I have lived in Wasilla, Alaska for the past twenty-five years."

She cocked her head. "Tell me something," she said. "Would you know a family from Wasilla who now lives in North Salt Lake, by the name of Rogers?"

"Hmmm. You know, I might. My parents were friends with a family by that name."

"George and Amy Rogers?" she supplied.

"That's right. I do know them! They have three daughters and a son. Probably all grown now. Sister Rogers was a professional ballet dancer if I remember correctly," Sam exclaimed.

"The very same," Marcia proclaimed. "We're staying with them."

"How do you know them?" Sam wondered.

"My sister is engaged to their youngest son."

"Wow, what a small world."

"Smaller than you think," she admitted. "They brought up your name several times in conversation. They take some boasting rights in remembering you as a family friend, the former lumbering teenager turned famous songwriter."

Sam had to laugh at this. Marcia seemed quite amused by it all, and laughed happily with him.

"Hey, I have a grand idea," she interjected suddenly. "If you are still in town, why don't you and your daughters come over tomorrow evening? The Rogers are having an open house to announce the engagement. They will be delighted to see you again, and I think you will enjoy yourself."

"I don't know. I hardly know them—they were my parents' friends."

"Please come. I promise you won't be disappointed if you do."

"Why would you say that?" Sam asked, truly perplexed.

"Take my word for it, Elder Mahoy," she said with such emphasis that Sam silently decided to go.

He looked at her more carefully. "Were you in South Africa while I was on my mission there?" he asked. This was all getting a little odd.

"Perhaps for a day or two. Take my word, it will be worth your while. Search your heart, Elder Mahoy. You need to come."

Her words echoed in his mind all the way home.

He arrived in a rented Ford, but it was curiosity that drove him there. They found the Rogers home tucked deep into an old subdivision of two-story homes and huge elm trees. Sam pulled up to the curb. The twins had insisted on coming, even when he had given them plenty of leave to stay home. They were his self-assigned companions on this trip, and probably wouldn't have left him for any reason.

Sister Rogers was exactly as Sam remembered her. She talked fast, laughed loud, wore too much make-up, and commanded attention in any room she was in. She was the life of the party, and her home buzzed with gaiety. Sam and his daughters were immediately absorbed into the happiness all around them. Introductions were made, and the twins found several young men their own age and disappeared. Sam found himself sitting somewhat awkwardly in a room full of strangers.

Marcia was sitting on the exact opposite side of the room, bouncing a baby boy happily on her leg. The child looked to be around a year old, and only partly pleased with his current lot in life. Marcia's voice drifted to Sam above the hubbub, and he suddenly recognized the lilting accent of one from Rhodesia. Twenty-five years ago he had known that accent well and could have picked it out of a room full of Englishmen. This far removed in time, it had taken this long for it to occur to him.

"Marcia, you're from Rhodesia!" he said suddenly. All conversation stopped in the room, and he wondered if he had said something forbidden.

"Yes, Sam. I'm from Rhodesia."

"Did I know you there? I was in Rhodesia during my mission."

She smiled oddly. "No, not in Rhodesia, more outside Rhodesia," she replied cryptically.

"Not in South Africa, you say. Not in Rhodesia, but outside it. This feels like a puzzle. I don't remember… oh wait—*on the train!"* he suddenly cried. "You're *that* Marcia. On the train!"

"Yes," she replied happily. She remained seated for about ten seconds then seemed to make a sudden decision, and set the baby on the floor. She jumped to her feet and ran toward him. He barely stood in time to catch her. He was amazed at her delayed, yet emotional response. She kissed him several times on the cheek as she held him tightly.

"I can't believe it," he said over and over. "You're really here, in America, right here! This is astonishing! This is wonderful!"

Marcia pulled away and smiled at him. "You will never know how greatly you have influenced my life, Elder Mahoy. If you had a week, and a box of tissues, I would tell you. Because of you, I joined the Church, although years later, and I'm married in the temple to a wonderful man. I'm so very, very thankful to you," she said emotionally.

"You didn't say a thing at the reunion. I don't understand? Why didn't you say something?" Sam demanded congenially.

"The Spirit stopped me. You had to come tonight on your own. And, I wanted you to meet someone," she replied.

"Who?" he asked happily.

"I think she means me," a soft voice replied from the far side of the room. Sam turned his head to see a beautiful woman standing in the doorway. She had long, curly auburn hair, beautiful dark eyes, a small upturned nose, and a face of exceptional beauty. He knew her immediately.

"Melody!" he cried, and she ran to him. By the time they embraced she was crying.

"Oh, Melody, Melody!" he exclaimed. "How are you? Are you OK? I've wondered a thousand times where you were, and what had happened after I left you there at the Pretoria train station."

She stepped away from him suddenly, and wiped her eyes with a cloth handkerchief. She seemed unable to speak. Sam was struck by her deep emotion at seeing him.

She looked around at the sea of curious faces. "Come," she said, and taking him by the hand, led him out onto the front porch.

They stood for a few moments gazing at one another as the elm trees swayed in the gentle breeze. It was a beautiful evening, and the moon was just coming up over the mountain. In the dimming light, some youth were playing soccer with a tennis ball in the road in front of the house. Their laughter was like music in the distance.

Melody turned toward him finally and took both his hands in hers. "Sam, I'm so pleased to see you again. I heard Marcia tell you how grateful she is to you. Any gratitude she feels is felt a hundred fold in me," she said, pressing her palm to her heart.

Sam gave her hands a squeeze. "It's wonderful for me, too. Do you know what the two hardest things I did on my mission were? Number one, walking away from you and Marcia at the train station; and number two, not seeing you at the airport to say good-bye when I left South Africa. I have felt an emptiness for years from those two things."

"I'm sorry," she replied softly without taking her eyes from him. "I think in a childish way I was in love with you back then. I cried myself to sleep many nights thinking about you going back to America."

"Oooh," Sam said with deep empathy. "In as much of a way as missionaries can, I loved you back then, too," he replied. This he said in all honesty, feeling those old feelings again more strongly than expected.

Melody seemed to stiffen when he said that, but quickly recovered and smiled. "I'm getting married," she said matter-of-factly. "Well, actually I'm getting engaged. Tonight is my engagement party, in fact."

"Marcia told me. Congratulations," Sam told her with a grin.

She glanced at her feet. "Thank you," she murmured softly and released both his hands.

A young man stepped out onto the porch. "Melody," he said happily, "we're ready for you to play."

"Oh, Brian. Come meet the man who introduced me to the gospel. Elder Sam Mahoy."

Brian shook his hand enthusiastically. "You're *that* Elder Mahoy, from the train?"

"I am." Brian was tall, and handsome in face and features.

"I had decided you were a myth, actually," Brian said almost cynically. "Tell me the truth. Were there really bombs going off and bullets whizzing around, and you were the only guy who was not afraid, but bravely gave Melody a priesthood blessing which promised that nothing would harm her?"

"That's entirely true," Sam confirmed, then added, "Perhaps except the part about my not being afraid. The peace of the Spirit was there, but I was otherwise terrified," he admitted with a smile.

Brian greeted this with some degree of triumph in his face. "I always suspected the story was punched up a bit." He slid an arm protectively around Melody's waist. She responded by taking his arm with a half-smile.

"Shall we go play?" she asked at the very moment an awkward silence threatened to engulf them. They all left the porch with relief.

In a room that had at one time been a large formal dining room, the Rogers had a very nice walnut-colored Steinway grand piano. Graceful Queen Ann chairs lined two walls of the room, while a large crystal chandelier hung directly over the large grand. On the far side of the piano, a sliding glass door led out onto a terrace, its glass covered by white lacy curtains. The elegant buffet cabinet that occupied the far wall was filled with photos, trophies, and the dozen or so brightly-colored ballet slippers. The room was a shrine to their life-long love of music and ballet.

Melody took her violin from its case and tuned it quickly. She stepped to the side of the piano and cradled the violin in her arms like a child. The guests stood or sat around the walls so that people surrounded her.

"Since this is a special occasion, rather than playing something showy, I've decided to play a love song. Since love is what fills my heart tonight, I hope you'll enjoy my selection. It's one of my most favorite in all the world."

She raised the violin, and after a long pause, began playing a haunting melody familiar to all present. Bonnie could not restrain herself, and whispered to the woman next to her, "That's my mother's song." Her words unexpectedly came during a pause in the music and echoed loudly in the room. Bonnie instantly realized her enthusiasm had caused her to speak too loudly, and clapped a hand to her mouth. But, the interruption was sufficient to cause the music to suddenly cease. Rather than being offended, Melody looked at Bonnie with open curiosity.

"Your mother?" she asked, genuinely interested.

Bonnie blushed but proudly replied, "Yes. Daddy wrote that song for my mother."

"How astonishing. I would love to meet him. Who is he? she asked brightly.

Instead of answering, Bonnie pointed directly at Sam. "Him," she said into the silence.

Melody followed the finger until her eyes fell upon Sam.

"Sam," she said quietly. The smile on her face slowly fell. She lowered the violin until it dangled from her fingers. For a moment it seemed as if she might drop it. Finally, she sat on the piano bench, apparently stunned. No one in the room moved. None, including Sam, understood her reaction to the revelation.

Sam took a step toward her after a moment, not really knowing what to say or do, but sensing he somehow had a part to play in this unfolding drama. She looked up at Sam with large, frightened eyes that stopped him in his tracks.

"This song," she said in a whisper too small for almost anyone except himself to hear. "I have always pretended it was written for me. There is so much love in the words, so much passion in the music. In some way, I suppose I always fantasized it was written by someone who loved me that way." She stiffened. "I'm sorry," she said and laid her violin behind her on the piano bench.

She stood and walked slowly toward the door. Sam walking around her and picked up the violin. He held it for a moment, savoring its richness before handing it to her with the bow. Melody had turned to watch him, and taking a step closer, took it as if in a dream. He sat at the piano bench and after raising the cover, played a soft introduction to the very song she had intended to abandon.

He paused, and heard Bonnie and Lisa clear their throats. As if angels had suddenly appeared in the room, the girls began to sing. It was only the second time Sam had played this song since Dawn's death. Suddenly it felt natural and beautiful again. In some way impossible to comprehend, the magic of perfect love settled upon him, just as powerfully as it had that day seventeen years ago, and he played the sweet melody with utter joy. He was not surprised when Melody's violin softly joined them, finding a delicate harmony—dancing, rejoicing, floating freely on the magic of love. Combined with the rich violin obbligato and the girls' angelic voices, Sam's love song was more exquisite than he had ever heard it.

In some way poetically beautiful, Sam knew they weren't singing for those assembled, nor were they singing for him; they were singing for Melody—and everyone in the room knew it. The moment was breathtaking.

Even after the music had ceased, it seemed to whisper in the room. Sam sat for a few moments longer, and quietly lowered the cover over the keyboard. There was dead silence, and no one dared move, as if some movement might mar the magic the music had just woven. He sensed Melody looking at him, and he looked up into her eyes. Where he expected to see happiness, joy, love—there was only pain. She laid her violin on the piano and ran from the room.

Melody never did return from the back of the house, and Sam left shortly thereafter to escape the awkwardness his presence had apparently fueled. He and his daughters returned to his sister's house, and quietly packed their bags.

The next morning the girls did not get up by themselves to leave for the airport. He urged them along, begging them to hurry. They missed their flight by twenty minutes. Sam was annoyed and began to give them a lecture. It would cost them $50 dollars per ticket to rebook, money that he did not want to spend. But he stopped mid-lecture, seeing the twinkle in their eyes; they were clearly not penitent.

Finally at their urging, he rescheduled their flight for three days away, rather than later that day. They hummed to themselves as he drove back home. Though the urge surfaced several times, he could not bring himself to reproach them. For some reason he did not even try to identify, he was strangely glad to still be in Utah, as well.

It was nearly nine o'clock that same evening when the doorbell rang. Emily, Sam's oldest sister and whose home it was, answered the door. "Sam, someone's here for you," she called.

Sam came to the door to find Melody standing outside. She was wringing her hands as if terrified. Instead of inviting her inside, he stepped out and walked with her down the sidewalk in the cool of the evening.

"I came to say good-bye. I didn't get a chance to say good-bye last night," she blurted out in a rush.

"Oh, yes," Sam said, surprised at how glad he was to see her. "Thank you, and I wish you every happiness in your upcoming marriage."

Melody swallowed hard. "I've called off the engagement, and have made arrangements to go back East," she confessed, twisting at a small handbag.

Sam's heart skipped a beat. "But—I thought you were happy? I thought you were going to stay in Utah?" he asked, genuinely puzzled.

"I only wanted to do that because it was near Brian's home, and we were planning…well, you know all about that. I've been offered a position teaching violin at a notable school of music in New York. I'm going to accept the position," she said with forced calmness.

"What changed your mind?" Sam asked, his mind a blur.

"Hearing you play that beautiful song," she answered with a sense of relief, as if he had finally asked an important question, one which she had repeatedly asked herself.

"Why? What difference could that possibly make?" he questioned her.

"I realized I was settling for happiness and security, rather than for love. I do love Brian, but not in the way your song describes. When I marry, I want to feel exactly that way. I want my heart to pound, and my palms to sweat, and my mind to hum with happiness. That's the way I felt as I stood there playing that song. I don't feel that way with Brian. He's a fine man, but I realized at that moment I'm not *in love* with him."

"I'm sorry," Sam replied.

"Whatever for?" she asked in genuine surprise. "As I heard your daughters sing, I could feel the love you have for their mother. They know you love her, and that knowledge came out in their voices. You saved me from a big mistake, Sam. Don't feel sorry. Your wife is an incredibly lucky woman to be loved so deeply. I envy her," she admitted honestly.

Samuel tried several times to say something, to explain, but each time he was stopped by the Spirit. They walked on in silence for almost half a block.

"Tell me, does love like that feel as wonderful as I have imagined it could?" Melody asked.

Sam glanced at her, then laced his arms behind his back. "It feels better than anything I can describe to you," he said softly. "It is life-giving, and soul-healing. It is the sweetest of all earthly gifts."

"Do you feel that your love is stronger now than when you wrote that song?"

"Melody, I need to tell you something…"

Melody stopped walking. "I'm so rude," she interrupted him. "I have no right to pry. Please forgive me." She did an about-face and began walking more quickly back the way they had come. He had to take a couple quick steps to catch up with her. When he did, he caught her by the elbow and stopped her directly under a street light. In doing so she turned to face him.

She turned quickly enough that her hair fanned out and fell in a rich cascade over her shoulder, onto her chest. He reached out and gently wove his fingers through it near her cheek. It was something he had wanted to do long ago, although until this moment he had not realized it. She caught her breath and closed her eyes as he slowly let the silken tresses slide through his fingers.

He laughed, a sound which surprised them both. "I think I've wanted to do that for a long time," he said.

"But…" she stammered.

"When I first met you, and then again last night, I wondered what your hair felt like." He brushed the backs of his fingers across her cheeks.

"Wondered if your skin was as soft as it looks." His eyes focused upon her lips. "Wondered if your lips are as warm and sweet as they appear."

"But, Sam!"

"Twenty years ago, I put you out of my mind. But now, I'm wondering again," he said as he took a small step closer to her.

Melody took a step backward. "Sam, this isn't…"

"I'm just wondering," he repeated as he slipped both arms around her waist.

"But you love your wife!" she nearly shouted at him, placing both elbows on his chest.

"My wife passed away nearly ten years ago," he said quietly.

"Oh…" was all she got out before his lips gently touched hers.

For many long seconds she stood rigidly in his arms, her eyes still open, her lips unyielding. Slowly, quietly, something melted inside her heart, and her arms found their way around his neck. She kissed him back—softly at first, then anxiously, then passionately. When he finally pulled away she remained standing with her face tilted upward, her eyes closed, a look of utter happiness on her face. He smiled and kissed her lightly again.

She opened her eyes, blinked twice, and blushed.

"Blimey," she said emphatically, her accent coming out. "Ah just realized I've nevah been kissed befo' - at least no' like that. Moah, please," she said and closed her eyes. It was a request he happily filled.

There is a gentle magic that turns the lock in one's heart, behind which hides love. Sometimes, if the lock is slammed closed too hard, it is painful to reopen. It had been so long since Sam had felt the magic, that its unexpected reemergence startled him. He simultaneously felt exhilarated, frightened, yet somehow unfaithful. He pulled away and opened his eyes in time to see hers open slowly, as if from sleep. She shyly lowered her chin and cleared her throat.

"It's been a long time since I kissed anyone," he told her.

"Ten years is a long time," she answered softly. Then she realized what he had just said. "You've not kissed a woman in all those years?" she asked a little incredulously.

"No, but that's not exactly what I'm talking about. It's been a long time since I…" he stopped, and she gave him a puzzled look.

"Since you?"

"Since I… felt so many startling feelings all at once," he finally told her.

"Does it feel good?" she asked coyly.

"I'm not sure."

"Oh." She was clearly disappointed.

Sam spoke quickly. "Sometimes things feel so good, they hurt," he responded, hoping to undo any hurt his last statement had caused.

She gazed up at him, even more surprised by what had just happened than he was. "In that case, one needs to keep doing them until they only feel good," she counseled. "At least, that's what I think," she said, her eyes alight with wonder.

For a moment he was back on the train, bullets slamming into the wall above, his hands just removed from her head. Her face held the same look of wonder now, as it had then. He realized with a start it was at that very moment he had first loved her. Being a missionary, he had forced all such feelings into a place not even noticeable to himself. Now, they were rushing back upon him so forcefully that he felt overwhelmed.

Sensing Sam's awkwardness, Melody took a step back. "It's late. I need to go home and pack. I'm leaving in a few days for the East coast." She said this with such regret that Sam's heart ached for her. New York was far enough away that it just as well could have been a different planet. He felt panic rise that she would leave and he would never see her again; then he felt ridiculously foolish to feel this way toward a woman he hadn't seen in so many years. Above all, guilt was screaming that he was being unfaithful to Dawn.

But above all the noise in his head, every fiber of his being wanted to stop Melody from going. Sam stood immobilized as she took another step back. She waited for him to say something, then took another step away.

"It was wonderful to see you again," she said sincerely, then added, "after all these years."

"Oh, yes, yes it really was," he replied with forced brightness, and then felt like an idiot for having nothing more meaningful to say—to stop her from leaving again.

Melody pulled a set of keys from her handbag and turned slowly toward her car a short distance away. Sam caught up to her in time to close the door for her.

She waited before starting the engine. She clearly wanted to say something. His own mind and heart were groping for the right words. When neither succeeded she started the car, smiled bleakly in his direction, and drove into the night.

Sam stood on the side of the road for a long time until the taillights of her car rounded the corner and were gone. He suddenly felt so completely alone that he had to suppress the urge to run down the road after her. Instead, he rubbed the tears from his cheeks in an angry gesture and walked slowly toward the house.

He was genuinely surprised to find Bonnie's and Lisa's faces pressed to the small panes of glass in the door. They were smiling broadly.

"Way to go, Dad!" they cried, patting him on the back and giving him hugs.

"What are you talking about?" he mumbled almost incoherently.

"You kissed her!" they cried in unison.

"How…?"

"You were standing under a streetlight, Dad. Didn't you even notice the light? It must have been quite the kiss!" they taunted him with glee.

Sam blushed. "It's been a long time," he said soberly, as if his mind had latched onto that one phrase, and it explained everything.

When they observed his sober mood the girls ceased their teasing. They glanced at each other and stepped aside to let him into the house. He walked slowly toward his room. They followed him like puppies on a string. He would have shut the door, but they were immediately behind him. He sat down on the bed.

"What's wrong, Daddy? Hey, we're sorry we teased you," Lisa said humbly. "We know it's been a long time, and we didn't mean to…"

"Honey, it's all right. You didn't do anything wrong. It's just that I feel so…"

Both girls looked at each other. "Guilty?" Bonnie filled in for him. Sam looked up at her as if seeing her for the first time.

"That's part of it, I guess," he admitted. In fact, that was exactly it, and it caused him to marvel at her perceptiveness. "So how did you figure that out? Is it that obvious? Shouldn't I feel guilty?" he asked as if they were someone other than the devoted daughters of the very woman he had just betrayed.

"Daddy, that's how I would want my husband to feel if he kissed another woman, even a hundred years after my death. You loved Mother, and I just knew you'd feel that way," Bonnie said lovingly.

"I know. I shouldn't have done it," he admitted, and let his mind go into lockup simply to avoid having to face his own guilt.

"Daddy? Daddy? Sam!" Lisa said loudly, snapping her fingers. He looked up regretfully at his daughter who looked very much like her mother. His eyes were red and sad.

"Daddy, listen to me," Lisa commanded. "I'm going to say something you need to hear, and I know it's going to hurt, but please listen to me. Are you listening?"

"Yes," he replied meekly.

"You are no longer married to my mother," she stated matter-of-factly.

"But, I am!" he objected.

"No, you're not," Bonnie said gently, picking up where Lisa left off. "You have an eternal bond with her, but you are no longer married to her. You can't betray her by falling in love with Melody. You just can't!"

"Then, if that's true, why do I feel so much like it's a betrayal?" Sam moaned.

"That's because you still love her," Lisa answered frankly. "And that's very sweet. But, you can't betray someone that doesn't exist."

"She exists in my heart, and in my memory. She is still a very important part of my life," Sam argued.

"Daddy, we love you for your devotion to our mother. But, you've got to snap out of your self-pity. I know for a fact that Mother wanted you to fall in love again."

"How could you know that?" he challenged.

"She said so in her journal," they said in stereo.

"What? When? You weren't supposed to read that!" he remonstrated.

Bonnie tried to explain. "Daddy, we have read everything she ever wrote. We've tried on every piece of clothing you kept of hers. We read your love letters to her, and we read hers to you. We even found her old scriptures and read them cover to cover just to see which scriptures she underlined and the notes she made in the margins. We even went through her recipe books to find what she loved to cook. If there is something our mother touched in this life, we have absorbed it as much as humanly possible."

"I had no idea."

Lisa shot a warning glance at Bonnie and stepped in. "Sorry, Dad, I guess we are a whole lot sneakier than you had apparently thought. But, that's not the point," she said, anxious to abandon that topic. "The point is that Mother is gone, and you don't have to stop loving her to love Melody. Surely you see that! Even Mother saw that before she died. She knew you wouldn't be able to understand, so she wrote it to you herself."

"She did, but it's so hard to think about," Sam admitted, then added forcefully, "And anyway, who says I'm in love with Melody?"

The girls looked meaningfully at their father. "Your eyes, Daddy," they droned dramatically.

"You two are impossible. You even use my eyes against me!" he said with a groan in his voice.

Bonnie put her hands on her hips. "I'll bet you a back massage that if you go stand in front of the mirror and say Melody's name three times, you'll see the sparkle yourself."

Sam chuckled, and reached to give them one of his big Daddy hugs. "You two go to bed. You've already got me confused enough without setting me up to go talk to the mirror."

"Good night, Papa," Lisa laughed, and kissed him on the cheek.

"We love you," Bonnie said for them both and kissed him on the other.

After they were long gone, he tried the mirror. They were right—he did see a sparkle, but it was a reflection of tears he could not blink away.

About noon the following day, Sam loaded his daughters and a picnic into their rental car and drove north out of town. He wanted to take them to his childhood home in the country. They were just approaching the last exit into Bountiful when he felt a sudden need to turn. All his life he had honed his soul to obedience, and recognizing the soft urging of the Holy Spirit, he signaled and turned at the last moment.

Ignoring the girls' questions, Sam drove into town on back roads, wound into a subdivision with big trees, and pulled up to a curb. It wasn't until they recognized the house that they began smiling broadly. Sam got out slowly and walked up to the porch, which seemed much longer than it had in the dark.

Sister Rogers took one look at him and turned away without saying hello. He hadn't even considered that he might be viewed as the one who had interfered with the wedding plans. A few doors slammed inside. Shortly Melody came to the door. She had several pieces of clothing over one arm. Her hair was tied back with a blue ribbon. She had no makeup on. Even so, her beauty took his breath away.

Because of the way the light was striking the screen door he could see her clearly, but she could not see who stood beyond until she pushed it open.

"Melody, I…"

"Sam!" she cried out in surprise, and stepped back, letting the door slam between them. She instantly realized what she had done and jumped forward to push the door open, hitting him in the shoulder. He stumbled out of the way and began to laugh.

"Melody. I'm sorry I didn't call. I didn't mean to startle you. Would you like to go on a picnic with us?"

"Us?"

"Me, Lisa and Bonnie. We're going to see where I grew up."

"Oh, uhm, well you see, I have so much to do. I'm not dressed. I haven't even taken a shower. I'm…"

"You're beautiful, and you're charming, and you're desperately needed on this picnic," he replied happily.

"I have to move out of the Rogers' home tonight. It's become very uncomfortable here, and anyway, Marcia's husband is coming for us in a few hours. They live in Logan. It's become awkward now that Marcia has left. You can well imagine, I suppose." She looked at him almost frantically. "I would love to come, but I've got to pack, really. I'm sorry, I really am sorry."

"Where are you going from here?" Sam asked, suddenly disheartened that she could not come.

"I'll spend the night in a motel, then fly out tomorrow evening. I didn't want to make my sister drive all the way back from Logan. It's such a long drive. They think I'm silly, but I insisted. I'll be fine. I've certainly stayed in worse places than motels, you know."

"Actually, I don't know, but I sure would like to… know more… about you…" His voice tapered to nothingness.

There was a long pause during which Sam's eyes drank her in. In a way typical of all females, she sensed what he was doing, and blushed. She shifted her weight onto another foot and smiled at him curiously.

"I have an idea," he said.

"OK, what is it?" she responded gamely.

"Why don't you let me and the twins help you pack up? They are true artists at it. Then you come with us on our outing. Afterward, you can spend the night with us at my sister's home. It'll be much nicer than a motel, that's for sure. I'll drive you to the airport tomorrow afternoon, and it will save you cab fare and a motel bill."

Melody shook her head. "It sounds fun, except I just couldn't impose on you and your sister like that. I just couldn't. I don't even know your sister."

Sam's mind spun at warp speed. Letting Melody just walk out of his life so soon did not seem like an acceptable option. "I'll make you a deal. We'll go to my sister's for a cup of Red Bush tea after the picnic. I won't say a thing to her about any motels. If she doesn't invite you to stay, I'll drive you to a motel myself. And," he added, using the same voice radio and TV announcers use when they are about to give you that 'but wait there's more…' pitch, "I'll still drive you to the airport tomorrow evening. How can you beat that?"

Melody's concerned expression slowly evolved into a tiny smile. "I guess I can't," she said at last.

Sam ran to get the twins. They quickly packed Melody's bags, scurrying around like Cinderella's magical mice, and before many minutes had passed, Sam was carrying her bags to the car.

At last, Melody came out holding a child in her arms. Bonnie was carrying a diaper bag, and Lisa a car seat.

"Won't Marcia want to take her son with her to Logan?" Sam questioned as Melody arranged the baby seat in the back.

Melody gave him an odd look. "This is *my* little sweetie," she told him.

"Oh—oh my gosh!" Sam exclaimed. "I was under the impression he belonged to Marcia. I'm sorry."

"For what? You apologize for the oddest things, Sam." Melody got the little one buckled into the seat. The twins climbed into the back, and Melody slid into the front seat beside Sam.

"What's your son's name?" Sam asked after the car was moving. It felt so odd that she had such a young son. He did some quick math and concluded that Melody was five years younger than himself. That would make her in her late thirties. Maybe it wasn't as odd as he thought. Still, he found it unsettling in the light that she was just getting married.

"I named him after a very influential person in my youth," she replied, and shot him a meaningful look. "His name is Samuel."

Sam almost drove off the road. When the car was under control once again he looked at Melody. Her eyes were shining. He didn't have to ask if he were *that* Samuel after whom her son had been named.

It took a few hours of driving to arrive at the country lanes Sam had known so well as a young man. He actually got lost several times. The low-lying farmland was now subdivisions full of homes. Only a few of the older streets had not changed, and he drove partly by instinct toward his childhood home.

When they arrived at his old home he was immediately struck by how much smaller it seemed. His memory of it was that it had been huge. In reality, it was not much more than an average-sized home with an extra room tacked on the back. It sat farther back from the road than any other house on the block. He could remember his Dad building it back that far to avoid being too near the street. Sam stopped the car in front of the ditch that bordered the home on two sides.

"Hey, I know this place!" Lisa exclaimed after a few seconds.

"Me too," Bonnie laughed. They opened the doors and climbed out. There was no traffic at that moment so Sam turned off the car, still in the narrow street.

"I don't think I have any pictures of my old house," Sam said more to himself than to the twins.

"No," Lisa said thoughtfully, "not in a picture. Someone described it to me."

"Yes, I remember, too," Bonnie said. She was silent for a minute. Then looking at one another meaningfully, they said in exact unison, "Our friend!"

"You mean your imaginary friend you used to play with?"

"Yes, only he wasn't imaginary," Lisa corrected him.

Melody turned to Sam. "Children often have imaginary friends. They seem very real to them," she said gently.

"I'm sorry," Bonnie objected, "but you don't understand, Melody. He was real. We could see him. We always thought our parents were just teasing us when they pretended they couldn't see him, too."

Melody was intrigued. "Really? How odd. Can you describe him?"

"Sure. He was about our age. He had bright red hair, freckles, and wore coveralls with only one strap over his shoulder. He almost never wore shoes."

Now they had hooked their father. "Truly?" Sam asked. "Did he tell you things? I mean, did he only respond to what you did, or did he initiate conversations, and tell you things?"

"He was very real, and acted exactly like a real little boy," Bonnie told him thoughtfully.

"Yes," Lisa agreed, "except, he acted much more mature. We always felt he was like our older and wiser brother. He often told us when we shouldn't do something, or that we should have minded Mom—things like that."

Bonnie nodded. "I remember being scared a lot as a child. Whenever I was frightened he was very calm, and always seemed to know what I should do. When I took his advice, things always turned out happy. I grew to trust him a great deal."

"I did too," Lisa agreed.

"Yeah, and then one day he described where he had lived," Bonnie observed.

Sam held up a hand as if instructing them to stop. "He said he had lived before? Like, on this earth?" he asked in amazement.

Both girls nodded, and Bonnie continued. "He told us he had. He said he had lived in a big house that had a brown porch and four big windows across the front, and a two-car garage. He talked about it more than once, in detail. He told us he really missed his home and his family, although I don't remember him describing his family."

"Me either," Lisa said with some irony. "I remember him talking about the ditch that was on two sides of the house. The description was exactly like this house here, Daddy," she told him excitedly.

"Did he ever tell you how he died?" Sam asked in a subdued voice.

Bonnie nodded solemnly. "Several times, actually. He said one day when he was still very little he wanted to go to milk the 'cowth.' He called them 'cowth,' like he had a lisp or something on that word. It was the only time I heard him lisp."

Sam had to lean against the trunk of the car. His legs seemed to no longer have enough strength to hold him up.

Bonnie continued, "He said he was upset because he didn't get to go milk the 'cowth,' so he picked up his kitty and tried to walk down to the barn."

"He was really mad at that kitty," Lisa interjected.

"He really was," Lisa agreed. "He said the kitty got afraid of the water in the ditch when he crossed the bridge, and scratched him real hard. When the kitty jumped away from him it landed right in the ditch. He said he was very afraid for the kitty, and tried to save it, but he slipped on the bank and fell into the water himself. He said the kitty climbed on his head and jumped out of the ditch. He was very happy about that."

Lisa nodded at her, and Bonnie continued.

"He told us his big brother drove over the bridge right at that time, and he was so sure his big brother would save him. But, he didn't even see him. He said nobody saw him as he floated right by them. He said he couldn't call to them because his mouth was full of water. He didn't know how to swim, and he died in the water. He said he felt very naughty because he was not supposed to go by the ditch. He was afraid he would be in big trouble."

"Yeah, I remember that story," Lisa said thoughtfully. "He told us about it, then he laughed, and said it was okay now. He said the kitty was sorry too, and they were still very good friends. He said he was happy now and living with us until we grew up."

There was a long moment of silence before anyone noticed that Sam had turned white.

"What is it, Sam?" Melody asked, suddenly concerned. "Are you feeling ill?" She placed a warm hand on his forehead.

"No, no. Lisa, did he tell you his name?"

"Sure. His name was Jimmy, the same as his father's name."

Sam grunted as if someone had slugged him in the stomach, and buried his face in his hands. It took him quite a few minutes to compose himself.

"Why does this story bother you so, Daddy?" Lisa finally asked him tenderly.

Sam was quiet for a moment before he spoke. "Did I ever tell you about my little brother who died when I was twelve?"

"You mentioned him, but no real details," Lisa said, looking at Bonnie, who was shaking her head.

"No one's told you that story? Not Grandpa or Grandma? Nobody?"

"No," they both said honestly. In fact, he had never spoken to them in any detail about Jimmy. It was a very tender subject with his parents to this day, and some unspoken decision had deemed it too upsetting to tell his young daughters. Now after all these years, Sam never thought to discuss it.

He sat in silence until something prodded him.

"Sorry, I was just remembering," he said quietly. "Do you recall which bridge your little friend fell from? There are three of them."

Lisa thought for a second before answering. "I think he said it was the one behind the house. By a chicken coop."

Sam turned to look down the lane toward the house. "Come with me," he said, and began walking down the lane. They followed without comment. They walked past the house, down a short lane with a picket fence on the left, and past a fallen-down chicken coop on the right. Beyond the coop, Sam turned right and stopped before a low wooden bridge. The cement ditch was dry now, but it was still there, and the bridge still showed evidence of being used recently.

"This is the bridge?" Melody asked breathlessly. Sam just nodded.

"Oh my gosh!" Bonnie exclaimed. "Are you telling me Jimmy, our little friend, was your brother? Your very own little brother? In real life?"

Again he nodded.

"And, this is the bridge? This is Jimmy's bridge? Right here? This one?" Bonnie blurted out, shaking a finger at the bridge and stomping her foot on it with a hollow, thumping sound..

"This very one," Sam replied soberly.

Then something unexpected happened. Both the girls began to cry. Their tears were not of anger, but tears of childhood grief. They had listened to a friend's tale of his own tragic death, and as little children themselves had thought it not much more than a fairytale. Now that the story had suddenly become real, the tears they might have shed years earlier came freely.

Melody comforted them, not totally sure what was going on. In a few minutes, they composed themselves with a few sniffles. A clean diaper served to dry tears.

"Excuse me?" a woman's voice called from behind them. "May I help you?" she asked in a loud, rather insistent tone. They turned to see a woman standing on the back steps of the house—her house.

Sam realized with a start that they were, in fact, trespassing. Having grown up here, his natural inclination was to still feel at home.

"I'm sorry," he called back. "I should have knocked. I'm Sam Mahoy. I grew up in this house. We were…"

The woman literally jumped through the door and down the steps. In seconds she was there at the bridge.

"I'm Gwendolyn Savage. I'm pleased to meet you," she said shaking Sam's hand vigorously. Sam introduced everyone by their first name.

"You have such a lovely family. Lovely daughters, lovely wife, and a beautiful baby. I'm so pleased you stopped by." Sam glanced at Melody, and from the look of amused pleasure on her face, decided not to disabuse the woman of the notion that Melody was his wife.

Mrs. Savage led them toward the back door, all the while talking excitedly. "You know, as long as I've lived in this house I've heard stories about you folks. There are lots of rumors. I'm just dying to know the truth. Did your little brother really fall from the bridge and drown in the ditch?"

"We were just talking about that," Sam told her.

"How sad. Oh, how sad. I was hoping that one was just a rumor," she said, shaking her head. Then she started again. "Is it true that…"

They spent over an hour satisfying her curiosity while she served them big chocolate chip cookies and cold milk. Sam thoroughly enjoyed himself. Melody listened with rapt attention, as did his daughters. Finally, Sam got to show them his former bedroom. The Savages had recarpeted and redecorated almost everything. He told them several funny stories from his youth that had occurred in the various rooms, including the time he had accidentally fired a hunting rifle through the floor of his bedroom and out the big front window below, shattering it to dust. It was a miracle no one had been injured. He also had the fun of showing Mrs. Savage the laundry chute. His father had built it into the linen closet in the bathroom. If you slid the handle sideways, it opened into a shallow cabinet. If you pulled forward, it tipped toward you to reveal a laundry chute.

"I have always wondered why that little closet was so darn shallow," she said with wonder. "Where do the clothes go," she wondered, peering into the darkness of the chute.

"Right into the cabinet over the washing machine," he informed her.

"Oh!" she exclaimed. "I had my husband put a couple of shelves in there. I could not understand why there was a cabinet with no shelves and a hole in the top of it. I never thought it might be a chute. That's so clever. All these years of carrying laundry! Well, I'll be…"

It was mid-afternoon when they were all once again buckled into the car. Sam drove away slowly. It had been an emotional, wonder-filled afternoon. Having Melody there had made it all the more special.

Sam had a sudden idea. "Hey, I remember there being a park not far from here. Shall we go picnic there?" It was quickly agreed, and Sam found the park without trouble.

"Look," Sam said as soon as they drove up. "They've added a transportation museum. After we eat, we can go look at the old airplanes and walk through the train. Sound fun?" They all agreed.

Sam felt somewhat subdued as they ate, the memories of his youth having been so poignantly awakened. He thought he had long ago resolved the pain of Jimmy's death, but found quite unexpectedly that there was still tenderness there. Still, the memories of his youth and childhood were warm and pleasant. By the time they had eaten, his spirit had lifted.

As he ate, he watched Melody. The more he was around her, the more impressed he was. She was sweet and loving with her son, almost to the point of being gushy. She laughed at his smiles and frowns, and talked to him as if she expected him to reply. As he watched he was struck by her graceful bearing. She was self-assured and calm, not at all shy or reluctant. She was assertive in a way that suggested confidence, not aggression. She seemed to radiate love. It all felt very familiar to him in a deja vu kind of way.

Even though caring for her child, Melody served everyone else, making sure they had everything they wanted throughout the meal. Her gracious kindness seemed from another age when people were chivalrous and gentile.

Lisa poked her dad in the side with her elbow and leaned over to whisper, "It's not polite to stare," she told him. Sam blinked a couple of times at her before comprehending what she was saying. He blushed slightly, and endeavored to look away. It was not easy to do.

The transportation museum was quite large, considering how far out in the country it was. They looked at World War II fighter planes, old bi-planes, and dozens of antique coaches, cars and trucks in various stages of restoration. There was even an impressive collection of old fire engines. They finally walked up to the big old steam engine. It sat almost as if asleep, yet imposing and powerful. It was attached to a coal car, a dining car, and two passenger cars followed by a caboose.

"This looks similar to the train we rode in Rhodesia," Sam said, mostly thinking out loud.

"It sure does," Melody agreed. "Probably, that engine in Rhodesia was made in America. I know lots of them were. They certainly weren't made in Africa," Melody ventured.

"Could be." He climbed aboard and admired the engine while the girls walked into the dining and passenger cars. After a while Sam climbed down and entered the dining coach. At one time it had been plush, richly appointed with velvet fabric and ornately carved wood. He could hear the twins talking excitedly one car away. He caught a glimpse of them through the doors between cars. Lisa had little Samuel perched on her hip.

When he entered the second car, the girls had already progressed to the third. He was suddenly struck by a sense of "having been here before," and looked around him. This was a sleeper car, very similar to the one he remembered from his mission. His cabin had been the third from the front of the train. He walked to that door and slowly slid it open. He was not surprised to see Melody sitting on the floor directly in front of the door, knees drawn up to her chest, her head tucked between her knees. It was as if he had walked back in time twenty years. All that was missing were explosions rocking the train, shattering glass, and bullets screaming overhead.

Sam stepped across Melody into the small room, then turned and knelt beside her. Except that twenty years ago Marcia had been huddled tightly against her, the scene was exactly as it had been so long ago. She looked up into his eyes, a look of grim remembrance on her face.

"I couldn't help myself," she explained. "I walked into this room, and I just had to sit down here. I remember the stark terror I felt then."

"It was a terrifying experience," Sam remembered aloud.

"My memory of it is that you were very calm. You said you knew Heavenly Father would protect you. Your strength and faith impressed me so much, Sam. The memory of that faith was all I had for a dozen years. It was my faith in your faith that finally led me to the Church, and to my own testimony."

"I'm so glad," Sam said quietly.

"Do you know I've only been a member for a little under two years?"

"No, I had no idea."

"It's true," she admitted. "Marcia joined the Church shortly after she moved to England. I got caught up in my life, and didn't have a real opportunity to freely investigate the Church until a few years ago."

"I would really like to hear about your life," Sam told her honestly. As a matter of fact, he was hungering to know everything about her.

Melody relaxed but did not move from her position in the narrow room. "I joined the Church shortly after Samuel was conceived. It was a big part of what broke up my marriage."

"I'm really sorry to hear that."

"Samuel was born after the divorce," Melody told him matter-of-factly. "His biological father does not know this baby exists."

Sam looked at her with awe. "I'm so amazed—so flattered—that you named him Samuel. I still don't really understand why."

Melody smiled. "Because it was my memory of your faith that gave me the courage to join the Church, even though I knew it would end my marriage. It was the only name I could name him," she said pointedly. "I wanted my son to have your faith and your courage. It gave me great hope."

"I'm truly honored. But, why did it have to end your marriage?"

"My husband was an Anglican minister and a rabid anti-Mormon," she said quietly.

There was a small moment of shocked silence. "That explains a lot," Sam said.

The painful memories bubbled to the surface, in spite of herself. "I think he could have forgiven me for committing adultery easier than joining the Mormon Church. He called it "spiritual adultery," and denounced me the following Sunday before the whole congregation. The only good news is that I had already left him, so I wasn't there to endure it."

"That's astoundingly heartless," Sam declared, feeling protective of Melody.

She looked at him with piercing brown eyes. "I'm not angry at him, Sam. He felt betrayed at the deepest level of his soul."

"I do know what betrayal feels like," Sam admitted.

Her eyes narrowed, and she fell silent.

"Do you still love him?" Sam asked suddenly, then wished he hadn't. He half expected Melody to be offended, but she wasn't.

"No," she answered without hesitation. "I loved him when I married him. But I also married him because I wanted the security and confidence that seemed to surround him. He was very charismatic, and he liked to help others, so people naturally followed him. I think I was just one of his pet projects that he decided to marry. I doubt he was ever really in love with me. He was in love with himself, and his calling. He was the most confident man I've ever known…"

Her voice trailed off, and Sam wasn't entirely sure she really didn't still love him. But, love is a strange phenomenon. It sometimes endures, even flourishes in the most barren soil. It's hard to stop loving someone, even when they no longer love you. These were things Sam knew very well himself.

Melody changed the subject. "Do you remember giving me that priesthood blessing that day?"

"I sure do. I don't remember any of what I said, though," Sam admitted.

"I was wondering, would you give me a blessing again?" she asked, her voice soft, almost frightened.

Sam's mind spun for all of a millisecond before his questions and fears evaporated, and peace settled upon him. He smiled gently. "I would be glad to."

"I mean right now? Right here?" Her eyes were bright with hope.

"I will," he said as the Holy Spirit gently washed over him. They moved closer until she was nearly leaning against him. He placed his hands upon her head, offered a silent prayer, and then he waited until the words of lasting truth flowed through him.

"Melody, in the name of Jesus Christ and by the power of the holy Melchizedek Priesthood, I give you a blessing this day of peace and comfort. You are a noble daughter of Heavenly Father, and a precious spirit in His sight. In order for you to fulfill the measure of your creation, adequately test, hone and purify your soul, you have been called upon to endure many trials, all of which you have endured faithfully and well. Though life is inherently fraught with trials, and ever will be, your present difficulties will shortly turn to a great blessing for you. I pronounce the days of your prophesied trials at an end.

"You were the last to inherit the curse of your fathers and the first to triumph over it. You were placed on this earth to purify and bring back a noble bloodline into the Kingdom of God, one upon which the Lord long ago placed a blessing in response to the righteous petition of a noble progenitor. Now, through your faithfulness, that blessing has been fulfilled and will be fulfilled until the Lord returns again in glory to place all enemies under His feet.

"Your quest has taken you to many nations and is now come full circle. You are home. God has granted you the desire of your heart, and it shall bring you lasting joy. In the name of Jesus Christ, Amen."

By the time he finished Melody was sobbing. He lifted her chin with his fingertips and saw them to be tears of happiness.

She began digging in her handbag. "Sam, I want to show you something. Do you remember writing the blessing on the train in your scriptures and tearing out the page to give to me?"

He nodded. "Yes, I remember it very well, like it was yesterday. I still have the book I tore it from, and occasionally look at the torn edge and wonder what happened to you."

She lifted an age-darkened envelope from her bag and pulled a piece of plastic from the envelope.

"I have carried this with me ever since that day." She handed it to him. It was a laminated sheet of paper that had been crudely torn from a book. In faded ink he could plainly identify his own script. He read it aloud.

"Melody, in the name of Jesus Christ and by the power of the holy Priesthood, I give you a blessing also of peace and comfort. You are a noble daughter of Heavenly Father, and a precious spirit in his sight. In order for you to fulfill the measure of your creation, you will be called upon to endure many trials, the present difficulties being a mere shadow of what will follow. You are the first and the last. You are the last to inherit the curse of your fathers and the first to triumph over it. Your quest will take you to many nations, and bring you full circle. When you finally find what you seek, you will have returned to this moment, and it will bring you joy. In the name of Jesus Christ, Amen."

"You see, it's the same blessing, almost word for word!" she exclaimed excitedly.

"It is," he had to admit. "Except the one today sounded like a fulfillment of the first."

"Sam, we have to write this one down too, before you forget it. Do you have a piece of paper?" About this time the twins returned, and they found a tablet in the diaper bag. Sam wrote down the blessing with her help. They worked on it until both felt it was recorded correctly.

Sam read the blessing again to himself as Melody watched him intently, her eyes sparkling in the dim light. As he read he kept glancing toward her. Each time he looked, her eyes were upon him. It made him feel as if she were the sun, and he a small planet orbiting it.

"I just have one question, if you don't mind telling me," he said. "What was the desire of your heart that you were searching for, and have now found, which has brought you joy?"

"I think I know," Lisa said meaningfully.

"Me too," Bonnie added almost reverently.

"I know now," Melody said emotionally. "I didn't until just a few minutes ago,"

"I seem to be the only one here who doesn't know," Sam complained amiably.

Melody winked at the girls. "Should I tell him, girls?"

"No, let him figure it out for himself," Lisa advised her.

Sam protested, "Come on, I'm dying of curiosity here."

Melody cleared her throat and placed a hand on his cheek. "I was searching for what you wrote about in your song."

"You mean, love?" Sam asked.

"Oh, Daddy, men are so dense sometimes," Bonnie said in mock consternation.

"Not just love, Daddy," Lisa corrected. "That song isn't just about any old kind of love, it's about *real* love—the kind of love that begins before time and lasts forever; it's the love every woman dreams of. Do you understand now?"

"Well," he faltered. He hated to be obtuse, but loving a woman and love, in general, were practically the same thing to him. He was about to say something to explain his confusion when the girls stood in apparent frustration.

"Melody, we're outta here. See if you can enlighten him." They piled from the room.

Melody blushed slightly. "Let me put it in a way you can't possibly misunderstand," she said in a quiet voice. She knelt up directly before him, wrapped both arms around his neck, and drew herself to him until only their faces were not touching. She slowly tilted her head and pressed her lips to his. About three minutes later, he understood completely, and it caused his fluttering heart to rejoice once again. She hadn't been searching the world over to find love; she had been searching the world over to find *his* love. Suddenly, sweetly, he understood, and for the first time in nearly a dozen years, he counted himself the luckiest mortal on earth.

Sam realized with a start that the twins had come to the door and were watching them intently, whispering and giggling. He reluctantly parted and Melody laid her head on his shoulder.

"Girls, you have a way of embarrassing your old man to death," Sam protested. Melody laughed and motioned for them to come closer. As the girls approached, a thought occurred to Sam unexpectedly. His question seemed like a departure from the special feeling of the moment, but it came with such force that he was quite certain it had to be asked.

"Did Jimmy ever say why he had visited you when you were little?" he asked.

"Dad, you're spoiling the moment!" Bonnie protested, punching him on the arm.

Lisa giggled, then answered, "He said we three had always been best friends. When he came to earth, he said we helped him until he came back home. He said we met him after he left his body in the water. And when it was our turn to come to earth we were afraid our lives would be short because his had been. We were afraid to come alone. So we asked to be born at the same time, and for Jimmy to stay with us on earth."

Sam had to smile. "That sounds like something you two would do. So, you were his invisible friends when he was little?" Sam tried to remember anything like that about Jimmy, but could not.

"That's what he said. We don't remember any of it."

"That doesn't surprise me," Sam said.

"He said he would take care of us, and he promised he would stay until we weren't afraid anymore," Bonnie added.

"That's amazing," Melody said. "When was the last time you saw him?"

The twins looked at one another before Bonnie answered. Something seemed to pass between them before she spoke. "We saw him at the airport in Anchorage just a week ago."

"What!?" Sam exclaimed. "He's still here, and you never said anything about it?"

"We hadn't seen him for many years, actually," Bonnie explained. "We were surprised to see him. He told us not to mention it to you yet, but that shortly we could. He told us it would be the last time he would visit us."

"Why?" Melody wanted to know.

Again they exchanged a glance before answering. Finally, it was Bonnie who gently ended the silence. "Because he said in a little while we wouldn't need him anymore."

Lisa finished by adding, "He said we were going to get a new mother very soon, and everything would be wonderful again."

Melody began to cry. Sam held her until little Samuel grew concerned and cried too. Finally, they all stood on stiff legs and climbed from the train. They were surprised to find the museum had closed. They walked through a turnstile exit and returned to the car.

It was now Melody who wanted to know more. "What did he look like?" she asked.

"He was tall, with neat red hair. His eyes were very blue, and he smiled a lot. He was about our age."

"He looked like a missionary," Bonnie added.

"Yeah, except he was wearing a light blue suit."

"And a dark red tie."

Melody peppered them with questions. "You saw him together, at the same moment? Did he look like a normal person? Did he just appear, or did he walk up to you from the crowd? Did you talk to him, or could he read your thoughts? Could you tell he wasn't a mortal person? Did he look like a spirit? Could you see through him, or was he transparent?"

The girls listened to this barrage of questions with a smile on their faces. When Melody paused to draw a breath Lisa simply said, "We already told you the best part—Mom."

7

UNCHAINED MELODY

Two months later Sam was once again kneeling at an altar in the Salt Lake Temple. His parents had flown down to be with him on this wonderful day. All his brothers and sisters were sitting there smiling with their spouses. Lisa and Bonnie were waiting in the foyer for them to come out. Cheryl and Fred had come to Salt Lake City to attend, and little Samuel was all dressed in white, waiting patiently on his new Grandma Laura's knee to be sealed forever to his new eternal family.

Sam was so taken by the celestial beauty of his bride that he could barely take his eyes off her to look around the room. Every face he saw wore a beaming smile. He looked into the infinite reflection of the mirrors beyond Melody's head, and somewhere in that eternity, he felt another person smile. For just a moment he felt the gentle presence of the woman he had loved before. He felt Dawn's love, felt it flow through him, warming him in a rich, familiar way. He felt her love so tangibly at that moment that he would never doubt, could never doubt that she took great joy in what he was now doing. Then her presence withdrew. She had set him free to love again, and he turned all his passion to the glowing angel kneeling before him. How it thrilled him to know once again he had someone upon whom to lavish his love.

When he had been married before, money had been no object, and no expense had been spared to make that day perfect. Life with Melody was much different. He was a struggling songwriter, and she not much more than a poverty-stricken refugee. Their wedding, and all things associated with it, were done with great attention to cost, or the absence thereof.

Sam actually knew very little about his new bride. All he really knew of her former life was a mere few days of terror on a train in Africa. All he wanted to know about her life since then was the fact that she loved him passionately, had a beautiful little boy whom he adored, that she was marrying him for all eternity, and that Heavenly Father approved. It seemed more than enough.

Melody knew even less about Sam. He was a mysterious stranger of great faith who had materialized when she needed hope most and vanished almost immediately thereafter. The difference for her was that all through the intervening years, the faith and confidence of her mysterious elderly benefactor had buoyed her up without ceasing. So many times she had faced threats more serious than those on the train: face-to-face with death, poverty, political intrigue, hatred, lies, devastating loss, and betrayed love.

The one thing that had given her the courage to survive was the image in her mind of a young man kneeling amid bursting bombs and screaming bullets, and calmly laying his hands upon her head. She had felt the power of that blessing, and had known without equivocation that she would be preserved, then and always.

For Melody, Sam was more than a memory; he was a dream, a far away, life-long dream. When they had walked away from each other that day on the train platform in Pretoria, she had torn off a significant portion of her young heart and given it to him. In a way too personal to describe, and too feminine for any man to comprehend, she knew in her heart of hearts that he had loved her too, had accepted her gift even without understanding it, and had taken it with him into his unknown future.

When she had heard Sam's song "I Have Always Loved You," it warmed her soul as no other music ever had. She now knew why. The first time she heard it she raced to her violin and played it over and over by ear until she knew its every harmony, every word, and every loving feeling. It had healed her in a way, and she had included it in many concerts over the intervening years. She had never seen a printed page of music containing her beloved anthem. She didn't need to, and had hardly even known the author's name, let alone suspected it could possibly be her long-lost Sam.

Thus it was that for Melody, Sam walking through the door on the day of her engagement party was an impossible lightning strike of epic proportions. He had become almost a myth in her mind; but seeing him standing there, alive and physically real, was nearly more than she could absorb. Yet, there he was with two lovely daughters, married, successful, and pleased (but apparently not overjoyed) to see her again. Seeing him again gave her a sense of quiet futility for her future, and she steeled her soul to accept what must be.

The lightning rod for her was when she had begun to play the precious music that had so often calmed her abused heart and had given her the hope to love Brian. At that moment when Bonnie had said, "That's my mother's song," the lightning struck, and was conducted directly into her soul. Without even knowing how or why, she knew that her world had just been blasted to dust, and it rendered her utterly helpless.

She knew then that she could not play that song for any reason, and sat down on the piano bench in utter desolation. Yet Sam had come toward her with genuine concern for her, just like he had shown so many years before. She had to stand, to force her body to move against the mountain mass of emotion weighing upon it. He held the precious violin in his hands, smiled, and handed it to her as if he were returning her soul.

When his girls had started to sing the beloved words, and the very fingers that had once composed it had blessed her ears with the precious harmonies, there was such love interlaced in its velvet tones that strength came, and courage, and music—her music and his music. She pulled the bow across the hallowed strings, and the rich tone reverberated through her body. Her music melded with his, and the words rang perfectly in her ears. She played, not as he played, not daring to move close enough to lose herself to him, not even in the ethereal magic of music; but high, aloof, floating above in precious harmonies, dancing, laughing, weeping in tones of ethereal sadness.

Sam had played with love, passion, and sweetness. She had played with love, passion, and bitterness. When the music ended, her soul was so aflame with the cold fire of sorrow that she could only run from the room in tears.

She had sought out Sam at his sister's home to apologize and to say good-bye, or so she told herself. In reality she had gone to feed her aching heart, to hear his voice one last time, and to finally close a chapter of her life that had been too long open to the ravages of the cold winds of unanswerable love. Somewhere inside, unseen and unrecognized, she was also desperately hoping to unplug the storm drain in her soul that she might not utterly drown in the torrential downpour of a shattered dream.

That night, Melody had asked foolish, intimate questions of Sam about love, and had run from him at last in embarrassment. But, he had caught her, had held her, and bewildered her by betraying his wife, the very love for whom he had written the song. But even as he held Melody in his arms, she heard words too tragically beautiful to be true: his wife whom he had loved was ten years gone.

Sam had kissed her then—beyond wonder, beyond hope, beyond dreams, he had kissed her. And she had been too stunned to do anything but stand there. She couldn't even form her lips into a kiss, or close her eyes; but he kissed her, and love flowed into her until a huge steel door evaporated in her soul, and the cold winds of despair ceased to ravage the landscape of her heart.

Then she had kissed him back, carefully, with breathless disbelief, then with wonder, and finally with passion fired by a desperation whose thunder voice had but a magic moment ago been rendered mute.

Now, just two short month-long eternities later, Melody was kneeling across the sacred altar of the house of the Lord, watching the one she had once thought most distant to her, gazing at her with the very love he had proclaimed to her a thousand times in a song. Her heart fluttered lightly in her chest; how fiercely her joy burned, how sweetly the Spirit of God enveloped her! A lifelong journey had come to an end. She was home, and her home was his arms.

They pulled away from the wedding reception slowly. Melody was kneeling backwards in her seat, waving out the rear window, shouting happy messages to those cheering them on, and especially waving goodbye to little Samuel, who seemed completely at ease in his new grandmother's arms. Sam waited until she was seated and had fastened her seatbelt around billowing flows of white lace.

As the miles rolled swiftly beneath the car, Melody's happy chatter grew quiet, and a feeling of intensity settled over her. She looked at her new husband in the dim light of passing cars, and Sam caught a look of hesitancy. He knew exactly what she was feeling, for he honestly felt it himself.

They had planned to drive back from the reception to Salt Lake City to stay at the new Marriott Hotel. Her sister had given them a gift of two days and nights in the hotel's bridal suite. Yet, the closer they came to the moment both he and his wife were anticipating, the more he grew increasingly certain it was too soon. He turned east just before the temple, pulled into the ZCMI parking terrace, and quickly found a parking place. It wasn't late, but it was Wednesday, and most shoppers had departed for home.

"Why are we stopping?" she asked, her voice both curious, and grateful.

"I have something I want to give you," he announced happily.

"A gift?" she asked excitedly. Something he had yet to discover about his bride was that she loved surprises, given and received. He answered in exactly the right way to titillate her.

"Sort of."

"Where is it?"

"In my heart," he answered cryptically.

"Then, why are we stopping at the mall?"

"It's the closest place I can think of where I can give it to you."

"You really aren't giving me very good hints," she said with a pout, then instantly brightened. "Is it big?"

"Not yet."

"Is it little?"

"It assumes the size of whatever it's in," he replied.

"Oh, that doesn't help. Can I wear it?"

"If it was the only thing you had on, you'd be arrested," he replied with a laugh. He reached into his briefcase and retrieved something which she could not identify. It was small enough to fit into his suit pocket.

"Can I eat it?" she continued to guess as they got out of the car and walked to the elevators. He punched the "down" button. They entered the mall with Melody still in her white wedding dress, and Sam in his rented tux. They didn't seem to notice, although a few passersby obviously did.

Sam's eyes were twinkling. "No, you can't eat it, my darling."

"I'm really not figuring this out. Is it something you bought for me?"

"No."

"Is it something you made for me?" Melody asked as she swiped for his hands behind his back.

"No."

She punched his shoulder and giggled. "Does it even exist at all?"

"No. Not yet, at least."

"Sam. stop it! You're such a big tease! What is it?"

"You'll see," he said, and led her out onto the ground floor of the mall. To their right a fountain bubbled cheerfully. To their left shops were quietly entertaining their last few customers before closing. People walked slowly above them on several stories of balconies surrounding the entire area where they stood. Quiet music played in the background. Sam took her hand and led her diagonally across the open court toward a stair on the opposite end. Just before the stairwell he turned and stopped at a large grand piano.

"What are you up to?" she asked suspiciously as he pulled its padded cover to the floor. Unknown to her, he had played here several times to promote his music during the LDS Booksellers Conventions, and knew the mall management well. He spotted a security guard looking over the railing at them. Sam waved. The guard waved back, then spoke into his radio. Just moments later the music in the mall grew quiet. Sam raised the big lid and seated himself at the keys.

He directed Melody to stand to his right, in the hollow of the big grand where he could look at her just over the keys. He took a small tape recorder from his pocket, clicked it on, and laid it on the piano.

He sat in silence for what seemed a long time, and was in reality most of a full minute. Finally, the stirrings came. The connection he had with the source of his music was fully opened to him, and his heart quickened pace. He placed his hands on the keys and quietly played a melody that had been turning gently in his mind for days. It was sweet, happy, and filled with flourishes and decorative runs uncharacteristic of any prior work. His canvas was the air, his brushes his fingers, and his oils the harmonies he carefully, lovingly brought to life.

His soul felt alive, and his canvas received his love in broad splashes of color, then delicate lace-like etchings of happiness. Then the music grow somber, and he spoke the sweet words of his love. Even when his heart was singing, his stubborn voice could not, so he spoke the words of love to her whose eyes watched through a veil of happy tears.

Neither Sam nor Melody heard the applause that drifted down from every level of the balcony above them. She walked behind him, leaned him back into her arms, and kissed him passionately. The people cheered, and clapped happily for the full duration of her kiss. Just before she released him a camera flashed. He sat up blinking away spots in his eyes. The owner of a camera shop had captured their moment of joy on film. When "Unchained Melody" was published some months later, that very photo was on the cover of the CD.

For both of them, it had been many years of quietly languishing without love's passion, without its sweet expression, without its fire. But before Sam and his new bride could completely close the door to their room, Melody abandoned herself to his arms, and their new life of joy began.

Where Dawn had been shy and demure, Melody was vivacious and uninhibited. Sam found himself swept into a world of love beyond his comprehension. Having only known one love, he had naively thought all love to be like that he had previously cherished. He found to his startled delight that Melody's love was completely different.

Melody was a breath of fresh air that energized him with life. Like the perfect Christmas, she wrapped her love in so many brightly colored packages, that after a time he could not even guess what they contained, but waited in breathless anticipation for her to hand him the next one.

In time Sam quit comparing, quit anticipating, quit guessing, and just loved her for all the sweet and wonderful things she was to him. But it took some time; Melody was not at all like his former love, and it startled him at first.

Dawn had been proper, regal, dignified, sober and genteel. She loved finery, had infinite patience, worldly wisdom, and valued sophistication and grace. She had loved her home, decorating it with care and precision. She had waged an unending war against dust, dirt and any form of uncleanliness. In all things Dawn was a princess, and her legacy was her noble spirit.

Melody was the opposite in almost every respect. She loved to play, and teased her husband to excess at times. She played practical jokes and saw little use for things not utilitarian. Though having been raised in privilege, she eschewed wealth, finery and society, preferring practical possessions, a steady job, and down-to-earth friends.

Dawn was high heels and diamonds. Melody was sandals and three-dollar earrings.

Dawn had been slow to ask for what she needed, and seldom said what made her feel loved. Melody was vocal about her desires, unabashed in telling him what made her feel loved, happy, or satisfied.

Dawn had been a genius at making money. Melody had trouble balancing a checkbook. Dawn had amassed a vast fortune before her death; Melody was quite literally penniless.

Life with Dawn had been challenging, somewhat confusing, and relatively complex. Sam had to try to sense her needs before he could fulfill them. She was the type of woman from whom a quiet hint was her only instruction, and Sam was constantly trying, with mixed success, to interpret what it all meant.

Life with Melody was turning out to be a joyful, dizzying spin on the merry-go-round of happiness. To Sam, the greatest compensation was that he never had to guess what she wanted.

But by far the greatest difference Sam enjoyed about Melody was her affinity for the gospel. She yearned for truth, sought it with hunger, and treasured it in an ever-expanding view of the eternities. More than being his love and his friend, Melody was his soulmate in all things, his musical equal, a perfect match, molded from the same divine forge. Loving Melody was like loving an extension of himself. He felt at one, at peace, and united with her in every way.

For Melody, loving Sam was the fulfillment of a once-forgotten dream. Her passion was to fulfill every sweet fantasy she had carried so long about him. Her fun was in realizing that the reality of loving Sam was much better than the fantasy she had quietly cherished all those years.

For them both, life had just begun.

THE GIFT

Though only two years and a few months had elapsed since she had fled England, true healing had begun for Melody that day she knelt across the altar of the Salt Lake Temple. It was at that moment that she summoned her heart from England to join her eternal companion in America. Melody had now found a reason to live, a reason to love, and a reason to hope.

So it was that Sam moved Melody quite happily to Alaska. Samuel had described the details of their long dark winters and endless daylight of summer, hoping she would not be too shocked by it all. She was completely willing to give it a try, assuring him she loved wind, rain, long dark nights, and mile-high snow.

A short time later the twins moved to Idaho to attend BYU-Idaho in Rexburg. They were nearly nineteen and anxious to attend college, but had been reluctant to leave Sam home alone. They saw their concerns sweetly answered in Melody's entry into their Daddy's life. They were right in their assumption that he would wither without family at home. Not many weeks after Melody moved in, they moved out. It was a tender but sweet transition for them all.

Melody and Sam had been married in April, and had moved to Alaska right after the honeymoon. Spring had yet to banish the snow and slush in Alaska. With no leaves on the trees and ankle-deep mud everywhere, Sam was afraid Melody would hate it. To his surprise she found the whole experience an unparalleled adventure, and immersed herself in creating her home in a new land, and in a new man's heart.

It was the second night after they had arrived in Alaska that Melody took out her violin. Sam heard the soft strains of violin music floating through the house as he sat in his study pondering past-due bills. He stopped his work, captivated by the sweetness and genius of her music. He went downstairs to find Melody standing before the piano, her eyes closed, music pouring forth from her like a fountain of pure water. He quietly sat down on the sofa and listened in a transport of delight. She played from somewhere deep within her soul, and it charmed him.

Then she lowered her bow.

"I have something to share with you," Melody said as she turned toward him. He was somewhat startled that she had even known he was sitting there. In time he would learn that she missed very little of what went on around her.

"I didn't mean to disturb you," Sam said a little sheepishly. "I couldn't help but come to hear you play. I don't know that I have ever heard you play like that before. Do you often just make up music as you go?"

"Occasionally, when the mood hits me," she replied. "I guess you inspired me."

"I hope it's an inspiration that visits you often," he replied happily.

"Me too. I want to play something for you, Sam. It's a song I wrote the day we were married."

"I don't remember you playing the violin that day."

"You weren't around me all morning, remember? I about drove your mother into a panic," she laughed. "I kept picking up the violin when I was supposed to be getting ready. She was hemming Bonnie's dress, and I was goofing around. It was kind of funny in a childish way. But, I had this song repeating in my heart, and I couldn't stand it until I had discovered all its parts. Would you like to hear it?"

"Absolutely. Does it have a name?"

"Humm, I think I'll call it 'Melody, Lost and Found.'"

"I like that. Play on, your audience adores you."

Melody winked at him. "I know! My audience is an obsessed sentimentalist, and I adore you right back!"

She raised her bow above the strings and paused. When she finally drew it across the strings a happy melody danced forth. It was cheerful, bright and wistful. He could almost envision her laughing as a child, dancing in fields of flowers. The music changed, grew gradually minor, and obscured the happy melody. At times the melody broke through, only to be swallowed up again. Then the music became heavy, dramatic, sweeping in its depth. Sam could feel the conflict, could sense the danger and compelling struggle. Again the music evolved and the melody triumphed and brought its brightness into the theme, stripping it of its minor qualities—lifting and coloring it in happy tones. With it all, the dramatic, sweeping nature of the theme remained unchanged, and the combined effect moved him.

He thought she was finished, but the music continued, growing soft without warning. He waited with anticipation as a single note sang long and serenely in the sudden silence. Then, quite unexpectedly, it danced away again, sweetly, cheerfully, more brightly than before, taking with it the flavor and grandeur of the dramatic theme. The music laughed in his heart, saying "I love you," in a way too personal to describe, then pirouetted to a happy end.

Sam was so moved he did not think to applaud. She correctly interpreted his silence as greater acclaim than any sound he might have made. More than any other person who would hear it in years to come, Sam understood the clarity and depth of the music, and it thrilled him. He stared at Melody, overwhelmed with emotion.

"What do you think?" Melody asked hopefully.

"It's breathtaking!" he replied, looking up into her eyes for the first time. She had found her way into a secret passage of his soul that he had never known even existed.

She giggled and carefully laid her violin on the piano; then she plopped onto his lap, looped her arm around his neck, and kissed his cheek playfully.

"I think you should publish it," he told her.

"Do you think so? Wow, I've never thought of anything like that. It would need other orchestra parts. And wouldn't it need words?"

"It already has words."

"It does? If it does, I don't have any idea what they are!"

Sam looked at her admiringly. "The words are the feeling the music calls forth. It doesn't need language; the message comes through loud and clear. Melody, this is a magical piece of music!" he said with awe.

"Well if you think so, I guess I'm all for publishing it." she told him.

Melody, Lost and Found, by Melody Mahoy, arranged for violin and piano by Samuel Mahoy, was published later that year to wide acclaim.

After a short time in Alaska, Sam and Melody settled into a happy orbit around one another. Everyone who loved Sam was relieved, especially his parents. They had wanted to move back to Utah for years but had delayed doing so until Sam found his way back to happiness. They moved from Alaska the following spring to a small farm near Brigham City.

By this time Sam's music was bringing them a moderate income. It would never make them rich, but neither he nor Melody had any great desire for such things. He had tried wealth, and found it no happier than poverty, and a lot more time-consuming. Sam listened and obeyed as the Spirit directed him to a steep course of righteousness; he felt strongly that the time for pursuing wealth had passed. Melody was delighted in his new focus, and she also dedicated herself to that same path. Their life together soon became a heavenly delight that neither had dreamed possible before.

It was during the days of sorting and unpacking while setting up their home that Sam had found Dawn's old journal. He almost set it aside, but felt compelled to open it. An odd feeling swept through him as he read her steady, flowery script. It had been twelve years now since her death, and the memories that remained were both bitter and sweet.

"You loved her very much, didn't you," Melody said softly from behind him. He glanced at her, suddenly feeling a bit guilty.

"It was a long time ago," he replied.

"I've often thought about Dawn myself," she told him. He was surprised to hear her say so, for he had said very little about his first love. "I confess that I found her journal not long after we moved in. I actually read parts of it."

"Oh? I didn't know that. Well, I don't mind."

Melody looked down for a moment, then back into his eyes. "I knew you wouldn't, or I wouldn't have read it. I was curious about what type of woman she was, because I knew you loved her deeply, and the girls loved her. In a way I guess I wanted to meet her."

There was a moment of silence. "We are very different," she finally said.

Sam nodded. "In the way orchids and roses are different," he admitted wryly.

"Which am I?" she wondered aloud.

"Roses."

Melody grimaced. "With thorns?"

"It's part of why I love you," Sam said. He placed a hand on her leg, then pretended he had been pricked by a thorn and drew back with a fake cry. She slugged him on the shoulder playfully.

"So which do you prefer, orchids or roses?" she impulsively asked him in fun. She immediately wished she had not asked. It was a loaded question, and one with no good answer. She didn't really want to know which of his loves he loved best—she really didn't! She opened her mouth to change the subject, but was not fast enough.

"I've learned something from you," Sam said.

Melody closed her mouth somewhat comically. "Oh, what?"

"I've learned what true celestial love is, the kind of love that predates this world and stretches into the eternities."

Melody's eyes grew wide, and a lump rose in her throat. She sat beside him and lay her head upon his shoulder. "Sam, you don't have to say that. Please forgive me for asking."

Sam touched her chin gently. "I do love Dawn, and I probably always will. And, even though I loved her very much, I have come to feel that she came into my life to lift me up, to prepare me for a deeper love, one that would become the greatest part of my Celestial joy. I am able to love you as I do, Melody, because I first loved her."

Melody was shocked. "Sam! That's so sweet!"

But Sam did not seem to hear her. "I didn't tell you this, but when we were in the sealing room of the temple to be married, I felt Dawn come and give her approval of my marrying you."

"No, you didn't tell me that. Did it make you sad?"

Again he did not respond directly. "I was filled with a sense of her love and of her approval, and then she departed. Since that time I have not felt her being involved in my life. I have come to believe that when she left that day, she left me forever. And now I think I know why."

Tears sprung to his eyes as he recognized the truth of what he was saying, even as he formed the words. "My darling, you and I share a passion for celestial music, in the deepest part of our beings. No one has ever shared that private part of me, no one. Oh Melody, it is this shared passion that predates our earthly existence, and forever bonds our spirits as soulmates."

He looked into her eyes, his own filled with new understanding. "Melody, don't you see? Doesn't your heart tell you this is true?"

This time Melody asked no questions, but placed her hand very gently on his back, and nodded with tears in her eyes. "Yes, Sam—I have felt that for a long time. But, why would you have been told to marry Dawn, when she was not to be your companion eternally?"

Sam's face was filled with peace. "I have a sense that Dawn came into my life to bless me until you and I could be together. I have come to the feeling that this arrangement was made by the three of us in the premortal world, and that she had other plans from the very start."

"But, why would Dawn agree to such a thing?" Melody asked, nonplussed. What he was saying sounded very atypical of her understanding of females.

"You have to understand that these things are all just impressions," Sam explained. "I can't say any of this with surety. But, I think it was in part because she was not going to be born into the faith. She was terrified at the thought, and because I loved her then, I think I promised to find her and teach her the gospel, and bring her into the covenant. But the Spirit tells me now that it was never intended for Dawn and I to remain together. I think she died because our contract had been fulfilled, and because my work with her was completed, as hers was with me. I now feel that she has set me free to get on with my eternal journey—with you."

"Sam, this is unthinkably beautiful! And a little scary," Melody added.

Sam nodded, then looked deeply into her eyes. "I am convinced that I have always loved Dawn, but that I have always been *in love* with you, my musical soulmate—and no one else."

Melody sighed and looked down. "Oh, my love. Thank you for that. I promise I will never feel insecure again."

Sam laughed and turned to Dawn's journal in his hand. "Let me read you something from her journal," he said as he thumbed through the last few pages. "This is part of her last letter to me. She knew she was not going to live much longer, and wrote this:

> It is my fond desire that you find another companion to love. I know the idea of it seems like betrayal to you now. But, in time, when the hurt has healed, you will come to understand why.
>
> Sam, you are a loving and gentle man, and you need to have someone to lavish these things upon in order for you to be well and happy. Besides, all that, it is the right thing to do. When you pray about it, you will understand this also.
>
> Sam, I know that you love me too much to fault me even in the things where I am very weak. You know I am not as spiritually alive as you are. I am quite certain that most, if not all, of my spiritual greatness came from you. I can't even guess what the eternities will hold. I only know that in this world, after I am gone, you need to love again.
>
> You will come to feel, as I do, that all the purposes for our meeting, loving and marrying have been fulfilled. I accept that it is my time to leave this world because of some grand premortal plan which has now reached an end.
>
> Don't feel like you have betrayed me by falling in love again. Feel that you have validated, and honored our love by not being able to live without love. Once true love has filled the soul, one cannot long live without it. I feel confident that I will love her too. Anyone you choose to love has got to be a wonderful woman—and a very lucky one indeed. I know!

"Oh Sam, how sweet! She was a woman of great character," Melody said quietly. "And she was physically beautiful, too, I've heard. The girls look just like her, don't they? Tall, blonde and blue-eyed?"

"They do," Sam responded absently. He was reading the postscript that Dawn had added. He hadn't thought about it until this very moment.

"Hey, I had forgotten about this. She added this postscript to her letter: 'Banque de Zurich 8521553-35 Zurich, Switzerland.'"

"What does it mean?" Melody asked, leaning over his shoulder.

"I don't know. It may mean nothing. The IRS cleaned out every account she had. However, this one wasn't associated with the business. I'm pretty sure whatever was in it is still there."

"How could you find out? Can you call them on the phone?"

"The only way is to go there in person."

"Fly to Switzerland? Just to find out the account has nothing in it?" She sounded dubious.

Sam sat pondering this until he stood and left the room. He was gone for quite a while before returning with a file folder. He rummaged through it until he found what he wanted. It was the original document he had signed when Dawn had first started Princess Gems. As a matter of fact, it was the only one in his name alone. All the others were in her name, or the business.

"This Zurich account she mentions in the journal is the very first overseas account she opened," Sam told Melody, his curiosity genuinely piqued. "She put my name on this account before we were married. When I asked her why, she just told me to trust her. She said she would explain when the time was right."

"What was the explanation then?" Melody asked, warming to the mystery.

"She never did explain. She died before she got around to telling me."

"I'll bet that whatever is in that account will explain why she did it. She apparently didn't intend for you to have the answer until after her death."

Sam nodded. "You are right, I'm sure. Dawn was nearly a genius at managing money. If she wanted me to know sooner, she would have told me."

Melody stared at him, then glanced back at the journal. "Sam, I think you should go to Switzerland," she said finally.

"It would cost thousands of dollars. We're nearly broke."

"I know. But it's important. I'll bet we can scrape up the money if we put our minds to it. I have a feeling you need to do this to close that chapter in your life."

She was silent for a moment in deep thought. "And, I think you owe it to Dawn," she finally added.

"Why do you think that?" he asked.

"It was basically her final request. It was the most important thing she had to tell you, and she saved it for the last. I think she would be disappointed if you never followed through on it. It was important to her. I think you should go."

It took three months to save most of the money for the trip. Finally, Sam borrowed the remainder of the money from his parents, who were very happy to assist.

The plane flight went more quickly than he had remembered. Previously it had taken days and days to arrive in Switzerland. Now, nearly twenty years later, he was standing in Zurich's main airport after a relatively few hours.

Except for being a little busier, Switzerland seemed the same to him. The roads were lined with huge walnut trees, the last remains of the great black forest once dense across Europe. He took a cab to a cheap hotel, and slept fitfully until the banks opened the following day.

Banque de Zurich turned out to be relatively small, a three-story brick building sandwiched between a restaurant and a clock store. Sam pulled open the heavy wooden door and felt as if he had stepped back in time. There were no teller windows as he had expected, but a row of four desks with men seated behind three of them. He approached the first.

"Hello, I need to check on an account," he said. The man muttered something in German, and left. He returned with a younger man a few minutes later, and stood by attentively, waiting for the younger man to translate.

"Good morning," the young banker said in a heavy accent. "I am helping you this banking problem. How may you assist me?" he asked, his voice trailing off in odd inflections. Sam suspected he had never spoken English to anyone other than his high school teacher.

"I want to check on this account," he said, handing him the account number on a slip of paper.

"Thank you, to please sit down." He punched the number into his computer and studied it for a full minute before speaking. "I am much needing to find what is this. I think very much it is being quite old. I am so questioning that we have not this numbers in our bank. Please to wait. Thank you." The men looked at each other and quickly walked to the back of the bank.

Sam took a seat on a very old wooden chair. He suspected it had been part of the original furnishings of the bank which, according to the plaque on the outside of the building, had opened in 1726. After half an hour, Sam was beginning to think he had forgotten all about him. In that length of time only a few people had come in and out of the bank. All of them had arrived in limousines. At least he was in good company.

When the bankers returned there were three of them, the original two, and another much older man. The older man spoke in German, and the younger man interpreted.

"I am Franz Plano, president of Banque de Zurich." Sam nodded and shook his hand. "This account number is much old. It has taken much time to find it in old books. Our computer was even not knowing it."

"Did you find it?" Sam asked, and had to wait for the translation to go and come back.

"Yes, happily. It is found."

"Very good," Sam said, and again waited for the translation and response.

"Yes, very good," the old man replied. Sam decided to keep his comments to a minimum or he'd still be waiting for translations when the bank closed.

"Please to show identification?" Sam pulled out his passport and handed it to them. The bank president sat at the desk and laid the passport atop some other document. Sam leaned forward and saw a yellow copy of the paper he and Dawn had signed that day so long ago. Apparently they were satisfied.

"It is good to meet you finally, Mister Mahoy," he said with a flourish.

"My name is Samuel Mahoy. My wife's name was Dawn—called Princess as well," Sam replied, then waited again for the translations.

"So sorry, Mister Mahoy. Do you now wish to see the box?"

"Yes. Is it a safety deposit box?" Again the translation lag.

"Yes. Did you not know this?"

"It has been a long time. I had forgotten," Sam said. He may have known at one time, but couldn't remember.

"So much true. A long time. But, come, we will go down. I will let Wilhelm show you. Go now, and goodbye." They shook hands again, and Sam left with the young interpreter. They were shortly joined by an armed guard.

Sam followed through a large double door and down a hall. A gate of thick steel slid into the wall and they passed through. After it closed, a heavy steel door nearly three feet thick opened toward them. They went down a long flight of stairs until Sam was sure they were a considerable distance underground. At the bottom of the stairwell was a large round vault door of the type Sam had seen inside banks in the US. It was partly opened, with an armed guard standing on either side. Another gate of thick bars separated them from the big vault.

Instead of entering through the gate, they turned left and the guard unlocked an iron door that looked like it had once been in a submarine. They turned a spoked wheel that groaned in protest. The hinges cried out as they pushed it open. Sam had to step over a high sill. Someone snapped on a light, and Sam found himself standing in a room filled with small lockers, each with a double set of locks. Back-to-back in the center of the room were two standing desks. Each desk had a shoulder high wall around it for privacy.

"This is old bank vault," his escort explained. "It is mostly empty now, but for very much older accounts such as yours."

"So, the new vault has been added since my box was rented?"

"Oh, yes. Long ago. One day, all old boxes will be empty, and it will not be opened any more. We often do not come here, as you see," he said pointing at the floor. For the first time Sam realized they were walking in dust dense enough to obscure the checkered pattern in the floor.

"Let me think of this," the young banker said, studying the numbers on the lockers. "I think… yes. This is the right one," he said, pointing to a small door to their right about chest high. The guard inserted a key and turned it. The banker inserted another, and turned it. The door opened with a little squawk. "The guard will wait in the hall to when you are finished. This box will now be not used. If you wish to keep these valuables in our bank, you will very much be purchasing a new one. Thank you," he said, and disappeared with the guard.

Inside the door Sam found a black tray about eight inches wide and eighteen inches long. He pulled the tray out and took it to the desk in the center of the room. He lifted the heavy steel lid to find a white envelope covered with postage stamps, and a small box not much larger than his fist. There were no stamps on the little box, so he assumed Dawn had placed it here herself. It gave him a moment of tenderness to imagine her in this very room, smiling to herself as she prepared this gift for him.

He opened the envelope and found a letter in Dawn's flowery script. The date on the letter told him she had written this letter on their honeymoon. Sam had no idea how she had managed to get it into this safety deposit box, since he could not remember her having left his side during their entire stay in Switzerland; she had hidden these things from him well.

My Beloved Sam,

I promised you an explanation when I first asked you to help me start the diamond business. I never intended you to hear that explanation during my lifetime. The fact that you are reading this now means I am now out of your life.

My explanation is simple. This is an apology. I never forgave myself for losing your diamond in England. I know you never felt that way, but I have felt badly about it for a long time. My main motivation in starting Princess Gems was to generate enough money to make it up to you one day. That's the reason my first act was to open an account only in your name. It was my way of dedicating myself to one day returning your stone.

I also wanted to leave you my love. Knowing you, it is probably now many years after my passing. I hope you haven't grieved a long time.

Perhaps my apology will be just in time to accomplish some greater good. Please take it and make something eternal happen. You were never one to build monuments to yourself on earth, so build one of an eternal nature. That way, it will be a part of us forever.

There is something else that I know that I must share with you. As I wrote this, and pondered the fact that you have most probably by now remarried, I expected to feel a little jealous. But, to my surprise, I feel a type of relief. I do not believe that I have ever been able to love you as deeply as you needed me to.. I have always felt that I was mostly holding your hand, desperately trying to keep up with you, until your real love could make her appearance in your life. But this is as it should be. Do not feel sad at my words, but rejoice! Rejoice that all is well. Rejoice that you are now where you needed to be from the very first.

With all my love I bid you adieu, and bestow my blessing upon your soul—wherever you go.

Princess

After the shock gave way to the whisperings of the Spirit, Sam's heart felt full. Dawn had sweetly confirmed that Melody was his "real love"—which he had sensed many times but had never fully admitted to himself. His heart filled with new gratitude for Dawn.

He took the small package and opened it with difficulty. He had to pick at the dried and brittle tape with his fingernails. When he finally pried it open he found a wad of tissue paper. As the tissue fell away, Sam gasped. Inside this he found a diamond about the size of his thumb. He could tell it was not the diamond from his mission, but it was similar in size, slightly larger perhaps, and considerably whiter. He held it up to the light and counted very few flaws. For a stone this size, it was exceptional in its clarity. Its color was very white, tending slightly towards blue. The cut was oval, and very finely executed. The light refracted perfectly from its many prisms.

Having worked with Dawn in the diamond industry, Sam had a good idea of its worth. However, he had been out of touch with these things for years, and couldn't be sure without the proper lens.

Using hand signals, Sam asked the guard to take him back upstairs.

"I need to speak to someone who knows diamonds and would be in the market for a large stone," he told the young banker with the broken English. He was promptly escorted back to the bank president's office. The request was repeated in German.

"Certainly," the older man told him. "I will write down address now."

"No. I need him to come here. I can't transport this stone. It's far too valuable."

The banker's big bushy eyebrows went up when he heard the translation. He picked up his phone and in a surprisingly short time, a man carrying a briefcase entered the bank. This man was introduced as a merchant whose specialty was rare gems.

Sam was seated opposite the diamond merchant at the bank president's desk as the man studied the stone through a loop. He produced an electronic scales and weighed it. Sam asked what it weighed. Twenty-five carats, he was told. Sam had not been far off. He had guessed twenty.

During all this time he had spoken to Sam only through the interpreter. Now he turned directly to Sam and spoke flawless, though heavily accented, English.

"I am Andrew Schwartz. I represent investors interested in quality gems," he said as he extended his hand for the first time. Sam had the impression that had the stone been smaller or less valuable, the man would have left without even speaking to him. Sam felt a little annoyed at what, in Sam's mind, was patent snobbery.

"Samuel Mahoy. Pleased to meet you," he replied without smiling, and shook his hand. Sam had associated with enough hoity-toity diamond merchants to know how to deport himself.

"You may not be aware that I sold this stone to your wife. It was almost twenty years ago, I think."

"I didn't know that," Sam admitted, leaning forward in astonishment, his eyes wide.

Mr. Schwartz made a dismissive gesture with his hand. "Almost all stones of this quality go through my hands at some point. I remember your wife well. She is a beautiful woman. I believe she said she was on her honeymoon at the time. I remember envying her new husband. I hope she is well."

All this was startling to Sam. They had stopped in Switzerland on their honeymoon for three days. He did not remember her being out of his sight for more than a few minutes. It was a mystery he would not be able to unravel in this life.

"Dawn died about twelve years ago," Sam said quietly.

"Such a pity." Mr. Schwartz said something in German and the other two men expressed regret in words incomprehensible to him, but in tones quite plain to understand. At least one of the old bankers remembered Dawn. Sam was beginning to think his former wife was a greater mystery than he had ever suspected.

"It makes sense then that you are here after the gem. She mentioned it was part of her estate. She expected at that time to hold the stone for a long time, as I recall."

"She died quite unexpectedly," Sam said. At least, he had not expected it, Sam thought grimly, despite how many times Dawn had tried to tell him.

"Quite tragic, I'm sure. What do you wish to do with this gem? Do you wish to sell it?" His voice was steady. Sam knew he was a shrewd businessman, probably quite wealthy, and certainly anxious to turn a profit from this transaction. He also knew he was not "inside" the diamond industry, or he would not be buying and selling stones this way.

"I wish to sell, if the price is right," Sam replied just as steadily.

"I have a buyer who will give you $500,000 American dollars in cash. I can have the papers drawn up in just a few minutes."

"That won't be necessary. I won't be selling it to you."

The man leaned forward, his eyes narrowing. "May I ask why?"

"Because you think me a fool," Sam replied evenly.

The man's eyebrows shot up. He steepled his hands under his chin and looked Sam squarely in the eyes. "My apologies. I did not mean to insult you. Perhaps you can suggest a price?"

Sam had only a vague idea of what its retail value was, but assumed Mr. Schwartz was hoping to double or triple his money. He was quite certain Dawn had put him in a vice and squeezed all but the tiniest profit from him the first time. Mr. Schwartz was now apparently hoping to make happy amends for that event by stealing the stone back.

"I will take four million," Sam said. It even sounded high to him.

"So, we trade insults," the diamond merchant said cheerfully, then grew somber. Sam knew he had blown way over the mark. "You understand that I must wholesale the stone. You ask me for its high retail value. The best I can do is one."

"Since we're insulting one another," Sam responded, "Do you think your time so valuable that you must make a million dollars for an hour's work? I will pay you for your time, and take the stone elsewhere," he said as he rose to his feet.

The merchant spoke quickly. "Come, sit back down," he urged. "We can do business yet. I will give you one and-a-half, no more."

Sam was still standing. He held out his hand for the stone. The diamond merchant looked at him as if in shock.

"One and three-quarter million. You must understand that I may not be able to sell the stone for much more than that."

"You aren't going to be selling it at all, so don't worry about it. Please hand me the stone."

"Mister Mahoy, you have me cornered. I don't think you understand the local diamond market, or you would accept my offer. Why do you refuse what is a reasonable offer? Don't you trust me?"

"It may be reasonable. And, no I don't trust you. I intend to verify that it is a fair offer, then I intend to sell it to someone I trust. I'm in no hurry to sell to you or anyone else. It's sat in this vault for over twenty years, as you are aware. I will have the stone appraised by two reputable houses, and then sell it to a third. So . . ."

"All right!" the man nearly shouted. "I went through something similar to this when I sold it to your wife, God rest her. For one so beautiful, she was more ruthless than a bandit. She must have gotten it from you."

Sam sat back down. He could almost see the wheels turning in his head. "I will give you two million. One million today, and one million after I sell the stone."

"I accept the price. But it must all be cash—today. As you suggested, I don't trust you."

"You *are* a bandit," he replied hotly. "I don't have that much cash!"

"Then give me the stone. I already told you, I'm in no hurry to sell."

Mr. Schwartz turned toward the two bankers. A flurry of words in German, and wild hand gestures passed between them before he turned back to Sam. His eyes seemed wary, but twinkled with exhilaration.

"I will have two million deposited into your account. I have arranged for credit with this bank. Will that be acceptable?" he asked with just a hint of sarcasm.

"It will," Sam replied. "You may now draw up the papers."

After they had both signed, and the funds transferred, Sam said, "I just have one question?"

"Yes, what is it?" the diamond merchant asked a little irritably.

"Why didn't you just offer me a fair price to begin with? I would have settled for one million if it had been your first offer."

It was probably the worst thing Sam could have told him. The diamond merchant slumped back in his chair, his face turning red. After Sam's comment had been translated, the older banker laughed. Even at that, the diamond merchant would make more for his one hour's bargaining than most Americans make in ten years of hard work.

Sam left the bank about noon, two million dollars richer. He had to admit, it was not a bad morning's work. He still had two days before his plane left for the US, and decided to spend the rest of the morning on a foot tour of Zurich. He was already in an older part of the city, and walked slowly down cobblestone streets, past fountains and buildings hundreds of years old. It seemed as if much in Switzerland had been built in the 1600's or earlier. Most of the buildings were constructed of heavy wooden beams with plaster in between. Most were several stories tall. Many of the more elaborate structures were constructed of stone. It felt to Sam as if he were walking through a picture postcard. In reality, the picturesque quality of that area of town was carefully maintained by law.

It was more of a city square than a park he had stumbled onto, but it was beautiful. He wished Melody were here with him. She had wanted to come, but they simply couldn't afford it. Well, he smiled to himself, that would never again be the case. He couldn't help think happy thoughts about blessings they could enjoy with this amazing windfall. He felt like the most blessed person alive.

Sam walked around the large fountain in the center of the square. Two large, bronze horses squirted water from their nostrils as a hundred jets of water shot up at them from the sides of the fountain. A larger-than-life soldier stood on the backs of both horses, a foot on each dashing steed. One hand gripped the reins, the other held a sword high over his head. It was an awe-inspiring work of art. Unable to read the time-darkened bronze plaque, Sam had no idea what it represented.

"It's beautiful, in a violent sort of way, isn't it," a man's voice said beside him. Sam turned to voice his agreement, but his words were sucked from his lungs in astonishment.

"Hello, Helaman," Sam finally managed to stammer. "I certainly didn't expect to meet you here," he said quite honestly.

"No, I suppose you didn't. It has been a while since that day high in Alaska's beautiful mountains. You were surprised to see me there too, though perhaps less so than now." The old man laughed in the same way Sam remembered well.

Sam's heart warmed, and it really did feel good to see him again. Sam had not given up hope of continuing his spiritual journey, but with all the challenges of life, a new marriage, and a new home, he had settled into a pattern of dogged obedience that didn't seem to be propelling him upward at any great speed.

Sam took some courage from Helaman's happy demeanor, and stuck out his hand. To his delight the old man took it without hesitation. In a way, Sam was almost surprised to find the hand corporal, the grip firm. "Do you mind if I ask you a question?" Sam ventured.

"That's actually why I'm here," Helaman replied, and took a seat on a bench facing the fountain.

"Why do you look like an old man? I thought translation would make a person young again."

"I look exactly the age I was when I made my request of the Lord. I haven't aged since that time."

"You carry a cane," Sam observed.

"Mostly out of habit. I used a cane most of my life—actually, right after I was killed by the Lamanites, and you sent me back!" Helaman laughed again, his eyes pointedly upon Sam. "But, it comes in handy at times. Like the time I delivered your sweet wife from a group of street thugs in Wales many years ago."

"You knew Melody in England!?" Sam cried, astonished.

"Wales. She was in Wales."

"Wales then. You knew her there?"

"My dear friend, I knew her well, and actually saved her life more than once. Ask her when you return without mentioning my meeting you here."

"But how . . . I mean . . . I guess I should just say thank-you."

Helaman looked at Sam and smiled. "You are most welcome. It was a pleasure."

Sam's mind spun furiously in this new information. "So, this was during the same time you first met me in priesthood meeting?"

"The same time. And, in answer to your next question, no, I didn't know she was to become your future wife. All I knew was that I had been sent to protect her and see that she made her way to America."

Sam nodded, "Which would have also given you to know that she was destined to become a member of your family."

Helaman smiled broadly. "You're beginning to see the larger picture, my friend."

"Wow. Again, thank you for protecting her. She is a true joy to me."

"It is my joy to serve you. And, it was a joy to see that you were Melody's link to my posterity. Did you know that I attended your sealing in the temple?"

"No kidding!"

"Remember when the officiator said, in the presence of God . . ."

Sam did remember. "Angels, and these witnesses. You were one of the angels!" Sam cried.

"As was your former wife, your brother Jimmy, Melody's mother and several others. It was a marvelous family event on both sides of the veil."

Sam was amazed. "I'm so grateful you told me. Thank you! That warms my soul."

"You're easy to impress," Helaman said with a chuckle. "You haven't seen anything yet—but you will. I'm sorry, but my time is limited. Is there anything else you wanted to ask me?"

"Oh, yes, I was wondering if you can change your appearance to look younger if you wanted to."

"Is that the best question you have for me?" Helaman asked, a note of gentle rebuff in his voice.

Sam grew serious in thought. "No. Actually, it was more for my curiosity. My real question is, what should I do next, Helaman? I'm anxious to continue with my progression."

"That's a better question," he said approvingly. "It's also a more difficult answer."

"Am I ready for it?" Sam asked, more of himself than of his visitor.

"Well, I'm here," Helaman answered simply. Sam nodded his understanding, ready to hear the answer. Whether Sam was ready to respond correctly was another question.

"So let me begin by saying, I have largely been engaged in the same field of labor for the last several centuries," Helaman told him. Sam nodded. Several hundred years seemed a long time to Sam, yet by his calculation this faithful servant had been laboring somewhere for nearly two thousand years. It was kind of mind-boggling.

"What you have yet to learn is that we labor under many of the same constraints the Saints of this dispensation do," Helaman explained.

"What do you mean?"

"For example, we can't use miracles to convince anyone of the truth of what we are saying."

"That makes perfect sense. Moral agency would always have to be paramount."

The old man nodded thoughtfully. "Most of the progress we make occurs by natural means. If we translated beings build a church in this telestial world, it is paid for with real money, or built with the sweat of real brows."

"I think I see what you mean," Sam said. "I suppose I had just assumed you did most of what you did by the power of the priesthood."

"Even Christ could work no miracles until after the people had faith. The laws haven't changed."

"But, you have come to me a number of times. Each of your visits was a little miraculous. Aren't those miracles?"

"Yes, but would you say that my visits increased your faith, or caused you to be more faithful than you would have otherwise been?"

Sam had to think about this. "I don't think so, really. I didn't have any greater faith after one of your visits than I had before. I think I may have had greater knowledge, though, and a determination to press forward. My understanding was certainly greater, but it didn't improve my testimony."

"That's right. I couldn't have come otherwise. All blessings, all miracles, all angelic ministrations, all heavenly visitations, all visions or anything like unto it come after the person has faith, or when it will not cause that person to be more faithful than they otherwise would have been," Helaman said emphatically.

Sam was confused. "Then what are these higher blessings for?"

Helaman rested a hand on his arm. "They are to inform and instruct. They almost always bring greater responsibilities, and consequently greater opposition into a person's life. It is actually a great test to have a heavenly visitation, Samuel. They are never given to build a person's faith. They almost always end up challenging it significantly."

"I hadn't ever considered that," Sam said, shaking his head.

"Few people do, and ask for things they are not prepared to receive. For this reason, almost all we do comes to pass by natural means, rather than through miracles."

"I'm beginning to think your job is harder than what most people think it is," Sam admitted. "Most people see translated beings like angels who can use miracles to accomplish their work with little effort."

Helaman chuckled. "Oh, we do work miracles—lots of them! But, most of our miracles are never seen by mortals. It is a miracle that I stand here at this moment, having mere minutes ago been on a different continent. It is a miracle that everyone here in this park can see me, but none will remember it, or anything they may have heard of our conversation. It is a miracle that when I leave here in a few minutes a hundred people will see me disappear from before their eyes, and none will observe or question it. Many such miracles occur unobserved by mortals."

The old man gazed intently at Sam. "The miracles that are consciously seen all come after the people have faith sufficient to behold them. For the most part, our work is to bring our posterity to the level of righteousness that they may work the miracles themselves."

Sam nodded. "Just as it is within the earthly church." Then a new question came to his mind. "I thought you said your work was to minister to people like myself who had qualified for certain blessings," he said, trying to remember the words exactly.

"That's the fun part of my assignment," Helaman nodded. "But what actually occupies most of my time is something quite different, and exponentially broader. We are working to prepare the world for the Savior's return."

Sam was intrigued. "Who are you preparing? Are they your posterity also?"

"Good questions! In our family there is a long tradition of righteousness, and many laborers. Because our family is in order, we also spend much of our time laboring among Father's children in general, preparing the world at large for Christ's return. But, when the needs of our family arise, their issues take first priority."

Sam pondered this. "That's very interesting—but why are you telling me all this?"

"I'm telling you this so you can begin your participation in the mission you will eventually labor in."

Sam felt a thrill throughout his body. "I'm anxious to begin," he responded enthusiastically. "What do you need me to do? I'm ready!"

Helaman looked at him for a long moment, then drew a breath. "I have been laboring for nearly a century to prepare a branch of the tribe of Levi to leave their homes and travel to Zion. They are very poor people, and it is difficult for them because they have such limited means."

"How can I help? What do you need?"

"Two million dollars," Helaman replied, his eyes steadily upon Sam.

Sam stared at him. Then he pulled a slip of paper from his wallet, wrote the name of the bank and account number, and held it out to Helaman. With a Swiss numbered account, that was all that was needed; to have the number was to own the money in the account.

"That will take care of it," Sam said, a look of satisfaction on his face. "I just acquired it today, and just in the nick of time, it appears."

Helaman did not take the paper. "Are you sure you want to give all that money away? Don't you need to talk to Melody first?"

"I'll explain it to her when I arrive home. She'll understand. She'll agree with my decision," Sam confidently told him.

Helaman took the paper. "You can't mention me, or where the money went. I'm sorry, but that's the way it has to be."

"She'll understand, I know she will."

"Then, I am extremely grateful to you. This will be a great blessing to those good people." His voice was heavy with emotion, and there were tears in his eyes, which amazed Sam in a way. Some part of him had imagined angels to be somehow aloof, or immune, from the trials of those to whom they ministered. Sam sensed in Helaman a heavy emotional investment in their welfare.

"I'm very grateful I even had it. That's a miracle in itself! I hope it's enough," Sam told him sincerely.

"It's exactly enough. God bless you," Helaman said as he stood.

"He already has," Sam replied, shaking his hand. Then Sam watched his visitor walk away from him toward the fountain. He watched him walk into a crowd of people on the far side of the square, but didn't see him walk out. Sam was not at all surprised. He stood there, a strange feeling resting upon him. He was both very happy, and very—the feeling didn't have a name, but was somewhat like being suddenly orphaned, and feeling peace about it.

The morning before he left Switzerland, Sam stopped by the bank to check the account. The balance was exactly zero. He closed the account. The only thing he kept from the bank was a single piece of paper with Dawn's script upon it.

All during his flight home he kept replaying the events of this trip in his mind. It had been so happily unexpected to be wealthy again. For a brief hour he had fantasized what he might do with so much money. Then, just as suddenly it was gone. Yet, it was happily gone, and he had parted with it without even having to consider his actions. It was simply the right thing to do, and therefore, what he wanted to do. Still, it was a lot of money to just hand away, and a tiny part of him felt emptied by its sudden departure.

But more urgently, he wondered what he would tell Melody? Of course, he would tell her the truth, but what part of the truth? He couldn't tell her about Helaman, or where the money had gone, so how could he possibly explain it to her so she would understand?

Sam knew it would be much easier to not mention the money at all, but that would be too small a portion of the truth. He was still pondering this as he walked up the jetway in Anchorage, and saw Melody's happy face in the crowd. She was holding Sammy, and pointing happily with his little hand toward "Daddy." It warmed his heart, and increased his dilemma. The loss of so much might well be a greater test for her than it had been for him. It was pretty easy to hand over millions of dollars when an angel asks you for it. It's harder to understand when all you know is that the money no longer exists.

They were lying in bed. Sam loved the way Melody fit into the curvature of his side. It was as if she had been molded by a master craftsman to reside there. He held her affectionately, wondering how to answer her last question.

"So, what are we going to do with all that money?" she had just asked him, a note of childlike wonder in her voice. He had just finished telling her of selling the diamond. When she got excited she rubbed her feet back and forth against each other, just as she was doing now.

"Do you care what we do with it?" Sam asked experimentally, still unsure how to tell her without mentioning his heavenly visitor.

"Certainly," she replied emphatically. "It could really help us, and help your music, and my music, and Sammy's college fund, and repay your parents what we owe, and think of the blessings of the tithe, and possibly a scholarship for gifted students, or poor children, or whatever. The possibilities are fantastic!"

Sam hesitated. "What if I decided to do something with the money that had nothing to do with our family's needs?" he asked, not knowing what else to say.

Melody's feet stopped moving. He felt her head turn up against his shoulder, toward his face. "What do you mean, darling?"

Sam swallowed hard. "I mean, what if the money needs to go to someone else—because the Lord wants them to have it instead?"

Melody was silent for a long moment. She looked at him intently. "I think I know what you're saying. Well, I guess it's really not *our* money after all—is it?" she said somewhat resolutely.

"Well, of course it's *our* money! Anything I have is yours as much as mine."

"I know you feel that way, and I love you for it. But, you misunderstood me," she said soberly. "I mean, it really is the *Lord's* money, isn't it?"

Sam said nothing, so she continued in earnest. "You know, as far as I am concerned, the Lord can have it. I can't imagine us having that much money anyway. We don't honestly need it, you know. So, I would be inclined to think this was more of a test, to see if we'll do something righteous with the money. What do you think?"

"I'm absolutely sure you're right," he replied a little too emphatically. Her feminine radar caught that, and she perked up.

She sat up in bed, pulling the blankets with her until he was almost without covers. She turned to kneel beside him, her knees touching his side. Her expression was inscrutable, and he was quite sure he was in big trouble.

"Sam?"

Oh no, I've had it now, he thought to himself. "What is it, my love?" his lips actually said.

"I just want to know one thing," she said earnestly.

"All right. Just one," he said, trying to interject some humor into what felt like a grim situation. He thought how many marriages had been torn apart by the loss of a whole lot less money than he had just given away. His heart felt burdened as he waited for her to reply.

"I'm serious," she told him.

"OK. I'll tell you anything you want to know."

Melody looked him right in the eye. "Do you still have the money?"

"No," Sam answered without hesitation. She studied him intently for a long minute.

"Well, then that brings up one more question," she replied finally as her eyes narrowed. He thought he knew what it would be, and it was the very question he didn't know how to answer. He prayed for help, and waited uncomfortably.

"Is the Lord pleased with where the money went?" she asked after some consideration. Her question so startled him that he sat up also.

They were nearly nose-to-nose when he said, "More so, I believe, than with anything I have ever done before."

Melody lowered her head, and he could tell she was praying silently. Finally she looked up at him. "Then, I'm pleased, too." She leaned forward to kiss him.

Sam received the kiss with huge relief. In that second he knew all over again that he was married to the most amazing woman in the world.

However, not wanting to press his luck, he changed the subject. "So I have a question for you, Mrs. Mahoy," he quipped.

"What?" Melody responded playfully.

"Were you ever in Wales?"

Melody nodded. "Oh, yes. It was where I landed after escaping from Rhodesia. Why do you ask?"

"I thought you went to England?" Sam questioned, settling back on his pillow as nonchalantly as he could.

"I probably just referred to it as England, but it actually was Wales. The city was called Swansea."

Sam pondered this for a moment, curiosity gnawing at his mind. "It must have been terrifying, smuggling away into a strange country."

She nodded. "It was, but not for so long. I met this wonderful old man who helped me."

Sam sat up. "What was he like?"

"He was maybe in his sixties, and walked with a cane. But, the funny thing was, he'd occasionally walk without a limp." Melody chuckled at the memory. "You want to know what else was strange? He never told me his name. Can you imagine that?"

"He was probably an angel or something," Sam offered carefully.

"He was an angel to me," she whispered, her voice reverent. "I think he saved my life, probably more than once."

Sam reached out to hold her. "I hope we get the chance to thank him some day."

"Me too, Sam." She smiled suspiciously at him. "What's that strange look on your face?"

"I was just thinking how beautiful you are." He stroked her cheek tenderly, then bent to kiss her.

"More please," she said, imitating little Sammy, and leaned into him for another kiss.

9

HOW THIN THE VEIL

In May of the following year, Sam and Melody moved to Utah to be closer to their family. They found a small split level-home in South Jordan, and moved their battered possessions in. The winter had not been especially good for music sales, and their finances were exhausted by the time they settled in. They had spent every dime of their savings on the down payment of the home, and had borrowed money against future royalties from music sales to finance the move. Still, it was an exciting time.

It seemed wonderful to be closer to the twins, who were still attending college in Rexburg, along with Sam's Mom and Dad, his siblings Emily and Cheryl, Benjamin, Angela and Beth and his youngest sister, Rachel—now with four kids of her own. One of them stopped by or called almost every day. It was especially sweet to see how graciously the entire family accepted Melody and Sammy into their hearts. Sammy, now six years old, quickly bonded with his extended family, and soon birthday parties and sleepovers were overflowing with lots of little cousins.

Out of necessity, Sam began looking for a job. The only problem was, now that he was in his mid-forties, few companies considered him imminently employable. He refused to be discouraged, and after many attempts at higher-paying employment, he and Melody prayed mightily for a solution. He immediately found a less-glamorous position that he knew was exactly what the Lord had in mind. Although it was a night job, it was more perfect than any he had ever imagined.

Sam showed up for the first shift of work at 8:00 p.m. He was introduced to five other workers and assigned a locker. They talked quietly as they dressed in their white uniforms. He followed them through a short subterranean passageway and into the building he would be cleaning.

"Brother Mahoy," his supervisor, Brother Tatum, said as the others filed off to their assigned jobs. "Welcome to the Salt Lake Temple. I hope your job here is as rewarding as mine has been." It was now 9:00 p.m. and the temple was closed for the night.

"I can't believe I'm here," Sam said. "I somehow thought the temple was so holy it didn't get dirty."

Brother Tatum chuckled. "I've heard that before," he said. "It is holy, and we treat it that way. Even when we are using a noisy vacuum in the most holy parts of it, we are reverent. We don't laugh or tell jokes, play pranks, run, or anything that would be disrespectful."

"I understand," Sam said.

"I'm sure you think you understand, and that's good enough for right now."

"I thought I understood, but now I'm not sure I do," Sam amended his answer.

Again, Brother Tatum chuckled quietly. They were still standing just inside the temple, near the sealing rooms. Sam recognized the room where he and Melody had been sealed not so many years before. "Let me just say that the temple is in use 24 hours a day," Brother Tatum continued.

"Oh, you mean the Brethren hold meetings here at night?" Sam questioned him. That would explain the need to be extra circumspect at all hours.

"Occasionally, but that's not exactly what I mean. What I mean is, it's in use 24 hours a day. It's used for sacred things on both sides of the veil. Just be aware that we are in the busiest building on this planet. It bridges two worlds—our natural world, and the world of spirits."

"I sort of understand," Sam said slowly, thinking about Helaman.

"If you work here very long, you'll understand completely. Come on. Let me show you what needs to be done. Each new employee starts by cleaning the temple annex rooms. I'll show you the ropes."

Sam loved his new job, and looked forward to each shift. It was true that he was a janitor, but he was a janitor in God's temple, and it pleased him. With his background in electrical and instrumentation, he also did many small electrical jobs, and eventually was called upon to supervise electrical renovations serviced by crews brought in for that purpose.

Sam had initially dreaded working nights. He hadn't done that since his Alaska pipeline days. More than just working nights, it was the separation from his family he dreaded. He hated being in bed while they were awake, and vise-versa. Melody saw the dilemma too, and quietly adjusted her schedule to overlap his. She and Sammy stayed up late. Sammy went to bed at midnight, and Melody waited up until Sam came home at 2:30 AM. She usually had a snack ready for him. They got ready for bed as they shared the events of their days. He especially loved telling her the spiritual experiences he was having, and she loved hearing them.

Just after his first year of working at the temple, Sam was assigned to clean the endowment rooms. It was a wonderful change for him, and he had looked forward to it ever since he had learned that one "worked up" to cleaning the actual working rooms of the temple.

There was a special feeling of reverence as he pushed open the big arched doors into the Garden Room. He wheeled his cart of cleaners and waxes into the room. Even the cart, and the bottles on it were white. He pushed his vacuum in and found a plug behind a potted plant. He looked around for a long minute, not wishing to mar the silence with the whir of the vacuum. Finally, he clicked it on. He carefully worked down each row. There was no visible dirt, yet he felt a special need to make the room spotless. It was his contribution to the holiness he felt glowing within that room.

At the front of the room he packed his things on the cart, and lifting the vacuum, climbed the three steps up to the big doors leading into the Telestial room. He pushed them open quietly, and began his work there. Even a more hushed feeling fell over him as he worked, and it seemed as if the whine of his vacuum was being swallowed up in an eternal vastness.

Sam finished this room close to his break time, and decided to skip the break. His heart felt at peace working in these rooms, and leaving them seemed like labor, not rest.

He rolled his cart to the steps leading to the Terrestrial room and stopped before the big arched door. He had never cleaned this room before, and felt a certain hesitation. This was the room where the veil of the temple was housed, and it seemed to him that eternity might be on the other side of the door. He lifted his vacuum in one hand and stepped up to the door, pushing it open. He took one step inside before he looked up, and quite unexpectedly found himself in a room full of people dressed in white.

Nearest to him was a young man with long, blond hair. The young man turned toward him and smiled. He was dressed in a white suit of an archaic cut, and while the others in the room were seated, he was standing, and appeared to be officiating, or at least observing in an official capacity. A look of serenity and satisfaction was evident on his face. Sam let his eyes sweep across the room. No one else had noticed him; their eyes were fixed on a group of three men standing at the head of the room near the veil. Sam could not hear what they were saying, even though he could see they were speaking. He considered this due to the unusual acoustics of the temple.

"Oh, excuse me," Sam whispered. "I didn't know the room was in use. I'll come back later." The man smiled, nodded and took a step toward the door, his hand out-stretched. Sam backed up as quietly as possible, making sure his equipment didn't clank against the doorway. The young man quietly closed the door.

Once outside, he stood for a moment considering what he might do. He would have to go tell the supervisor that the room was in use, and get another assignment. The Terrestrial room just wouldn't get cleaned tonight. He left, taking his equipment with him, and quite unexpectedly found his supervisor coming toward him through the Garden room.

"How's it going Brother Mahoy?" he asked in his usual reverent voice.

"I would be almost done, but the Terrestrial room is in use. No one told me, and I just barged in on them," Sam admitted, still feeling a little embarrassed.

"Really?" Brother Tatum asked. "Let's go check."

"But, I already disturbed them once," Sam said. Still he followed his supervisor to the big doors.

Brother Tatum quietly pushed open the door not much more than a foot, just wide enough for Sam to see inside.

The room was empty.

"But?" Sam stammered. "They were… I was… I just . . ." He stopped to collect his wits. Brother Tatum had quietly closed the door. "Well, I guess I might just as well finish it now," Sam finally mumbled, and lifted his vacuum. He was afraid the boss might suspect he had made it up to get out of cleaning the room.

Brother Tatum held up a hand, standing directly between him and the door. "Let's just leave it for now."

Brother Tatum took charge of his cart, and Sam carried the vacuum until they were standing in the service hallway outside the Telestial room. "I don't understand," Sam told him once they were outside. "Why didn't you want me to finish the room?"

"Like you said, you already disturbed them once."

"So you do believe me, that there really were people in there," Sam said somewhat triumphantly.

"Of course I do. It's not at all uncommon."

"I'm not even sure what I saw in there," Sam admitted meekly after a moment of silence.

"Yes you are," his supervisor said, "You just haven't seen it before. The first time it takes a little while to believe your eyes. Most of the rest of us have seen it before, and we just quietly leave. Sometimes we don't even mention it to the other workers unless it's to keep them away too. It's a sacred experience to be allowed to actually see."

"You really believe me," Sam repeated again.

"Of course I do. That's the reason I was coming down the hall, to tell you to leave that room undone tonight. I had a feeling it was in use."

Sam was quiet for a moment which he spent studying the restful pattern of the carpet under his feet. Finally he looked up, and his boss was waiting patiently for him to speak. "Why did you open the door when you knew there were people using the room?"

"So you would know for certain that they were not mortals using the temple," he said, and patted Sam on the shoulder.

"I'm grateful you did. They looked just like normal people. I assumed they *were* just people."

"They were just people," Brother Tatum corrected.

"They sure were," Sam agreed. "I'll never think of spirits quite the same way after this."

"Now you understand," his supervisor said poignantly.

"Do I have to go home tonight?" Sam asked in a childlike voice.

"Yes. Now let's get you finished up so you *can* go home."

"Please?" Sam begged with a sad look on his face.

"Sorry, you have to go home, just like all the rest of us."

"Ok," Sam said reluctantly. "But, I'm coming back early tomorrow."

"Now you understand," his supervisor repeated quietly.

Sam and Melody loved their new home, their new ward, and friends. They labored in many callings, and rejoiced in each of them.

"Do you know what I like about working in the temple?" Sam asked Melody as they sat together in the early morning reading the Book of Mormon together. Sammy would be getting up in a few minutes to get ready for school. Sam would not go to bed until after he was off to school, and would be awake and getting ready for work about the time he returned from school.

"Let's see," Melody said, setting down her copy of the scriptures. "There must be a thousand things, like seeing angels, and feeling the Spirit while you work, and rubbing shoulders with worthy men and women."

"That's all true. But, I was thinking of something else."

"Please tell me," she smiled at him, and laid her glasses on the end table.

"I'm not sure I can put it in just one sentence."

"I'm not in a hurry," she assured him.

"It has to do with purity of heart," Sam said, choosing his words carefully.

"The pure in heart shall see God," Melody rehearsed.

"You know, I hadn't made that connection. But, yes. It has been coming to me that this type of purity is not the same sense as mere absence of sin."

"Really?"

"I don't think so. The sense I'm getting is that the purity which opens the doors of the veil is a purity far richer than sinlessness. It is a purity of principle and precept. To be pure is to be free from false belief and false concepts, to be filled with truth and light."

Melody thought about that. "You mean, this higher purity is how we believe?"

"Well, yes. I've been realizing that purity cannot exist in the face of lies."

"Lies?" she asked.

"Lies—like having the idea in your mind that you are unloveable, or that you are not good enough to be loved by God, even though you have repented. The lies could be incorrect thoughts that place grand spiritual experiences beyond one's own personal reach. Or thinking you're fat, or stupid, or boring. Believing even the smallest lie renders us impure, and thus unprepared to meet God."

Melody nodded excitedly. "You're talking about a deep holiness, an infusion of truth so complete that it purifies on the most intimate levels, and replaces all darkness with light, and all fear with faith."

Sam nudged her knee with his hand. "My dear, that is better stated that I could have ever put it! Yes, that's exactly it. It is the purity of coming to see yourself as God sees you, accepting the closeness of heavenly beings, and beholding the angels all around us. It is the purity of the simple acceptance of your endowed right to behold God and the workmanship of His hands, even in this life if it is the Lord's will. It is the purity to possess faith to move mountains, faith to work miracles in His holy name, and faith to enjoy the perfect felicity of His love forever—worlds without end."

Melody leaned toward him, her face lit with the Spirit. "It is to know that eternity is the safe harbor of your eternal companion's love; to understand your place in the patriarchal priesthood, in the family of Christ, and in the eternal order of perfect, familial love. It is to rejoice day and night in His unending grace, and to send your voice to the heavens in strains of praise that ascend to the very throne of God."

Sam could not keep tears of joy from his eyes. "Oh my darling, you are right! It is to find your eternal lover in this life, the soulmate you never thought existed, and to know your place with her is forever secure. It is to know your marriage is sealed in heaven, that it will endure forever. It is to know that more than my soul can even comprehend, I love you."

A tear slipped down Melody's cheek. "I love you so much," she whispered.

Sam was halfway through his second year when he was given the task of cleaning the Celestial Room, and the landing behind the large potted plant that blocks the way to the outer room and then up the stairs to the actual Holy of Holies. As far as he knew, this outer room and stairs were only cleaned a few times each year. He did know that if the interior of the Holy of Holies ever got cleaned, someone besides his crew did it.

He approached the holiest of all rooms on earth through a service hall covered with deep red carpet. One thing that impressed him was that even the service hallways, back rooms, and smallest closets were carefully finished and decorated almost as beautifully as the main halls and great rooms everyone saw.

He carefully vacuumed the hall and steps, opened the small arched door with a key, and let himself into the Celestial Room. The deep spiritual quality of this room always made him feel as if he had stepped into someone else's vision, almost as if he were vacuuming the sacred grove while Joseph was talking with the Father. He vacuumed the landing and the long stairs leading down to the floor of the room. As he worked, the nearer he got to the outer room of the Holy of Holies, the more profoundly he felt the awkwardness of being there. He always felt odd running a vacuum in sacred rooms, but here, tonight it was more pronounced. He chalked it up to his own sense of awe.

Quite distinctly he had the prompting that he should leave, but shrugged it off as his own nervousness. He continued to work around the steps until he was within a few yards of the door behind the plant leading to the outer room of the Holy of Holies. He was looking forward to stepping within that area for the first time in his life.

Unexpectedly, Brother Tatum hurried into the room from the same door Sam had entered. He walked right up to Sam and switched off the vacuum.

Brother Tatum's face was actually pale. "We've got to leave. Now!" he whispered urgently. Sam knew enough to trust him, and quickly gathered up his things. Brother Tatum helped him out through the door, and quietly closed it.

"What's going on?" Sam asked, expecting an explanation something along the line that the prophet was coming into the temple. The only answer he got was a motion to follow him. Sam followed him to his office where Brother Tatum flopped into his chair. For the first time Sam realized his boss was sweating profusely.

"Brother Tatum, what's wrong?" Sam asked, greatly concerned. It took a few minutes for his supervisor to calm down sufficiently to speak.

"Brother Mahoy," Brother Tatum began. "I was so startled, I almost choked."

"What is it?" Sam asked again, truly perplexed.

"I was sitting right here eating an Oreo cookie," he said, "when a man I have never seen before opened the door to my office and stepped in. I was really surprised to see him standing there. He was dressed in a white suit like the temple officiators wear. I was about to ask him what he was doing there, because he's definitely not on our crew, when he said, 'Please go ask Brother Mahoy to leave the Celestial Room. The Lord is coming tonight.'

"I was so startled that I dropped my cookie on the desk. I glanced down and right back up, and he was gone. I hadn't looked down more than a second. Needless to say, I jumped up and came running to get you. My heart's still fluttering in my ribs," he said, patting his chest and breathing deeply.

Sam nodded. "I had a feeling like I should leave, but chalked it up to my own sense of awe at being in the Celestial Room so near the Holy of Holies."

"Any time you feel like you should leave—just leave. Don't make the Lord send an angel to tell me to come get you," he said loudly in mock sternness. "It's too hard on my heart!"

"Yes, sir," Sam responded emphatically. After a moment's thought he asked, "I wonder why He didn't send that angel directly to me?"

Brother Tatum thought about this for a moment before replying. "I think because they observe the line of authority in all things, even in custodial work."

"That's good. I was worried that perhaps I wasn't worthy," Sam said.

"Actually, it was I who wasn't worthy," Brother Tatum said as he reached for a paper towel from Sam's cart, and began wiping his shaking hands.

"But you're the one who saw the angel!"

"Right. It took an angel opening the door to my office to get my concentration off of an Oreo cookie. That's not what I'd really call in tune, would you?" he said, wadding up his towel and throwing it into the can with perfect timing.

"And I felt the impression, but I didn't respond to it," Sam responded, mostly to himself. "I guess we both need to work on obedience." They sat in silence for a minute.

"Well, all I can say is, I *do* love my job," Brother Tatum said with a broad smile. They both knew exactly what he meant.

The effect all these things had upon Sam was to change his perception of the spiritual realm. Where previously the unseen world of spirituality had been an insubstantial, almost mist-like concept, it was now one of solidity. He had shaken hands with a heavenly minister, and spoken with him as normally as one might speak to a friend. He had seen a room full of spirit beings as substantial as any sacrament meeting congregation. He ceased to think in terms of "us" and "them," and began to think of them as one with us in the great work of the latter days. No longer were they "angels in heaven;" they were "angels among us."

As the years passed in his new work, Sam's faith almost imperceptibly changed from belief to irrefutable knowledge. He simply *knew* the grand truths of angelic ministration. His knowledge was a powerful confirmation of his previous faith, and a key to the massive door separating man from the veil of eternity. Without even understanding why or how, he had turned the key, and found the door feather-light upon divinely-oiled hinges.

Sam looked forward to each evening that he came to work, but mostly appreciated the opportunities to go into areas of the temple that not even the temple workers visited. Such was the opportunity that befell him the evening marking his fiftieth birthday. For some reason, the Spirit had directed him to fast that day, and Sam had not broken his fast before going to work. Perhaps for that reason, he felt especially humbled to be in the temple that night.

Brother Tatum knew it was Sam's birthday, and had a special assignment for him. "There are still parts of the temple you have not seen," he told Sam. "You've been on the third floor and worked in the rooms set aside for the Quorum of the Twelve, and the First Presidency. You've cleaned the Assembly Hall, and nearly every ordinance room. But there is one area you have never been in, and tonight it needs a good cleaning."

Following Brother Tatum's direction, Sam took the hall past the office into the Celestial Room. His task was to clean that holy room, along with the adjacent sealing rooms and halls.

He vacuumed the Celestial room in silence, basking in the solitude and rich spirit there, and enjoying the power of nearly-perfect prayer as he labored in the house of the Lord. Then he climbed seven steps and stopped before a heavy door on the far east side of the room. He found the right key on the special key ring he had received for this task. When he opened the door to this little-used upper sealing room, he was surprised to find himself no longer alone.

"Hello," Sam said quietly.

"Brother Mahoy. It's such a great pleasure to see you again." The old Nephite stood from where he had been sitting in one of the white velvet chairs lining the outer wall of the room, and stepped up to him. He opened his arms and embraced him. Sam felt his heart flooding with joy.

Once again, he was pleased to find his heavenly friend very solid in his embrace.

"I'm so pleased to meet you here," Sam told him with great warmth. "I have missed you."

"And I you," his friend said, and motioned toward a seat beside him. Sam turned it so they were facing one another.

Sam spoke first. "I have anxiously awaited your next visit. It has been three years, I think. Even though I have cried out to Father with greater faith than ever before, I have felt my life slipping away without seeing you. I was beginning to fear I haven't yet become all that I needed to be, or consecrated every part of my existence, or partaken enough of the grace of the atonement. I hope you've come to teach me more. I'm so anxious to learn the Lord's will!"

"Brother Mahoy, I've come to share with you the most wonderful part of my mission on this earth. Every once in a while it becomes our privilege to stand with someone as they experience the greatest blessing available to mortal man." This he said with a sense of wonder and joy.

Sam understood immediately. "Am I ready? Finally, am I ready?," he whispered beyond hope. Then he lowered his head. "But I can't be! I'm weak, I'm prideful, and I flounder at the simplest things."

The Nephite smiled. "No mortal is perfect in this life," he reminded him. "It isn't possible, or expected. What is expected is obedience. It is true you are not perfect, but you are obedient. In this respect you have been true and faithful in all things, and now I am here to give you your next instructions."

"What is it you will teach me?" Sam asked, barely able to believe how blessed he was. He was actually sitting before a messenger from God in the holy temple, on the very cusp of learning some great and eternal truth. His whole soul resonated with joy unspeakable.

"I am here to instruct you in how to part the veil," Helaman said, his eyes alight with joy.

Sam stood in silence, praying fervently. "I am ready,"he heard himself say, almost as if he were listening to someone else speak those words. It surprised him how ready he felt, given that just moments before he felt himself unworthy. Yet the Spirit descended upon him with great peace. Knowledge, more than any other gift, was what Sam had most desired and sought with all his soul. The privilege of parting the veil had been the focus of his fasting and prayer for a decade.

For the next hour they knelt in that small room, and Sam was taught the method whereby every being from Adam had parted the veil. Sam felt as if he were caught up into another world, and it seemed as if the little room grew larger until the walls were so far distant as to be imperceptible.

Finally, still kneeling, Helaman turned until they faced the same direction. Helaman bowed his head and spoke in a voice of quiet authority. The fabric of the air seemed to coalesce and part vertically. As it parted, a beam of light streamed outward, illuminating Helaman's form. Sam heard a rich chiming as if a massive, divine bell had pealed a long way off. It rang three times. Helaman stood, as did Sam.

Sam heard a voice of rich and deep timbre so filled with love he instantly knew from whom it came. He felt both awed to immobility, yet as excited as a child on Christmas morning. He stepped forward just as his Nephite friend moved aside to reveal an opening in the air from which emanated a light of inexpressible whiteness. Under any other circumstances he would have been blinded by the incredible intensity of the light. Yet, its startling brightness was pleasant and infinitely healing to behold. The opening continued to expand until it was the size of a man.

Within the light Sam could discern a man walking slowly toward him. The masculine form, the power, the grace, the emanation of eternal love were all familiar to Sam from a long-forgotten memory. His soul began to sing in harmony to symphonic music which he immediately recognized he had heard before. His heart took flight, his head seemed to become weightless, and his arms lifted as if on their own. His arms rose high over his head then reached outward in an expanded stretch, as if opening himself to the greatest possible exposure to the light. As he did this he felt the light amplify, warming first his skin, then his muscles, then his bones, then passing through him as if he were transparent. As it passed it took Sam's natural telestial man with it, washing away everything that was impure and unneeded. He wondered if he had just passed from mortal life, and he didn't care.

Sam suddenly understood that now, this instant of his life, was the fulfillment of everything he had worked for for a billion years or longer. More a memory than a thought, he understood how long he had labored, how many years, centuries, and millennia he had sought to come to this very moment. The sheer eternal significance of this moment both weighed upon him with almost planetary mass, yet buoyed him to perfect weightlessness.

The nearer the personage in the light came toward him, the greater was Sam's comprehension of the overwhelming love that surrounded him. He instantly comprehended things not previously even contemplated. And, these truths all came to him not as new knowledge, but as memories—long forgotten, yet previously cherished.

Sam willingly allowed the light to penetrate him. He rejoiced in it, and basked in its power. Every impurity it burned from his soul lightened his mortality until he no longer even knew if he were alive in the flesh or not. Yet, he felt more awake at that moment than he had at any point in his life.

Perhaps it was mere seconds, perhaps several eternities before the Personage stepped through the opening before Sam and into the small room. Had he been able to see from Helaman's vantage, Sam would have seen that he himself had been filled with light almost as brilliant as the being walking toward him. Sam had seemingly become like his Savior Jesus Christ, as the scriptures promise. In reality, it would be vast millennia before Sam would even began to approach the glory and perfection of his glorious visitor. But, for this instant in time, because of the grace and elevating power of God, through the infinite atonement, Sam had become sufficiently like Him who is perfect. The veil no longer served a purpose, and the glorious promises were at long last being fulfilled!

Sam gazed up into Jesus's eyes, for He was taller than Sam. His face was as familiar to Sam as his own. Sam felt the Savior's love permeate his being, and he comprehended his Lord's name, His sovereignty, and His glory. And yet, Sam was not able to open his mouth to utter a word, or even to fall to his knees.

"Samuel, my son," the Savior said and held open His arms. His voice was soft, yet like the movement of a mighty wave, or the rushing of a river. His voice was vast and eternal, melodic and peaceful, and it penetrated Sam's soul to its very core.

Sam could stay himself no longer, and simply fell into His Savior's arms with such joy that he felt aflame, as if he were literally being consumed by joy. He sensed the familiar contour of his Lord's chest, and the once-loved shape and strength of His arms as He wrapped them lovingly around Sam.

"My Lord!" Sam exclaimed with profound emotion. "My Master!" The Lord held him tightly as Sam's tears fell on the Master's chest. Sam felt such exquisite love flowing from his beloved Savior to him, that he was completely overwhelmed; he was sure the very marrow of his bones had melted. He was home.

Strength was quickly slipping from Sam, and he slid to his knees, overcome with love. His eyes fell upon the feet of his Savior, and Sam ran his trembling fingers across the prints of the nails, bathing them in tears and kisses.

In that instant, he at once fully comprehended the depth and breadth of his own personal sins, those whom he had hurt, and the deep shame and grievous consequences of his fallen state of nothingness, for which this glorious Being had willingly died. The pain he felt was excruciating, the guilt overwhelming. He looked into Jesus's eyes, begging him to take the pain away and at the same time such profound sorrow that he had caused Him to suffer.

Jesus smiled down at him. At that moment, the pain of Sam's awful comprehension of sin and guilt was no more. Jesus Christ expressed without words that He would gladly do it all over again for his son Samuel, if that were needed. In the end, all-consuming, eternally-encompassing, and forever-healing compassion were all that was left, and all that mattered.

Finally, the Savior raised Sam by his shoulders and held him at a short distance. Sam gazed into those eyes so piercingly blue they seemed to be flames of fire, as if all eternity were contained within them. Sam noted how familiar his great Friend's face was, yet how different from all paintings he had ever seen. The Lord's face was more masculine, far more powerful and perfect than any painting could be made by the hand of man. His hair was a rich deep golden hue, His robe the purest white, open slightly and tied at the waist with a blood-red sash.

"Samuel, I want to thank you for so many kind deeds you have performed in my name. I love you, my precious son, and I have come to bless you and your posterity for all eternity. I have come to fulfill the promises I made to you—the covenants we made before the world was."

"I am not worthy of anything, my Lord," Sam whispered, astonished that the first words from his Savior's lips were words of thanks—thanks to *him*. "I am truly nothing. Literally nothing!" He started to sob, remembering his sins, his obsession with the world, the pride he still used to cover his weakness. "It is *your* infinitely kind forgiveness, dear Lord—your merciful grace on my unworthy head; it is surely all done through *your* righteousness, not mine!" he said hoarsely, barely able to speak around the lump in his throat.

"You have proven yourself true and faithful in all things," Jesus said gently. "You have served me faithfully despite every trial. You have chosen to forsake the world and its riches for my sake. How wonderful it is that you have found the faith and obedience to join the faithful of many generations!"

Sam wept deep sobs, and buried his head again on the Savior's shoulder in bewildered gratitude. The Lord continued, "Through the blood of my atonement, through my grace and the infinite price I paid for you, you are at this moment made perfect in Me. Henceforth, Samuel, my son, you are redeemed from the fall, for you are brought back into my presence.

This day you have entered into my rest, and that rest shall be forever glorious. Never again shall the adversary have power over you; his temptations shall never again divert or confuse you. In all things you have triumphed through me, and my joy is full because of you."

Sam looked into the Savior's eyes, and saw that He, too, was weeping. Jesus motioned for Sam to stand upright before Him. Sam was able to do so because of the strength flowing into his body from the Savior's hands upon his shoulders. Sam wanted to shout praises, to sing some new and glorious song, to write vast eternal music, to stand upon the housetops and proclaim the glory of the Lord! But more than all that, he wanted to stay exactly where he was at this very moment, for all eternity.

The Savior smiled at him, and Sam knew that Jesus understood his son Sam's every desire and deep longing, and was actually delighted by them. Jesus looked at him with twinkling eyes, and Sam felt a new wave of perfect love envelop him.

"What do you desire of me, my son?" the Lord asked.

Sam's heart knew this was an invitation for him to seek knowledge. He dared not speak at first, then took hope in the Lord's smile of encouragement.

"I know I am a weak man, and I pray thou will forgive me if I ask amiss," Sam began.

"Ask whatsoever you will," his Savior replied kindly.

Sam lowered his head. "I wish to see the workmanship of Thy hands. I want to know Thy glory first-hand, and to know Thy perfection, so I will have power to proclaim Thy majesty to all who will hear me. I long to know Thee and all Thou hast done for me, that I might worship Thee in righteousness and in truth."

The Master nodded. "Look," He said, turning Sam slightly to his right, and pointing in the same direction. Where once had been a wall, Sam now saw an endless void. He sensed its scope, its unending vastness, and even with the full glory of the Lord upon him, he found it difficult to comprehend. As he watched, he saw a place filled with uncountable spirits, each searching for greatness far beyond themselves. He watched as they were loved and taught. How his heart thrilled to see them learn, to rejoice in truth, to marvel at the continual stream of heavenly gifts they received. He saw himself, his family and friends among those that were spirits. It was as if he were there, and he felt his soul joining his beloved brothers and sisters in their joy of progression and ascent.

Sam then beheld the formation of a great Council, and watched as the numberless spirit children of heavenly parents gathered to a single place.

Sam looked and saw that they stretched on seemingly forever, seemingly beyond the limitations of even perfect sight. They came to hear the formation of Father's plan to fulfill their greatest desire.

Having lived for billions of years in the presence of perfected, exalted Parents whom they loved, everyone there desired more than any other thing to become like their Progenitors. Sam watched as an exalted being more powerful and glorious than all the rest stood forth, accompanied by another equally as exalted as He. Sam felt his heart soar with love at the familiar sight of the Father and Mother of his soul! Had he been able to, he would have rushed into their arms in sweetest bliss. Standing with his dear friends, he felt a wave of reverence, expectation, and excitement wash through all assembled.

The plan was set forth. There was a way, a plan eternal in origin, whereby they might prove themselves, acquire a body of temporal flesh, and eventually become like Father and Mother. How great was the shout of joy which burst spontaneously from them! Sam profoundly felt their excited elation. The thought thundered through his mind, as with all present, "We can become like Father and Mother! We can become like Father and Mother!" Over and over it echoed in his soul, and he rejoiced as never before, aware that all creation was rejoicing with him.

As the plan was described, however, a sense of fear swept across the vast throng. There would be failure. Some would not return. A single sin, a small omission, any act of weakness would disqualify them from their eternal reward. How bleakly Sam felt the eternal weight of that loss, for all there knew that no one could live up to such high ideals in the fallen world.

But, wait, what was this? A Savior would come? One who would take upon himself those very sins? We can be forgiven? It's true! It's true! We *can* succeed! We *can* become like Father and Mother! Oh how glorious the joy, how supreme the wonder, how sweet the truth!

"Yes! Yes! Yes!" he felt his soul resounding with his brothers and sisters. "Hosanna! Hosanna! Hosanna!" they all shouted with one voice, and the very fabric of all eternity cried back, "Hosanna! Hosanna! Hosanna! to God, and the Lamb!"

They clasped each other, vowing they would go, and that earth would be their temporary home. They would be faithful, fearless, repentant, and they would be saved by the love of One so perfect that He himself would suffer for their sins—and the only One who indeed could. It was a perfect plan, and once again all rejoiced with a single voice.

The panorama shifted into starry darkness. Distant suns and planets slipped by at incredible speeds until the image stopped at an area of space littered by unformed matter. Before him, Sam saw a vast repository of broken and twisted elements. The largest of these was the size of a planet. It was dark and lifeless, sitting motionless in the emptiness of this planetary graveyard.

Sam watched the great Jehovah and many others move to organize, to reclaim and renew the unformed matter. The Creator and His laborers brought with them a spiritual pattern—an earth created of spirit-matter, perfect and pristine. They positioned it in a place amidst the elemental matter and commanded all to be like this spiritual pattern. Creative powers, which to Sam's eyes appeared to be light so dense it had mass and form, worked upon the elements and they obeyed the call, all within the design and timeframe commanded. Layer upon layer of matter assumed its place within the pattern, and the earth began to form.

Astonishment grew in Sam's mind. All that occurred, all the power that was expended, all the infinite genius came from the Son of God, who at this moment stood beside Sam in the temple. Yet, in the vision before him, the Son of God stood foremost in the creative periods. Christ was the Creator; yet every creative act was attended by millions of laborers, organized and sent forth to execute the will of the Master. Sam suddenly knew with an electric start that he had been one of those.

When the earth was finally assembled, Sam was given to know that the matter from which the earth had been formed was precious and loved, that it had been used many times before on many similar worlds, and that this would be the last, and the greatest world of them all. When the work was completed, the earth was pronounced very good; and he comprehended that one day far in the future it would become a celestialized sphere, thus fulfilling the measure of its creation.

In each successive stage, further spiritual patterns were brought, and increasingly progressive life was organized around it. Sustaining atmosphere, trees, flowers, grasses and grains, then animals and insects and every form of life were organized this way.

Sam had no way to estimate the time involved as man would reckon it, but it was vast, and accomplished according to God's timetable, foreknowledge, and obedience to His law. When the earth was finally complete and ready, a beautiful man and a woman in the terrestrial image of Father and Mother, took their place in God's newborn world.

The vision changed rapidly, and time swiftly progressed. Sam watched the Savior of mankind take His place among men. Sam saw Him being born in the lowly manger, and he thrilled to see himself singing with the angelic choir as they joyfully announced the Christ child's birth. Sam watched Jesus's childhood with reverent wonder, and saw Him as a young man growing in grace and truth. He saw Mary and Joseph, and their tenderness in raising their God Son. Sam marveled at His humility and singular wisdom. Sam laughed at the Teenager's gentle humor, was much amazed at His early understanding and astonishing knowledge of the world He had once created.

Sam wept as he beheld His sorrows and pains as a rabbi and teacher of His beloved people. He watched Christ instruct with love and power—not as others taught, but in pure truth that only a few could comprehend or accept. Sam felt frustration as he watched the Son of God struggle against evil, darkened minds, and yet still teach them with such plainness as they could endure. Sam wept as His closest friends and family denied and abandoned Him. Sam's soul cried in triumph as Jesus found the worthy few, taught them, and bestowed upon them the profound blessings now familiar to Sam himself.

Sam suddenly found himself standing in a garden of stunted trees and large stones. For a moment Sam walked alone, feeling the loose gravel beneath bare feet that was still hot from the now-absent sun. Stars twinkled overhead with unusual clarity. Larger stones which had been placed there long ago to define and beautify the garden lined a narrow gravel path upon which he stood. Sam turned to his right and saw that the path wandered lazily among the larger trees, skirting a few boulders until it ended at great, gnarled old olive tree.

Sam knew in an instant that this was the mother tree; this was the ancient, the first, the wellspring of life, planted by the hand of some itinerant farmer many centuries ago. Its trunk rose thickly from the ground at an angle, eventually bending back down to the ground as if it had been struck by a great force in its tender and green past. Sam could see evidence that a fire had long ago blackened the trunk, nearly killing it. Yet, the tree had lived, and had grown upward from the blackened trunk to form a singularly knotted and stumpy tree. Many branches had been sawn from the old tree to be transplanted elsewhere, leaving legions of knots and knobs, until it looked more like a warrior's club than a tree. Yet, between the symbols of its sacrifices to give life, tender young branches grew in lush profusion, jutting into the darkened sky. Evidence of a heavy yield of fruit, now plucked, lingered on the branches and lay on the ground.

Sam immediately saw in the old tree the living metaphor for the atonement. The stump and blackened saddle formed by the twisted body were worn smooth, as if generations of children had come to play upon the old tree, to ride it in their games, and to stand upon its knobs as they reached for the precious fruit above them.

As Sam pondered this, the sound of crunching gravel told him of nighttime visitors. Sam stepped back, moving behind a nearby tree. Four men came down the path in the darkness. They bore no lanterns or torches, but came quietly, obviously intimately familiar with the garden. They said nothing, and seemed to be in a deep anguish of sorrow.

They were all dressed similarly, in loose garments the color of camel's hair which extended nearly to their knees. The older men wore a type of pant beneath this, while the smallest, and apparently youngest, appeared to be bare from the knees. Just recently having seen His face, Sam immediately realized the nearest to him was Jesus, who was half-a-head taller than the others. Whisperings of truth told him that the youngest was John; the large, muscular man with the massive beard was Peter, and the clean-shaven disciple was James.

Christ was the only one there whose garment had a mantle, which He had pulled upward as if to ward off the night chill, although it was not cold. At that moment Jesus looked up, and Sam realized that His face was stricken with grief and streaked with tears. Sam realized He had hidden His face to spare His disciples the vision of His excruciating suffering.

Tears sprang to Sam's eyes, and he wanted to rush forward, to embrace his Savior, to warn Him of the approaching betrayal, of Judas's duplicity, and of His impending death. But, Sam's feet would not move, and he watched in stunned silence.

After asking His friends to watch and ensure His privacy, Jesus made His way to the tree. He laid a hand upon its gnarled trunk like an old friend, looked up into its branches and smiled. He turned so that Sam could only see His back, then fell to His knees as if they had suddenly lost all strength. He leaned against the trunk, held His head in His hands, and with a trembling body, prayed in an anguished voice.

The words pierced Sam with intimate grief. Many times he wanted to look away as the awful payment was made, but did not. For hours he watched the Savior of mankind descend into infinite depths, and it racked Sam with exquisite sorrow to view the bloodied sweat, the depth of sorrow, the excruciating agony, and the incomprehensible anguish of the Son of God. So horrific was the vision to his eyes and spiritual understanding that he finally could bear no more, and the vision shifted once again.

But it was not over. Sam's heart pounded, his hands wrung in terror, and his forehead beaded with sweat as he watched them lead the greatest of all mortals from mock trial to mock trial. Sam's voice cried out as the bone-laced lash fell upon Jesus's sinless back, again and again. It felt to Sam almost as if all eternity were being flogged, and he himself cried in horror as each blow landed; but the Savior of mankind uttered not a sound, and bore it with willing grace.

Unable to watch, Sam closed his eyes as the hammer fell, and flinched at the ring of steel-on-steel which signaled the tearing of trembling flesh of His hands—hands that had loved, blessed, healed and raised from the dead. Then almost as an afterthought, in a perverse and demented desire to inflict additional pain, and because the nails in the palms might not hold the Savior's weight, they peevishly selected two more rusted spikes, and drove them through his wrists.

Sam watched the Roman executioners move to Jesus's feet. Sam was startled to watch the Savior, paralyzed with pain, lift His feet onto the cross to assist them. The soldiers looked at one another and shrugged. They bent His knee, so that he could gain no relief upon his arms by lifting himself upon his feet without great effort, then drove the spike through the side of his ankle, nailed first one foot to the side of the beam, and then the other.

Sam marveled that this last act of love was lost on his executioners. The most gracious of all mortals not only willingly died for the sins of those driving the nails, but also graciously assisted them in their despicable task. In all things, even in death, He was the Way, the Truth, and the Life. Sam understood as never before what it had cost the Savior to become his personal Redeemer. This act of redemption was pure, unstained, unrestrained, and performed in infinite love—such love as no mortal can comprehend, even when gazing upon it with immortal eyes.

The vision then mercifully shifted. Sam's strength failed him, and he fell forward into the Savior's arms, weeping bitter tears. It was more than he could comprehend or endure. But it was still not over. Strength from the Savior flowed into Sam again, and he stood on his own. The scene had changed, and Sam saw the garden tomb. He watched the angels roll back the stone, and saw the risen Lord Jesus Christ step onto the earth, the first fruits of the resurrection.

Sam watched the grieving Mary come to the tomb, and witnessed that tender moment when the her Lord spoke her name with gentle affection. He watched Peter and John rush to the tomb, and heard the angel say, "Why seek ye the living among the dead? He is not here, but has risen." How those familiar words now filled his soul with renewed everlasting safety!

Sam watched it all, heard every word, saw every act, felt every truth the Savior taught, and then watched Him ascend into heaven. Sam stood there with Jesus's disciples, gazing up into the clouds, wondering, waiting for the Christ to come again.

In rapid succession, the vision changed again, and Sam beheld the history of the earth, the rise and fall of the Nephite civilization, the restoration of the Gospel, and at last the glorious Second Coming and millennial rest of the earth.

Then, with ever-increasing speed, the scene changed to other worlds. As rapidly as grains of sand fall from the hands of a child, Sam comprehended every world, and knew their place in the grand scheme of eternity. When this infinitely inclusive vision finally closed, the walls of the temple room were once again around him, and it was over. In a way more marvelous than Sam could ever have conceived, the Lord had answered his request. He could not ask for more, for there was nothing remaining he had not seen.

Sam felt every cell in his body enlivened as never before. His soul resonated with the glory of God, and his mind felt expanded to embrace all truth and all knowledge. His soul mourned, rejoiced, and marveled at it all.

Even as the minutes ticked away from the closing of the vision, Sam felt the mortal veil closing upon him, and the once-godly comprehension began to melt into a homogenous whole. In mere seconds, he was left with a sweeping memory, but with few of the staggering details he had just moments before comprehended in their entirety.

Sam turned his grateful heart and mind back to his beloved Master. His request had been fulfilled. Sam understood as completely as it was possible for a quickened mortal to understand, what the Savior had done, and why. His praise would now be forever full, joyous and perfect.

"I will come to you again," Jesus's loving voice proclaimed. "I will come and make my abode with you, and my Father and I will bless your home with our presence. Great shall be your joy, and eternal your reward. But first, Samuel, I have a glorious task for you to perform, and I commission you to its accomplishment before you return to my glory."

"I will, my Lord," Sam said earnestly. "I will do anything you ask!"

"I know," came His reply. "Because of your faithfulness, I desire to bless you. Is there a special gift that I may grant?"

Sam felt his heart soar, and then immediately sink. This was his moment to ask the very thing of which he had long dreamed! Yet, he could not speak what was in his heart. He did not feel unworthy, because the

 Savior had just proclaimed him as such; but he felt presumptuous, and could not voice his deepest desire.

The Savior smiled patiently, "What do you want, my son?"

Like a trusting child, Sam gazed longingly into His eyes. Jesus spoke for him. "You desire that which John, my beloved disciple, asked of me," he told him gently. "It is the loftiest gift one may receive on earth. Remember, Samuel," he said, as He placed his hands on Sam's head, "that I called you to this blessed ministry in your Patriarchal blessing—indeed, in the premortal world. And this is granted you. From this day you will live free from the aches and pains of mortal life, immune to temptation, disease, suffering, sorrow, pain and death. I grant you power to accomplish the last great task I require of you. When it is done, and I have come again in my glory, I will receive you unto myself, that your joy, and your glory may be even as mine, that we may together inherit all My Father hath."

Sam's heart was satisfied, and he wept again openly for joy. But even amid the sweetness, while trying to comprehend the glorious words being spoken, Sam felt the glory all around him beginning to fade. With deep regret, he sensed the Savior withdrawing. Sam wanted to rush into the light with Him, to remain with Him forever; yet he knew he could not.

"I will come to you again," Jesus assured him lovingly as the light gathered around Him. The opening through the veil slowly grew smaller until it closed entirely, and Sam was left alone.

He sank to his knees a few inches from where the Savior of all mankind had just stood. He reached out and ran his fingers across the deep pile of the carpet which still held the precious imprint of two bare feet. Sam marveled that mere seconds before, He had been here. Just seconds ago! Many minutes had elapsed in deep, reverent contemplation before Sam was snapped back into reality by a hand on his shoulder.

"It is time to go," Helaman told him gently. Sam looked up into the old man's eyes. They were moist with emotion, and aglow with righteousness. Sam stood effortlessly, with surprising ease and confidence, and they embraced.

"Your shift has ended," Helaman told Sam. This statement seemed rich with double meaning. "Come, I will walk you to the stairs."

Sam gathered up his things, and after a long look into the small room, snapped off the light and locked the door.

"As I said," Helaman told Sam, "that which you have just received is the most glorious of all earthly blessings. I am honored I could be here with you."

Sam walked slowly away, stunned to reverent silence. He had no idea what the actual ramifications were going to be of what had just occurred. He felt entirely different, yet he also felt exactly the same. He only knew that he was now, to some degree at least, immortal. He was immune to all that the world could throw at him, and yet he still was mortal enough to be hungry. He humbly realized that this was a process that would take teaching, learning, and getting used to.

"Will you still come and teach me?" Sam asked as he carried his bundle of tools down the steps. The heavy tools seemed weightless now. "I really need help. I don't have a clue what I'm supposed to be doing now!"

Helaman nodded emphatically. "My most important work with you is just about to begin in earnest. There is a great deal I must teach you. You must learn quickly, for the time is growing short. There is just enough time for us to complete your preparations for the great labor awaiting you."

"May I tell Melody what has happened tonight?" Sam asked as they reached the bottom of the stairs.

"Of course you may one day, but only in due time. Right now just be patient, say nothing, and all things will work for your good. The Spirit of the Lord will teach your sweet wife all she needs to know. In time, she will understand what has happened to you, and she will rejoice in it."

Sam sighed. "I'm relieved. I ache to share this marvelous joy with my wife! But I can be patient." He chuckled to himself. "Even if I could just blurt it all out, I can't even imagine how one goes about telling his wife that he's no longer a mortal!"

Helaman grinned. "I shall be interested to hear how it goes when you get home."

Sam smiled back, but did not immediately reply. They continued walking slowly down the hall. Sam sensed that Helaman was shortly going to leave him, and quite unexpectedly, he felt reluctant to be without heavenly company. After a moment he asked, "Heleman, can you tell me what my task will be?"

Sam wasn't prepared for what he next heard, and had to lean against the wall to steady himself.

Helaman turned toward Sam, his voice rich with meaning. "I can now. You will bring a remnant of the great tribe of Levi out of the north countries. You will walk with them from the lands of their captivity to the temple at Cardston, Canada. As you do so, you will teach them the gospel, baptize them, ordain them to the Priesthood, and prepare them for the temple. In time this group will become part of a marvelous latter-day exodus, which future generations will say was greater than the exodus of the children of Israel from Egypt."

Sam was silent for a long moment. "It feels like more than a man can do," he finally whispered, overwhelmed.

"It is," Helaman said, then leaned very close until Sam could see nothing but his face. "But, you are more than a man."

Sam pondered this. He knew it was true, but also doubted he would ever think of himself as anything more than a small servant in a very large world. "Will you go with me?" he asked, still feeling intimidated by the magnitude of the task.

Helaman smiled reassuringly. "You will discover in powerful ways that no earthly thing can harm you. From time to time I will assist you. But, even when I am not there, you will never be alone. The Holy Spirit will be your constant companion and witness of all truth, even as it was before this day. It will empower you to do all things required of you. Everything you need will flow without compulsion. Angels will assist, and Christ Himself will come to you if you call. There is nothing to fear, my friend, and vast reasons to rejoice!"

Sam felt the fear evaporating at his mentor's words.

Helaman continued. "After you are prepared, I will have completed my work with you; then it will be up to you in the power of the Lord. Fear not, Samuel, you will be ready. And, remember, you will never be alone!" Sam felt this truth resonate throughout his body. A surge of warmth coursed through him, and he suddenly felt fearless.

Sam straightened to his full height. "When do we begin my training?"

"Immediately," his heavenly friend replied.

THE MIGHTIER CHANGE

Sam drove home from his custodial job at the Salt Lake Temple, glowing in profound remembrance and awe of what had just happened. As he neared his neighborhood, he had to smile as a question suddenly came to his mind, which he had never before anticipated. How do you come home from work and tell your wife you are no longer mortal, but a translated being? Even the formation of the question stunned him, let alone any attempt at an answer.

He and Melody had now been married five years, and he considered her the greatest joy in his life. To Sam, Melody was springtime, laughter, and the song in his soul If any mortal deserved the name of Melody, it was his dear wife. She brought music into his life both from within and without. She energized him with love so vivid, so colorful, it sometimes robbed him of rest as he lay watching her sleep. She would often awaken and see him watching her; then she would smile and move so close to him he could no longer watch, and sleep would come in gentle waves of happiness. Seeing his wife tonight gave Sam a thrill of happiness, along with the nagging thought: how could he *not* tell his beloved sweetheart everything that had happened?

Sam arrived home at midnight, much earlier than usual. Melody and Sammy were waiting for him in the kitchen. Sammy was seven going on seventeen, a fiery little bundle of curiosity. Though not his blood child, which the boy vaguely knew but did not yet comprehend, Sam loved him as powerfully as either of his twin daughters. And for Sammy, his Dad Sam was the only father he had ever known.

"Daddy's home! Daddy's home!" Sammy cried happily as he climbed from his chair to greet him. When Sam had gotten the job at the Salt Lake Temple he had been obligated to work at night. Melody and Sammy had adjusted their schedules to match his, staying up late to eat dinner with him. It was just one of the thousand thoughtful things Melody did without comment, and one of the myriad reasons he loved her.

"Hi ya tiger!" Sam laughed as he whirled Sammy around in a circle at arm's length, the boy's legs flying outward. Sam hadn't done this since Sammy was four, and wasn't sure why he did it tonight. His earlier excuse for stopping had been that the lad was just too big. He went faster and faster until Sammy's eyes changed from glee to fear. Sam quickly stopped, and set him down.

"Daddy, you scared me!" Sammy complained happily, on the verge of asking for more.

Melody had come into the room just in time to see all the fun. "Hey, you're home early! Did something happen at work?" she asked, grinning.

"Actually, yes," Sam admitted, and having so said, knew he couldn't tell either of them what it was. He followed her into the kitchen.

"Well sweetheart, welcome home," Melody said as she kissed him, carefully holding a bowl of salad off to the side. "Let's eat, and you can tell us all about it."

"Well," Sam said as he took the salad, grateful to break his fast. "I guess I have to say it was just a wonderful shift, and I came home with a happy feeling,"

"So, nothing special happened?" Melody asked. Sam could tell from her voice that she was going to eventually get it out of him, and it frightened him a little. In five years of marriage he hadn't been able to bring himself to withhold anything from her except rare confidences that weren't his to share. He wasn't sure where this fit.

"I'll tell you later, Honey," he replied, averting his eyes. It was enough to forestall her quest for the truth she suspected was lurking just out of sight. "How was first grade, my man?" Sam asked, turning his attention to his son. What followed was an animated description of Sammy's entire day in first grade. Melody watched intently as the two men most precious to her discussed the very real world of a seven-year-old, and it made her heart soar.

It was 2:00 AM before they were all quietly in bed. Sam didn't feel tired. Usually, he fell asleep no more than ten seconds after his head hit the pillow. Tonight he lay in bed pondering, waiting for Melody to do all the wiggling she needed to become comfortable. He seldom noticed it, usually being sound asleep before she even clicked off the light.

Seeing he was still awake, she slid back against him spoon-style, and he wrapped his arms around her. He really didn't feel like sleeping.

"So—what happened at work?" she asked curiously, almost as if two hours had not elapsed since the subject had originally been broached.

"Oh, something wonderful," Sam replied, still unsure how to describe it without disobeying the injunction against telling her. He had had just such a dilemma once before. That time she had resolved his problem herself. This time, he felt no fear as he had before. He was serenely comfortable with the fact that no obvious solution to this question was known to him.

Rather than pumping him for details, Melody lay silent for a while, enjoying being in his arms. "It must have been something really, really wonderful," she said softly.

Sam laughed gently. "Why do you say that?"

"Because you're different."

"In what way?" he asked, a little surprised. Surely, whatever difference she had detected in him could have nothing to do with what had actually occurred. But, that was the last time he would underestimate the powers of his wife's intuition.

"Do you need me to tell you?" she asked, her voice a little teasing.

"Go ahead," he urged her, interested to know in what way he seemed different.

"Let me ask you a question," she began. He nodded.

"If someone got plastic surgery so they looked like you…"

"Why would anyone want to do that?" Sam interrupted doubtfully.

Melody laughed. "That's beside the point," she insisted. "Suppose there was a good reason, and they did it?"

"OK. So now there's two of us," Sam conjectured.

"Not really, there is only one of you, but there's another person who looks like you."

"OK, sure."

"Let's suppose that other person came home to me and pretended to be my hot, adoring husband."

He laughed at her imagination. "I'd be mad and jealous," he replied, feigning anger. In his mind, the example was as impossible as a sofa sprouting wings and flying.

"That's also beside the point," she insisted.

"Not to me," Sam returned.

"OK, not to you, but this is just a 'what-if.' Anyway, don't you think I'd know the difference? Don't you think there would be differences between the two of you, even if they were subtle?"

Her question intrigued him. "Well, I guess so. What are you saying? Do you think I'm someone else?" He expected her to deny it vigorously.

"Yes," she said unexpectedly.

Sam's eyes grew big. "I'm an impostor?"

"Yes," she repeated calmly.

"Should we call the police?"

"No," she replied quietly. "I think we should call a brass band."
Sam remained silent for a long moment. "I'm confused," he admitted.
"No you're not," she replied. "You think *I'm* confused."
"You're talking in riddles."
Melody laughed. "OK, let me speak plainly. Just answer true or false. Can you do that?"
"True," he answered, already playing the game.
"All right." She thought for a second and confronted him. "Something happened at work."
"True."
"It was wonderful."
"True."
"You are not going to tell me what it was."
Sam paused before saying, "True." His voice was small, but she didn't seem to notice.
She thought again. "You were told not to tell me."
"Uhm, true," he replied somewhat reluctantly, wondering if this game was going too far.
Her eyes rolled to meet his. "Because if you were able to, you would, and we wouldn't be playing true-and-false games."
"True," he said emphatically.
She grimaced and patted his shoulder. "You're lucky you answered that one right," she said seriously.
"True," he said, understanding perfectly what she meant. " But why are you asking all these questions?"
Melody sat up in bed and faced him squarely. "All right Sam, true or false: You swung Sammy around and around until he was actually frightened."
"True."
"You weren't tired or dizzy after doing that."
"I hadn't thought about it, I…"
She gave him a nudge with her elbow. "True or false, my dear?"
"True," he said.
"You quit swinging him around three years ago because he was getting so big that it made you tired and dizzy."
"True."
"And, here you are wide awake at two o'clock a.m. and not tired, even after all that."
"Well, ummm, oooof!" he grunted as she elbowed him again.
"True or false?" she reminded him.

"OK, true," he laughed.

Melody was silent for another few seconds, putting the pieces together. "I'd have to say that whatever happened tonight was deeply spiritual, deeply renewing."

"True." he admitted, quite amazed at her intuitive reasoning.

"I'd also say it occurred in the temple, since that's where you were."

"Also true."

"And, I'd say it is something so unexpected that you are energized with the Spirit, and too excited to sleep."

"True, again," he admitted.

She yawned and lay back down next to him. "Last question. You're the guy who's so energized now that you're going to get up and take Sammy to school at 9:00 o'clock tomorrow morning, true?" she said.

"True," he said after a brief pause.

"Good answer," she grinned sleepily, and fluffed her pillow. In a matter of minutes she was sound asleep. The subject of what had actually happened that night never came up again. He wasn't sure what she thought she knew, but whatever it was, she was satisfied. Or, at least she was willing to respect that fact that he would tell her when he could.

If he could have seen inside her, he would have seen great contentment in the fact that whatever the change was, he wore it well. She just knew that she loved him, no matter what. In her mind, that was all she really needed to know.

After another sleepless hour Sam carefully slid his arm from under her neck and slipped out of bed. Since he still wasn't sleepy, he decided to read a bit in the scriptures. He was anxious to read the account of the three Nephites' request of the Lord. He pulled on a pair of sweatpants and slipped into a robe.

He walked into the living room and was startled to see his friend sitting on the piano bench.

"How did you.... never mind." Sam said all in one breath.

"Good evening," Helaman replied jovially. "You might say, I let myself in."

"You are welcome of course—any time!" Sam said as casually as he could.

"Thank you, Sam. Are you ready to begin?"

"Sure!" Sam exclaimed. Then he had another thought. "Won't Melody hear us?"

"No," Helaman answered simply.

"Then, let's begin," Sam agreed excitedly. He took a seat in the armchair opposite his friend, and gazed at him expectedly. He had a million questions, but Helaman spoke up first.

"I need to give you some instruction about your new state-of-being. As you can tell, you aren't sleepy."

"I noticed that," Sam laughed ruefully. "I thought I was just excited."

The old man chuckled. "That's what I thought at first, too. It took me a while to figure out that I just didn't need sleep like before. It was different for us Three Nephites than it will be for you. Since everyone around us knew of our change, there was no need to be secretive. We just happily discovered the different aspects of the change as time went by. It was a delightful time for me and my loved ones," he said a bit wistfully.

"I can imagine," Sam agreed.

"In your case, you must keep these things to yourself. For that reason, I need to tell you what to expect, and how to keep it from being obvious."

"Alright, I'm excited to hear about it."

Helaman smiled broadly. "I was too. At any rate, there are some things that are now very different about you. As this process settles fully upon you, you will need less and less sleep. Actually, you will soon need no sleep at all. But, you will still enjoy brief naps. I know I do! You also won't need to eat, but you can if you choose. You will become nearly tireless; if you do tire, you'll recover very quickly."

"Wow, you mean I could go for days or weeks without eating?"

"Longer if you wish. I only eat for the pleasure of experiencing taste."

"That will take some getting used to. How can the body exist without food?" Sam asked.

Helaman leaned in his chair. "There is a principle that is very obscure, which I will explain. The human body doesn't actually feed on food as mortals commonly think."

Sam stared at his friend. "You would get some argument from scientists on that subject, but okay, I'm willing to go with it."

Helaman laughed, then continued. "What the human body exists on is actually energy as it emanates from God. For mortals, the process works like this: God lets the sun radiate a portion of His power. The plants of the fields absorb that energy, and are in turn eaten by humans. Or, in the case of meats, there is another step involved, in that the energy also passes through the animal. Each additional step that is needed renders the energy less life-giving. The further one gets away from the original source of life-giving energy, the less pure it becomes. By the time you eat a piece of meat, very little of the original purity remains. Hence, you must eat three times a day to remain alive."

Sam nodded in understanding, and his friend continued.

"This energy which powers the sun is actually present throughout all creation. It is the Light of Christ, or the Light of Truth. The sun is but a small manifestation of that power. When the mightier change of translation occurs in someone, the body is given the ability to absorb energy directly from the source, without the necessity of having it processed through plants or other life forms. The reason that humans age, become diseased, and eventually die, is because they starve to death and decay for want of a pure source of energy. When the change to translation is made, the energy we absorb becomes sufficiently pure that the aging process stops indefinitely. Once it stops, one is essentially non-mortal. Not immortal, but what some of us think of as super-mortal."

Sam had to ponder this, and his friend waited until he spoke. "So, I'm able to absorb power to sustain life directly from God. That's incredible. But why do I still feel hungry then?"

The old Nephite chuckled. "That takes another explanation. Are you ready to go on, or do we need to talk some more about the power of God? I barely scratched the surface of that subject. The things I don't tell you tonight, the Spirit will teach you as time goes by. I just need to give you the basics tonight."

"I want to hear it all, but I'm curious about why I still get hungry."

"The reason is habit. You are used to being mortal, and haven't progressed beyond that memory. Let me show you something. You perceive me as an old man, right?"

"You have always looked the same to me—like an older man."

"I usually choose that appearance because it's what I looked like when I was changed. However, since my life isn't dependent upon any particular body shape to exist, I can look like whatever I choose, if it is righteous."

Sam watched with amazement as Helaman changed before his eyes into a young man. His hair grew dark, almost black, his eyes an intense brown, and his skin a shade darker, supple and more muscular.

"This is what I looked like on my wedding day, many years ago. I was twenty-three. Not bad, eh?"

"Not bad at all," Sam exclaimed enthusiastically. "Can I learn to do that?"

"If you don't consume it upon your lusts, you can—with some practice. There is something else to know first. All of our abilities come from God. What you just saw me do is actually a miracle of God. He intended it. It would literally be impossible to perform a miracle contrary to the will of God. I was able to show you this because God wants you to know these things. Had it been otherwise, I could not have done it, and I wouldn't have tried. I also couldn't, for example, change into a bird or horse, because that would defy the law and will of God. Do you understand?"

Sam nodded slowly. "I'm beginning to. I just never thought of angels having such power. It certainly broadens my perception of things. I suppose the important part is that everything I do must be in harmony with Heavenly Father's will, or it simply can't be done. So, how does that apply to my getting hungry?"

"You get hungry because you choose to. To stop, simply choose the opposite. The same is true of all normal body functions, including breathing. Personally, I choose to live a fairly normal biological life. Some of my brethren and sisters shut their biology down almost entirely so they can concentrate on their labors. It's really a personal choice."

"How did you ever figure out you didn't need to breathe? Why would one even experiment with something like that?"

Helaman frowned, then shook his head and smiled. "The Lamanites buried me alive one time. That's how I learned that breathing was not necessary."

"Didn't it hurt? Weren't you frightened? Why didn't you just leave?" Sam blurted, feeling a little sickened.

"No, nothing hurts physically. I was not frightened because the power of God was upon me, and I didn't leave because they didn't know I was one of the three, and I chose not to show them otherwise. I let them think they had killed me. It was actually to my advantage to be thought of as dead. It freed me to do my work more completely."

"Did you ever go back to your family after they thought you were dead?" Sam wondered.

"Oh, they had all passed away a long before that time. I had watched them all grow old and die. That's probably the only real disadvantage to being non-mortal," he said with some introspection. "You have to remember that there was two hundred years of peace after I was changed. Most of my close relatives were gone before that glorious era came to an end."

"I had forgotten about that, I guess," Sam admitted to the young man sitting before him. He couldn't help but be excited about his friend's new youthfulness. "When will you teach me how to change my appearance?"

"When you need to know!" Helaman replied pointedly. "My dear friend, there is so much that is far more important to teach you before you learn that. It isn't just your appearance that you have power over, Sam.

Every aspect of your body is under your control. You will find that you are impervious to pain, but not to injury. If you are cut with a knife, you will bleed just like anyone else. You will feel the cut, but it will not be painful. In as much time as it takes to form a thought you can heal the cut if you choose. This is important because we often must appear to be injured like any other mortal. But no injury can be life threatening, regardless of how severe it is."

Sam pondered this before asking. "Even if I were completely blown to bits, and couldn't think—I could heal myself?"

Helaman smiled and shook his finger reprovingly at Sam. "You are still thinking like a mortal, Sam. *You are not your body!* You are an intelligent, powerful spiritual being who is housed in a body. Even if your body is completely vaporized, your spirit cannot be harmed. For a mortal, any time the body is severely damaged the spirit departs. The change you are experiencing makes it impossible for your spirit to depart prematurely. You simply reassemble the elements of your body, and continue to function. This has happened to me several times, especially with my assignments in wars. I spent four years in the Civil War, and was twice hit by cannon balls. As you can see, I bear no scars from the experience."

"This is all quite astonishing," Sam admitted. "I'd like to hear your Civil War experiences someday."

Helaman's voice was subdued as he spoke. "Actually, I could show you several books where I'm mentioned, particularly during those dark days of the American Revolution. During that first winter when Washington's troops were deserting him, and those who remained with Washington were starving and freezing to death, I was sent to bolster the men who were so disheartened. I spent that winter blessing them by the power of the priesthood, even though not one of them ever heard me mention God or religion. I worked more miracles on that assignment than … but, that's another story," he said reflectively, then quickly grew cheerful again.

Sam's curiosity was piqued. "Was Washington as spiritual a man as some say?" he asked.

Helaman hesitated as if waiting for permission to reply. At last he smiled, apparently satisfied, or perhaps just accepting that their conversation was derailed for the moment. "Sam, I served close to that man for four years. He was as great a man as ever lived. I will answer your question by saying there were four mighty angels who stood on either side of him at all times, protecting him with flaming swords. They stood by him in battle, and hundreds of times turned aside bullets intended to kill him. Does that answer your question?"

Sam nodded. "Thanks for indulging me," he replied. "I'm glad to know that. Many people doubt Washington's divine commission to do what he did."

Helaman sighed and gently turned the conversation back to the present. "Yes, but they are wrong. And we still have some time before your family awakens, so I need to teach you something very important before then. I'm going to request some help from another brother—do you mind?"

"Certainly not," Sam responded. As he spoke a person materialized in the room, surrounded by a bright glow. The light dissipated quickly, revealing a young man who smiled at Sam and then immediately walked to Helaman and embraced him. It warmed Sam's heart to see their obvious love, and he felt honored to be among them.

"My name is Daniel," the young man said, holding out a hand to Sam. Sam took it and smiled. He suppressed the urge to ask why he could know Daniel's name, but not Helaman's real name. Daniel smiled. "Daniel is my other name," he confirmed, "not my given name."

Sam almost laughed that Daniel had perceived his question and answered it. "I'm honored to meet you," Sam replied.

"No, the honor is mine. It is so beautiful to us when we are joined by a new brother or sister. It happened seldom in the past because the times were not appointed for many new translated mortals to join us. We have long awaited the day when Zion would be rebuilt. The very fact of your joining us indicates that these times are beginning, and we have great joy in you!"

Sam nodded. "I had also realized that my being changed was significant in the timing of things. I am deeply honored to be here."

Daniel smiled broadly and laid a warm hand on Sam's arm. "We knew you would be joining us since before you were born, and have been waiting anxiously for you to find your way through the process that leads to us. Welcome, welcome, my brother," he said with deep emotion, while still holding Sam's hand in a firm grip. Sam felt humbled and overwhelmed as he pondered what he had heard. His mind spun with a thousand questions, none of which he felt he should ask.

Helaman stepped closer and laid a hand on both their shoulders. "Samuel, Daniel is a member of Enoch's Zion, and was in that great city when it was taken up to heaven. He has had glorious experiences serving the Lord. I am honored to have him here to help instruct you. Daniel is a specialist in teaching new people how to travel, so I've asked him to join us tonight. He can teach it so much better than I. Actually, it was Daniel who taught me, wasn't it, my friend?"

"You were a quick learner, Brother Helaman," Daniel replied warmly.

Helaman laughed and clapped his friend on the back. "I was so afraid I would end up at the bottom of the ocean or something, I could scarcely bring myself to do it. But I've got my bow strung now, I think," he quipped, using a colloquialism at one time common among the Nephites.

"You are far too modest. You're one of the best. Now, let's help Samuel learn."

Sam spoke up. "Brother Daniel, why do you both call me Samuel rather than Sam?" he asked, his voice almost shy.

"That is your name," he replied simply.

"I prefer Sam."

"Sam is the name of your body. Samuel is the name of your soul. If you knew yourself as the Lord does, you would call yourself Samuel. This name predates this mortal world, and has been a part of you for many thousands of years."

"I see," Sam said thoughtfully. His mind was reeling. "This is all giving me far more questions than answers," he told them both. However, at that moment he silently determined that he would henceforth go by the name of his soul—Samuel. It sounded right.

"You can ask all your questions in time," Daniel replied kindly.

"I'll forget half of them by then," Samuel said ruefully.

"No, you won't," they both said in exact unison, then looked at each other in silent recognition. Sam had little time to ponder their answer, for Daniel immediately turned his attention to teaching Samuel how to "travel."

"Focus on me for a moment," Daniel began, "and I will explain this as plainly as I can. Close your eyes, and let me show you the pattern of existence," Daniel instructed.

Samuel closed his eyes, and immediately saw a complex image of overlaid three-dimensional patterns, each blending perfectly with the others, yet never losing its distinctiveness. "What you are seeing," Daniel said, "is a graphic portrayal of the fabric of mortal existence. There are many layers, or spheres of truth, each with its particular properties and laws."

Samuel nodded, frowning in concentration. "It appears to be many colored spheres of different sizes sharing the same space, like balls of light. Is that right?" he asked.

"You see truly," Daniel replied patiently. "What you are seeing is how the properties of mortality exist in their present form. God is able to order them in an infinite variety of ways."

Samuel watched as all but one sphere disappeared. Daniel continued his explanation. "This sphere possesses only one law, or property—that of distance." Another sphere appeared which seemed to surround or engulf the first. "This one possesses the element of time. By the power of the Lord we are able to stop the operation of any of these spheres we wish."

Samuel then watched all the layers reappear. "What you are seeing is the actual fabric of mortal existence. As you can see, it is a complex junction of many spheres of existence. Combined in this way, an area of mortality forms. The one you are seeing actually belongs to this earth."

"That's amazing!" Samuel cried. "It's fantastically beautiful!"

"Yes, it is. Many people comment on that when they first see it. Everything Heavenly Father has created is beautiful if it remains unpolluted," he answered him, and then turned again to the lesson. "If we step outside any one of these layers, that element or property of existence ceases to function for us, while continuing for everyone else."

Samuel was fascinated to watch one image move out of one of the layers, but remain within the whole. Daniel continued. "For example, if we leave the sphere of distance, all things, all places in the universe as you understand it, become immediately present. In other words, there is no space between places. We become everywhere at the same time."

Samuel did not need to ponder his words, for under the illuminating presence of the Holy Spirit it all made perfect sense to him. He instinctively looked one direction and saw familiar images of his own world, then he looked at another and saw other things that were in fact far distant, yet now immediately before him. He had the impression that he had only to look at a sphere to arrive at wherever he desired.

"You are right, Samuel," Daniel said. "All you need do is hold the location you desire in your mind and reactivate the sphere of distance to immediately be there."

"It seems so simple now that you explain it," Samuel replied. Yet his mind reeled, because he had no idea how to do it.

"It *is* a simple concept, Samuel, but much more demanding to actually accomplish," Daniel instructed. "Now, let me mention the sphere of time. If one were to exit that sphere, one would be every-when, or at all times, at once. In other words, just like one could step out into any place through the sphere of space, one may step out into any time through the time sphere."

"One could essentially become a time traveler," Samuel stated with awe in his voice.

"That is exactly right. You must understand, though, that as angels we are not generally allowed to travel through time. Having once been born in this life, we are mostly subject to time. In other words, unless directed to do so, we dwell within the earth's time sphere by divine decree, just like all mortals do."

"So, can we manipulate time?" Samuel clarified, eager to learn more.

"Yes, in a small way," Daniel told him. "We do have the power to step outside of mortal time for brief periods. When we do that, we are able to accomplish whatever is needful, while the rest of existence appears to us to come to a stop. In actual fact, it continues on; we just no longer perceive the passage of time, and can act any way we need to during that period."

Samuel thought about this for a long moment, his pulse racing. "This all seems incredibly difficult!" he exclaimed. "What if I make a mistake or something?"

"Moving through any one sphere is challenging," Helaman said calmly. "Moving through two or more is even more difficult. But don't worry; you aren't able to harm yourself or anyone else by mistake. If you try to do something and get it wrong, it simply doesn't work. The only harm of any mistakes is that they render us temporarily ineffective in our service to the Lord.

"This is true; you need not worry about mistakes," Daniel picked back up.

Samuel was visibly relieved, so Daniel continued. "In addition to these two spheres, there are spheres that control different elements of nature, such as gravity. Stopping the operation of that law would cause someone, or something to become weightless. There is a sphere governing light, sound, inertia, mass, power, heat, cold, wetness, the actual process of life, chemical and physical laws—every other element of existence you are used to, and an eternity full of others you could not have conceived of in mortality. You can see why careful training is necessary, can you not?

"It's all mind-boggling," Samuel admitted.

"It is at first, but you need not fear. You have been chosen for this path," Daniel said encouragingly. Then he motioned to Samuel. "Let's try a simple exercise. I suggest you lie on the floor here," he directed, pointing at a spot in the center of the living room. Samuel did as instructed. Daniel lay down beside him. "We are lying down so you don't need to even think about standing up. You will need all your mental ability to concentrate on what we are going to do. Are you ready?"

"For what?" Samuel asked.

"For your first experience in being everywhere at once."

Samuel watched the spheres and opened his mental perception so that he could clearly see which one contained the element of distance. He watched Daniel stop the operation of that sphere. Something unexpected happened as soon as they were no longer subject to distance. Everything in existence was immediately visible. Samuel tried to shut his eyes to stop the mind-boggling influx of information, but it made no difference. It wasn't so much that everything was before him, but that everything was *inside* him. Since all existence occupied a single point in space, he was there too, and he felt as if he were being crushed. He began to pant in terror.

Daniel patted his arm. "Relax, there is nothing to fear. The only thing that has changed is your perception of where everything is. Nothing is actually occupying the same space as your body; it is only that these things are no longer defined by distance. You are everywhere at once only in your perception. As a mortal, you do not comprehend all things at once, but you see linearly. That isn't necessary here. You can comprehend all spaces as a whole, or limit your perception to a single place."

He sat up and looked at Samuel intently. "I want you to find your living room. All you need do is desire to see it. Focus on that location alone. Can you do that?"

"I see it," Samuel replied, greatly relieved to have just one place to see, rather than a seemingly infinite number.

"Good. Now let your focus move several feet toward the sofa. Tell me when you are there."

"I'm there," Sam said after a moment.

"Good, now let's come back in." Samuel felt himself re-enter the realm of distance, and his perception narrowed until he was only looking at the ceiling of the living room. He sat up slowly, and realized that all three of them had reemerged on the opposite side of the living room.

"That was a little frightening," Samuel admitted.

"It can be until you realize that no harm can come to you," Daniel agreed. "If you get confused, simply desire to return to your original location and you will. If you accidentally attempt to do something dangerous, it just won't occur. So, relax and let yourself enjoy this experience. Being able to freely move from one place to another is very important to our work."

He stood and helped Samuel up with a smile of encouragement. "You did a great job for your first time! And also, don't worry about appearing or disappearing within a mortal's sight. If you try to do that, it simply will not work."

Samuel was shaking, and walked to the couch to catch his breath. "I never dreamed that I would be entrusted with power like this—at least not in this life!"

Daniel considered his next words carefully. "Compared to the unlimited Power, Light and Truth of God, this spiritual technology is altogether crude and rudimentary. But we rejoice in the Savior's grace in letting us use it, and in the marvelous gifts we have been given, as imperfect as we are in implementing them."

A deep silence followed these humbling words. Helaman decided to speak. "Samuel, do you remember when I met you in Sacrament meeting that Mother's Day in Alaska?"

Samuel nodded.

"After we spoke, I walked away and disappeared from sight a moment later. This is the reason I seemed to leave when you glanced away. The way that works is that I just initiate the travel and wait for it to work. As long as you are looking, it doesn't happen. As soon as you glance away, I move on. It's really quite simple, and is actually a function of the justice of God. Justice and its accompanying law, the agency of man, simply will not allow these things to happen any other way, for they could potentially violate the agency of others."

"What about all the other people who were in the chapel at that time?" Samuel wanted to know. "Didn't they see you, too?"

"Most of them were not aware that I was there. Because you could see me, you automatically assumed everyone else could too. In actuality, anyone who was not supposed to see me could not. Perhaps it would be more accurate to say, they could see me, but were unaware I was there."

"That's almost more than I can take in," Samuel said mostly to himself. Then he had another thought. "But, they must have heard me talking to you, and yet they couldn't comprehend you?"

"They were not able to see it. If they would have looked directly at you, they would have seen you speaking to me, but would not have perceived it. I know it's a fine line, but it gives us the ability to appear to someone in a crowd of people, and not interfere with those other people's agency. Mortals don't receive a heavenly manifestation they're not prepared for."

Samuel sighed in relief. "So, basically, it's impossible for me to goof up. If I try to do a miracle that is wrong, or that incorrectly influences someone, it won't work. And, if I am doing the Lord's work, other people simply don't observe it as unusual. Is that right?" he asked.

It was Daniel who replied. "That's an over-simplification, but yes, you are pretty much right." Then his voice became reverent as he spoke. "Our

 Lord has many laborers, of which we are but a few. However, we all serve Him under the same laws. We can do only what Jesus Christ desires, in the way He desires it. It is impossible for us to inappropriately influence someone. It makes it much easier for translated beings to have these God-given abilities, because even in our non-perfect state, we can't use them incorrectly."

Samuel pondered this for a second, then asked, "Doesn't that take away our agency, to not even be able to make mistakes?"

"No, because this is a matter affecting all mankind. If you don't want to obey the laws associated with these privileges, you are free to leave," Helaman responded. "You have used your agency to arrive at these blessings. You can exercise it to leave. However, the rights of the priesthood are inseparably connected with the powers of heaven. And, the powers of heaven can only be exercised according to the principles of righteousness. That is divine law," he concluded.

Samuel shook his head. "But I would never want to leave! Why would anyone quit this glorious work? It all seems so incredible!"

Daniel took a seat in the armchair, and Helaman sat cross-legged on the floor opposite Samuel. "Some tire of the work after being in it for centuries, and they long for the rest of paradise," Daniel explained. "Sometimes they miss loved ones so badly that they wish to leave. Sometimes they grow discouraged by the wickedness of the people. Occasionally, their mission simply comes to an end, and they are done. If such a thing happens, the Lord allows them to come to Him without delay, and they are welcomed home. They lose nothing, and receive a glorious reward for their additional labors. We are here by our own request, and are free to leave this life of service at any time."

"This is very comforting, actually," Samuel admitted soberly. He could see how any, or all of those things could happen to him, and though he certainly didn't feel trapped in this new life, it did feel merciful to know there was a way to honorably move on to a place where loved ones waited.

"I have another question," Samuel asked presently.

"Please, ask it," Helaman urged.

"Can we go to the world of spirits and visit loved ones? Are they in one of these spheres that you showed me?"

"They are in a sphere not unlike the mortal sphere. As a matter of fact, there are few differences between them, and only a thin veil separates the two," Helaman replied. "Let me answer it this way: We would not go there to just pass the time and chat. They are very busy, as are we. If the need arises, we work together as fellow servants. It all depends on what task we are assigned, and who else is working with us. The possibilities are truly limitless."

Helaman paused as if collecting his thoughts. He glanced at Daniel, who gave him a tiny nod. "One of the things you cannot remember, is that as children of the covenant, most all our labors are directly related to our families. When we live on the earth, our yet-unborn children and future grandchildren watch over us. After we pass, although we remain greatly interested in the progress of our mortal children and their posterity, our primary task is to teach the gospel to our deceased family awaiting the resurrection. It is a huge task! You can imagine that there could easily be millions in your family who desperately want to be taught the truth, so that they may accept the ordinances performed by mortals."

"So, who do translated people minister to then?" Sam wanted to know.

"We labor with a different subset of the children of Father than either those in the premortal or the postmortal world," Helaman said. "Translated persons are assigned first to help their mortal families, but then to expand their ministry to all the people of the earth. These things that are happening to you, Samuel, are far more vast and glorious than you can comprehend at this point. You will probably not be in this assignment long enough to learn of all the celestial ramifications of your calling."

Samuel nodded with new understanding.

Daniel spoke next. "All these understandings will come to you as you grow in your new assignment. For now we need to return to traveling. Shall we try it again?"

The three men lay back down on the floor. They worked on the various steps of traveling, and after multiple tries Samuel finally grew more comfortable with the experience.

"All right," Daniel said, still lying beside him on the floor. Helaman stood and sat on the sofa. He was apparently going to sit this next one out. "Now you try it alone. I'll come with you, but you choose the destination. Just pick a spot somewhere in this room. Let's go."

Without having any time to reconsider, Samuel easily moved into the now familiar realm devoid of space, and picked a spot a few yards away. He returned to the normal sphere, and found himself flailing in the air. He thudded to the ground to find himself sprawled on the floor beside Daniel, who had returned correctly. Helaman was laughing uproariously, slapping his legs with glee. Daniel shot him a reproving glance, and finally clapped a hand over Helaman's mouth to stifle his laughter.

Ignoring Helaman, Daniel turned to his student. "Nice try. You came back, but you forgot to focus on exactly where you *wanted* to be. You are used to seeing places from your eye level, and quite naturally picked a position at that height. Fortunately, you can no longer be injured by such an error. It just lacks dignity," Daniel said seriously. This statement had the effect of eliciting another peal of laughter from Helaman. Daniel shot him another glance. Helaman shrugged, and still laughing, vanished from the couch.

They repeated this exercise many times until Samuel was able to control his return to what he considered the normal sphere every time. Next they stood up, and did the same thing until Samuel was able to pick any spot in the living room and go to it exactly. They even did a couple trips to isolated places outdoors. Their furthest excursion took them to a small island where the sun was high in the sky. Samuel could only wonder where it was, but figured it was somewhere on the opposite side of the globe, since it was nighttime back in Utah. It took no more effort to go there than to move to the opposite side of his living room.

When they returned, Helaman was waiting for them in the living room. He seemed to have regained his composure.

"I'll be leaving now," Daniel informed them. "It was a good session, and you're learning quickly. I will ask you to make no attempt to practice these things until I return tomorrow evening." He shook Samuel's hand. "It really has been a great honor working with you. Until tomorrow then, God bless you," he said, and disappeared.

"Thank you Daniel," Helaman said into the empty air with obvious affection, then turned to Samuel. "Sorry about laughing so much," Helaman said. "I have a confession to make though. I did the very same thing, but from a considerably higher place. I was so startled to find myself falling, I actually screamed. It struck me as funny tonight because I saw the expression on your face as you were falling, and I could only imagine myself looking just the same, or worse. I couldn't help laughing! Sorry, I meant no disrespect."

Samuel chuckled back at him. "I imagine it was pretty funny. I'm glad to see that we can still enjoy our lives. I like to laugh!" He glanced excitedly around the room, remembering all that he had just been through. "This has been a wonderful experience—the most amazing day for me. I appreciate your help, and your friendship, Helaman."

Helaman smiled warmly at him. "Ah, you are welcome, my friend. Your life is just beginning, my young brother, and it gets more fantastic with each moment. Before long you will wonder how you ever survived as a mere mortal. As you learn to exercise these new priesthood powers, you will realize that you knew them all before. What you are doing is relearning skills you perfected long ago, in our premortal days. Your blessings are truly vast, my dear friend. Praise God for His mercy to us! All glory to Him!"

Helaman held out his still-youthful hand, which Samuel clasped firmly. "I'll be back tomorrow evening after your family is asleep. You'd best go to bed now. They'll be awakening in a bit. See, it's already growing light outside. It wouldn't hurt you to have a few minutes sleep, either. Farewell, Samuel, and God bless you," Helaman said, and disappeared. Samuel could feel the opening and closing of the fabric of existence, but could not tell where he had gone.

Samuel returned to bed and actually fell asleep, only to be awakened a short time later by his alarm. He slammed it off and started to roll over for a few more minutes of sleep, but discovered quite unexpectedly that he was fully awake. He climbed from bed completely free of any lingering effects, and happily started the new day.

It was actually the start of his new life.

11

HOPE REKINDLED

It was with deep regret that Samuel quit his job at the Temple. He had worked there for four years, and had enjoyed the most profound experiences of his life within those hallowed walls, even while pushing a vacuum. Yet, without even knowing why, he knew he had to leave. There was a greater task awaiting him.

It was difficult explaining to Melody how he was going to support the family with no job, and little likelihood of finding one. Besides all that, the Church had a decent retirement program which he would no longer be a part of. He was now fifty-one and not in the prime of his earning powers. His resume read like a patchwork quilt, no block of which was extremely impressive. He had spent a few years as a diamond merchant, (now defunct), a technician on the Trans-Alaska pipeline (now mostly manned by computers), and as a janitor in the Salt Lake Temple (recently retired). Of course he was a successful songwriter—still in publication, but not producing enough to completely support his family. Samuel wanted to transfer to Melody his confidence that all would be well, even though he hadn't a clue how. The thing that was strange about her response was that she didn't pry, and his vague attempts to explain it to her simply died out for lack of a concerned audience.

It was even more strangely difficult to explain to Melody why he wanted to take a week and drive into the high Uinta Mountains—by himself. She didn't argue with him—she never did; she just helped him pack, and kissed him goodbye.

"It's no wonder I love her so," Samuel thought to himself as she and little Sammy enthusiastically waved him goodbye. She hadn't even stated the obvious, that he had taken far too few provisions to spend a week in the mountains. Her belief in him was evidently so complete, that if he felt he could live on almost nothing for a week, she believed that too. His heart hummed with happiness as he drove away in their old station wagon.

Samuel headed south, then east toward Uinta National Forest. Four hours later he pulled the tired old car into an isolated state campground near Moon Lake, slung a backpack onto his back, and locked the door. His was the only car in the parking lot as he picked the trail marked "Tokewanna Peak."

“The mountains are beautiful this time of year,” he heard a voice say beside him. Samuel wasn’t surprised; he had felt the opening of the veil a few seconds earlier.

“Hello, Helaman,” Samuel said happily. “I’m so pleased you could join me.” He silently noted that Helaman had resumed his former appearance of being rather aged, which was actually a comfort for Samuel.

“My pleasure, Samuel. I do love the mountains.”

In less than three minutes they had quickly climbed out of sight of the parking lot. In ten more, they were in a dense pine forest. The smell was rich with life, and filled Samuel’s heart with joy. They walked in the dappled sunlight for another few minutes before Helaman stopped.

“May I guide you to our destination?” the old prophet asked.

“Please,” Samuel said. He felt the now familiar opening of another reality, and saw his world visually collapse into a single point. He watched as Helaman quickly found a secluded spot far into the wilderness of Idaho, and deftly moved them both there. Even knowing as much as Sam did of this type of traveling, he still had to marvel at its sheer power. He was only vaguely aware that they had moved somewhat short of five hundred miles in the blink of an eye. Five hundred miles, or five hundred light-years—it was all the same.

Sam found himself standing on the grassy shore of an alpine lake surrounded on all sides by rugged mountains. The granite peaks and massive pines growing on the opposite shore cast a mirrored reflection of green and gold in the placid water. Sunlight, now angled into afternoon, made the scene all around him etched with fingers of heavenly light. He could not imagine a more beautiful place on earth.

Sam was pleased to find that traveling this way had left him with a clear understanding that he was standing among the rugged, unexplored mountains in Northern Idaho.

Moments after they arrived, Daniel stepped into view with a young woman at his side. Samuel could not help observing that she was flawlessly lovely. Her hair was sandy brown, and her eyes a colorless clear gray. Her robe was silken and flowing, a luminescent blue. After embracing Helaman and Samuel, Daniel turned to his companion. “Samuel, I want you to meet Islana.” Samuel took a step toward her to shake her hand. She bowed slightly at the waist and straightened with a smile on her face, but did not extend her hand.

“Islana is formerly of this world, and is awaiting the resurrection,” Daniel explained quickly. “It is not lawful for her to offer to shake your hand.”

"Oh, of course!" Samuel exclaimed, embarrassed. She looked exactly like any other person, and he found it unnerving to be this close to an actual spirit. "I'm sorry, I'm not used to all these things yet," he explained nervously.

Islana smiled broadly and then laughed, her voice musical and enchanting. Sam realized that he had heard the sound of her voice in his soul, not with his ears. "This is a first for me as well, Samuel," she admitted, looking around her. "I only left mortality a few weeks ago. This is indeed a beautiful place. It reminds me very much of my home."

Daniel nodded, and took a step closer to them. "Islana accepted the gospel while yet a mortal, and thereby became a spiritual leader in her family. It is among her brethren that you will labor."

Samuel's eyebrows raised slightly. "Uhm, I hardly know what to say, Islana. I'm very anxious to be of service to your people."

"They're not just my people," she replied, suddenly sober, "they are my family."

"I understand," Samuel assured her.

Daniel shook his head. "Samuel, those people are her parents, her older brothers, and her baby sister, as well as aunts, uncles, and many others—not just distant relatives. Her grandfather is the leader of the group you will serve."

Samuel cried. "Oh! I understand now. It will be my pleasure to do everything I can to help them." Then, turning to Daniel he asked, "What is the purpose of our meeting here today?"

It was Islana who answered. "I have specific knowledge which will help you in your mission. Daniel has instructed me in how to pass this on to you." She smiled a little sheepishly. "I've never done this before, but Daniel assures me I won't harm you. I'm ready whenever you are."

Samuel was astonished with all this. Here he was, in fact, speaking to an angel, standing among translated beings, yet the whole conversation seemed normal. He found himself liking Islana very much, and a great desire to help her people filled his heart. No sooner had this thought occurred to him than Islana smiled broadly, as if she had heard his thoughts.

Sam looked at Helaman, who nodded. "I'm ready," Sam told her.

Islana closed her eyes partway, and instructed Sam to do the same. Almost immediately Samuel felt his mind open; and in less time than it would have taken to form a thought, a fully-developed understanding permeated his soul. He saw—or rather vividly remembered—a harsh, snow-covered land, with towering mountains, spruce forests, and icy rivers. He 'remembered' a small city lying separate and lonely a safe distance from a much larger city. He saw wooden homes joined together into a commune of sorts. He felt the bitter cold, the desolation and the oppression of the place. Vast chronicles of history, both personal and general, settled deeply in his mind. He felt Islana's love for all of it. Inside the wooden homes he knew the people by name: their relationships, their lives, their hopes and faith. He knew them as if he were one of them. Yet, he did not know what it all meant.

"Thank you Islana," Daniel said. "You were wonderful. God bless you."

"Thank you Daniel, and especially thank you, Samuel," she said as she shimmered into non-existence.

Samuel couldn't take his eyes from the spot where she had just stood, his mind still groping with the incredible events of the last few days. "Was Islana really able to hear my thoughts?" Samuel asked after she was gone.

Daniel nodded. "And you were hearing hers. It is the only way beings without a body can communicate. What she heard filled her heart with hope and joy. She will forever be grateful," he added gently.

Samuel nodded, his eyes upon the ground in contemplation. "I perceived that it wasn't my physical ears that could hear her voice. But, I was surprised when she responded to my thoughts. That did surprise me, but more than anything else, it just highlighted that there is so much for me to learn. It's very easy to feel overwhelmed . . ." His voice tapered to silence.

Helaman stepped up to Sam and placed a hand on his shoulder, which caused Sam to look into the old Nephite's eyes. "Believe me when I say, we understand how you feel. We both have gone through this process. But remember, we are here with you, and won't leave until you are prepared. Beyond that, you have a full endowment of the Holy Ghost, the ability to receive any degree of revelation you need, and the power to summon angels, myself included, to assist you. It is hardly a position of weakness," he concluded with just a hint of remonstration.

Sam smiled and squared his shoulders. "I know. I don't feel overwhelmed emotionally, I just feel overwhelmed . . ." He paused, searching for the right word, "overwhelmed by all the new information. I'm afraid I might forget something."

"Oh!" Daniel laughed. "Of course. We haven't dealt with that, so I can understand why you feel overwhelmed."

Helaman nodded. "Now is a good time, then."

Daniel stepped directly before Samuel. "The night of your change in the Temple you stopped at a stop sign on the corner of first west and sixth south."

"That's the onramp to the highway," Samuel agreed. He had turned at that intersection many times.

Daniel nodded. "There's a gas station on that corner."

"Yes, I remember."

"To the left of the entrance is a blue metal box."

"It's a newspaper vending machine," Samuel said, seeing the image in his mind.

"Yes, and what was the headline on the paper?"

"I didn't pay any attention, and it was in a shadow . . ."

"Samuel, just read the headline from the image you are seeing in your mind."

In Sam's mind the image grew larger until the headline was clearly visible. "North Korea Resumes Nuclear Testing."

Daniel smiled broadly. "And, the story?"

"I can see it clearly! All of it!" Samuel laughed, and was about to begin reading it line by line when Daniel stopped him.

"No need to read it. The point is—you can't forget."

Helaman quickly added, "Unless you want to, of course."

Samuel drew his mind from the image of the newspaper. "It's true, isn't it! Now, all I have to do is make sense of it all so that my new life seems normal to me, rather than so incredibly amazing all the time."

Daniel and Helaman exchanged a knowing look. It was Helaman who said, "I'm still working on that one myself. When I think about it, my life still seems unbelievable. I think it's this fact that makes it so wonderful, so unendingly delightful and engaging. I haven't experienced a single moment of boredom in the last thousand years," he said, and then laughed out loud at his words.

Samuel's eyes grew wide, but then he suddenly felt at ease and burst out laughing with his friend. Sam felt that he had come home, home to a new life that was more glorious than he could even yet imagine. His laughter was a mixture of joy, gratitude, and a very large dose of relief.

The mood grew sober again, and Sam's mind returned to Islana and her message to him.

"I now know a great deal about a group of people in a snow-covered village. Can you tell me why Islana showed me these people?"

"These you will bring from their ancestral home back to the temple in Cardston, Alberta, Canada to receive their temple blessings. From there, they will go to the New Jerusalem in Jackson County, Missouri to help build a temple to the glory of the Lord. Your labor will be not only to bring them from their home in the far North, but to teach them the Gospel along the way, and baptize them. You will also ordain them to the priesthood and prepare them for their temple blessings," Helaman told him.

Samuel pondered the mission before him. "I am willing to believe anything is possible, but these people are proud and deeply suspicious, as well as firmly rooted in their own religious beliefs. From what I know of them, it seems, if not impossible, at least improbable that they will yield to any form of missionary labor," he said thoughtfully.

"It is a great assignment, one that no mortal could accomplish. But, with the gifts you now possess, and with the guidance and power of the Lord, you will succeed—even if they choose to fail." Daniel told him.

Once again his teacher's words stunned him. "I will be glad to go and serve these people," Samuel said solemnly, then paused before adding, "But I will need lots of help preparing. I'm not presently up to the task, I think."

Daniel smiled. "That is why we are here. In a week's time you will be ready," he said with great confidence.

The following week was one Samuel would never forget. He learned things previously incomprehensible to him. As the days came and went, he spent hours enthralled by instruction from various personages from the unseen world. Each had a message essential to his success. Each delivered their precious information with solemnity, and left as soon thereafter. Most of the messages were delivered without words, as a vision, or burst of understanding which washed over him. Many of those who came were ancestors of those to whom he would now go.

Samuel also learned something quite startling to him, something he should have already known. There was every possibility those he served may choose to ignore him, and their opportunity to return to Zion. It would be their choice, and he could do little more than nudge them toward their spiritual birthright.

Something else that startled Samuel was learning that he could not assume leadership of the exodus. He could only advise them *after* they had asked him for help. Until then, he had to remain silent, not suggesting or volunteering any information. Even in desperate and life-threatening situations, he had to wait for them to ask. He could not teach them the gospel until after they asked. Nor could he ever let them know he was more than a man. It was a truly daunting task laid out before him—and it humbled him to the dust.

Near the end of the week Daniel handed him a book which appeared to Samuel to be a textbook. "This book contains the knowledge you will need to secure the employment that will take you to the country where they live. You will seek a job as an electrical engineer specializing in oil fields. Your new job will be your introduction to these people. The Lord placed a great abundance of oil in their frozen land for this very purpose," Daniel explained.

Samuel took the book. No sooner did his fingers touch it than a staggering flood of information poured into his mind. He almost dropped the book it startled him so. After a few seconds he handed it back, shaking his head. "I always thought the idea of learning that way was just a myth."

Daniel laughed and nodded. "It would have been nice during our mortality, I admit. It is the way we learned prior to becoming mortal. In our current state of blessedness, this is one of the things the Lord has allowed us to do again. This book is like those we studied in the premortal world. Normal books will not have this effect on you," Daniel assured him.

Samuel stood there, his eyes moving back and forth as if examining new memories in his mind. He found he had a complex and comprehensive understanding of electrical engineering and design. "The odd thing is that it all feels very comfortable, as if I have known these things all my life."

Daniel nodded. "Of course, none of us remember the premortal world, but we have come to believe this knowledge feels familiar because we understood all these things prior to this life. We have come to accept the idea that what you just experienced is more a matter of lifting the veil on a prior memory, than actually learning something new."

This experience and many others left Samuel with no doubts at all that he could fulfill his duties with courage and exactness. His doubts, if that is even the right word, all grew from his intimate knowledge of their stubborn will. It would take something of great consequence to humble them sufficiently that they would even consider asking someone outside their own private world for advice on anything. He knew for a fact that these proud people would not consider asking an outsider for a breath of air if they were suffocating, let alone how to make a journey to a land they despised, to dwell among a people they feared and hated, to a place they doubted even existed. But Sam also had a profound testimony of the power of Christ burning within him, and this was more than enough.

When Sam returned to his car it was putrid with the smell of rotting food. He had forgotten that he had left it all there. He dumped it all in a dumpster. It was only during his unloading the car of spoiled food that he realized he had not eaten during the entire week, and felt no need to do so now. He drove home, his mind laden with precious knowledge, his heart alight with joy.

For Melody these had also been days of happiness. Even though Sam's sudden urge to go camping was atypical of him, she felt a quiet sense of peace as he drove away. She had waited patiently for him to return. Then, although he had given her no idea of how long he might be away, she awoke on the day of his return with a happy certainty that he would shortly be home.

Sam drove up to his modest rambler home in South Jordan filled with happiness. Sammy ran from the house to greet him with great enthusiasm, with Melody just a step behind.

After an affectionate hug, Melody helped her husband unpack the car. She could tell he was bursting with joy and yearning to express it. She also instinctively knew that he could not—not to her, not to anyone. For this she felt a sadness which had no true definition, and no remedy. It simply was.

As she helped empty out the car from his "camping trip" Melody quietly pondered the many incongruities she observed, even while he happily told her of the beauty of the woods this time of year. The food containers were empty and unwashed, but his paper plates and silverware were all untouched. His sleeping bag had not been used, nor had his several changes of clothes. The clothing he had on was crumpled and dirty. He had a full weeks growth of beard, complete with smudges of gray at his temples; yet he had no body odor. His shaving kit and toothbrush had not been removed from the baggie she had packed them in, yet his breath was fresh.

It never occurred to her to suspect anything amiss or afoul. This was not about her; it was about him. In her heart of hearts she knew something was very different about her husband, and it brought her deep personal satisfaction to know that it filled his life with joy.

The following day Sam felt impressed to make a phone call to a company in Texas engaged in electrical engineering. The following day he was on a plane at their expense to interview for a job. He was not certain how he would successfully apply for this job when he had little experience to show them but his few years on the pipeline. When he arrived at their Houston office he was impressed to find them occupying the top twelve floors of a skyscraper. Their offices were richly decorated; the company was obviously doing very well.

The man who interviewed him did not ask to see his resume, but asked him two questions. "How confident are you of your knowledge of electrical engineering?"

"Very," Samuel replied flatly. He realized grimly that it was unlikely any living man on earth knew more. His interviewer arched his eyebrows in a "we'll see about that," type of look.

His second question was quite different. "Are you willing to sign a one year contract to work in Russia?"

Samuel felt a flood of knowledge from the Holy Spirit. "I am," he replied but added, "if the pay is right. For a one year contract I expect a minimum take home of $25,000 dollars per month, a $50,000 dollar signing bonus, and the same upon completion. I expect all expenses, including my housing, to be paid by the company. I will also require a management position with considerable freedom to complete my work as needed. In return I guarantee a thorough and accurate project, superbly executed, and finished on time."

When he finished saying all this, the man's mouth was hanging open. He closed it and said "I don't think we can offer anything that substantial. I'm sorry to have wasted your time."

When devastation should have surged in, Samuel felt only peace. "You'll be even sorrier if you don't hire me. At present you have no other prospects, and the project is already behind schedule. I'm your man, and you know it." Samuel said all this because it came into his heart to do so, not because of anything he actually knew.

"Well, I don't know about that, Mr. Mahoy, but I can tell you that not even our top managers make that large a salary." He eyed Samuel with suspicion. "I'll take your demands under advisement if you wish—but with expectations like that, you might as well bundle on back to Utah," he stated arrogantly as he stood up, signaling the end of the interview.

"In the meantime," Samuel said, still remaining seated, "I will give you one hour before a review board of your top engineers. If they can ask me any question I can't answer in an hour's time, I will accept minimum wage for the position, and drop the bonus. Are you up to the challenge?"

"If they can ask you anything you can't answer?"

"Anything related to electrical engineering," Samuel amended.

"So, let me get this straight. If they can ask you any question relating to electrical engineering that you can't answer, you'll take the job at minimum wage?" the interviewer asked incredulously.

"Correct," Samuel replied.

He considered this with a wry smile. "It would almost be worth it just to be able to drill you into the ground. I've never met someone so insanely confident of his abilities, Mr. Mahoy. I almost said arrogant, but that doesn't fit you, really. You just seem confident to the point of sanity. You know, even I wouldn't submit to what you propose. Are you serious?"

"Are you willing to give me what I ask if I pass the review board?

"I will try," he said guardedly.

"That's not good enough. Give me your word on it, and yes, I am serious."

The man considered this while he chewed his lower lip. Finally he left the room and was gone nearly fifteen minutes. When he returned he held open the door. "This way, Mr. Mahoy. You have a deal, and your review board is waiting for you."

Samuel followed him to an elevator and up to the twentieth floor. He was taken into a conference room where six men and two women were hastily assembling. They each had a stack of books before them through which they were hastily leafing and inserting slips of paper. He was directed to a seat at the far end of the table.

After a brief introduction which was punctuated by stares and some frowns, the first man to Samuel's left began with a question. "Mr. Mahoy, would you please give us the formulas for capacitive reactance and inductive reactance and explain their relevance to electrical conductors in free air or conduit, and explain how the formulas were used to arrive at the charts in the National Electrical Code governing allowable conduit fill?"

Sam looked him in the eye just long enough that his examiner's smile began to grow triumphant. "The formula for capacitive reactance is two times pi times capacitance in farads. The formula for inductive reactance is one over two times pi times induction in henrys...." For the next twelve and a half minutes Sam explained every element of the question until the man who asked the question closed the book and leaned back in his chair with a stunned look on his face.

The woman to his left was anxious with her question. "Would you please give us the concept behind explosion proof wiring methods, their application as relating to oil production, and draw all relevant charts on the board and their reference numbers in the Code, as well as cite all the relevant sections of the National Fire safety code that apply?"

"You expect me to do this from memory?" Samuel asked, and she flashed him a dangerous smile. "Actually, what I meant to ask," Samuel interrupted himself, "was, do you really have enough time for me to draw all twelve charts, or do you just want to pick two or three?"

"All twelve," she said. She stopped him fifteen minutes later as he was drawing the third one. "That will be quite sufficient," she told him in a defeated tone.

"I have one question," the man at the end of the table said. All eyes in the room turned in deference to him.

"Yes, Mr. Albright," Samuel said. "What is your question?"

"How did you know my name?" the man demanded impulsively.

"There is a large inlaid wooden door six offices from this room with the name Allen Albright, Senior Engineer / Vice President, written on the door," Samuel replied. "It's the biggest office on the floor. You are sitting at the head of the table, and everyone here obviously defers to you. You're also the oldest and best dressed person at the table, and the only one wearing a gold watch. Who else would you be?" He had only observed all that because the Spirit had instructed him to make note of them as they walked down the hall.

"Mr. Mahoy. You have yourself a job," the senior engineer told him. "Everyone else get back to their projects. Sam, may I call you Sam?"

"I prefer Samuel, please."

"Samuel, I would like to speak to you in my office. Would you like a cup of coffee?"

Melody wept as they sat in the Salt Lake Airport. Her husband was leaving in a few minutes for Russia. "I don't understand why this all has to be so sudden, and why you have to be gone for a whole year! Can't you even come home for a visit? Can't we come visit you? It isn't right!" she said, her face streaked with tears.

Samuel hadn't anticipated this aspect of his leaving on this mission. He had blindly assumed Melody would be as enthusiastic about it as he was. She was devastated and hurt. She saw Sam taking this job and living for a year apart, for no better reason than to make money. The truth was she would rather live in absolute poverty than to make money this way. As a matter of fact, those had been her exact words.

Samuel tried to comfort his sweetheart. "Honey, I honestly can't say when we will see each other again. But I have several things I need to say to you before I leave. Will you listen very carefully? This is important."

"Please, please explain this craziness to me," Melody blurted through tears.

Samuel kissed her on the forehead and sat her down. He knelt on the ground in front of her and held both her hands. "Please remember everything I'm going to say now in the smallest detail. It's important, OK?"

"OK," she said softly.

"I'm not going for money. This is a mission for the Lord. Don't forget that."

"You said that, Sam Mahoy, but you still won't explain it!" she complained. Samuel took Melody in his arms and held her close, stroking her hair and kissing the tears from her cheeks, until the tears finally subsided.

"Okay. I won't forget. I guess," Melody finally mumbled, sniffling loudly.

"I will be safe. No matter what you hear, no matter what the company tells you, I am safe."

"You better be," she said emphatically.

"You're not listening to me," Samuel said earnestly, yet kindly. She blinked twice at his words, then nodded. He repeated himself. "No matter what you hear to the contrary, I am alive and well. That's all you have to remember."

"I believe you," she said with more courage than she actually felt. Samuel slowly released her and stood as if to go.

"Wait!" Melody cried, retrieving a notepad from her purse. She quickly wrote down what he had said, and looked up at him expectedly for more details.

Sam took a deep breath and obliged. "If things get rough while I'm gone, ask my family for help. Stay close to them, and when they move, move with them. Alright?"

"Why in the world would they want to move?" Melody demanded. Then she saw his dismayed expression, and assured him, "Okay—okay Sam, I will."

"Melody—I will be gone longer than a year."

"What!? Why!?" she demanded.

"Just write it down, and remember."

"How long? How do you know? Why would you do that?" she wailed, her face streaking with fresh tears.

"Please listen. It's almost time to go," he urged, but she was inconsolable.

Sammy placed a hand on his mother's shoulder. "Mama, you should listen to what the old man says," Sammy told her.

Melody looked up at her son, a look of bewilderment on her face. Sammy was nine now, and she had never heard him refer to Samuel as "the old man."

"Sammy, don't talk to you father like that!" she remonstrated with more emotion than the situation warranted.

"Not Daddy—him," he said pointing behind Samuel. Three pairs of eyes followed his finger to an old man leaning on a cane. Sam recognized

 Helaman instantly. Sam was at a loss to explain his presence, and didn't know if he should pretend to have never seen him before, or what.

"Hello, Samuel," Helaman said brightly. That took care of that question.

Samuel shook his hand warmly, "Hello uhm . . ."

"Helaman. Don't tell me you've forgotten my name!" the old man laughed.

"No, of course not. Sorry, Helaman. I just wasn't expecting . . . we were just saying goodbye, and having a hard time."

Helaman turned to Sam's wife. "Hello Melody. It has been a very long time."

"What? Who…are you?" she stumbled.

"It is I, remember?" he replied. Now it was Samuel who was in the dark.

"From the park! In England! The violin!" she cried in short bursts, and jumped up to embrace him. He received her into his arms and held her as she laughed and cried. Sam could not tell if her new tears were for happiness at meeting Helaman, or sadness at leaving Samuel. Perhaps they were for both.

"That was over …" she did a mental calculation, "twelve years ago!" she finally finished with awe. "I thought I'd never see you again."

"There was no need until now."

"I never did get to thank you! I'm so glad you're here. What are you doing in America, and especially here at this time?" she exclaimed, her attention now focused on Helaman.

"I'm here to help you again," Helaman exclaimed.

"That sounds pretty deliberate," she said suspiciously, but happily.

"Melody, you need to listen to your husband. He must depart in just a moment. Listen to him. I will explain further after he's on the plane."

Melody turned to Sam. "So how do you know Helaman? I knew him years before I ever met you! He saved my life—more than once, actually!"

Sam gave her a grin. "I'll let Helaman explain that. Right now you need to write down what I tell you."

"Alight. Let me sit… OK. I'm ready, Sam."

"ANNOUNCING ALASKA AIRLINES FLIGHT 422 TO ANCHORAGE WITH CONNECTION TO MAGADAN RUSSIA…" a voice announced loudly.

Sam spoke slowly so that she could write his instructions. "I'm going on a mission for the Lord. I will be back when it's done. I'll let Helaman tell you all he can. The important thing is to remember that I am alive and well. Even if it takes up to five years, or longer, I will return, even if it seems impossible. You must remain faithful. Seek the greater spiritual blessings.

You have barely scratched the surface of your profound spiritual potential. I will come to you as soon as I can. Don't ever give up," Sam reiterated forcefully.

"I have it. I don't understand it, but I have it written down," she said as she finished her note.

"Let me write one more thing down for you," he said, reaching for her pad.

"I LOVE YOU," he wrote in big letters. She blushed and slugged his arm.

"ANNOUNCING FINAL BOARDING CALL FOR..."

"I have to go now," Samuel explained as he straightened up.

"I love you," Melody said, rising to hold him hold him rightly. He drew a last, deep scent of her hair, and wasn't surprised to feel tears gathering in his own eyes.

"I will miss you, my darling, but I will be back," he told her emotionally. He felt Sammy run into him in a strong, impulsive embrace.

Samuel knelt quickly and gathered his son into his arms. "Goodbye my precious Sammy. I love you, son! You have to be strong and take care of Mommy. Be an obedient boy, and please do what Helaman asks, okay?"

Sammy stood a little taller "I will. I really will. I love you too, Daddy. I won't let Mom lose hope, I promise." he said. Samuel heard those words, and felt the Spirit confirm that it had wrought upon the young lad to instill that truth within him. It brought peace to Samuel's soul.

Helaman shook Samuel's hand firmly. "I will stay with your family as long as they need me, and they will be safe. On this you may rely," Helaman assured him with a smile. "Go now. Go serve the Lord."

Samuel nodded and turned his face toward the gate, and an uncertain future. He was aware of his wife's lingering sniffles as he handed the stewardess his tickets. He looked back at the last moment. Even while wearing a stoic smile, Melody's shoulders were trembling. Helaman wrapped an arm protectively around her shoulder. She waved bravely. Samuel turned and was gone.

Just as the plane was lifting off the end of the runway, Helaman turned to Melody who was just about to be overcome by another wave of grief. "I have a message about Theodore and George," he told her. Her head snapped up.

"What!?" she demanded.

"Theodore and George, your sons."

"A message, a message—from my babies?" Melody asked, her voice trembling.

"They're no longer babies, and it's not from them, but about them. When I realized they needed your help, I came here as quickly as I could. I lived near them in England, as you recall, so I kept an eye on them for you. They need you desperately, my dear."

"They do?" she asked in a daze.

"Yes, very much. Theodore is entering his second year at ministerial school. He's turning twenty-two this fall. He's about to lose his way in life."

"Oh!" was all Melody could say. There was not a day gone by that she did not think of them, but they were always little boys in her mind.

"And George is turning nineteen. He's a rebel, and is talking about joining the Mormon Church."

"George is? George wants to join the Church?"

"He does, but his father has disinherited him, and he has no place to go. His grandfather has made it impossible for George to obtain work. He's living on the street. I haven't seen him for weeks. Even the missionaries teaching him don't know where he is. Come, we must hurry. We have to pack and go to England," he urged her.

"But, I will have to buy tickets, and arrange things. It could take days, or weeks. I don't have passports, or money, or…"

Helaman reached into his coat pocket and withdrew two tickets. "I have them already. I hope you don't mind, but I knew you would need to hurry. The tickets are for about this time tomorrow evening."

"Oh my!" Melody said, clapping a hand to her mouth. "Oh good sir, I don't know what to say, I am so grateful to you, so eternally grateful! I will pay you back just as soon as my husband gets a paycheck." She stopped to think and calm herself. "We'd best hurry. I'll leave Sammy with Grandma Mahoy…"

"Mama, I want to go to England!" Sammy complained loudly.

"The tickets are for Mr. Helaman and me. You have to stay home, dear."

"Melody," Helaman interrupted. "You misunderstand me. I bought these tickets for you two. I have my own right here. See?" He said, holding up a third.

Melody's eyes grew fearful. "You are more than kind, sir! But, won't they try to take Sammy away from me? They are very powerful, you know," she cried. She knew very well that they would try.

"No, he's Samuel's son, and your former husband has no claim on him," Helaman assured her.

Melody turned to her son. "Go watch the planes, Sammy. We need a few minutes alone," she said as she turned Sammy toward the big windows. As soon as he was out of earshot she turned back to her friend.

"Sammy is indeed my former husband's son. If I take him to England they will surely try to keep him away from me."

"Well, I made a mistake then," Helaman admitted. He pulled a passport from his other pocket and handed it to Melody. She thumbed it to the picture on the first page of she and Sammy. She was quite impressed when she saw her own signature on the bottom, knowing full well that she had not signed it. The passport described her son as the offspring of her current husband, Samuel Mahoy.

"I'm impressed," she said. "This is good work. Is it legal? I don't mean to be rude, but is this for real?"

"It is." Helaman replied honestly. "Sorry about the mistake."

"Oh, I think it's for the better," she said. "This must have cost a fortune!" she realized, clapping a hand to her mouth. "I'll do everything I can to repay you, but I'm afraid…"

"My dear, I have more money than is good for me. If you must repay me, you can. If you don't ever, I'll just consider it a debt partly repaid to your husband. I owe him much more than two plane tickets."

"Mr. Helaman, you're an angel! Come on Sammy, let's go home to pack."

"Me? An angel?" Helaman laughed heartily. "Where did you ever get that idea? So, would this trusty cane pass for a flaming sword?" he said with a curious smile as he walked quickly behind them, his cane barely touching the polished floor.

Melody smiled. "It saved my life once."

At that moment Sammy suddenly realized what was going on. "Yippee!" he cried as he pranced beside his mother.

Melody was grateful for his exuberance. It masked her own aching sense of loss. She turned to the old man. "Helaman, do you have a place to stay in Salt Lake?"

"I do not." he replied evenly.

"Come, stay with us. We will all leave tomorrow. Please?"

"Very kind of you, and I accept. Besides, I promised Samuel I would stay with you until you no longer needed me."

"That may be a long time," she said, casting him a quick glance over her shoulder as she strode toward the elevator.

"Oh that's no problem. I have all the time in the world," he said. She could have no idea how true his words were.

12

INTO THE BREACH

Samuel climbed down the airplane ramp to the concrete runway. The runway was cracked with tall weeds growing through. The plane was a good hundred yards from an old gray concrete building. He watched as his luggage was tossed onto the ground from the door of the plane. His bags bounced twice and rolled onto their sides. He picked up both bags and carried them to the terminal. With his briefcase tucked under one arm, and a bag in each hand, it was quite a juggling act. "To Russia with love," he thought wryly.

The Magadan terminal was in a dismal state of disrepair, with broken furnishings and worn carpets everywhere he looked. It looked as if someone had played rugby inside the terminal for years. The air smelled of mold and stale tobacco. It took a few minutes to get through customs. The guards seemed to hardly care who he was, or why he was there. They opened his passport and slammed a lightly inked stamp onto the page. He noticed later that the stamp was upside down.

"Hello," a man in a fur hat called to him from the side of a dark blue Honda. The car was not new, but it was in good condition. "Are you Samuel Mahoy?" the man asked as he drew near, offering a hand.

"Hello, I sure am."

"I'm Troy Fletcher," he said in a Texas drawl. "I'm your superintendent on the job. I've come to bring you to the site. We've been hurting for an electrical engineer for months. I've begged them until I'm blue in the face. They say you're pretty good."

"I can get by," Sam replied modestly.

"Good, 'cause we're months behind, and the Ruskies are yellin'. You don't want to hear a Ruskie yell. They usually do it with their hand on the butt of a pistol."

"I'll try to avoid that," Samuel said as Troy led him to the Honda. They jammed one bag into the trunk, one in the back seat, and they drove away. A cold wind was blowing out of the north even though this was late May.

The airport was a long way out of town. They drove on a two-lane road which was alternately pavement and dirt.

"Magadan and the airport were built with Korean slave labor," Troy was saying. "The airport was one of the last to be built. They built it way out here because it's too foggy in Magadan, and not enough open space. After they built the airport, they didn't need so many Korean slaves. Tradition says that they dug a deep trench a full mile long beside this road in about this area, shot most of the Koreans and buried them here. The stories claim as many as 20,000 prisoners were killed and buried in a single day. If you watch to the left, the land sinks here and there. They say those are the graves." Sam felt oppressed as he watched the terrain dip and heave. Every low spot seemed like a mass grave to him. Even worse, he found out later that the stories were true.

When they finally arrived at Magadan he found it surprisingly drab and run down. All of the buildings were of gray concrete with various colors of paint peeling off in long strips. Some of the apartment buildings were four or five blocks square. Sam was intrigued. Most were built in a square with all the apartments facing an inner court, almost as if it had once been a prison. He could see that many of the iron doors into the courtyards were torn from their hinges, or completely missing.

Perceiving Samuel's interest in the arcane architecture, Troy explained. "Magadan was built by Stalin as a prison city. These apartment complexes were designed to be able to lock the tenants inside if necessary. I don't know if they were ever used that way. Probably were. During the purges if someone found disfavor with Stalin or his boys they sent them to these prison cities. Like I said, Magadan was built by slave labor, mostly Korean, and lots of Russian dissidents."

They drove up and down hills past almost endless buildings of exact similarity. As they neared the center of town the buildings grew taller, and the colors peeling from them were more pleasing and artistic. Samuel found himself looking down long streets that once held parks in their meridians, but were now strips of dirt, their trees and shrubs dead and standing ghost-like with barren branches jutting accusingly at the sky.

Magadan was on a peninsula with the ocean on three sides. Everywhere, every day, the wind blew. Everyone Sam saw was wearing a warm coat and heavy hat.

"The arts are really strong in Magadan," Troy was saying. "Almost everyone in Magadan is an accomplished artist of some sort. That's because Stalin sent thousands of artists, painters, sculptors, dancers, musicians, and anyone else with any talent who fell into disfavor into this prison city. Consequently they married, had kids, and the arts still flourish here. We'll go to some concerts if you like. They are very good. The art museums are world-class good."

"I'd like that," Sam said. "Is the whole of Russia run down like this?" he asked.

"The whole @#$* place is a mess," Troy said.

"Troy, forgive me, but I find that type of language offensive."

Troy was mildly contrite. "I apologize. I do too, actually. But, damnation, these Ruskies drive me to drinkin' and cursin'. Excuse me for saying so, but I'm about to quit and go home just from tryin' to work with them. They seem to think it's their job to place endless obstacles in our way, then to demand that we get it done ahead of schedule. Fifty years of communism has made 'em all drunkards, and the ones that aren't drunk think they're little Stalins," he said hotly. "But since you asked, I'll try not to curse."

"Thanks," Samuel said with a chuckle. "Tell me about the job. I haven't seen any plans."

"There almost aren't any. The plans are somewhere in Southern Russia still being reviewed by some committee. In the meantime, we're building a refinery from memory and some drawings on napkins.

"It's a refinery?"

"You didn't even know that?" Troy asked incredulously.

"Actually, I never asked. It doesn't matter."

Troy sighed. "It's probably good you didn't ask. Yeah, it's a refinery about a four-hour drive from here. The countryside is pretty bleak, so you might as well settle back. I'll keep you entertained with horror stories about Russian inefficiencies."

Samuel leaned back in his seat. "Let me hear the worst of it," he said.

So their long drive was filled with long tales of a country gone awry. Once there, Samuel learned for himself that the site consisted of an eighty-acre tract of land cleared to gravel. It had been excavated with huge bulldozers which pushed the rubble into huge piles on all four sides of the compound. These rubble piles were a nightmare of twisted trees, remnants of buildings, and soil. Later when he saw them, the word "rape" came to Samuel's mind as he surveyed them. The compound felt like a prison surrounded by walls of dirt.

On the south end was a grouping of eight ATCO trailers. Sam had been in many ATCO buildings on the North Slope of Alaska. Beyond the trailers was a yard full of building materials of every conceivable type. Sam could see mountains of pipes, lumber, equipment skids still covered in plywood, and row upon row of shipping containers. He could only guess what they contained. Sam had been told they had everything needed to complete the project. So far not a single slab of concrete had been poured. He shook his head. It was no wonder his employer was willing to pay him almost any price to get him here. He found out later that the previous four electrical engineers had taken one look and returned to America. With winter coming on in just a few months, the possibility of getting back on schedule was nil to none.

Sam surveyed the plans available to them, a sketchy bundle of a mere 43 drawings. The entire set, which was lost somewhere in the bureaucracy, consisted of over 1200 drawings. Sam studied what was available until it became clear what they were building. The refinery was actually an older design gas knockdown recycle system. The main towers had been built in Oklahoma. The systems were older technology, assumedly to make it easier for the client to operate and maintain. All the components had been prefabricated, packed on barges, and sent to Russia. In reality, the refinery was like a giant jigsaw puzzle without a picture on the outside of the box to go by.

Sam's room was next to the dining room. It was moderately large with an attached private bath on one side. A door led directly from his bedroom to the office. His superintendent, Troy, had a room on the opposite side of the hall. A mechanical engineer, Vladimir Alexandrovich had a similar office down the hall.

Valdamir, a local Russian Troy informed Samuel, was in Magadan getting drunk. There were several offices for a petrochemical engineers, secretaries and draftsmen down the hall, which were presently all vacant. Sam stayed up that night pouring over the drawings. His office had a state-of-the-art computer with AutoCAD and a fast D-size printer. There was no dial tone on the phone.

Hour after hour Sam made drawings of the footings and concrete pads. Everything he produced was miraculous, with information flowing into his mind as he needed it. His fingers moved across the keyboard at lightning speed, as his hands guided the puck across the drawing tablet faster than humanly possible. By morning he had enough drawings to begin pouring concrete.

Vladimir was up and about early, and for having drunk himself into a stupor the night before, seemed rather chipper that morning. He came into their meeting with a huge mug of steaming coffee. He loved American coffee because it was not as bitter, and the Americans always had sugar. Vladimir spoke with a booming voice, even though he was barely thirty, and of medium stature. He had a full beard but no mustache, and looked like a Quaker. His attitude was superior and condescending. Sam liked him immediately.

Vladimir spoke very good, though heavily accented, English, was trained in soils and structural engineering, and served as their translator and liaison with the Russian government. In reality, he was completely dedicated to the project, and would have done nearly anything to see it finished, as it promised to breathe life into the stagnant local economy.

"I like this drawings," Vladimir said loudly. "Where did you find them?" he demanded.

"They're on the computer in my office," Samuel said quite truthfully.

"Humph. I didn't see them. It makes no difference. I will review them today, and we will begin construction in three days," he told Troy. "You will arrange for the start-up of the concrete plant in about ten days, I think."

Troy sat up, his face beaming, as if he had just been given a huge raise. "I've been waiting for these #$@&% plans for months," Troy complained, "and you just found them on your computer? Well, if that don't beat the hell out of me, I'm . . ."

Samuel interrupted. "Sorry, Troy, but I'll need to take the drawings back. It seems there's a problem with the language on the prints."

"What language?" he demanded hotly.

Vladimir's eyes grow wide, then narrowed with understanding. "I think our new electrical engineer is having difficulty with the language from your foul mouth, not on the drawings," he said, his eyes fixed upon Samuel with an unreadable expression.

"Well, I'm . . ." Troy began as if preparing to launch into a tirade. ". . . I'm just so *dang* pleased to get these drawings. I'm sure we can fix the *language on the prints*," he said forcefully.

Vladimir was nonplussed. "I have complained many times, and you never . . ."

"Shut up, Vladimir." Troy groused. "Can we proceed with the project," he asked Samuel sarcastically.

"I think so. We'll work on the language at a later time, I guess."

Troy gave him a face, then turned to the others of his scant team. "Why didn't ya'all find these drawings before? I told you to look on every computer."

Vladimir threw up his hands. "Wvy vould vee look on an electrical engineer's computer for structure drawings?" he demanded.

Troy turned red. "Wve vould look because I told voo to," he shouted, attempting to mock Vladimir's accent with comical results.

Rather than growing angry, Vladimir began laughing until he was forced to leave the room to regain control.

They began pouring concrete two weeks later. During that time Sam labored as much as he dared to see the project get under way. He had to be very discrete about working late into the night, and had to feign tiredness the following morning. He fell into a routine that ground on in seeming endlessness. The other engineers fell into step, and the project came to life. By the end of the third month they had placed the first pump module and bolted huge distillation towers to their concrete pedestal. The whole crew celebrated by getting drunk for two days.

One interesting aspect of their engineering crew was that they got along well, except when the subject of religion came up. When it did, everyone in the room seemed to attack Vladimir. When this happened, Vladimir simply walked from the room. They couldn't even get him to comment on his beliefs. Sam waited for an opportunity to add his beliefs to the frequent discussions, but waited in vain, for the Spirit never did prompt him to join in. He contented himself with answering questions as simply as possible, and leaving the room when the tone turned rabid against "Mormons."

There was a fair-sized branch of the Church in Magadan, and Samuel consistently made the long, bumpy drive in each Sunday. He drove alone. The third time he drove, there was snow on the road. Since the State had no money, the roads remained unplowed. It took six hours that Sunday for Samuel to make the four-hour drive.

To his surprise, Samuel found the Russian people delightful. They were friendly, loving, and full of faith. Though the meetings were conducted in Russian, Samuel had no problem understanding them through his new gifts; but he made it a habit to sit next to a set of Elders who "translated" for him. He found the Saints' testimonies rock solid, and their faith was sure. The only sadness was that a full three-quarters of the active members were women and children. It seemed that few men could stay away from their vodka long enough to remain active in the Church. Samuel quickly found himself drawn into the branch and given assignments such as a foreigner who doesn't speak the language, might perform. These he did with zeal and joy.

Winter landed with ferocious suddenness. Wintertime was bleak and miserable, even for someone who could not experience the pain from the cold. Sam remembered well his former years in Alaska, and shuddered. Temperatures settled around twenty below zero and the winds howled out of the north. The project ground to a stop by the sheer fact that working outside was life-threatening. Sam's only entertainment became working on drawings and electrical systems that would be needed when the project began again in the spring. Every day seemed to mark the beginning of another century away from Melody, and he longed to get back on a plane and return to Utah. There were two reasons he could not. His contract specifically prohibited him leaving for even for a break for one full year, and even more importantly, the Lord wanted him to stay, though the Lord's reasons were completely obscure, since nothing he did seemed of religious significance.

As the weeks dragged by Sam became so increasingly fixated upon his engineering tasks that it actually startled him when Helaman walked into his office as if from nowhere. Helaman was handsomely dressed in a dark blue suit with a maroon tie.

"Oh, my gosh, you startled me!" Sam cried, then laughed at himself.

"I'm sorry," Helaman said, then placed a firm hand on Samuel's shoulder. "We have an appointment to keep. Why don't you put on your suit and tie." It was not a question. Samuel hurried to change and returned to his office about ten minutes later. Helaman was still waiting.

"What appointment are we going to?" Samuel asked.

"In about ten minutes we have a meeting with the Prophet."

"The Prophet of the Church?" Samuel asked with some amazement in his voice.

"There's only one Prophet," Helaman said with a smile.

"In Salt Lake City?"

"Of course."

"But, that's several days travel from here—Oh!" he cried. "I'm still thinking like a mortal. We have tickets on a different plane. Perhaps I should say, a higher plane."

This earned him a smile from Helaman. "I was wondering why you hadn't gone back home to visit Melody and your son all these months."

"Oh nuts," Sam exclaimed. "You know, it didn't even occur to me that I could. I just assumed it would not be appropriate, and never tried. I really could have done that?" he questioned in wonder.

Helaman chuckled. "I'm sure the Lord wants you here. I was just surprised you hadn't tried to do it."

"I was so focused on completing my assignment here that I never considered doing otherwise," Samuel admitted, mostly to himself.

"You certainly are single minded. Are you ready? You look fine. Would you like to practice your traveling skills?"

"Sure. Where are we going?"

"I'll indicate the correct spot, you do the work."

"I'm ready."

It took two tries before he successfully brought them to their new destination. Samuel found himself standing in a small, serenely quiet room with thick white carpet and white velvet chairs. Helaman indicated a chair for Samuel which he took. Moments later a gentleman dressed in a white suit quietly entered the room.

"Good, I see your companion has arrived. I didn't see him get off the elevator. If you will follow me, I will escort you to the President's office." Having said this, he stepped back into the hall.

Samuel had seen these rooms before, and felt at home. Being back in the Salt Lake Temple was like returning to his childhood home. He had on occasion cleaned these very offices, but had never been here on official business of course, or even when the offices were in use. Samuel also knew these particular offices in the temple were only used for special meetings. Now that he was here on apparently-official business, he had no idea what business it was.

Their escort led them to a large office with a polished walnut desk and large leather chair. All around the room were large paintings of the Savior, the Prophet Joseph Smith, and scenes from Church history. There were exactly fifteen chairs around the walls of the room. A large chandelier hung majestically from the center.

Sitting behind the desk was the Prophet of the Church. Samuel felt his heart skip a beat. He had never had the honor of meeting any prophet face-to-face. As soon as they entered, President Andrews stood and walked quickly to Helaman. To Samuel's astonishment, they embraced.

"Welcome, welcome my brother Helaman," President Andrews said. "How wonderful to have you back among us. This certainly is a grand day, is it not?" They smiled at one another as if sharing a glorious secret; then the Prophet turned kindly eyes on Samuel.

"And, you are Samuel," he said, extending a hand. Samuel took it and was pleased to find it firm and warm, but much more significantly, he found in the living oracle of God an outpouring of love and virtue. Something deeply spiritual and marvelous passed through him the instant their hands touched. Whatever testimony he had of this man being the chosen of the Lord before this moment was quadrupled and then again, and again, until his witness was absolute that this man was *the* Prophet of God in every sense the term could convey.

"I am honored to meet you," Samuel said solemnly.

"And I you," he said emphatically. "Certainly, I am honored, and not unaware of what a privilege it is to be among two of God's great and special servants."

"You do me more honor than I deserve," Samuel protested softly. "I consider myself among those who love the Lord, of only common abilities and accomplishments."

"Now, it is you who do yourself less honor than you deserve," President Andrews said amiably, but with a hint of reproof in his voice. This was not pleasant banter; it was a lesson in truth.

"I agree Samuel," Helaman interjected with great love in his voice. "Humility is a gown of the finest linen, and worn by you it adorns like royalty, but you are hardly giving yourself your due—or the Lord His due either, for that matter. You are highly favored of our Savior, and you must never forget that." He turned back to the Prophet. "But of course, Samuel is in the dark on why he is here. Perhaps you should explain, since it is your stewardship," Helaman said softly. The President motioned for them to sit, and he began.

"Thank you. Samuel, as you are aware, I hold all the keys necessary to prepare the earth for the return of our Lord. One of those most important to the preparations is the gathering of Israel, and the return of the ten tribes to Zion. As the sole possessor of those keys, I bear the stewardship in this matter. I and my brethren of the Quorum of the Twelve have long and diligently petitioned the Lord to let the times begin when the long dispersed of Israel will be gathered home. Helaman and I have met on numerous occasions to discuss the preparations and means whereby these things must come to pass. Your name has often been included in those discussions, and your progress and preparations watched with great interest and satisfaction. You have brought many people on both sides of the veil great joy because of your righteous desires."

Samuel lowered his eyes, feeling the Lord's grace upon his head. President Andrews continued.

"I know you have paid a dear price for your current standing before the Lord, and that you have dedicated your whole life to the service of God. All of us have paid similarly, so we understand your sacrifice, and your humility before the Lord. We also understand the joy you treasure in your heart because of these things. For that reason I will not ask you any of the usual worthiness questions as I extend to you this call, which is as it should be."

The President fixed his gaze on Samuel as he spoke. "Brother Samuel, acting in my capacity and calling as the living oracle of God, I formally issue to you this call to commence the gathering of God's dispersed children. It is a weighty matter, and one for which you have been preparing for millennia. Yours is not the first, nor will it be the last call to gather Zion. But, hundreds of faithful servants like yourself are positioning themselves to accomplish this mighty work."

The Spirit in the room was palpable, and Samuel swallowed hard.

"I feel to warn you that your glorious standing before the Lord notwithstanding, it will be a task that will demand every measure of faith and endurance you possess," the Prophet admonished. "The reason this call comes to you as a translated servant of God is that no mortal man could survive the physical punishment of this mission. Aside from that one thing, your translated status will be of little advantage to you."

Samuel glanced over at Helaman, who was solemnly listening to every word.

"What is of great and lasting benefit to you is the road you have faithfully walked to arrive there. You have, by your faith and obedience to the voice of the Spirit, qualified to be given this great mission. The power of these things lies in your unquenchable faith, and your demonstrated willingness to sacrifice all things to accomplish Father's will. Always remember this, Samuel: *Your strength is in Christ.* You truly will be able to do all things in Him. This is how you will succeed—in the strength of the Lord. Do not rely upon anything or anyone but Christ—even upon yourself. Do not assume that being an angel of God will insulate you from failure. There is still that sin which begins with pride and eventually becomes unpardonable, and which could strip you of all you have gained. Though Satan has no power over you, you know it is because you have ceased to hear his dark voice, not because he has ceased to speak to you. Never yield. Never forget."

Samuel was both amazed and frightened by his words. He had never even guessed the very truths he now heard. The fact that his blessings were only sustained by his continuing faithfulness in Christ, rather than by his faithful standing had never occurred to him. Neither had the possibility of failure ever occurred to him, nor the unthinkable loss of returning to within Satan's dark voice. It caused a shiver of revulsion to cascade through his soul.

Grimly, with absolute determination, Samuel recommitted his soul to the true course. He was pleased to observe that it changed nothing. It neither corrected nor improved his previous commitments to utter dependence upon the Lord. Still, he was taken back that such a warning should be issued under inspiration as part of this great call. He wondered if he actually could fail—after all this, after all the joy, after all the sacrifice.

President Andrews paused for exactly as long as it took Sam to ponder these things before continuing. "Will you accept the call to gather a portion of Christ's dispersed children to Zion, to act as His steward in this matter, and to faithfully discharge this calling as He directs you?"

"I will," Samuel said, and felt a burst of joy which originated outside himself, and which he rightly attributed to jubilation somewhere on the other side of the veil. Without understanding what he had even agreed to do, he immediately felt a flood of warmth and peace in this decision. In reality, there had been no decision, except the one Samuel had made decades ago to obey the voice of the Spirit at any cost. Today's acceptance of the call was but an extension of that life-altering choice so long ago. What he could not know, as one still subject to the veil of mortality, was that he had made that very decision thousands of years ago under circumstances not entirely unlike those of this day.

"It is well," President Andrews said, and stood. "If you will take a seat right here," he said, turning a chair to face Samuel. "This is a great day,"the Prophet proclaimed with a smile as he placed his hands on Samuel's head; yet one by one Samuel felt the placement of other hands, until it seemed as if prophets from every dispensation stood around him. He could not see them, yet they were there. President Andrews perceived this as well, and waited a long moment until all were assembled. For a small moment it felt as if all of eternity paused, and they were at the epicenter of history.

Samuel savored the words of the blessing which was sweet in its promises, and powerful in its pronouncements. He felt the power of the priesthood penetrate every atom of his soul, and he rejoiced in it. As the prophet spoke he felt a new mantle of authority settle upon him. It seemed to Samuel like a great weight, yet it felt light upon his shoulders. After the blessing was over he stood and the Prophet of God embraced him, and held him for a long moment. Then a most startling thing occurred. Still holding him, in a very soft voice President Andrews said, "I love you."

Samuel was stunned, and unable to reply. What had rendered him to silence was that the words were true in the most literal sense, and spoke the feeling of that wonderful man, and every other who had participated on both sides of the veil. It was more than a confession of brotherly love; it was the outcry of a thousand righteous participants who had awaited this momentous time since the plan was first laid millennia ago. Now, at this precious moment of fulfillment, their joy could be summed in those simple words. "I love you." This was the essence of the great jubilation which Samuel could feel, but not hear.

A few moments passed as Samuel brushed away tears from his eyes. President Andrews took several steps back and sat upon the edge of his desk. He smiled gently as he waited for Samuel to regain his composure. When that moment came Samuel expected something other than what next occurred. The Prophet looked him square in the eye and said, "Now, what was it you wanted to ask me."

For just a moment Samuel had no reply, for he had no conscious memory of wanting to ask him anything. Yet, as the prophet quietly waited, a host of questions came to his mind. It wasn't until this very second in time that Samuel realized he yearned for answers; not answers to justify or underpin his faith, but answers to ease his soul.

"When I was called to be bishop," Samuel began, "I had a wonderful spiritual experience wherein I met the former bishop in a heavenly apparition. He gave me certain instructions which I followed." Samuel paused here to formulate the exact question but never got that far.

"So," President Andrews inserted into that brief silence, "if this were truly a heavenly experience, and you were being obedient, why were you drummed out of office, so to speak, and subjected to all the pain and embarrassment that followed? Is that your question?"

"In a nutshell," Samuel replied.

The Prophet placed a kind hand on Samuel's arm. "It is interesting that this is the very question most people in your position ask me. Does that give you any clues?"

"That this happens to almost everyone?" Samuel asked incredulously.

"Not almost. Something much like this happens to *everyone*."

"But, why? It just doesn't seem like the way the Lord's Church should operate," Samuel objected, a small bit of passion flavoring his voice.

"In fact, it is exactly as it should be. Everyone who seeks the highest of blessings must pay the highest of prices to obtain them. One of the ensuing tests must include the opportunity to apostatize. Further than that, the motivation to apostatize must be justifiable. In other words, some great injustice or offense must be the driving cause of the spirit of apostasy. How else can such an offense come but from within the Church you know to be true?

"If you examine church history from the time of Christ onward, and probably back to Adam, you will find accounts of many rising above apostasy, and many falling. The offense, either real or imagined, nearly always originates with someone in authority over them. Look at Joseph Smith. Though he was innocent of the charges leveled against him at the time, he was accused of being a false prophet. His decisions and actions to protect himself rang like lead in the ears of his accusers. Imagine being excommunicated from high office while you were certain your accusations were invalid. It would be a terrible test.

"I'm grateful to understand all this," Samuel replied humbly.

The Prophet was not finished. "Do you remember the incident with Brigham Young and Joseph Smith?"

"Not very well," Samuel admitted.

"It was during a session of the School of the Prophets. All the leaders and dignitaries of the Church were present. Without warning Brother Joseph stood and began to accuse and verbally chastise Brigham. This went on for many minutes. Every accusation was false, and yet, only Brigham knew it. Everyone present believed him guilty because they trusted Joseph.

"When the tirade ended, Brigham stood. Everyone thought he would storm from the room. Instead, that great man bowed his head and with tears in his eyes, begged Joseph for forgiveness. Mind you, he was begging forgiveness for sins he had not committed. He finally asked, "Joseph, what would you have me do?"

"Joseph walked to him slowly and embraced him. He said 'Thank God Brigham, you have passed the test.' It was merely a test! In that era, many others were similarly tested. Heber C. Kimball was asked by the prophet to give him his wife to be Joseph's second wife. Brother Kimball struggled over this for days, and finally led his wife, whom he dearly loved, by the hand and presented her to the Prophet. Brother Joseph embraced him and thanked God that they had also passed. Many there were who did not survive such tests, but apostatized. The list of names who passed is famous in our ears, and the list who did not, infamous. You are in very good company, Brother Samuel," he concluded.

"Thank you for explaining that to me," Samuel said, his mind reeling a bit. It was true. It made sense. It was still amazing. "May I ask one more thing?"

"Please do."

"Was every part of my life orchestrated to bring me these blessings? Or, did I just happen to walk down this path?"

"It was all planned," President Andrews said, a wry look on his face.

"By whom?" Samuel asked.

"Why, by yourself!" he replied with a chuckle, almost as if everyone but Samuel knew the answer.

"You know, that's exactly what I thought," Samuel said. "Knowing me as I do, I would probably do something like this to myself. I'm the only one who could have planned such trials and have them be perfectly just and not infringe upon my agency. But, hearing you say it, President, solidifies what was before just a matter of faith."

"Oh yes, we certainly planned our lives," the Prophet explained. "Of course, we did it under divine influence, and with an eye upon the promised rewards. I'm certain that Father and our Elder Brother consulted with us carefully, and inspired us in our decisions. Hands were laid on our heads to foreordain us to each a grand mission. And because we planned the events of our lives, our agency was not violated; we were acting in our own behalf."

Samuel nodded and his eyes filled with tears of spiritual confirmation. President Andrews continued, "Just as in this life, some of us there were more ambitions in our planning than others. Perhaps, ambitious is the wrong word. Some of us knew what joy service could bring, and in making our plans we spared ourselves no pain to reach the greatest blessings in mortality. Along with beloved companions, parents, children, and dear friends, some of us plotted a course designed to school us very well, which would spare no trial, and bring about the full promises of the Father. You, Samuel, were one of those."

"I wonder what I was hoping to overcome?" Samuel asked, mostly to himself.

"Pride," the Prophet replied gently. "Your greatest liability was your pride. Every trial you endured, from those of your mission, to the loss of your wife, to your financial ruin, to being reduced to poverty and working as a janitor, was all to deal with your pride."

Samuel nodded in recognition. "It's true," he said. "It took me years and years to understand that. I was never disdainful of others, but I had a far worse form of pride. I just thought my worth was because of what I had, what I possessed, what I did, rather than who I was in Christ. When I had all that money, I measured my self-worth by it. When I wrote beautiful music, I measured myself by it. When I had a beautiful wife, I measured my own beauty by hers. Even worse, when I was the bishop, I was certain I had found my true value to the kingdom."

He glanced at Helaman, who was enjoying this confession immensely. "It wasn't until all that was stripped away," Sam continued, "and I had absolutely nothing, was poverty stricken and broken-hearted, that I was able to come to know what my worth truly is. When I was reduced to nothing in every worldly sense, that was when my blessings were the sweetest. When I found that Heavenly Father loved me without all those things, then I came to know who I am, and where my worth truly lies. I had to come to know what a truly broken heart and a contrite spirit is through grueling lessons of adversity. But it was then that I learned what joy is! It was a horrific lesson for me, but I am eternally grateful I learned it."

Samuel voice shook as he continued. "Grateful is such a small word! What I mean is that my soul rejoices night and day, and I shout praises unto God regularly for these great gifts of His grace unto me—the lowest of all men! These words and a thousand others that require the Tongue of Angels to express, are the burden of my joy!"

President Andrews stood and clapped Samuel on both shoulders, then turned and embraced Helaman. They held one another for a moment longer, and then stepped apart. Helaman nodded to Samuel, and they vanished from the Prophet's presence in a silent flash of light.

It was already turning spring, and the project was nearly back on schedule before Vladimir interrupted Samuel one afternoon. He unexpectedly strode into his office and pulled a chair up to where he could watch Samuel's drawings quickly take form on the computer screen.

"It almost seems like magic," Vladimir commented. "American technology is so advanced to Russian computers. I think if the old government knew you had this, it would be taken away by the KGB long ago." He laughed in his characteristically hearty voice.

"Probably," Samuel agreed. "Is there something I can do for you?" he asked, turning his attention away from the screen.

"It is a question which is wanting me to ask you," he said. "Why are you so much different from the others who say they are Christians and get drunk and go whoring? You say nothing of your religion, but you are more Christian than all of them. I know of the Mormons, and think they are not pushy like some American religions. Those others are very aggressive in proselytizing us poor lost Russians," he said sarcastically with a sad voice and bowed head. "But, if you have the Christian virtues, then why do you not pound your fists upon our heads to awaken us from deep sleep of darkness? Why are you not like the others?" he asked intently in a near-shout.

Samuel got up from his desk and moved to the armchair to answer him. "I suppose I'm different because I know it isn't I who bears the gospel to the Russian people, but the Holy Spirit. Therefore I wait upon the Spirit to lead. So far, it has led nowhere, and I have kept my silence."

"I like this saying," Vladimir said heartily. "I also have a faith in the Holy Spirit of Jesus Christ, and I wait upon His words to lead me."

"You don't really go into town and get drunk nearly every night, do you?" Sam asked.

"Ah, you are wise too. No, I don't even go into town. My village is but a short drive away. I go home to my wife and children. It was just easier to let the Americans think I am typical Russian drunk," he said with an ironic laugh that came out a little forced. "That way they feel superior, and tell me many secrets which they do not know they say," he said, wagging a finger in the air.

"Someday I would like to meet your family," Samuel said warmly.

"I will take you, then. I told you I have read somewhat of the Mormon American religion. I don't want to know more because it is a false religion for Russians. I think it could be true enough for Americans who have motorcars and TV in the bedroom. However, I think you are an honest man, and I would ask you if you might want to know what I am believing."

"I would like to know what you believe," Sam said, his heart resonating suddenly with the Holy Spirit.

"Would you be welcome to come to dinner with my family this tonight? We will have small meeting for our religion after eating. I will translate for you, and you will learn a little about what is true Russian religion," he said proudly, yet sincerely.

"I would like that. What do your people call your church?" he asked sincerely.

"We do not call ourselves a church. We say to one another that we are the "Children of Christ."

"Who started your religion?" Samuel asked, quite interested now.

"Jesus Christ, of course," he replied. "But, I will let you learn this for yourself tonight. Will you like to drive your Honda car?" he asked hopefully. Vladimir's was a Russian-made vehicle that looked and drove like an army tank. The Honda at least had a heater that worked. Samuel heartily agreed.

Vladimir's village was not much more than a cluster of wooden buildings surrounded by a single dirt road. The buildings were built side-to-side in a cluster, with a dirt road circling completely around them. Samuel felt as if he had walked into a dream. He recognized it as the cluster of buildings Islana had shown him in vision.

Vladimir directed Samuel to drive to an unpainted and weather-beaten building that appeared to be at least three smaller homes joined together. They parked and walked to the door. As they approached, Vladimir grew increasingly uncertain, until he stopped near the stoop and turned back to Samuel.

"I am concerned that the elders may not like that I brought you here. I was not able to call since they have not a telephone. I hope you will not be offended if they do not let you in. It is not up to me."

"I won't be offended," Samuel assured him, and they proceeded to the door. Vladimir knocked twice, and waited. Shortly a young woman opened the door, glanced at Samuel, said something in Russian, and closed the door again. A moment later a gray-haired man appeared and held a conversation with Vladimir which quickly turned hostile. Understanding perfectly, Samuel knew that the old fellow did not appreciate him being there. Finally Vladimir turned to Samuel.

"He insists I ask you why you are here."

"To learn," Samuel replied simply after being nudged by the Spirit. Vladimir relayed his answer, and the old man stepped aside for them to enter.

The room inside was much larger than it appeared from the outside. Apparently some of the interior walls of the houses had been removed to make a fairly large hall. Inside were rows of wooden tables and wooden benches. Samuel estimated they could seat nearly a hundred adults and almost that many children at a collection of smaller tables to his left. The room had wooden floors, papered walls, and no coverings on the floor. The ceiling was plaster with chunks missing. Yet, the room was tidy and warm. People were arriving in a steady stream. Everyone took note of Samuel's presence, and many sought out the same old man with questions, and obvious objections. Each time they finally deferred to the older gentleman's words.

Vladimir finally approached Samuel and with an apologetic look, showed him to one of the children's tables. "You will sit here please," he said, motioning to a small wooden chair half the size of the others in the room. "I apologize for the rudeness. Please endure until I can straighten it out."

"Don't become concerned," Samuel told him. I will be fine." He took a seat at the end of the little table.

There were already children sitting at the table, and they eyed him openly. Directly to his left sat a little girl in a pale yellow dress with faded yellow roses. She was about six, and as cute as any child could be. Her dark hair was pulled back and braided. Her face sparkled with innocence. She sat primly on her little bench, staring at him in open curiosity.

Presently everyone was seated, and the old man stood at the head of the center table. Everyone bowed their heads, and he said a prayer—a blessing on the food, Sam interpreted. As soon as the old man concluded, a murmur of conversation fell over the room. Almost immediately a small army of teenage boys and girls began bringing in kettles of stew. The boys carried the kettles, and the girls ladled the stew. Each person also got a thick slice of nearly-black bread.

When they went past Sam they ladled him a child's portion, and left a half slice of bread on his plate. He ate carefully, enjoying the denseness of the bread and its pungent flavors. It tasted somewhat like pumpernickel, and had a hint of dill and garlic. The stew was salty, mostly potatoes and carrots in a thin broth. He was glad to have only a small plate of it, and had to force himself to eat it all. There was almost no meat in it, which was a plus to his thinking.

After dinner the same army of teens whisked away the dishes. Samuel was watching the front of the room as the old man stood. He had a look of consternation on his face, and it seemed aimed at Samuel. At that very moment the little girl next to him stood and hopped onto Samuel's lap. She sat on his left leg, with both her legs across his right, then laid her head against his chest. She squirmed into a comfortable position, and grew still. She periodically looked up into his face. Samuel felt his heart swelling with love, and looked down at his new little friend. He brushed a rich brown strand of hair from her face. He wanted to speak to her, but had to continue feigning a language barrier.

All this did not go unnoticed by the aged leader of their group. Seeing his granddaughter in the stranger's lap softened his heart, and he made a decision. He turned to Vladimir and said something quietly. Vladimir also stood, and began to translate. The old gentleman interrupted himself periodically to allow Vladimir to catch up.

"Tonight," the old man said through Vladimir's translation, "we have gathered together as is our custom, to eat our evening meal, and to teach and pray. For generations we have done this, many years in fear for our lives; but we have endured, and today we worship with little fear.

A little smattering of clapping interrupted his speech, then he continued. "This evening I was prepared to hand the time to Alex, my son, yet I feel impressed to tell the history of our people instead." As soon as he said this a murmur of dissent arose. He waited until it died down, and continued without comment. "We have a guest tonight, and he is unaware of our history. He says he is here to learn, so let us teach him what we can. Perhaps it will be enough to save his soul. It is an exceedingly rare thing that we ever speak to outsiders of our beliefs. To my knowledge, this is the first time it has occurred in my lifetime.

"Our history begins with our ancestors making a long journey to escape captivity. Our records say they came from the ancient city of Jerusalem at the time of its Babylonian conquest. In time they escaped from the Babylonians, or rather, were let go. The holy record describes in rich detail their travels of many years to find a new homeland. They were led by Holy men of God, who would not suffer them to return to Jerusalem, but took them to a new land then unpopulated.

"Their prophets heard the words of the Lord, and wrote them down. They taught them to the people every evening, much as we do yet. Except that now, the words of the holy books they wrote for us are obscure in an ancient language, and only a small portion of its words are known to us today. We know they came to a land of lush summers, and terrible winters, and knowing the land undesirable to any others, were instructed of the Lord to settle here. They flourished, and became a great people, and forgot their heritage.

"Generations passed until a godless people rose up from among them and conquered almost every other nation of this continent. Once again our people found ourselves in bondage, and persecuted for our faith. However, the persecution made us stronger, and we grew in our faith."

At that, many in the congregation nodded resolutely. The old man continued, "All this time we have had the ancient prophecies that no other people on earth possess. God saw fit to give unto us this ancient book to guide us through these dark times. But, with our own apostasy, we have forgotten the old language, and cannot read those precious words. As you all know, what we have today to guide us is an oral history preserved in living memory of what our dear prophets taught and wrote for us. These memories we have written down, which we study each evening together. The rest of the sacred words await a date when God shall again send a seer among us to restore the words we cannot read. Until then, we believe, and we wait."

Samuel listened to all this with a growing sense of wonder. As the old man spoke, his heart burned brighter and brighter with the Holy Spirit until he felt consumed. The history continued.

"Because of the persecutions, thousands of us were sent to prison in this very city. Thousands more died from the forced labors, and still we grew stronger in our faith. When the last of the Korean brothers were killed by our captors, we felt sure we were next, and we rejoiced in our pending deliverance. However, when they saw our calmness, and the peacefulness with which we faced death, they stopped slaughtering us before they were done, and those remaining returned to our homes. Ever since we have labored in their factories, and served in their government, and done their bidding for barely enough food and shelter to stay alive. And still, our faith has grown."

The congregation nodded at one another in agreement, and then turned their attention back to their leader. "Now that our captors have lost interest in persecuting us, we have become a relatively free people, and we cautiously experiment with our freedom. Our faith continues to grow, for we refuse to forget the terrible price we have paid to come this far. Yet, as the holy books say, we must not stand idle, for when the cry goes forth 'peace and safety upon the land, do not be deceived, for the work of destruction is a breath away, and you will flee again to escape destruction, and the peace of Zion shall be your reward. Then in that day will I come to wipe away your tears, and dry your eyes, and heal your wounds. And, I will be your God, and you will be my people.'" he quoted, his eyes closed in reverence.

He waited a long moment before continuing. "So, in keeping with our custom, I invite any who would speak to stand, and address us." So saying, he sat back down.

No sooner had he done so than Samuel felt himself propelled to his feet. He gently set the little girl on her feet, and looked around the room. All eyes were upon him. Vladimir approached him, shaking his head.

"It is not allowed for you to speak," Vladimir said in a whisper, motioning with both hands for him to sit. "Please to sit down, and not make an embarrassment for us," he pleaded. But the power of the Holy Spirit was upon Samuel, and he could not have sat back down to save his life.

Though speaking to Vladimir, Samuel's eyes were upon their aged leader. "I must speak. What I have to say is of great importance to your people. If you judge otherwise, I will leave you, and never return." Vladimir translated this for the old man. A storm of protest erupted around the room. After listening to every objection, the old man stood.

"Words are not our enemies," Vladimir translated, "truth comes in different clothing at times. The stranger may speak."

Samuel walked to the front of the room and stood near their old leader. He cleared his throat, not knowing what he would say, yet knowing he must deliver a message they needed to hear. Almost a full minute ground by slowly as those in the room grew increasingly more curious. When he finally knew what the Lord desired of him, he spoke softly, yet with conviction.

"I am here by invitation, a stranger among you, yet one who has come a long distance to stand here. I have heard your history, and felt the pullings of the Holy Spirit as you spoke. You know who you were, and where you came from. I am here to tell you who I know you are, and where you are going. You are of the house of Israel, of the priestly tribe of Levi. The time is upon you for your return to Zion, and the reception of your blessings at the hands of Ephraim."

As soon as his words were translated, pandemonium broke out. Men flew to their feet crying out, shaking their fists at him. Some were so angry that spittle was flying from their lips as they cursed. Some women were weeping openly. Many faces displayed a look of relief and joy, while others were a reflection of fear and dread. Samuel could not make sense of it all, and contented himself to know that he had delivered the message the Lord desired.

Vladimir grabbed him by the arm and hurried him outdoors. He returned inside to retrieve their coats, and then hurried him to the Honda. "You cannot understand the great uproar your words created," he proclaimed. "But I think it wisdom to leave. Perhaps this is best? Yes?" he asked. Samuel obliged, and they quickly departed.

It was nearly a month later before Vladimir spoke of anything more than their work. He came into Samuel's office and sat nearby once again. Samuel turned his attention to the Russian. "What is it, Vladimir?"

"I have most difficult to understand news. My uncle, the old gentleman who leads us, has requested you should come back to address us again this tonight. I do not understand, for your words have caused a crisis among us, with many crying out against you. However, calm has come upon us, and they wish you to now returning. If you are as much willing, I will take with you this tonight, together."

"I will come," Samuel said. It was what he had been hoping, and gladness filled his heart.

The attitude inside the big hall was very different this time. They gave him a seat near Vladimir at the head table, and brought him an adult-sized plate of steamed cabbage and rice. He forced himself to eat all of it. It was actually quite good, but he was growing unaccustomed to eating, and found it a nuisance, and the resulting feeling of fullness unsettling, if not uncomfortable.

As soon as the meal was completed the old man stood. Once again Vladimir translated.

"One month ago this stranger who calls himself Samuel came uninvited into our lives. Many of us were angry, and cried out against him. However, he spoke to us, and I permitted it because I felt the turnings of the Holy Spirit of Jesus Christ working inside me. I have searched the holy writings of our prophets and found the words I remembered. Let me read the translation of them in our own language. As you know, we do not understand all because we have lost the use of the old script, and must rely upon later writings in our own tongue. These are the words." He pulled a pair of reading glasses from his shirt pocket, and opened a very old, hand-written manuscript close to his face. Everyone in the room waited patiently, reverently.

"Behold, I am a stranger among you, yet one who has come a long distance to stand among you. I know your history, and I am familiar with the Spirit among you. You know what you were and from where you came. I am here to tell you who I know you are and where you must go. You are of the house of Israel, of the priestly tribe of Levi. The time is fully come for your return to Zion, and the reception of your blessings at the hands of Ephraim. I have come to lead you home." With the exception of the last sentence, it was word for word of Samuel's extemporaneous statement a month ago.

The old man closed the book slowly, a look of solemnity upon his face. The room was heavy with silence. Samuel waited for his next words with anticipation. "As you recall, the stranger, Samuel, spoke these very words to us. These are the prophesied words "the one sent by God" was to say to us that we might recognize him. The sign is given. Samuel is the one to lead us to the lands of our freedom, to receive our blessings at the hands of Ephraim, to the temple of God that we may once again officiate in the office of our birthright. There we will build a great city to our God, and worship in His temples. There we will await His coming in glory."

The entire room was transfixed as the words were spoken. "I do not know all of what this means, or how it will come to pass, but the time is now fulfilled, and we will be going home at long last." This he said with great emotion. Men and women alike began to weep for fear mingled with joy, for they sensed that many of them would not survive the long trip home.

At that very moment of great emotion, a young man frantically burst into the room, his face flushed with fear. "We are going to war!" he cried with a loud voice. "Our country and China are joining forces, and gathering armies to fight against the world! A general conscription has been ordered. Every female between eighteen and forty who has no children, and every male between fourteen and fifty is ordered to report to active duty—on penalty of death!"

13

DAY OF MIRACLES

Melody could not make her restless heart sleep on the plane. By the time she touched down in England she was so nervous she could hardly think. She let Helaman find her a hotel and get them settled in. Of course, since he lived in England, he returned to his own house for the night, but promised to check on her tomorrow, at which time he would escort her and Sammy to her sons.

Though it had been a dozen years, her former husband was still pastor of the same little church. He and his new wife still lived in the small brick home she had occupied so many years ago. It was evening when she knocked on the heavy door to the cottage. A moment later it creaked open, a boy about eight years old smiled up at her.

"Is Pastor Tennison at home?" she asked him. He nodded enthusiastically, and scurried away without closing the door. She could hear muffled words, and heavy footsteps that rang familiar tones in her ears.

"Hello, how can I help…" the pastor's voice trailed off, and his smile dropped. "Melody," he said, as if speaking the name of a dead person. He seemed stunned, but recovered quickly. A small smile returned to his face, and she was surprised to feel it was sincere. "Melody, how very unexpected to see you at my door. Won't you come in?"

"I would like that," she said, and walked awkwardly into the familiar rooms. Very little had changed. She met his wife, a heavy-set woman named Anna. She seemed perfectly happy with her life, and hurried back to her tiny kitchen after they had been introduced.

"Tell me all about yourself," Theodore insisted as soon as they were alone. Melody took the seat he indicated, and tried to relax. "Where did you go after you left England?" he asked a little too enthusiastically.

"To Utah, actually," she said.

"How perfect for you," he replied smoothly. "Have you remarried? Do you have children?"

"I have remarried,"

"Splendid! Did he come to England with you?"

"No, he's away on business overseas," she said a bit guardedly. She surely did wish Sam were with her at this moment.

"So, children? Any more little ones?"

“I have one son who was born in America. His name is Samuel, named after my husband,” she said.

“I see. Named after your husband? I was perhaps mistaken in my impression that you were pregnant when you left England? But you named your son after his father,” he interpreted, somewhat incorrectly. She saw it as divine intervention and made no effort to correct him.

“You know I wouldn’t get pregnant by someone I wasn’t married to, and he is named after my husband.”

“Of course, so rude of me to even ask. Forgive me. May I ask what brings you to England, and to my door? Not that I’m unhappy to see you after all these years, but I am curious a bit, you know.”

“I’m sure you are. I have a friend who lives in England, and he contacted me with the news that George Alexander is in trouble. I had been wanting to return to England to visit anyway, and this seemed an opportune time.” She paused for a moment and looked intently at him. “How is George?”

Pastor Tennison stood and walked to the opposite side of the small living room. He leaned against the rock hearth of the fireplace and seemed to contemplate his answer. “I honestly don’t know,” he replied.

“How could that be?” Melody demanded in as even a voice as she could.

Theodore sighed and looked away. “He left home months ago, and hasn’t contacted me. I have tried to find him, and failed. He is almost twenty years old, an adult now, and I have put him out of my mind.” His voice seemed disappointed as he spoke. “However,” he said more brightly. “Theodore is due home any moment. He’s just enrolled for his second year at the seminary. He’ll be most surprised to see you.”

Melody got the clear impression that Theodore was the pride of his father’s life, and George was a great disappointment for him.

As if on cue she heard heavy footsteps outside, and Theodore Sr. pulled open the door with a smile. “Good evening son! We have a special visitor.” Her son stepped into the room, his head almost brushing the top of the doorway. He had her blond hair, and his father’s dark eyes. He was taller than Melody by a full head, and she immediately thought him handsome. It took every ounce of her strength to restrain herself from rushing into his arms.

“Son, this is Melody, your mother,” he said, pointing toward her with an open hand.

“My mother?” he asked. His voice was deep and clear. It was more than she could endure, and with a strangled cry, she rushed to him, wrapping her arms around his broad chest. As she wept, he stood there unsure what to do with his arms.

"Oh, Theodore! I have missed you so. I'm so sorry I had to leave. So sorry," she said between sobs.

"Mother?" he said again, his voice growing cold.

Melody's words tumbled out. "Oh, son, you don't know how awful it was to leave you. I have thought of you every day since, and wanted so badly to see you."

"So, you are my mother . . . my mother. Well, if you are my mother, why have you suddenly decided to come back after all these years?" he asked, still not returning her embrace. "You have no idea how many nights I cried the whole night through, begging God to send you back to me. The only way I could survive you leaving was to hate you. I'm sorry, Melody, but you aren't my mother. My mother wouldn't just walk away and leave me!"

"Oh, Theodore," she cried. "Oh my precious baby. I didn't leave you, I was thrown out. Don't you remember. Don't you remember the fights, and the hitting, and the police? Don't you remember?"

"There was nothing of the sort," the older Theodore said calmly, forcing himself into the exchange. "You left us for another man and went to America with him. You weren't thrown out, you abandoned us. Now, if you are going to lie, you must leave. We took our leave of you years ago, and we'll not have you come back to wound delicate feelings again. See here? There's the door," he said firmly, though not loudly, pointing at the door.

Melody looked from father to son, each with a frown on their face. "Son, you were eight years old at the time; surely you remember! Don't you remember coming to my sister's house, and the police coming to take you and George away? Don't you remember my cries, my screams, my fighting the police and almost being taken to jail for hitting them?" she cried, her voice nearly hysterical with renewed loss.

The pastor's voice remained calm. "He remembers no such thing, because there was no such event. Now, you have overstayed your welcome. Go back to America. Go back to your Mormon man and his dozen wives—or however many he has."

"Please, Theodore, please remember! I'm not here to hurt you, I just want to tell you I have loved you all these years, and I want to see you again. Please don't throw me out of your life. Your father threw me out once; don't you repeat his mistake," she begged through tears. "Please!"

"Leave! Now! Or I will call the police again! Do you understand me?" Theodore bellowed at her, his calm demeanor evaporating.

"Again?" the younger Theodore asked, turning suddenly toward his father. "You will call the police *again*, Papa?"

His father was flushed with anger. "It is only a figure of speech, son. Now, leave here at once." Theodore briskly took Melody's elbow and escorted her toward the door.

"Why didn't you write?" her son called after them.

"I did!" Melody cried as she whirled around. "I wrote every day for months, then every week, and then every month for years."

"I never received a single letter!" the young man retorted accusingly, his eyes misting with tears.

"Here!" Melody cried as she began digging in a big bag she was carrying. She pulled out a handful of letters with blue and red striped edges. "Here are your letters—take them!" she pleaded as she held them out to him. When he did not move, she dropped them at his feet and pulled out more from her bag, then more, until the floor around him was covered with letters. "There are letters, birthday cards, Christmas cards, silly cards, photos of me and Sammy. There are even more at home, I couldn't bring them all. Look at them, they are all marked RETURN TO SENDER, or REFUSED."

"But…" her son whispered in shock.

"Anna! Anna, call the police!" the pastor shrieked through the house at his wife in the kitchen.

"I have to go," Melody told her son. He let her place a hand on his cheek. She brushed away his tear with her thumb. "I'm staying at the Centre Street hotel. I'm sorry this is the only tear I've been here to wipe away. I have to go. I love you," she said, and strode quickly away.

Melody, Sammy and Helaman spent the remainder of the day searching for George, her nineteen-year old son. The closest they got to him was to find the missionaries who had been teaching him. They said he missed his last appointment, and had not rescheduled. They weren't sure where he lived, but they promised to call the hotel if her son contacted them.

Melody spent the next few days visiting old friends and showing Sammy a little of England. It was late on the day before their departure from England when they heard a gentle knock on the hotel room door.

Melody pulled it open to find her son Theodore standing there. She blinked twice, then lovingly opened her arms to him. This time he held her, and breathed deep breaths to keep from sobbing. Finally, she released him and pulled him into the small room.

"Theodore, I want you to meet your brother, Sammy. Sammy, this is your big brother, Theodore."

"Wow!" Sammy said, and pumped his big brother's hand enthusiastically. "Are you really my big brother?" he asked happily.

"I sure am, Champ. I go by Theo now." He pronounced it Tay-oh.

"Okay! I like to be called *Sam*," he said importantly. Then his native conversation skills went into high gear. "Do you like it here in England? Do you have sports here? I play sports, even though I'm not too good, I guess. Do you play stuff like football?"

"American football?" Theo asked.

"Yeah, what other kind is there?"

"I do like it, but I like soccer too. That's what we call football in England."

"Hey, that's cool! I play soccer! I'm going to be on a team next spring. Are you good?"

Theo smiled. "I used to be on the college team. Perhaps we can go bump a ball around some time," he suggested.

"That'd be great!" Sammy said. "Wow, my big brother is a famous college soccer player from England! All the famous soccer players are from England—or somewhere," he proclaimed.

"Not famous, Sam. But, I'll show you some tricks, and you'll be famous instead, OK?"

"Yeah! I can't wait!" he cried happily. Theo ruffled his hair, and straightened to look at his mother. She was beaming so happily that he felt his own eyes cloud with tears. He blinked them away.

"I read the letters," Theo told her simply.

"All of them?"

"Every single one. I cried a lot. I laughed a lot. I was mostly angry."

"I'm sorry you feel angry at me. I …"

"No! No, not angry at you," he interrupted her. "Angry at Papa. Every one of those letters came to our home, and he sent them all back. I still don't understand why he didn't just burn them. They all have English stamps over the American ones and RETURN TO SENDER, written all over them. Why would he do that?"

"Because he knew each letter that came back was like a sword going through my heart. It was his way of reminding me that he had you boys, and I would never…" she let her voice trail off. "Let's just say that it was the way he was at the time."

Theo shook his head. “That’s far more charitable than what he said about you all these years. And, infinitely more charitable than what I said to him this morning,” he said emphatically.

“I hope you weren’t mean to him,” Melody said gently.

“Why would you care? I would think we owe him some meanness.”

“No, no Theodore. Don’t stoop to meanness. That’s what drove me out of his life. Don’t make the same mistakes he made.”

“You really are my mother, aren’t you,” Theo said quietly, his voice rich with emotion.

“I am,” she said slowly. Her eyes were tender. “I’m so sorry I wasn’t there to raise you. Did you have a good childhood?” She really wanted to know. She realized it was an odd question for a mother to ask, but it was something only he could answer.

“I think so,” Theo said a little more kindly. “Papa was strict, but he raised us to be good. I was happy, but I think George never got done being angry that you left.”

“But, I didn’t leave.”

“I know, Mama,” he said. Hearing him call her Mama again sounded so good to her that her eyes misted with another wave of tears. He laughed, pulled a handkerchief from his jacket, and wiped them away. “No more tears now. I’m not going to let you leave me again. Let’s get that settled here and now. I know you didn’t leave me on your own. I had to think a long time, but I do remember Papa beating you, and driving you out. I remember the police, and screaming as they pulled us out of that apartment. I remember you fighting the police, and my wondering why you didn’t stop them from taking us.”

“It was an awful time, now long past,” she soothed.

“I know, mother. But, even after reading your letters it took me a couple days to remember. Papa had told us the story another way so many times that I actually remembered it the way he said. It wasn’t until I read your account of that day in one of your letters, that I began to remember.”

“I’m so sorry…” she began.

“You need to quit saying that. It’s not your fault. Quit apologizing for something that was beyond your control. Let’s just move on with our lives.”

“That’s good counsel,” she admitted. “I’m just sorry… I mean, I just regret this chapter of my life more than any other. I have thought about you boys constantly, and longed to be with you. But I thought it was useless to try to get you back. Now, I’m not prepared for how big you’ve become, and how handsome!” she exclaimed.

"Spoken like a true mother," Theo proclaimed happily. "There's something else. You remember Uncle Tennison?"

"Yes, certainly," Melody said guardedly.

"Well, I remember great-uncle Tennison saying awful things about you after you left. I know Papa spoke to him after you left, and I know for a fact that Uncle Tennison is petitioning the court today to have little Sammy here DNA tested, and to have you deported! It is going to be ugly again," he concluded sadly.

Melody thought about this for a moment. "I have tickets to go back to America tomorrow evening. Your father won't have time to do anything that soon. The thing that really concerns me is that I only have today to find George. I'm worried about him. I was told he's living on the street."

"Surely not!" Theo protested. "Papa says he's sending George money every week. He constantly complains about still having to support him."

Melody shook her head. "Your father told me he hadn't been in contact with George and doesn't know where he is. Both statements can't be true. I was told by someone I trust that he's destitute and living on the street. Will you help me find him?"

"Certainly!" Theo cried, jumping to his feet. I know a few places to try. Can we begin right away? I have a car downstairs."

"I'm ready," she said.

Theo turned to his brother. "Come on Sam, the game's afoot!"

"Cool!" Sammy cried, and grabbed his coat.

They hurried through the small lobby to observe traffic inexplicably at a standstill outside the small hotel. What should have been a melee of swirling traffic, screeching tires and blaring horns was an eerie scene of almost total silence. The people seemed to be sitting in their cars stunned to immobility.

"What's news, chum?" Theo asked the first man who hurried passed on the sidewalk. He looked up as if in a daze of disbelief.

"The Russies are invading Europe! They're in cahoots with the Chinee'!" he said in a stunned voice. "The whole bleedin' world's goin' te war!"

With the news of war, the pandemonium in the community hall grew so all-consuming that Vladimir quit interpreting for Samuel, and joined into the shouting. Samuel had no choice but to wait for Vladimir to begin translating again. All he really knew was that the Soviets expected every able-bodied man and woman to report to active duty, immediately. The news of the war was disturbing enough, but the fact that Russia was drafting everyone with two legs made their situation grim if they did not comply.

Samuel longed to be able to switch on CNN and learn what was going on, but had no such luxury to indulge in. He only knew that the events of the last days had just jumped from a holding pattern, to a terrible war destined to eventually end in the death of as many as two-thirds of mankind.

At the center of all this shouting was the old man whom they revered as their spiritual leader. Though Samuel had never asked, he knew his name was Alexei. He was Islana's uncle. It was Islana who had come to him, and given him her intimate knowledge of their lives. Islana was Vladimir's oldest sister. One day, Samuel would tell them about meeting her, but for now, they had more than they could assimilate as it was.

Finally some order was restored, and they fractured into small groups, still arguing among themselves. It was then that Alexei came to Samuel. Vladimir translated for them.

"Did you hear the news?" he wanted to know.

"I did. It is not good."

"It is a desperate time. The prophecies speak of a terrible war at the time of our departure from this land. But we could not have known it would be so soon."

"What will you do?" Samuel asked, trying to keep his questions short to facilitate translation.

"That is an odd question from you," the old man said.

"Why?"

"Because it is you who will lead us away to our new home in Zion."

"Do you believe this?" Samuel asked him pointedly.

"You know I do," he replied, then said, "We must leave immediately. What shall we do to prepare?"

As if a window had suddenly opened in his soul, a burst of understanding flooded into Samuel's mind so vivid it included details, visual images and sounds. He had, in reality, seen in vision the answer to their question. Seconds before he knew nothing of this mission; now, having been asked by those he was to assist, he knew the answer.

"You have stored food," he said. It was not a question.

"Some."

"Gather the people. They must prepare all through the night. Collect everything necessary for the trip. We will leave no one behind who wishes to come. Bring nothing but food, clothing, bedding, and necessary items. If you have any livestock or dogs, bring them. Other pets stay behind. Leave all else here. We will not take weapons of any kind. We will not take furniture or other possessions. We meet at first light tomorrow outside this building. This is what you must do," he said.

Alexei seemed energized by Samuel's words, and immediately turned toward the others in the room. He began shouting orders as people began running in various directions to begin their preparations.

The following day's first light found a long line of people assembled outside. Samuel estimated there to be upwards of 2500 people of all ages. Under Alexei's direction, several dozen men began at the near end, and inspected every parcel. Under their leader's direction they took toasters, VCR's, TV's, radios, pictures, portraits, jewelry, and a host of possessions—mostly worthless, some priceless—and set them beside the road. Among those things left behind was a Faberge egg of intricately wrought gold worth a king's ransom. They were not picked up again. Even stuffed animals and children's toys were abandoned.

By midday they were ready. They began loading into old trucks and cars; even a tractor was driven with a wagon behind it. People packed inside the vehicles until they were over-full. Samuel, Vladimir and Alexei climbed into the blue Honda, and Vladimir started the engine.

"Which way do we go?" Alexei asked. As if he had always known, Samuel answered with great certainty.

"East, then north to the sea," he said.

Alexei shouted the word from the car, and it passed quickly down the long rag-tag caravan. Vladimir gunned the engine and they pulled away, a long line of homeless refugees behind them.

Vehicles began breaking down almost from the start. However, the people proved adept at making them run on almost nothing. They came to the first small town an hour later. The owners of the tractor and trailer were not able to purchase fuel, and were obliged to leave their vehicle behind. The remaining vehicles became more crowded, and children began to cry for want of food and sleep. Just outside the city Alexei signaled them to make camp. They parked the vehicles off the road in a circle, and tents were pitched inside. The wind picked up, and it snowed for the first time that year. It was just September.

Samuel slept in the Honda, and was aware of Vladimir shivering in his sleep. Samuel was not cold, and he almost gave his friend his own thick down coat to put over the top of him. He did not. Anyone without a coat would have frozen to death in a short time. Samuel could not raise anyone's suspicions in such a way.

Morning was still just a gray smudge across the horizon when they were awakened by the honking of a horn. Samuel sat up and stretched. Vladimir struggled to make his stiff limbs move.

"What is going on?" Alexei asked from the back seat.

"Someone is honking a horn," Samuel said. They climbed from the car and found a young man jumping on the running board of one of their trucks, honking the horn and pointing down the road. They looked in the direction he was pointing to see a row of headlights heading toward them. It quickly became apparent they were military vehicles.

"What does it mean?" Alexei asked.

"They are definitely military. What do you think? Are they coming after us?" Vladimir asked.

"They were probably alerted by the townspeople of the last city," Alexei surmised. At this point a spotlight blazed to life, and flooded across their tattered convoy. The lead truck slowed, then sped ahead. After a moment a loud speaker blared.

"Identify yourselves," the voice boomed in Russian. "Be prepared to show your papers!" the voice called.

"We have no papers!" Vladimir said to Alexei urgently. "We are fleeing the country, and we'll all be considered traitors!"

"I know, I know," Alexei said. "We need help from God, and we need it now!" he said. He turned to Samuel. "What should we do?" he asked urgently.

Samuel bowed his head in a silent prayer. "Cheer!" he cried as he looked up, almost before the thought had materialized in his mind. "Cheer them, and curse the Western pigs. Quickly!"

"Pass the word, raise a hearty cheer," Alexei told Vladimir, then began spreading the word. In a few seconds a small cheer arose from a few voices, then was joined by many others. By the time the trucks roared to a halt the people were screaming and dancing up and down, their faces streaked with tears. The military men could not know they were tears of stark terror.

"Who is in charge?" he demanded over the speaker. "Come forward!"

Alexei trotted forward clapping his hands and thrusting his fist into the air. "I am leading this people," he said loudly. "Power to the union!" he cried.

"What?" The man asked, his voice booming across the snowy landscape. The speaker clicked off and he climbed from his truck. He walked toward Vladimir, his hand on his revolver. "What did you say?" he asked.

"Power to the Soviet people, and damn the Western pigs! We cheer you and our certain victory!" he cried enthusiastically.

"Well, yes," he stammered. "We will stomp them into the ground, and send them back to their filthy homeland."

"Yes!" the people cried. "Hurrah, Hurrah. Victory, victory, victory!" they chanted.

"We will destroy the Western pigs!" the soldier shouted triumphantly.

"Destroy them, destroy them, destroy them!" the chant came up.

"You people, where do you go?"

"To fight the war!" Alexei cried.

"All of you?" he asked incredulously.

"We all come to this glorious cause. Drive them out. We will drive them out!" he cried.

The people echoed. "Drive them out, drive them out, drive them out."

"Do you have travel papers?" he demanded.

"Our hearts are our travel papers. We travel to the aid of our country!" he shouted.

"You are true patriots. I wish you were younger, and I would take you with me and make you my general. You people, follow your leader, and he will bring you glory!"

"Glory, glory, glory!" they cried with one voice.

"Victory!" the soldier cried as he climbed back into his rig.

"Victory, victory, victory!" they screamed as he drove away.

As soon as the last taillight disappeared from view they fell to their knees as if on a signal, and voices that had seconds before cried for victory, now prayed for thanksgiving. They were delivered, and every soul knew it was a miracle.

"We can't remain here," Alexei suddenly said, his head jerking up from his prayers. "Our deception will not last for long. We must leave now! Signal the camp. We must travel cross-country from here. We will only take the farming roads. We depart in ten minutes!" he cried.

Melody's first thought was of Samuel when she heard the news that Russia was invading Europe. She immediately tried to dial his number in Russia, and after repeated attempts, was told by an operator with very poor English that the number had been disconnected. A moment of panic swept through her, then she concluded that it was in fact a good sign. They must have closed the office, and her beloved husband would be coming home. He might even be home already! She dialed her own home, and got nothing but prolonged ringing.

It was impossible to estimate how many Eastern Bloc citizens had died in the two weeks of invasion. The international uproar was tremendous and immediate. Every country on earth condemned the action in the most violent possible terms. Nations formerly friendly to Russia, including the U.S., withdrew all ties and unforgiving economic sanctions were slammed into place. NATO ponderously swung its dragon head toward their new enemy, and fire screamed from Russia in billowing threats of absolute destruction. The great Soviet bear stood on its borders and roared to shake the whole earth, and the world trembled.

International opinion confirmed the absoluteness of the Russian conquest, and the resulting sanctions and threats should have calmed the Russian blood-lust to which their invasion had given life. However, it seemed almost as if someone had shot an arrow into the great beast, only wounding it, and feeding its fierce anger to white-hot intensity. Feeling justified beyond discussion, Russia cut all diplomatic ties and communications in or out of Russia, throwing great clouds of dirt into the air in its rage. As the world watched in stark terror, Russia unleashed their arms build-up which mobilized its vast citizenry as never before. Their great, once-hidden military machine pushed their advanced weaponry forward at unmatchable speed.

While the world tried to respond in kind, the United States found itself politically unable to match the pace of rearmament. Recently returned from expensive and emotionally crippling campaigns in the middle-east and North Korea, the people of America could stomach war no longer. Not wanting to spark a nuclear holoaust, the U.S. tried to remain neutral for as long as possible.

As the minutes ticked into hours, one thing seemed immediately obvious to Melody: she absolutely had to find her missing son and return to America. Even though England had no logical reason to fear a military assault from the frothing giant, they were a paltry thousand miles away—the blink of an eye from possible total annihilation.

She didn't dare miss her flight out, for prices and availability were already astronomical. They searched all that day and late into the evening, all without success, and returned late that evening to the hotel. Theo was as devastated as Melody, but for a different reason. They had spoken to enough people who knew George to come to the inescapable conclusion that he was living on the street. With the outbreak of war, George would be one of the first to be swept into the conflict if England joined the war. Assuming war in Europe was inescapable, England's involvement was guaranteed.

Theo feared for his brother's life. As for himself, he would almost surely get a deferment due to his divinity studies. The churches and their ministers were considered untouchable during times of war. Popular opinion would quickly turn against any government who began drafting "men of God" to do their killing.

"I'm so sorry, Mum," Theo was saying. He had begun calling her Mum, and her heart warmed every time he did so. "I had no idea he was on the street. I just don't know where we might look, especially this late at night."

"We'll begin again first thing tomorrow," Melody said quietly, with little hope. There were only a few hours in the morning before she had to hurry to the airport or miss her flight. With her husband no doubt on his way home, she surely didn't want to miss the flight. "Would you like to spend the night with us?" she asked almost without thinking. Then she realized he was twenty-two years old, and hardly in need of her putting him up for the night. His own home was a short drive away. She drew a breath to apologize, but he interrupted her.

"Thanks," he said. "I would like that. What do you say Sam, my good man? Should we have a sleepover?"

"Yipee!" Sammy cried, and began jabbering and dancing from foot to foot.

"Come on Sport," Theo said putting an arm across his shoulders, "let's go get a bite to eat."

They arranged for a trundle bed to be moved into their room. Sammy got the "bed with wheels," and Theo and Melody took the two twin beds. Theo was about to switch the light off when Melody and Sammy knelt beside her bed. It took him a moment to realize what they were doing, and he quickly joined them.

"Heavenly Father," Melody began after a moment of silence. "We thank Thee with all our hearts for bringing us together again. Oh, Heavenly Father, Thou knowest how deeply I have missed my boys, and how dearly I love them. Now Theo is here, and he's so wonderful, and handsome, and good. I'm so proud of him, as I know Thou art. Please bless him Father, and fill his heart with all the love I was not able to give him…" her voice cracked here, and she had to wait.

"Father, I know Thou knowest all things. And I know that Thou will keep George safe. I pray that we can find him tomorrow, if for nothing more than to say goodbye. I love him Father, and I miss him, and as the world seems on the brink of war, I pray Thou will allow us this last farewell.

"I pray for my beloved husband in Russia, that Thou wilt keep him safe, and bring him home to my arms. Forgive us for our weaknesses, I pray in Christ's holy name, amen."

"Amen," Theo said quietly. He clicked off the light, and slid onto the mattress. They lay in the darkness for a long time in silence.

"Mum?" Theo asked.

"Yes honey?" Melody's voice was sweet with love.

"When you prayed just now, you closed your prayer in the name of Christ."

"That's right."

"But, why? Why use Christ's name if you aren't a Christian?"

"Why do you say I'm not a Christian," she asked, her voice a little wounded.

"Because Mormon's aren't Christians, they're… Mormons, I guess."

"Who told you that?"

"Well, Papa, and my seminary professors. It's pretty common knowledge, I'd say."

"Then, it's false common knowledge."

"Why would you say that, Mum? How could so many good religious people be mistaken about Mormons?"

"What would you say is the definition of a Christian?" Melody asked.

"Well, one who believes Jesus is God, and that he died for our sins, and that he is part of the Trinity. I would also say that a Christian believes in the Bible, and tries to keep the commandments of Christ. There are probably other things, but those are the basics, I think."

"Sammy, are you awake?" Melody asked quietly.

"Yeah," a small voice said in the darkness.

"Do you remember the first article of faith?"

"Yeah," he said again.

"Say it, would you?"

"We believe in God the Eternal Father, and in His son Jesus Christ, and in the Holy Ghost."

"Thanks, honey," she said warmly. "That's what we believe about Jesus Christ. Even a nine-year old knows what we believe. And, I have a deep and personal love for my Savior. I owe him everything! It is my fondest desire to live with him again someday."

"Do you believe he died for your sins?"

"The ones I repent of, absolutely." she replied.

"Well, I do know Mormons try to keep the commandments; their commitment is almost legendary," he said with a tone Melody interpreted as approaching reverence. He fell silent, thinking.

"What about the Bible? Haven't you replaced it with the Mormon gold bible?" he asked suddenly.

"There's no such thing as the Mormon gold bible," his mother replied cheerfully. "We read and love the Bible, both Old and New Testaments. We also have the Book of Mormon."

"That's what most people call the gold bible," he informed her. "You believe it over the Bible, don't you?"

"No," she said. "We believe them equally. The Book of Mormon has clearer teachings in some subjects, and the Bible in others. The two harmonize with one another, and both testify of Christ. They are both deeply important to my faith. The Book of Mormon is also called 'Another Testament of Jesus Christ.'"

"I didn't know that," Theo admitted. "So, you consider yourself a Christian," he said a little stiffly.

"Even more importantly, Christ considers me a Christian. I joined the Mormon faith because I felt it brought me closer to Christ. I did it knowing full well that I would meet severe opposition from my husband, your father. I never expected that it would make me lose my boys…"

Theo thought about this. "Had you known it would do that, would you still have joined the Mormon church?"

She paused for a full minute before answering slowly. "It would have been much harder, but I think I still would have. I knew it was true, and I trusted Christ to make everything else work out right if I did His will and was baptized. In a way, I really had no choice. It was simply what I had to do."

"That's more faith than I would have," Theo said, a note of wonder in his voice. Then, his voice grew accusatory. "I find it hard to accept that any mother who loved her children could leave them, for any reason, even for God."

"I agree with you, Theo," she said gently, her voice rich with love. "I couldn't have left you boys for anything."

"But, you said…"

"Perhaps you don't perceive faith the same way I do. I believe if God asked me to leave my children, or anything else for that matter, both I and my babies would be better off for it. It is only this great hope, this faith that I have, that allows me to believe that good will comes of every act of obedience, without exception. Without that inner peace, I could never have joined the Church—not in a million years."

"You are certainly right about the fact that I don't perceive faith at all like you do," Theo conceded. "As a matter of fact, I am slowly coming to the conclusion that I don't understand it at all. I have spent countless hours sitting before the most learned men of theology, and heard every conceivable description of faith the human mind can conjure. I must draw the somewhat disheartening conclusion that not one of them ever described faith in this way. When you talk of your faith my heart burns, and my soul listens. When they spoke of faith, my mind burned, and my fingers took notes."

Melody laughed at his unexpected humor. "Don't be too hard on yourself, son."

"I know I'm keeping you up, but I may watch you get onto a plane tomorrow and depart out of my life forever.," he said softly. "Would you mind terribly explaining to me how you came to possess this great faith?" he asked.

"I would be thrilled to explain it to you. It all began in 1820 in upstate New York. A young man by the name of Joseph Smith had questions quite similar to your own…"

Dim morning light was coming through the small window of their hotel room before they fell asleep in a room filled with the Holy Spirit, and enormous amounts of love. The last words she heard her son say were, "I promise you this, before I die, I will have this great joy of which you speak, even if I have to become a Mormon to get it."

Her last words were, "Before I die, I want to be sealed to you in the holy temple." A few hours earlier this would have elicited from him a snort of disdain. Now it brought a feeling of warmth which seemed to wash over him from head to toe.

A few hours later they sleepily awoke to a gentle but insistent knocking at their door. Theo awoke first, and opened it part way. It was an older gentleman whose name he did not know, but who seemed to have a familiar face.

"I have something for your mother," the kindly old man insisted. Theo relented, and opened the door. By this time Melody was awake.

"I'm sorry to awaken you so early, but I felt impressed to bring you something," he said, holding out an old violin case. Melody gasped as she took it from him, and snapped it open.

"My old violin!" she cried. She turned to her sons. "I brought this with me from Rhodesia to England, and then took it with me to America, but it mysteriously disappeared during our move to Utah. How in the world did it ever get back in England?"

Helaman shrugged. "I can only tell you that it came into my possession a while back. Can you imagine my pleasure when I found your name written on the underneath side. Why, I felt compelled to acquire it, and bring it to you. Imagine after all these years, what miraculous circumstances must have transpired to bring it back into your possession," he said amiably.

Melody hardly heard his explanation before she was tuning the violin. She blew the dust from the strings, paused, and brought down the bow in a long, sustained note whose tonal quality seemed like liquid joy. She closed her eyes, and with a sudden motion the bow danced across the strings in a fiery Bach quartet. She played for nearly five minutes before lowering the beloved old violin. She stroked it as it lay in her lap.

"Ah, it seems like only yesterday when I first saw you playing that very violin in the park," Helaman said wistfully.

"It was a long time ago," Melody said. "As a matter of fact, I first met your father in that park, Theo."

"He told me the story," Theo said happily. "Both George and I used to go to the park and sit in the bowery where you used to play. We went there when we were upset. It helped us to know you were there once." His eyes lit up. "Mother—do you suppose!?"

"The park!" Melody cried.

"George," Theo said suddenly. They grabbed their jackets and ran for the door.

When they arrived it was still early, and few people were in the park. The bowery was just as Melody remembered it, though it had seemed somewhat larger in her memory. George was not to be found.

"Please, my dear," Helaman urged. "Play for me as you did once before. Perhaps George will hear, and it will call to him. Play, my dear. Play with all the love you possess."

Melody removed the violin from its case, and stood just inside the bowery. The music wafted sweetly across the park, and like the rising of the sun, brought sweetness and warmth to all who heard it. She sent her love in those notes, wrapped in eloquent ribbons of harmony which pierced the darkness lurking in the dirty corners of the streets, and into the ears of their ragged inhabitants.

Theo and Melody saw him at exactly the same moment. George walked slowly toward the bowery, drawn as if by a magnet to the delicate lace-like beauty of her music. He found a spot on the first bench, and sat in rapt silence. His hair was tangled, his face smudged with dirt, and his clothing rumpled. Yet, his face was pristine with sweetness as he listened to her. He did not see his brother, and certainly could not have recognized his mother. He had only come because his soul hungered for beauty, and here it was freely given, and hungrily consumed.

She played on for nearly a half-hour, her heart content that he was here, and that he had found beauty in her. She remembered Theo's comments that George harbored great ill will for her. So, before he knew who she was, it thrilled her that he thought of her, at least in terms of her music, as someone of inner beauty.

As was her habit of many years, she closed her concert with a medley of beloved church hymns, the last being "Come, Come Ye Saints." As soon as she started, George sat bolt upright, and stared at her with great wonder. As soon as she lowered her bow, while people were still clapping, he raced to the steps of the bowery, then climbed them deliberately until he stood immediately before her. She struggled to keep a cascade of emotions from her face. She could hardly believe he was actually standing there, completely unaware of who she was.

"Your music," he said, his voice grave, "touched my soul."

"Thank you. May I ask your name?" she said, not quite sure what else to say.

"George Tennison, Ma'am," he said politely, and bowed slightly.

"A pleasure to meet you, George. My name is Melody," she said quietly, and began putting away her violin.

He seemed to ponder this in deep silence as others came up to compliment her on her music, and to offer her coins. She accepted them graciously, so as to not damage the impression she had begun. When she turned back toward him, his eyes were intently upon her.

"My mother's name was Melody as well," he said with heaviness of heart. "She also played the violin in this park. People say she was very good, and very beautiful as well. I can't imagine anyone playing as beautifully as you though…" his voice grew almost inaudible as he spoke.

"You sound as if your memories of your mother are sad for you," she said, and immediately wished she could take her words back.

"Sad?" he asked. "I don't think sad is the right word. Bitter, perhaps? A little angry, possibly a lot angry. But, I didn't intend to burden you with my memories. I just wanted to thank you for the music. I don't have any coins to give you. I'm sorry," he said as he turned to go.

"Please wait," Melody said hastily. "Please tell me why you are angry with your mother. You see, I'm a mother too, and I'm sorry to say that I have a son who is angry with me too. I feel so tragic in my heart. Please tell me. Perhaps it will help us both."

He turned back toward her, a hard look in his eyes. "There's not much to tell. She left me suddenly when I was quite young. I was devastated by it. My father told me that she simply walked away because she was deceived by the Mormons. That's about it. She apparently loved the Mormons more than her own sons."

"That sounds terrible! Do you believe that?" she asked, struggling to keep from bursting into tears.

"I did for years. I'll admit that I went through periods of hating her. But not anymore."

"I'm glad to hear that," she admitted with obvious relief. He looked at her oddly.

"Why?" he wanted to know.

"I told you, I'm a mother too." He nodded. "What caused you to stop hating her?"

"Well, it's because my memories of her, though sketchy and incomplete, made me not want to believe she could ever walk away from me. I just didn't believe it."

She waited for him to continue. "So what did you do?" she finally asked.

"I found some Mormons, and I asked them to teach me about their religion."

"Why would you do that? Weren't you worried you would be deceived, just like she was?"

"No. My father's a minister, and I had heard so many things about how to resist Mormon lies that I knew I could handle any argument they had."

"Oh, well that's good. But why would you study with them?"

"I wanted to know what was so enticing about the Mormons beliefs that she would leave her own children. I wanted to discover if they were capable of enticing a young mother to leave her family. I'm not sure what I wanted to find. I think I was just looking for truth."

"What did you find?" she asked quietly.

"I found a group of people with great humility and faith. I found people who love the Lord, and who would never entice a young mother to leave her baby. But I also found further rejection, and I found deep, utter confusion."

"I can see why that would be confusing," Melody admitted.

"I went to talk to my father about it, and instead of speaking to me gently and reclaiming me, or convincing me of my error in loving words, with logic and scripture, he confronted me with violent anger. I was so utterly taken aback that I lashed back at him, and told him he was less of a Christian than the Mormon missionaries." Melody had to suppress a smile. She could well imagine how her former husband reacted to that.

"What did your father do?" she asked.

"He threw me out of the house," he said bitterly. "And, my rich great-uncle has seen to it that I can't find any work unless I return to my father and renounce what I think is true. I'm daily forced to decide between eating, and living a lie."

"I'm so sorry, George. How long have been living on the street since then?"

"Nearly six months now," he admitted. "But, I've completed my studies of the Mormons, and I think I'm going to be baptized." Then he gave her a wilted smile. "Does that make you think less of me?" he asked.

"Certainly not!" she replied forcefully.

He smiled wearily. "You're a Mormon, aren't you."

"I am. How did you know?"

"From your music. You know, I recognized one of the Mormon hymns you played! And also from the fact that you aren't against my wanting to join the Church."

Melody blushed at his detection. "So, are you going to try to find your mother?" she asked, and again wished she hadn't.

"No," he said with finality. It caused her heart to sink.

"Why not?" she asked, unable to keep despair from her voice.

"If she loved me, she would have come back years ago. My father was right about the fact that she did leave me. And for whatever reason she left, she hasn't even attempted to come back. My father…"

"Lied to you," a young man's voice said behind them. George spun around to see his older brother. George ran into his arms, and they slapped one another on the back with gusto.

"Big brother!" George cried. "I have missed you, Sport! How did you find me? Why did you come looking? I thought you and Papa had disowned me."

"Never!" Theo said. "We came looking because we finally heard the truth, that you were destitute. Melody and I had to find you before she left back to the States."

"You're with Melody? How odd. We were just…" Then he stopped amid sentence, his mind quickly piecing together the elements of their former conversation.

"But… I'm… are you…?" he stammered.

"I am, George," Melody said sweetly, quietly. "I *am* that Melody, your mother. I never wanted to leave you, and I've come to take you home," she said, and held her arms out to him.

George stood there staring at her with open mouth and blank eyes. For the longest time he merely stared as emotions drifted across his features: anger, fear, distrust, grief, and finally, love. During all this time she held open her arms until her shoulders ached. Finally he lowered his head, sobbed once and walked into her arms, lowering his head onto her shoulder. He stood there and sobbed like a little child. She wept silent tears of sadness, and tremendous relief, all the while stroking the back of his head and humming a tune that leapt happily into her heart. It was the tune she used to hum when she rocked him to sleep so many years ago.

It was Helaman who interrupted their reunion. "I'm sorry to intrude," he said. "But your plane leaves in but a few hours. I'm afraid you need to get packing."

"You're leaving? But you just got here. You can't leave now!" George cried, his eyes brimming with tears.

"I have to leave. I must. There's a war on, and I may not be able to get out later. My husband's at home waiting for me."

George lowered his head as if someone had shot him through the heart, and his body had yet to fall to the ground. "I understand," he said, and turned away to walk back into the park.

"No you don't!" Melody cried, and grabbed his elbow. "I'm leaving, but not without you. You're coming with me!"

"But, I can't leave. I don't have tickets. I don't have a passport. I'm certainly going to be drafted into the military. And, I'm not sure I want to go with you anyway. England is my home, and she needs me now that there's a war."

"I can't make you come, of course. But you must understand that I came back to get you. I couldn't come all these years for fear that your father would take away your brother. Now I…"

"Our brother?" George asked.

"Yeah," Theo said. "Come here Sam, old chum. Come meet your other big brother George. Well, your half-brother," he said as Sammy came forward and shook George's hand. George was so stunned to find out he had a little brother that he could scarcely shake hands. Sammy was in heaven. Two big brothers!

Melody motioned to Helaman, and he immediately took the boy's hand and said, "Come on, buddy, let's go throw some coins in that fountain. I think your Mum needs some time with your big brothers."

When they were beyond hearing distance Melody turned to her sons. "You're only half right," she said.

"About what, Mum?" Theo asked.

"He's not your half-brother."

"So, he's really not our brother now?"

"No. You're going the wrong way. He's your full brother. You all have the same father, as well as the same mother."

"What!" Theo cried, and looked from Melody to George, and back again. "He's our father's son! If Dad finds out about this he'll go friggin' bonkers. He'll have the army attack you instead of the Russians!"

"I know," she said. "That's why I never came back all these years. I knew if he ever found out Sammy was his son, he'd never rest until he had him, too. He'd have taken him away to spite me, even though he didn't know or love Sammy. With his uncle's help, he has enough money to do it, even from England. I couldn't stand the thought of losing my youngest son. He was all I had to remind me of you two."

George turned toward Melody with sudden determination. "Mother," he said, his voice catching on his own words. Melody began to cry again, and held open her arms to him. George rushed into them with a strangled sob. His voice was muffled against her shoulder. "Mother, I understand, and I'm so sorry. I don't know what happened all those years ago, but I know you did what you had to do." He stopped suddenly and took her hand. "Mother, I want to come to America with you. Please, can't we work it out? Are you coming Theo?"

Theo spoke slowly. "I must be bonkers myself, but I think I do want to come. I want to go to America, and maybe even become a Mormon, I think. That'll fry Father's tongue in acid," he said in bitter humor. "But, I'm under the same constraints you are. I doubt we can leave."

Helaman and Sammy were just walking up to them, a big smile on Sammy's face as he reached out his hand for Theo. Melody turned to her friend. "Is there any way you can help me get these boys to America? They want to come. Oh, I know it's asking an awful lot, and you have no great compelling reason to come to our aid, but if you are able, I beseech you for help. I'll pay you back anything it costs, and more."

"My dear Melody, I have every reason to help. I promised your husband I would stay near you until you no longer needed me. That is as compelling a reason as any on earth. I'll see what I can do. I'll meet you at your hotel room in an hour. I suggest you boys do not return home to pack. If you say anything to your father it will greatly reduce your odds of leaving the country. Your only hope is to apply for exit visas on the strength that your mother is an American citizen. I believe they will let you out on that alone. Let me work on the passports and tickets. In one hour then!" he said, and marched away toward his home.

It was more of a miracle than either Melody or her naïve sons could have known that Helaman produced two additional serviceable passports and tickets. He handed them to her and urged her to flee to the airport. They arrived just forty-five minutes before departure, every second of which was spent in passing the heightened security now everywhere imposed. They barely succeeded in getting her two English-born sons on the plane, and only their American parentage and the fact that their tickets seemed to have been purchased prior to the outbreak of the war, finally secured their passage. In fact, had the harried officials thought to look up the new customs laws but hours old, they would not have let them leave at all. As it was, they passed through on the barest of margins, which margin was nothing less than divine intervention on their behalf. Helaman remained by their side, calm, determined and unflappable.

They boarded the plane mere moments before it taxied away. They were still shoving bags under their seats and tightening belts as the big jet roared into the sky. Their departure was so hasty that the stewardess had already given the safety briefing and instructed them to buckle their seat belts. The plane pointed at the sky, and pushed home the throttles.

THE WAR OF WARS

Scarcely a week had passed. Each day the caravan of refugees traveled another thirty miles or so on muddy, rutted farm roads. Every dozen miles another vehicle either ran out of fuel, or broke down. Those vehicles still operating were loaded beyond capacity, and sure to not survive such rough service for long. Alexei sent word that all the camp should gather together prior to supper. He looked over his small group with sad eyes as they gathered before him. Their heads were wrapped in rag scarves, their coats patched and worn, their faces gaunt with fear and hunger.

"My dear people," he called to them loudly, his voice filled with confidence that even Samuel had not anticipated. Again Vladimir translated for him, although Samuel assured him that he was slowly learning the language. "We have made a goodly trek today, and I wanted to speak with you before you retire.

"We are still in danger of being discovered by the military. Our vehicles will not last much longer the way we are using them, and we have no more fuel. Tomorrow we will select four of the best trucks. Onto these we will load our food and those who cannot walk. We will drain the fuel from all other vehicles and abandon them here. The trucks will go in their slowest gears, and take every precaution to use the smallest amount of fuel possible. All of us will walk beginning tomorrow. We will continue in this manner until God opens before us a new way."

The murmur that arose from the people was more of disappointment than disagreement. Samuel surveyed their faces and saw less fear than resolve in a sturdy people who had grown tired from a hundred years of soviet oppression—not from this sudden exodus.

Alexei continued, his voice resonating sharply in the harsh cold. "I feel compelled to caution you to strict obedience to our beliefs. Whatever people we encounter along the way, and whatever villages we enter, we will not steal their food or fuel. If we have more, we will share with them. If they have extra, we will trade for it, but we will not steal. Anyone caught breaking this commandment will be exiled from our group, and will not reach Zion. Remember your prayers. Our people will make it to Zion, of this I am sure."

His voice grew silent, and not a soul made a sound. He looked at the ground as he continued. "You all know the prophecies. Many of us will not survive the journey." He looked up, his eyes sober. "So, let us be humble and prayerful. We are on God's errand, a journey we have anticipated with longing all of our lives. Now, go eat your meals and sleep safely. God bless you," he said and stepped down from the log on which he had been standing.

The people turned away slowly, talking quietly among themselves. Samuel did not detect murmuring or dissent, but he also detected very little hope. Their faith was largely centered in long-held dreams, rather than the workings of the Spirit, and consequently it brought them no peace.

They possessed few tents, and what shelter they had was scarce. Accordingly, Sam gave up sleeping in the Honda to allow some children the luxury of sleeping out of the wind. It had always been the case among these people that they slept in unheated, or at best, poorly heated homes. As a result they traditionally slept together: husband with wife, brother with brother, sister with sister, friend with friend. Those who had no one either slept cold, or were assigned someone to be their bedfellow. This was known to Samuel, and was of some concern to him. He could not think of a situation where he could be comfortable sleeping with anyone. And besides, he actually did not need to—even if they did not know why.

Alexei, however was of another opinion, and not willing to let one sent from God to lead his people suffer while he had anything to say about it. As a result, the first night Sam slept outside the Honda he and Alexei had a spirited, though friendly argument in Samuel's broken Russian on this very topic. Alexei concluded his part therein by turning around and walking briskly away while growling, "We'll talk about this later."

Since sleep was not a necessity for Samuel, he stilled himself and prayed. Except fleetingly while yet a mortal man, it was prayer unlike anything he had experienced, and it caused his heart ascend nigh unto heaven. It was far more than speaking humble words, it was communication of the highest order of spiritual attunement; it was a two-way interview with Heavenly Father on a celestial scale, and something which relaxed, warmed and healed, and gave him the courage to carry on.

His translated status notwithstanding, he was still Samuel, and what courage and resolve he called upon came from within the reserves of his soul. His was not a walk in the blinding light of perfect understanding. His was not to know every answer, to solve every sorrow and concern with piercing insight. His was often a walk in the shadows of faith. Except for when Alexei asked, and pure knowledge flowed, he spent much time seeking answers. These came during the nighttime hours when his soul soared upon the wings of sweetest prayer.

About the time Samuel could hear the Northern Lights crackling overhead in the far reaches of morning he finally fell asleep. The first sound he heard was a distant thrumming of the wind. Yet, far more disconcerting was the instantaneous cry of alarm that arose from the camp. Instantly awake, he slipped from the blanket and stood.

Having never heard the distinctive sound of a Soviet-armored ground-assault helicopter, he did not appreciate the sudden terror that swept across the hapless refugees. He watched with little understanding as they dived for cover beneath vehicles and whatever safety the rugged terrain offered.

When the first chopper arrived, its very appearance struck fear into his heart. It was larger than any craft he had seen in American skies, and was flying low and fast. For a moment it looked as if it might simply fly past them, but then it swung in a wide arc to come about. When it finally faced them it was fearsome. Its nose was studded with guns, its stubby wings were heavy with a double row of rockets, their red tips plainly visible in the first light of morning.

Alexei and several others ran up to Samuel. "We have been discovered! They believe we are traitors!" Alexei cried, while his people watching the helicopter in terror.

The craft hovered there until another identical chopper thundered over them and swung around to join its brother of death. They menacingly remained there for a full thirty seconds, which seemed an eternity. All around him people screamed and scattered. The question of what they intended to do ended abruptly with a burst of machine gun fire that roared in a prolonged explosion. Samuel could plainly see fire belching from rotating barrels on either side of the narrow ship. The bullets cut a path of death and destruction through the refugees, killing hundreds of innocents in mere seconds.

As if on cue, the remaining survivors bolted helter-skelter across the snowy landscape. At this point, a rocket belched flames and roared into a cluster of vehicles. Samuel watched his blue Honda leap into the sky as it came apart into a thousand fragments which spread further death. He knew for a fact that a little family with three small children had taken refuge there. It caused his heart to cry out in anguish and anger. He had never seen such violence, such wanton destruction. The helicopters were close enough that he could clearly see the bug-like helmet of the forward pilot. For a moment he forgot himself, and looked around for a weapon to fight back. There was none.

Samuel realized with a start that he was not alone. Both Vladimir and Alexei stood beside him as if rooted to that spot by his own refusal to flee. He turned toward them to urge them to seek cover.

"My people die like pack dogs," Alexei said with deep sadness. "Pray to God, Samuel," he said, his eyes filling with tears, "and ask him for our deliverance. Tell me, man of God, what shall we do to escape utter destruction?"

Samuel waited for Vladimir to translate. The answer came to him with startling clarity, yet it made no sense. Still, he shouted the message above the roar of incoming rockets. "Tell them to run toward the enemy!"

No sooner had he given these instructions than both Alexei and Vladimir bolted simultaneously toward their people. They began shouting in Russian. All who were not too frightened to hear, obeyed their words, and in less than one minute, all those who could run were surging forward. Those who did not obey, turned and ran away from what appeared to be a dash to certain death.

At that moment in the frenzy, Samuel looked down and saw Sarah, Alexei's little granddaughter who had befriended him. She had been critically shot and was crying weakly. In a single move he cradled her under one arm, and began to run. He caught another terrified young woman under his other arm, and literally lifted her off her feet as he ran. She looked down in amazement at her feet off the ground, touching the ground once for every three of his strides. Samuel was surprised at his speed, strength and endurance. This was his first experience with pressing his body to its limits, and he found to his amazement that those limits were well beyond his present urgency.

For a terrifying second the choppers seemed to not understand their utterly foolish response to their attack, and they hovered there without firing. The people were too close now to come under direct fire, and the choppers began backing up in a jerky, zigzag effort to stay ahead of the fleeing people. Several bursts of fire flew over their heads, killing those disobediently fleeing from the scene of death. This had the dramatic effect of flooding life into winded lungs and exhausted legs. The people flew forward on the wings of abject terror. The choppers continued to back up, trying to get a better shot.

Finally, the chopper on the left grew weary of trying to fly the big machine in a direction it was not well-designed to go, and banked hard to his left. At that exact moment, the other banked hard to its right. Their intent was to circle around the fleeing people and get behind them where they could complete their destruction. Mere seconds of life remained for the people, except for the strange fact that as the big ships swung ponderously around their tail rotors passed within one another's arc, and in a flash of sparks and tortured metal, they ground each other's tail rotors into flying slag.

Both machines spun out of control immediately. One chopper gunned his big jets to try to regain control. It vanished from sight, quickly rising into the sky in tight circles. The other machine quickly cut his engines and crashed to the ground with a solid thud that Samuel felt in his legs and feet. Oddly enough, the big machine sat there in a billow of dust and smoke, but it did not explode as all were expecting.

Still pointing toward them, it fired another burst of bullets that ripped a path through the survivors, killing more dozens of them. The people ran away from the path of the big guns. Dozens of men dashed toward the downed chopper, quickly covering the two-hundred yards separating them. Samuel watched them pounding on the windows with rocks and moments later, they were pulling the two pilots from their seats. The shooting stopped immediately. By the time Samuel arrived at the big chopper, the two pilots' bodies were already being dragged away.

Samuel felt his stomach turn as he surveyed this gruesome scene. He was saddened the two pilots had been killed; yet he also knew their deaths were justified. These two had killed hundreds of innocent men, women and children for reasons that were not fathomable to Samuel. Their death machine, which towered as high as a two-story building, was now still and foreboding.

Samuel released the frightened woman he had been carrying; she walked away in a daze. He kept wounded little Sarah cradled in his arms as he looked for Alexei or Vladimir. He could not see them. People were returning to their dead families, and wails of grief began to rise from the camp behind him. Still carrying Sarah, he trotted to the scene of carnage and felt a sickness in his soul that would have otherwise translated to an urge to retch, which was gladly not possible for him.

He soon located Vladimir, who was holding Alexei in his arms. A large red stain was spreading around a gaping hole in the old Russian's abdomen. From the ashen color on his face Samuel knew there were mere seconds of life left for him. Samuel had never been exposed to such carnage, and the incredible stench of death was so overwhelming that he fought the urge to run away. Even in his altered state, it was almost more than he could endure.

He carefully placed Sarah on the ground and knelt beside the old man, who immediately took Samuel's hand. His hand was slick with blood as he clasped Samuel's tightly. "My people," he rasped, his words thick with pain.

"Many survived," Samuel told him in broken Russian, with as much optimism as he could muster.

"They will scatter without me," Alexei said through clenched teeth. "You must lead them on. You must take over for me," he said urgently.

"I cannot!" Samuel said. "It is forbidden."

The aged Russian narrowed his eyes at Samuel, and skipped all the questions his statement must have generated in his old heart. What was impossible was just that— impossible.

"Then heal me!" he cried, and coughed. The sudden movement caused blood and stench to spurt from the gaping wound in his gut.

Samuel waited, unprepared for the old one's request. He was not waiting for faith, or courage, or anything like unto it. He was waiting for permission to honor this request.

"Do you have the faith to be raised up?" Samuel asked.

"I know God sent you to us. If God wills it, I have the faith. Tell me what is God's will, and I will rise up and lead this people to their home. Speak the words of God, my brother, and I will…" His words died in his throat as his spirit departed his body.

"No!!!" Vladimir cried in deep anguish. "Don't die! Not now! We need you! Oh, God, God, why have you allowed our only hope to die. Oh please…"

Samuel slowly straightened as Alexei's bloodied hand grew slack and slipped to the ground. He turned to Vladimir, and felt the power of truth flow into him. Vladimir looked into Samuel's eyes with deep anguish. "Why did God let him die?" he demanded. "His faith was strong enough! I felt it! I knew it! Why must he die?"

"It was not Alexei's faith that was the deciding factor," Samuel told him quietly. "It was yours."

"What?" Vladimir demanded. "It was his life, not mine! Why would God abandon him because of my lack of faith?" he asked with a quivering voice, tears freely flowing onto his friend's face over whom he yet crouched.

Samuel spoke calmly. "It was God's will that you should lead this people with Alexei. Your faith was not ready to see him raised up. Tell me something. Set aside your grief, and reason with me a moment,"

"I will try. I will try," he said between sobs.

"Consider with me that God cannot show something unto his children which gifts them with something He does not give to all other of His children. As one who lived under communism, perhaps you can understand that God gives equally to all of his children. He could not give to you the vision of Alexei rising from his wounds."

"But why? I do not understand this!"

"What would you have done had you watched the wound in his belly heal, and seen him restored to perfect health before your eyes? Would you have reordered your life, and sought God with greater diligence than ever before?"

"Yes!" he cried. "What is wrong with such a thing?"

"What is wrong is that to do this would change you and make you greater than you would otherwise be. This would give you an advantage that others of God's children have not received. This would not be just, and God can do nothing that is not flawlessly just. Can you see this?"

Vladimir looked away. "In a way I can. If this is true then I have killed him as surely as the bullet that passed through him."

"No! He isn't dead, he yet lives. Don't you understand that it is no more miraculous to close the wounds of a dying body, than to raise the same body from the dead? The reason for his death is irrelevant. The reasons he cannot come back are extremely important, and they all have to do with you!"

"What must I do?" he asked, his head lowered, his chest heaving in silent sobs.

Samuel spoke the words that filled his mouth, marveling as he said them. "Look at me!" Vladimir raised his head as if it weighed several tons. "This day, this moment in time must be the pivot point in your life. If you will set your whole soul in the service of God, and covenant with Him to walk unerringly in His path all the remainder of your life, just as you might have had you seen this great miracle, then seeing a great miracle will not change the outcome of your life. Do this, and there will be no difference in whether Alexei lives or dies. Can you do this?"

"I can." he said simply. "I have always known that one day I must. Now is the moment of my greatest need. Alexei is dead, and I must take his place. I will walk in his shoes, and in God's light." He placed a hand on his beloved friend's body. "Forgive me my Uncle, my brother, that my faith comes too late. Forgive me," he said. He stood slowly, took a deep breath and turned his face toward his people. Samuel watched him square his shoulders and arrive at a decision. He walked to the nearest grieving survivor and knelt beside a young father rocking back and forth with a teenage girl in his arms. Samuel could hear faint words of comfort being spoken at a distance.

"Samuel," a voice said nearby. He looked up to see Helaman standing on the opposite side of Alexei's corpse.

"Helaman," Samuel said quietly. "Assist me, please."

"I am here to strengthen you. But, you must do this alone."

"It overwhelms me, Helaman," Samuel groaned. "I have never before seen such carnage, such useless slaughter." Samuel looked up across the bloodied remains of an already-fragile people. "My soul is grieved, and I feel so inadequate. I am only one, and it is not enough," he cried quietly, but urgently.

Helaman fixed his eyes upon him and urged him: "See, Samuel, open your eyes, and see." Samuel bowed his head and prayed until power flowed through him, he looked up and saw the snowy fields of carnage filled with heavenly beings leaning over the grieving and dying. All around him stood a dozen men and women, adorned in glorious white, their faces serene and glowing with righteousness.

"I see them," Samuel said. One of them he recognized instantly, partly because he was the only one not in billowing white garment. Though many years younger in appearance, Alexei stood just beyond the ring of angels. They were all there for a purpose, and as firmly as he had ever known anything in his life, he suddenly knew what that purpose was.

Samuel picked up the bloodied hand he had just dropped and in a quiet voice of authority said, "Alexei, In the name of Jesus Christ, and by the power of his eternal Priesthood, and through his infinite grace, I command you to return to your body. Arise. Arise and lead your people to Zion."

Samuel plainly saw one of the heavenly beings step aside. Alexei hastily finished a conversation with a woman and turned his attention to Samuel. He stepped past the others, and paused before his body. He glanced at Samuel, then in the blink of an eye seemed to enter the lifeless corpse through the crown of the head. Samuel watched the wound close. The body took a breath, and seconds later, he sat up. Alexei placed a hand on his abdomen, and finding himself completely healed, looked into Samuel's face.

"I know you now," he said quietly, a look of significance on his face. "Thank you for being here. And, thank God," he said in a fervent whisper, looking up into the sky. Samuel wondered if he could see the many angels who stood rejoicing around them. If fact, he could not, but he clearly remembered what had been for him a long and empowering visit to his heavenly home. His eyes sparkled with joy, peace and purpose.

"You will need a clean shirt," Samuel smiled matter-of-factly.

Alexei shook that off. "A shirt can come later. For now, my people need me."

Samuel watched as Alexei walked over to Vladimir and placed a hand on his shoulder. The younger man glanced up at his uncle, and for a long moment suppressed the urge to stand and cry out in joy. His heart was filled with exquisite gratitude and praise to God for this miracle of miracles, but here in this place he could not call attention to anything extraordinary; in front of the others, there could be nothing more than a nod. Vladimir glanced at Samuel in gratitude, then up again at his uncle, a look of new-found faith on his face.

Then Samuel turned his attention back to Sarah, who was lying on the ground near them. She was not breathing, and two large pools of blood had gathered near her lifeless body. Alexei felt for a pulse, and cried out. "My precious flower, my little Sarah! She is gone!"

Alexei looked up at Samuel, his face grim and streaked with tears, but calmly resolute. "I know my faith, that it is sufficient to ask you to heal my granddaughter. But, I do not know the will of God." Alexei said solemnly.

Samuel closed his eyes and poured out his heart to God. He knew if he asked with all his heart that God would heed his call, and the child would live. But, more than the life of this faithful child, he feared to ask amiss. His prayer was for understanding, for sanction to exercise the vast powers that had been granted to him. When the answer came it thrilled him.

Taking Sarah by the hand he said, "Daughter of Israel, in the name of Jesus Christ, I call you back. Your mission is not finished in mortality. Sarah, come back. Come back and be whole," he said with quiet authority. Sarah's eyes flickered open. She smiled at her grandfather, and then at Samuel, the color returning to her cheeks. She looked down at her wounds, and gasped as she watched the holes fill with smooth white flesh. It was a manifestation of the power of God she would never forget.

Alexei cried out "Hosanna!" and gathered his granddaughter into his arms. She embraced him for a long moment before he straightened.

"We must soon leave this place," Alexei said as he stood, tenderly releasing Sarah. He stretched his back, and with a sly grin said, "Too bad you didn't heal my old age, too." Then he grew serious. "I was overjoyed to be free of my body for a time, and coming back was startlingly painful. But, my people need me, and I thank God for His mercy!" he said, and walked stiffly away with Vladimir.

Samuel walked side-by-side with Sarah until she stopped beside the body of her mother. Words of tragic sorrow spilled untranslated from her young lips.

"I know, Sarah," he said. "I know it hurts, it really hurts," he whispered to her, hugging her tightly. As if she understood his every word, she listened, nodded, and understood.

Then Samuel saw the spirit of Sarah's mother. She was bending over her daughter, whispering words of comfort and instruction. "Your mother is happy now," he told her. "She is warm and safe, and has left me to take care of you."

Again Sarah nodded, and stood, her hand in his. They turned aside to comfort and bless others. He was never sure why, or how his words passed the barrier of language, but they did, and from that moment on, Sarah stayed by his side.

Samuel's eyes remained opened to the world of spirits for several hours afterward, as he walked among the dead and wounded, and healed everyone that the Spirit directed. As he assisted the survivors in their grief, he marveled at how many from the other side of the veil also labored in their own way to comfort those who suffered.

Of the four hundred wounded or dead, one-third were restored to perfect health. All the others passed on, their reward glorious and sure. Word quickly spread through the camp of the healings that had occurred, and a feeling of solemnity settled over them as they pondered this powerful example of God's deliverance.

But the most dramatic effect of this encounter occurred with Vladimir. The changes within him were powerful. A deep inner confidence previously unseen in him now seemed to illuminate his entire frame. He strode forth with confidence, and worked among the people with gentleness and compassion. Probably the most startling of all was that his faith was now absolute.

In much less time than Samuel would have dreamed possible, Alexei got his people loaded and ready to go. They carefully laid their dead inside the very machine that had brought them death. A fire was set, and they walked away slowly, their pathway brightly lit by the funeral pyre of their loved ones.

Having just arrived in Utah, Melody began the joyful task of finding room for her three sons. Their home was not large by American standards, merely three bedrooms and an unfinished basement, but to her older sons, it was a mansion at least five times the size of their childhood home.

Her greatest disappointment was in arriving home to find Samuel still gone. Her heart had danced with happiness all the way home from England, anticipating their joyful reunion. When he was not to be found, and with his phone in Russia still disconnected, she began calling his employer in Texas. After the third call she could no longer get past the switchboard operator. She knew something was terribly amiss. But the joy of having all her boys home comforted and soothed her.

One might assume a general state of economic chaos would swamp the nation, but such did not immediately occur. Slowly at first, then in increasingly greater steps, inflation began to influence the cost of everything from a can of beans, to homes. Though the inflation quietly eroded the value of the dollar, it was not nearly as dramatic as the increase in real property values. People who at one time owned a one hundred-thousand dollar home, now owned a two hundred-thousand dollar home. People who were making seven dollars an hour were now making seventeen.

Contrary to inflationary trends of the past, interest rates remained relatively low. Businesses flourished, were built upon and expanded. Personal wealth appeared to expand as everyone seemed to have money to spend. No one really minded that they were paying more, because they had more. Work was plentiful, and easy to find. War related industry was everywhere. People were offered half a year's salary up front just to come to work. It was not uncommon for skilled craftsmen and blue-collar workers to change jobs every six months due to offers they felt they could not refuse.

A spirit of speculation gripped the entire nation, as well as the Saints across America. People with any type of nest egg, and even a little foresight, parlayed their holdings into considerable sums of money. The Prophet warned the Saints to avoid the temptation to enter into speculation, to borrow or expand their businesses by borrowing. He urged the people of God to get out of debt, prepare spiritually, and store food. Yet with few exceptions, like the click-clack of a train rumbling by, his words became background noise to the happy chatter of a people fully engaged in mammon.

Almost with a united shrug of indifference, the world ignored his counsel. Few within the Church understood why they should not ride the gravy train to financial safety. The minority who heeded the Prophet's counsel were slowly left behind economically. They became an underclass who were seen as stupidly choosing poverty in a time of prosperity. Class distinction and division seemed to take a thundering step inside the Church.

The news hit the world like a nuclear explosion, and it had nothing to do with the war. The U.N. passed a resolution not unlike the US Freedom of Information Act, but much more forceful. The law was drafted and supported by certain parties in the US as critical "progress" to allow the world to benefit from private stores of knowledge held by religions, governments and private persons alike. No longer would modern, historical or technological secrets be withheld from public scrutiny. It seemed like a noble idea at the time, and the loss of privacy and freedom loomed small against the mass of knowledge and truth potentially gained.

Without even breaking stride, with the new international law passed, the U.N. targeted religions first and descended upon the vast libraries sequestered in the Vatican at Rome and even those maintained by the Church in Salt Lake City. There was an outcry from everyone from the Pope to the President of the United States; yet it seemed that although it violated our sovereignty and our constitution, it was justified in the name of freedom of information and social progress and little harm was actually done. Soon the matter was if not forgotten, at least dramatically minimized in the media and the minds of the people.

However, the actual effect of this seemingly minor storm brought high-water floods of confusion, and eventually proved devastating to almost every living Christian on earth.

Not many weeks after the U.N. researchers forced their way at gunpoint into the LDS Church libraries, they began publishing documents long considered too sacred to share. Aside from members and critics of the Church, few people took notice. Of far greater interest were the Vatican archives. The U.N. began publishing discovered documents, and their translations, that had apparently not seen daylight in thousands of years—if ever. What emerged was a scandal that built in crescendo until the resultant clamor was heard around the Christian world, which actually drowned out the noise of war.

The researchers published what appeared to be conclusive, irrefutable, undeniable, and incontrovertible evidence of a vast Christian conspiracy. Thousands of documents from around the time of Christ spilled across the world proving—not just accusing, but *proving*—that early Christian authorities did not believe Christ was divine. Beyond this, the ancient conspirators privately spoke among themselves that Jesus, the man, the lowly prophet of Galilee, never himself claimed to be anything more than a man whose gentle soul and unique perspective on human relations were peace-giving and uplifting.

Found among the archives were the original, hand-written accounts by Matthew, Mark, Luke and John, Joseph the father of Jesus, James the brother of Jesus, and many others. Without exception these documents painted a much less-positive picture of Jesus than the biblical versions of their stories. They spoke of Mary and Joseph's plan to cover up the unplanned pregnancy that resulted in Jesus's birth. They pressed their clever deception to great success because of the fervor and heightened desire for a Messiah of the day.

To their complete surprise, their little son believed them, bought into the ruse, and lived the life of the "Son of God" as authentically he could. All the gospel writers spoke glowingly of Jesus the man, and darkly of their own dismay at finding him to be little more than the farcical outcome of a lie. He was actually insane, they said, and believed himself to be the by-product of a virgin birth; and though he was hardly divine, they deemed him a prophet nonetheless. After Jesus died, those seeking power over the growing Christian movement greatly embellished the stories removing any flaws and inserting so-called mighty miracles and worked to ensure the original documents were never found. Acclaimed academic researchers authenticated the documents and verified they were from antiquity. Renowned psychologists confirmed Jesus suffered from acute schizophrenia with many documented episodes of delusions of grandeur.

Many letters of Paul, the supposed Apostle, were widely published. It became apparent that Paul wrote two sets of letters, one to his proselytes to Christianity, and another set to his Jewish puppet masters in Jerusalem. Paul, it turns out, was a plant, a spy of sorts, whose mission was to spur the early Christians to such fervor that they would incur the wrath of Rome, so that eventually Rome would annihilate them as they did all their enemies. Paul's final letter to his handlers in Jerusalem was a bitter cry for rescue. Paul, it seems, had played his part too well, and was about to join his victims in their destruction. His friends at Jerusalem decided the net "effect" of Paul's efforts would be enhanced by his own martyrdom, and asked their contacts in Rome to ignore any "information" they might have received earlier that Paul was innocent. Thus, Paul was abandoned by his Jewish friends and killed along with the other early Christians.

But, perhaps more damning than any of these was an official report written by the hand of Pontius Pilate himself, relating not one, but four interviews with Jesus of Nazareth. The first three were almost word-for-word transcripts of Pilate's conversations with Jesus, whose worldly views Pilate considered to be partly, if not wholly insane. The only reason Pilate washed his hands and pronounced him innocent at their final, much publicized trial, was because Pilate considered the man beyond rational thought, and innocent by reason of insanity.

The broad effect of this drama was one of nearly decapitating Christianity. In less than a year, entire sects of Christianity folded and evaporated. Christian megachurches emptied across the U.S.. All remaining Christian groups were dramatically marginalized and even considered dangerous. Traditional Christian schools of thought and philosophy were at first suspect, then publicly decried, then abandoned en masse, and in time—outlawed. Persecution against Christians became so severe that it became dangerous to say anything in favor of it. Violent beatings were common in the cities and churches were constantly vandalized and the target of arsonists. Secularism and atheism swept the nation as scientific enlightenment finally seemed to triumph over the deluded and dangerous so-called yoke of religion, for which atrocities have been committed against mankind for millennia.

Among the members of the Church of Jesus Christ of Latter-day Saints, a full one-half simply threw up their hands in despair and ceased to consider themselves either members or Christians. Among the other churches that actually survived, the toll reached as high as seventy-five percent.

During all this dissemination of such damning information, the Prophet and Quorum of the Twelve repeatedly urged their faithful to ignore the growing tide of negative information. Before long they openly claimed the information false, fabricated, and Satanic in origin. They labored day and night, visiting the Saints, praying with them, reasoning, quoting scripture that prophesied this very thing, all with little effect. Those without a personal relationship with Christ and acquainted with His voice were simply unable to stand against the unrelenting avalanche of scientific proof, persecution and unrelenting opposition.

Before long many wards simply dried up and blew away. Every stake lost large blocks of their members, and many lost their entire leadership. Some stakes collapsed. Of those remaining, those who chose to pay a full tithing fell to fewer than one in a hundred. Temples closed from lack of volunteer staff and patrons and lack of funds. Several stakes filed claims of ownership of their church buildings and won in civil court. Seventeen temples in the U.S. and most temples overseas were likewise lost into private ownership. In a year's time the Church membership lurched to a stop, reversed itself, and almost faltered entirely. From a worldwide membership of twenty-plus million, fewer than two million would publicly count themselves LDS. The Church finally lost its tax-exempt status, and within a short time, financial ruin gripped the Church in an iron vice.

At this very moment in time, those few who had faithfully remained true to the Prophet's warnings grew deeper in their convictions. Buffeted from every side, they sought greater blessings, and an outpouring of faith overlaid their sorrows. Priesthood power increased. Miracles became commonplace, and it was widely known that angels walked and talked with many.

In a short time the flood of miracles met head-to-head with the calamitous flood of lies and persecutions, a spiritual detonation occurred.

It had been nearly a year following their return to Utah. Melody had found herself unexpectedly in the front lines of a civil war— not a war of bullets and bombs, but a war of faith and ideology. When she perceived the perils around her, Melody quietly aligned herself with the Prophet. To her joy, so did her three sons.

Sacrament meeting was nearly empty, with fewer than one hundred people in attendance. Bishop Snow was newly called, a young man of great faith, though still in his twenties. He had no counselors to assist him.

"Brothers and sisters," he began following the opening song and prayer. "I apologize that we don't have a sacrament meeting program today. Brother and Sister Prevost informed me last evening that not only would they not be speaking, they would not be returning to church."

A murmur of sadness rolled across those assembled. Melody fought back tears, as she sensed Theodore shaking his head in disbelief. George had been baptized almost as soon as they had returned from England, while Theo had decided to wait.

At that moment the doors in the back of the chapel opened and an older man and woman, and their teenage son entered the room. Seeing Bishop Snow's eyes flicker up, all in the chapel turned toward them. Melody recognized them as Brother and Sister Huntington and his son. They had lost their home months ago, and had moved from the area. It was good to see them again.

"Forgive us," the man said quietly. "We ran out of gas and had to walk the last couple miles."

Bishop Snow smiled. "Brother and Sister Huntington! Come up here," he said happily. "Come up here and address us. Would you be so kind?" he asked with obvious relief, and then took his seat.

Brother Huntington straightened, but did not register surprise. He simply led his little family to the stand, and then himself to the podium.

As his family took a seat, Brother Huntington slipped off his battered coat and laid it across the seat behind him, then turned to the podium. Brother Huntington was all of seventy years old. He had a full head of white hair, and an equally white beard several inches long. His clothing was tattered, but his face was bright with faith. Melody could not remember him having served in any visible capacity in the ward or stake. It seemed as if the Huntington family had merely lived a quiet life somewhere on the outskirts of LDS society.

Their aged speaker steadied himself with both hands upon the pulpit, yet remained silent for almost a minute. When he finally spoke his voice was quiet, yet strong. "I left for church with you this morning feeling a deep urgency to worship with you today. We knew we didn't have enough fuel to arrive here, and merely trusted in God to get us here. By the way, I had no idea I would be speaking," he said with a smile, "or I might not have been in such a rush to get here."

This elicited some laughter from the audience.

Brother Huntington ran his fingers through his perfectly white hair, then smiled, seemingly at a loss as to what to say. His eyes fell upon a young woman in a wheelchair three rows back. He seemed to gaze at her for a long time. The young lady was fourteen, and had spent her entire life as an invalid. She had long, light brown hair that her mother had carefully combed and braided. Hair clips shaped like butterflies held her hair out of her face. Though her body was wasted and withered, her face was astonishingly beautiful. Melody realized everyone present had turned to look at the young woman.

"I think I'm going to speak about miracles," Brother Huntington said, and promptly walked from the stand until he stood before the young girl.

He knelt before her and took both her hands in his. He turned to her mother. "What is her name?" he asked, his voice trembling.

"Her name is Vicky Ann," her mother replied.

"How long has she been like this?" he asked, looking back into the child's eyes.

"All her life," came the quiet reply.

Brother Huntington stood, still holding the youngster's deformed hands. His voice was soft and utterly calm. "Vicky Ann, in the name of Jesus Christ I command you to arise," he said, and gently lifted her hands.

Vicky's head lolled back, her mouth open and wet with saliva. The sounds of the congregation's polite concern were unheard by Brother Huntington, who merely stepped back still holding her hands. The chair rolled forward. Someone coughed poignantly.

"Come on, Vicky," Brother Huntington said with a kindly nod. "Hold her chair," he said to the mother, who quickly set the brake. Whispers of disbelief arose all around them.

"This is ridiculous," someone said and was greeted by a murmur of agreement. A dozen people stood and with flailing arms and stomping feet, left the chapel.

To everyone's surprise, Brother Huntington smiled broadly. He looked down at Vicky. "OK, the faithless ones have left, and you can do it." With a sound something between a growl and a laugh, Vicky stood, looking down at her feet. A look of joy lit her face. She looked up and rushed into Brother Huntington's arms.

"Well done!" Brother Huntington cried. "I knew you had the faith! We just had to wait for a few doubters to leave." He turned her toward her mother who was gasping in utter amazement.

Brother Huntington looked around and saw a large woman nearby who was stooped with age, sitting next to a portable oxygen bottle. "Sister Abigail Foster, aren't you about tired of lugging that bottle around with you?" he said forcefully.

"I surely am!" she said, and stood painfully, her back deeply bowed.

Brother Huntington raised an arm to the square and placed the other on her shoulder. "Sister Abigail Foster, in the name of Jesus Christ, I command you to be healed," he commanded in a voice Melody could only describe as utter joy. He stepped forward and slipped the mask from her face, then taking her hands, quietly said. "You have to do your part, Abigail. Stand up straight. Just do it," he instructed. Melody was close enough to see a look of determination on Sister Foster's face give way to a look of faith. Sister Foster straightened to her full height. Melody was startled to see her clothing collapsing around her.

"Praise God," Brother Huntington cried, his voice cracking with emotion. "I'm sure the Relief Society sisters will help you tailor your wardrobe," he said with a joyful laugh.

Sister Foster gasped, and turned toward the audience. Her face was devoid of the ravages of weight and disease. Some began to weep openly.

Brother Huntington returned to the pulpit where he stood for a long moment in complete silence. He gazed out across the faithful whose faces were now streaked with tears of joy. He nodded once, then spoke. "All done through the grace, power, and merits of Him who is mighty to save. In the name of Jesus Christ, Amen." Then he sat down beside his wife.

The battlefield whereon human lives were being lost paused to catch its breath, and the world waited to see what Russia would do next. Some years earlier the so-called "struggling democracy" in Russia had ceased to exist, if it had ever really existed anywhere but in U.S. newspapers. All the foreign missionaries were expelled. Every church, temple and other Church-owned property, LDS and otherwise, was absorbed by the state, and religious meetings were strictly outlawed. As the fear of war in Europe grew, air travel became severely overbooked and ticket prices skyrocketed.

In the threat of imminent war, other countries ordered the missionaries to leave. The first missions affected were the former Eastern Bloc nations, then France, Italy, Germany and Spain. The missionary force fell from a high of nearly 100,000 to less than half that number overnight. The Church could no longer bring so many missionaries home with limited airtravel and now-astronomical plane fares. When families in the U.S. could not finance their return, young men and women had to take jobs and earn their own way home, many on ships.

Completely against the odds, with miracles attending, all the missionaries eventually made it home. None were lost. Many were blessed by the charity of beleaguered local members in their missions. Most worked as much as a full year for their ticket home, daring to share their testimonies to those who would listen. As they arrived home, they knew there was no likelihood of ever completing their formal missions, but every likelihood of being sucked headfirst into a world-wide war.

What was strange about all this was that these returning missionaries came home with fire in their souls impassioned by the Spirit of God. Their sense of loss in their missionary assignments was turned to rekindling the waning faith of their families and wards. It was, in fact, the thousands of miracles Heavenly Father had wrought to bring His sons and daughters home that kept the remaining saints' eyes opened to belief. Had the Church been able to simply bundle them all onto aircraft and bring them home, these faith-anchoring miracles could not have occurred.

What appeared to be a tragedy was in fact theirs and the Church's salvation. Nobody could explain away the awful riptide of so-called proof against Christianity. Neither could they explain away the powerful deliverance they had beheld in their miraculous return home. As much as any miracle wrought by the hand of God, this tidal wave of faithful missionaries returning home saved not just the Church, but its floundering population from impending spiritual extinction.

The stage for world war set, Russia relentlessly advanced their vast armies and weaponry into Eastern Europe, while China had its eye fixed on South Asia and ultimately the United States. As NATO allies cried for help, and under threat of worldwide domination, the U.S. was finally forced to enter the war. They began an involuntary draft, instituted liberal rationing, and began enforcing laws against hoarding food. Stock markets including the Dow Jones Industrial Average were rocked amid rumors and global speculation and fell nearly four thousand points in a single day. Long-abused entitlement programs and even some food stamp programs were discontinued as riots erupted around the country, with many larger cities forced to enact martial law. The Church "suggested" all members bring their food storage beyond three months necessities to their local Stake Centers, where it would be stored and redistributed to the needy. The government immediately insisted the Church turn over all collected food. The Church refused.

Melody found herself in greater difficulty as each day passed. At first her two older sons were able to avoid going into the military simply because they were not U.S. citizens. She watched as thousands of young men and women were conscripted into the army, or went underground to escape. A general conscription order was issued for all able-bodied persons ages sixteen through forty-five. No longer was gender or citizenship an issue. The penalty for avoiding the draft was death. Eventually, the penalty was enforced on the front lawn of the offender's home. As soon as this became general practice, the mood darkened further and ranks of the armed forces swelled with reluctant conscripts.

Never before had so many nations combined for so great a unified cause, or so great a threat. World opinion soared in favor of the war, and national pride became the religion of the day. The old ethnic dividing lines flared in hatred. Food distribution centers were set up in former grocery stores, and armed troops checked ration stubs.

In a last-ditch attempt to avoid defaulting on its staggering national debt interest payments, the U.S. devalued the dollar beyond the breaking-point and runaway inflation ensued. The bond market imploded as the nation's national credit plummeted. Soon money became worthless, and unemployment was rampant. Huge companies folded overnight, or switched their production to wartime needs. Everything became scarce. Millions of families lost their homes when payments could not be made. The black market roared to life, and food became of far greater value than money. Barter became commonplace as people avoided the distribution centers except for items available nowhere else.

Laws were enacted to stem unemployment and put every citizen to work. Factories bustled with labor paid largely in food and housing rations. To ensure that food was distributed only to those employed in the factories or other "authorized" jobs, a small microchip was implanted under the skin of the right hand or just above the hairline on the forehead. Nearly overnight it became nearly impossible to obtain food unless one had the chip implanted. For a short time, a government-issued credit-card type ID card was allowed instead, but most chose the implants simply out of fear or sheer convenience.

The Church issued a general announcement urging their members not to get the chip implants. They said nothing about carrying the ID card. A full two-thirds of the members ignored their leaders' warnings and got the chip. Those with faith understood its significance and considered it the mark of the beast.

To heavily entice conformity, a law was passed erasing all mortgage debt for those who accepted the implants and worked in war preparations. Black-marketers were hunted down and imprisoned until the underground barely existed.

Soon after however, receiving the chip became absolutely mandatory. Even worse, membership or allegiance to any organization not approved by the government had to be denounced in order to get the chip and receive food and housing.

It became easier and easier to tell the "Good Mormons" from the "Bad Mormons" by the fact that everyone without the chip implant weighed an average of 25 pounds less. The "Bad Mormons" were those who obeyed their leaders, and refused the chips, in the face of massive pressure and fear of survival.

At this time the former economic structure of the world finally collapsed. State currencies became worthless overnight. The value of gold and silver coins skyrocketed but could not be traded without significant risk. Everyone, not just some or a few, but everyone who had refinanced and expanded their homes, or purchased larger homes with remaining high mortgages, inevitably lost their properties. But those who had the chip implanted were told they had nothing to worry about. The government-influenced banks still repossessed their home, but they were "given" another home to live in. It was generally a smaller home, but it was a roof over their heads. The government allowed them to occupy it as long as they remained productively involved in the new economy and the war effort.

Only those who had no, or very small mortgages on their homes escaped the loss of their properties. The "new socialized economy" eventually required that all banks turn their assets and functions over to the government. With all homes with outstanding mortgages now in government ownership, the new socialized banks did not have the will or manpower to search out the few who were still privately owned or with small outstanding balances. Those who had obeyed the Prophet's warnings to become debt-free quietly retained possession of their homes.

Small businesses that could adapt to the emerging barter system and who had not used the hyper-inflationary years to build and borrow remained somewhat intact and in private ownership. Those owners, especially among the saints who had ignored the Prophet's warnings about debt, lost everything.

One morning, Melody received a letter from Samuel's employer in Texas. They regretted, the letter said, to inform her that her husband had been found dead in Russia. The letter was a mere two curt sentences.

Melody shook her head in disbelief, and then anger. Life these days it seemed was incredibly cheap—not worth more than a few casual words! She did not tell Sammy, but took the letter and burned it. Though anguish tugged at her soul, Samuel's last words to her to not believe his employer if they reported him dead, sustained her. Fear often haunted her dreams at night; but when she awoke, her faith in Sam and pure trust in God kept her hope alive for one more day.

A few weeks later, largely because the Church had refused to enforce the chip implants and to turn over it's food and assets, the U.S. government passed a law targeting all dissenting organizations, considering the Church of Jesus Christ of Latter-day Saints now to be an enemy of the State. Many local Church leaders were arrested or killed. The First Presidency went into hiding, and the Quorum of the Twelve scattered underground. All Church property was confiscated, and the Salt Lake Temple was seized by the state and permanently closed.

Melody was never entirely sure why the government simply gave her small home to another family. Most people in her circumstances kept their homes. Melody had refused to let Sammy be implanted with the chip, and he could no longer attend school. And although Melody had an ID card, she had refused to receive the implant. She had a chair in the Utah Symphony, but was told she was not contributing sufficiently to the war effort to have a four-bedroom home and had refused to get the chip. The new family awarded her home had five kids, all of whom were implanted and the father was working for the government.

Melody and Sammy, who was now eleven years old, were given 24 hours to move out of their home and into the street. The new family who moved in had been civil enough to let them stay in the garage a few days until they could make other arrangements. She was not allowed to take anything away except a few personal items. Theo and George had left months ago, at Melody's insistence, to avoid fighting in the war. She had no idea where they were now, but firmly believed that the Lord would protect them, and they would meet again. They had both joined the Church by then, their faith burning brightly. Both had refused the mark of the beast, and had been forced underground to survive.

It was late in the day when Melody and Sammy were finally forced to leave the relative safety of the garage. Except for one small bag of clothing, a journal and a few photos, they left everything behind. It was October, and the weather had turned cold that night. Melody could think of nowhere to go, so they just sat down on the curb outside their former home, shivering as they clung to one another, and prayed a fervent prayer for deliverance.

Moments later an old school bus with darkened windows screeched to a stop before her. The door clanged open to reveal her father-in-law sitting in the driver's seat.

"All aboard!" he announced cheerfully.

Melody cried out with joy, and climbed in with Samuel's aged parents, his sisters and their children. She praised God for this merciful answer to their prayers. All phone communication between the family had been cut off months ago, and only the Lord's intervention could have brought Jim Mahoy to her rescue. Melody looked around at her beloved inlaws, and smiled as Sammy talked excitedly with his cousin across the aisle. This was a happy bundle of exiles, though mostly women and children, since their boys had been drafted for the war. Melody boarded that bus solely upon faith, but was so overjoyed that she did not even ask where they were going. Jim aimed the bus northward.

Jim had heard that a few faithful members of the Church were eking out a safe existence in the rugged hills of Northern Idaho. They had no choice but to attempt to find them. Besides the refugees, the battered old bus held large containers of water, emergency supplies, quite a bit of bedding, a small stack of books, a few cans of gas, and a few meager boxes of canned food. The gas had been collected from motorcycles, lawn mowers, chain saws, even a few kerosene lamps.

Melody was surprised to find everyone cheerful, upbeat, and full of faith. The fountain of their hope flowed almost exclusively from Jim Mahoy, her husband's righteous father. He actually seemed to be filled with joy that they were worthy to be persecuted for their faith. Anyone who did not understand the kind of faith Grandpa Mahoy possessed might quickly think him quite insane. Yet, he was rock solid in both his faith, and his sensibilities. Besides all this, he was perfectly willing to ignore any "proof," incontrovertible or otherwise, that flew in the face of his burning testimony of Jesus Christ, and a lifetime of profound experiences with the Spirit.

They drove past every government checkpoint without much trouble, even though the guards knew they were likely "Bad" Mormons because they didn't have the chips. Persecution of Christians and especially members of the Church had been severe, but now there really was no longer a Church for them to belong to. Though they could detain or kill anyone without the chip, those who manned the gates finally waved them through. After all, it was their own foolish choice to be poverty-stricken and starving. If they had received the chip, they would have food like everyone else.

Somewhere near the Idaho border they heard over the radio that Washington D.C., New York, Boston, San Francisco and Los Angeles had been attacked by tactical nuclear weapons, wiping out the majority of elected government officials. No one was sure who had launched the attack. All civilized life in the United States came to an immediate halt. An emergency shadow government took control, which had been prepared for such an event. Martial law was declared, and all civil liberties were suspended.

People began desperately pouring from the major cities into the suburbs and farmlands. Looting, murder, and ruthless gangs became commonplace. So many people tramped into the farmlands of California and the Midwest what little remaining food was stripped from the land and there was serious doubt there could be a crop the next year.

In the face of starvation, people went berserk in search of food. Those wielding true power in the world had carefully worked to weaken and polarize the United States for decades. With society now in chaos, the new President called upon the Secretary-General of the United Nations to deploy U.N. troops to help, who had been pre-staged all throughout the country over many years. These troops emerged almost as if from the woodwork wearing the blue helmets and began patrolling the streets in armored vehicles, shooting suspected looters on sight. Troops wearing the blue helmets did not speak English and appeared to be Asian. Most claimed they were Chinese; in fact, many were North Korean.

The righteous raised their voice to the heavens, and pleaded fervently for divine intervention. God was their only hope.

15

THE CAMPS OF GOD

A thunderclap was heard around the world as a vast Russian army breached its southern border into Turkey and swept across Syria and Iraq in a surprise attack. Nobody could believe their sudden aggression and advanced nuclear weaponry. All three countries immediately surrendered their armed forces when threatened with annihilation. Russia captured their supplies and troops and thundered toward their former ally, Iran. All U.N. attempts at diplomatic negotiations with the Russians were summarily rebuffed.

Within days, Russia and China and their close allies suddenly left the U.N., announcing their new "Eastern Coalition." Struck with fear, the United States and the rest of Europe created the hastily-formed "Western United Nations."

Threatened with war, Iran amassed troops on its borders and declared a potential nuclear attack against Russia, Israel and the United States. Israel vowed a preemptive strike if the word "nuclear" were ever used in the same sentence with "Israel" again. The whole world hoped the collapse of Turkey and Iraq would placate the Russian juggernaut. For about a week it appeared to do so.

However on the first day of May that year, and completely without warning, Russia leveled Tehran and Baghdad in a shower of nuclear warheads and then swept across Iran with little opposition. They paused long enough to install a puppet government and outlaw the practice of Islam. Russian soldiers began going from city to city looting and demolishing mosques who opposed them. Wave after wave of Arabs surged against the Russian desecrators in what they saw as the greatest "holy war" ever fought. All resistant Muslims were slaughtered by the thousands.

As a matter of survival, the Muslim tide of resistance fled the homeland of their fathers and poured into Saudi Arabia. Refugees were given food, guns and hasty training. In less than three months, Saudi Arabia commanded the third largest standing army in the world.

With the fall of Iran and almost all radical Islam in general, Israel considered this the fulfillment of prophecy and immediately began dismantling the sacred Dome of the Rock mosque, and reassembling it on another site. Muslims around Israel revolted and attacked in all-out hatred. They were summarily repulsed and slaughtered without even slowing the construction project. Construction of the Third Temple at Jerusalem began immediately. In less than a month's time the outer walls were standing at their full height, and the wall around the temple compound was nearly completed. Materials for the temple had been carefully prepared for decades. Such fervor gripped the souls of the Jews to build the temple anew that quotas were set and passes allotted for those with skills to join the holy construction project. Tens of thousands of Jews and Gentiles, including willing laborers were kept out by sturdy, electrified fences.

Once free of the Islamic occupation of the temple mount, excavation began in earnest. Since the days of Rome, no Jew had been allowed to excavate beneath the historic temple site. The system of underground caves and tunnels was far more extensive than ever imagined. The tunnel leading to the Holy of Holies was finally discovered, and a free-flowing well directly underneath the temple was found and uncapped. Water quickly filled the three man-made caverns beneath the temple and flowed outward for the first time since it was capped by the Romans nearly two thousand years earlier.

During all this, Russian troops simultaneously blitzed into former Soviet Bloc nations and quickly reestablished themselves in absolute rule. Martial law was declared, labor collectives rebuilt, major-city factories refurbished, grocery stores were restocked—and the people rejoiced. The state religion of labor was once again elevated to godhood, and the Soviet communist machine groaned to life. With a renewal of red pride, the new Soviet state began churning out munitions at an unimaginable pace. A full 75 percent of their national budget was poured into the war.

It was then that China finally unleashed its unending hordes into Asia. Nearly one million Chinese soldiers on a vast number of ships left their eastern shore and headed straight for an easy victory in Taiwan which they had been planning for decades. With no time to respond, they took the island in mere days. China and their long-time puppet North Korea then joined forces, and three million combined troops with tanks and warheads surged across the border of South Korea.

The Western Coalition fired a pre-emptive tactical nuclear missile into the oncoming surge. The vast enemy army was temporarily reduced, but more waves of troops surged behind them. Within two weeks of warfare, the reinforced Chinese-North Korean army still outnumbered the coalition four to one in manpower. Unable to use more nuclear weapons without fear of killing themselves, the Coalition was forced to meet wave after wave of heavily-armed Chinese and North Korean troops on the ground.

Day after day the hordes came. Day after day the Western Coalition forces released an unending stream of conventional bombs, trying to avoid getting in the way of their own death. The Chinese died literally by the millions. But because of their sheer numbers, in less than three days the Chinese broke through; hand-to hand-fighting ensued, and the seemingly endless Chinese troops surged forward. By the end of the week there was not a single organized Western Coalition survivor left in South Korea. The loss of Chinese and North Korean life had been staggering: more than seventy-five percent of their army was dead.

Having secured the entire Korean Peninsula, the combined Chinese forces cheered their immense victory over the West. Because the military takeover of South Korea was over so quickly, nearly every Western Coalition military machine there had remained intact. The Chinese picked up these weapons and with two million new reinforcements from home, they continued to sweep into the remainder of Asia in unrelenting conquest. Executing their plan for world domination, China then surged into vulnerable ports all over Africa which they had purchased and secured over decades.

With Russia's overthrow of Iran, the rest of Islam soon surrendered to the brutal Eastern Coalition. Their only condition was that their combined forces would first focus on destroying Israel, and all else later. Russia was by now in need of more armaments and reinforcements, and they called upon their Chinese allies who readily agreed. The vast combined Russian and Isalmic forces then moved toward Jerusalem.

The line was drawn in the ancient sands, and soon every nation on earth would gather outside the Holy City.

The world economy was in shambles. To sustain their war effort, the remaining Soviet economy was now completely occupied in supporting the war. As every able-bodied citizen had been recruited into the army, many of the smaller Russian factories were abandoned to funnel enough workers to man the massive military production plants in Moscow and St. Petersburg. As a matter of survival, families were obliged to leave the empty factory cities and migrate to the country. Mercifully, after that time Samuel and his little band of refugees encountered no further attacks from the military.

It was full-blown winter when Alexei's band of rag-tag refugees arrived outside such a factory city. As they had been trudging onward for three months, exposure and starvation had dwindled them from over 2,500 souls to fewer than 750.

No one bothered to tell Samuel the name of the city, or even if it had a name. All he knew was that it sat in a narrow mountain pass, with a river against its eastern wall, and a mountain against the western side through which they needed to pass. It was an old-style factory city, built not only to contain the factory, but to form a compound for imprisoning the workers. From the outside it looked like the backside of massive, windowless warehouses a half-mile or more wide. The buildings were constructed of sturdy gray concrete. The only way into the city was through a large gate which was now piled deep in junk vehicles and rubble.

There was no sign of life within the walls, and much damage was evident on the outside of the buildings as if they had been under sustained attack, and yet had somehow endured. Alexei stopped a short distance from the towering walls and pondered their options. Snow was falling heavily as the people milled around, miserably looking for anything to make a fire.

A large hole about fifteen feet above the ground had been blown through the wall near the gate. After some effort a makeshift ladder was constructed and Vladimir, Alexei, Samuel and three other men climbed the rickety ladder.

"It's an old flour mill," Vladimir told him after looking around in the darkened interior. Though no milling equipment remained, Samuel could see the metal chutes that once guided the grain on its journey through the mill. The floor on which they stood had been used to bag the flour and prepare it for shipping.

"Hey, look at this," Samuel said in broken Russian as he stumbled over something soft on the floor. "Flour bags," he said as he picked up several dusty, gray bags. Others helped search until they had literally hundreds of fine-linen flour bags. They were in better shape than the clothing most of them wore. They tossed them out the opening to those waiting on the ground. The people received them with a cheer and immediately began cutting them into badly needed clothing.

They discovered that the only doorway leading from this room had been solidly blocked. They were about to give up when Alexei turned to Samuel. By now Samuel felt he could comfortably carry on simple conversations in Russian, without bringing undue attention to the language gifts he had acquired with his "change." He asked Vladimir to translate only when the conversation grew complex.

"We need guidance once again," Alexei said. "What shall we do? We can't go around the city, and therefore must pass through. It is unlikely we shall do so without resistance."

The familiar feelings of truth flowed, and an answer presented itself in his mind. Samuel walked to the right until he found a large ramp covered with sheet metal. The metal had been worn shiny from years of sliding bags of flour down it. He pointed down the chute. "This is the way out, or inside, in our case."

Alexei was the first one down the ramp. He sat on the edge and shoved off. He zipped from sight into the darkness. Samuel heard him swishing around corners, then he came to a stop. Alexei called back up to say he was now on a street. Vladimir went next, then Samuel, and six other men.

They found themselves standing on a loading dock about four feet above a concrete street. It was dusk, and snow was falling heavily. Samuel jumped to the street and immediately saw the flicker of a torch a short distance to his left. The street was blocked by two huge pieces of factory equipment. They were covered with chipped green paint with rollers and large gears on them as if they may have been used for rolling steel. They had been pushed end-to-end across the street so that they formed an impenetrable barrier a dozen feet high. Samuel doubted that even an army tank could push its way past. As they watched, some men climbed onto the machines carrying torches and rifles. When they were assembled there were about ten of them. One of them fired a shot which hit one of the refugees in the shoulder. He spun to the ground with a cry of pain.

"Go back!" one of the men yelled. "We will not let you into our city. If you do not leave immediately we will kill you where you stand and eat your bodies for food!" he said. This produced a demonic howl from the rest of those on the machines. Samuel heard several more rifles cock.

Alexei stepped forward. "We only want to pass through and be on our way. We will not take your food or bother you. Your factory entirely blocks the road!"

Their answer was another shot which chipped the pavement in front of Alexei and lodged in the leg of another of their men.

"Please, we have women and children who will perish if…" he was cut short by a bullet whizzing past his head. He ducked, but did not run. He turned to Samuel.

"God moves mountains. Pray to God, and ask him how we shall move these mountains," Alexei begged him.

Never in his life had Samuel felt what next flowed into his soul. As if he were immersed in liquid fire, the power of God swept through him.

He stepped forward with a perfect knowledge of how God would deliver them. A gun fired, and the bullet slammed into his chest. He took a step back and looked at the wound in his chest. In less than the blink of an eye it closed up and the bullet rattled on the pavement.

Sam looked again at the monstrous machines before him, and raised his left hand before him. A feeling of peace settled over him so powerful that he felt compelled to close his eyes. He slowly moved his hand to the left. Immediately a terrible screeching and grinding noise assaulted his ears. He opened his eyes and watched the machine on the left quickly slide out of the way. He raised his right hand, and moved it to his right. The huge machine scraped to the right so quickly that sparks flew off the pavement. Those who had been on the machines either fell off, or were too terrified to speak.

Now visible, nearly a hundred men with guns and clubs were standing in the street. There were only six with Alexei, two of whom were wounded, and none of them armed. Alexei stepped forward once again and raised his hands in peace. The men on the machine screamed in terror, and many of those in the street dropped their weapons and fell to their knees.

"We mean you no harm," he said in a loud voice. "But, as you see, the power of God is with us, and we must pass through your city. Please make way, and we will shortly leave you in peace. You know this is true, or our God would not give us the power you see."

A cry of fear arose from those in the street. People began running in various directions until only a few remained. When the street was nearly empty a group of four men walked toward them. They were all carrying guns.

A stocky man who appeared to be in his sixties took one more step after the group stopped. He was wearing a tattered coat that came to his knees, a fur hat and boots lined in fur. His hands were wrapped in strips of cloth that seemed to be an attempt at homemade gloves. He stood there a moment, apparently collecting his thoughts, or bolstering his courage.

"I am Motyvich, the mayor of this city. I have never seen the power of God before, but know this is what it must be. Besides, I felt my old heart sing within me with great joy. I will grant you passage through our city if you will teach me of your God, and why you have this power. I wish to know where you are going and why. Will you bring your people inside our protection and take dinner with us? I will trade you food for wisdom. My food, your wisdom," he added with a smile.

"It is a good trade," Alexei said and shook the old man's hand vigorously. "Vladimir, go bring the people into the city."

"How many of you are there?" the mayor wanted to know.

"Besides us, about seven hundred fifty."

Samuel glanced back at Vladimir who had turned and knelt beside their wounded men, praying. Samuel felt a flow of the power of God coming from their direction, and a moment later both men stood. Samuel smiled. Vladimir's faith truly was growing.

Motyvich was still speaking to Alexei. "We are also about that number. Come, I will show you something that will make your old eyes pop from their sockets," he said merrily. As Vladimir and the others climbed back outside, the old man led Samuel and Vladimir down the street. A short distance later they stopped before an iron door large enough to drive a truck through. There were four guards with machine guns standing before it. They unchained and pulled open the big door. A sweet, wholesome smell rolled out of the dark room.

Motyvich took a flashlight from his pocket and clicked it on. In the dim light it made they saw pallets stacked to the ceiling full of sacks of flour and grain.

"It is a beautiful sight, is it not?" their guide exclaimed happily.

"I am having trouble keeping my eyes inside my sockets, as you said," Alexei proclaimed.

"I told you such would be the case."

"How came you into all this food?" Alexei asked.

"We grew much of it with our own hands and brought it here and milled it. When the war broke out more was brought here on its way to Saudi Arabia. When the army ceased to exist, everyone forgot about it, and here it sits."

"Someone will eventually remember it, and come after it." Samuel said in broken Russian.

"You are English, yes?" Motyvich asked.

"No, American," Samuel replied.

"Ah, our old friends the Americans. I will say we are more lucky to be in Mother Russia than in New York today," he said solemnly.

"Why is that?" Samuel asked. He had heard no news of America for months.

"Because the nuclear bombs have leveled it to the ground!" he said emphatically.

Samuel thought about this and the prophecies that it would be destroyed. "It was bound to happen sooner or later," he said.

"Ha!" the mayor cried. "I like this American already. Come, we must make arrangements for your people." He began walking briskly down the street. "We have much food, but very little coal or wood. So, I think we must put you into our homes with our people. Not so comfortable, but much warmer, I think."

"We appreciate your hospitality," Alexei said.

Motyvich leaned close to Alexei and whispered quietly. "It was the American who moved the great machines with the power of God, was it not?" he asked as quietly as he could.

Alexei leaned back and whispered. "His name is Samuel. He is the man of God whom the prophets said would come to lead us to Zion."

"I have heard of these prophets, and of this 'Zion'. But, never have I believed it could be true. Always I thought it was stories from the hearts of superstitious old dreamers," he said more loudly.

"I will tell you the prophecies, and you will see that they are all true!" Alexei proclaimed.

"After you have told me all this, will Samuel, the man of God not teach us also?"

This struck Alexei almost as mightily as a baseball bat between the eyes. He stopped walking suddenly. It was as if the idea had never occurred to him that Samuel might have more knowledge of God that he had not yet taught.

"But, of course it is so," Alexei marveled, as if answering several questions he had asked himself in silence. He turned to Samuel. "You are a man of God and must know the true words of God. How stupid of me to not know this. Samuel, forgive me! But, why did you not tell me? Why did you not teach me? With all my soul I seek the things of God, and day after day I walk next to one who lives with God, and you say nothing?"

"I'm sorry, Alexei. I could not," Samuel replied earnestly. "In all things you lead this people. I am here to assist only you. If you ask, I will teach you. If you do not ask, I can do nothing."

"This I will remember!" Alexei proclaimed. "We waste no more time. Tonight we sleep, tomorrow we assemble the people, and tomorrow evening, you will teach us. If it pleases God, that is."

"It pleases God," Samuel assured him.

The following evening they built a large fire of broken crates in the middle of what appeared to be a large parking lot near the center of the city. Other smaller fires were built beyond to warm the surrounding area. About dusk the people came slowly and found seats on pieces of wood and chunks of concrete. A few brought chairs from their homes not far away. There were about twelve hundred people sitting with expectant faces turned toward him. Samuel could see them all plainly in the flickering light of the fire. There were very few old or very young people. In harsh conditions such as these, only the strongest had survived. Besides a few older people like Alexei, they were mainly in their teens, twenties and thirties. More than two-thirds of them were women. Besides Samuel, Alexei and the mayor were the oldest ones there.

"My fellow citizens," Motyvich called out loudly. It was unlikely those further back could hear. "Our friends have brought with them a prophet of God, and one who possesses the power of God. You all know of the moving of the big machines. It was the prophet Samuel who moved them, and God who gave him the power. He has agreed to teach us. Hear him, my people. Hear the words of God from one who knows Him well!"

Samuel waited as those words were relayed to the people further back. "Thank you, and God bless you," Samuel said, not knowing for sure what to say. He spoke in English, and waited for Vladimir to translate, and for the translation to be relayed back. "I wish to correct only one thing your mayor said. There is only one prophet, and I am not he. I am a servant of God, and one whom he has tasked with aiding this great people in returning to Zion. In time I will teach you who the prophet is, but it is not I."

"I perceive that you are a noble people, long oppressed, and long lost from your heritage. You are the children of Israel, and those whom God has taken in His heart to bring back after their long dispersion. If you wish, I will teach you how to come home." He waited until all had heard the message.

"Oh, yes! Teach us!" they cried almost with a single voice.

Samuel nodded. The crowd grew still. Only the crackling of the fire broke the stillness of the night. As he spoke his voice was punctuated by puffs of vapor in the harsh cold of the night. "There are two great gatherings happening here today. One is of the soul, and the other is of the body. Alexei has been given the job of taking your bodies to your rewards in Zion, and I to assist him. I have been given the great honor of leading your *souls* to Zion."

"Tonight you will come to understand that your body cannot go to Zion and receive your reward there until you have gathered your soul to Zion first."

"What this all means is that you must learn the truth, and embrace it completely in your hearts. You must be baptized and receive the priesthood of God. Then, when you at long last return to the doorsteps of God's temple, you will be permitted to enter. Only then will your journey will be completed, for your body and your soul will have both come home."

"What does Zion mean?" someone cried out, giving voice to the question of a thousand people.

Following Vladimir's translation, Samuel replied. "Zion is God's people, the pure in heart. The people of Zion dwell in the presence of God. They are safe and use the power of God to defend themselves, much as you have seen in your own journey. By the time we arrive at His holy temple, we will be a part of Zion."

"Is Zion then a people, or is there one place called Zion?" the same man cried loudly.

Samuel's voice rang strong. "We will be Zion when we become pure in heart, and when you are each baptized by authority into the gospel. There is also a place called Zion. It has been prepared for all those who become Zion people. When the time is right, I will tell you, and I will take you there, if it pleases God." A spontaneous cheer came from those assembled.

"Then let us be baptized!" someone cried, and hundreds of voices agreed.

The fire seemed to burn hotter at his side for a moment. Samuel rejoiced as he waited for their voices to grow still. He finally held up both hands and a hush fell over them. "You shall, but first you must be taught. First you must know where the power of God resides. You must understand His latter-day work, His true church, and His true doctrine. After you know this, then I will baptize you for the remission of your sins, and you shall receive the gift of the Holy Ghost, and thereafter, His priesthood power. When we arrive at the holy temple each of you must be full of truth, and cleansed of your sins in order to enter and receive the blessings of the temple, including marriage for all eternity, and the sealing of the family so that it will endure forever."

"You must teach us!" they cried, their voices almost desperate.

Samuel waited as their anxious cries grew still, and then paused in the resulting silence as the warmth of the Spirit spread across them and peace healed their fears. When all that could be heard was the crackling of the fire, he spoke again.

"In the spring of 1820, in a state within the United States called New York, there lived a young man whose name was Joseph Smith…" he began. His final words tapered into the night three hours later. The fires had burned to embers, and the people were shivering. But they hardly noticed their frozen limbs for they were alive with the fire of testimony bourne of God.

Samuel prayed in love with them, then sent them to their beds with the promise that they would meet again tomorrow. His heart sang with great joy as he slowly walked back beside Alexei, Vladimir and Motyvich.

"It is a great day," Motyvich said quietly.

"A glorious day," Alexei agreed.

"A blessed day," Samuel proclaimed.

Alexei quietly motioned for Samuel to follow him as they left Motyvich at his door. They walked a short distance to where one of the trucks was parked, carefully guarded by faithful members of Alexei's people.

"I have something you should see." Alexei stepped onto the bumper of the truck and lifted a large metal chest from the truck which he handed down to Vladimir. They carefully set it on the crumbling concrete street. Alexei undid six screw-type clamps with large wing nuts. From the symbols on the box, Samuel surmised it had at one time contained nuclear material. It was both water and airtight. Samuel hoped for their sakes it was free of nuclear contamination.

Upon opening the box Alexei removed a delicately carved wooden box, which he then opened with a key hanging from a silver chain around his neck. Inside was a leather-bound book of obvious antiquity. He lifted it carefully and handed it to Samuel.

"These are the writings of our prophets," he said with reverent awe in his voice.

The book was quite heavy, and apparently fragile. Vladimir stepped up and held the book so that Samuel could examine it. One of the guards switched on a bright loading light attached to the rear of the truck and aimed it at the book. The ancient book itself was about the size of a photo album, approximately twelve inches square. They were bound with leather-covered wood of very skillful craftsmanship. It had a hand-sewn binding. The cover bore bold script completely illegible to Samuel.

Samuel carefully opened to the first page containing writing. The pages crackled ominously as he turned them. Samuel looked up from the book into Alexei's eyes, which were sparkling with happiness. The pages were unexpectedly thick. A moment's inspection suggested they were animal skins rather than paper. The book gave off a peculiar smell, a mix of cedar and antiquity. The rest of the smell was something akin to mothballs.

The book was written in a language Samuel could not read. The lettering was small and careful, with flourishes at the beginning of the sections of text. The flow of the text appeared to be in three columns from left to right. There were occasional hand-drawn pictures scattered among the text. Most of these graphics were skillfully executed. Others were little more than line drawings that could as easily have been crude maps as something else.

"What does it say?" Samuel asked after many minutes pondering. The Spirit was burning brightly within him, and his every sense told him this was a volume of great worth to the Lord and this people. He longed to know what its message was.

"We do not know," Alexei replied with a carefully studied response that Samuel was true. "We have lost the old language."

"But, I heard you quote some of it earlier," Samuel replied.

"We have an oral version which has been passed down from father to son for many generations. Even those who possess this knowledge have great doubts concerning its accuracy."

"Why?"

"Because it is so fantastic, so utterly unbelievable," Alexei answered

"Yet, you believe it," Samuel added.

"I do," the old patriarch replied emphatically. "It seems to be a part of me to believe. I always have."

Samuel pulled the book open midway, and found the flow of the text had changed, as if the writer, or scribe had changed. He studied pictures on the pages and thumbed to the end. There was a score of blank pages at the end as if the scribe had intended to write more. He closed the book carefully and held it out to Alexei, but Alexei did not reach for the book.

"Part of what I do know about this book," Alexei said instead, "is that you are to help translate it for us."

Samuel blinked in surprise, and retained possession of the book. Though completely unexpected, his words had the ring of truth. He opened the book again, and still the pages clung to their message with a tight fist. Then, suddenly, he knew what to do with the book. "Our living prophet is a seer," he said as much to himself as to Alexei.

"This I know. You must take him the book," Alexei said with finality. "He will read its words to us. Will you do this?"

"Alexei, we will hand it to him together. Until then, your fathers have kept it safe for over a thousand years. I suggest you continue to guard it until we come to Zion."

"This is a good thing," Alexei said, and took the ancient volume with obvious respect. He rolled it back into the black cloth, closed it in the wooden box, and packed it away in its airtight chest.

At this same moment on the opposite side of the globe, Melody's first hint that something was terribly wrong was when the old motor home suddenly screeched to a halt. She had been holding one of her little nieces, and the sudden stop started the child crying again. She carefully set the little one down and made her way to the front. The road before them was blocked by old cars and trucks. A group of men was doing something on the ground not far from the bus. With a start she realized they were beating someone. From the energy they were putting into their work she was forced to assume their victim was either dead, or shortly would be.

"We can't let this continue," Grandpa Mahoy cried, and jumped from his seat. At 87 years old, he was just barely able to walk, let alone fight. A dozen hands restrained him. He was the only adult male in the motor home, and he was desperately needed where he was. They urged him to wait, even to back up and find another way. Certainly, it was not their fight.

"All right," he said, shrugging off their hands. "I'll handle this another way. Everybody sit down." They just barely had enough time to take their seats before the boxy old vehicle lurched forward. He laid his hand on the horn and roared toward them. A dozen startled faces looked up, then bolted for the sides of the road for safety behind their barrier. He swerved and slammed on the brakes, just barely missing the body in the road.

"Grab him!" he ordered, and Melody and several others jumped from the door. They yanked up the unfortunate soul and hauled him inside. Before the door was even shut Grandpa backed the motor home up and then raced forward. At the last instant he swerved off the road, through a barbed wire fence, and then back onto the road. People, bedding, babies, pots and pans flew in every direction. They lurched back up onto the road, and roared down the street. For a few minutes it looked as if the men were going to chase them, but they gave up, apparently thinking it not worth the gas it would take to catch them.

"Help me," Melody ordered as she and Grandma Mahoy struggled to roll the person they had picked up onto his back. He appeared to be an older man, his hair sprinkled with gray. The man was unconscious, his face bloodied and smeared with mud. Melody carefully dabbed away the grime to survey the extent of his injuries. No limbs were broken, and no serious cuts could be found, though his flesh was black and blue everywhere they looked.

As Melody was wiping his forehead his eyes flickered open. They were the deepest blue she had ever seen.

"Hello, Melody." The old man said happily in a British accent. The combination of the eyes and the accent suddenly brought the impossible truth full force.

"Mr. Helaman!" she cried, and wrapped her arms around him. "Thank God we stopped, and that you're all right!"

"Why yes, thank God. And, thank you, sir," he said, turning stiffly to address Grandpa Mahoy in the driver's seat. He had slowed the motor home back to a slow pace to conserve fuel.

"You're sure welcome. I'm glad we came in time. Melody, do you know this man?" Grandpa asked.

"Oh Grandpa, yes, I know him very well! This is the man who helped me get my sons out of England. He bought us tickets both ways, and got us passports on a moment's notice. I practically owe him everything in this world!"

Grandpa smiled warmly at his new passenger. "Melody has often spoken of you, brother Helaman. God bless you for all you have done for this family," he said as he continued to drive.

"The debt is repaid," Helaman said with finality. "Here, would you help me stand, please?" he asked, and the women clustered tightly around him helped him up. "I hate being on my back surrounded by people. It seems to happen to me a lot," he added ruefully.

"I can understand that," Grandpa empathized. "Those folks back there didn't seem to like you very much, brother. Why were they beating on you?"

"I had nothing to give them. They said I either had to give them food, gold, or my life. I told them I had none of the former, so they proceeded to take the latter."

"The world is falling apart," Grandma said with disgust.

Helaman snorted meaningfully. Melody interpreted it to mean something similar to "You ain't seen nothin' yet." She was exactly right.

"Helaman," Melody said, suddenly curious. "The last I saw of you, you were getting on a plane for England. Shortly thereafter all international travel was suspended. Now, here you are in Idaho. I don't mean to pry, but why are you here, and where were you going?"

"Why, I was coming to see you," he said matter-of-factly.

"What? Why?"

"Because I made a promise to assist you if you needed me while Samuel is away."

"You've more than fulfilled your promise," Melody assured him earnestly.

"It won't be fulfilled until Samuel returns to you. Until then, you need me again."

"What makes you say that?" she demanded, not willing to believe she was once again in desperate straits.

"The truth," he replied simply.

She had to think about that for a moment. "Okay, the truth then. But how did you know I was headed to Idaho, and then found me even before I got there! You would have never met up with me…."

"And…. here we are," she echoed weakly.

Helaman laughed and sat near her, facing the back of the bus. "Since I'm here to help you, may I make a suggestion?"

"Certainly," Melody replied without enthusiasm. She was still pondering his former words.

"Good. Ask Brother Mahoy to take the next dirt road to the right."

"What? Why? How do you know there's a dirt road. What's the reason?"

"So many questions," he responded, then would say no more. All the women stared at him in wonder.

Melody called up to the front. "Grandpa?"

"Yes dear," Grandpa replied, unable to hear the conversation going on.

"Grandpa, is there a dirt road on the right up there?" Melody asked, trying to see out the windows.

"Don't see one, Melody."

She looked back at Helaman, whose eyes were closed as if to block out the pain of his bruises. She continued, "Grandpa, if you see one on the right in the next few minutes, will you please turn off on it?"

"Why Honey? We won't make much time on a dirt road, and we need to get further away from those men."

"I'm sorry, but I need to go to the bathroom," she said. It was a truth, but not *the* truth. Helaman opened one eye briefly, then closed it. A small smile formed on his old face.

"Here's a dirt road," Grandpa suddenly called from the front. Melody still could not see out the windshield from where she sat. The motorhome veered right, then bounced down the road a short distance and screeched to a halt.

"Farther," Helaman said quietly.

"Go a little farther please, Grandpa," Melody called. They moved ahead slowly as the lane grew more rutted. After a little farther they suddenly dropped down a short hill and came to a stop.

"Well, I'll be! Look at that!" Grandpa said loudly.

Melody made her way to the front. "It looks like an old barn," she said, staring in disbelief at the low structure built into the hillside. It had a dirt roof overgrown with weeds. Heavy timbers defined a door large enough to drive the motor home through.

"It's an old potato cellar," Laura Mahoy said from the passenger seat. "We used these when I was a girl. We kept potatoes in them through the winter and sold them in the spring. They were completely underground just like this one. I wonder if…"

"These things haven't been used in nearly a hundred years. Are you thinking there might be potatoes in it, Mama?" Grandpa asked. "No way. No possible way."

"I suppose you're right," she said. "Besides, if there were, whoever put them there would have come back for them already with this food shortage we've got going. Silly idea," she said mirthlessly.

Grandpa looked at Melody and asked, "So girl, are you going to use the bathroom?"

Melody looked up in surprise, then smiled sheepishly. "Oh, sure. I'll be right back. Let's let the kids run a bit while we're stopped, okay?"

"Good idea," Grandma said.

"Stay within sight of the motor home, kids." Grandpa Mahoy urged. The children streamed out the door and across the snowy ground. As open as it was here they could wander for miles and still be visible.

Melody was nearly the last one out the door when something occurred to her. She turned back to Helaman. His eyes were upon her intently. She took a step backward toward the outdoors. "I'll check the root cellar," she said, and stepped onto the ground. His only reply was a small smile.

Melody found the big doors old and battered by time. They were padlocked shut with a very large, but surprisingly new padlock which had been painted brown to look old and rusty. Her curiosity got the better of her and she searched until she found a big rock. She raised it up and heaved it against the lock. The rock bounced off sharply and nearly landed on her foot. She did this several times before Grandpa came up behind her. She showed him the lock, and he grew curious as well.

It took most of an hour to batter-open the lock. They pulled the heavy door open to reveal a cavernous room with a dirt floor wide enough to drive the motorhome and several others into. It was completely empty. Melody felt devastated, angry, and hungry. It had taken energy she did not have to help batter open the door. She was about to return when she remembered all Helaman had done for her, and how he had never let her down. Still, it did seem horribly unfair. In frustration she picked up the big rock and heaved it into the empty room. It hit the dirt floor and bounced with a hollow *thunk*.

"Hey, that didn't sound like a dirt floor," Grandpa observed, his eyes wide. He walked to the spot and scraped with his heel. About six inches down he scraped across wood—new wood. They dug away the thin layer of dirt and found an access door, which they pulled it up to reveal a wooden stair. Someone fetched their only flashlight from the motor home, and Grandpa descended slowly, flashing the dim beam back and forth. He disappeared from sight, but they could hear him bumping into things down there.

He returned suddenly with a bag in his arms. "Potatoes!" he cried, and pushed them over his head. A dozen eager hands grasped the bag and pulled it up. "Carrots!" he yelled. "Cabbage and pumpkins!" A cheer arose from every throat. He passed an armload of each up to those above then climbed the stairs.

"Is that all of it?" They asked almost in unison.

"No, there's a lot more," he proclaimed happily.

"Let's get it all!" someone yelled.

"No!" he said forcefully.

"Why? We're practically starving!" they cried.

"It's not ours. We will take enough for a few days, and we'll leave something in exchange, and a thank you note."

"But!" they cried.

"Go get that big quilt Grandma made, and those extra flashlight batteries. I think we can spare a shaker of salt and some pepper too. And bring me that piece of paper and pencil."

Someone hurried off to do his bidding. They carefully buried the trap door and closed the big cellar. They rubbed old grease mixed with dirt on the door and lock to make it look old again. It was still battered open, but the cellar was as invisible as before.

The women were just gathering twigs to light a fire when Helaman lowered himself painfully to the ground. "What did you find?" he asked.

"Food!" the little ones cried happily. "We're going to roast potatoes and carrots," they exclaimed.

Melody looked at her old friend with misty eyes. "Thank you, Helaman. I'm sorry I ever doubted you," she said as she slipped an arm through his.

"You think I knew this cellar was here?" he asked, amazement in his voice.

"What I think is that you always show up when I need you most," she said lovingly.

"A pretty good coincidence, I'd say!" he laughed. Then he became solemn. "What *I* think is that building a fire isn't such a good idea," he warned, nodding toward those kneeling around the brush. A small fire was already sending bluish smoke into the air.

Melody understood immediately. "Hey wait!" she cried out to the others. "No fire! Put it out! Those bad men will see it and follow us here. Hurry, put it out!" Everyone immediately hustled to extinguish the fire, and then watched anxiously as the last black puff of smoke curled into the sky. They knelt and offered a prayer that no one would see the smoke.

"Back into the motor home, everyone," Grandpa announced, clapping his hands to hurry them along. In a few minutes they were back on the highway and making their way toward Idaho. As they drove they ate sweet, crisp carrots, raw potatoes and cabbage wedges. Melody could not remember eating anything so delicious. Mothers chewed pieces of carrot until they were very soft, then gave them to their babies, who ate it like candy. Even Helaman exclaimed how wonderful it tasted as he nibbled on a carrot.

Besides food, their next pressing need was fuel. They were probably going to travel upwards of 500 miles during this trip, much of it up and down hills. They had begun their journey with a full tank and about ten gallons in cans. Now the cans were all empty, and the tank read less than one-quarter full. Except for when they were deliberately putting distance between them and those who had attacked Helaman, they drove around forty miles an hour to get the best gas mileage possible. The miles crept past slowly, but the heavy vehicle's gas gauge seemed to move steadily downward with perceptible speed.

They made it as far as Hazleton, Idaho before they ran out of gas. They coasted into town on the last fumes in the tank, and the old bus died before an abandoned filling station and garage. It was just before noon, yet the town was completely deserted. Hazleton's main drag consisted of a single narrow street about four blocks long, with ramshackle businesses on both sides. It was evident that the little town had not fared well economically for many years prior to the present collapse. Still, it did them little good either way, since there was no fuel to be found or purchased—even if they had had any money.

The children jumped out and started exploring the abandoned buildings, carefully avoiding those locked tight and shuttered. They saw no one for over an hour, and the kids were glad to have a chance to play. It was almost three in the afternoon before one of the teenage girls came running back.

"I found an LDS church building," she said between breaths, "and there are people inside."

"What were they doing?" Grandpa asked with interest.

"Singing," she cried happily.

Grandpa looked at his wife and shrugged. "I guess that's not against the law," he muttered.

"Grandpa, they were singing "Come, Come Ye Saints!"

He straightened up. "Really? Church meetings have been outlawed for years! Lead us to them, will you? Come on everyone, let's go to church!" He had no difficulty convincing even the smallest among them to come along. Some of the younger ones couldn't even remember going to church in their entire lives.

The chapel was a large rock and brick structure about six blocks from the center of town. The grass was brown and frosted with snow. Oddly, the windows of the church were all intact. In Utah, most every church building had been vandalized. They pulled on the doors and found them unlocked, and without the usual red placard declaring that this church property had been seized.

There was indeed music coming from the chapel, and the sound of an out-of-tune piano. Of course, all the lights were off, but the smell of candle smoke was strong. They quietly opened the chapel doors and found about a hundred people near the front singing with full voices. As soon as those inside heard the doors open, about half of them stopped singing and looked back toward them suspiciously. Upon seeing the family, they soon turned back and resumed their singing. The whole Mahoy clan quietly took the first empty seat behind them, and began singing as well—first, with a feeling of doing something, if not wrong, at least illegal, and then with as much vigor as they possessed. It felt so good to feel the power of that beloved hymn again.

The music came to an emotional end, and a young elder stood at the pulpit. In the dark interior of the chapel only the candle he set on the podium illuminated his face.

"Brothers and Sisters welcome to Sacrament meeting, and a very special welcome to our weary guests. May God grant us peace this day while we worship the Lord. Sister Anderson will offer the opening prayer, and then we'll bless and pass the sacrament. Do any of our visitors hold the priesthood?" He smiled when several heads nodded. "The two older brethren, would you bless? Thanks. And you young man," he said, indicating Sammy. "Do you hold the Aaronic Priesthood?"

"No, sir," Sammy said quietly. "I turned twelve last year, but there's no more…" his voice tapered off.

The young man at the podium surveyed Sammy carefully before he spoke. "There will be a slight modification to the program," he announced. "After the opening prayer, the Spirit directs that we ordain this young man to the Aaronic Priesthood. Are you worthy, young man?"

"Yes sir!" Sammy cried in delight.

"Are his parents here?"

"I'm his mother," Melody said, tears of unrestrained joy gathering in her eyes.

"Is this alright with you then, sister?"

Melody nodded vigorously. "It certainly is. Thank you."

"Sister Anderson," he said and sat down.

The sister in question was old and feeble and had to be helped to the stand. Though feeble of limb, her faith was not, nor was her relationship with her Heavenly Father.

"Our Father who art in heaven," she began, then paused as if awaiting Him to answer. "Great and glorious art Thou, and unto Thee we give all praise and all glory, and confess before Thee our great love, and utter dependence upon Thy goodness to sustain and succor us.

"Beloved Father we bow our heads in most humble reverence to worship Thee, and partake of the sacraments of Thine only begotten Son. It is with the fondest hope of being worthy of that great atonement that we do this, and we beseech Thee in the name of our dear Lord that Thou would forgive us of our sins, and consecrate this day of worship unto our souls.

"Forgive us dear Father for our sins, and sanctify our hearts and souls before Thee that we may find the courage to live a righteous life, even when it is illegal to mention Thy precious name in public.

"We pray for those who oppress us, that Thou would bless them, and through the workings of Thy Holy Spirit, call them to repentance and cause their hearts to swell with compassion regarding us, Thy children.

"Father, we trust Thee, in all things cast our lives at Thy feet, and…"

She got no further than this before the doors of the chapel burst open and two asian armed men in blue helmets stomped into the room. One of them aimed an automatic weapon at the floor and let off a deafening burst of fire. The roar of the weapon was like a sustained explosion. When it suddenly stopped only the tinkling of brass casings hitting the ground came to their ears, ironically like sleigh bells at Christmas time. Acrid smoke filled the room as people screamed and gathered loved ones into their arms.

The soldier's faces were twisted in anger, and their stance was belligerent and threatening. The one who had fired the gun screamed at them, "What you are doing here is *against the law!*" he bellowed. His voice was so twisted by rage that his words were barely understandable. "I have authority to execute anyone who defies the law and meets in a Mormon church. I will give you one minute. Anyone who is not willing to die has one minute to leave. After that, all who remain will be shot down where you stand, and the building burned to the ground!" he screamed.

For a full two seconds people sat rigid with terror. Finally a young woman cried out, gathered her two small children and ran from the room, heedlessly dragging her screaming babies. The guards stepped aside. Thereafter, a few more left, then an old man, then a young couple with a baby.

"Thirty seconds left!" he screamed, and cocked his weapon. About a dozen more people left the room. Melody looked at Sammy, and saw fear mingled with faith. She held out her hand and he laced his fingers into hers in an almost iron grip. Neither of them even looked at the exit, and their only hope of life.

She watched Helaman scratch his head, then turn around and sit so that his back was toward the intruders. He pulled a hymn book from the rack, thumbed to the very song they had just sang and began to sing in a surprisingly beautiful tenor voice.

"And should we die," he sang, "before our journey's through…"

A woman's high soprano joined him. "… happy day, all is well." Melody joined in the sacred hymn, and sang the words with such meaning as they had never before held for her. "Happy day, all is well!" the words kept ringing through her heart. "Happy day, all is well!" Others joined in, and as they joined, they also sat back down, until all were seated with their backs to those who in seconds would take their lives.

"Brrrrrrrrtttttt!" the machine gun belched with a deafening roar above them. It made everyone jump, but they looked at one another and continued singing louder than before. This last burst drove three more adults and one child from the room at a hard run.

"Close the doors!" the one in charge cried. "Close the doors, and let's get this business over with!" With weapon lowered at the backs of the heads of those still singing he stomped forward, his boots falling heavily on the floor. He and his comrade stood for several seconds, and then stepped into the bench just behind Helaman. They laid their still-smoking weapons on the floor at their feet, and began singing in heavily accented voices.

"And if our lives are spared again, to see the Saints their rest obtain,

Oh how we'll make this Chorus swell, all is well. All is well!"

The music ended, but the strains of praise lifted heavenward. Every person in the congregation turned to look at the two soldiers seated behind them.

The one who had fired the weapon smiled weakly, and in broken English said. "We are so sorry to make loud scaring noise. We from Korea. But, we wish to worship with only true saints of God."

A stricken silence endured long moments before the soldier tried to explain further. "You who stayed to die are true saints who love God more than life. It is necessary that we know you will not betray us. It is the only way we can be in army, and also worship Jesus Christ in Restored Gospel.

He stared at them, chagrined and apologetic. "Please to see, we shoot only guns with big noise, and not bullets. Not to make much bullet holes in God's church. Please, forgive. But, we have but a short time. Let us worship God."

A bewildered silence followed, and would have continued except that Sister Anderson, who had remained at the pulpit during all this, bowed her head and continued as if she had never stopped.

"... and we thank Thee for those whom Thou hast sent here to join with us this day, and ask Thee to bless and prosper them in their sorrows, their needs, and their journey.

For a moment her voice grew silent, then in an entirely different, very personal and familiar tone of voice, inserted, "Father, just speaking for myself, I want to thank You for sending the soldier boys and allowing me the privilege of choosing to shed my blood for Thy Son. I was ready to die... and happy...and yet I live..." she concluded, her voice filled with wonder. Twin trails of tears glimmered on her cheeks in the candle light. She sniffled, and after a moment her voice returned to formal prayer.

"Father, into Thy hands we consecrate our lives, and give unto Thee to preserve us or call us home. Either way we shall with grateful hearts ever cry unto Thee, All is well! All is well! In the name of Jesus Christ, Amen." A cry of "Amen" echoed with such vigor as to make one wonder if the only voices speaking this holy benediction were mortal, or if angelic voices had joined them.

The young elder who had opened the meeting stood. "Would the young brother please come to the stand? Do either of you soldiers hold the priesthood?"

"We both do," the one who had not yet spoken replied. "We are both Elders in the Church. If our commanders ever found out we would be executed. This is the first time we have dared meet with the Saints for three years. Please forgive us."

"Would you like to help us ordain this young man?"

They looked at each other as tears sprang to their eyes. They quietly, meekly walked to the stand. Grandpa Mahoy clasped each of their hands as they came toward him. The second of them fell on his neck and held him in a prolonged embrace as he openly wept. When they finally separated they all laid their hands on Sammy's head, and Grandpa ordained him a Deacon in God's true church.

Melody had never felt such a profound outpouring of the Spirit in a sacrament meeting. There were no assigned speakers, and it was not a testimony meeting; but the spontaneous worship they experienced was something entirely new to her. After the sacrament, which Sammy helped pass, the young brother stood at the pulpit again, and pointing at Helaman said, "The Spirit directs that this brother here will please address us on the subject of Christ's atonement." He then pointed at a teenage girl. "Sister Linda Phillips will then bear her testimony on the power of prayer. Then we will hear from our two soldier brothers, and ask them to bear their testimony, and tell us briefly of their conversion. Then, young brother Timothy will bear testimony. We'll go to that point," he informed them, and sat down.

Every talk was extemporaneous, and so energized with faith, testimony, and humility that Melody felt as if her heart might burst open. She sensed the periphery of her vision growing white, almost as if she might pass out, but felt gloriously well. Brother Helaman's talk was like nothing she had ever heard before. He spoke with such deep love for the Savior that the congregation wept. He quoted scripture after scripture with such joy that her heart leaped into her throat. He bore testimony with such power that she wanted to stand on her feet and shout "Hosanna! Hosanna! Hosanna!" and barely restrained herself from doing so. He spoke with deep, penetrating understanding, and in so few words, laid open the atonement of Christ to her view, and what it meant to her personally, in such a way as she had never contemplated. Again and again, she felt herself rejoicing and inwardly crying, "Of course. Of course this is true!"

When Helaman finally drew his remarks to a close, her heart was pounding with inexpressible joy, and her testimony was aflame such that her entire body felt engulfed. Her skin tingled from the tips of her hair to her toes, and she felt as if she understood the gospel of Christ for the first time in her life. She would have run to Helaman and fallen into his arms had not decorum restrained her. As it was, a smile to him was her only communication of the deep emotions within her. Oddly, Helaman did not smile back at her. As soon as their eyes met he jumped as if he had been stabbed from behind by a needle. His eyes grew wide as he studied her face. She caught this strange reaction and raised her eyebrows in query, to which he smiled, and forced his eyes away from her. She longed to ask him what he had seen that so startled him, but which he could not, at least for the moment, divulge to her.

Sister Phillips stood and with trembling hands told of the day when her home was searched by the blue helmets for illegal food. They had a basement room stacked with food and canned fruit. Her husband, and most likely all her family, would have been killed on the spot had they found it. The soldiers repeatedly walked right past the food as they uprooted furniture and smashed holes in the walls in search of food and weapons. During all this time she had prayed for deliverance with great fervor, and faith such as she had never before experienced, and knew this was a miracle of salvation for her family.

The two soldiers bore testimony in deep humility. They told of the death of their families because they would not deny their membership in a Christian church. They told of the destruction of everything Christian, and their brutal induction into the army as the Chinese swept across North and South Korea. Only by pretending to be communists had they escaped execution. For reasons they could not fathom, they had never been asked if they themselves were Christians, for they surely would be dead now if they had. They told of tens of thousands slaughtered for no crime greater than having a picture of Christ in their homes, or bearing a non-Korean first name such as Paul.

Young Brother Timothy was barely fourteen. He stood and bore powerful testimony, speaking briefly of the loss of his family who had been arrested and then killed by the blue helmets. Their crime was that his father had been the Bishop of their ward. There was no bitterness in his voice, only peace. He spoke longingly of the day when they would be together, and expressed deep faith that the day of resurrection was not so far away. He wept as he bore his personal witness—not testimony, witness—that Jesus was the Christ. Melody felt electrified as the Spirit bore witness to her that this young man's sacrifice had prepared him to receive the most supernal of all mortal blessings.

The small congregation then sang "The Spirit of God Like a Fire is Burning" with such volume that Melody and many others looked around the room toward the source of invisible voices. At times she could even hear a mighty organ joining in the joy of that celestial anthem.

When it was time for the closing prayer Melody felt as if she had been to church for the first time in her life. Her heart was aflame with faith, and bursting with joy. So significant was her glorious faith that had the Spirit directed her to raise the dead by her faith, she would have done it, and watched death flee in the face of unshakable faith. It came as no surprise to her when she heard their young leader ask her to give the closing prayer.

"Oh God, our Eternal Father," she raised her voice in perfect prayer and love. "How glorious, how precious, how divinely perfect it is to worship Thee this day. Our hearts are filled to overflowing, our souls rejoice, our minds expand to the very heavens, and our faith fills us with perfect hope. As if the veil had burst open, and heavenly angels had filled the room, we feel ourselves consumed by Thy glory, and overpowered by Thy love."

"Father, we pour out our hearts unto Thee in the greatest strivings of worship we can express, and dedicate our lives unto Thee in the presence of Thee, Thine angels, and these witnesses. Ever after, in all things, in every walk of life, at every hazard, in every circumstance, throughout time and for all eternity, regardless of the cost to ourselves, we covenant and consecrate all that we are, all that we possess, all our time, our talents, our very lives unto Thee, for Thee to do with us as Thou wilt. With joy do we stand with open arms to deliver unto Thee our all!

"All this we do in the holy and beloved name of Thine only begotten Son, our beloved Savior, Jesus Christ, Amen I say, Amen!" The congregation shouted Amen in a single voice, a virtual detonation of praise.

She stood there at the pulpit, her face awash with tears, her eyes tightly closed, her mind lifted up on high, her heart burning with pure fire. It took her a moment to realize her arms were raised over her head, and her face was turned toward heaven. She was not aware that no one in the room had stirred, and every eye was likewise bathed in tears of joy. She did not move until someone placed a hand on her shoulder. She lowered her arms and turned to look into Helaman's eyes.

"Come," he said. "I have someone I would like you to meet."

JOURNEY OF FAITH

Helaman led Melody to the Relief Society room, allowed her to enter alone, and closed the door between them. She was too caught up in the joy of the Spirit to even wonder who she was going to meet. She assumed this would be some local person who might be able to help her family on their way. The room was warm and dim, full of sweet feelings and quietude.

"Melody!" a familiar voice said with such love that she spun around to gaze at a person she had not noticed standing in the shadows near the piano.

"Samuel!" she cried, and ran toward him with outstretched arms. After two steps she drew up short, unsure. He held out his arms to her and smiled, and she slowly stepped toward him, never taking her eyes off his, until their arms were around one another but not touching, their faces inches apart.

Slowly, carefully, as if fearing he might not be real, Melody closed her arms around him until at last they touched ever so lightly. With a cry of joy she hugged him in an embrace fierce with happiness and relief. She kissed him long and passionately, drinking deeply from the well of his love. At long last their lips parted, and she laid her head on his chest. He held her tightly, almost fiercely in his arms, the familiar contours of her body causing his blood to boil with longing.

"You *are* real!" she exclaimed in joy. "I was afraid you were a spirit! They said you were dead!"

"I know," he whispered. "I'm sorry for your sorrow."

Melody was laughing and crying at the same time. "I didn't ever believe you were dead though! You promised me that you would be OK, and I believed you, not them." She looked back up at him questioningly. "But why didn't you contact me sooner?"

"I couldn't," he answered softly.

"I suppose things were pretty bad, huh?"

"Things are really difficult over there," exhaling deeply.

Suddenly she stopped, her brain finally realizing how illogical it was that he was actually there in front of her. "How *did* you find me?" she wondered. "We're way out here in Idaho, lost and hungry. How *did* you find us?" she said out loud.

"Helaman brought me to you," he said simply.

"But he's been with us for the last week or so!" she protested. "How could he . . ."

"He gets around," Samuel said with a chuckle.

At that Melody nodded and laughed with him. "Wow, isn't that the truth!" she giggled. Then she spoke in earnest. "But—how did you get here? Oh, Samuel! You should have come sooner to the meeting with us! The Spirit was *so* powerful, and I gave a closing prayer that is *still* giving me goosebumps."

"I know," he said. "That's why Helaman came to get me. He knew I'd want to be with you on this glorious day."

Melody was now more confused than ever. "How could he have come to get you? He was sitting next to me all during the meeting. What are you talking about?" she asked him in a daze.

"The prayer—you don't know what it was, do you?"

Melody thought for a moment. "Well, it was glorious, but other than that…"

"Do you remember the covenant?"

"Well yes, I do. But …"

Samuel took her face in his hands. "Melody, it wasn't just an ordinary prayer, or a simple covenant. This covenant is the one every person must eventually make to be sealed up unto eternal life."

"You mean in those exact words?" she questioned, trembling.

He shook his head. "No, sometimes there are no words involved. It's not the words, it's the intent. The rock solid, unchangeable covenant, in the face of all hazards. You did it!"

"I don't know what it means," she said, quietly perplexed.

"Search your heart, honey. How do you feel? What does the Spirit whisper about your relationship with God; about your place in his kingdom?"

Melody pondered this briefly and slowly said, "I know as surely as I know you are standing here that my place in His kingdom is assured," without pausing to think about it.

When Samuel didn't reply she thought upon her own words. "Oh my…" she said. "Do you mean this was my calling…"

"It was, my Love. It was! And that's why I was able to come to you. I am so very overjoyed to be able to come back, and to share this joyful moment with you. Don't you see? I have been allowed to come to you to confirm this great blessing, this marvelous change that has occurred in your life."

Melody's voice trembled as she looked up at him. "If such a thing were even possible," she said, "your being here makes it doubly sweet. It adds a dimension to my joy I cannot describe, but which makes this the most perfect day of my life!" she cried.

Samuel released her and began to search his pocket. "I brought you something in honor of this occasion," he said, retrieving a stunningly beautiful white flower. It looked like an orchid, but larger, with a brilliant pink center. Its fragrance filled the room with sweetness, and she took it with wonder.

"It's beautiful! Where did you get it?"

"I picked it just before I arrived," he said.

"But, you're talking as if you just got here."

"I did. Just a minute ago."

"Where were you just a minute before that?" she asked, her voice a little suspicious.

"Somewhere just beyond Siberia," he answered truthfully.

Melody sat down on a nearby chair, and contemplated this for a long moment.

"That's what the change was that day in the Salt Lake Temple, wasn't it?" she said slowly. "You have been . . . what is it called?"

"The scriptures call it being translated. We refer to it as the 'Mightier Change,'" he said softly, then added: "I couldn't tell you back then."

Melody cried again, this time with tears of relief and understanding. "That's all right, my darling. I finally, finally understand! And, I confess, I love you now more than ever before!" She stopped to brush the fresh tears from her sunburned cheeks. "Oh Sam, tell me all about it! Is translation truly marvelous? I mean, do you feel very much different? Is it everything a mortal can hope it could be?"

"It is far beyond wonderful," Samuel said, then added thoughtfully, "yet really in some ways, not all that different. I am the same. I think, I hope, ponder, pray and yearn just as always. I am physically very different, but my soul is as it always has been." He scooped her back into his arms. "Oh my sweet Melody, I love you, and have missed you with all my soul," he said fervently.

"I love you with all my soul," she replied with deep feeling. She gazed into his eyes, searching his face and finding joy mingled with sadness. She understood. "You will be going back," she said. It was not a question.

"In just a few minutes," he admitted.

"Oh Sam, I have missed you terribly. I am happy in the Lord, yet I feel so incomplete without you," she said softly, her eyes pooling with tears of love.

"Not for much longer, my love," he said. "Only for a little longer."

"But now that I understand, I think the waiting will be less painful …" she replied a little dispiritedly.

Samuel straightened up. "I have some instruction to give you before I must leave." But Melody was not interested.

"I just want to go with you," she said, burrowing into his chest again.

Sam stroked her auburn hair. "I wish you could. Just remember that I am perfectly well. Remain utterly faithful and obedient, my precious wife. Stay near my family, and let Helaman help you."

"Is Helaman also…?" She didn't know what word to put there.

"You'll have to ask him that question," he replied.

Melody shook her head. "I really don't need to. I already know the answer."

Sam wrapped his arms around her in one last embrace, and kissed her lips tenderly. "I must go, sweetheart. Give my love to Sammy, but please don't tell him I came here. He must also be ready before he can know. I love you … forever," he said. Then he slowly took a step back and simply faded from her sight.

She was sitting on a chair holding the beautiful white flower when Helaman quietly opened the door and entered. Melody knew full well nothing like it grew in Siberia. It was a delicate tropical flower, and it had been picked mere minutes before. With a deep sigh that was far more happiness than regret, she stood and followed Helaman. She was so lost in thought that Helaman silently looped his arm through hers and led her gently from the darkness of that unlit building. When they emerged into the dimming light of evening, a wisp of candle smoke swirled behind them as if they had emerged from another world.

When she rejoined her family they were talking with the two soldiers who had driven an armored vehicle onto the church lawn.

"Melody, the Korean brothers have given us fuel and food. We should have just enough fuel to reach our destination! It is a great blessing," Grandpa Mahoy exclaimed joyfully, and turned again to thank their Korean brothers, who brushed aside his gratitude with confessions of humility and regret.

"It *is* a day of miracles," Melody agreed quietly as they walked together towards the motorhome still a few blocks away.

"Who did Helaman take you to meet?" Grandpa asked.

"Oh, just another miracle," she said wistfully, and held up the tropical flower still vivid and glorious in the chilly afternoon.

Samuel returned to his frosty blankets in the bitter cold of Mayor Motyvich's small apartment. Sarah, Alexei's granddaughter, was tossing and turning on the cold floor a few feet from him; Samuel draped his warm coat over her and she soon slept contentedly. The night dragged on endlessly as he listened to the others sleep. Himself lacking that need, Samuel lay awake the rest of the night, his heart fondly rehearsing each moment of this evening's great joy. He and Melody had been separated for a little short of two years now, without any communication between them since he left the job site a year ago. Helaman regularly brought him word of their welfare and had been faithful in watching after them. But Samuel could send no message to her, nor could Helaman even mention they often met.

Now that she had pierced the spiritual veil separating all mankind from God, he knew he could be with her as occasion allowed, and as the Lord willed. As a translated being, one of his main functions was to minister to those—especially those of his family— who were heirs of salvation, and whose calling and election had been made sure. What a glorious blessing it was that Melody had succeeded against such incredible odds! Yet, in a broader sense, he knew of no one who had gained this great blessing who had not done it against seemingly insurmountable odds, willing to sacrifice all. This was the only way it could be done.

Helaman often commented on the general condition in the world, and being involved with aiding and ministering to the saints, especially those very recently blessed with this great gift, he was quite aware of the condition of mankind, and of the Church. His reports were startling. Since the Church had been outlawed nearly eight months ago, the number of individuals qualifying for their election had quadrupled. Extra heavenly beings were being assigned to minister to them as their numbers steadily increased. Far from tearing down the work of the Lord, this great persecution had the unexpected effect of exponentially spurring the faithful onto greater glory. Humbled by their circumstances, those whose hearts were true found their full spiritual greatness, and the heavens opened extra lanes on the highway between heaven and earth to accommodate this great outpouring of faith and righteousness.

As the faith of the faithful grew, so did the occurrence of miracles. Healings, restoration of life and limb became daily occurrences. Visions, dreams and angelic visitations were commonplace. In a matter of a few months first the Church, then the world, became polarized into diametric opposites.

Of course, there were those who could not face the opposition, and who ran to join the forces of evil to preserve their lives at all costs. As opposition in all things must remain equal, with the great increase in miracles and manifestations of God's power, so a corresponding increase occurred among those whose damnation was evident as well. As the weeks slowly clicked by, those whose faith had once been bright now took intense delight in persecuting those whom they had formerly called brother and sister. Many innocent lives were lost, both spiritually and physically, and innocent blood shed by those whose hearts had once been at least content with the religious status quo. It was tragic now to see a great sifting take place when the names blotted from the book of life were friends, loved ones, admired ecclesiastical leaders, and beloved family. Many of the persecutors were incensed by the miracles taking place, while others drew lines in regard to social issues, which were hotly contested by those who felt they were more enlightened than the Prophet.

However, one report Samuel delighted in was concerning the Brethren. Helaman reported that the Quorum of the Twelve and First Presidency had all remained faithful and true, and were in fact secreted away, very much engaged in running the Church, and preparing the people for the Lord's triumphant return. Helaman spoke of them in first person, having often met with them. He said they daily communed with angels, and with the Master himself. All was as it should be, he said, and no unhallowed hand could stay the Lord's return.

Alexei decided to allow his people to spend the winter in the great factory city. There was food there, shelter and new friends. He did not ask Samuel what the Lord desired, and Samuel did not volunteer to say. Had Alexei asked and obeyed, they would be trudging through knee-deep snow making their way slowly toward Zion. That would have brought them the greatest blessings, and poured out miracle after miracle upon their heads—marvelous blessings not otherwise available. Staying in the city gave them time to become comfortable, to lose their determination, and to succumb to the temptations that idleness brings. Samuel silently grieved for them, knowing that when they left that next spring their hardships would be greater, even though the weather would not be the source of it.

The one great blessing staying in the city afforded them was the opportunity for Samuel to teach the people. Each evening that it was not snowing or blowing they met in the great open square at the center of the city. It seemed odd to Samuel that they met in the open when surrounded by cavernous factory floors and warehouses. But, he soon learned that only non-Russians see the indoors as preferable. None of the buildings available to them were heated, and during the day they radiated the intense cold of the night before, making them colder inside than it was outside. Inside it was dark, musty, and often dirty or greasy. Outside, the sun lit their days and large fires lit their nights. No one would be foolish enough to build a large fire inside a building and not expect it to fill with smoke and burn to the ground. It was common understanding among them that if one building burned down, so did every building, since they were joined side by side to form the large square compound that was their city.

Each night was an excursion into faith and righteousness. Samuel oftentimes arrived at the bonfire with no knowledge of what he was to teach them, only to be filled as he opened his mouth. These were the best times, and the Spirit of truth was poured out upon them in rich measure. As the evenings progressed, however, fewer and fewer attended, until less than half of those in the city seemed interested anymore. Most of those who came each evening were Alexei's faithful refugees. Most from the city lost interest, or took offense, or simply grew weary of the routine.

Samuel rejoiced as he taught the faithful. He rejoiced in the great truths that came forth, but as much as this, he rejoiced in their simple faith and believing hearts. He praised God for their growing testimonies, and in the blessing of being their trumpet call to truth. His all-night prayers were symphonies of praise for the Lord's tender mercies to all His far-flung children, and joyous marveling that God would use the weak and simple, such as Samuel knew he was, to help accomplish this mighty work.

Weeks passed, and still they came faithfully. Samuel organized a special Sabbath meeting where they met earlier in the day. He selected those of the strongest faith to stand forth and testify before their brethren. As they did so their own faith was magnified a hundred fold, and those who heard their own revered loved ones testify were changed as well.

By the time the days grew longer, and the winds turned warm and sweet with the scent of new life, the band of wanderers were anxious for one simple rite of summer to occur: they desperately wanted the river beside the city to flow ice free that they might dam it up, and be baptized. It was the desire of every faithful heart, including Samuel's.

When the day finally came that the ice gave way and clear waters flowed, a cry of joy arose from the people as if food had arrived for the starving. Men, women and children labored to stack logs and rocks in the rushing stream that formed beside the larger body of ice still remaining to make a pool deep enough. Samuel tested the water, and found it far too cold to endure. Yet, they would not wait. "Tomorrow," he told them. "Tomorrow at noon, come with fasting and prayer, and I will baptize you into God's true Church, and you will take upon yourselves the name of Christ. Then after you have been warmed and built fires in the square, I will give you the gift of the Holy Ghost." They cried aloud for joy, and danced in one another's arms like children.

When the appointed hour drew near, the people moved in a great congregation to the water's edge. Samuel pulled off his shoes, walked across the ice still on the bank, and waded out into the water. He looked up into a sea of faces standing above him at the water's edge. For almost half a minute no one stirred.

"Who will be first?" Samuel asked in a loud voice. "Who comes first to the waters of purity?"

"I will," a small voice said from far back in the crowd. Samuel watched the sea of people part for the person who walked toward him. His heart radiated with joy to see that it was Sarah, Alexei's granddaughter. It was she who had first befriended him that night when he had been forced to sit at the children's table. It was she who had been raised from death at the helicopter attack. It was she who now walked toward him with sure steps. She stopped by the water's edge and stepped out of her shoes. She unfastened her coat and dropped it to the ground. She had made rough baptismal clothes from flour sacks. The cut and stitching were crude, yet Samuel had never seen so gloriously pure a vestment even on an angel, and he had seen many angels.

Samuel held out a hand. Her eyes fastened on his, she walked through the flowing ice water without any indication she felt its stunning cold.

He turned her toward the people and raised his hand over her head.

"Sarah Caterina Antoyov, having been commissioned of Jesus Christ, I baptize you in the name of the Father, and of the Son, and of the Holy Ghost, Amen." He lowered her into the water, and as he did so he heard a great cry of "Hosanna! Hosanna! Hosanna!" go up from a hundred thousand angelic voices. He knew the people on the riverbank had not raised the shout, but those who loved little Sarah from the world of unseen family. He pulled her from the frigid waters as quickly as he could. The warmth of her body caused the cold water to evaporate suddenly, letting off a billowing cloud of steam which curled slowly around her head.

At that very moment a cloud parted in the heavens and a brilliant shaft of sunlight fell upon her, illuminating the mist. People on the bank gasped, and held hands to their eyes. For a full minute Sarah looked as if she were engulfed in billowing waves of fire which seemed to form into the shape of a dove alighting upon her.

No one dared move until Alexei stepped into the water and led his granddaughter to the shore. Others quickly wrapped her in blankets. She refused to leave the water's edge.

"Pray God," Alexei said quietly, "and ask him if a sinful old man may beg a remission of his sins in the waters of Christ's sacrifice."

"What you ask is the very desire of your Savior's heart," Samuel said in a voice that only Alexei heard. Tears sprang from the weathered old face, and he bowed his head in strong emotion.

"Then if it pleases God let it be so, and for all eternity ..." thereafter he spoke a phrase in Russian that was unfamiliar to Samuel. He looked with puzzlement at Vladimir who stood on the very water's edge, his torn coat removed in preparation for his baptism.

"Roughly translated," Vladimir said with great significance, "it means Phooey the Darkness."

Samuel baptized Alexei, who too was greeted into the kingdom by a halo of fire. Samuel saw people on the bank looking around them, or gazing up into the sky trying to determine the source of the spiritual fire. They did not understand what eternal significance this event held in the heart of God. He had long awaited this very moment when His scattered people once again came unto Him with humble hearts and true faith.

This was the gathering of Israel that was in the Father's heart, when they took upon them the name of His beloved Son and entered into the kingdom via the straight gate of baptism. Their journey to Zion was but incidental to this, the greater gathering. God had held this day in His heart for millennia, and today was a grand day of days, on both sides of the veil.

Samuel baptized over a hundred people before Alexei insisted he come from the waters to save his life. They had built a fire upon the bank, and Samuel rubbed his blue legs until they turned pink again. It was somewhat amazing to see his flesh chilled to solidity, and still feel no pain or stiffness. When Alexei was content, Samuel returned and baptized another hundred, then another, until all who desired it were washed pure and holy in the blood of the Lamb. It was indeed a glorious, glorious day!

By the time the big fires were crackling in the square they had all dried and changed. Samuel brought a chair and set it before the people. He spoke to them briefly about the gift of the Holy Ghost, and then motioned for Sarah to be the first. Samuel was certain all present could hear the angels singing as he spoke the sacred words bestowing upon this faith-filled child the greatest gift God grants the living, second only to the bestowal of eternal life. She stood and turned toward him.

"Did you hear them, great one?" she asked breathlessly, her eyes sparkling in the firelight. "Did you hear the angels singing?"

"They sing for joy, Sarah," he told her. "They sing for you."

"I wish I could sing with them the song I hear in my heart," she said, her eyes bright with joy.

"They can already hear the song in your heart," he whispered.

"Thank you, great one," she said, and stepped aside for the next. Samuel had had a difficult time allowing them to call him 'great one.' It was actually a compound word which as near as he could tell meant "the one whom God sent, but is not a prophet." Vladimir told him to think of it as an honorific, and not an undue homage. Samuel had trouble seeing the difference, but it was apparently clear to them. He restrained himself from out-and-out forbidding them to use the term. Had he done so, they probably would have persisted anyway.

It took three evenings to confirm them all. Each blessing was recorded word for word by several people Alexei had instructed to do so. When all the baptisms and confirmations were done, a detailed record existed.

Alexei's people reluctantly left the walled city soon thereafter. They began their journey ankle-deep in mud, and filled to overflowing with profound faith and hope.

Just as Alexei's people had wintered in the factory, Melody's family had wintered in Hazelton. There was such love and faith here that they immediately accepted the first offer they received to stay. This had come from Sister Anderson, who lived alone in a small home not far from the chapel. Her little home had been built prior to central heating, and still had a cookstove in the kitchen. Sister Anderson's quiet grace and genuine hospitality was so marvelous that before they were all tucked in that first evening, they knew they were not just "at home"—they *were* home. Here they healed both physically and spiritually as they awaited the advent of spring.

Spring had already broken in Idaho, and a skiff of green was visible across the abandoned fields when the Mahoys began their journey once again. It was hard to leave, yet they knew they must. Reasons uncertain, and Helaman's gentle assurance drove them on. Their slow journey through Idaho was much less eventful the farther north they came. The smaller the town they passed through, the more helpful and accommodating were the people there. In one small town they had to drive down several residential streets to pass through. Several times they were stopped and given a few wrinkled apples, a quart of old motor oil, or much-needed encouragement.

These country people seemed much less oppressed by the hatred all around them. When they passed the small LDS church there, they found it had been burned to the ground; only the spire remained standing as a stark testament to the fact that even here they had not escaped persecution.

Their journey took them beside a river. They were never sure what its name was because all road signs had been destroyed. They gradually descended as the canyon walls grew taller and further apart. As they traveled along the river for several days, it had grown to be almost a mile across, the walls of the canyon hundreds of feet above them. They believed this to be the Columbia River. The family came to two large cities on opposite sides of the river. The big bridge that used to connect them was gone. They could see ocean-going barges sunken in the harbor. They passed through without incident, grateful to be beyond any large population center.

They left the Columbia and turned toward the mountains. The canyon narrowed almost to nothing, then opened back out again. Nearly vertical cliffs miles apart surrounded them. Above the cliffs stretched the great Idaho desert for hundreds of miles. Down in the protection of the cliffs the rolling hills were just turning green with approaching spring.

The first major building they came to was an LDS church. They found it standing and in good repair. The most remarkable thing of all was that an electric light burned brightly in the foyer. They had seen no electricity anywhere for at least a year. Two men stood by each door. They had no weapons in their hands, but their expression was determined.

The family stopped in the church parking lot and climbed out wearily. They stretched their legs by walking to the front door of the church.

"Good afternoon," one of the guards said. "Have you come a long way?"

"We have been on the road since last fall. We started just outside of Salt Lake City," Grandpa Jim Mahoy told them.

"Would you mind if we asked you a few questions?" the guard said.

"Of course not."

"Who was the last prophet in the Book of Mormon?"

"Moroni," Grandpa replied.

"Who was his father?"

"Mormon."

"What position did Mormon hold in the Sanhedrin?"

"He was a general in their army, and a prophet of God. There was no Sanhedrin."

The guard smiled. "Would you please bear us your testimony?" he gently asked.

Grandpa squared his shoulders and paused to collect his thoughts. Tears came to his eyes as he said, "I know..."

"That will be sufficient," the guard said. "I don't mean to be rude by interrupting you, but there is a testimony meeting going on inside right now. Perhaps it would be more enjoyable bearing your testimony in there rather than standing out here. Please come into the Lord's house, all of you! You may remove your shoes just inside the door." Then he paused and said with a smile, "Welcome home."

Samuel and the "Camp of God," as the people began to call themselves following their baptisms, left their winter home in the spring with confidence they did not feel upon entering. Almost two hundred people from the city joined their march to Zion, swelling their ranks to a little over 900. They took with them sufficient food to sustain them for almost six months. They could have taken more had they the means of carrying it. As it was, they were afoot, with only two military trucks, with a good supply of fuel. Both trucks were ruggedly built and in excellent condition, but they were hardly sufficient to carry so many people's basic supplies. They were loaded until their springs groaned under the weight.

After leaving the factory city they turned north, and avoiding any obvious roads, traveled cross-country, intent on encountering as little civilization as possible. Small factory cities and villages dotted the landscape, so they moved as far away from these as possible. They frequently met small bands of people moving without purpose across the wilderness of Northern Russia. These bands brought disturbing news of the world's perilous condition. They willingly shared their food with these wanderers, taught them the Gospel as opportunity afforded, and moved on. Almost all of those they encountered joined their migration, probably as much for the food on their trucks, as for any hope of actually reaching the mythical place called Zion.

The terrain was vast with dense birch forests hugging surging rivers of water, ice cold and clear. These forests quickly gave way to vast stretches of sparse brush lands and tundra that was spongy underfoot. They followed the rivers as much as possible, only crossing the open ground when the geography they encountered demanded it. They were forced to choose a route that their two trucks could traverse. Even so, they frequently found themselves pulling the trucks from dense mud bogs.

It was early one afternoon that both trucks became stuck in mud up to their floor boards. Every effort to free them only dug them deeper into the mud. The men strung ropes onto the chassis of the vehicles, but even with enough people pulling on the ropes to snap them in two, the trucks would not budge. With great reluctance Alexei ordered that the trucks be unloaded of their precious cargo. They would be left behind. Samuel watched all this from the near bank, his own sense of the situation declaring them hopelessly stuck. By now the heavy mud was so high that one could only enter the cab through the windows.

For the first time since leaving the factory city Alexei approached him. "I have endeavored to do all in my power without calling upon the Lord for deliverance. I know all I need do is ask, and God will speak to you. What shall we do that we may continue our journey with our trucks?"

As if viewing a motion picture in his mind, a complete vision arose wherein he watched the trucks being easily freed from the mud. Even seeing it with his spiritual eyes, he could hardly believe it was possible. Yet, his faith was absolute, and he began describing how the Lord would have them retrieve the trucks.

They went to a nearby stand of birch and cut long narrow trees. They trimmed the limbs from just one sides. They laid these on the mud, limbless side up, parallel to the truck on both sides, then tramped on them until they settled into the mud. They laid another layer, and another, until they could tramp them no deeper into the mud. They next cut long poles and cleared them of all branches. These they forced under the trucks until a pole extended from both sides of the truck every few inches from bumper to bumper. A hundred strong men got a grip on the poles and upon Alexei's cry, lifted the truck above the mud.

At that moment Samuel wished he had a video camera with all his heart. It was one of the most incredible things he had ever seen: that truck suspended upon poles held up by a hundred men barely straining their muscles. A cry of joy escaped every lip in the camp as they walked forward on the logs beside the truck, and set the big truck on solid ground. They quickly carried the second from the mud in the same manner.

Afterwards they all knelt and thanked God for their deliverance. It was a miracle in their eyes, and in Samuel's as well. He tried to calculate the weight of the big truck, and quickly discovered that rather than being a miracle of levitating the trucks by the power of God, it was a miracle of obedience. Each of the men on the poles was lifting a little more than fifty pounds each. Yet, without the aid of a loving Heavenly Father, they all would have walked away from them, never having even considered such a means of deliverance.

Every evening Samuel taught the people more of the Gospel. He allowed his Russian now to be excellent, and no one suspected that he had known it all along. Alexei spent all his time walking among his people, encouraging them, praying with them, answering their concerns, and weeping over their losses. Every day there were losses, and each loss devastated someone.

Hardly a day went by when they did not bury some faithful soul. Usually it was the very old, or the very young who could not endure the rigors of the march. Babies began to be born along the trail. Mothers often did not survive, and their babies usually did not. The cry of a baby in camp became a talisman, a sign of life, survival, and continuity. When one of these tiny voices of hope was stilled, all mourned.

A division was slowly developing in the camp. There were those who rejoiced in the outpouring of truth that God delivered via Samuel's tongue. And there were those who listened curiously, hesitantly, suspiciously, even skeptically. The greater the truths he taught them, the greater the dichotomy grew, until there were those who openly opposed, even debated what he taught. When the spirit of dissension was present, the Spirit of God departed. Thus, as time went on the moments of teaching grew fewer and fewer, and the truths grew less and less profound.

It was now mosquito season with a vengeance. It was almost as if the jaws of hell had snapped open and vomited demonic mosquitoes to eat them alive. Thick swarms of thirsty insects attacked with single-minded hunger. All suffered, their exposed skin puffy with accumulated venom from thousands of bites. Morale grew at first feisty, then rebellious. First they complained, then they rebelled—not so much against Alexei, or their new faith, as against the whole concept of their bitter experience. They entirely forgot their previous joy in having repeatedly escaped destruction through the providence of God in the face of powerful enemies they could not combat.

Against Alexei's urging they stopped, made camp, covered themselves with blankets, and wept loudly. Nothing Alexei or Vladimir could say would move them from their smoky fires which kept the mosquito hoards at a distance. They would not come to hear Samuel teach, and fought to pull supplies from the trucks in quantities that would quickly exhaust the group's provisions and render their onward trek impossible. Short of beating them off with clubs, there was nothing Alexei could do. Those who would still obey Alexei's voice were becoming a dwindling minority.

For three days Alexei went from fire to fire, urging, begging, even threatening, yet the people would not obey. Finally, he retreated to his own fire and knelt in prayer. Samuel joined him, as did a few faithful others. They were still on their knees when the first cry arose. The voice was that of a man, yet so shrill it sounded like a small girl. Above his screams there came a roar as if the very gates of hell had been opened within the camp.

Alexei sprang to his feet and ran toward the sound, dodging tents, fires and screaming children. They came to a stop a mere stone's throw from a scene of terrible carnage. Before them a great grizzly bear stood upon its hind legs, its front paws raking the air as if intent on killing the very air. Samuel had never seen such stark ferocity, such shear rage. The bear's roar was like the scream of a demon mingled with the roar of a hundred lions. It dropped to the ground and charged. Bodies flew into the air as the great beast ripped at everyone in its path. It again reared up and roared.

As if answering a call, another mighty roar came suddenly from their right where a beast even larger than the first was tearing through the people with even greater ferocity. Then a scream of a woman, and an identical roar to their left. In all there were five bears, and all seemed possessed by a demon of terrible wrath. Men grabbed clubs, shovels, knives, anything they could find to fight the threat to their families, and were in a single swipe tossed into the air as effortlessly as one might toss a tissue.

Exquisite terror gripped them all, and the people began to run helter-skelter across the camp seeking any means of escape. There was none to find, and there was no way to get past the bears without suffering the awful wounds of death.

As if on a signal from their collective will, the bears caught sight of Alexei and his small group of faithful. Forgetting for the moment their rage against those surging all round them, they fell to their fours and bore down upon the small band of men. Samuel watched in astonishment as the people fell back, ran and then as if pricked in their conscience, turned back to gaze upon the fate of their leaders. Now a double arena had been formed. A large group of men, women and children formed a circle twenty yards in diameter. Inside that ring was a circle of five frothing bears, and inside that, four men.

The largest of the five dropped to its front feet with such force that the ground shook beneath their feet. It roared and shook its head back and forth, spraying the men with acrid foam. Its fangs bared and snapping, it charged for Samuel. When it was about three feet away it stopped suddenly, screamed, and jumping like a rabid dog, bounded back. Others did the same, coming within a few feet of one of the four under attack. Screams came from the people watching from a distance with each attack. Samuel saw hundreds of them fall to their knees in prayer, others turned on their heels to race even further away. Someone started one of the trucks and began driving it away as quickly as it would go on the rough ground.

A dozen times the bears charged, sometimes getting as close as six inches from tearing flesh. Samuel knew why he felt great calm, for he knew absolutely the bears could not hurt him. Yet, the calm that exuded from Alexei, Vladimir and Karl, Vladimir's teenage son, was so incredibly steady that it astonished even Samuel. They stood facing the bears as they charged, not even bringing their hands up to protect themselves as the enraged beasts fangs snapped inches from their face and foul, foaming spittle sprayed in their faces.

After many minutes of this, Samuel sensed a change in the bears, as if the time had come to make good their threats. Killing passed across the minds of the bears, and the thousand others who watched. Where the bears had until now made their lunging attacks separately, randomly, they now paused, cried with a single collective voice of rage, and charged.

At that very instant Alexei raised his right arm to the square. A voice of complete calm, yet as mighty as a thunderclap rang out across the bears, and fell upon the ears of all.

"In the name of Jesus Christ, I command you to depart," Alexei said. The bear closest to him came to such an abrupt stop that it appeared to have hit the end of an invisible chain. Each of the others did the same. The bears seemed so unnerved by this sudden event they stood immobilized for many seconds. Then they turned their backs to the men they had only seconds earlier intended to rip to ribbons, and walked slowly away. The bears continued to walk, occasionally looking back at Alexei, until they came to the wall of frightened people, who quickly parted as the bears walked down the corridor of human bodies opened for them, and disappeared into the low brush.

Alexei stood without moving for many minutes. Samuel had often tried to imagine the many glorious moments in human history: Moses upon the banks of the Red Sea as it opened before him; Nephi before his rebellious brethren as they fell stunned by the power of God; Samuel the Lamanite upon the walls of the city prophetically crying to the people. But he had actually seen true human majesty but once, as it fearlessly rebuked the jaws of death in the unfathomable power of the Master's name.

The people slowly returned, their faces stunned and shamed. Alexei waited until silence was upon them. "We break camp immediately," he said loudly. "We march through the night and into the next day, and into the following night. God will go with us!" He turned and walked back to his own tent to pack his meager possessions.

As they traveled the little band of seekers grew until their numbers were over one thousand. With the fall of the Soviet empire, hundreds of thousands of Russians took to flight, the vast majority of them heading south toward warmer climates and richer soils. Every day Alexei's group met bands of people moving in the opposite direction. A hundred times they escaped destruction through divine intervention. Each group they passed added to their numbers a little at a time. They fully expected to find the whole northern coast abandoned of human life by the time they arrived.

Of all the obstacles they knew they would encounter, the most impassable was the Eastern Siberian Sea. All Samuel knew of their journey was that they must arrive there before the waters turned to ice.

It took them the entire summer to travel to the Northern coast. They were twice blessed to be able to load their whole band on trucks, busses, or trains and cover as many miles in a few days as they might have in months. The reason such things occurred was that the bands of south-bound refugees willingly traded busses or fuel for food. Oddly enough, those fleeing south seemed to have large supplies of gasoline or diesel fuel, and almost no food. They, on the other had been blessed with abundant food, and no fuel. It made for many interesting evenings of bartering. It was amazing to Samuel to see how many liters of gasoline was worth a liter of wheat or rice.

They arrived at the coastal town of Likhalkin in August. The city was virtually abandoned with no electricity, water, or economy, and very little food. The people who still clung to their city did so with the bleak hope something would change before winter seized them in its icy jaws.

Likhalkin sat on the mouth of the Vladensko river. It was a sprawling jumble of concrete buildings and wharves. Judging by the size of the docks, at one time the sea port must have been quite busy. Now, it stood silently waiting for better times. The few people remaining in the city looked at them suspiciously, yet from a distance. They walked en mass down the main street of town in grim silence. It was somewhat like walking through the bleached ribs of a monster that only a short time ago would have devoured them in a single bloody bite. Now the monster was dead, and with its death they knew safety.

As they approached the ocean with its tumble-down piers and great steel cranes jutting into the sky like the accusing finger of a skeleton, a feeling of desolation came over them. They had come a long way to find the final, and furthest point in their journey so very uninviting. They could journey no further North, as their destination had always been the sea. To turn East and Northward would be to journey into increasingly more arctic territory until life simply could no longer exist. This was as far as anyone, including Samuel, had ever thought of going. Now that they had arrived, their journey seemed futile indeed.

In need of shelter from the winds blowing off the ocean, they searched warehouses and other buildings. Every run-down building they found offered little protection from the wind. They finally settled for a long warehouse tightly enclosed on all sides, which at least housed them from the wind. There they found a large stack of wooden crates and broke them into firewood. As evening closed in upon them, Samuel stood beside Alexei gazing out across hundreds of small fires. The people were quiet, a few mothers sang quietly to children. Here and there a child cried, or laughed in youthful innocence. It was a bleak time. They had exhausted their food supplies trading for fuel and transportation. They had but little food left, and there was none to find here in Likhalkin. Yet, the people did not complain, and their collective spirit, though subdued, remained faith-filled.

Nearly a year had elapsed since they wintered in the factory city, and Samuel had taught them the gospel as extensively as the Spirit directed they were able to bear. With few exceptions, they had gathered every evening of their journey and had listened sometimes for hours as he taught them the truths of the restoration. Every evening the Spirit fell upon them until they sometimes shouted for joy, or stood up and sang in spontaneous verse, singing new songs no one had heard before, yet all spontaneously knew. He had heard people stand up and prophesy in a loud voice, even speaking in tongues. It was all new and unique to Samuel, yet it was how the Spirit manifested great joy in these people. He knew it was of God, and rejoiced in it. They were, after all, the blood of Israel, and they were worthy of the greatest blessings.

In their journey a great sifting had occurred. Those who murmured or rebelled either abandoned them, or in time died. Those who had faith, who sought righteousness, lived. Though this great sifting process was opaque, unobservable to the people, it was not lost on those faithful who now stood beside Samuel gazing across at the people. Of the thousands quietly milling around at his feet, there was not one among them who was unworthy. Acting in the authority he had been given prior to leaving on this journey he had baptized them, and had given them the gift of the Holy Ghost. Now, at journey's end there was a final task he needed to do.

"Alexei, call the attention of the people. I have an instruction to give them," Samuel said. Alexei gazed at him with surprise. In all their journeying Samuel had not once instructed him in anything. Never had he done more than provide guidance when asked to do so. In the many minutes it took to gain everyone's attention they walked until they stood in the midst of the people. More wood was brought and the closest fire kindled bright enough that all could see.

"My people," Alexei said, his voice ringing out in the cavernous interior of the warehouse. "We have come a long distance, and have endured many things. I do not know what awaits us, yet I feel the power of God in my soul, and my faith confirms in my soul that we are on God's errand, and He will take us safely to Zion. It is not necessary to know how this will occur, only necessary to enjoy the peace that it will be." A ripple of agreement drifted up from the sea of dirty faces before them.

"All through this journey Samuel, whom we all love and look to as a man of God, has asked nothing, and given no word of advice or instruction except when I have asked for it. For the first time he has stepped beyond this divinely-imposed limitation, and requested that he might address you. My soul trembles with joy to hear what words God has given him that are so important that he does not wait for us to ask for them. Hear him, my people," he cried softly, and turned toward Samuel, his eyes moist with emotion, his face beaming with anticipation.

Samuel gripped his friend's shoulder in love, then began. "That which I now do is something no man may request," he said. "Yet, the time has fully come, and I am instructed to give unto you one of Jesus Christ's greatest gifts. You understand well the principles of the Priesthood of God. Until this moment I have received no commandment that any of you should receive it. Yet, as the days draw to a close that you will remain upon the soil of your homeland, and as you walk upon the final leg of your journey to Zion, I am given to know that you will not set foot upon your new land until you bear the Priesthood of God."

"Praise God!" a hundred voices cried out in simultaneous joy. Then a thousand, then thousands joined in, until they were all chanting, "Glory be to God, and the Lamb!" Samuel waited for them to grow quiet. As if by a signal the chanting came to an abrupt end.

"The first to receive the priesthood will be Alexei, thereafter Vladimir, Karl, Masik, and others by my own hands. Thereafter, Alexei and those I ordain will go forth among you, and this very evening, all worthy brethren will hold the Priesthood of God. Bring forth the books, and let there be a record of these things kept beside the records of your baptisms."

People scrambled to bring forth the big ledger book they had found in the factory city. Someone brought a small wooden box and placed it before Samuel. Alexei took a seat and a dense silence fell across the people as Samuel placed his hands on their aged leader's head.

"Alexei Antoyov, in the name of Jesus Christ, and by the power of the Holy Melchizedek Priesthood which I hold, and according to the will of God, I confer upon you the Aaronic Priesthood and ordain you to the office of Priest therein. I confer upon you the Melchizedek Priesthood and ordain you to the office of High Priest therein. I give you the authority to ordain others to these two priesthoods as you shall be directed by God. I say unto you to be faithful in all things, and great shall be your reward. I bless you that you will complete your journey to Zion, and live to see the Savior of all mankind standing upon the steps of the Temple in the New Jerusalem. This I do because of your faithfulness, and according to the covenants you made with God before the world was formed. In the name of Jesus Christ, Amen."

The sun was just coming up when the last deacon was ordained and set apart. It was such a glorious outpouring of blessings that few felt tired. With the rising of the sun the final scraps of wood had been burned, the last few bites of food consumed, and the chill of the night held back primarily by the warmth of the Spirit.

"Hey!" a voice echoed back and forth across the vast emptiness of the warehouse. Samuel spun around to see a tall, bearded man stomping toward them, a clipboard tucked under one arm.

"Hey!" he cried again as he grew closer. "You can't stay here! This is a private building, and you must leave!" the man roared as he stopped a dozen feet from Alexei.

"We are children of the motherland," Alexei explained. "We have as much right to be here as anyone. Besides, we are only pausing here before moving on."

"Wrong!" the man roared. "This warehouse and the assets of this company were all sold about five years ago to an American company. This is not Russian property, and you are not welcome here. Look, you have burned up valuable crates, and you are lucky there are no longer police or I would have you all arrested and jailed. You must leave, and take all your crying babies with you!" he bellowed, his voice echoing back and forth across the building.

"We have nowhere to go!" Alexei explained in a loud voice.

"That is not my concern. I go now to get the guards. When I find them, they will return with clubs and guard dogs to drive you out!"

Alexei turned to Samuel. "My friend, I suppose now that I, too, hold God's holy priesthood, I should know within me what to do, but I do not. Pray, ask God what we shall do."

"There is an order to God's kingdom, Alexei," Samuel admonished him. "The order as long as I remain with you is that you ask me. When I am gone, you will know what to do as you ask God. You have done exactly as you should."

"What is your answer then?" Alexei replied, puzzled.

"Ask him the name of the company who owns this building," Samuel suggested.

By this time the man with the clipboard had nearly gained the outer door of the warehouse. Alexei cupped his hands to his mouth and shouted, "What is the name of this American company?"

"Why do you care," he called back, his voice hollow and echoing.

"I may wish to pay rent or restoration for the crates," Alexei replied loudly, and truthfully.

"I do not understand Americans," the bearded one yelled back. "They call the company Princess's Gem. It is a foolish name, but who understands capitalists?" he said loudly.

Alexei again turned to Samuel who was standing with his mouth agape. "What does it mean?" Alexei asked.

Samuel whispered something, and Alexei nodded and shouted back at the man, "Why are you still here in Likhalkin?"

"I was told the American would come and I was to meet him!" the frustrated man bellowed, then turned into the door to leave.

"Wait!" Alexei cried. The man froze with one foot across the threshold. "How were you to recognize this American who is coming?" he asked. "Do you have his name?"

"No!"

"How then?"

"I have only a picture," he replied, shaking the clipboard in the air.

"May we see it?" Alexei insisted. The man seemed undecided, then finally turned back and began stomping toward them. Alexei, Samuel, and a small knot of others moved toward him. As he walked he was flipping pages on the clipboard. When they met he held up a large picture of the American who owned the company.

"Satisfied?" the man demanded, and dropped the pages over the picture.

"Have you studied the photograph?" Alexei asked him, a smile on his face.

"I have, but who understands Americans. They all look alike to me," he said, and flashed a grin that was missing several teeth.

"Would you recognize your employer if you saw him then?" Alexei asked, his voice even more humorous.

"Absolutely," the man insisted importantly.

"Then I suggest you take a look at my companion here," Alexei said, pointing at Samuel. The man turned a bored expression upon Samuel, and after an instant his face dropped. He flipped back to the picture and studied it, his eyes darting between the photograph and Samuel's face.

"What? Is this so?" he finally cried. "I think it *is* you! You are the American. Say something in American!" he demanded.

"Give me a cheeseburger, fries and large Coke," Samuel said in English, and smiled at his choice of words. It was the only thing he could think to say, not having spoken much English years.

The company man dropped the clipboard. It was still rattling on the concrete as he switched to English himself. "It is you!" he exclaimed. "The old man who gave me this picture and my instructions said the first thing you would say in English would be about American food! Thank the patron saint of weary travelers! I am so much crazy to finally have you come. Now, I will go with you to America," he cried. "The man said I could come too, with my family. Is this not true?"

"It is true," Samuel replied, then switched back to Russian. "Where is my ship," he asked, not even sure there was a ship.

"My instructions two months ago by the old man were to anchor it offshore and wait for you. Come. Come. We will light the signal fire, and it will return. The radios do not work without electricity, but we have a signal. Come, you will see!" he urged, taking Samuel's elbow and directing him toward the door. The others followed him down the waterfront for half a mile until they came to a big pile of old furniture. "My name is Andryev Moskov," he explained as he fumbled with a book of matches. "I have waited here for over three years for you to come. But, I have done everything as you instructed, you will see. It is all ready."

He struck the match and a big fire soon was burning on the pier.

"There!" he suddenly cried, pointing at the horizon. "There, they signal back!" Samuel could see a blue light flickering on and off in the early dawn. They stood on the dock as a dark shape slowly materialized. The closer it got the more sure he was that they were looking at a fish processing ship. By the time it was close enough to see the white smoke billowing from its twin stacks, he had decided it was indeed an old floating factory ship.

The ship's lower deck consisted of a ramp like a ferry might have for loading automobiles. Samuel could not see inside that deck, but assumed it was, or at least had been filled with canning equipment. The decks above that were row upon row of small windows. He knew the factory ships had enough room for a full crew to live on the ship. Their numbers would be greater than this ship was designed to accommodate, but with some care, they could make do. The only question was of food and fuel.

As if Andryev had read his mind, he began speaking excitedly. "As I was instructed, the ship has now been fitted to house four thousand. There is food and fuel aboard for a one-month voyage. The factory has been stripped, and the equipment you requested is in the main hold. The food and water were replenished two months ago, waiting for you to arrive. This has been no small task, but the American dollars you gave us speak loudly. It is a good thing you have arrived, though, for the money is all but gone. Yes, it is a very good thing," he concluded happily.

As soon as the ship was tied to the pier they began moving the refugees aboard. Alexei and Samuel went ahead to determine what accommodations they now possessed, and were pleased to find the old ship in reasonably good condition. Much of the upper decks were small ward rooms with a big dining room and kitchen. The kitchen was heavily supplied and ready to begin production. At one time the old ship had been quite nice inside. The walls and floors were all hardwood, and crystal chandeliers hung in the main dining room. Samuel found a plaque stating the ship had been built in 1949 in Boston as a ferry. He could only guess what ill fate had brought it to be a factory ship in the Russian fishing fleet.

The main hold, which was once the parking area of the ferry, was now filled with old gray busses. The large fish freezers in the lower deck were packed full of food, and the engine rooms below were clean and efficient. The big ship had a crew of twelve who had lived on it and kept it in good condition, waiting for their arrival.

There were many pieces of the puzzle missing, but now Samuel at least knew what Helaman had done with the money from the gem he had recovered in Switzerland. He had come to this place and purchased the ship, all in preparation for this very day. It filled Samuel's heart with deep gratitude to see the bigger picture of the workings of the Lord, which had been hidden to him for so many years. He was lost in happy memories when Alexei approached him, and a man in a faded captain's uniform walking beside him.

"Samuel, this is Captain Anestiv, and he wishes to know where we sail, and when."

"When—as soon as we are aboard. Where—to Prudhoe Bay, Alaska."

"To America?" the captain exclaimed in disbelief.

"Yes, to America," Samuel responded quietly.

"But won't the American submarines sink us, or the American fighter planes attack us? The Americans will not let any Soviet ship near, I think not," the captain replied hotly.

"They will not stop us, and we will go safely."

"It cannot be. I will not pilot my ship and these thousands of good people to their deaths!" he insisted, and stomped away.

"What should we do?" Alexei asked Samuel quietly.

"You and Vladimir teach him the Gospel. Take as much time as you need, but we must leave tonight before sunset."

Alexei smiled. "You sound like a Russian now," he said. "We will do as you say. I already feel the power of the Holy Ghost upon me. That Russian captain better look out, for he is about to become baptized," he said earnestly. Samuel gave him a grin and a clap on the back.

The ship pulled away from the harbor a few minutes before sunset, just an hour after the captain's baptism in the frigid waters of the East Siberian Sea.

They sailed northeast, then due east toward the coast of Alaska. Although this was significantly farther than a direct course would have been, it was the route the Lord directed. It took five days to reach Wrangle Island, some 500 miles from Likhalkin. From there they continued east until they crossed into U.S. waters three days later. As the Captain announced their entry into the waters of the Americas, a cheer arose that was heard in every part of the ship. It took three more days and approximately 500 more miles to round Point Barrow. From there they sailed through choppy waters for five days before sighting the first artificial oil drilling island of Prudhoe Bay, Alaska.

Far across the boiling gray waters of the Beaufort Sea, the amber lights of Prudhoe Bay's sprawling complex were plainly visible in the night. Seeing those lights brought a surge of happiness to Samuel, for he had once worked there, and their familiar warmth was like seeing the distant flickering of a candle in the window of your home after being lost at sea. Yet, seeing it also indicated it was still in operation, making it unlikely they could land there without difficulty. Since the outbreak of the war, Prudhoe Bay was one of the most secure sites on the North American Continent. They would not welcome a boatload of Russian immigrants, no matter how righteous their cause.

As if to validate his dark ponderings the first mate cried out, "Captain, I have a large shape materializing directly ahead. It is emitting a strong radar signal. Captain, it is an American Submarine!"

"I told you this was foolish!" the captain accused loudly without turning toward Samuel or Alexei. "What do you want me to do now?" he added, his voice lowered. There were countless rumors of the American navy sinking shiploads of fleeing Russian citizens. Sadly, many of them were true.

"Captain, I have a strong sonar blip directly ahead. I believe the sub has fired a torpedo!" he cried.

"Hard to Port! Full speed…" the captain cried, but was interrupted by a commanding voice.

"No!" Everyone turned toward Samuel. "Come to a full stop," he commanded quietly.

"But…" the captain objected.

"Do it, please."

"Full stop," the captain said, then added. "Now, we die."

"Twenty seconds to impact, fifteen, ten, nine, eight, seven, six, five, four, three, two, one…"

17

WARS IN YOUR OWN LANDS

Melody, Helaman and those with them found the new little Idaho town to be open and friendly, and deeply spiritual. Their initial introduction to their temporary home was like walking into the embrace of a loving family, and they rejoiced to be there. Worship services were held every day, and fasting and prayer brought each soul the comfort and joy they so desperately craved in these hard times. Helaman saw that Melody was settled, he excused himself to work elsewhere. Thereafter, they saw him but seldom. When he finally did return, he brought disturbing news.

A general conference of the Church had just been concluded wherein a few general authorities had urged all present to cooperate with the government forces, and to embrace the new monetary and political systems that were being enforced by the government. These mixed messages confused and divided what was left of Church membership. However, the Prophet stood and boldly declared that Christ is the head of the Church, and he urged the Saints to follow him as the prophet and true mouthpiece of the Lord, no matter the consequences.

Even more frightening was the news that a huge army had crossed the border of Mexico and had invaded dozens of cities in Southern California, New Mexico, Arizona, and Texas. The army was made up of the combined armies of a dozen repressed South American nations, including Mexico. They were well organized, well supplied, well led, and fierce. The reports were that all it took to receive a bullet in the head was to have a white face. Thousands of Americans died within the first month of the assault, and millions of others fled north in stark terror.

With little or no food, the fleeing hordes of American refugees looted as they went, causing nearly as horrific a devastation as the armies behind them. It seemed the "American Liberation" army, as the invaders called themselves, was in no great hurry to proceed, and waited until the fleeing bands of Americans devastated their fellows before moving in to complete the job. They even went as far as to announce which cities they intended to attack next, simply to allow the terrified population to depart. Behind the conquering army came another army of foreign women and children intent upon inhabiting the vacant homes of the vanquished.

With its entire military forces committed to the war overseas, the U.S. government had very little to throw in the path of the invasion. What small forces they did muster were quickly swept aside by superior weapons and soldiers. A frantic call went out to the front lines for some portion of the committed troops and National Guard to return home to defend their own soil. A reverse convoy was quickly formed and sent homeward. In its haste, it was intercepted en route and destroyed almost without resistance. A dense fog of desperate fear settled upon the inhabitants of the western United States, and without hope, they struggled to throw together whatever rag-tag resistance they might invent.

The invaders split into three forces without warning. One prong continued its conquest up the California coast, another pressed into Texas where it met heavy resistance, and a third headed directly for Salt Lake City, conquering every city in their path. As they rolled across the desert they gathered up American Indians of every tribe, training and outfitting them. Most of them willingly joined in the promise of sweeping the white man from off the face of the land. A great cry of self-righteous vengeance arose from their collective throats, and they marched with solemn hatred toward everything that represented their long oppression and expulsion from their native homelands. Their single watchword was "Purge the land of the white plague, preserve all else." Consequently, their warfare was as much of the mind as of arms.

It was their practice to capture a few hundred of the enemy, publicly execute them in a brutal fashion, and watch the remaining citizens flee in terror. Though reports were everywhere believed to the contrary, the death toll in the recent days of their offensive grew very small compared to the vast reaches of land they conquered almost without opposition. Exponentially greater numbers died from the looting and frantic exodus of the invaded, than from the bullets of the invaders. Almost without opposition they swept northward, clearing the land as they went. Thousands ran from their homes in near nakedness seeking refuge further north. Others sat calmly waiting for the armies to pound on their doors.

Somewhere outside St. George, Utah the great, unstoppable army paused, passed around that city, and following Interstate 15, quickly made their way toward the capitol of Utah without entering any other cities. Their journey to the heartland of Utah's capital that was expected to take weeks in fact took but a few days, and without warning, the invaders swarmed into the valleys of the mountains. Here, their tactics radically shifted; they sought and received an audience with the exiled President of the Church. The meeting lasted several days. Afterward, they departed toward the East in peace. Their army was so large it took two weeks for it to pass through the city. They left a large body of troops just outside Salt Lake City.

Almost immediately, the Church surged back to life. The temple at Salt Lake was cleansed, refitted and rededicated. With the total collapse of government, the Church became the defacto authority in the desert West. Thousands returned to their homes illegally confiscated during the dark days of their persecution. The only utilities restored were sewer and water. However basic medical services became largely available. Cooperative farms were formed to produce food for the people. In less than six months, Utah was one of the few places on earth where hunger and fear were not the norm.

The first general announcement made by the true Prophet was an explanation of why the South American armies had spared them. It was quite simple. For years the Church had loved, fostered, and cherished the South Americans as the children of Lehi. The Mormon Church was one of the few things in North America they did not despise. Hence, they spared it, in fact continued to guard it with their army.

Those who had abandoned their principles and joined in the persecutions had largely left the valley when the Lamanite armies had arrived. Food and missionaries were sent to the armies guarding their borders, with the result that nearly all were baptized.

However, peace was far from settling upon the country. Without warning, ships containing Chinese and Russian troops began landing on both the California coast, and the Eastern seaboard. As they threatened to overthrow the entire nation, they brought with them the terror of foreign invasion. As their numbers grew, the people flocked toward middle America, abandoning most major cities to the invaders without a struggle.

At first there was gladness that these foreign armies did not seem to pursue them, but their elation was soon violently crushed. As soon as a city was subdued or largely abandoned of its people, Chinese planes flew over the huddled masses and dusted them with a pink cloud of death. The Chinese had spent decades developing a powder which slowly decayed to release its deadly toxic gas for this very assault. People took one breath of the pink horror, rolled their eyes into their sockets, and died in a choking anguish just minutes later. Thereafter the pink powder began decaying their bodies until there was nothing recognizable after a mere three days. Thus, without firing a bullet, the depopulation of the American coast lands proceeded in its gruesome wake. The only thing that stopped the invading armies from annihilating every living being was that there simply was not enough pink death to do so.

From that day, people of every area and religion flocked into the Utah valleys in an unending stream. Those who came were mostly women, many children, and an occasional pre-teenage male. They came contritely, not as a conquering army, invading hoard, or roving band of desperadoes, but as a conquered people beaten into humble, hopeless submission. As if the Church had always known they would come and had prepared for years, tent cities were thrown up in orderly chaos. Medical needs were met, food was provided, productive labor assigned, and peace established.

Then came the missionaries—thousands of them teaching day and night, comforting, blessing, healing the sick bodies and wounded hearts. Large groups of baptisms became a daily event, and the Spirit of the Lord was poured out upon the valleys of Utah as abundantly as during the dedication of the Kirtland temple.

Priesthood holders were assigned to each tent city. Wards were organized, stakes formed, and order reigned supreme. It was then that the Church set aside a portion of the BYU campus and reignited the School of the Prophets. Reignited was the correct term, for those who emerged from its holy walls were aflame with righteousness. For the first time in this dispensation, the priesthood was commonly understood in its fullness, and its powers fully enjoyed. Men and women emerged from that sacred experience with great faith and great power.

It became nearly axiomatic to say upon seeing someone aglow with the Holy Spirit, "Behold a priest (or a priestess) of the Most High," with a holy, warm embrace. As the righteousness of the people grew so did their joy, and their general communion with God. So common did the tales of great miracles, healings, and outpourings of priesthood power become that all rejoiced, and all believed. For the first time in nearly two hundred years, the children of God were in fact one in heart, with no poor among them. They were Zion.

In her Idaho haven, Melody felt the continual outpouring of the Spirit like a warm breeze blowing from the south. A kind family had invited her, Sammy and Helaman to stay in their small home, and for that small season she had found peace. Now, a restlessness stirred within her so powerfully that she could not stop pacing. The voice of the Holy Spirit whispered constantly in her heart until one evening halfway through dinner she stood suddenly at the table and announced in a forceful voice, "I leave tomorrow for Utah."

As if her own words had voiced the restlessness which had settled upon the entire community, a cheer arose from a thousand throats as multitudes of righteous were moved upon to speak the same words. Not all left, but those who did went by twos and tens, forming into determined little caravans, heading south. There was no general announcement by the Brethren, no great call, no public debate or discussion; they simply heard the voice of the Spirit, and obeyed.

It was early spring when they departed their cherished mountain home, and mid-summer when they stumbled into the Salt Lake valley, singing songs of joy. They were amazed to see every square foot of that valley covered in tents. Everywhere they looked, s a newness of life had come upon the once-tired people. All was order, peace and righteousness. How glorious it seemed to be home. How strange the cities seemed, being so dark without electricity. Yet, a feeling of security literally bathed the night in peace.

Home! For the first time in years Melody suddenly remembered she had a home of her own in South Jordan. Even with the quiet industry of the valleys of the mountains of God there was very little gasoline, and few functioning vehicles; so she, Sammy, Helaman, and a few others used a little horse-drawn cart to travel the freeway south. A day later, she was standing outside her former home, gazing with gentle longing at what was once hers. It was painfully obvious that another family lived there now. The warm, unsteady light from candles danced softly in the interior of the house. Rippling laughter of children emanated from the walls that had once separated her from the cold. She turned aside, lifted her head to the sky, and laughed. It was a laughter of happiness, and of peace. She strode back to the cart that had brought her and was already seated when a familiar sound told her that someone had opened the door to her home—her former home that is.

"Drive on," she said quietly to Helaman, who held the reigns. He snapped them softly and clucked at the horses who were munching on the unmown grass.

"Wait!" a man's voice cried after them.

"Just keep going," Melody instructed. "We'll find some other place. They need this home now." She smiled as Helaman nodded and prodded the horses again.

"Please wait!" he called. But, Melody did not wish to even discuss to whom this home might belong. It was theirs now.

"Mother! Sammy!" the voice cried in desperation. Melody turned in her seat and gasped.

"Stop! Stop!" she cried, and jumped from the still-moving cart. She ran toward her oldest son Theodore, her arms outstretched. They fell into one another's arms so passionately it should have hurt, but neither of them felt anything but joy and wonder.

"What?!" the captain cried. Did they miss us?"

"No, Captain," the first mate replied. "They shot under us! Our draft is too shallow!"

"They won't miss a second time. We must turn about and run. Now!"

"Let me have the radio," Alexei said. The anxious captain handed him the mic. He promptly handed it to Samuel. "Say something amusing in American," he said, and smiled.

Samuel keyed the mic without having a clue what to say. He opened his mouth and this is what came out. "Whoever shot that one's gotta be from New York. No other American would have the gall to shoot another fellow American without even saying hello. On the other hand, I suppose a New Yorker would have at least taken my wallet before blowing me away. I take that back—you've gotta be from California. The last time I was there they were killing each other at stop signs just for smiling wrong."

"Please identify yourself," a flat voice boomed across the speaker.

"Texas!" Samuel cried. "I should have known. I have a brother in Texas."

"Who are you? Identify yourself, or not. Either way I have orders to sink any foreign vessels entering American waters."

"The fact is, we are an American vessel. This is the USS Princess's Gem, registered in California. US Merchant Marine registry 0722515." This he read from a plaque above the radio.

"I never noticed that there," the captain mumbled, rubbing his chin and pondering the plaque as if it had just materialized out of nowhere.

"Please remain at your present location while I check your identification…" silence crackled across the waters.

It took several minutes for the voice to return. "Your ID checks out. I have instructions to order all traffic out of these waters. While we apologize for shooting at you, we still can't allow you to stop here. Please turn around immediately and depart. Have a pleasant journey."

"Captain," Samuel said. But there was no answer.

"Captain?" Silence still.

"Perhaps he does no longer wish to talk to you," the Russian captain said in broken English.

"Captain Bill Hamilton!" Samuel said loudly into the mic.

"How did you know my name?" an angry voice boomed out of their speaker. "Are you a US intelligence vessel? State your business immediately, or I will open fire. My name and the mission of this vessel is classified!"

"Captain. I only wanted to ask you if you set the safety on that torpedo before you sent it into the night."

"That is also classified…." there was some background noise of people speaking all at once that came across as gibberish over the radio. "What…"

"Captain, I only ask because our instruments indicate the torpedo has circled back toward us. It will pass under us as before. Your sub is the next thing on its list. I suggest you…"

"Right full rudder! Release countermeasures! Full…" the radio clicked off to the sound of shouting.

Samuel turned to his captain. "Now, Captain, bring our ship to dock as quickly as possible. This is the only chance we will have to get past the sub."

"Aye," he said, and began shouting orders to his small crew.

Samuel whirled to address Alexei. "Alexei, I suggest you prepare everyone to disembark. We will need to be ready to get off the ship in just a few minutes. Get the buses loaded and running. Load all the extra food and clothing. We have to be off the ship minutes after it pulls to the dock."

Alexei and Vladimir hurried away, shouting orders. About thirty minutes later the old ship nosed up to the concrete pier. The big ramp was lowered to the ground and the gray busses began rumbling off the boat. They didn't even take time to tie the ship, but Captain Anestiv kept the engines running to hold it firmly against the dock. Samuel took his place in one of the buses and they drove off into the sub-arctic night of Prudhoe Bay. They had gone less than three miles when a clap of thunder and enormous explosion of orange fire erupted into the night sky behind them. There was no one on board the faithful old ship when she blew.

Samuel's bus took the lead as they wound their way toward the exit road from Prudhoe's vast complex of oil wells, gathering stations, gasification plants, power generation and pump buildings.

"I remember this place. Turn right here. See that complex over there to the right? That's Pump Station One. I worked there a few times." Samuel felt as if he were giving a tour, rather than fleeing for their lives.

There was a guard gate a short distance ahead. Four marines were standing outside the little building, their guns lowered. The crossing gate was lowered. Samuel could see their breath in the frigid night. They were breathing rapidly, adrenaline coursing through them in anticipation of a fight.

"Let me drive," Samuel said. Vladimir stood up and Samuel slid into the seat while the bus was still moving. He slowed and crawled to a stop beside the first marine.

"Good evening," the guard said. "I have orders to hold you here. As far as we're concerned, you are an invasion force, and we have orders to shoot to kill."

"Good evening Sergeant," Samuel responded, not sure if he was a sergeant or not. "I appreciate your concern. Would you take a look into the window just behind my seat?" The sober face in the helmet nodded once and he took a brisk look into the window. Samuel knew a young mother, a three year-old boy and an infant were huddling in the cold bus. The soldier continued on down the line until he came to the last window. He walked slowly back to Samuel.

"Did you see an invasion force in this bus, Sergeant?"

"I don't know. I'm not responsible for the decisions, I just have my orders."

"Weigh this alongside your orders, then," Samuel replied. "These people have spent the last two years walking through hell to get this far. For every adult you see on this bus, four others have died along the way. For every child on this bus, six others have died. If you stop us, we will either be executed, or sent back to where we came from. We must continue on."

"If I let you pass, I will be executed," he said forcefully, yet with regret.

"That wouldn't be good either," Samuel said. "We wouldn't want that. Where should we wait?"

"I suppose, right where you are." The soldier's voice softened. "Thank you for not forcing us to shoot. We would have shot you, you know."

"Yes, I know. That would be even worse for you than if they had shot you for letting us escape."

"I don't understand how that could be," the soldier said, stomping his feet against the cold.

Samuel flashed a smile at him. "Well, you know as well as I do that killing an innocent man is a no-no with God. Killing one of God's anointed is even worse. I'm afraid you would have had a very unpleasant eternity as a result."

"What do you mean, anointed?" the soldier asked.

"You should understand that. You're a deacon in the Priesthood," Samuel replied. His words surprised even himself.

"Be quiet!" the soldier whispered urgently. "If anyone knew that..." His eyes flashed from side to side, but none of his fellows was paying any attention. Relieved, he looked back at Samuel and cocked his head to one side. "How did you know that I'm a deacon?" he asked.

"The same way you know I'm an innocent man, and one of God's anointed. You sense it in your heart."

The soldier's voice grew brisk. "Look, I'm sorry you're in trouble here, but I can't do anything about it. Who are all these people, anyway?"

"The ten tribes, or at least part of them."

"You mean these are the…"

"Yes."

"But, I always thought they'd come from the stars, or across a highway cast up from the ocean."

"We just came across the ocean," Samuel replied.

"I know, but…"

"Ah, you do know. And you know that my words are true, my young Deacon."

"Maybe I do. But, even if that was so, I still couldn't let you through without getting myself shot for disobedience. There is zero tolerance for such things these days."

"There is a solution to this," Samuel said quietly, almost under his breath.

"What might that be?" the young soldier asked suspiciously.

"Come with us."

The soldier took two steps back as if he had been slugged in the chest. He gasped for breath and blinked his eyes rapidly, pressing a gloved fist to his chest as if his heart hurt.

"That's impossible," he hissed, trying to keep his voice very low.

"It is both possible, and the right thing to do. You know that. As a matter of fact, you already knew you had to leave, you just didn't know how."

"But, how?" he cried under his breath. He stole a look at the three other soldiers who were paying more attention to some teenage girl on the second bus than to this hushed, treasonous conversation.

"How did I know about your decision to leave?" Samuel asked. The fellow shrugged, a look of terror on his face.

"I didn't, actually. But the Lord did, and He just whispered it to me. Come with us. The time is short, and we must leave quickly or we will never reach Zion. Soon, other soldiers will come, and we will be trapped. Come with us, and take your place in the greatest migration of God's people since Moses departed Egypt."

"I… I…" he stammered. A frowned expression creased his face, then he marched away. He barked orders to his three comrades. "I am escorting these buses to the parking area at Central Control Facility. Have them follow me. Make sure they all follow. Tell the others to meet us behind CCF in the morning."

"Yes sir!" they barked.

The young man marched to the door of Samuel's bus and pounded on it with the butt of his assault rifle. "Open up!" he ordered. Samuel pulled the handle and let the young man aboard.

"Drive straight until I tell you to turn," he instructed as he lowered his weapon at Samuel's head. "Don't try anything."

"All right, son," Samuel said, and put the big bus in gear. He gunned the diesel engine and lurched out as the heavy gate was raised. They turned left two miles later on the road to CCF and ground slowly down the snow-packed road. After they turned, Samuel could see a long line of headlights following them. A few miles later they came to a "T" in the road. They should have turned left to go to the CCF.

"Turn right here," he said, and for the first time, lowered his weapon. "I hope you realize we are now an enemy of the United States of America."

"Son, what's your name?"

"I'm Lieutenant Hollis. Randy Hollis," he replied smartly.

"Brother Hollis, I'm Samuel Mahoy. This is Alexei, the leader of these people. I want you to understand that we are not an enemy of this great country, and in a while they will realize that. For now, we had best put as many miles between us and Prudhoe Bay as possible.

"Yes sir," he agreed.

"Brother Hollis, what's the local time?" Samuel asked.

"Well, it's just a little after five in the morning, sir," he replied after consulting his watch.

"Then daylight will soon be upon us. What do you know about the Mormon Church?" Samuel asked.

The lieutenant shot him a withered glance. "Well, I had just been ordained a Deacon when the Church was outlawed. I haven't been to church for nearly eight years since then."

"Has it really been eight years?"

"Yes sir."

Samuel was misty-eyed as he spoke. "I haven't been home for seven of those eight," he said slowly, his mind filling with a mental vision of Melody, Sammy and the twins.

"So, are you a prophet, or something?" Randy asked.

"I am—something like that," he replied without thinking. His usual modesty would have prevented him saying this, but something about the circumstances elicited a direct answer. He wasn't *the* prophet. But there could be no doubt that he was sent from God. The distinction seemed insignificant at that moment.

"Randy?"

"Yes sir?"

"Would you like to know more about the Church that you just committed everything to, including your life?"

"Well, yes sir, I guess I would. Being as how I'm going to die for my convictions shortly, I'd like to know what they are. Will you teach me?"

"I'm going to drive the bus. Vladimir speaks excellent English. And, he has a powerful testimony."

Vladimir was still bearing testimony when the ice fog settled in upon them. The darkness of night was just giving way to the gray of dawn when it came.

Crystalline ice fog is something difficult to visualize until one actually sees it. The best way to describe it is to imagine a windless cold day, so cold your breath crackles as you exhale, so cold that exposed flesh turns white with frostbite in less than a minute. Now imagine taking a thousand tons of silver glitter made of ice, and suspending it in the air. The headlights of the bus hit the slowly swirling crystalline fog and glared back into Samuel's eyes in dazzling flashes of color. No longer able to see the road, Samuel pulled to a stop and turned off the lights. All the other busses did the same, and their drivers dozed off amid the crystalline beauty surrounding them.

In less than an hour the sun began to rise. As it rose above the horizon it penetrated the ice fog in a burst of light. In the deep arctic winter the sun hardly rises above the horizon, yet, reflected as it was off the ice fog, it was dazzling. A halo formed around the sun in stark white too bright to look at. It was truly a halo, for it completely encircled the sun.

Some distance further out a second halo appeared, then still farther away, a third. Connecting the sun with each of the circles of light was a tapered shaft of light going up and out in all four directions. Each beam of light was broader at the ends where it touched the halos, and tapered in the waist. It formed an image a thousand feet high in the shape of a brilliant, double cross. The bottommost beam of light appeared to continue from the sun directly to the front of the bus, so that they might have stepped on it and walked directly into heaven.

"Is this the Second Coming?" Vladimir asked after Samuel aroused him from a deep sleep. Soon everyone on the bus was awake and gazing in wonder at the spectacle. Still the fog swirled around them so thick that they could not see the bus directly behind them.

"No, it's not the Second Coming, but it *is* our salvation." Samuel said.

"What do you mean?' Vladimir asked.

"Listen!" Alexei said urgently. "Listen." Everyone grew silent so that the low idling of the bus sounded loud and persistent. In the silence another sound thrummed above them.

"Helicopters!" Randy said urgently as he recognized the thrum-thrum of the mighty war machines above them. They listened in stark fear as the sound came toward them, grew very loud, then passed off into the distance.

"They didn't see us," he finally said as the sounds faded. A few minutes later the monstrous helicopters came across from a different direction, and again passed overhead without stopping.

"Why doesn't the radar work? Surely radar can see through the fog," Randy asked Samuel.

"Because God has closed their eyes. They see what He wants them to see," he replied.

"Then, we *are* going to make it safely to Zion?"

"Oh yes, we are going to make it to Zion," Samuel rejoined. The word "safely" was conspicuously absent from his reply.

The ice fog lasted about an hour longer than the fuel in the helicopters. Shortly after their ominous searching ended, the fog lifted to reveal a barren expanse of ice that stretched as far as the eye could see in all directions. Only to the south was a hint of a mountain range visible on the horizon. These were part of the mighty Brooks range. The only evidence of man having been there was the raised roadbed upon which they were slowly driving.

It took them two hours to sight Pump Station Two of the Trans-Alaska pipeline. Built in the seventies, the pipeline still carried crude oil along its 800 mile length to the fresh water port of Valdez, Alaska. Forty-eight inches in diameter with wall thickness varying from a quarter inch to well over a half, the pipeline had outlived its designed life of twenty years by over triple. Not only was it a marvel of engineering, it was a marvel of maintenance as well.

For several years in the nineties Pump Two had been mothballed due to lack of flow through the pipeline. But when the new world war had broken out, all environmental concerns had been tossed aside and the huge oil reserves of the Arctic Wildlife Refuge had been hastily drilled and plumbed. Now, the pipeline carried in excess of two million barrels a day to the ragged remains of the U.S.

With the absolute dearth of middle east crude, the Alaska oil range took on critical importance. The shipping lane from Valdez to Seattle was the most heavily guarded sea corridor on the globe. Given all that, it was not surprising that the road paralleling the pipeline should be the most jealously guarded gravel road in the world. The shivering refugees' only hope of salvation was in divine intervention. But of this they each had personal knowledge; divine providence had stayed with them throughout their journey.

About the time the great plumes from the twin jet engines of Pump Two came into sight, it was beginning to grow twilight again. The ice fog settled in rapidly around them. Samuel directed the buses to remain nearly bumper to bumper as he felt his way past the station. On the left side of the road were white reflectors every hundred feet, and on the right, yellow. By following the closely-spaced reflectors, they could pick their way down the highway using a flashlight rather than the headlights of the bus. As long as the reflectors remained white on their left, they were on the road. If a reflector on their right side was white, they were about to drive off the left side of the road. If a yellow reflector passed on the left, they were about to drive off the road on the right.

They inched their way past the station without being seen, climbed the low hills just north of there and found the ice fog non-existent on the far side of the hill. They gratefully switched on the headlights of the buses and continued on. An hour later they crossed a bridge over an unnamed river, and drove parallel to the river for many miles.

It was deep into the night when Samuel had the strong impression to turn down a sideroad. Though not plowed of snow, the road was passable. They drove up a narrow canyon between low hills, wound past numerous 55-gallon drums scattered along the sides of the road, and finally came to a closed gate. Samuel pushed open the gate with the bus, and drove into a large yard surrounded by large steel buildings. It was a construction camp used recently during repairs to the pipeline. In better times it would have been torn down and cleared away. In these times of pragmatism and financial hardship, they had been left standing.

They opened the doors to the big sheds and found ample room inside for their buses. Crews were sent out to sweep fresh snow over their tracks. The crews were just returning when the thrumming of helicopters was again heard in the distance. They finished their work and pulled the big doors shut on the sheds moments before the big black harbingers of death slid past.

At that moment in time a breeze whipped the yard around the sheds, in mere seconds moving tons of powdery snow. One of the big black birds swung up the canyon and hovered outside the big construction camp complex. With no visible sign of the invaders it shortly lifted higher and roared away. Samuel had watched it hovering a mere stone's throw from the building he was in. The crack in the door was large enough that he could see the big machine guns under its stubby wings, and the dozens of rockets nestled against its side.

"The only problem with being inside the sheds is that we can't idle the engines. We'll soon freeze to death," Randy said, his breath creating ice fog with hung around his head like a cloud. "We can't light a fire. Besides, there's nothing to burn. And if we idle the engines on the buses through the day we'll run out of fuel before we reach the next Pump Station. When we reach the next station they'll see us, and call for the helicopters. And," he drew a deep breath. "we'll starve to death about the same time we freeze to death."

"I must say--it is very refreshing," Vladimir said without looking at Randy, but obviously responding to the young soldier's concerns. ". . . to once again be in the jaws of death."

"I don't understand why that would be refreshing," the younger man replied bleakly.

"Because it gives us the chance to exercise our great faith. And, it gives our loving God the opportunity to show His hand in some great miracle to preserve our lives."

"I can certainly agree it would take a miracle to do that," Randy replied hotly.

"Young man," Alexei said, walking past Vladimir and taking the soldier by both his shoulders. "You must understand that we have been on this journey to Zion for over two years now. We have seen miracles aplenty. We have watched God shut the mouths of bears, destroy helicopters who were slaughtering our people, even raise the dead. In every way we have great faith in our God. In time you will join us in these feelings."

"In time I hope I will still be alive to have faith."

The old man smiled. "It is my opinion that you will be. Now, come and I will show you what we do when it appears we are about to die. Come..."

For himself, Samuel longed to find a quiet spot where he could not be seen for a while.

"Alexei," Samuel called after the old man.

"Yes, my brother?"

"I am going to walk outside for a while, and will return in a few hours. Don't send anyone after me."

"As you wish. God speed," the old man said in Russian.

"And you," Samuel replied with bowed head.

Samuel stepped out into the daylight of the arctic winter, in reality not much more than twilight. The sun was not visible in the shallow canyon they were in. He walked until he came to a very hard patch of ice. He continued walking until his tracks were not visible in the ground. He called upon God in mighty prayer, and in seconds was no longer in Alaska.

Randy followed the old leader between the buses to where a large area remained open. There, in the midst of the busses and abandoned equipment in the sheds a few hundred people knelt on the ground in a circle within a circle within a circle. All waited for Alexei to arrive.

"Vladimir, my son. Since my English is weak, would you lead us in prayer so that our young soldier friend will understand?"

"Gladly," Vladimir replied, and took a position in the center of the people. Randy knelt beside Alexei far back in the crowd.

After a long silence Vladimir raised his hands high over his head and looking up into heaven cried out, "Our Father who art in heaven, hear the pray of Thy children."

All the people repeated in broken English. "Our Father who art in heaven, hear the pray of Thy children." Few of them actually understood the meaning of the words, but the warmth of the Spirit they knew well as it settled upon their collective souls.

Randy looked up with a start, for it appeared to him as if a bright light had formed all around Vladimir and those closest to him. He blinked then lowered his head, thinking it must have been his imagination.

"Oh Father, we give Thee thanks, and honor and praise and glory." Vladimir began reverently, and the people echoed each word. "But most of all we thank Thee for the atonement of Thy Son, and for the deliverance His great sacrifice has brought into our lives." Again the people repeated, but this time, they began speaking before Vladimir had finished.

"Great is Thy glory, and endless is our joy in Thee, and ever and ever shall we worship Thee, Thou who are most holy above all, and in whom we take infinite delight." Randy was startled to hear many voices speaking in exact unison with Vladimir's. No longer was there an echo of voices, but all seemed to be speaking as one voice.

"Holy Father, we raise our voices in Hosanna's unto Thee, and pray Thou will hear our cries of joy and adoration and worship, that our voices might join with those of the angels in making a joyful sound unto Thee." Randy found his own voice loosened as an intense burning welled up inside his soul. Without knowing how, he knew every word Vladimir would say, for the phrases formed in his own heart as they were spoken by the congregation.

Vladimir raised his hands high. "Beloved Father, we confess before Thee our weakness, our sins, and our impurity, and pray Thou will look down upon us in mercy, and apply the atoning blood of Thine only Begotten Son, to purify us with fire. Especially we pray for our young American soldier…" At that moment a pause in the collective voice caused Randy's own to cry out as if the sound of a trumpet.

Randy's voice reached into the heavens: "… and forgive me, oh Father, and purify me with fire, that I may humbly attend to the great task before me, willing to give my all, my life, my hopes, my very being in service to Thee. Father, beloved Father, unto Thee I consecrate my all, willingly, joyfully, with great longing to be of service unto Thee, and unto this people." These words the people did not echo, but cried in response, "Amen."

Vladimir continued once again, but Randy could not tell the words did not originate with himself. As far as he could feel, his was the only voice in that large temple of steel and snow, and his voice ascended unto the throne of God in mighty worship for the first time in his life. He did not notice the hours pass, nor the stiffness in his body, nor the cold seeping into his flesh, for he was afire with the Spirit of truth, and the power of the Holy Ghost was working a mighty change in his soul. He was literally a different person.

When the young man stood stiffly, his eyes were puffy from prolonged tears of joy, his face was aglow with light, and his soul felt as if it were on fire. He looked around to really see the world for the first time in his life. A new and glorious feeling surged through him suddenly, powerfully, and he fell to his knees again. A dozen people joined him in silence as he poured out his heart in mighty prayer. The feeling that had brought this sudden undeniable urge to commune with his Father was a feeling of love so powerful, so healing and life-giving that the only way his soul could answer was in sweetest prayer and gratitude.

All around Randy the work of caring for so many people, sharing their meager food, and providing for the very demanding rigors of their journey went on unnoticed. For most of that day he remained where he was, surrounded by a handful of fellow worshipers who waited upon him, covering him with blankets, keeping his knees upon padding, making sure he did not lie on the frozen ground. All this was unseen by him, for he was elsewhere. When he finally came back to the world of mortality he was exhausted, unable to stand or walk, and filled with the Spirit to the consuming of his flesh.

"Take him to a place in the bus where he can sleep." Alexei instructed. "See that he drinks and eats a little. He is our brother now."

ESCAPING BABYLON

Melody found it difficult to release Theodore. They were both laughing and crying so loudly that neither of them could speak.

"Mother!" another voice cried from the steps of the house. "Mother!"

"George Alexander?" she cried in wonder. Her younger son from England, much older and taller than the last time she saw him, bolted down the steps three at a time and ran to her. Theodore stepped aside just as George ran into her arms. They embraced and kissed one another over and over.

"Mother! Mother, it's so wonderful you're actually here. I knew you'd come! I just knew it!" George shouted with joy. "I want you to meet your grandchildren. Mama, I have two beautiful little girls, and Theo has two boys and a girl. We're going to the temple just tomorrow to be sealed. Mother! It's just too wonderful!"

Sammy had waited behind his mother until this exact moment, when he strode around her and grabbed both his brothers in his arms. Now a strapping sixteen year-old, he was as tall, and definitely stronger than either of his siblings. They cried out in happy surprise and hugged him fiercely.

About this time, children and wives came pouring out of the little house. In all, over a dozen people were living in her former home. She was amazed to see the changes inside. Someone had completely removed the electric stove. In its place stood a big makeshift wood-burning cook stove. It was the ugliest thing she had ever seen, but it was radiating a warmth that completely redeemed it. The smell of baking bread added to its ugly charm. The furniture was all handmade. The kids slept on three-tier bunk beds. There was one room for boys, and one for girls. A third bedroom had a normal bed with soft mattress. The fourth bedroom had quilts on the floor for beds for the rest of the adults. The married couples took turns in the only private room a week at a time.

One by one Melody was introduced for the first time to her daughters-in-law. She instantly adored them. Their faces were full of love and light, and she found herself completely charmed. The grandchildren were precious beyond gold. It was late into the night before their excited laughter and stories were hushed and put to bed.

Melody finally had some time alone with her boys. After briefly mentioning some of her own adventures in Idaho she asked, "What happened to you boys after you left home? I was so afraid you would be caught and punished by the blue helmets for not getting the mark and joining the army."

Theo spoke first. "Mom, it's a long and wonderful story. We can't tell it all to you now, but when we left here we didn't know where to go. We finally made our way into the mountains, and there we found a large community of Saints. Mother, it was wonderful. They were full of the power of the Lord, and faithful and true. They were living off of their food storage and moving every day or so. They lived there in the mountains. Day after day their numbers were growing. Many times the soldiers would come and walk past our camp without seeing us, or they'd fly right by overhead. Even though we had campfires burning, they wouldn't see us. We were truly living and being preserved by the power of God.

George nodded and excitedly continued the story. "In our group we had one of the members of the Quorum of the Twelve Apostles, Mother. Imagine it! A prophet and an apostle among us! Every day he sent some of us into town to get supplies, and to preach the gospel. In the nearly four years we have been apart, George and I have been on a full-time mission. We have baptized hundreds of people. By the time the enemies of the Church left the Salt Lake Valley, we were Zion, and fully ready to partake of the glories of the Lord."

Melody clapped her hands in joy. "Oh, I'm so proud of you! I want to hear all about that time. As a matter of fact, I feel strongly you two should write it down while it's still fresh in your minds."

Theodore and George looked at one another meaningfully, then back at their mother. "We were instructed by Elder Andrews, who is the apostle I mentioned, to do exactly that," Theo said. "When we're not working to feed our families, we write everything we can remember." He winked at her. "What about you, Mom? Have you written down your experiences in Idaho?"

Their mother chuckled. "So you want to know if I practice what I preach? Well my dears, actually I have. I kept a diary the whole time." Then she grew more serious. "I want to know something else. Have you boys found your joy in the Lord? Have you truly found and dined upon the fruit of the tree of life?"

"We have," came their emphatic reply.

"We are ready and anxious for the Lord to come again," George explained.

"Do you believe in the ministering of angels?" Melody asked.

"Oh, we do. You do too, don't you, Helaman?" Theodore said, directing his comment to the older man sitting a short distance away. Helaman looked up from the Book of Mormon he had been reading all evening.

"Why do you ask?" he wondered.

"Because I have this strong feeling about you. I always have had a strong feeling about you. I think…"

"I think there's someone I'd like you to talk to, rather than my poor self," Helaman interrupted. "Come with me you three."

"But, aren't you going to answer my question?" Theodore asked, already knowing the answer. He had tried many times to pin Helaman down, and had been unsuccessful every time. It was almost a game with them now. Yet, he had known Helaman in England almost twenty years ago. The man was older and walked with a cane then. Now, when Helaman should have been much more frail, he was exactly the same. He still walked with a cane, most of the time without a limp. He still looked ancient, yet still had the ability to move like a cat when he needed to!

Helaman walked to the front door without a word, opened it and walked through. He held it open for Melody who was followed by her two adult sons. Sammy had already gone to bed. They followed Helaman who walked quickly to the edge of the front lawn, then turned around to face them. Since there were no street lights, it was very dark out. The only light on Helaman's face came from a single kerosene lamp in the window of the house.

"Who did you want us to meet …" Melody asked, and gasped. She ran forward and into the arms of the familiar man who was walking briskly down the sidewalk at that very moment. He was dressed in a heavy down coat and thick boots, even though it was hardly that cold in Utah

"Hello, my love!" Samuel cried with great affection. He kissed her over and over as he held her in his arms, savoring the smell of her hair and the warmth of her body against his.

"Sam," Melody sobbed against his shoulder. "Oh darling, I've missed you every single day since you left!" She pulled back to gaze into his face. "Oh my goodness, Sam Mahoy, you are a sight for my sore eyes! Can you stay long?"

"I'm sorry, Angel, I can only stay for a few hours," he replied.

"Dad!" Sam Jr. said, having waited as long as he could before running into his father's arms. "Oh Dad, you are really home! I've missed you so bad!"

The two Sams wept for joy as they held one another, and Samuel ruffled his sixteen-year-old's hair as he had done since Sammy was a child. Then Samuel turned again to Melody. "Will you please introduce me to my other sons?"

Melody put her arms around her boys. "Theodore, George, meet my husband, Samuel Mahoy."

Samuel embraced them each in turn. It was the first time they had met face-to-face, though they had heard much about him from their mother as well as from Helaman. While he held them in his arms, Samuel told each of them he loved them, and thanked them for their care of their mother. They both pulled away from their stepfather with deep affection for the stranger who called them his sons. They knew, as did Melody, that he had now included them in his celestial family.

Perhaps it was this obvious love that put George at ease so quickly, or perhaps it was a question he had wanted to ask for a long time. Whatever the reason, George asked the first opportunity he got. "So, you work with Helaman?"

In fact, he had asked the same question of Helaman, and had received a kindly, but blunt sidestep to his question. Whatever he expected his stepfather to say, it was not what he had heard, and it quite startled him in its directness.

"I do," Samuel replied, his answer given by the Spirit. "And, rather than have you ask questions one after another, let me just answer them here. I am what in some ages is called an angel. I received my commission from the Lord and was translated to my present state many years ago while you boys were still in England. Helaman and I have been working to bring a portion of the tribe of Levi of the lost Ten Tribes from the North. Is there anything else you want to know?"

Both boys stared at Samuel before they found words to speak. Finally, George blurted out, "Heck yes! There's a lot more I'd like to know," he exclaimed. "To start with, why couldn't Helaman just say what you just said?"

"Because I'm not your father. It wasn't my place," Helaman interjected. "However, now that you know, you must also respect the idea that only your father may inform another of his blessings. You may never speak of it, not even to your Mother or each other. Do you understand?"

"Yes, absolutely," they both said.

"This isn't our first exposure to heavenly beings," Theodore replied. "We had many experiences being assisted by strangers who saved us from impossible situations on our missions, and then simply disappeared. We know the importance of sacred silence."

George nodded in agreement as Theo continued. "I have never had the opportunity to actually ask what it feels like to be so blessed, to actually converse with angels and to live so close to Heavenly Father," he explained.

Samuel smiled. "You're talking to an angel now," he said.

"Good point!" Theo replied, somewhat astonished at his own lack of insight. "But I guess it isn't quite the same as having the angel Moroni appear above your bed in a cloud of glory," he observed wryly.

"True," Helaman replied. "It's better! Before you ask why, think about it. Here we are, conversing with you as one friend converses with another, telling you things that few mortals have heard. We are under no mission to appear, deliver a message, and depart. You may actually ask anything you feel is appropriate. The fact that this is the case is a direct result of your worthiness in Christ to receive this blessing, and the great price you have paid to be obedient to His voice. You are both greatly blessed—actually, far beyond your understanding. Don't let the realization that this great man is your father cloud the fact that he is in fact, one familiar with the face of the Lord, upon whom lies the most profound of blessings: an angel in every sense."

This all had the effect of causing the boys to ponder what had been said in deep silence.

Samuel smiled at them warmly. "Your faithfulness in Christ is the main reason I have come today. You two have a great work to do, as does Sammy, your brother. You need to work with him to help get him prepared so I can come to him soon. My coming to him has little to do with his mission, but I miss him very much. So, do all you can to hurry him along. Teach him about your struggles, and your great faith. Teach him about Jesus Christ and the empowerment of His great atonement. Sammy will come around quickly; he has strong faith already. In a short time you all must leave this place and begin your journey to Zion."

"Is it really that close?" Melody asked her husband, gazing up into his face.

Samuel took her hands and kissed the top of her forehead. "Yes, my love! In just a few months the group I lead will cross Canada and head for Missouri. Your leaders here will begin your journey from Utah in a short time. Finalize your preparations now. As soon as word arrives that a group has arrived at the Cardston temple from Alaska, that will be your signal to begin the journey."

"We will, Father," George promised. Samuel smiled at his words, especially his calling him "Father."

"Where is the group you are with?" Theodore wanted to know.

"They are just beginning down the Trans-Alaska pipeline."

"That is a heavily guarded road. It will take loads of divine intervention to bring them safely here," George said knowingly.

"They have great faith," Samuel assured him.

"As do we," Theodore added. "Perhaps we should go inside and let you and mother talk?"

"Thank you," Melody said gratefully. The boys returned to the house with Helaman. They were deep in conversation as the door banged shut.

Samuel turned to face his wife. He bent down and kissed her lips tenderly. "I have missed you, Melody—really, really missed you."

"Oh my darling, I have missed you terribly," she replied sadly.

Samuel paused, then smiled broadly as if a wish had suddenly come true. "If you'll come with me, I'll show you one of my favorite places on earth." She nodded happily as Samuel took her hand. They walked into the darkness of the night.

It was several hours before Melody pushed open the front door and walked inside. Samuel was now gone. She walked slowly into the room and sat softly on the love seat, a faraway look in her eyes. Her face was aglow with happiness, her cheeks flushed and rosy. Her hair was loose around her face, and she smelled of lilacs and exotic flowers.

Even though it was very late, her sons had waited up for her. Though not worried about her, they had been anxious for her to return.

"Where have you been, Mother?" they asked.

"I'm not sure," she replied softly. "To heaven I think…" was all she would say. They never did find out what happened that night. But, until the very end of her life, whenever someone mentioned that evening, the same sweet smile would cross her face, and she would get a faraway look in her eyes.

Samuel returned to the snowy landscape with some regret. His whole being longed to stay with his beloved wife and children, to go with them to Zion. However, the Lord had commissioned him with another task, and with all his heart he chose to obey. He knew Helaman would stay with his family as much as needed, and they would arrive in Zion safely.

He retraced his steps to the big steel sheds only to find the buses loaded with people and backing out into the yard. It was nighttime, and time to journey once again. The air was bitterly cold with a brisk breeze blowing.

Had he been able to appreciate the cold as a mortal, he would have buried his head in his coat, and shivered fiercely. The wind chill was nearly seventy below zero. As it was, he pulled his coat around his neck, and trotted to the first bus.

Alexei and Vladimir smiled at him as he climbed aboard. Neither said anything to him about his long absence, nor the possibility that he might not return on time. He took his place behind the wheel and glanced at the fuel gauge. There was less than a quarter of a tank left. They would have to find fuel before the morning came.

The convoy of noisy buses turned left onto the snow-packed haul road, and continued their slow journey toward Pump Three. The road from here was hilly, tucked between a river on their right, now frozen, and hills on their left which grew in height and ruggedness as they pressed forward. They drove slowly, partly to preserve fuel, and partly to ensure that no accidents claimed any of their numbers. The old Soviet buses were at best utilitarian, yet extremely sturdy. The same engine that powered the vast fleet of Soviet (now Chinese) light armory also hummed under the hoods of these old gray buses.

Finally, the gentle rise of the ground dropped away steeply, and they could see Pump Station Three glowing brightly at the bottom of a broad valley. Dense plumes of heat were visible billowing into the sky from the four, square exhaust stacks of the big turbines. Samuel pulled to a stop and turned off the lights.

"From here, we must walk," Alexei said. They had run out of fuel, and there was no other alternative. This came as a terrible shock to those on the bus. They had walked literally a thousand or more miles across their frozen homeland. Now, to be once again afoot in an even harsher world, one unknown and frightening to them, was almost more than their weary bodies could accept. Still, they began gathering up their possessions, and moving toward the front of the bus. None complained, even those who knew their depleted bodies could not make the remainder of the trip afoot.

"Alexei," Samuel said quietly as he watched the people filling the road. "It is unthinkable to see these people afoot again. I'm afraid many of them haven't the strength to go the hundreds of miles we have left."

"I know this," Alexei said, his eyes tearing in spite of himself. "My dear brother, I don't know how, but we must go into the station below us and obtain fuel and food. I need you to petition Heavenly Father again, and gain His word. As so many times before, we need His aid!"

Sam nodded humbly, and waited for the Spirit to accord. When it did, he placed an arm on the old man's shoulder. "You are right. I must go alone into the station. You will wait here for my return," he told Alexei, his mind clear on what he had to do, just no idea yet of how to do it.

"We will wait for your return. God speed," the old Russian said.

Samuel began the long walk toward the pump station without much idea of what he should do. As he topped a hill on his slow journey and dropped over the crest, he realized that the pump station was all but abandoned. As soon as he was out of sight, an odd vision filled his mind. It was of a hallway with a gray steel floor. The hallway was lined with lockers on one side, and fire-fighting equipment on the other. He had seen many like it, but not specifically this one. Suddenly, in as much time as it takes to think a thought, he was standing in that hall. A sudden warmth flooded over him, and he pulled open his coat to let the cold escape. Billows of frigid air rolled downward and across the floor from his frozen clothing. He took a step and slid forward. He looked down to find his snowy boots melting into puddles of water. On the painted steel floor it was quite slick.

He took three careful steps to a rubber mat that ran before the row of lockers. He walked down them slowly reading the names. He came to one which read "GRIZZ." This startled him, because he was quite sure he knew the man who owned this locker. He smiled to himself just thinking about "Grizz", who worked at Pump Two years before. This fellow was a three-hundred pound festering package of profanity. He could insult anyone over anything, find something vile and profane in any situation, and curse in a way few benighted heathens ever considered.

Tonight, Grizz's locker was securely locked with a very large padlock. It was unusual for the locker to be secured, since theft was nearly unheard of at the pump stations; this was because everything they used at the station had been given to them by the company. Nevertheless, this evening Grizz's locker was locked tight. For reasons Samuel could not explain, he felt that the very thing he needed was inside that locker. He took hold of the lock and it simply clicked open in his hand. One of the laws he did not have to abide as a non-mortal was the law of opposition. As long as he was doing God's ordained work, nothing in the material world could oppose him—a sturdy lock as well.

The locker contained a gigantic pair of coveralls, a down parka, two large boots, and a collection of tools. Although Samuel didn't realize it until he had it is his hands, on the shelf under a white hard hat he found what he needed: a clipboard with a maintenance schedule, and a set of keys.

Samuel pulled down the clipboard and was not surprised to note that the service schedule for two remote gate valves was due in the morning. It would not be at all unusual for someone to begin this maintenance the night before. He grabbed the keys and the clipboard, and hurried out into the freezing night.

He marched undetected across the yard to where the fuel trucks were stored in a big garage. The truck he sought was a large red tanker truck with a capacity of four thousand gallons of diesel, and five hundred gallons of regular gas. He found the truck, inserted the key, and the engine coughed to life on the first try. He let it idle as he climbed from the cab and stabbed a finger onto the "UP" button to raise the garage door.

Samuel shifted the big truck into gear. No one at the pump station saw him drive smoothly out into the night; it was a miracle, he knew, as the station would normally be heavily patrolled. When he arrived at the guard gate it was already open; he drove to the haul road and turned left. In less than a half-hour he was trying to figure out how to turn on the pumps to transfer the precious fuel to the buses.

It took most of the night to pump the fuel. By the time Samuel was finished it was just growing twilight. As the morning grew lighter a dense fog had rolled into the low valley. He drove the big truck past the pump station and honked twice on the air horn. Behind him, unseen in the fog, a convoy of refugee buses rolled past, barely able to see more than the bumper of the bus in front of them.

They drove all that next morning and passed Pump Four about midday. They saw no further helicopters. Samuel could only assume that there had miraculously been no reports of strange vehicles on the haul road, or anything unusual the night before.

From Pump Four they began the slow climb toward Atigun Pass. Here the terrain changed dramatically from rolling to rugged. To their left the rock formations were breathtaking. A great jutting of granite in one spot formed a jagged mountainside. Right next to that another great peak jutted in the opposite direction, and between them a giant stone dome as smooth as a bowling ball. The combinations of stone formations seemed impossible to all exist in the same place. As they climbed the air grew colder, and the road more treacherous. Near the summit, the visibility was nearly zero. Samuel slowed the fuel truck as much as he dared without going so slow that he could not start again on the slick road.

The only thing that gave it away was a single flash of light that caught his eye. Samuel stopped and studied the blinding snow where he had seen the dim flash. In a moment he saw another, and realized it was the unsteady movement of a dim flashlight off to his right. He pulled a little farther ahead and stopped. Unwilling to stop on the long slope, the busses passed him and continued up the hill until they reached a flatter area. By that time Samuel, Alexei and others were climbing through a deep drift toward the light.

"Thank God you saw my light!" a weary voice cried as they pulled open the passenger door of a big supply truck leaning on its side, stuck on the side of the road. "I've been here for nearly 24 hours, and had just about given up hope."

"Come on, we'll help you get warm. I have a bus here," Samuel told the man.

"Who are you?" he demanded through chattering teeth. "I didn't think any buses were running up here anymore."

"Well, if I told you we were the ten tribes returning from the North, would you believe me?"

"No, I'd say you're insane," the half-frozen driver asserted.

"Right," Samuel chuckled. "The bus has my crew in it. We just left Prudhoe on our way to Fairbanks. Our fuel truck is just a few yards away. We'll drop you off at Pump Five on the other side of the pass. The crew in the bus will see if they can get your truck out of the snow. It doesn't look like it's damaged, mostly stuck I think."

The driver was beyond relieved. "That would be wonderful," he gasped between coughs. "I'm afraid my feet are almost frozen. I can hardly feel them anymore."

Samuel helped him into the cab and climbed in himself. "Pull your shoes off and let me rub your feet," he instructed.

The driver looked at him suspiciously, then began unlacing his boots. He had worn regular work boots in the truck, not expecting to have to endure the fierce cold for any length of time.

Samuel began rubbing his feet and found them frozen solid. His heart lurched in sorrow. He would probably lose both of his feet. Samuel prayed silently and in that moment the Spirit flooded him with peace. He gratefully extended God's gifts to the man. His toes immediately softened and flexed.

The man sighed. "Oh, thanks, that feels much better," he said and lay back in the warm cab. "I guess they weren't frozen after all."

Samuel turned up the heater to full blast. "I think they'll be fine," he said. The driver's eyes closed in relief and he quickly fell asleep. Samuel put the big truck in gear and drove past bus after bus of Russian refugees.

Alexei and Vladimir began examining the cargo of the truck while Samuel took the driver to Pump Five. Samuel already knew what was in the truck. On the door of the truck were the words, "Carr Gotstein," Alaska's largest food wholesaler.

Atican pass wound steeply downward with many tight turns, but the scenery was breathtaking. Samuel enjoyed the drive as the lost driver snored deeply. A few hours later he dropped the tired man off at the base of the hill leading to Pump Five.

"I've got to continue on, but it's just a short walk to the station," Samuel said.

"You can't just drive me up the hill?" the man protested wearily.

"I can't," Samuel told him. "I have to go back to get your truck out of the snow."

"Okay, I do appreciate you doing that," the driver said in a sort of daze.

Samuel looked him in the eye. "I will deliver your truck and its contents to where they need to go."

"Sounds good," the driver told him sleepily. "Thank God you saved my life—I know you did."

"Yes, God *is* good! I am indeed glad we found you," Samuel said. Then he added, "We'll take care of your truck. If anyone asks, just tell them the Lost Tribes of Israel have it."

The driver laughed loudly. "I'll do that. Thanks, and so long."

There was an element of danger in returning the man to Pump Five. He would surely report that he had arrived at Pump Five in a fuel truck. That would put to rest the mystery of the missing fuel truck from Pump Three. The odds were they wouldn't send helicopters after a missing fuel truck. But, they probably would send a security vehicle, or set up a roadblock.

Samuel pondered all this as he found a place to pull off the road just beyond Pump Five. The terrain was less rugged here as the road leveled out quickly. There were once again trees—that is if the stubby, black spruce of the far north can rightly be called a tree. Still, it seemed wonderful to be in less-barren country. When the first trees appeared they were sickly looking, barely alive, and less than the height of a man. In just a few miles they became taller and thicker until the forest was dense with robust spruce.

It took the buses an additional three hours to catch up with him. But, when they did, there was a semi-truck filled with food in the convoy. Now they had more food than any of them had seen in years. It was a miracle, and they all rejoiced.

With plenty of food and fuel the only thing to slow them in reaching their destination was the treacherous journey south. Samuel knew that only the power of God would deliver them once they reached Fairbanks, which housed the largest military base in Alaska.

A pink fog settled over Salt Lake and Utah valleys without warning, and its work of death began instantly. With an almost complete breakdown in communication, people had only heard rumors about the "pink death." What they had heard, even the most horrifying rumors, was less than the reality—because none who actually experienced the pink cloud ever lived to tell about it.

The war waged by the Chinese and Russian forces against the United States was never intended to be easy. They knew before they loaded the submarines that brought them to the American homeland that resistance would be fierce, and strongly doubted they would be able to use their pink horror more than once or twice before they were rebuffed. To their delight, they arrived in the East without opposition and dispensed their death with nothing but isolated, ineffective resistance. When it became evident they had underestimated their chances of actually conquering their hated enemy on their own soil, they had dispatched urgent requests for backup and supplies. In the meantime, they stormed from city to city subduing and killing as many as they could.

Somewhere in the Midwest they came to the startling conclusion that there was almost no one left for them to kill. The deep South was heavily engaged in a war against troops from South America, and far too well-defended for them to engage. The far north was too sparsely populated to waste their dwindling supplies on, and the West coast of California was already in the hands of the South Americans. The major population centers of the West were now teeming with frightened refugees. Salt Lake City made the perfect target.

The Chinese loaded the last of their deadly supplies onto a stolen plane and argued for three days over whether to drop it in sufficient quantity to kill on contact, or to spread it over a vast area in the hopes of killing more in the long run through the lingering death it left in its wake. In the end a compromise of sorts was reached. They would dump sufficient on the city center to kill a few tens of thousands, and spread the rest south as far as it would go. Sick from exposure to their own chemicals, they took off knowing they would not themselves survive long enough to even land the plane.

When the drone of the plane was heard above the quiet city, every eye looked up in wonder. A plane had not over flown their homes in years. As the billowing pink cloud began forming behind the plane, they knew something was terribly wrong. When the first people in the streets died after three choking breaths, the population screamed in panic, ran a few steps and died themselves.

Theodore was rocking his youngest child and humming an English tune to her when his head suddenly snapped up.

"What is it, honey?" Melody asked.

"Do you hear that, George? Do you hear it, Helaman?" he called loudly. The baby in his arms began to whimper. He handed her to his wife and stood. At that moment George came running up from the basement.

"We have to go into town," he was calling. When he saw Theodore he looked at him solemnly. "We have to go into town."

"I know. I was just coming to get you. Where's Helaman?"

"I'm here." Helaman said as he walked in from the back of the house. "We must leave. But first, we need to leave a priesthood blessing on this home."

Theodore nodded. "Mother, Rachel, everyone! Come, gather in a circle and hold hands," Theodore instructed. It was a few moments before all the kids could be gotten from their beds. It was still early in the morning, and the house was chilled from the winter night. They came protesting—but they obeyed.

Theodore surveyed the small group to make sure everyone was present. Thereafter he raised his right arm to the square, as did George and Helaman. Melody had never seen anything quite like it.

"In the name of Jesus Christ, and by the glorious power of His priesthood. I rebuke the destroyer and place a blessing and promise of protection upon all present, and upon those we love no matter where they may be. In His holy name, Amen."

A chorus of "Amens" was followed immediately by a barrage of questions as the three priesthood holders pulled on their coats.

"Please, tell me what is going on," Melody pleaded.

"Mother, the plague is come. I heard the Spirit of the Lord plainly speak in my ears to tell me to make haste into the city. We must hurry before there are none left to help."

"What plague?" she demanded.

Theodore threw open the door. Already a light dusting of pink powder was on everything in sight. "Behold, the hand of death," he said soberly as he surveyed the landscape.

"What is it?" a dozen voices demanded sleepily.

"Get together. Sweep it into the streets. Go help the neighbors, and show them that your faith and the Priesthood has delivered you. Our only hope is in the mercy of God. Go now, there is no time to lose," he commanded. "Come George, we have a long walk ahead of us."

Every house Theo and George passed they pounded on the door and prayed with them, leaving a priesthood blessing. Some of the houses they entered were already filled with choking people. These received priesthood blessings. Many recovered instantly. Many died before their words were finished. Death seemed to be very selective, taking whole households, whole kinships, while completely sparing others.

The nearer they walked to the city the greater the number of dead. They walked up and down the rows of homes, often meeting other groups of priesthood holders doing the same task. They did little more than call a greeting, and pronounce a blessing upon the other faithful brothers they passed, who then joined their ranks. Many of the groups of righteous also included women who went out boldly to minister and heal through their faith, and by power they had received through their temple ordinances.

The outskirts of the city seemed to be the hardest hit. As they walked up the quiet streets they stopped by each body. At each body they paused, listened, and either walked away, or knelt down to bless them.

"My beloved sister in Christ, in the name of His holy Priesthood I command you to return to this world and complete your sojourn here," one of them would say when inspired to do so. Without exception the black, sunken eyes would flicker open as color and vitality returned to the festered flesh. Never once did those restored to life seem surprised, but calmly stood, thanked them in two or three words, sometimes with a hug, then strode off to continue administering to others. But fewer than half of those they encountered were they allowed to heal in this way.

All through the day, George and Theo worked their way closer to the Temple. As they labored up and down each street they were met by more and more who had heard and heeded the call to redeem Zion just as they had. It took most of that day before they came to the outer walls of temple square, and the great granite Salt Lake Temple. They walked into the square to find throngs of righteous in the attitude of singing praises and worshiping in songs of joy. They raised their voices with those already there for hours. As if the veil grew thin at that place, many saw visions, spoke with angels, and prophesied of glorious things to come.

It was well past midnight when the men again climbed the concrete steps of their home. Their walk home had been much more disheartening than their march into town. Almost every front lawn they passed had mounds of dirt marking the graves of loved ones whose faith, or whose destiny had not been sufficient to keep them on this mortal sphere. It was not correct to say that only those who were unrighteous died that day. For all knew of people with great faith who simply were not ordained to survive that experience. It was true to say, however, that none who were not righteous survived the desolating sickness.

For reasons no one quite understood, on the following morning a loud rumbling awakened everyone in the house. Children ran from their beds in terror, wondering if the house had come alive, or was going to be destroyed by another earthquake.

"It's the furnace!" Melody cried. "I can't believe it—the electricity is back on!" It had been several years since a light bulb had burned in the valley. Many children had not seen such a marvel in their young lives, and stared into the lights until their eyes ached. Realizing that light bulbs would be impossible to replace, every fixture with more than one bulb was quickly stripped of all but one, and children were schooled intensely on the evils of leaving a light running for no reason, or even worse, turning on a light during the day, even if it was dark in the room. The family gathered around the radio, anxious to hear any news from the outside.

The following day muddy brown water began burping from the taps. In a few days it became sweet and cold. A few days later someone brought an old television back into the room and plugged it in. They watched as the picture flashed to life. The first image they saw was the face of their Prophet.

"Brothers and Sisters, I repeat. Now that we have running water in most parts of the valley, I urge you to plant gardens in every available space come spring. If you do not have seeds, contact your home teachers. Some will be made available. Every chapel will hold classes on gardening between now and spring. Your gardens must be successful the first time. If you have no garden plot, join with neighbors at their invitation and share their space. Dig up your lawns and flower gardens if necessary. You don't need fertilizer, all you need is faith. Pray for your gardens, do as the Holy Spirit directs, and they will flourish.

"The supplies of food the Church and many faithful members have stored against this very time are nearly exhausted. Come next fall we will live on whatever we raise this summer. Fear not, for all this is known to the Lord, and he will bless your efforts with bounty from the earth. As He did when feeding the 5,000, Jesus Christ will multiply your faithful harvest with food sufficient to feed your families and neighbors.

"I leave you this last prophecy to warm your hearts and strengthen your backs against the times just ahead. In the not far distant future the Lord will sound His trumpet, and a few blessed and chosen ones will begin the journey back to the lands of our inheritance in the East from whence our fathers were driven by the hand of unrighteousness. There they will build a Holy City."

"Many of us will remain here to receive and teach those who will flock to us for aid. It will be a great missionary labor, and we will baptize millions. As we prepare the people they will be gathered to Zion. In time we will all go to Zion. Except for those who go first, we shall not walk, but shall go upon the wings of the Spirit."

"We will build God's Zion and will meet the Lord Jesus Christ as He returns to His temple. There we will watch in awe as He comes in Glory to subdue all enemies under His feet, and to establish the millennial reign of peace so long awaited by the righteous of every age. This I prophecy in the name of Jesus Christ, Amen."

That message was repeated every half-hour throughout the day. In the evening speakers from among the General Authorities spoke on subjects of great interest. The topics were as basic at times as obedience, baptism, faith, and repentance. At others, they were as lofty as the ministering of Angels, the washing of feet, and the second endowment, the fullness of the priesthood, miracles, the law of consecration, and a host of other topics previously unmentioned in such a large forum. It was almost as if General Conference were in permanent session. The Spirit rested upon His people in rich abundance, and Zion began to emerge among them. The temples were open twenty-four hours a day. It was truly a time of rejoicing among the faithful.

Samuel and his convoy of Lost Israelites reached Fairbanks late at night in the last days of January. The air was almost brittle with cold as they lumbered down unplowed roads toward the city they most feared. The nearer they drew to the city the broader the roads became, and road signs counted down the miles before they would arrive. The first street light they encountered was not lit, nor any thereafter. They came to the main gate of the massive military base that now encompassed the city. No lights glimmered in the crystalline fog. Strangely, no one was at the guard gate, and they passed into the city.

Fairbanks was a city of ice. Every structure, every tree, every sign was completely encased in thick frost so that some structures were not even recognizable. Cars were stalled in the middle of the freeway where they had been abandoned, and nowhere was there a light to be seen. Nowhere was a person to be found.

Samuel turned off from the main highway and drove slowly down a wide street, its name obscured by ice. Turning left down another street and then right again they found a row of houses. Buses began stopping as families stomped through the crusty snow up to the front doors and into the empty homes. In less than an hour everyone was inside and snuggled under blankets. Of the hundred homes they occupied that night, not one was missing furniture, beds or bedding. The only things that had been taken were food and photographs.

All else had been left behind.

19

A ZION PEOPLE

Peace, such as can come upon a people of tremendous faith on the ragged edge of starvation, settled over the Salt Lake Valley and its environs like a down comforter. As food grew more scarce and less varied, the people fasted as many as three days a week, giving their surplus, if they had any, to those without. That which they lacked in physical needs was abundantly replaced in spiritual manifestations such as had not been previously known among the people in this dispensation. It became commonplace for people to see or hear angels in sacrament meeting, for children to speak prophetic words, and for talks given in church to be as powerful as anything that ever rolled from the tongue of a prophet.

Another interesting change was that the Saints did not consider anything they possessed as their own. Most families had not actually built or paid for the homes they lived in; few had purchased the food they ate with any kind of money. All they possessed was "ours," rather than "mine," and a simple equality of stewardship blessed the people. Every day those able to labor did so with all their energy. In return they were given sufficient for their needs, and even some of their wants. The streets were clean, the schools staffed, and the businesses manned. The bishop's storehouses were stocked as much as possible, and public utilities were maintained, all through the Church distribution. There was no jealousy, class distinction, or wealth except as was common among all of them.

For the first time in several hundred years, Zion blossomed upon the desert soil. For the first time in as many years the condemnation was lifted off the Church, which condemnation had been because of their worldly walk and prideful hearts. With the lifting of that heavy burden, the Spirit of the Lord moved freely and powerfully upon the people in all they said and did. The emotions most common among all who dwelt in Zion was peace, and undiluted joy.

When summer finally came at long last all hearts and hands turned to the soil. A hundred thousand gardens produced bountifully, and food was no longer scarce. Trees that had ceased to give fruit for years now sprang forth with limbs heavily laden. Nothing was wasted, all was preserved, and there was enough, and to spare.

The long-awaited call finally came to prepare to trek east to the center place of Zion, but it did not come over the television, radio or any address given by the Brethren. It came into the hearts of those who listened. Melody simply began collecting things they would need. As if some internal mechanism had chimed the hour of preparation, the work began in quiet earnest through out every reach of Zion.

Melody was just finishing stitching the border on a quilt when a firm knock came to the door. It was just turning cool as summer gave way to fall. She was sitting in the house with all the windows open, a pleasant cooling breeze moving gently through the house. The children were all at work or play outside. She laid aside her work and walked down the steps to the door. She was not prepared for what she saw.

"Mother!" the tattered visitor cried, and rushed into Melody's arms.

"Lisa! My sweet girl! I can't believe you are here! Oh Lisa, I have prayed so hard that you would come home. Come in, come in." she urged.

Lisa turned around and picked up a little boy two years old, who was hiding behind her. A small girl not much older than four had been holding his hand. "These are my babies," she said happily. "Monica and Timmy, meet your grandmother," she said, holding Timmy forward. Melody knelt down, smiling at him so broadly that he smiled back immediately, and looped his arms around her neck. She then held out a loving hand to Monica, who took a happy skip and slid a small hand into her grandmother's.

"Come inside everyone. Welcome home!" Melody exclaimed with joy. Lisa smiled back at her with relief and love. It was the best thing Melody could have said.

Everyone having eaten and the little ones happily off to play with cousins, Melody turned her attention to Lisa. Her stepdaughter was still lovely, although her tired eyes were puffy and strained. Her hands were severely chapped, her dress torn and tattered, and her short hair looked like it hadn't been washed in months. It broke Melody's heart to see her this way.

"Lisa, the last I knew of you, you were in Texas with your husband," Melody said as she reached out to rub her daughter's shoulders.

"That's right. It's a long, long story," Lisa said wearily.

"I'd like to hear it. When your father returns, he'll be most interested to hear everything that's happened to you. He loves you so much!"

"Oh Mama, how is Papa?" Lisa cried. "Is he well? Where is he? I had so hoped he would be here!"

"Your father is much more than well. I saw him last winter for a few hours. He's off on a mission for the Lord. He's doing fine. Come to think of it, I don't think he's aged much at all in the last dozen years. He sure looked good to me," Melody said wistfully.

"You haven't aged either, Mama."

"You're sweet honey." In fact, Lisa was right. Melody wore her fifty-seven years with elegant grace.

"As a matter of fact, if I didn't know any better, I'd say you're pregnant! Sorry, but it's true," Lisa giggled.

Melody blushed. "You're far too observant," she said, running a hand across her slightly distended abdomen. "I am."

"But, aren't you kind of…" her daughter said, and then stopped, not wanting to be rude.

Melody laughed. "Old? Normally, I would say yes. But, I'm different. Something has changed in my body these last few years, and I feel as strong as when I was twenty. I have simply loved being pregnant again. I'm so happy I can hardly express my joy."

"So, you are all right with being pregnant? I mean, you're happy about it?"

"I'm positively overjoyed," Melody said with such fondness that Lisa was left without a doubt that it was so.

"So, since you're expecting, obviously Daddy came home a few months ago." Lisa winked at her mother. "When is your baby due?"

"Just three months. I can hardly wait."

Lisa thought about that. "So when can I see Daddy again?"

"That depends mostly on you," Melody said slowly.

"What do you mean?"

"I'll explain later," Melody said, trying to avoid a real answer. "He is on a special assignment, and can come back if we have sufficient faith. Otherwise, I'm thinking we will only see him when we finally make it to Jackson County,"

Lisa shook her head. "I don't understand."

Her mother good-naturedly patted her knee. "Oh sweetheart, I'll explain it all to you in good time. Now, tell me about you!"

Lisa settled into the couch, savoring the warmth and security of her new surroundings. Melody joined her. "Well, as you remember, Alvin and I left Salt Lake just before the Church was outlawed. How long ago was that now?" Lisa wondered.

"About five years ago, I think."

"Seems like longer," Lisa said quietly.

"It does indeed."

Lisa sighed and continued her story. "So anyway, we moved to a small town outside of Houston called Huntsville. It was beautiful there. The economy was still good. People were optimistic, the Church was growing, and it was wonderful. Alvin got a job with a small crating company and quickly moved up into management. We bought a house and were doing great—until the Church was outlawed."

Melody nodded in sympathy. "It came as a total shock," Lisa confided. "The changes it made in people's attitudes were severe. Since we were new in Huntsville, few people knew we were Mormons. Alvin decided to try to keep it a secret as long as possible. I was worried about doing that, like it was betraying our faith or something. But, Alvin insisted he'd lose his job if he didn't pretend to not be a member."

Lisa stopped, her voice becoming emotional. Her mother nodded for her to go on. "Everything seemed to go along fine for a few months. But, it was awfully hard for me to stand by and watch as other Church members were persecuted and driven out of their homes. I could hardly stand to keep quiet. The only reason I did was because Alvin insisted. He was adamant that we should not let anyone know we were Mormons. I tried to go along as best I could. I salved my conscience by helping other members, giving them food or clothing, and housing them whenever I could. It was truly pathetic. The members were so destitute. My heart ached for them," she remembered, her eyes pooling with tears.

"The worst part came when the monetary system changed and paper money was outlawed. Everyone was forced to get the microchips in their bodies, or to go hungry. Of course Mormons who wouldn't renounce their religion could not get the chips. Alvin came home one day and announced that he had gotten the chip implanted. He said it was so that he could feed me. At the time I was three months pregnant with Monica. He said it was the only way."

"Your poor husband!" Melody told her softly.

"I was frightened, and didn't know what to do. He pressured me to get the chip also so that I could have the baby in a hospital." Lisa paused with emotion. "I refused," she whispered.

"You are indeed a brave girl," her mother told her with a nod.

"Maybe too brave," Lisa told her. "What happened next was so sudden… I had no warning. It was really bad for the other members of the Church. They were leaving Texas as fast as they were able, but many of them were destitute. I had found three teenage children digging in our garbage can. I convinced them I was their friend, and took them in to hide them and feed them. They said they were Mormons, and that if I took them in I could get in trouble. I told them I was a Mormon too, and not to worry."

Lisa stopped, her voice breaking. "Oh, Melody, but they weren't Mormons!" she cried. "They were spies. They turned me in to the police. Some men came in blue helmets, and without saying anything more than that I was an outlaw, they threw me out into the street. When Alvin came home they let him into our home, but I couldn't go through the door of my own home. The police went inside and talked to him for over an hour. When they came out they loaded me into a jeep and drove me over fifty miles away from my home and dumped me off on the side of the road. They told me not to try to return home." Lisa paused as tears rolled down her cheeks. She looked up tragically. "I have never seen Alvin since, and that was over six years ago."

Melody held Lisa tightly for a few minutes before her daughter could go on. "What happened next, my dear?" stroking her back.

Lisa sniffed and bravely resumed her story. "I was close to the border of Louisiana, and was able to hitchhike to the town called Leesville. When I arrived I was nearly starving. It was a small town and a lady saw me stumbling down the street and gave me food and a place to spend the night. In time I got a job as a nanny and housekeeper for a family named Allen. They were very good to me. I took care of their two younger kids and kept house. They were fairly well-to-do, and seemed to not care that I was homeless, or that I was pregnant."

"Everything went fine until it came time to have the baby. They drove me to the hospital for a prenatal checkup. I hoped to get the checkup in spite of not having the chip. I had been able to do other things fairly easily without a chip in Louisiana, and hoped to get by. When the hospital found that I didn't have a chip, they offered to implant one. I refused, and they reported me to the authorities."

"It was late that night when the police came to the Allen's. I had gone to bed early with light labor pains. They got me up and brought me to the police station. The police grilled me until I finally told them I was a Mormon. The Allens were shocked, and ordered the police to punish me then and there. So the police took me out into their truck. All this time I was in labor, and terrified. It was raining and cold, and all I had on was my nightgown. The only other clothing I owned was the dress I was wearing when they found me, but it was far too small now. The Allens let me keep the nightgown; otherwise I would have left their home naked. As it was, I was shivering in the back of their truck, sitting in the rain in a wet nightgown, terrified, cold, and in hard labor."

Lisa was crying again, and stopped to compose herself. "I was actually hoping they would take me to prison where at least I might receive medical help. My biggest fear was that they would just dump me somewhere. If they did that I was quite certain that I or my baby would die—and probably both of us."

"Oh Lisa, that's terrible!" Laura cried.

"It really was, Mama. The police drove to the outskirts of town and stopped on the side of the road. I could hear them arguing for a while about what to do with me. One of the policemen was actually compassionate. He argued I was young, and pregnant, and that I would die if they left me there as they had been instructed to do. The other said they had no choice. I could hear them arguing loudly in the cab of the truck. They both seemed desperate. Neither wanted to cause my death, but neither knew what to do with me. All the time I was sitting in the back of their truck in the rain. While they were arguing my water broke, and I knew the baby was coming. I had heard of the government taking babies from other Mormon women. I knew I couldn't wait for them to decide what to do with me. I climbed out of the back of the truck as quietly as I could and ran away into the night."

Melody took her daughter's trembling hand. "I was still close enough to the truck to hear their conversation when they realized I had escaped," Lisa continued. "They just shrugged, and said me being gone made it easier on them. They drove away and left me huddled behind a bush. If they had looked for me they could have found me in seconds."

Melody rose to get a handkerchief for her daughter, who was almost incoherent by now. Lisa wiped her tears, then continued. "After they left I knew I was in worse trouble than before. I prayed like I have never prayed before, and suddenly I felt a warm hand upon me. Somehow, Mama, I was guided through that delivery, even though I don't know exactly how it happened! It was a pure miracle, I know that!"

"Praise the Lord!" Melody exulted.

"It was a miracle, let me tell you," Lisa told her. "I was just exhausted, and wrapped little Monica in my nightgown, laying her on my belly to keep warm. Luckily it was a warm night, and I was so exhausted that I slept and fed Monica until morning."

She paused here to reflect, then concluded. "As I look back on those events, I'm surprised I survived, and Monica as well. Actually, I know we survived only because Heavenly Father was watching over us very carefully. Ever since that miraculous experience, I have felt more faith than I've ever had before."

Melody's eyes were brimming with tears, and she put her arm around Lisa. "What happened then?"

"Well, when I could walk, I went back to the Allen's and was able to hide us in their garage for two days," Lisa said.

"What did you eat?" Melody asked.

"I ate from a bag of apples and opened some jars of bottled fruit on the shelf. When Mrs. Allen found me, she screamed and ran back into the house. She began throwing things at me and ordering me to leave at the top of her lungs. She threw shoes, blankets, food, clothing, all kinds of things! She even threw a big laundry bag for me to put them in. She was 'screaming" while I loaded all that stuff into the bag while saying, 'Thank you, thank you.' She was also weeping, and I knew she hated herself for what she was doing. I left with enough food and clothing for a few days. It was nighttime and rain was starting to fall."

Lisa shivered as she thought about it. "That very night I heard the news that Mexico had invaded Texas. Suddenly, the police quit worrying about Mormons. I no longer had to hide for fear of being arrested, or having my baby taken away. I joined the army of people who were leaving Texas. I was able to get a ride up into Oklahoma. There were so many refugees now that I was no longer different from anyone else. It was hard to get food, but when people saw that I had a tiny baby, they usually shared. It was an awful time, and terrifying."

"I can't imagine how you survived," Melody said, her eyes filled with pain.

"I'll tell you how I survived—by divine intervention. I know that now."

Melody nodded solemnly. "I have prayed with great faith concerning you and Bonnie," she told her. "I had no idea you were struggling so! But I always felt you were being preserved."

Lisa smiled in gratitude. "Your prayers were undoubtedly a big part of my survival. Prayers—and an older gentleman I met in Oklahoma."

Melody cocked her head. "Older gentleman? Was his name Helaman, by any chance? Does he walk with a cane?" she asked.

Lisa's eyes grew big. "How did you know? He does use a cane, and his name is Helaman!"

Melody laughed out loud. "He is a friend of your Father's, and seems to be heavily involved in our family's survival," she grinned.

"I had no idea. If it hadn't been for my bumping into Helaman in Oklahoma, I would never have survived," Lisa exclaimed.

"Oh no! Please tell me about it," Melody encouraged.

"It's kind of a funny story!" Lisa began. "I arrived in Oklahoma in the hot afternoon. It was extremely muggy and unpleasant. Monica was hungry, and I didn't have much milk for her. I probably would have if my diet had been better, or if I even had more water to drink. By this time, Monica was five weeks old and I was pretty much skin and bones."

Melody shook her head. "Oh, you poor dear!"

"The people I was with tried very hard to help, but they didn't have anything either," her daughter continued. "I had decided I was going to die about the time we made it as far as the rest stop. We were driving an old beat-up van, and it overheated and died. We coasted into the rest stop with steam billowing out of the engine. There were lots of other people there, refugees like us. When we arrived there was a big fight going on. It appeared to me as if a big bunch of them were beating someone up. It made me so mad that I left Monica on the floor of the van and ran toward them, yelling my head off. Somewhere along the way I had picked up a branch, and was waving it around. I must have looked insane running toward them like that."

She stopped here to shake her head. "When I arrived, this poor old guy was on the ground bleeding. They had worked him over pretty soundly. I clobbered the guy closest to me with the stick and knocked him to the ground. That got their undivided attention, and they actually backed away. I asked them what this man had done wrong. They said he was a Mormon, and Mormons were responsible for the invasion of Texas. I asked them why, and they said because everyone knew they were. So I told them I was a Mormon—as a matter of fact, I screamed it at them! I told them that I was an advance scout for the Mexican army and that they were going to be here before sunrise and kill everyone who had ever touched a Mormon."

"You're kidding!" Melody cried.

"No! That's exactly what I said," Lisa laughed, her face beaming for the first time.

"What did they do?"

"They believed me! They took off in every direction."

"No!"

"It's true. They did!" Lisa insisted. They laughed together, and Lisa turned contemplative again.

"I helped the old man to stand up, but it was he who practically dragged me back to the van. In spite of the beating he had taken, he seemed pretty strong to me. I tried to clean up his wounds, but he insisted on helping me. He said his name was Helaman. At that moment the people at the rest stop started coming back. I knew we were in trouble when the first rock hit the side of the van and broke out a side window."

"Whoa!"

"Richard, the guy who owned the van, jumped back in real quick. It started right up, and we drove away. Whatever had been wrong with the van before, it seemed perfectly fine after that. Honestly, it was another miracle," Lisa said quietly.

"Helaman seems to be surrounded by miracles," Melody observed wryly.

"Well, Richard drove us several miles from the rest stop and pulled over. He told us we had gotten him into trouble, and ordered us out of the van; then drove on with us standing by the road: an old battered man, a sick mother and a baby. I started to cry. Then Helaman says, 'Oh, let him go. He would have just wanted part of my apple.'"

"'Apple?' I asked. So he reaches into his coat pocket and pulls out this big red apple. He handed it to me, and I bit into it after he told me to. Mama, I have never tasted anything so amazing in all my life! I chewed until my jaws hurt and then swallowed. I handed the apple back to him, but he wasn't interested. I finally ate the whole thing. While I ate, he played with Monica. She seemed to love him, and stopped crying for the first time in days. It was strange, too, because I felt the milk flowing into my breasts then, and was able to nurse her for a full year after that. That was a miracle too; I had been dry for weeks."

Lisa took a deep breath and continued. "Helaman stayed with me and began taking care of me. He always was somehow able to find food and transportation, or whatever else I needed. He was very kind. But, he was so solid in his faith that I literally fed upon his love of the Lord. He began inviting me to pray three or four times a day. We never traveled on the Sabbath, and he never passed by a fellow sufferer. He gave of everything he had, no matter who was in need or how little we had ourselves. I learned something new and wonderful from him every moment of every day. If he had been forty years younger I would have fallen hopelessly in love with him right there on the dusty streets of Oklahoma."

"I know what you mean. Helaman is a marvelous man, and a Christian of the highest caliber," Melody affirmed.

Lisa stared at her mother. "How long have you known him?"

"Honey, I've known Helaman for over twenty years. Your father has known him about the same. And, I met him in surprisingly similar circumstances."

"Who is he? I mean, why does he have such a great involvement with our family?" Lisa wanted to know. "I spent years with him, walking from Texas to Utah. And, how could he also have been here with you too?"

"I don't know, but he was." Melody asserted.

Lisa's eyes grew wide. "Well, when I see him again, I'm going to ask him!"

Melody laughed and shook her head. "No, don't ask, it won't do any good. I've asked a hundred questions he just didn't answer, and he may stop coming if we try to pin him down. Just accept him for what he is, and praise the Lord for it. Maybe he's your guardian angel!" she suggested smilingly.

"Yes, I've often thought that maybe he is!" Lisa declared.

Melody got up and motioned for Lisa to follow her into the kitchen, where they began making dinner. "What happened the rest of the time? Six years is a long time to walk," Melody asked as she and Lisa peeled potatoes for the soup.

"Well, we didn't walk the whole time, of course. We spent days, even weeks at a time in some places, waiting for my health to return, or for some opportunity to continue on. During it all he never insisted on anything. If I said I wanted to sleep for several days, I slept. If I would have said I wanted to go to the moon, he would have taken me, I think! But all I could think of was making my way back home to you and Daddy."

"We're so glad you're finally here," Melody beamed at her, leaning across the table to give her daughter's hand a squeeze.

"Where is my twin sis, Mama? Where's Bonnie?" Lisa asked suddenly.

"I..." Melody suddenly interrupted herself as a sudden understanding flooded into her heart.

"Is she OK? Where is she? Is something wrong?" Lisa asked in a rush.

Melody felt the Spirit flood over her. "No, everything is as it should be."

"Where...." Lisa asked, but was cut short by Melody's reply.

"She's with Helaman." Her answer was so powerfully true that Lisa instantly believed her. Of course—Bonnie was with Helaman!

"Where do you suppose they are?" was the only final question to be asked.

"I have no idea. But it really doesn't matter. They'll be here in time."

"In time for what?" Lisa asked, perplexed.

"In time to begin walking back to Zion," her mother answered with a note of wonder and awe in her voice.

"Walking?" Lisa asked, as if she had just heard a death sentence pronounced.

Melody patted her arm. "You'll be up to it, my dear, and filled with joy at the prospect by the time we leave."

Lisa frowned then said, "I kinda doubt it. But I have experienced so many tender miracles, I would do anything the Savior asked."

Melody decided to change the subject. "Since you left your husband in Texas, how is it you have two children?"

"That's an interesting tale."

"I'd love to hear it," Melody said, bringing out some garden carrots for the two to peel and chop.

"Well, I didn't know this, but right after I was taken away from Alvin, he immediately tried to find me. He had no idea where I was, but never gave up looking. He finally left Texas looking for me and headed north. He assumed I would try to go back to Utah if I was still alive. He searched for four years and finally found me just outside Denver, Colorado. We spent one night together, and I got pregnant," Lisa said, rolling her eyes.

"Why isn't he with you now?" Melody asked gently.

Lisa frowned and stopped peeling. Melody felt horrible for having asked, but didn't know how to retract the question.

"When we met again he had no light in his face," Lisa answered. "I knew that he had completely lost his faith. But, he was so overjoyed to see me again, and see Monica too, that my memory of my love for him overwhelmed me, and I let him sweep me off my feet. Literally."

"I see," Melody said quietly.

"The next morning he was angry with me for leaving Texas, and fumed about the four years he had spent searching for me. He insisted we go into Denver, that he could get work and food and medical care for me and Monica. I tried to ask about his faith, but he wouldn't talk about it. When I finally insisted that we talk, he said that he had lost his testimony. He said he had seen too many awful things, and that if God really was alive, he was an awful and heartless being who didn't deserve to be worshipped. He said he just preferred to not even believe there was a God. He told me I was a fool to put myself through all this hardship because of a false belief in a false religion."

Melody shook her head sorrowfully. "What did you do?"

"I bore my testimony to him as powerfully as I could, and he answered by cursing at me, at the Church, and at God. He told me if I didn't come to Denver with him, he would take Monica and go without me. I told him I would think about it, and that I would give him his answer in the morning."

Lisa's voice grew happier. "Late that night Helaman returned from—well you know how he is; he's inclined to come and go without warning."

"I know exactly what you are talking about," Melody affirmed.

"Anyway, Helaman returned quite late and I asked him to take me away from Alvin. He bundled us away that very night. We went way around Denver, and walked across a mountain range on dirt roads. Sometimes we had no roads to follow. When we descended the other side about a month later it was winter, and we were in Vernal, Utah. I had Timmy in Vernal. The odd thing is that when I arrived in Vernal I was in perfect health, and seven months pregnant."

Lisa finished peeling her last vegetable, and rose to get a glass of water. "Sweet little Monica was just two years old and full of energy and happiness," she went on. "She just thought her life of being on the road, sleeping in the open, and never knowing where our next meal would come from, was perfectly normal. Helaman was just wonderful with her, and he treated her as tenderly as any father could have. He was stern at times, but never harsh. Even though I have repeatedly told her otherwise, I know Monica thinks of Helaman as her father. She loves him dearly."

Lisa stopped to think about what she said next. "I have come to the conclusion that Helaman is more than a man, because no mortal in his sixties could have done all he did for me. Still, I can't imagine why I should be so blessed to spend six full years being guided by someone who may in fact have been an angel of God, when all around me millions of people were perishing. I just don't understand why I was so blessed."

"The best I can explain it . . ." Melody began quietly, then changed her mind. "Well, I will just say that Helaman told me he had made your father a promise about our family, and he was going to fulfill it."

"He did all this because of a promise to Dad?" Lisa asked, astonished.

"Maybe it was more than a promise; perhaps it was more along the lines of a covenant."

Lisa sighed. "I think I know what you mean. Well, one day I would sure like to know. In the meantime, Helaman left me before I could thank him properly. I wanted to give him a big hug and tell him I love him."

"I am sure he already knows that," Melody mused.

She was more right than she knew.

Samuel and his little band of refugees left Fairbanks several weeks later. It had been a time of rest and renewal for the weary travelers. Samuel could not imagine what had happened in Fairbanks to cause every man, woman and child to leave so suddenly.

He prayed mightily about where they were to go next. He was instructed that they needed to travel in an almost straight course southeast through Alaska, down through the Yukon Territory, across a corner of British Columbia, through the heart of Alberta and straight south to the Cardston Temple. In all, their remaining journey still involved over 2,000 miles through a foreign country quite possibly unwilling to let them peaceably pass through. Even peaceably, a thousand people eat a lot of food, and the task of feeding them would certainly require drawing upon the local resources. It was unlikely in such a devastated world, that any local economy could stand such a strain for long.

Samuel was still pondering these questions as they were pulling away from Fairbanks in the faithful old gray buses. When he brought his bus to a sudden stop just south of town, several buses behind him actually rammed into his back bumper. Alexei followed his eyes to where he was looking. Through the dense ice fog it was nearly impossible to see what it was.

Alexei let his gaze follow Samuel's out into the frozen world. "What are you looking at, my friend?"

Instead of answering, Samuel turned the heavy bus right and drove a half-block before turning into an Alyeska yard full of ice-covered trucks. There were literally hundreds of Chevy pickups, all of them crew cabs, all of them new, or nearly so, all of them red. There were even two large motor homes, four greyhound-type buses, and a host of trucks, tractors, cranes, generators, bulldozers and numerous other vehicles.

"I think I'm looking at our way through Canada," Samuel said.

Alexei immediately understood. "Of course! We will go through in small groups," he cried, relief in his voice. "In this way we will not threaten anyone, or bring upon us an attack from the Canada army. God truly is wise and good," he said humbly.

"God is good," Samuel agreed. "And the pipeline was very accommodating to leave us all these nice red trucks. Let's go see if we can find keys." Not only did they find keys, but they found a very large repair shop with four more greyhound-type buses inside. In the end they loaded most of the sick and elderly onto two buses. All of the other refugees were given a new truck with enough fuel to make it to Whitehorse without difficulty. The exodus began two trucks at a time every half-hour. It took most of the next week to get everyone on the road south.

Along with the buses they took two additional fuel tankers. They were empty of course, but Samuel was certain he knew how to remedy that problem. Just outside of Fairbanks was the North Pole refinery. It used to produce most of the fuel consumed in Alaska.

When they pulled up to the main outer gates of the refinery they found the lights blazing brightly. It was a good, and a bad sign—good in the sense that it absolutely meant there was fuel still being produced at the refinery, and bad because it also meant it was manned and guarded, perhaps by the US military.

It was still foggy as they approached. Samuel went first in his bright red tanker and slowly approached the guard gate. Two armed men in US Army uniforms in protective masks stepped out into the cold. By the rapid puffs of frost coming from their masks Samuel could tell they were frightened.

They waited for Samuel to climb out of his truck and approach them. He was still wearing his Alyeska parka, and his stolen ID badge. They didn't even look at it.

"Go back where you came from," one of them said after angling his rifle toward Samuel's chest.

"We need fuel…" he began to explain, but was cut off by the first guard leveling his weapon at Samuel and flicking off the safety with his thumb.

"I'm not going to say it twice," the first guard said.

"All right. I'll leave," Samuel said walking backwards toward his truck. Without this fuel they would still likely make it to Whitehorse. With it, they might have made it all the way to Cardston.

"Wait," the Spirit commanded, and Samuel obeyed. The first officer raised his weapon, his finger tightening on the trigger.

"Wait a minute," the second guard ordered, and held his radio mic to his ear. The guard did not lower his weapon.

After a moment the other guard looked disappointed. "The boss wants to know what your name is."

At that very moment the Spirit brought a memory and flash of knowledge to Samuel's mind. Years ago he had known the man who ran the North Pole refinery. He smiled broadly. "Please tell Brother Richards hello from Brother Mahoy," he said.

The message was repeated over the radio, and a voice radioed back.

The guard looked at Samuel oddy. "You can enter on foot," he said less gruffly. "Just go over to that big building with the flashing red light. Someone will meet you there."

Samuel left the big truck sitting before the gate and walked a considerable distance until he was met by another armed man. He was scanned with a type of beeping device and led through a winding maze of halls until he came to a double set of doors with a plaque overhead labeled "Control Room." Just as he was about to reach for the door it flew open and a familiar face came stomping out to meet him.

"Brother Mahoy!" his old friend cried happily, and scooped him into his big arms. "What in the world are you doing up here?"

"Brother Richards!" Samuel laughed. "It's a long story that you wouldn't believe." He regarded his friend with a smile. "Wow, you've lost some weight, my friend!"

"Well, you can't eat crude oil," Brother Richards chuckled. Then more seriously, "We live on pretty slim rations around here."

The last time Samuel had seen Brother Todd Richards was over twenty years ago. In that era Brother Richards had weighed in excess of three hundred pounds. While not close friends, they had served together on several Stake callings, and Samuel had always liked this big man whose face was always pulled up in a happy smile.

Brother Richards shut the door and motioned for Samuel to sit.

"Where has everyone in Fairbanks gone? The entire city is deserted!" Samuel blurted out.

Brother Richards looked incredulous. "Didn't you hear, Samuel? The military was installing a small nuclear power plant on the base when the power grid was sabotaged. The reactor overheated and resulted in a catastrophic core meltdown." He shook his head sadly. "The city was immediately evacuated, and everyone was ordered not to return because of the danger of radioactive fallout. It took weeks to contain."

"I'm surprised you are still here!" Samuel said.

"So am I," Brother Richards agreed wryly. "I was going to evacuate with my family, but the military refused to let me go. I finally cut a deal that I would stay if they took my family all the way to Utah."

"I'm sorry you have to be separated," Samuel empathized.

Brother Richards nodded sadly. "It's been hard, but at least I know they are safe. The military keeps our skeleton crew safe here as this facility is considered critical to national security. The fallout was largely localized and we have decent protection from the radiation. Also, as soon as air travel out of Alaska was shut down, I was stuck here with no way to leave."

"That's awful, Brother Richards. Is there anything I can do to help?"

"I'm surprised you're still working for the pipeline yourself. I thought you retired a bunch of years ago," Brother Richards said, ignoring his offer for help.

"Well, I'm not actually."

"Then, what are you doing in Fairbanks?"

"I'm on my way south. I've spent the last three years bringing a group of Russian Israelites from their country on their way to Zion. We've been here for a few weeks living in the empty houses in town with no apparent issues. Now we really just need fuel," he finished simply.

"Is that right?" Brother Richards said enthusiastically, and leaned forward in his chair.

"How many of you are there?" he queried.

"Over a thousand."

"None of you have had effects from the radiation? Wow!" he cried, then leaned back again. "Three years you've been traveling?"

"Not quite three, actually."

"Who put you up to this? I mean, how did you get involved?"

"The Lord put me up to it. A prophet of God sent me."

"Holy cow!" he intoned again. "So, this really is it, isn't it? The ten tribes are returning from the North." He looked dumbfounded but pleased. "Where are they at this moment?"

"On their way south as we speak." Samuel replied. The conversation was going faster and faster.

"Where did you get enough vehicles…."

"The Lord, and the pipeline provided."

Brother Richard's eyes grew wide. "You didn't! You took all those trucks in the vehicle pool yard, didn't you!"

"We didn't take them. The Lord gave them to us."

"I doubt if the military will see the fine line there," Richards commented ironically.

"I'm not concerned about the military."

"Why not?"

"Because they that be with use are greater than they that be with them," Samuel replied, quoting the prophet Elisha.

Brother Richards gave him an odd look. "You really believe that, don't you."

"Believe? Is it proper to call an absolute certainty a belief?" Samuel asserted.

"What are the odds you will actually make it to Jackson County, Missouri?" Brother Richards asked with sincerity.

"One hundred percent," Samuel replied quietly. The answer resonated in the office more loudly than if he had shouted it from a bull horn.

There was silence before his friend spoke again. "Do you have room for one more?"

"If that one is a faithful Latter-day Saint, we do."

"Sam, I have to confess that I've not been able to be faithful with the persecution of the Church, and all. But, in my heart I do still believe, and have a strong testimony," Brother Richards told him honestly.

"We need fuel," Samuel said again as if all the intervening conversation had not occurred.

In response, Brother Richards picked up a portable radio and keyed the mic. "Control Room to George, come in?"

"George," the radio crackled.

"Take the trucks parked outside the gate and fill them. Have them ready to leave within the hour."

"Yes sir," was the muffled response.

He turned back to Samuel. "I'm going to go grab a few things. Do you need any warm clothes? We have lots."

"Anything you can spare would be wonderful," Samuel admitted.

After the trucks were fueled, Todd's nerves were calmed by Samuel as they walked past the guards who didn't seem to mind they were leaving. As as soon as they were found to be missing, the guards grabbed as much food and fuel as they could carry, and quickly left themselves. When the pipeline authorities investigated the surprising silence from the refinery, they found the place totally uninhabited.

Brother Richards, or Todd as he preferred to be called, was driving the tanker when they rolled up to the Canadian border guard house two days later. They were startled to find several dozen red trucks parked in long rows on both sides of the road. None of the trucks had passengers in them.

"This doesn't look good," Samuel said.

"Let me handle this, Samuel," Todd requested.

"I would love you to," Samuel said after the Spirit stirred his soul.

Todd pulled up to the gate and waited for the guard to walk slowly out to the truck.

"Where you headed?" the guard asked.

"South," Todd replied.

"We are not allowing any traffic into Canada," the guard said sternly.

"We're here to pay the toll fee for all these red trucks and their passengers."

The guard looked behind him at the parked vehicles, and chuckled. "Those people are all in jail."

"I'm willing to pay five gallons of diesel for each truck you let past."

"I don't need to accept your bribe. All I need to do is shoot you, and all the fuel is mine anyway," the guard threatened, putting a hand on the butt of his pistol.

Todd smiled faintly. "I was fairly certain you'd say that, so I brought you a surprise," he said, and reached into his pocket. He carefully pulled a grenade from his pocket and held it up so the guard could see it. "You see, a truck load of fuel this size would make a crater about a mile across I'd guess."

"What the…" the guard cried and took two steps back as if hit in the chest by an invisible hand. "Wait! Hold on. What do you want?"

"I already told you. I want to pay the toll of five gallons per truck."

"Uhm, ten gallons," the guard said weakly.

"Four," Todd countered.

"All right! All right! Five. But, I'll have to call my boss, and all those people are on their way to jail…"

"Get them back." Todd ordered.

"I can't…"

When Todd pulled the pin in the grenade, Samuel began to doubt his sanity. He had never been a part of a Mexican standoff, and didn't like it at all. He thought grimly that he had come too far and shed too many tears to see these wonderful people die in a mile-wide crater. He was about to intervene when the guard suddenly stammered, "I'll have them back here in an hour."

"You better start rounding up some gas cans, too," Todd said calmly. "I want to be on the road before dark."

"Yes sir. Uhm, excuse me, I've got to make a radio transmission," he said, and hurried away.

Samuel shot a daggered look at his friend. "Put the pin back in that grenade!" he hissed.

Todd smiled cooly. "Okay, don't get so upset."

Samuel was serious. "I have a job to finish here, and I can't let you blow the thing to kingdom come the first few days you're with me!"

"Relax, it's a smoke grenade," Todd assured him. "We drop them from helicopters to mark oil leaks on the pipeline. I think this one is orange."

"It's not—you mean—you were bluffing a man with a gun and taking a thousand people as hostage!?"

"Yeah," he said, and grinned like he had just eaten the canary and gotten away with it.

"Well, you have just alerted what's left of the Canadian military to stop us," Samuel said, more serious now. "We must pray and ask for the Lord's forgiveness for relying on our own strength, and for safe passage."

After the people returned and they were a few minutes beyond the checkpoint, Samuel and Todd humbled themselves and prayed aloud together as a warmth entered the cab. Several times they heard helicopters in the distance but did not seem to come any closer.

This type of situation occurred at nearly every town or village along the Alaskan highway but they seemed to know just what to say and do in the moment. While few towns would only let them pass safely in exchange for fuel, their bountiful supply of fuel turned out to be liquid gold. They were able to purchase nearly everything they needed along the road. In fact, the word went ahead of them as much as the limited communications still allowed, and people lined the roads to offer whatever they had for sale. Samuel thought they might be met by armed men intent on simply stealing the fuel. But, Canada had years ago confiscated every gun the citizens owned. What few guns actually left were far more valuable for hunting deer or moose than for making the unwise choice of shooting at a loaded fuel truck. They made sure that one of the things the rumors included was tales of their generosity.

Their 2,500 mile trek across Canada lasted well over a month. What should have taken five days stretched into weeks as they slowly negotiated their way across Canada. This was true both in the sense of barter, and in making long detours around portions of the Alcan highway that were impassable. But the Lord was with them, and the weather was beautiful by the time they arrived into Cardston.

Nearly the whole city was waiting along the road to welcome them, rejoicing at their arrival. Somehow they knew they were coming. The Cardston Temple was without electricity when they arrived, but had been safely guarded by faithful members. Because of the need to purchase everything with fuel, the three tanker trucks ended up in the lead of their convoy. Thus, Samuel's rig was the second to pull into the large parking lot outside the temple.

This was a historic moment, one foreseen and foretold for thousands of years. He could almost hear Jesus Christ, Isaiah, Ezekial and a host of others speaking the words that would echo through the generations regarding this moment.

As vehicle after vehicle pulled into the parking lot until it was full, Samuel stood facing the Temple of the living God. He pondered the faithful sons and daughters who would now fulfill their spiritual journey, in one of the greatest exoduses ever conducted by mortals. It was not possible to calculate exactly, but his faithful few had traveled in excess of 10,000 miles in a little over three years.

Beloved friends and leaders joined him in his silent vigil: Vladimir, Alexei, Sarah, Karl, and a hundred others. Without preamble or explanation, Alexei knelt upon the brittle grass in front of the majestic temple and raised his arms over his head. The people fell to their knees, their faces streaked with tears of joy.

"Oh beloved Father!" he cried, as if his heart might burst if the great gratitude within was not given voice. "How everlastingly grateful we are for Thy almighty providence, love and gentle care over these, Thy people. Surely, Father, we shall worship Thee and take Thy name upon our lips with reverence all our lives, generation upon generation, in remembrance of Thy great providence in bringing us out of the lands of our long captivity and unto this holy edifice."

"Purify our hearts, O God, that we may enter into Thy house with humble hearts, and partake of those covenants which have long been denied us. Father, into Thy hands we commend our lives, and covenant all that we are, or ever will become, in joy and in honor of these great blessings. Hear our prayer, Holy Father, and accept our offering, we pray in the name of Thine only begotten Son, even Jesus Christ, Amen."

"Amen!" rent the air like the battle cry of a mighty army. Then a sweet stillness settled over them.

The refugees outside the temple grounds prepared to rejoice in this transplendent day of deliverance. "Look!" someone shouted, and they all turned to see a man in a white suit and tie walking quickly towards them. Samuel stepped forward, prepared to explain why these thousands of people were there. But there was no explanation needed.

"Welcome, O House of Israel!" the man said. "We have been awaiting your arrival for many years! After we secure your housing and food necessities, we will ask you to follow the following procedures." He waited for the translators to finish before he spoke again. "Each of you will have two interviews. The first will be to make sure you have been baptized and ordained. If not, these ordinances will be attended to first. The second interview will be to determine worthiness to enter the House of the Lord. We ask that those who speak English come first. They will then be instructed and set up to help and interview those who do not speak English. We estimate it will take several weeks to complete all these ordinances."

The people stood in humble rapture as his words were again translated for them. The man in white then continued.

"May I ask, which of you is Samuel?"

"I am," Samuel said with some surprise.

"I am President Arkin. I have been instructed by our Prophet to defer to your leadership regarding these people. He asked me to thank you personally for your long and faithful service."

Samuel bowed his head, cleared his throat and answered with a voice made unsteady by deep joy. "I am well blessed for my service, and if you speak to him, tell him thank you for the opportunity to serve in this capacity."

"Actually, I will speak to him this night over the Church's short wave radio. He will be most pleased that you are finally here. We have reports of many others coming after you. It seems as if the floodgates are finally open, and Israel is coming home."

"Praise the Lord," Samuel declared heartily. And as if his words had triggered a blazing fire, the entire congregation cried, "Praise the Lord!" in Russian, as if with a single voice.

President Arkin smiled and gazed around him at the sea of tear-streaked faces. He sighed happily, then turned back to Samuel. "Come, then. We have much work yet to do. I need your advice on many matters. I know of your special status, and I am most honored to work with you." President Arkin stood with his hand outstretched toward the temple waiting for Samuel to follow.

But Samuel stood still. "Give me just a moment to say goodbye, please." he said. Brother Arkin bowed his head, a puzzled look on his face, and stepped back two steps. The faithful temple president had no idea that Samuel would not see his friends again for many years. Samuel spoke in his now-unbroken Russian.

"Alexei, Vladimir, my friends, my brothers and sisters. I must leave you here."

"What!" they cried out, tears starting again in their eyes. "But why? There are still thousands of miles for us to go!"

"It is true, but now you are in the land of Zion, and in the care of the Prophet. You are no longer strangers in a strange land, or wanderers in exile. The curse is lifted, and the long dispersion of Israel is finally over. Your people will no longer be hated, hunted or persecuted. No longer shall you be killed and imprisoned by the Gentiles. No longer shall you lift up your heads under oppression, but shall from this day be protected of God. Now is the long-awaited day of your deliverance. Now, my beloved friends, you are free!"

A cheer arose from the assembled thousands, "Free! Free! Free!"

When it died down, Samuel continued. "I did not realize it until this moment in time, but this is the extent of my mission among you. I have assisted you, taught you, baptized you, ordained you, and brought you to the steps of God's holy temple. My work is done. I have another work to do. I must take my leave of you."

"No, no!" a thousand voices cried at once. "Will we see you again?"

Sam raised his arms in victory. "We will! In Zion! I will be with you when the Lord comes to His temple. We will meet again in Zion! Until that glorious day, farewell my dear friends."

The resulting chorus of "Hurrah for Israel!"and tears was unintelligible, yet heartfelt. From out in the crowd a familiar form raced toward him and ran into his arms with great energy. It was Sarah—not so little anymore, but a beautiful young woman almost fourteen, full of faith and vitality. She was Alexei's granddaughter, and for Samuel, the closest to family he had among them. She was the daughter of Islana, from whom he had learned so much of this people during his training in the Idaho wilderness school. She was also the only survivor of her immediate family. Sarah's devotion and love to Samuel were absolute and unshakeable.

"Samuel!" she cried, her voice almost shrill with fear. "You aren't going to leave me, are you?" she cried.

Samuel opened his mouth to explain when a shimmering light just behind Sarah drew his attention. He looked up to see Sarah's mother Islana standing behind her, a glowing hand upon her daughter's shoulder. Samuel smiled. Sarah sensed something and glanced over her shoulder but saw nothing.

"Dearest Sarah, my task is finished. I promise you will be safe. Your mother will watch over you after I leave, I testify of that to you."

Sarah again glanced over her shoulder. "Is that my mother I feel warming my soul?" she asked breathlessly as peace settled all around her.

Samuel brushed her long blonde hair away from her face with a tender smile. "You look very much like you mother," he whispered. "She has also joined God's true church and is anxious for you to receive your blessings in the temple one day."

Sarah looked at him with belief and adoration, although she was openly weeping. She pulled Samuel down to her and kissed both his cheeks in formal farewell.

"Goodbye," she said almost inaudibly. "Then we will meet again in Zion."

Samuel brushed the tears from his own eyes and struggled to be brave in front of this valiant soul as precious to him as his own daughter. He could not say goodbye easily, and was spared the necessity of doing so by Alexei, who was distraught.

"No! I cannot say goodbye, my brother," Alexei cried, and fell on his neck in tears.

"Then, let us say what your ancestors long ago said. It is a greeting, as well as a benediction. 'The Lord bless Thee, and keep Thee,'" Samuel said slowly, tears now streaming down his face.

Alexei replied in a whisper. "The Lord make His face to shine upon Thee, and be gracious unto Thee:"

Samuel could hardly reply. "The Lord lift up His countenance upon thee, and give thee peace."

Before he was persuaded to remain forever with his beloved people, Samuel spun on a heel and marched with President Arkin into the temple. He smiled to himself as he heard Vladimir's steely voice command someone to bring up a generator and find a way to power the temple.

"So, your mission is complete?" President Arkin asked as they walked briskly together.

"It is. I have loved it, but I am anxious to go home. I haven't seen my family for almost five years."

"You have living family?" President asked incredulously.

"My wife and all my children are living."

He stared at Samuel. "When I heard that you are—well you know—I just assumed you had lived centuries previously, I guess."

"It feels like that long ago," Samuel said, and laughed to himself.

President Arkin nodded and smiled broadly. "I can imagine. Well Brother Samuel, we will take good care of your people. We have been preparing for this very day for nearly a hundred and seventy-five years. We have food, lodging, medicine, temple clothing, and everything but electricity, it seems."

At that exact moment a generator rattled to life and a great cheer from the crowd went up..

"And, now, we obviously have electricity," the President remarked, completely amazed.

Samuel shook his hand. "Thank you, and God bless you, President. You have your work cut out for you."

"I know. We will go with God's hand upon us."

From where they stood, the front doors of the temple were now plainly visible. Two young men stood before the doors, guarding it with great solemnity. Samuel stood facing them for a full minute in contemplation before turning back to the Temple President.

"A word of caution," Samuel told him in parting.

"Please," President said.

"Not all who came with us are worthy to enter the temple. You must not let them enter until they are ready. You will need to hold some church courts and rebaptize some. Not many, but some—more than I had wanted. However, I am confident that before this people leave your area, all who I brought will be in the group of faithful who continue on to Zion."

"I pray to God it is so. Thank you for the warning."

Samuel sighed. "I suddenly feel very tired in spirit. I shall take my leave now. Fare thee well, President."

"And you," President Arkin replied quietly.

Samuel nodded, shook his hand again, then turned and faded quickly as he walked away.

20

NOW AND FOREVER

Samuel wearily arrived upon the mountain top to find Helaman waiting for him. A young woman and a young man Samuel did not know were standing beside him. A gentle spring breeze was blowing, and the song of a faraway bird was in the air. It was one of Samuel's favorite places on earth, and not accessible by any means other than helicopter or the power of God. As far as Samuel knew, no mortal had ever set foot here.

The fact that other heavenly servants were here was unusual, but not unexpected. Helaman seemed to always know where Samuel was and what he needed. At the end of this long and difficult assignment it was a pleasure to be with his dear friend once again. It brought him peace, and placed an appropriate conclusion to this chapter of his life.

Samuel greeted Helaman silently with a warm embrace. They turned to look out across the emerald-green sea as it rolled steadily toward the long stretch of white sands far below. The scent of exotic flowers greeted his senses like expensive perfume. He had been here only three times prior to this. Once was with his wife, and sudden memories of Melody arose sweetly in his mind.

"Well done, my brother," Helaman said at last.

Samuel sighed deeply and turned toward his Nephite friend. "Thank you, Helaman. And, more than I can express, thank you for your long service on behalf of my family."

Helaman smiled broadly. "It has been a joy," he replied happily. Indeed, it had been exactly that for him. Having dealt with several generations of disbelieving and stiff-necked heathens, it had been a pleasure to work with people whose hearts were tender and teachable, and who wanted with all their soul to be worthy and obedient. In fact, it had been more of a vacation than an assignment.

Helaman turned to the woman beside him. She was as tall as Helaman with dark brown hair to her waist, exquisite brown eyes and luminous skin. Her face was aglow with goodness. She radiated light and had every appearance of being an angel. She possessed that timeless beauty that spoke of youth and great age; the appearance of one yet to be born. She was dressed in a radiantly white gown that reminded Samuel of a temple gown, with the exception that a lei of exotic flowers was draped over her shoulders. She smiled at him with perfect teeth and rich ruby lips, and eyes that twinkled in ways that suggested deep inner peace, and a healthy sprinkling of mischievousness.

"Samuel, I would like you to meet someone who loves you very much. Her name is too complex for a mortal to pronounce. In your language her name would be Star."

"Forgive me that I don't remember you," Samuel said almost shyly, and held out a hand. She did not offer hers, but bowed from the waist. He knew she would not shake his hand. However, Samuel had learned that it was still polite to offer. Had she extended her hand and he felt nothing when they touched, he would have raised his arm to the square and commanded her to depart. Her response was exactly appropriate and indicated her worthiness and the appropriateness of her appearing.

Star had been smiling broadly and recomposed her features into seriousness. "I have long awaited this moment, and have asked this special blessing from Father that I may come and speak to you before my mission begins," she said, her face radiant with joy.

"In what way may I be of service to you, Star?" Samuel asked, his heart fluttering in his chest with anticipation and wonder. He had never known a creature of such exquisite elegance before, and yet he felt a bond and connection with her that confused and delighted him.

She laughed, a sound which came more to his heart than his ears. "You already have blessed me much more than you know. I was granted this great blessing only because of your standing before the Lord, and because my stay on earth would be..." she paused here and smiled. "... brief," she concluded, as if searching for words.

"Who is this young man with you?" Samuel asked her, sensing she had said all she would on the former subject.

"This is my dear brother. He and I go everywhere together," she responded as she turned to smile at her companion. The handsome young man bowed slowly, but said nothing. Samuel felt a great outpouring of love for the young man, and from him back to Samuel.

"We must go." Star said quietly, and immediately began to grow transparent.

"Wait, please," Samuel said softly. They remained with him, neither coming nor going. "I don't remember you, but I feel with all my heart that I want to tell you, both of you, that I love you."

"We love you too, Samuel. When you meet our mother, please tell her I love her and am so grateful for her giving me life. Now and forever..." she said, the last of her words coming into his mind after his eyes could no longer behold her. He wondered what circumstances might bring him to recognize who this precious spirit's mother was. It was a mystery in his heart, but a sweet one.

Samuel turned back to Helaman and taking a deep breath, turned toward the ocean. Helaman never took his eyes off of Samuel. "Who are they?" Samuel asked.

"They said all they could," he replied.

Samuel nodded, familiar with the sometimes cryptic nature of divine things. He knew no more would be said, so he changed the subject. "Is my family well?" Samuel asked. "I'm anxious to return to them if there is time now."

"They are well, and gathered. Your youngest daughter Bonnie is still on her way to join you. I will continue with her until she returns, and until you are ready."

"Ready for what?" Samuel asked.

Helaman smiled mischievously. "Your next assignment, of course."

Samuel squared his shoulders and nodded. "Can you tell me what it is, or do I have to wonder for a while?"

"I can tell you now," Helaman grinned. "Your next assignment will be to accompany your family, and many others, to Zion."

Samuel was elated. "You mean, I get to stay with my family! This makes me so happy! I have missed them very much!" he said with a happy sigh. Then he glanced at Helaman with a smile. "This sounds much easier than my previous assignment."

"In many ways it will be much more difficult."

"Why is that?"

"Because, the more you love those you serve, the harder it is to see them suffer and die," Helaman replied, his voice heavy with emotion, with deep personal understanding of the truth he had just spoken.

"I'm beginning to understand why some ask the Lord to take them speedily into his kingdom when they grow old," Samuel replied, with no hint of regret in his voice.

Helaman nodded. "I know what you mean; I have thought the very same thing. Yet, all you need do is ask to be taken home, and your assignment as a special servant will end immediately."

"I know, my friend," Samuel replied solemnly. "I'm nowhere near ready for that. You have been at this for over two thousand years. Do you ever wish to have another assignment?"

"Never!" he replied forcefully. "I love what I do, and feel the importance of my assignment. I wouldn't want to do anything else. I sense this is also the case with you, my young friend."

"Nobody's called me young for a long while," Samuel replied with a laugh.

"In the work we are both engaged in, you are but a babe—albeit a powerful one."

"I am sure I'm but a child in the eternal scheme of things." Helaman mused, as he thought about the incredible mission he had just completed. "It really is glorious, isn't it, my friend, serving the Lord like this?"

"Beyond anything man can comprehend," Helaman replied, his voice resonant with supernal happiness.

Helaman stepped back slightly. "I need to go now to complete a few things before I bring Bonnie to you. You need to get home to your wife. She needs you."

"Is everything all right?" Samuel asked, suddenly concerned.

Helaman shook his head slightly. "Everything will be fine as soon as you get there."

"Farewell my friend," Samuel said, and immediately departed.

"God bless you," he heard Helaman's voice reverberating back.

Samuel was in the nowhere between everywhere that traveling by the power of God is, when a sweet instruction came to him. Without hesitation he returned to the early morning hours just outside the Cardston Alberta temple. He arrived just out of sight, not three paces from Alexei's tent. He lifted the flap and said a single word, "Sarah."

Sarah was kneeling on the ground beside her bed roll, talking with Alexei. She was fully dressed, making spiritual preparations to begin her day's labors. She turned her head so quickly that her hair flew out in a halo of golden tresses. "Samuel!" she cried with a sound that was both an exclamation of astonishment, and a cry of joy.

Samuel looked at her grandfather's startled face and said the only thing he needed to, "I will take good care of her. May I?"

Alexei nodded silently, fully aware that Samuel would be taking his granddaughter with him, and lovingly embraced her. Then Samuel took Sarah's hand, and they both were gone. Alexei sat there for several moments before he opened the tent flap and followed their footprints in the grass to where they ended without a trace just beyond the trees.

It was early morning when Samuel and Sarah arrived just outside the Mahoy home in South Jordan, Utah. There were street lights glowing in the early dawn, and several lights on inside the home. He could see shadows moving around inside. He stepped up to the door and heard a cry of anguish.

"Helaman! Where is Helaman?" a feminine voice cried out.

Samuel yanked open the screen and grabbed the doorknob. It was locked, but as usual opened without resistance to his twist. He quickly escorted Sarah into the house, and asked her to stay downstairs; then he charged up the stairs, turned right and ran into the master bedroom. He found his wife propped up in bed, her knees elevated. Two women he did not recognize were huddled near the foot of her bed, also on their knees.

"Melody, sweetheart, I'm home," he announced urgently, and sank down beside her.

"Oh, oh, Samuel!" she cried, grabbing both of his hands. "Samuel, I was so afraid. I need a priesthood blessing. The baby is coming, and I'm not able to deliver it. My body won't let this baby deliver, Samuel! I think it's stuck! I need help, or the baby will die. Please, Samuel! Beg the Lord to spare my baby, and take me instead. Please…" she begged on the edge of hysteria.

From her pale and exhausted face he could tell she was beyond endurance, and near collapse. A profound peace flooded through him—sweet, pure peace—and he knew what he should do. He sat on the edge of the bed. His wife rested her head in his lap and cried weakly. He laid both hands on her sweat-soaked head and blessed her.

"Beloved and precious wife, in the name of Jesus Christ I rebuke your fear, your weariness, and your physical limitations. I command your body to function correctly, and to bring forth this child. I promise you in the name of Jesus Christ that you will be delivered of a healthy child this night, and you will raise him to maturity in righteousness. This I do in the name of Jesus Christ, Amen."

Melody's trembling stopped, and she pushed herself up with determination.

"I'm ready," she said to the two women. "Bring towels. The baby will be here shortly," she said. The two women scurried to comply.

"Thank you my love," she said to her husband, turning her now-confident face toward him. "I feel better now. I can feel the baby moving. Thank you—and thank you, Father!" she said, looking heavenward. Then she turned her face away as she moaned with the onset of renewed labor.

"The baby's coming," one of the midwives said. "Wait for the next contraction and push!"

About ten minutes later the baby came into the world with a tiny cry.

"It's a girl!" the midwife cried. Then there was silence as they worked with the little one to open her throat and dry her off.

"Oh, she is glorious!" Melody marveled breathlessly. She turned weakly to her husband, who still held her hand. "Hey, you said I'd have a son," she chided him with a small smile. "But I always wanted a daughter, and she is perfect," she said breathlessly, and lay back against her sodden pillows.

The attending sister appeared anxiously at Melody's bedside. "Melody, there's something wrong with the baby. She's not breathing right. I'm afraid she was too slow in delivering. I'm afraid we're going to lose her. Here…" she said, and brought the little bundle to lay in Melody's arms.

"Oh no!" Melody cried, her face distorted with disbelief and sorrow. "No. No. No!" she repeated over and over. But the child in her arms appeared lifeless. "I tried, my baby girl, I tried to give you life. Please stay with me!" she begged the little soul in her arms. Then she turned to her husband. "Oh, Sam, I know you have power with the Lord. Ask Him for me to spare our precious daughter," she cried, her face streaming with tears. "Bless my baby," she begged, then looked up. "Oh, please, dearest Father, take me instead of this sweet baby, I beg Thee…" she cried in deep anguish.

Samuel, his face coursed with tears, gently opened the bundle to gaze upon the little face ringed with a halo of dark hair. Two little lids flickered open to reveal her clear eyes, and startling intelligence in that tiny face. She gazed deeply at her mother, and then at her father before closing her eyes. Samual placed his hand on her tiny head and prayed.

"Heavenly Father, in the name of Jesus Christ and by the authority of His holy priesthood, I give this child of Thine, and ours, a name and a blessing. The name I give her is Melody Star Mahoy. The blessing I give you, Star, is the knowledge of our love, and the promise that err long, your mother will hold you in her arms, feed you from her breasts, and raise you in a time of glorious peace. Until then, I commend you to Heavenly Father's care and to His love. In the name of Jesus Christ, Amen."

Melody Star took a shallow breath and seemed to relax. She quietly departed mortality.

"Oh, no, no! Oh Samuel! Oh my precious daughter! Don't die, don't die!" Melody mourned. She wept uncontrollably for many minutes before she spoke again. "I don't understand, Sam! I wanted her so badly, and I loved her ever since I felt her inside me. She was the child of my old age, the child of our love, and the witness I had that Heavenly Father loves me and heard my prayers. I have yearned to bear your child, Samuel, to have this binding seal upon our love and our eternal marriage."

Melody's voice gave way to more sobbings, then she spoke again. "Sam, I don't understand why you said she would be a *son!*" She paused as her face contorted with pain while silent tears fell on the still bundle in her arms.

Her face twisted again. "Oh, oh, another contraction!" she said, her attention diverted to her own physical pain. "Why do I have more pain?" she asked the midwives.

"Sometimes there are a few contractions to expel the placenta," one of them replied. "It's nothing to worry about."

"It was stronger than that," Melody asserted. "I think … oh! Here comes another contraction. This one is strong!" She reached down and palpated her stomach. "My tummy is really firm. I think I'm carrying another baby!" she cried incredulously.

"But there was only one heartbeat," the midwife protested, and lifted a stethoscope onto her abdomen. She listened for a second, moved the instrument to a new location, then pulled them down in wonder. "There's still a strong heartbeat!" she cried in wonder. "You do have twins!"

At that moment a strong contraction bore down, and the ladies scurried to find more towels. In about ten minutes another child entered mortality. "It's a boy!" they cried in unison. "A healthy, strong little boy," they laughed and cried, barely able to contain their happiness sufficiently to perform their office. They bundled the little one up without even wiping him thoroughly, and happily, joyfully, laid him in Melody's arms. They silently took Star's little tabernacle away.

Melody had never felt such exquisite pain, and now such exquisite joy. "God has heard my prayers, and blessed me with the child He promised. Oh, Samuel, oh, my love, we are so blessed!" she cried happily, and laid her head upon her husband's chest in exhaustion and joy. She opened the little blanket so she could gaze upon her son's tiny face; but her thoughts were still with her daughter.

"Why did you name her Melody Star?" she finally asked.

"That was her name," Samuel replied simply.

"When I heard you say it, I knew it was her name; but how did you know?"

"I'll tell you about it later. Just know, darling, that your daughter Star fully understood she would only be in mortality for a few moments, and she accepted that. I also feel impressed to tell you how perfectly she loves you."

"I sensed that while I held her. I wish I could tell her how much I love her," she said wistfully, a note of both joy and sadness in her voice.

"You just did, my love," he replied. He looked to the opposite side of the bed and watched Star smile; with a radiant smile she leaned forward and kissed her mother on the forehead. Then she slowly vanished without straightening from the kiss. In his mind he heard her musical voice say, "Now and forever..."

Melody and Samuel named their son Helaman James Mahoy. With the birth of little Helaman a new sweetness fell upon their home. Melody was radiant with love, and seemed at times to have difficulty deciding which of her boys she should be gazing upon with absolute adoration. Sammy, now eighteen years old, held his little brother hour upon hour.

Samuel pondered the great bond between his sons, and remembered the fierceness of his own love for his little brother Jimmy, just prior to Jimmy's death. The thought was not unsettling to him, for he knew that love was the nectar of life, a sweet fruit he had been blessed to savor many times.

It felt so good to be home.

21

APPROACHING ZION

It would be a dramatic understatement to say that Melody welcomed Sarah into their home. From the first moment they met, the day that baby Helaman was born, a bond of love formed between them that astounded everyone except Sarah and Melody. In a very healthy way, Sarah became her lost baby girl, and Melody became Sarah's lost mother. They wrapped their love around one another so completely that to see them interact was to be charmed to the core. Melody was no longer young to be the mother of an infant, and Sarah lavished upon her new mother such attention and assistance as few mothers ever experience.

Though Sarah knew little English, and Melody absolutely no Russian, they communicated by the power of love. It wasn't long before Melody's sweet new teenage daughter was mimicking oft-repeated phrases in tortured English and bombarding both Samuel and Melody with myriads of questions. Even something as simple as a flushing toilet had to be explained in detail, and pronounced slowly in English. It was a fun and fascinating time for them all.

For Sarah this was the childhood she had missed, and she followed Melody around like a two-year-old. However, she was anything but childish in her interaction with her new mother. Raised to work, and expected to do so without complaint, she served with quiet zeal, and when not helping take care of baby Helaman, often invented jobs to keep her busy hands occupied. Melody urged her to slow down, a thing she seemed incapable of doing. Yet, for Sarah, these simple chores were a delight, and far easier than anything she had known as a child.

Best of all, Sarah had Melody's complete love. For many weeks Melody was the sun, and Sarah's tiny planet revolved around her in tight circles. As the weeks grew to months and beyond, Sarah's universe expanded to include everyone she found within it. Equally as wonderful was the fact that all who came to know Sarah, loved her.

Samuel and his family spent all that summer growing and preserving food, along with making clothing and gathering other necessities. Some things were impossible to find, among these shoes, medical supplies, and anything mechanical or electronic. Still, these things hardly seemed important in the face of the quest they were contemplating. Spirits were high, almost jubilant, as preparations were made in a world fast crumbling all around them.

Almost all the inhabitants of Zion saw these times as a period of happy privation. It felt to them as if they had returned to pioneer days, and they struggled to adapt their minds and hands to scrubbing clothes by hand while using their washing machine as the tub of water for doing so. The Zion dwellers learned the art of cooking by fire, sun oven or cook stove, and many began to produce excellent dishes, as the meager ingredients would allow.

Sarah was by this time a scant fifteen-years-old, yet she seemed far older. Had anyone been able to look beyond the immediacy of their own lives, they would have seen the Lord's wisdom in placing Sarah among them. This little girl with broken English and busy hands knew things vital to their survival. Having lived all her life in relatively primitive circumstances, she accepted as the normal what the "saints" saw as hardships.

Sarah quietly demonstrated her skills by simply doing them: baking bread outdoors without an oven, washing a whole family's clothes in just a few gallons of water, cooking, cleaning and bathing with an economy of effort and supplies. She also knew how to sleep warm, which was something most had yet to figure out, and how to make her own thread, needles, soap, yeast for raising bread, treat a wound without medicine, and a seemingly inexhaustible list of other skills desperately needed by her new family. As much as they gave her, she gave more in return.

Without even knowing it, Sarah became the epicenter of a tidal wave of change. What she taught her willing and attentive mother was quickly spread throughout the community. Aided by the Holy Spirit, some essential truths took little time to become common knowledge.

It was tempting to think that because a relative peace had settled upon God's mountain home, that the world had also found peace. Nothing could have been further from reality.

While Samuel had been on his four-year mission to bring lost children of Israel from the north, much had happened in the world, and most of which he had not been aware. The combined armies of South America had invaded the United States and claimed much of California, Arizona, New Mexico, Texas and all of Cuba. They had sent armies as far north as Nevada, Utah and Colorado.

The initial South American zeal to retake what they viewed as the lands of their fathers from the hands of the "white devils," was satiated with their collective capture of countless property. That portion of the army which had invaded Utah was unique in that nearly every member of its forces was a member of the Church. They had quietly banded together and when the opportunity arose, they marched into Utah with the single-minded purpose of ridding their spiritual homeland of those who had banned, outlawed, and persecuted those they revered as their spiritual brothers and sisters.

The South American soldiers in Utah were successful beyond their own hopes. Once having accomplished their self-assigned task, the soldiers took up station outside of Salt Lake City and stood sentinel against armed incursion by any others. In time, food, missionaries, and love called them in from their self-imposed sentry duty, and they became one with the Saints. Even so, they stubbornly remained separate, an autonomous and unique people, retaining their weapons of war and standing ready to use them. When the spirit of preparation settled upon God's people, it landed squarely upon them as well. They positioned themselves to march before the caravans of faithful to clear the way and ensure their safety. It was a noble and needed thing, but unbeknownst to them, one which they could not possibly accomplish with the arm of flesh.

It is probable that the South American armies would have continued northward in their conquest had not the Chinese and Russians landed on both the East and West coasts of America. The only metropolitan area that escaped extermination was New York. With the fall of the American constitutional government, the Western U.N. claimed all of the state of New York as sovereign territory of the Western United Nations. For reasons unclear, the Chinese and Russians bypassed that entire region.

After sweeping the Eastern seaboard clean of most of its population, the combined Chinese armies bypassed most of the abandoned cities of middle America and targeted their fury on the Salt Lake valley with chemicals of death. Having then exhausted their chemical resources, they joined with their forces from California and attacked Arizona's teeming cities, a land now physically and emotionally claimed by the South American invaders. The two forces clashed in the vast deserts of Arizona, and having underestimated their enemy, were caught in a South American surprise attack. This brought an unexpected end to the majority of the Chinese threat on the American continent. Even so, it exhausted both the means and the will of the South Americans to wage war any more. They settled into the impossible task of retaining and living upon the vast regions they had conquered.

Before they could even restore electrical power to their cities, Texas organized themselves into a separate nation, elected a Confederate-style government and attacked their South American squatters, reclaiming all of Texas and large amounts of New Mexico. Demoralized by this unexpected defeat, the South Americans retreated from Texas and after a year of continued bloody conflict, finally signed a treaty with them. Texas boldly annexed Oklahoma, Arkansas, Louisiana, Mississippi, Alabama, Georgia, South Carolina, Florida, and eventually Cuba.

Without opposition or even comment from what little remained of Washington D.C., the new Confederate Nation of Texas began the arduous task of rebuilding. Their first official act was to cut all ties with the Western United Nations.

With the United States in chaos and the Western U.N. weakened, a new face appeared on the European horizon, challenging the domination of the world through his high position as Secretary-General of the Western United Nations. Quiet and charmingly calculating, Secretary-General Aleksander Sarkus suddenly rose to supreme power within a matter of weeks. In a bold move, he and his inner circle secretly launched a covert nuclear terrorist attack on the Western U.N. building in New York City, decimating the area and killing the remaining world leaders who were gathered there for a Western world summit.

At this point forward, any possible threat to Secretary-General Sarkus's domination was eliminated. Now unopposed, he swiftly took control of the Western U.N. and moved its headquarters to Switzerland, renaming the organization the "United World Order" and giving himself the title "Supreme Commander." Using his new position and seductive powers of persuasion, he began meeting with western world leaders to amass an army capable of controlling the remaining splintered nations. He also instigated a cashless world monetary system, which the nations gratefully accepted because their own economies were falling in rapid succession.

After the bombing in New York, the federal government of the former United States ceased to exist in any official capacity. Food was not regularly delivered to the cities, and hungry bands soon began foraging for food. Communities and churches banded together and actually built walls around subdivisions and small communities. Once they felt secure, they themselves roamed out and preyed on smaller communities or farms for tribute of food or young men. Large groups of families gathered into feudal tribes, as local populations began to recover to a small degree.

Only among the Saints in the Mountains of the Lord did the Constitution of the United States, in its pure form continue as supreme law. With happy acquiescence from the remaining citizens of the former United States, the inhabitants of Utah, Idaho, parts of Nevada and surrounding areas elected a new President, Congress and Supreme Court. Their first legislative act was to repeal the many amendments to the constitution. Elections were scheduled again in three years with an eye to the fact that they did not fully represent the population of the land governed, and that changes would occur as greater areas fell under the protection of their peace. Until then, they rejoiced in liberties and freedom unknown since the late 1700's.

Shortly after the reestablishment of the U.S. Constitutional government among the Saints, the now-strengthened Church again called missionaries into the states now occupied by South America, as well as into the new Confederate Nation of Texas. Their commission was to preach unto the house of Israel. The times of the Gentiles were past, the Church proclaimed. They went forth with faith, like unto Ammon and his brethren, into a hostile land, among a bloodthirsty people. The inspiring reports that filtered back from these intrepid missionaries was that the people of Israel were flocking to the waters of baptism. But, the glorious news was not without its cost. Dozens of faithful missionaries died at the hands of evil men, giving their lives in the cause of the Master. They were speedily replaced.

The nations of Europe thus far had fared slightly better than the United States. Though their land was devastated by war, their compact population and smaller land mass made it possible for most local governments to survive somewhat intact, in large part due to governmental and monetary assistance by Supreme Commander Sarkus and the newly-formed United World Order. Unexpectedly, the one thing that did largely survive all this destruction was television—if one had electricity to view it. Every day news agencies both official and renegade, broadcast disturbing news of the world condition.

It was then the unthinkable happened. As China's domination of their occupied countries solidified, their thirst for domination became unquenchable. Under the guise of assisting their Russian allies at the European eastern front, the Chinese marched a massive army north through Ukraine to bolster Eastern Coalition forces. As the army entered Belarus they suddenly swung eastward and unleashed their full might upon Moscow. The Russians were caught completely by surprise, and within two days Moscow was brutally overthrown. Knowing that Russia was now burning with rage at this Chinese treachery, Supreme Commander Sarkus offered military aid and the former Soviet Bloc in exchange for the Russian juggernaut's unconditional alliance.

In the wake of the horrific devastation of worldwide war, a full one-third of the population of the world had died. In the ensuing war another one-third had died either of wounds of war, or of the indirect results of war upon the weakened populations. The land was poisoned by the mindless use of nuclear weapons, chemical and biological warfare, whose poisons were ultimately washed to the sea where they killed vast regions of life beneath the waves. Some estimates placed the death toll in the seas as high as a full two-thirds of all life therein. The very ability of humans to inhabit the planet was at once called into question. To the western world, including many in the U.S., their only hope glimmered in the United World Order, and the promise of help from Commander Sarkus.

It was during this world-wide turmoil that Samuel and his family, and thousands of other faithful Saints turned their heads and hearts toward the east. They had been warned by the Prophet that Commander Sarkus was the prophesied Anti-Christ, and the true followers of Christ were determined to follow Him and none else, no matter the consequences. Amid the world chaos, they began to sing and rejoice as they quickly made preparations for the journey to Zion.

Having brought a small group of refugees through a much longer trek, Samuel could not envision the journey from the valleys of the mountains to Missouri with any great anxiety. This group of Zion people was prepared both physically and spiritually for the journey. They were led by men of God and accompanied by angels and translated beings. Beside himself, Samuel was aware of thousands of sisters and brothers now among the Saints who were likewise translated and endowed with this special calling and power.

Samuel knew that the journey east would be protected and sanctified by God, but also hallowed by the blood of many he loved. It had ever been thus, and would be once again, that the price some would pay to redeem Zion would be their own precious blood. Just as Christ Himself had paid with His blood to purchase redemption, so there was a cost for this redemption. Helaman had taught him that this was a pattern that could not be defied.

The first company left in the early spring of the following year. Their caravan consisted largely of horse or hand-drawn wagons and carts. Even a few ancient handcarts from former days had been pressed into service, more as a matter of emotion than necessity.

Since there were few automobiles upon the nation's formerly grand highway system, Samuel and his group left walking down the middle of Interstate 80 East. As if a silent trumpet had been sounded high above the desert valley, hundreds of groups just like his started that very day for Zion. Their horses hooves clopped steadily on the hard asphalt as they slowly made their way east. Most wagons they pulled were the frames of small cars stripped of their engines to make them lighter. They rolled easily, and proved adequate protection from wind and rain at night.

By far the most popular wagon was the ubiquitous mini vans, now stripped. With everything but one or two seats removed, they held the belongings for several families, and rolled easily on the hard surfaced roads. It became common practice to unhitch the horses at the tops of long hills, and after loading as many people inside as could fit, allow the vehicles to roll to a stop as far as they would go. Besides being a welcome change of pace, it gave the horses a needed rest, and added hundreds of free miles to their trek.

Familiar cities passed slowly: Fort Bridger, Green River, Rock Springs. Each day they felt the Spirit of the Lord strengthen and push them onward. Every day difficulty darkened their journey, but not their hearts.

After two tragic mishaps with vehicle brakes failing while coasting down a mountain pass, it became the practice to chain three vehicles together before allowing them to coast. That way, any brake failure could be overcome by the other two. This backfired one day when the center vehicle blew out a tire, lost control, and caused the other two to crash into the side of the mountain. The three cars rolled side-over-side down the long mountainside, strewing baggage, food and bodies as they rolled. However, for reasons of providence not understood by any present, all survived without injury. Only the vehicles themselves were left by the way. Toddlers who had been thrown from the tumbling vans simply stood up and cried for their mothers. Teens were pulled from the twisted wreckage still laughing from the experience. Old people were dragged from the wreckage, alive and unharmed. It was impossible to understand why they had been miraculously spared, but it was a joyful relief nonetheless. There were special prayers of thanksgiving that night at camp.

The practice changed again, and single vehicles made the dizzying spin down the steep grades alone. However, they were thoroughly checked by someone who understood mechanics and piloted by an adult driver before being allowed to go. Vehicles of questionable quality were chained to a fallen tree at the top of the hill. Once this practice became common they were unharmed—until they approached Cheyenne, Wyoming.

Cheyenne had declared itself an independent city-state, organized a militia and closed its borders to the world. With enough citizens to provide for their needs, and sufficient arms to enforce their will, they possessed an arrogance and determination on a par with an invading army.

Their terrible demands to pass were simple: one-half of any traveler's food and clothing, one-half of their young men, and all male children under three years old would be required as tribute to ensure safe passage. Any attempt to turn back, bypass Cheyenne, or to fight would be met with deadly force.

The leaders of the caravan to Zion called a council around a large bonfire to consider their options. In their midst were two of the Quorum of the Twelve, including the President of that quorum who now addressed them.

Samuel stood near the fire; though he had no leadership voice for the company, he did speak for his family. He waited with some anticipation to hear what would be decided. Many options were discussed, including fighting. They had with them one hundred armed soldiers, with more coming in groups behind them due to arrive each day for weeks. In time, they would be strong enough to force their way through.

Others were in favor of negotiating a lower settlement, reasoning that some price would be required no matter the solution. Others favored leaving during the night and heading north to Torrington before heading east again, thereby going around Cheyenne. There were even a few who favored slinking back to Salt Lake City and abandoning the journey until a compromise could be negotiated with their enemies.

President Johnson, senior apostle and President of the Quorum of the Twelve, listened with polite interest to all comments. Somewhere in his early seventies, he was spry and energetic. He was of medium build and somewhat tall, bald except for what he called his "putting green" around the sides of his head. He wore a short beard of gray, which was unusual among the Brethren. His appearance was at once noble, yet open and friendly. The saints loved Elder Johnson without exception. Even more importantly, they honored his priesthood keys, and trusted his ability to speak on behalf of the Lord.

After hours of dissertation and some debate had passed, he stood and thanked everyone for their comments.

"Brothers and Sisters," he said with deep affection in his voice, his face luminous, "I understand your concerns, and share them. However, as I have listened to your excellent ideas, I have been struck quite forcefully that none of them are what the Lord wishes us to do. Here is what I propose. We will divide our food so that each brother who holds the Melchizedek priesthood has three day's supply. They will then go among the people of Cheyenne and preach the Gospel of peace."

A few whisperings and coughs punctuated the air. The President went on. "I believe it was Nephi who observed that the word of God was more powerful in subduing their enemies than the sword. The brethren will preach, bless, prophesy, and share their food with whomsoever they meet. In one week's time they will return. I promise you in the name of the Lord that if they are fearless and faithful to this charge, we will pass through this city at that time without loss of life, and without tribute except as we choose to render.

Samuel's family looked at one another with hope. President continued, "Remember, these people we call our enemies are the Lord's children. They are frightened and hungry, and probably see us as a grave threat. Let us answer those fears with kindness and show them Christ-like love, and they will let us pass."

The sounds of consent and accord arose from all assembled. Samuel felt his heart burn with conviction of the inspired wisdom of this course of action.

"All in favor please signify," President Johnson called out. Every hand arose.

"All brethren who wish to answer this call please remain by the fire to be set apart. All others please attend to your families. We will call evening prayers by the bugle as usual. Go now, and God bless you for your faithfulness."

Samuel joined his sons Sam, Theo and George, and a host of others. One by one they were set apart by Apostle Johnson. When he laid his hands upon Samuel's head, he jerked them back off as if they had been burned. He stepped aside to see Samuel's face and looked down at him.

"I see you have already been given an unusual and glorious mission to perform," he said so quietly that none but he and Samuel understood.

Samuel actually blushed. "I would like to answer the Lord's call through His Apostle," he replied.

President Johnson nodded. "I feel impressed that there is something more you must do in Cheyenne."

"I feel it too," Samuel said.

"Then, let's get you set apart," the President said, and pronounced a brief, but powerful blessing upon him.

When it came time to set apart Sammy, Samuel ordained him an Elder, and President Johnson set him apart as a full-time missionary. It was heartwarming to young Sam that his entire family could be there to witness his ordination.

By the first light of day Samuel, Sam Jr. and others of the Saints were slowly approaching the ramshackle barricade of upturned cars and busses that blocked the road.

"What do you want?!" a woman's voice called shrilly from the barricade. Previously, it had been a man who had made their demands. "Have you come to surrender?"

It was Samuel's voice they heard in answer. "We have come to share our food and to pray with you. Or, if you do not wish to pray, we wish at least to share our food." Samuel pulled a small red apple from his backpack, and held it up for them to see.

There was a long moment of silence before a woman with bright red hair stood up on the side of an old school bus. "Throw me the apple," she demanded. Samuel walked the short distance to the bus and carefully tossed it up to her. She caught the apple in a swift movement and carried it to her mouth.

"What else you got in that bag?" she asked, her mouth full of apple.

"I have some other food, and my scriptures."

"Throw me the whole bag," she ordered.

"I cannot," he replied. "I wish to save some for the others. But if you wish, I can give you a potato."

"I'll take it," she responded hastily. Samuel sorted out a potato not much bigger than the apple and tossed it to her. This she tucked into her pocket. "For my kids," she explained a little forlornly.

"How many kids?" he asked.

"Three," she replied cautiously.

Samuel tossed her two more potatoes which also went into her pocket. Others of his group stepped forward following his example. There appeared to be about a dozen lightly-armed people. Only one of them was male, and he appeared to be in his early teens.

"Thanks," the woman said. She looked at him suspiciously and asked, "Why are you feeding us? We expected you to attack, or to go around."

"We have no desire to attack, and no time to go around. We are the people of God, and feel no malice toward you. We hope to be able to share our faith with you," Samuel replied in complete candor.

"We're not interested in your faith. We know you're Mormons. Mormonism is outlawed in Cheyenne," she replied in an accusatory voice.

Samuel smiled and held out his arms in surrender. "Then, we will baptize you all, so you will have no choice but to decriminalize your own faith," he replied loudly. She could not know that his words were in deep earnest, and profoundly true.

"Haha! A bold plan," she said with a laugh and smirk on her face. She took another bite of her apple. "This apple is the first fruit I've eaten in months."

"What do you usually eat?"

She didn't answer, but gazed at him with wary eyes. "Grass," she finally replied quietly.

"You survive by eating grass? I wasn't aware the human body could survive on grass," he said, somewhat amazed.

"It can't for any length of time," was her reply. "But, it fills the belly, and does have some food value, especially when it goes to seed. It's harder to chew, but makes into a green tea. It isn't so bad once you get used to it." She bit into the apple again and spoke through her chewing. "The city does have a few farms running, but there isn't enough seed to get them producing soon enough, so we eat grass and a little bit of wild game—but not very much."

"I'm sorry for your trials," Samuel responded softly. "We have been a little more blessed in that we had our food storage to fall back on for a couple years."

She stared at him hard. "Yeah, I had heard that the Mormons have a bunch of food. It doesn't seem fair."

"We prefer to be called Latter-day Saints."

"Whatever," she replied curtly. Then her voice softened. "I used to know some Mormons. They were fine people, actually."

"Why do you say 'were'?" Samuel asked.

"They disappeared after the Mormons were outlawed."

"Fortunately, those times are past," Samuel said happily.

"They aren't past here!" she insisted. "The remaining Mormons are being rounded up to be executed, if the rumors are correct. You people should have stayed in Utah. I heard you have your own peaceful government, and even have electricity and running water again. Believe me, if I had a peaceful home with food and water, I'd stay put."

"I see your point," Samuel said. "However, we are going back to Missouri to build the New Jerusalem."

This took the woman back. "I heard of that in my church. Isn't that where Jesus is supposed to rule the world in the Millennium?"

"It is. Who told you that?"

"Oh, I read the Bible," she said nonchalantly. Then her voice lowered. "I even have a Book of the Mormons," she added in a whisper, as if she were revealing some dangerous secret. It was still illegal to own that book, so her whispering was probably a wise precaution.

After some silence, Samuel spoke. "There's something else you want to tell me," he urged.

"Nope."

Another silence. "OK, I'll tell you," Samuel challenged. "You were baptized a member just before the Church was outlawed."

"I was not!" she insisted hotly.

"You left it shortly after that, and even persecuted some other Mormons."

"You are crazy," she said angrily.

"And, now you are sorry."

"I'm not either!" she cried.

"Not guilty, or not sorry?" he asked calmly.

She did not answer immediately. She looked around, and finding her companions totally engaged in receiving food from the other Mormons, turned back to Samuel. Her voice grew soft and regretful. "Okay, I *am* sorry," she said finally. "I was afraid, and I got caught up in the feeling of the time, and didn't want to be identified as a Mormon myself. I did some bad things."

Samuel gazed steadily at her. "The Apostle Peter did something similar when he denied he knew Christ for fear of his life."

"That's right, he did," she replied, and gave her head a toss so that her bright red hair fanned out across her shoulders. If she had been something more than skin stretched over bones, she might have been attractive. "I don't wonder why he did that anymore," she said quietly.

"Then, you've learned something quite marvelous from your experience."

She shook her head vehemently. "I look upon it with loathing, not as something marvelous."

"I suppose," Samuel allowed. "Would you like to know what's going to happen once we get to Zion?"

"Got nothin' else to do," she said with a bored voice. "You fed me, so I'm yours until I get hungry again."

"What's your name?"

"Shirley," she said after some hesitation, as if she were leery of telling him.

"Shirley, do you understand what Zion is?"

"Don't know that I do. Is it a place, or a people?"

Several hours later he and Shirley were deep in conversation while they walked toward town. He accompanied her to her home, which was in fact a small apartment not far from the barricade. There he found over a dozen very hungry people. He gave them all his food, most of which they used to make into a thin stew. They invited him to share their meal. He ate a little while he taught them the Gospel.

That evening more came to hear him, and the following morning they had to move into a larger apartment to make room for all who wanted to hear. He taught with joy and conviction, and bore down in testimony as strongly as the Spirit gave him utterance. By that evening many in the group either admitted they were former "Mormons," or requested baptism. He invited them to join their band in a few days. They immediately began making preparations to do so.

That evening as Samuel lay awake with Melody in their tent pretending to sleep, he was suddenly aroused by a fierce voice.

"Where's the Mormon?" a male voice demanded. A gunshot went off and someone screamed nearby. Samuel jumped to his feet, hoping to act as a decoy for the rest of his family. He walked quickly towards the two men and three women who were waiting outside. He silently prayed that Melody and young Helaman would not be detected; they were miraculously unseen.

"Come with us!" a man ordered him at gunpoint. They escorted Samuel to an army jeep idling by the curb. It was the first running vehicle he had seen since leaving Cardston, Canada. They sped down darkened streets toward the center of town. After zipping around numerous corners they came to a school surrounded by a high fence.

"Out!" the man ordered. Samuel complied and let himself be led through the fence and into the school. The air inside was dense with the smell of body odor and feces. The stench was overwhelming. Through the classrooms and larger rooms were literally hundreds of prisoners kept in squalid conditions. It was the middle of the night but few of those inside were asleep. They looked at him through narrowed eyes.

"Welcome," a thin woman in the near darkness said as she approached him. "Are you one of the Mormons camped outside the city?"

"I am," he replied.

"You should have left rather than come into this city."

"Why is that?"

"Because most of you have been rounded up already. Come with me." Samuel followed her down a hall stepping over bodies all the way. Finally, she turned into a small classroom and stepped aside.

"Father!" a weary voice called. It was Sammy, his son, and many others he recognized and loved. The woman was right: they were almost all here. She was also wrong though; they were exactly where they should be.

"See," the woman said in weak triumph. "You're all in the same sinking ship as the rest of us."

"Who are all these people? Why are they locked up?" Samuel asked.

The woman narrowed her eyes bitterly. "We are the misfits, the out of favor, the ones who dared question or oppose the new government. There are lots of Mormons here who thought it was suddenly okay to be Mormons again. They were sadly mistaken," she said with deep irony.

"Which are you?"

"I fit into several of those categories, even the Mormon one."

"We're here to help you," Samuel said.

She laughed. "You're in prison too," she reminded him, "and not a moment too soon. They told us just today that there were too many of us, and at least half of us would be executed tomorrow morning, starting with the Mormons. Your timing is impeccable," she said, her voice heavy with sarcasm.

"Then, there's still time," Samuel told her.

She shook her head as if Samuel were insane. "Time for what?"

Samuel ignored her question. "First, is there a woman here named Bonnie?"

"I have absolutely no idea," she said with anger in her voice.

"She would be in her late thirties. Blond hair, blue eyes, and probably among the Mormons."

"Do you really think she's in here, Dad?" Sammy asked. He didn't really expect an answer since it was apparent Samuel did think so.

The woman shrugged. "Come with me, and I'll take you to the rest of the Mormons. They stick together, so they're easy to find."

She led the way to a large room with wide raised steps that had once been the band room. When they entered only the very small children were asleep. Everyone else watched them with thinly veiled fear.

Samuel stepped forward. "I'm looking for a woman named Bonnie Mahoy. Do any of you…"

"Daddy!" a hoarse voice cried out. A young woman came running down the steps toward him. She fell into his arms with a cry of joy and wept as if her whole soul had been rent. "Daddy, Daddy," she said over and over. "I knew you'd come for me. I knew it!"

"Are you all right?" he asked, forcing her to look at him.

Bonnie clung to him, nodding weakly. "I am, I think. I'm awfully hungry and sick, but honestly I'm better than most. My husband is really bad off though. He was beaten by the guards for insisting they give us food. He's over here," she said, leading the way around many supine bodies.

She came to a far corner of the room and stopped. "Daddy, I want you to meet Steven, my husband." A young man in his late thirties was huddled in a fetal position on the hard vinyl floor. His only comfort was a rolled up piece of cloth under his head. His face was battered and cut. One eye was swollen shut, and dried blood was visible in his hair and on his face. His skin was pasty and damp. He was obviously in shock and severe pain.

"Steven. I'm Samuel, Bonnie's father. How are you doing?" Samuel inquired, surveying his injuries as much as possible in the semi-light.

He couldn't look up for long before his eyes shut again. "I'm pretty battered, I'm afraid. I've got two broken arms, a broken collar bone, several broken ribs, and probably a concussion," he said with a slur. "I haven't even thought about what internal injuries I might have. But, I'm doing OK other than that," he laughed weakly, and winced from the effort.

"What you did was a very brave thing," Samuel started to say.

"Futile and foolish, you mean," Steven replied. "I just couldn't stand to see my wife and the people starving."

"How long have you two been married?" Samuel asked Bonnie. He hadn't even known that Bonnie was married.

"Less than a year, Daddy," she said. "We were married secretly by our bishop. The authorities found out about it, and killed the bishop," she said, her heart heavy with regret. "He was such a wonderful man, Daddy. You would have liked him. He had tremendous faith. Steve and I feel horrible because it was all our fault!"

"His death was not your fault, Bonnie. It was the Lord's will," Sam comforted her. "So, this was a year ago?" he asked.

"About a year ago, I guess. It's hard to keep track of time," Bonnie replied. "I just wish we had our strong bishop with us now."

But there was only a little time to do what must be done. They would talk of loss and sorrows later.

"Steven, how is your faith?"

"Very strong, sir."

"Strong enough to be healed?"

"Yes sir," he said emphatically.

"Then take my hand, Steve," he directed. With a small groan Steven raised his broken arm high enough to take Samuel's hand.

"Steven, in the name of Jesus Christ, and by His holy priesthood, I command you to be healed, and arise." This he said solemnly, in a calm and commanding voice. He slowly pulled on Steven's hand, coaxing him to a sitting position. Steven grunted in pain as he pushed himself upward with an elbow by sheer willpower. He gave Samuel a look filled with hope, and intense pain. His face was beaded with sweat.

"Stand up Steve, you can do it. It requires faith, not a tolerance for pain. Stand up."

"I will!" Steven cried. He came to his knees with a groan, then pushed himself to one foot, and then to standing. Samuel began undoing the makeshift slings supporting his arms. Steve reached up and stripped a bloodied bandage from his head. There was no wound beneath.

"Don't say anything," Samuel instructed just as he was about to cry out for joy. Bonnie gasped and rushed to her husband. He held her tightly in arms that had been useless and festering just moments before.

Samuel looked around. "Sammy?"

"Yes sir," his son said, coming to stand beside his father.

"You see that lady sitting by the piano?"

"I do, sir."

"She has faith to be healed. You're an elder. Go heal her as you saw me heal Steve. Stay with her long enough to offer a prayer of thanks, then return and report to me."

"Yes sir," Sammy said and marched away.

"Steve, you're an elder as well, aren't you?"

"I am. I am indeed," he replied, keeping his voice as low as he could.

"You take the far side of the room and begin healing people in Christ's name," Samuel instructed.

"Yes sir!" he cried, and hurried away with Bonnie on his arm.

"You, good brother," Samuel said, motioning toward a man lying in a puddle of his own vomit, yet whose eyes were burning with fire at what he had just seen. "Do you have the faith to be healed?"

"I do!" he cried hoarsely.

"Then in the name of Jesus Christ, arise."

The man jumped to his feet as if he had been shocked by a cattle prod.

"I'm a high priest," his face aflame with faith. "Tell me who's next," he said humbly.

"That sister there with the three kids huddling around her. The smallest one there has died. Bring the little one back, then heal the others," Samuel directed.

"I will go and do as the Lord commands," the man said, and turned toward the sister. At that very moment Samuel heard a cry of joy as the woman by the piano received the promised blessing from Sammy. To his left he could hear the quiet words of Steven, and sobs of joy all around him.

Samuel turned back toward the thin woman who had escorted him to this room. She was on her knees praying. He knelt beside her and curved an arm across her shoulders. She laid her head on his arm.

"I don't know your name," he said.

"Grace," she said with some irony in her voice.

"Grace, are you ready to be healed?"

"I'm not sick," she replied without looking up.

"I wasn't referring to your body," Samuel said. "Your sickness is within your soul."

"I know it is. I'm afraid I have sinned too bad to be forgiven. It would be better for me if my sickness was in my flesh. I think I have sufficient faith for my body to be healed. But, the wounds of the soul are more permanent, I'm afraid."

"What makes you think that? Don't you think the Lord is able to heal all wounds, and bind up all sorrows and afflictions?" Samuel asked her gently.

"I do," she said, and looked at his face through tearful eyes, "if the person is worthy." She paused poignantly. "I'm not. I'm the worst of the worst. Don't you wonder why I'm not sick like the other Mormons?" she demanded.

"I know why," Samuel said. "So does everyone in this room."

"What? How? I mean…"

"You sold your integrity for some food," Samuel said.

"I sold more than that. I sold my friends, my self-respect, my body, my very soul," she lamented.

"I know," Samuel replied. "Listen to the sounds of joy in this room tonight. How does it make you feel?"

"Like shouting praises to God," she said honestly.

"Then, you haven't sold as much as you thought. There are those who would order us all shot after what you are seeing. I'm going to leave you here. You seek God, and ask Him to forgive you," Samuel said as he stood up.

"How will I know when He has?" she asked as she looked up at him, tears coursing down her face.

"You will know when peace floods in upon you. Then you will know," he said. She didn't answer, but lowered her head.

Just as the first rays of morning were beginning to light the walls of their prison, the last of those with faith to be healed stood upon solid legs. Sometime during the night Grace had been taken out and released.

"Shortly, the guards will come for us," Samuel said, his voice solemn and steady. "This morning some of you will die. If you are afraid to die, seek help from God those around you. If you are not, then give your strength to others. At some point we will all die. It is a rare opportunity to be able to die for your faith. Lift up your hearts and be glad," he said brightly.

"If we die with our hope bright in Christ, happy day, all is well!" an old man cried. A chorus of "Amens" filled the room.

Samuel gazed at them in love. "You have great faith. Do not fear, but let your hearts be full. The hour is upon us." At that very moment the door banged open and four armed guards stomped into the room.

"All you Mormon vermin—out!" the only man among them ordered. They obeyed meekly. They were led out into a fenced enclosure that surrounded four tennis courts. One wall was made of cement blocks, the others were tall chain link.

"You are to be shot for being Mormons, and enemies to the state," the man cried out, his voice bitter with hatred. "Your only hope of survival is to renounce your religion and swear allegiance to the state of Cheyenne! Anyone who refuses will die! Do you understand?!" He waited until he was certain his threats had reached their greatest possible impact.

You!" he said, pointing at a young woman with a four-year-old girl clinging to her neck. "You and the child. Against the wall!"

The mother adjusted her sobbing child and walked to the wall where she turned to face the four guards. She was one of those healed just hours before. She had been severely afflicted with festering skin lesions. Her face was now clear of all blemishes, and free of all fear. She comforted her baby until she grew still.

Willing to make an example of her, the guard marched up to the young woman and shouted in her face. "Are you still a Mormon? Or, are you going to renounce?!"

"I will not renounce," she said calmly, looking him squarely in the face.

"Shoot her," he said with utter disdain in his voice. "Shoot her and the brat!" he bellowed, and took a step back. The three guards, two women and one man, looked at one another as if unsure what to do. Finally one of the grizzled women stepped forward and pulled a pistol from her holster. She cocked it and aimed it with a steady hand at the mother's heart. She was barely ten feet away. Samuel felt his heart racing. He wanted to run forward and stand between them, but he was constrained by the Spirit. He looked at his son, and saw tears streaming down his face.

"Fire!" the guard cried, and the gun bucked in her hand. The young mother slumped against the wall, followed by her baby.

With a satisfied grin, the guard marched back to the prisoners and pointed his pistol at Bonnie. "You," he cried, "to the wall." Bonnie walked soberly to the wall and stood next to the two bodies at her feet. She didn't seem to notice.

"No!" a young man's anguished voice cried out, and before Samuel could stop him, Steven ran to his wife.

"All right fool, you can join her then," the guard said, and shoved them together. "Will you renounce your false religion?"

"No," they both said in unison.

"Guards take aim," he commanded. The same woman who had shot the first two raised her pistol. Her eyes were glassy and numb, a look of hatred on her face, then a brief wince. The other two guards stood as if paralyzed by shock.

"Last chance Mormons. Renounce your religion, or die."

"No," they said again.

"Shoot her first, then him," he commanded, and stepped back two paces to watch them die. Steve turned them so that he was between Bonnie and the guards. She closed her eyes as he lowered his head to kiss her with great tenderness. This infuriated the guard who screamed, "Fire!"

"He's in the way!" the guard screamed, her voice nearing hysteria.

"Then shoot him first!" he screamed back in demonic rage.

As if sudden understanding had just hammered into her mind, the guard blinked her eyes, turned the pistol slightly and fired. The male guard fell to the pavement. Everyone's eyes were riveted on this unexpected development, and were shocked to hear another gun discharge. They looked around in time to see the female guard who had fired both times slump to the ground from her own bullet. The other two guards quietly took their guns from their holsters, dropped them to the ground and slowly walked out of the building, leaving the doors open behind them.

"Steve," Samuel said, drawing his son-in-law's eyes to his own. Steve was dazed, and not sure that he had not actually been shot himself. He stood looking into Bonnie's eyes with deep shock on his face.

"Yes, Father?" he said meekly.

"God has spared you. Please administer to the young mother and her child. Their death was untimely."

It took a moment for comprehension to dawn. Steve's eyes brightened. "Yes sir!" he replied with certainty, and knelt by their bodies. Two other priesthood holders joined him. Soon the only lifeless bodies left behind were those of the two guards.

Moments later a rattle of gunfire interrupted the quiet of the morning. Shouting and more gunfire came to them from across the yard. Former prisoners began streaming out of the school building. They passed through the gate and out into the city without opposition. Samuel and the others waited where they were, just a little beyond the tennis courts. Finally, a small group of four armed people approached them from one of the buildings. The second among them was Grace. They stopped a short distance away, at which point they holstered their weapons.

"You're free to go," Grace told them happily.

"Where have you been, Grace?" Samuel asked.

"Trying to redeem my crimes," she said.

"That's the Savior's job."

"I know, but I felt like I had to act or my soul would be lost forever. You said I should pray until I felt peace. I pondered every possible way for me to be forgiven by God. When my mind happened upon the idea of going for help from the resistance, I felt such a feeling of peace that I ran the entire way to get them. It may not have been what you were meaning, but it has brought me the peace I had lost. Now, I can begin to petition Jesus to take away my sins with some faith."

Samuel threw his arms around her. "He will hear your prayers, Grace. We are very grateful to you for bringing help," he said, overjoyed.

The woman in front cleared her throat, and all eyes shifted from Grace to her. She was young, perhaps in her late twenties, but her face was steely and hard. Her dark eyes sparkled with keen intellect, but her countenance was nearly devoid of light.

"I'm the leader of the resistance, such as it is," she informed them. "We're going to go from here to the standing government's headquarters and call on them to surrender. They have a lot more people and guns than we do, so I don't really expect to be successful. I suggest you people return to your caravan and find a way around the city."

"Tell me something," Samuel asked as she was about to turn away. His question brought her eyes back upon him. "Why are you doing this? Why are you willing to fight them?"

"Because they are wrong and we are right," she snapped back.

"That is not the right answer, and you will fail," he said solemnly.

"How do you know that?" she demanded.

Grace interjected into the conversation. "Listen to him, Jean, I told you, he's a man of God," she urgently told her leader.

Jean glanced in her direction. "What makes you say that?"

Samuel stepped toward her. “A new era is upon the land, and the times of tyranny are past. God will not allow any form of government to prosper unless it is founded upon righteousness, freedom, liberty, and true constitutional principles. The main reason our own nation was toppled was because as a people and a nation we had abandoned these very things”

“Then, you’re saying we should fight for liberty and freedom, and the outdated constitution?” she asked, her voice somewhat ironic, as if such a cause were impossibly naïve.

“Not just fight for it, cherish it, pray for it, and seek God’s help in establishing it. Be willing to spill your blood to obtain it, and be willing to step aside and let it rule in your stead.”

The woman spat and turned away. “What you suggest is the philosophy of a fool. Others have dreamed, and they have all died.”

“Not all,” Samuel countered. “Consider that our founding fathers were just a few, yet they changed the course of a whole nation. Their task was more difficult than yours. You fight for something the people already believe in. In their day as well, the majority of the people did not understand freedom.”

Jean thought for a moment. “I suppose most people do remember and dream. But, do you really think such a thing is possible? I find my heart yearning for what you say, but I’m too afraid to hope. We are just a few hungry survivors, and there are so many who have a different agenda, who don’t trust the old ways. And, it seems they all have the guns,” she said, her voice a little hopeless.

“This is not a battle of guns,” Samuel assured her. “It is a contest between truth and error, between freedom and captivity. God established this nation and this constitution once in the face of great opposition. If you fight for another form of control, you are outnumbered and you will lose. If you fight for freedom, to establish the constitution and guarantee liberty and freedom of worship, then you fight with God, and they are outnumbered.”

“Are you sure you’re not a politician?” she asked with mock suspicion, then added, “I do believe in the constitution. I was studying to be a nurse before the war. All this killing and hatred is toxic to my soul. I detest it, and yearn with all my heart for freedom and liberty. I really do,” she said with deep emotion.

“Then, set your goals there. Fall on your knees and pray until you are certain you are doing as the God of all liberty desires of you. Once you are on His errand, you will succeed,” Samuel instructed.

“Do you really think so?” she asked.

"I am certain of it," Samuel replied.

Jean pondered these words for many moments before a look of resolution crossed her features. "I will do as you say," she said quietly. Then she nodded at Samuel, turned and walked away. The haughtiness was gone from her gait.

"God bless you," someone called at her back, and a hundred voices echoed the cry. She stopped walking, hung her head for a moment, then without turning around continued on with greater determination and hope. In that brief moment she had come to know that what Samuel had told her was true. They would triumph as long as their cause was just and inspired of God.

Jean did not go directly to battle as she had planned, but returned to her tent where she confronted the Lord for many hours through the night and following day. It truly was a confrontation, for it was the only powerful form of communication she understood. She at first accused, then demanded the Lord get on their side of the war; then after many hours, she finally wept and pleaded for forgiveness. As the Spirit slowly permeated her soul she softened, repented, and humbly asked God to show her what her place was in His war.

When she reemerged, Jean was serene and confident. Her small band of rebels had never seen this fiery leader at peace. Much more than any warbling battle cry, her serene confidence energized them. When they finally made their way to battle, there was no one there to fight. The account of their victory at the school yard the day before had been told and retold with such inflation that they were more fiction than fact.

For those standing in the hijacked seats of power, the delay of the expected attack of the rebels created a state of deep anxiety within their ranks such that during her night of prayer, the military force that gripped Cheyenne had quietly dissipated. When morning came those in command of the city found themselves in command of themselves alone. The transition in power was accomplished overnight, without bloodshed.

Within seven days, the newly-elected democratic government of Cheyenne let the Saints pass through their city unmolested. It had taken exactly one week for the miracle to occur, exactly as President Johnson had proclaimed. President Johnson gave the new government enough wheat, barley, and corn to seed several large fields. If they were careful, in a few years there would be no more hunger in Cheyenne.

Almost as if Interstate 80 had been constructed for the express purpose of transporting the Saints home, they followed it due east across Nebraska, stopping only as necessary along the way. At every major city they encountered, a drama similar to Cheyenne was replayed. Every day they rejoiced, every day was filled with miracles, and every day they buried more faithful saints along the way. They were periodically attacked, robbed, persecuted, ridiculed, or driven away at gunpoint. Each time they responded the same, by teaching the Gospel of Jesus Christ. Each time it cost them more lives; each time many were healed or brought to life; each time it delayed their journey; each time they moved on with more people accompanying them, and more joy than they had had before. The very ones who had persecuted them often begged to join them. These they taught, baptized, and happily embraced.

The further east they traveled the fewer people they encountered, until at Lincoln, Nebraska they found no inhabitants at all. The city was intact, there were just no living people. The streets were littered with human remains. Samuel thought of the Nephites finding and naming the Land of Desolation because of the heaps of bones they found there. It was impossible to describe the feeling of desolation they felt as they passed through, knowing each of those deceased had not so long ago been a loving being, with families, dreams, and lives. As they passed children hid their eyes, women looked away with heavy souls, and grown men wept at the tragic end of so many.

They left I-80 at Lincoln and continued east on side roads until they came to the Missouri River. They found an intact bridge and crossed over into the upper parts of Missouri.

The rolling hills of Missouri were green and lush. Every town, every home, every farm was abandoned. In some places there was evidence of warfare. In others, human bones lay in the streets, undisturbed since they had died from the "pink death" plague years before.

It took seven days to travel from the Missouri River south and east to Adam-Ondi-Ahman, the place where Adam would meet the Lord in the greatest Priesthood meeting of all time. They could feel it's sacredness as they entered the small valley, surrounded with lush trees and rolling hills of verdant green. The valley itself was devoid of any human structures, seeming to them to be as pristine as when it was a part of the Garden of Eden. They camped there for several weeks waiting for the remainder of their people to catch up with them. From there it took six days to travel to Independence, the actual place where they would build the New Jerusalem. They arrived at the ancient cornerstone of the temple late on the afternoon of April 6th, and fell upon their knees and prayed until the shining moon bathed the glorious hills of Zion in light.

They were home at last.

THE NEW JERUSALEM

When the Saints arrived in Jackson County, Missouri, they were the only human inhabitants of the region. They first blessed the land, casting out all disease, darkness, and evil that may have lingered there. Plans were then quickly developed to accommodate the influx of people that must shortly follow. Crews were assembled to lay out tent cities. For now there were enough empty homes and buildings to house all who had come to build up Zion. The brethren set up Church headquarters in the LDS visitor's center which stood a few blocks from the temple site. It served as both an office building and a chapel.

That next day the building site of the temple was staked out, and work was immediately begun to clear the ground. The old corner stone was carefully removed and set aside. It was crudely cut, and though historic, would not serve to support the corner of the structure the Lord intended them to build. It would be laid symbolically at the corner, but it would not bear the weight of the mighty structure.

Through foresight and inspiration, they had brought with them a communications system able to transmit sound, video, and data. It relied on a system of satellites owned by the Church which had been put in service just three years prior to the war. The destruction of communication satellites had been one of the fronts of the war, so the Church's system was rare and highly prized. The equipment was set up and switched on. In a few seconds the link was complete and fully functional. President Andrews, the Prophet of the Church prayed with them, then announced plans for the greatest temple ever built.

While skilled architects studied the plans under the direction of Elder Johnson, crews set out in all directions to acquire building materials. There was a vast plenitude of everything they would need—tools, lumber, and machinery of every type. This was due to the fact that this land had been heavily populated before the war. Their death and destruction had been so swift they had left behind everything of worth. It stood in construction yards intended for other buildings, banks, skyscrapers and homes. It now awaited any hand willing to make use of it.

Others set out to find fuel and construction equipment. Some went in search of a quarry from which to cut the stone. In the meantime, a thousand men cleared top soil and gravel with the power of willing muscle.

 Samuel labored day after day to dig the foundations of the new temple. His was a tireless task. Able to work almost indefinitely and recover with little or no rest, he had to pace himself to keep from working the non-translated beings to death.

He was amazed to find that dozens of men and women in the crew were capable of similar feats of tireless labor. He began to suspect that a considerable percentage of their number were, in fact, like himself. It was an odd fact that he was unable to identify a fellow translated being any easier than anyone else. Except on special occasions, and for reasons only known to God, none in that state could discuss their present circumstance; Samuel honesty did not know which of his brothers and sisters were, in reality, angels.

Perhaps as startling as the number of people working faithfully on the temple was the fact that a full two-thirds of them were women. They came each morning and labored side by side with the men, even stepping in front of them to ensure their participation in the fullest extent. What was most odd to Samuel and many others, was the strength they possessed, equal to, and at times greater than a man. Yet, they were not hard, nor masculine. They worked, walked and spoke with gentleness and feminine dignity. In every respect they were saintly and gracious, yet they worked like draft horses for the Lord.

When the plans they had received from the Prophet were fully understood and drawn, they were laid out for all to inspect. Samuel, and a thousand others stared in wonder at the tremendous scope of the mission ahead of them. It was a daunting task that could well take decades to complete. The main building was circular. Radiating outward were twelve rectangular buildings arranged like the spokes of a wheel. Each of these was connected to another circular building at its end which formed a twelve sided building completely enclosing the spoked wheel. The spaces between the spokes held gardens, fountains, outdoor libraries, outdoor ordinance rooms and offices. It was truly magnificent in every respect. When completed the entire structure would be a little short of a quarter mile in diameter.

The main building was to be four stories high with an additional four stories of spires and steeples. At the very top of the temple was to be a statue of the Angel Moroni with his trumpet held by his side, indicating that the trumpet had been blown, that Christ had returned to the earth. Each of the spoke buildings was stair-stepped, beginning at three stories nearest the temple proper, and stepping in graceful arches and flowing lines to a single story at the rim.

The outer rim was two stories tall with row upon row of steepled windows, graceful arches and tall towers. Each of the twelve outer buildings were identical with three prominent steeples above the main arched doorway. The inner hub of the temple was to be paved completely in marble, with an inner Holy of Holies paved on its floor in pure gold. The workmanship was to be exquisite, finer than mortals can build without divine assistance. The materials to adorn its interior were to be brought in from the four quarters of the earth. The building was, in fact, designed by Christ himself.

Not attached to the great Temple of the Living God were twelve buildings for preparation to enter the temple, schools to teach the people the ways of God, and vast "parking lots" that appeared more like parks. An obvious oddity was that none of the parking lots connected to any roads, and could only be accessed from the air. In all, it was a vision of grandeur never before attempted by mankind.

Stone began arriving from the quarry before the crews had dug the foundation to bedrock. A bulldozer rumbled onto the site and finished in but a few days what would have otherwise taken months. The cornerstone arrived, a massive block ten feet square and three feet thick. Upon all six sides were chiseled the words "Holiness to the Lord," in Gothic letters. The great cornerstone was laid a full two stories below the natural level of the ground. There would be a great underground system of rooms with twelve fonts dedicated to baptisms for the dead.

With much effort and manpower, it was lowered into place by a massive system of cables and cranes. Once set, it was at once discovered that it sat several inches out of place. The arduous task of resetting all the slings, cables and pulleys had just begun when four men in white stepped out from among the workmen. No one had noticed them previously. These four walked up to the stone. Each placed a hand upon the stone and slid it the necessary distance. While the stone rumbled its way to its permanent position, the workmen fell to their knees in humble gratitude. They would not build this mighty structure unaided.

The enormous stones began arriving with every hour, each cut to an exactness that defied mortal skill. Each stone was placed with deftness so that the building began taking shape even as they watched. It soon became obvious that every part of the construction process was accelerated. The workers sent three great stones from the quarry, and six would arrive. They would strike the stones with a crude chisel, and a polished surface would emerge. Miracles became so commonplace that a scribe was assigned to attend each phase of the work to document every such occurrence of divine aid, so that every generation thereafter might give glory to God.

Weeks, rather than years saw the outer wall rise to ground level. Workman completed the stone floors of native white granite in several weeks and the walls continued climbing toward heaven. Six days a week they labored from sun up to sun down, never pausing for more than a few minutes to eat or drink. Samuel found himself almost outworked by mortals who seemed to have the strength like himself. They sang, prayed, and shouted praises as they worked.

As the outer walls of the Temple grew in height so did the inner structure. After six months the intricate bridge stones were set arching from the inner walls to the outer, and the spires began to rise above them all. The first stone of the center spire was cut from a different vein in the quarry. Where the other stones were uniformly lustrous white in color, the spire stones were brilliant and sparkling, as if with white diamonds. The spire stones required longer to dress. Intricate in design, and delicate in shape, they required special care. A single mistake could cost a week's work by ruining a nearly completed stone.

Each night the workman laid down their tools, and returned the following morning to find some intricate part of their work completed. The precious stones were then carefully transported to the temple and lifted into place. The center spire rose to a certain height, and stopped. A different construction method completely unknown to them would be used to craft the upper spire. Undaunted, they turned their labors to other areas.

Once this sparkling white vein of stone was found they felt impressed to use it to frame every arch, window and doorway. The effect was stunning. The same brilliant stone was also used on all floors, columns and ceilings. The effect was so striking that there was no need to plaster the exterior of the building. The structure was magnificently beautiful.

The architecture was uncommon in that the inner walls, arches and ceiling were to span the full distance from wall to wall without benefit of trussing to hold the outer walls. Not being an architect, the engineering impossibility was lost on most. All arches push outward on the walls that support them; without some means of countering that incredible force, the walls would collapse of its own weight long before the structure was even finished. This miraculously did not occur.

The plans called for an intricate network of long, graceful walls that flowed outward from the main structure in a design so lace-like they appeared almost to be huge doilies cut from stone. The effect was gloriously beautiful, and impossibly complex. No single architect could completely understand how they transferred the incredible weight of the great stone ceiling of the temple through these walls and to the foundation. The construction was similar to the obscure renaissance design called a flying buttress, yet it was an adaptation of that concept never before contemplated, nor attempted by man.

His eyes opened to things of the Spirit that few mortals were able to see, Samuel watched in awe as a thousand angels labored on the Temple. He watched as a mortal would place his shoulder against some task too great for any man or woman, and several unseen angels would gather on each side of him. With a mighty shove and shout of praise, the object would move, apparently against the laws and logic of nature. This explained the phenomenal strength the women possessed. It also explained why once they left the temple site, their strength was once again only equal to their mortal stature.

One beautiful sunny afternoon, Samuel was helping set a long white stone in a broad stairway when he heard a sustained scream. Everyone looked up to see a worker falling head first from one of the highest walls of the Temple. She hit the ground with a low thud while everyone ran to her in great concern. Then she immediately stood up, dusted herself off, and climbed back upon the wall. She was uninjured, undaunted and back at work almost without comment, except for the thousand prayers of gratitude uttered.

Perhaps even more amazing than all this was the steady influx of people into Jackson County. Thousands from many tribes streamed in the course of the summer, and the number of workers swelled. Skilled artisans of every craft and trade arrived. There were carpenters, painters, plasterers, workers of gold, gems, and a hundred other trades.

The Temple was soon expertly wired for electricity. Provisions were made for elevators, escalators, and some designs and constructs within the Temple no one was sure what function they served. The Holy of Holies was built without a ceiling, directly below the center spire. The center spire itself contained a circular cavity exactly twelve feet in diameter which penetrated its exact center. No one was sure why it was there, or how the open ceiling would be sealed, as it was presently open to the sky.

But, by far the happiest moment for Samuel came when the School of the Prophets was once again convened, and he was asked to preside over it. He set down his tools, handed his thick gloves to another, and left the Temple never to return as a workman. His heart was full of gratitude as he walked slowly away, marveling at how much they had accomplished in a single summer.

The central structure was nearly complete on the outside. The system of spires was about half-erected. A thick vein of gold had been discovered at the quarry, and enough had already been mined to cast the Angel Moroni of solid gold. He had seen the plaster model from which the solid gold statue would be cast. It stood twice the height of a man and would eventually weigh more than the structure of the temple spire could normally support. This, however, did not concern them.

The School of the Prophets held its first class in the Visitors Center chapel. Those who initially attended were brothers and sisters in leadership positions, taught and assisted by immortal beings. The class lasted six weeks, during which time they ate and slept at the Visitors Center. The goal, almost universally accomplished, was that each student leave after that six weeks with their Calling and Election made sure. What a joy, a supernal privilege it was for Samuel to stand amidst righteous women and men, angels and resurrected beings, and call upon the powers of God to work the mighty changes within the souls of his students. He considered that no greater blessing could have come to him, or those over whom he presided.

His calling to preside over the school, and his standing before the Lord as a translated being himself, gave Samuel an unusual perspective on things. As the spiritual power of those attending the school grew he was able to gather speakers of great uniqueness. Though they spoke of these things not at all, toward the end of the first session of the school they were taught day after day by glorious visitors from the past. Imagine what one could learn about the law of Moses, when the class was taught by Moses himself! Or, what one could learn about faith from the Brother of Jared! It was a time of such rejoicing that Samuel felt as if his very soul was aflame night and day.

The leaves had turned to shades of yellow, red and orange, and the nip of fall was in the air when a new caravan arrived. Samuel was standing near the back of the chapel listening with great joy to a lecture on love being delivered by John, the disciple whom Jesus loved, when he felt compelled to leave the hall. He passed by the guards standing at the doors and hurried out onto the front steps of the Visitor's Center. The Temple, a dozen blocks away, dwarfed everything around it, its brilliant white spires reflecting the afternoon sun. As he approached, he saw a vast ragged group coming steadily toward the temple.

"Samuel!" a voice cried with such joy that he instantly knew who it was.

"Alexei!" Samuel cried in return and ran toward his old friend. They met halfway across the lawn and fell into one another's arms with great joy. Vladimir and a host of others joined in the embrace until they were laughing out loud in the overwhelming joy of reunion.

"You are finally here!" Samuel cried happily, clapping his back.

"Yes, we are here to build that portion of the great temple dedicated to Levi," Alexei explained. "It was never known to us until we had our experiences in the temple at Cardston, but each of the twelve outer buildings must be built by their respective tribes of Israel. There are twelve, one for each."

"I knew that must be the case," Samuel agreed. For this reason and others like it, the inhabitants of Zion joyfully welcomed each new arrival to Zion.

"We will help finish the center building, then we alone will build our temple," Alexei said humbly, tears of joy gathering in his eyes.

"How many tribes are represented by your people?" Samuel asked.

"We have people from three tribes," Vladimir explained excitedly. "We will build three of the great temples in the outer temple ring."

"How many tribes are we still missing, I wonder?" Alexei asked aloud.

"The Lord will provide," Samuel said with complete faith.

"Of course He will," Alexei agreed.

"We have brought something else of importance," Alexei said urgently, and motioned for something to be brought forward. It was the carved box containing the box of their scriptures. "When can we see the Prophet?" he asked excitedly. "We have something important to give him."

"President Andrews is in Utah, but I believe he will be here in a few days. In the meantime, do you want to give your scriptures to President Johnson?"

Alexei shook his head. "I think not. When President Andrews arrives, he is the Seer; we will give them to the Prophet," he said, then after a moment added, "A few more days out of several thousand years isn't so long." This brought a smile to all their faces.

The following day after Alexei's group was settled, ground work began on three of the outer buildings. Alexei and his people provided all the labor for these structures. Everyone else assisted with technical direction, or in getting them materials.

During this time, industry began to operate once again. Food became plentiful, though basic. Clothing was largely handmade, but cloth was loomed now and easier to obtain. Medicines were scarce, but were rarely sought after. The power of the priesthood was so prevalent that sickness was rarely treated with medicine. Doctors of medicine worked on the Temple and delivered babies, but not much else. Even after community water was restored, there was still no electricity, and no reason to believe it might begin any time soon; there were no working power generation plants anywhere nearby. But the power of the priesthood made up exponentially for any lack of electrical power.

From the day they arrived in the New Jerusalem, a system of consecration and community economy was established. There was no money in circulation. Whatever was needed by a family to live was freely available. There were two large stores in Zion, one which dispensed food, another handling clothing, furniture, and building supplies. It was extremely common to go to the store with one's arms laden with surplus items or items in excess of your own needs, and on the way out to pick up the several items needed.

Samuel's family occupied a house a few miles from the Temple site. It was an older home with four bedrooms. Since they had no gasoline, there was no need for the double car garage, so it was converted into an apartment for Lisa and her two children: Monica, now six, and Timmy, age four. Melody's sons and their wives each had their own homes. Bonnie and Steven temporarily occupied a bedroom in Samuel's home. Since they had no children, their need for a separate home was delayed and many larger families that arrived almost daily were given the much-needed housing first. But Bonnie and Steven loved living with their parents, so they were in no great hurry to have their own home.

Little Helaman turned two that spring. He was the delight of his Mommy and Daddy, who were both shamelessly infatuated with their little one.

Despite the turmoil of the world, for the Mahoys a new season of joy had begun.

BONNIE'S STORY

The one member of the Mahoy family who was yet a mystery was their twin daughter, Bonnie. She said very little about her experiences of the past six years. Steven, her husband, also chose not to say much about those years until his wife finally broke her self-imposed silence. Samuel often wished she would find her peace so they could know what had occurred that still caused her pain.

That day came unexpectedly one afternoon while everyone but Bonnie and her mother were away working at the Temple; the babies were asleep, and they were washing dishes side by side.

"Mama?" Bonnie began." It tickled Melody that her stepdaughters called her "Mama." It was the girls' way of constantly reaffirming their love and acceptance of the woman who had married their father.

"Yes, honey?"

"The reason I haven't said much about the years we were apart is because I'm so ashamed."

Melody didn't look up from her work. "Do you want to talk about it?" she asked as casually as she could.

"I do, desperately, but I'm just so ashamed that I can't." She shook her head. "I don't want to keep it a secret anymore, though! What should I do?" Bonnie asked, her voice soft and pleading.

"Do you need to talk with the bishop, honey? Is there something you still need to work through in that respect?"

"Oh, no. Mother, I've paid the price for my mistakes, and Heavenly Father has forgiven me. I just can't forgive myself."

"Bonnie, if you feel comfortable with telling me, maybe that will help you come to terms with it. I'm a good listener," Melody urged her gently.

Bonnie took a deep breath. "Okay Mama. I'll try and see how far I get." She handed a wet dish to her mother and began. "Well, as you know, I had left Lisa in Rexburg and was attending BYU in Provo when the Church was outlawed. When that happened, I refused to get the microchip implanted, since I was certain it was the mark of the beast. Without even being able to go home to say goodbye, I was then ordered to leave Utah Valley. They drove us about fifty miles north of Salt Lake and dumped us off in the desert. There were about a dozen of us college kids. We began walking along Interstate 80, living off of whatever we could beg from passing motorists. There was still a lot of traffic in those days."

"I feel so terrible, because we didn't know anything about this!" Melody told her sadly.

"Mama, there was no way for you to know; I couldn't get ahold of you! Anyway, we finally made it to Cheyenne without dying in the desert, only because we didn't admit to being Mormons. We had hitched a ride on a semi-truck and got a ride all the way to Cheyenne. The driver said we could probably find work there, so we went that far with him."

Bonnie was washing one plate over and over, her mind riveted on the story. "To avoid suspicion my friends and I parted company in Cheyenne to find work and a place to live. We were afraid that a group of us without the chip implanted would be labeled as bad Mormons and exiled again. It was the most terrifying experience I have ever had. I remember walking down the back streets of town wondering where I would ever find help. I was terrified someone would rob or rape me, or something worse, and was afraid to go near groups of people. I tried begging from house to house, but everyone I begged from asked me why I didn't just go to the food centers? I didn't have a good answer, and they suspected I was an illegal. And it was illegal to give food to someone who didn't have the microchip."

Melody nodded with deep understanding. "It sounds completely awful, Bonnie!"

Bonnie's shaking hand handed the plate to her mother to dry. "It was, Mama, it was. I had gone without food for most of a week, and was too weak to hardly even walk. My clothing was dirty and torn. I was sick. I had lost so much weight I was practically skin and bones. I was certain I would die. Finally, I could stand it no longer and stumbled into a food center and asked them to give me a microchip. They asked me why I hadn't gotten one earlier. I told them my family lived in the country. I told them I had walked into town to get a chip because my family was starving."

Bonnie started to cry in shame. Melody waited. "They happily implanted the chip in my right hand and gave me food and a job. It was so easy and so painless that it didn't take me very long to get over my guilty feelings for having done it. Whenever I was hungry, all I had to do was to wave my hand under the scanner and I could take anything I needed from the store. In a short time I began berating myself for having thought it a bad thing. I actually started to think that those who still refused to get the chip were stupid beyond belief!" Bonnie said.

"I can understand why you would think that," Melody soothed her. Bonnie just shook her head.

"I was pathetic, Mama. Anyway, during this time I met Steven, and fell in love with him. He was my age, handsome and super sweet. He worked at the Food Center and helped me get a job. He had been there longer than me, and worked in management. I was flattered when he showed an interest in me because I was still very skinny and had not yet regained my strength. Nevertheless, he was kind and complimented me, so it was easy to love him. I was terribly lonely, and he was the first guy who saw beyond my awful appearance."

Melody stopped her. "Bonnie, you could never look awful!"

"Oh Mama, if you had seen me, you'd never say that!" Bonnie laughed ruefully, and continued. "So we dated for almost a year, during which time I said nothing about the Church to anyone. I actually began to almost forget it even existed. That's why I was so startled when Steven asked me if I would like to go to church with him. I naturally assumed it was an approved church, and after thinking about it for a day or two, I told him I'd go with him.

Bonnie dried her hands on the dish towel and took a seat at the countertop facing her mother. "Steven took me to a house not far from our work. The meeting was held in the basement, which I thought was odd. But, these were odd times. Imagine my total surprise when we sang an LDS hymn for the opening song! I was both overjoyed, and terrified as it became obvious to me that these were Mormons, and I was stupidly sitting there with them! I sat in stunned silence as the meeting progressed. All this time Steven was watching me with anxiety—I could just tell. The words "Mormon" or "LDS" were never used until the Branch President spoke. Steven told me later that if I would have objected or acted offended in any way, they would have immediately shut down the meeting. They would have moved their meeting place, and Steven would have found other work where I would never see him again. It was super risky for him to take me there."

Bonnie looked down at her hands and frowned. "I am ashamed to say that I seriously considered turning them in, and I actually may have."

"What changed your mind?" Melody asked, her voice subdued.

"The branch president. I don't suppose you knew this, but everyone in the underground Church always used a false name. The branch president went by the name of Helaman."

Melody looked up sharply, her eyes narrowing. "Helaman, huh? Describe him, would you dear?"

"He was perhaps in his fifties, though still very energetic. He had quite dark brown hair and dark brown eyes. He almost looked as if he might have a little Indian, or Hispanic blood in him."

"Did he use a cane?" Melody asked.

"Yes, he walked with a slight limp. Why do you ask?"

"You just finish your story. I'll tell you later."

"Sure. So Helaman was the only speaker at church that night. I have to tell you that I have never felt the Spirit of the Lord more powerfully than I did then. He spoke with such conviction and powerful testimony that I found myself hanging on his every word. He was truly not ashamed of the Gospel of Jesus Christ! He openly and proudly spoke of his love for the prophet Joseph Smith, and bore powerful testimony about Jesus Christ."

Melody took a seat at the counter with Bonnie, listening intently. "Do you know what, Mama?" Bonnie said excitedly. "He said that all those proofs from the Vatican documents disclaiming Jesus Christ were just a clever fabrication by the U.N.—a scheme of Commander Sarkus, and a deception of the adversary! And Helaman said he knew with *firsthand* knowledge that Jesus is the Christ!"

Melody nodded knowingly. "I always believed that someday the real explanation of those documents would come out," she said. "Their deception was the perfect storm, wasn't it? And yet, your Helaman saw through it!"

"Oh yes, Mama, he did. I had the distinct feeling as he bore testimony that he couldn't have loved the Lord Jesus Christ, nor the Prophet Joseph more if he had known them personally." Bonnie paused her as if reliving that sacred evening again in her heart.

"What happened next?" Melody asked after a brief silence.

Bonnie shook her head. "Nothing, really. I started attending church every week after that. It was held on a different night of the week and at a different place every time. Steven and I found great joy in it. My testimony returned and I was so grateful to Steven for having the courage to invite me there. He saved my life that day."

Melody smiled. "He is a wonderful man, that husband of yours! So, you were happy then?"

Bonnie took a deep breath and looked away from her mother. "Well, everything went along just fine until I started noticing that Steven and I were the only two at church who were not thin from hunger. I began seeing the thin, ragged appearance of the children, and the tired look in the faces of their skinny mothers. After that, every time I looked in the mirror and saw my plump, healthy cheeks, I hated myself. Steven and I talked about this for hours, and decided that we had sinned by getting the implants so that we could eat. We concluded that we would remove the implants, but that before we did, we would smuggle food to our brothers and sisters."

Melody's eyes widened. "That sounds pretty brave—and risky!" she noted.

"Well, it actually worked! That very next meeting we showed up with extra food for them. They were very happy, and extremely grateful. However, they begged us not to do it ever again. But you know, Mama, bringing them food seemed to atone for my sin of being full while they were starving. It somehow made my feelings of guilt less powerful, I guess. I talked Steve into taking food each time we met.

"This went on for nearly a month before Steve's supervisor asked him why he had started taking home more food than he could eat. Steve acted surprised, but his boss showed him a computer printout that indicated the number of calories he had been taking home. We had no idea the computer calculated how much each person ate. About a month ago the number had nearly tripled for Steve. The computer had triggered an investigation. They also told him that I was going to be investigated because I was also taking home more than four times the food I needed. Steve told them that we were in love, and that I was pregnant, and eating like a horse."

Melody laughed in spite of herself, but Bonnie did not reciprocate.

"His supervisor said that made perfect sense. He told Steve not to worry about the extra food, but to keep it down to what was absolutely necessary. Steve agreed that he would." Bonnie rolled her eyes.

"Well, now we had two problems. First of all, I was not pregnant, and in a few months it would be obvious that Steve had lied. The other problem was that we could no longer take home enough food for the children. The only solution I could think of was for Steve and I to stop eating so much, and to take the surplus food to our friends. We immediately began to do that. When our supervisor saw that I was losing weight, and pregnant as he thought, he insisted I go see a doctor. I refused, which caused him to really become suspicious."

Melody nodded. "I can see that."

"We were in such a tight spot that we didn't know what to do. Finally we decided that our only course was for me to actually become pregnant. If I did, the people at work would quit being suspicious. If I did not, they would assume we had been hoarding food and come search our apartments. When they found that we were not living together, they would force me to have a pregnancy test, and one thing would lead to another until they found out we had been giving food to Mormons. It was all so ugly…" she said with a shake of her head.

"So, what did you decide to do?" Melody asked with great curiosity.

"We asked Helaman to marry us so that I could become pregnant."

Her mother's eyes widened. "That seems like a drastic solution," she observed dryly.

"It was, but I really did love Steven, and he loved me. We actually wanted to be married, and would have eventually chosen this course. We just felt trapped at the time."

"Well, I'm glad to hear you loved each other, at least," Melody said with relief.

"Yeah, I guess that's true," Bonnie admitted with a small smile, and continued. "So we made arrangements to be married that next Friday right after Sacrament meeting. We were so excited, it must have showed in our faces. Several people asked us what we were up to, and we denied that anything was going on.

"Friday came and we hurried away after work to be married. We told Helaman our plans just before Sacrament meeting, and he became very concerned. He asked us to wait until we could think this over some more, but we were determined. He said he didn't feel good about it for some reason, and again asked us to wait. We pressed him to marry us, and he consented, but said he wanted to do it immediately, rather than after church. We agreed to that."

Melody looked worried. "I wonder why he didn't want you to marry?" she mused.

"You'll see why, Mama. So we met early before church and had a quick ceremony in one of the back rooms of the member's home. We had already begun as people were arriving for church. Brother Helaman gave a beautiful talk on marriage, and pronounced us man and wife. We were just kissing for the first time as a married couple, when we heard the commotion outdoors. The door banged open and the police stormed into the room."

"Oh no!" Melody cried.

"It was just awful, Mama. The officer went directly to Brother Helaman and arrested him. They clubbed him unconscious and dragged him out of the room. Then this guy ordered me to hold out my right hand. I did so and he held a small electronic device over the microchip in my hand. No sooner had he done this than the chip began to heat up. I had heard stories about them doing this, and knew that I had only a few seconds to save myself. I tore away from them and ran. The only thing I could find in the old house was a bent fork in the kitchen. I used one of the tines from the fork and dug the chip from my skin…"

Bonnie sat there for a moment in silence, her face pale. When she began again her voice was bitter. "I dug that thing out of my skin and dropped it on the floor. As soon as it hit the floor it exploded with a tiny blue flame and a liquid oozing out."

"I've never heard anything like that," Melody exclaimed in horror. "What would have happened if you hadn't gotten it out?"

"I would have died! The little battery is made of some material that is really poisonous. It causes the person to die within just a few hours. They actually pronounced a death sentence on me because I was a Mormon!" Bonnie slowly held out her right arm and showed her mother a ragged scar on the back side of her hand.

Melody was repulsed by the size of the scar and the obvious pain it would have caused to create it. "I'm so very sorry, honey," she said softly. "You know, I'm surprised they didn't try to stop you from digging it out."

"Oh, no! They did at first but then stood there and laughed at me thinking I would fail."

"That's so cruel. What about Steve?"

"They did the same thing to him. He had a pocket knife, and insisted that I use the knife and give him the fork. To be honest with you, I don't even remember him saying a thing to me, I was so focused on saving my life. He finally took care of himself and got his out just in time too."

"What happened next? What happened to Helaman?" Melody asked with some urgency.

Bonnie sat quietly for a few long moments, rubbing the scar on the back of her hand absent-mindedly as she relived the horror of those days. When she did speak again, her voice was hollow, as if a part of her mind was not there.

"I don't remember what happened next. I think I was in shock. I know I had lost a lot of blood. I remember standing in the snow and being shoved around and accused. I think I denied something, I'm not even sure what. Someone kept shouting at me. I was cold, and sick to my stomach, terrified, and bleeding, and I just wanted the screaming and terror to go away. I finally just told them whatever they wanted to know. I remember looking at Steve and realizing he was shouting at me to not say what I had just said. It was all like a dream, a very bad dream."

She paused for another long minute without speaking, her voice ragged. "The next thing I remember is a gun going off. I looked up and Helaman was lying on the ground. This guard was saying, 'You are free to go, and take your garbage with you so I don't have to arrest you for littering.' Mama, he had killed Helaman because of something I had said, but I don't remember what it was!" she cried, burying her face in her hands, her body shaking with sobs. It took her many minutes to compose herself.

"With that he and his troops drove away, and left us standing in the darkness of the darkest night I have ever seen. I was grateful for the darkness because I couldn't see the faces of my friends. All I could hear was their weeping and mourning as they picked up Helaman's body."

Her shoulders shook with weeping as she continued. "Mama, Steve and I tried to help, but our Mormon friends, or who used to be our friends, refused to even let us touch his body. They asked us to leave them. Steve tried to tell them it was not my fault; he begged them to listen. But, they just ignored him, and walked into the darkness until all I could hear was their voices mourning their dead friend."

Bonnie was completely undone; her heart had broken and would not be healed. Melody consoled her and waited for her to speak again. Finally Bonnie continued. "I just stood there for a long time, sick to my stomach and hating everybody. But mostly hating myself. In my mind and in my heart, I knew I was responsible for Helaman's death. Steve tried to convince me otherwise, but I wouldn't listen. As far as I'm concerned, I am totally responsible! I'm guilty of murder, and even worse—the shedding of innocent blood!" she cried piteously, her voice filled with self-loathing.

"Oh, no, Bonnie. That's not true. You can't think like that. I'm sure …"

Bonnie appeared to have heard nothing Melody was saying, but cut her off to continue her narrative. "Later that evening we went to both our apartments and found them locked and guarded. They wouldn't even give us our own clothing. Even members we knew wouldn't let us in. We slept that night in the alley behind Steve's apartment."

Melody decided to remain quiet, though her heart was crying out to comfort her sweet and sensitive daughter.

"It was kind of ironic, actually. After that, everywhere we went we were rejected and threatened. After four days surviving on rotting food from garbage cans, we decided we could not survive much longer, and held a fast."

"But, you were already starving," Melody protested.

"Yes we were, but we desperately needed Heavenly Father's help, and Steve and I both felt we needed to fast. I was just numb, and felt like I wanted to die; fasting seemed a type of poetic justice to me at the time." She laughed ironically. "It was very difficult, because we were already hungry, but we fasted that whole next day. By the end of the day we were too weak to go find food, so we just knelt together in an alley and prayed for help. Our prayers were answered when we heard someone behind us."

"Who was it?" Melody asked breathlessly.

"It was Tarah, one of the members of the Church. We told her who we were, and told her to leave us alone."

"'I know who you are,' she said. 'We've been looking for you.'"

"Really?" Melody said, and slipped around the counter to put an arm around her daughter.

"Mama, we were so amazed, we asked her why they would try to help us.

'Because we love you,' she said simply."

"What a saint!" her mother marveled.

"I tried to protest, to remind her that I was responsible for Helaman's death. She just shushed me, and handed me a piece of bread from her pocket. I couldn't eat it. I wanted to die, and I just couldn't eat it. The fact that it came from someone who had also loved Helaman made it impossible for me to swallow the bread. I told her I couldn't eat her food."

Melody was crying. Bonnie patted her arm, grateful to not be judged, but merely listened to. She looked lovingly at her mother, and continued.

"'My dear sister,'" the lady told me quietly, 'it was wrong that you were treated unkindly. Two days ago, I held a special fast in the Church to help us find you and Steven. I personally decided that I would not break my fast until I had found you. So, you see, if you die from your fasting, then I will too.'"

"I cried out, 'But, I killed Helaman!' She just smiled at me, and said, 'Helaman knew his days were numbered, and spoke often of how few days he had left. We were not prepared for his death, but we were expecting it.'

"I told her that didn't alter the fact that my words caused his death! Then she asked me if I remembered what I said. I told her that I did not. Then she said, 'Neither do we,' and then she held out the bread to me again."

Melody put her arms around Bonnie while they wept together. "I opened my mouth like a little baby and let her feed me, Mama. There was such love and compassion, and genuine forgiveness in her face, that I let her actually feed me," Bonnie sobbed. "I have never felt such pure love from anyone in my life!"

"She must have been a wonderful woman, and filled with the pure love of Christ," Melody nodded at her with joy.

"Mama, do you know what? She was Helaman's *wife!*" Bonnie cried, as if the whole burden of her guilt was embodied by that single sentence.

Melody sat stunned, rigid with deep irony until fresh tears sprang to her eyes. They held each other for a long embrace.

"Mama," Bonnie said after she regained some control over her emotions. "Tarah and the other Saints took care of Steve and me for nearly a year. They fed us, and loved us, and taught us what it means to be a true disciple of Christ. If ever a group of people deserved to go to the Celestial Kingdom, they do."

Melody nodded through tears, and silently expressed her gratitude to God.

"A short time after that we were all captured and thrown into the prison where Daddy found us," Bonnie continued. "By the time he got there, we were all nearly dead from the beatings, from sickness, starvation, and exhaustion. We all longed for the peace and rest of being in Paradise with Christ whom we all loved."

Then Bonnie's face brightened. "But there was something incredible about that prison. Even though we were absolutely destitute, the one thing which we had in abundance was faith. I know you've heard how Daddy, Sammy and Steven used their priesthood to heal so many, and to even raise some of us from death. What you don't know is that the whole reason those miracles took place was because of their perfect faith in Christ. Those miracles were blessings long overdue those wonderful Saints of such purity. I just wish I could claim to be like them," she said sadly.

Melody straightened up, and took her daughter's hands. "My dear child," she said softly, her face a perfect image of gentleness and love. "I have several observations to make about your story."

"What?" Bonnie asked quietly.

"Do you have a testimony of Christ?"

"Oh, yes!" she cried passionately.

"Were you among those who were healed that night by Samuel and Sammy?"

"I was," she said softly.

"As I recall, you were suffering from a bleeding ulcer, which was in fact, life threatening."

"Something like that," Bonnie admitted.

"Is it possible that such a miracle could have happened if you were, in fact, such an awful person?"

"Oh but I am," she insisted.

"Just answer my question."

"I don't know," Bonnie said weakly.

"Yes you do. It *isn't* possible! In order to receive such a glorious blessing one must be worthy, through their faith in Jesus Christ. Oh Bonnie, none of us is worthy on our own; we all are sinners and fall short of the glory of God! But through Christ, you are worthy, I am worthy, and no one is worthy in any other way! I can feel the power of your convictions, Bonnie, and I can see the light of Christ in your face. Is it possible that light could be present in a person so unredeemable as you proclaim yourself to be?"

"I…"

"If you had it to do over again, would you do anything to contribute to another person's death?"

"No, never!" Bonnie cried.

"That's right. I know you wouldn't, because you would rather die that let anyone die in your place, or because of your words. Don't answer, because you know it's true. My dear Bonnie, I proclaim before you and all the world, and every angel who is listening, that you are free from the crimes that are burdening your soul!"

Bonnie blinked her eyes, a glimmer of hope emerging. "I wish I could believe…"

"Sweet Bonnie, you do believe! That's the point! You believe as firmly as any prophet of any age. Such belief comes from God, wrought by the atonement, through your faith in Christ. This makes you worthy, Bonnie! Let your heart rejoice, let it be lifted and soar unto the heavens. God holds no guilt against you, why should you?"

"Oh, Mama!" Bonnie cried, and threw herself again into Melody's arms. "I'm so sorry! I want to believe you, but even if it's true, Helaman is dead. Even if I didn't do it with malice, even if I am forgiven, I still spoke the words that resulted in his death!" she cried.

"Not everything is as it appears," a low voice said from near the door. They both started and turned toward the unexpected voice.

"Helaman!" Bonnie screamed for joy, and rushed toward him. Helaman caught her in his arms and held her as she sobbed. His eyes were filled with love and gentleness as he stroked her hair. Helaman appeared thirty years younger than when Melody had seen him the first time in England. But, there was no mistaking who it was.

When Bonnie finally got to the point where curiosity overcame her tidal wave of emotions, she pushed back from his embrace. Before she could voice a single question, Helaman turned to Melody.

"Helaman, how wonderful to see you again," Melody said happily, and accepted a warm embrace. "We were just talking of your tremendous help to Bonnie and Steven. Once again our family owes you a deep debt of gratitude, my friend."

"It was my great joy to be involved with Bonnie and Steven, and the other Saints of Cheyenne," he said with quiet enthusiasm.

"I thought they killed you!" Bonnie exclaimed, still in shock.

"Many people have tried to kill me," he said with a chuckle. "It's actually not that easy to do."

Bonnie took his hands into hers. "Oh Helaman, I have felt so awful all these years because I thought I got you killed! I thought . . ."

Helaman stopped her with a smile. "Oh, they did shoot me, my dear, and under normal circumstances, I would have been very much dead."

"So, what I said *did* get you killed—or at least, it should have?"

"That is correct," Helaman said soberly.

"So I am guilty," Bonnie said with lowered head.

"That is not correct," Helaman said again with equal force.

"But…"

Helaman patted her arm. "Let me explain, if I may. I only have a few minutes before I have to go. I was there in Cheyenne to accomplish several things. Only one of them was to help you and your wonderful husband. I promised your father Samuel that I would watch out for his family while he was on his mission. There were many other reasons I was there, too—not the least of which was to build up the struggling Saints in that city and to help them find the faith sufficient to be worthy to come to Zion. The only way I could accomplish that was through giving them a greater cause than their own hunger."

"Steve and I were that greater cause?" Bonnie asked, perplexed.

"You were a part of it. The larger task was teaching them Christlike forgiveness. For you and Steve, it was the process of abject humility, and powerful faith."

"Those were difficult and painful lessons," Bonnie said thoughtfully, her head lowered.

"Yes they were, and yet you learned them, and here you are, talking to an angel. So you must have learned them very well."

"An *angel?*" Bonnie gasped.

"Bonnie, honey," Melody interrupted. "I knew Helaman over thirty years ago."

"But, he's hardly thirty now!" Bonnie marveled, her understanding beginning to dawn.

Helaman turned to leave. "Your mother can explain it. I only came to complete my promise to your father, according to his faith," he said, and took a step back. As he did so, he seemed to become brighter, as if a light had come on within him that shone through his skin.

"Why did you come back, Helaman?" Melody asked. "You already got Bonnie safely to Zion."

"That is true," Helaman said. "But my job was not done until the scars in her heart were also healed. Now, Bonnie is whole in body and in spirit. My work with her is done," he said, and grew brighter still, until he vanished in a silent burst of light. Melody and Bonnie stood for a long time looking at the spot where he had just been.

Finally, Bonnie sank down on the couch. "I can't believe I've just seen an angel," she marveled, mostly to herself. Then she thought for a moment and asked, "How could he have been married to Tarah if he were an angel?"

Melody prayed silently for the right answer before she spoke. "Tarah was Helaman's wife when he was alive on the earth," she said, as the thought entered her heart with great force.

"You mean Tarah was an angel too? She really was his wife?" Bonnie asked in total wonder?

"*Is* his wife," Melody corrected quietly.

Both women sat silently contemplating these startling truths, which the Spirit was now confirming. It was Melody who broke the solemn silence. "Look out the window and tell me what you see," she said earnestly to her daughter.

Bonnie complied and knelt on the couch before the front window. It was late in the night, and Bonnie expected to see nothing but blackness. Melody drew open the blinds.

"It's still light outside!" Bonnie exclaimed in surprise.

"Oh, good," Melody said happily. "Your eyes are still open from seeing Helaman. Come quickly. I want you to see something before it passes."

"What?"

"Just come. It's wonderful!" Melody quickly led Bonnie out onto the street before the house. From where they stood they could see the partially-completed temple, even though it was over four miles away.

"It's lit up!" Bonnie exclaimed. "Is the electricity back on?"

"No, it's not electricity. Look closer. Can you see them?"

"You mean the people working on the temple? That's incredible! Mama, I didn't know there was a night shift. Where did all that light come from? That's amazing!"

"Bonnie, it is the glory of God, and those people working on the temple are not mortals. You're seeing a host of angels at work! The mortals are working inside, while the brilliantly-lit angels are working outside."

"Oh Mama, I can see them! There are so many! It's no wonder the work on the temple is going so quickly. I never knew. This really is the New Jerusalem, isn't it," she said with awe.

"You know it is," Melody confirmed.

"Yes, I do, I really do!"

Melody pointed to the street. "Now, look away from the temple. Look anywhere. Look at the end of the street by Elder Parker's home. What do you see?"

"Nothing," Bonnie said with disappointment.

"Keep looking, look with your heart, and with your faith. Tell me what you see," Melody urged.

Bonnie stared into the darkness, and then brightened. "People! I see people walking up and down the street. There are lots of them. Some of them are carrying books. Others seem to be searching from house to house." She turned to her mother. "Who are they, and what are they doing?"

"They are the righteous who are awaiting the resurrection. They are here to prepare for the coming of Christ to His temple. The books they are carrying are the genealogy of their families. They are preparing to have their temple work done," her mother said with a smile.

Bonnie was beginning to understand. "How wonderful! But why are they walking up and down the streets?"

"They are searching for their living relatives. When they find them they wait near them for the time when their relative's eyes and ears will be opened, and they can begin their long-awaited work in the Temple. This is a glorious time for them. See how they are all smiling. Listen, and you will hear their voices. Listen…"

Bonnie listened carefully and could hear a distant melody. It sounded as if the workers on the temple were singing. As she listened it became more distinct until she was surrounded by the most beautiful music. It was as if all of creation, the trees, the houses, the angels of heaven were singing with one accord.

"I hear them! It's all beautiful beyond description," Bonnie said as she listened, her hands pressed to her chest. "Why am I hearing and seeing all this? What does it all mean?"

Melody clasped her daughter's hand. "It means your eyes are opened, that you have become a part of Zion. It means that you are the pure in heart, because only the pure in heart can see the things of God. It means that you have a tremendous responsibility ahead of you. And, it means that the days of sorrowing are over. My dear, you just joined the innumerable company laboring day and night in preparation for the Lord's return!"

Bonnie let out a cry of joy. "It feels so—alive! I feel as if my very soul is on fire! I feel like if I don't start singing too, I'm going to explode with joy!"

"It is a marvelous feeling, is it not?" Melody whispered.

"Can everyone in Zion see and hear this?" Bonnie asked suddenly.

Melody nodded. "Some. Every day a few more. In time, everyone will, I believe."

Bonnie was so excited that she got up and started pacing. Then she turned back to her mother. "How did you come to see it, Mama? Who showed it to you?"

"Your father did, honey. It took quite a while for me to see. Of course, it was while we were still in Utah, and the heavens were not yet opened like they are today. But, it took me a long time, and much prayer and fasting to see with new eyes."

"What is the difference between here and Utah? Why are these marvelous things happening here and now? Why hasn't it always been this way?"

Melody thought for a minute. "I'm not entirely sure, Bonnie, but it has to do with the purity of the people. Even one telestial-minded person in a city can limit these types of spiritual manifestations. As the people collectively grow more righteous, the heavens open in response. In time, we will be ready to walk in the presence of Jesus Christ Himself. In time, there will be a wall around this city so that no unclean thing can enter in. Even one evil or worldly person in such a city would either be burned up by the glory of the Lord, or the Lord would have to depart. That's why the scriptures say that after the New Jerusalem is built, no unclean thing can enter in. Zion will be pure as much by the repentance and obedience of its citizens, as by the fact that those who will not repent will be required to leave."

Bonnie stopped her pacing and turned to her mother. "Oh, Mama, we have to tell everyone! I don't think people realize how wonderful the message of Zion is! We have to warn them. Is it too late to begin now?" she asked in a rush.

"Dear, it's early in the morning. Everyone is asleep."

"*They* aren't!" Bonnie said, pointing to those working on the Temple.

"Oh, they don't need sleep—but I do!" Melody laughed. "Come dear, let's get our rest so we can begin fresh tomorrow."

"I don't think I *can* sleep," Bonnie cried, but unwillingly let herself be led back toward their house, her eyes still upon the heavenly beings.

Melody laughed and gave her a good-night hug. "Everything in its proper order, Bonnie. Sleep now; warn later. Let me give you a warning, though, my darling daughter. You must say nothing of this until you are moved upon by the Holy Spirit to do so. Do you understand why?"

Bonnie stopped, suddenly sober. "Actually, I do. I had that exact thought just come into my heart. The teaching and warning must be done in its proper time, according to the timetable of God. I must wait for the proper moment, which may not come as quickly as I might want."

"That's right," her mother said soberly.

"Have you seen these things for a long time?" Bonnie asked.

"Several years now."

"It must have been very hard to not shout it from the rooftops!"

"It was at first. Now, I know there is a greater joy than shouting it from the rooftops."

"I can't imagine what *that* could be!" Bonnie said in astonishment.

Her mother gave her a kiss on the cheek. "As the Spirit accords, whispering it to someone you love, and watching her heart change as the truth of your words echoes in her soul. That is the greater joy."

Bonnie slid her arm through Melody's and walked with her back into the house, her heart full of joy. "I can see," she said, her eyes sparkling with joy, "that this truly would be the greater joy. Thank you, Mama. Thank you, and thanks be to God!"

"Hurrah for Israel!" Melody said with quiet fervor.

"I still don't think I can sleep," Bonnie giggled as they quietly closed the door behind them.

"Sounds like a good night to spend in prayer," Melody winked at her.

"It does indeed," Bonnie grinned.

Then they climbed up the stairs together, arm in arm.

THE STARS SHALL FALL FROM HEAVEN

Work was well underway on the interior of the temple. The entire interior floor was polished, white marble. Because gold was now plentiful, a six-inch strip of solid gold was laid around the perimeter of every room to set off the white floor. The walls held beautiful scenes carved in relief on the marble. Since there was no electricity, and at the direction of the Prophet, there were no light fixtures. The interior rooms were dark unless lit by lanterns or candles. Without understanding why, each exterior room had a perfectly round stone conduit a foot in diameter leading from the center of each room to the Holy of Holies. Below the large opening in the ceiling of the Holy of Holies would one day hang a large crystal chandelier. For now, work on the innermost rooms proceeded slowly due to the difficulty of working by lamp light.

Through the winter, a project was underway of which few of the Temple workers were aware. A huge kiln had been crafted outside the stone quarry. Its construction was entirely unique in that it was able to fire an object over fifty feet in height and the same in diameter. It had twelve forced-air furnaces around its base, and a circulation system inside to disperse the heat in a uniform fashion.

Just a dozen feet from the kiln a large temporary building was constructed. Inside, a mold of the spire was filled with an unusual mixture of sand, lime, crushed stone, flux and diamond and gold powder. The design was kept secret by guards day and night. Once the mold and mixture was dry, it was covered in an outer plaster several feet thick. The whole object was dried for weeks and moved on rollers into the kiln. It barely fit inside. It took one week to bring the kiln up to temperature. The services of two-hundred men and women were needed around the clock to stoke the mighty furnaces and run the blowers. Once up to temperature it was held at a steady 2500 degrees for eight hours. Thereafter, it took an additional week to slowly lower the temperature until it returned to normal.

Samuel was present when the doors of the kiln were opened to reveal a shapeless mass fifty feet in height and nearly that wide across the base. It was slowly, laboriously rolled out into the daylight. Its weight was massive, and caused the heavy planks laid for the rollers to groan and sink into the soil. Its surface was covered with gray ash.

Workmen began chipping away the exterior shell. When they first caught a glimpse of what was inside the shell, a cry of wonder arose from all present. Work proceeded quickly to reveal a crystalline structure of such surpassing beauty as to boggle the mind. Its appearance was glass-like, though not transparent. If one had to ascribe some color to it, one would be forced to pick opalescent white with a shimmer of gold. Anywhere light hit the structure it caused a shimmering rainbow of colors which appeared alive within it.

What was even more astonishing was the impossible delicacy of the structure. It was artwork of divine origin, more beautiful and astonishing than any masterpiece before produced on earth. Thousands of intricate curves, fluted columns, spirals and shapes too numerous to catalogue formed a colossal monument to the glory of God. And, this was only the base of the great spire. Even those who had shaped the model according to the plans were astounded at what had been created.

A month later, the upper section rolled slowly from the kiln. Formed in the exact design of the base, it was just as stunning, delicate and fragile in appearance. The final spire was a mere twelve inches in diameter and gracefully ended in a small platform upon which the twenty-ton Angel Moroni was to stand for all time. It was unthinkable, impossible and bizarre to even attempt to put the massive statue atop such a slender and delicate pedestal. Yet, it was the way the very creator of the earth designed it, and His children labored with absolute faith.

All the pieces of the spire were moved to the Temple site on huge wagons drawn by horses. Even if the modern world had used all its machinery and cranes, it would have been a daunting task to move these monolithic monuments to the top of the structure. Today, with little more than muscle power and faith, it should have been impossible. Yet, a stair-stepped ramp was built of scrap lumber that rose steeply from the ground to the roof. Another rose from the roof to the base of the spire. One hundred forty-four men and women, twelve from each of the tribes of Israel, stood around the glittering spire base.

On a signal, and with a shout of praise, they hoisted the spire to their shoulders. To Samuel's eyes, and in fact to many present, they also saw a legion of angels lift at every point and protrusion of the great spire. Less than an hour later it was situated atop the temple, spanning the opening above the Holy of Holies. Before lunch the ramp was expanded, and shortly thereafter, the upper spire was in place. A set of ladders was leaned against the spire and a dozen workers, and a thousand angels, carried the

Angel Moroni to its resting place atop the spire. They set it in place to a shout of "Hosanna!" that echoed across the valley for miles.

"Sisters, brothers—look at the windows!" a cry arose. Samuel turned his eyes toward the windows of the temple and gasped at a bright glow coming from every opening. A concourse of people filed slowly up the steps and into the partially-completed inner rooms. Each was lit by a column of light that seemed to pierce the darkness like a laser beam from the hole in each ceiling.

When Samuel arrived at the door of the Holy of Holies, he had to raise his arm to shield his eyes from the bright light. The room was ablaze with light so intense that the doors had to be closed to shield the mortal eyes among them from destruction. The great glass spire seemed to collect the power of the sun, rather the very power of the Son, and bring it undiminished into that holy room. From there, the light passed through the system of conduits to each room. In time, when the crystal chandeliers hung in each room, they would catch and disperse the celestial light into the rooms. The temple was, in fact, to be lit by the power of God.

From that day on the interior rooms were lit, and work within the temple progressed with accelerated speed. Gold was brought in abundance and lovingly laid according to the plans. Wearing protective clothing and goggles to shield their eyes from the brightness, workers covered the divinely designed floors and walls of the Holy of Holies with gold an inch thick. The circular column in the ceiling was overlaid with silver, inlaid with gold.

Even though the temple was not yet dedicated, and in reality mortals could enter the room that would one day be the holiest place on earth, it was nevertheless blocked off and guarded. This was done as much to protect some innocent from being blinded by the sheer brightness inside, as to begin its transition to the purity that must exist in order for the very God of heaven to dwell there.

The Holy of Holies itself was circular with seven broad steps leading to a raised platform exactly twelve feet in diameter. A throne of pure gold with white luminous cushions was constructed in the exact center of the platform, directly below the spire. Below this, on the next lower level, were twelve smaller thrones facing outward. Six positioned on the left side of the room, and six on the right. The next three levels were unoccupied. The sixth step held twelve altars facing the center of the room, again with six on each side. Each had dazzling white cushions upon which to kneel. In golden letters the names of each of the tribes were inscribed upon the altars. On the lowest level stood a large altar also with padded top. It had a padded ledge upon one side, sufficiently large for three people to kneel.

A veil of very thin material hung between this altar and the only door leading into the room. The veil had no openings in its fabric, and could only be passed by walking to the right or left around its ends. The veil would never be parted accidentally, so that some unprepared individual might inadvertently glimpse its inhabitants, and thereby be destroyed in the flesh. Though the veil was almost as translucent, once the glorious light was upon it, it was as impossible to see through as stone.

Every element of the temple had deep significance. The plans specified every design, every minute detail, every element of every part of the temple. The entire structure was a profound testament to the glory of God.

Scriptures were rendered in gold-overlaid stone. The murals on the ceiling of the Celestial Room contained prophecies of the entire future of the world. The trim around the doors leading into the Celestial Room contained the keys to entering the presence of God while in mortality. The patterns in the carpets taught concerning the earth and the eventual purification it would receive to become a great Urim and Thummim. The symbolic patterns woven into the veil of the temple spoke eloquently of the laws governing the veil separating men from God.

The chandeliers in each room were layered testimonies concerning the order of heaven, the government of God as it exists in heaven, and the place of mortal man within it. To understand the total significance of a single chandelier in that building would be to understand more than God had ever before revealed concerning the order of His eternal dominion. It was the first time that a glimpse of the beauty of that kingdom, which would later be called Celestial, had been displayed within the view of mortal man.

There was no detail in the temple that was random or without meaning. For hundreds of generations to come, the children of God would study the truths constructed into its very stone, layered with deeper and deeper meaning, and marvel at the workmanship of God in every age of man. Forevermore, angels would wander its halls, and gods in embryo would ponder its message as they prepare themselves to emulate the very God of all that is.

What was completely unknown to all, including translated angels and mortals, was that an exact duplicate of this structure stood at the heart of the Heavenly Jerusalem, the holiest of all places, the center place of the infinite and glorious Kingdom of God the Eternal Father.

Of course, all these vast and eternal correlations were obscure to the workmen and women who placed them there according to their instructions. Had they known the full meaning of what they crafted, and were able to implement it in their lives, they would have become gods themselves.

It was hard into winter and a light dusting of snow lay across the Missouri landscape as Samuel walked side-by-side with several brethren toward the Temple. It was just growing light, and the sounds of construction were again beginning to fill the air. It was cold enough that Samuel could see his breath. The brethren beside him were shivering and walking briskly to warm up. Without electricity, the only way to heat their homes was by burning wood or coal. Few homes were equipped to do so, and families spent their days and nights bundled up in all the clothing they possessed. Even though they were warm enough and had plenty to eat, there were problems with pipes freezing and other issues endemic to cold weather. Still, the joy of Zion was constantly upon them, and while they struggled with the affairs of their lives their voices were raised in frosty shouts of joy.

Four of the buildings forming the spokes of the wheel of the Temple were complete and in use for administration. It was toward one of these buildings Samuel turned as he parted company with the others. He spent a few minutes gazing at the Temple. Even in the dim light of early morning the spire seemed to contain lightning inside. At last he climbed the steps and entered the Temple. He removed his shoes and slipped on a pair of thick slippers.

President Johnson and most of the others were already seated at the long table. After singing a hymn, and a prayer offered, President Johnson stood.

"Brethren, it is with joy that I stand before you today and announce that we have received further instructions from President Andrews. But before I detail that, I want to introduce Sister Jennifer Evans, and Brother Tom Jamison."

The two people walked into the room, and the brethren stood as they entered. Four young women pulled a cart into the room and then departed, closing the doors behind them. The object on the cart was about the size of a television set and covered with a tarp. It was apparently fairly heavy, as the four who pulled it into the room were straining.

"Sister Evans, why don't you explain what you have brought to show us," Elder Johnson said, his voice taut with suspense, as if he could hardly restrain himself from blurting out the news.

"Actually, the original idea came from Tom," she began. "He came to me because I have a degree in electrical engineering, and together we were able to construct this prototype. I'm going to let him initially explain what it is," she said, and stepped aside.

Brother Tom Jamison was in his early twenties, with light sandy hair and freckles. He was slender to the point of being willowy, and stepped to the end of the table with confidence. "Without telling you the whole story for now, I want to say that this idea just spontaneously occurred to me the other day. I want to give full credit to Jesus Christ for it. Beyond that, it is probably better to just show you than to try to explain what it is." With that he and Sister Evans pulled the tarp from the object.

It was apparent from the first glance that their creation was inside the enclosure of a small refrigerator. Tom opened the door to reveal a device not unlike three cylinders on their sides stacked atop one another. Wires ran from the cylinders to a small control panel above them. Tom flipped two switches and a light came on. Having spent the last several years without electricity this stimulated a cry of amazement from those watching. Jennifer stepped behind the device and set an electric heater on top. Tom flipped a switch on the heater and the coils quickly turned red. A flood of warm air swept across the room.

"It's an electric generator. It functions on a completely unique principle. The process is actually very complex, but the Lord guided our efforts every step of the way. It uses the earth's magnetic field to produce electricity in the coils. In order to build this machine we had to first create a super-conductor which functioned at room temperature. That was the real triumph, and was only possible through God. Once we had that, it was simply a matter of constructing this device."

"What is the fuel it runs on?" President Johnson asked.

"There is no fuel," Jennifer answered. "It is like an electric generator that uses the earth itself as the armature. As long as the earth keeps spinning on its axis, the coils will continue to produce electricity. That's the best we can explain it at this time. It has no moving parts and a generator with three coils like this one would be sufficient to heat an average home. It is entirely safe and will run indefinitely if not overloaded."

"It is a gift from God," Tom concluded humbly.

There was an audible gasp from everyone in the room. "How difficult are they to make?" Samuel asked incredulously.

“Not hard, given the Lord’s instructions,” Tom said. “The hardest part is making the super-conductor wire. We have set up a small shop to produce it already. We should be able to produce about two generators a week at first, more as we get geared up. We hope to have one of these machines attached to every home in Zion before the winter is over.”

President Johnson spoke next. “We are going to use the first few out in the tent cities. They are suffering from the cold more than those in homes. The next few will go to essential services such as refrigeration at the food stores. The next ones will come to the Temple to provide heat and light in the outer buildings. Then we will begin fitting them to businesses, and finally homes.” He surveyed their excited faces with a grin. “Can I see a show of hands for all who approve this action?”

A hearty vote of approval followed. The two young inventors left the heater running and departed, smiling broadly. Even with his inability to experience discomfort from the cold, Samuel felt a thrill of physical pleasure as his body accepted the welcome warmth.

He paused and breathed deeply. “Now, Brethren, we have a far more pressing matter.” All eyes turned from the heater back to their leader. “President Andrews, our Prophet, has given us an instruction from the Lord that must also be interpreted as a warning. He has instructed us to call twelve groups of twelve faithful priesthood holders. They are each to travel one mile from the Temple in every direction north, south, east, west, and equally spaced between those positions, until they form a two-mile perimeter around the Temple. We are to bring all our people within that two mile circle.”

“What does it mean?” someone asked.

“President Andrews did not say. But, he did say we must have these brethren in place by tomorrow evening.” This brought a rumble of anxious comment from the brethren. “Please, Brethren, your attention still. I have here a list of twelve men from this body who will preside over one of the groups. You are to call and have set apart the other eleven in your group and depart tomorrow morning.” Again a flurry of comments and questions arose, all of which President Johnson ignored.

“Brethren, I was also instructed on a matter of utmost sacredness. Each member of these groups will be given an additional priesthood power under my own hand. Up until now the Lord has graciously given us the spiritual Priestly power of the Melchizedek Priesthood. As such we have been authorized to administer in all matters of the kingdom and establishment of Zion.”

"The Lord has now authorized the transferal of the Kingly powers of the Melchizedek Priesthood. You will recall that in the Temple we are promised that we shall become Priests and Kings, Priestesses and Queens unto the Most High God. Today these brethren, in connection with their worthy wives, are to be given the fullness of the Priesthood with power to command the elements. Brethren, the times are upon us when we will defend Zion with pillars of fire. It is a great and terrible day. Let me read the names the Lord has chosen to preside over these groups," he said, and began to read.

Samuel's name was sixth on the list of leaders to be called. Immediately his mind began to fill with names of the eleven others in his group. He pulled a scrap of paper from his pocket and began jotting names as quickly as they came to him. He was pleased to see his oldest son, Sammy, his stepsons Theo and George, son-in-law Steve, and many from Alexei's people—Vladimir among them.

The following morning before the sun arose, Samuel, Melody and all those with them were assembled inside the temple to be set apart. The faithful priesthood holders with their wives waited reverently for their opportunity to be set apart, beginning with those called to preside. It was a marvelous gathering, and the Holy Spirit rested powerfully upon them. When the time came, Samuel took a seat before President Johnson who placed his hands upon his head.

"My beloved brother, Samuel Nephi Mahoy. By virtue of the holy Priesthood of God, I lay my hands upon your head and in accordance with your special calling by the Savior Himself, I give you the authority to confer the fulness of the Melchizedek Priesthood, which grants the power to command the elements and the earth according to the will of God in defense of His people."

"Great has been your service in Heavenly Father's name. You have been faithful in all things wherewith you have been charged. Now, lead in the defense of Zion. Let your faith be absolute, and you shall rejoice in this great opportunity to serve God. Though this profound power has not been exercised upon the earth by mortals since the days of the great Nephite Prophets, the keys have been held by every prophet and apostle since the Prophet Joseph, to be exercised at this time and those with the special calling you now bear."

"You have been privileged to hold this holy commission once again in this era. In time, this power will become commonplace. Today, it is unique and glorious, and it has been your privilege to be among the first to call upon this great power of God in this latter-day dispensation. Teach those you lead how to exercise this great gift. By your example shall Zion survive, or perish. In the name of Jesus Christ, Amen."

Samuel stood from the chair a little stunned. Even though he had exercised this great power many times since his translation, the authority to confer it to others was profoundly humbling to him. He knew he must have absolute trust in God as the safety or destruction of Zion depended upon his example. He smiled, embraced President Johnson and quickly departed to find the other brothers and sisters on his list.

It was not surprising that Vladimir was waiting for him at his home when he returned. He quickly explained and gave Vladimir half his list. They parted in search of the others. By late evening they had all had been found. All humbly accepted the call. Without exception, they derived courage from the fact that Samuel would lead them. With increasing certainty Samuel knew the words President Johnson had pronounced in the blessing to be profoundly true. If his faith was not sufficient to exercise this priesthood power, neither would theirs be. It was a burden more weighty than any he had known before.

It was a unique and unsettling idea, that even as a translated being, it would require all the faith he possessed to act in this new mission. His heart called out in mighty prayer, seeking strength he did not have. Even knowing he could not experience hunger, and in fact did not require food at all, he began a fast for the first time in almost a dozen years. To his surprise, his stomach knotted in a spasm of hunger. It was not painful, but it was sufficient to constitute a fast, and he rejoiced.

Samuel joined President Johnson in conferring the fullness of priesthood power upon each of the others. Samuel's group was assigned the area due east. With a strange foreboding hanging in the air, they set out before daylight the following morning and bid farewell to their loved ones and friends. By the time they departed all in Zion knew the time had come, and with one accord, they entered into a united fast and began crying unto the Lord with great faith for their safety.

After mighty supplication, the brothers and sisters walked the short mile to their assigned location. They stopped in a subdivision of middle-class homes and took up station in the center of the street. Others passed their group headed further east to spread the word of warning to gather into the circle of safety. By noon people were streaming past them, carrying bundles of their possessions.

The first indication of a threat to Zion came suddenly above them with such savageness that no one, including Samuel, was prepared. As evening approached it did not grow dark. It seemed as if the sun were rising in the east even as it was setting in the west. They watched with astonishment as a bright ball of light rose in the eastern sky. When they could actually see the source of the light it was immediately apparent that this was not the sun, nor the Son of God. It was some massive object approaching the earth, about a third the size of the moon in the sky, growing larger and larger by the minute. Samuel and his small group watched in awe as the celestial body entered the upper atmosphere. As it approached it suddenly burst into a fiery ball too bright to look at directly.

Panic filled his bosom as Samuel realized the magnitude of this calamity. The doom that was quickly approaching had the potential of wiping out all life upon the earth, let alone destroying Zion. Quelling his momentary panic, he fell to his knees and fervently petitioned his God, crying with all his energy for understanding and direction. He waited for the familiar feeling of calm to wash over him, and when it did not, he increased his strivings. He heard several of his group cry out in fear as if from a great distance away. He looked up into the eleven frightened faces surrounding him.

"My dear brethren and sisters, kneel with me in prayer. God will deliver us," he said, and with his own words, knew they were true. "When the moment comes, we will know what to do, and we will be spared. Until then, we wait upon the Lord. Have faith, and be at peace," he instructed, receiving a witness again that these words were profoundly true. Though his heart was pounding in his chest, an element of certainty settled upon him. Not the peace he had prayed for, but it was a beginning.

Samuel looked into the sky to see the great ball of fire streaking toward them. It was difficult to tell where it might impact. Though it appeared much larger, it was several miles across, but decreasing in size. Slowed by the atmosphere it broke into several pieces as it continued its westerly path, then arched away from them, turning slightly north. In what seemed to be an acceleration of its speed, it quickly fell out of sight.

"We are saved!" someone in his group cried.

"Not yet," Samuel said with absolute surety. He stood up from praying, as did all the others. Within seconds they felt more than heard the first wave. The earth trembled violently beneath their feet. Then, as if someone had shaken a huge rug, the ground started convulsing far away to the east. Within thirty seconds, all could see debris as large as houses being thrown into the air as the deadly earthquake approached in slow motion.

"Brethren, bring your arms to the square," Samuel said as the peace he had so earnestly sought finally swept through him. They did as he instructed. "In the name of Jesus Christ, by the power of His mighty priesthood, and through the merits, mercy and grace of Messiah, I command you to pass beyond us," he said in a quiet, commanding voice. The approaching wave of destruction rolled onward for another five seconds, then suddenly submerged. They felt it rumble far below their feet. They would learn later that it emerged about one mile beyond the temple and continued on its path of destruction. It again submerged just outside the Utah valleys, and appeared again beyond the Rocky Mountains. When it hit the coasts of California and Oregon, it had fanned out and picked up a 500-mile strip of the western coast at the fault lines, rolling it into the sea. Ocean water rushed in to fill the sudden void.

It would not be known until years later that the asteroid had fallen three miles off Long Island, New York. The resulting shock had lifted the ocean floor a mile from shore and rolled it atop the desolate cities all along the Eastern coast. Years later when people finally went to investigate the damage wrought, there was nothing but wilderness with no trace of mankind ever having been there.

"Praises be to God," one of the sisters cried out when it became apparent that they had been spared. The cry was echoed by all, and redoubled by the thousands within the two mile circle of safety.

"It is not over," Samuel said quietly. He did not know why he had said that until the sky grew dark in the east. It was a massive shockwave consisting of a dense cloud of sea water, mud and debris. It was potentially more devastating than the quake in that it could render the land uninhabitable for years, and darken the sun so crops could not grow for decades.

Without being told, all twelve couples faced the cloud now close enough they could clearly see flashes of lightning on its surface. It boiled toward them like the fist of Satan, accompanied by a continuous roll of thunder. They raised both arms over their heads.

"In the name of Jesus Christ, let the winds blow, and the mighty hand of God turn aside the destruction of the wicked, for there are no wicked here," they all cried in unison. It was the first time Samuel had heard twelve people speak an entire phrase as one, through divine inspiration. A thrill of faith and peace surged through him. A mighty wind instantly began to blow at his back, which struck the approaching cloud with great force, causing the approaching cloud to rear up like a charging horse thrashing its hooves.

After a moment the wind continued just above the level of the trees. They watched the titanic forces battle for a long moment. Finally, the great storm parted, and passed on either side of Zion. They watched in calm wonder for many minutes as the winds continued to part the tide of destruction. For weeks thereafter the winds blew until the threat was gone. While all around them the land languished in darkness, the city of Zion was bathed in the warmth of sunshine.

Everywhere but in Zion and her sister cities, day after day further destruction from the sky rained down. Some days the asteroids were small and numerous and burned up in the atmosphere. Others were huge and struck the earth with great destructive power. During that time the priesthood of God stood guard along their perimeter which was expanded to five miles from the Temple, and nothing harmed their tranquility. It was a time of intense wonder for all, including Samuel. Miracles of divine intervention became so commonplace that people lived in a constant state of rejoicing. It was the greatest day of miracles ever wrought by the hand of God upon the earth since its very creation.

When Samuel and the other brethren walked away from their posts that day, the danger from this assault was past, and their faith in God was absolute. Where once they had trembled before the titanic forces of destruction, now they strode away in the humble majesty of Kingly Priesthood power.

A phenomenon no one had anticipated was that a few television stations continued to broadcast news of world events. How they had survived could only be described in terms of divine intervention, for every part of every continent, east or west, was one continuous scene of destruction.

As electricity became available in some homes, and with the widespread use of generators, pockets of people around the world availed themselves of these daily broadcasts to hear of the condition of the nations. What they reported was appalling and distressing to watch, for it chronicled the collapse and destruction of the entire fabric of society.

Unknown to the Saints was the fact that the remnants of the United States Army persisted in its involvement in the war. This was only possible because of the huge store of arms they had cached all over the globe prior to the collapse of the US economic base. Even though every notable nation in Europe and England had largely been overrun by Chinese and Russian forces, the tiny nation of Israel was yet intact in spite of relentlessly being under attack. This was so because nearly every western nation on earth saw tiny Israel as the only toe hold in the Middle East, and pressed every resource at their disposal into its defense. From the shreds of information the news media reported, it was apparent this resistance to the Ruso-Sino juggernauts was temporarily effective.

Also startling was the now apparent fact that the Russian push across Europe had been for the sole purpose of attacking England. For reasons every future history book recorded, Russia considered it a moral duty to destroy the British Empire and the vast system of world banking that had so long held the Communist nations in chains of poverty. Their assault on England was single-minded in its ferocity. They cut a ten-mile wide path of total obliteration from the English Channel to London, where their fury spent itself in destroying everything associated with culture, government and banking. Needless to say, the British Royalty ceased to exist—nor would it ever rise again.

It had taken the Russians and Chinese six years and six months to conquer England and its allies. Immediately after those days the war changed dramatically. The Soviets unexpectedly withdrew most of their forces from every conquered land except for vast tracts of Eastern Europe. Now that they were completely purged there of their former enemies, the agreement was that China would send wave after wave of Chinese to settle the land. Just as startling as this withdrawal was the fact that they left behind nearly half of their military hardware. At first everyone thought this an oversight, or some concession to local sovereignty. It was perhaps the most pernicious act the Russian-Chinese forces had perpetrated to date, and was born of Satanic brilliance.

Crazed by prolonged war, failing economies and the incalculable death count, the inhabitants of these lands picked up those weapons and began carving out little empires for themselves in hopes of securing some peace. Instead of gaining any security, they created a feudal system of small city-states jealous of every neighbor's holdings. The war that ensued was far more terrible than the former threat, in that families were divided by the happenstance of their physical locality. A prolonged war of father against son and mother against daughter ensued, ignited by a universal hatred that seemed to know no bounds.

This withdrawal of the Russian and Chinese armies from most of the Middle East and Europe dropped the checkered flag on the race to finally conquer Israel. With one accord the remnants of the nations of Islam united, picked up the scattered pieces of their armies, and attacked Israel with demonic fury. Faced by a far more determined assault than the Chinese or Russians had ever brought, the combined forces of the defenders of Israel were pounded back to within their own borders.

Their hatred was fanned to white-hot intensity by the recent removal of the Dome of the Rock, and the nearly-completed reconstruction of the Third Temple described by the prophet Ezekiel. The desecration of Islam's holy shrine fanned their hatred, and it simply was not possible for them to wage war any more violently. If anything, the assault waned briefly as the collective spirit of Islam mourned what they considered an irreconcilable spiritual loss.

On the American continent a similar, though different, dynamic occurred with the end of Russian and Chinese aggression. As if orchestrated by an invisible commander, the nation fractured overnight into a dozen tiny nations. Florida combined with Cuba to form New Cuba. The Confederate States of Texas retained Texas, Louisiana, Oklahoma and Arkansas.

South Carolina reformed the Confederate States of America upon lines almost identical to those of the South during the Civil War. What was left of the destroyed eastern seaboard above New York was annexed by the new Canadian nation of Quebec. The former states of Utah, Idaho, parts of Nevada, Colorado and Wyoming formed into the self-proclaimed state of Deseret, with allegiance to their newly-elected Congress convened in Salt Lake City.

Previously conquered by the South American Liberation Army, California, parts of Nevada, Arizona and New Mexico split with their mother countries and formed the nation of New Mexico. Immediately upon this defection, a war commenced between this new nation, and their South American motherland.

Under these circumstances it was hardly unexpected when each new nation-state began sending ambassadors to Zion in former Jackson County, at first inviting, then demanding Zion's political union with each new nation. Because of the central geographic location of Missouri, and because it was intact and completely undamaged from recent events, it soon became the hub of anxiety among the new nations. They reasoned that whoever controlled the powerful state of Zion controlled the corridor to either annex other non-aligned states, or to defend against aggression from the other nations vying for the vast resources and fertile farmlands of central United States.

Every offer was politely refused. Every refusal brought a myriad of threats for speedy retaliation. As the pressure mounted, only one question remained: Would this Zion be righteous enough to maintain independence of every nation on earth, or would this generation falter?

The faithful knew that glorious answer.

A NEW DAY OF PENTECOST

It was never clear how President Andrews came to Zion—the New Jerusalem. All most knew was that he was suddenly there. It was a great joy to have the living Prophet among them at last. Somehow, Zion had been incomplete prior to his arrival. From that day onward he would remain in Zion. A special conference was scheduled for the sixth of April, only one week away.

Upon arriving in Zion, President Andrews immediately asked to see Alexei. President Johnson had inquired among his aids to find out who Alexei was. When he learned that Alexei was the leader of the Levites from Russia, he sent word immediately. When the worthy Levites arrived, men and women alike came with Samuel, carrying with them their sacred records in their carved wooden box.

Introductions were hardly over when President Andrews asked to see their scriptures, a note of anticipation in his voice. Alexei carefully presented the leather volume to the oracle of God. President Andrews removed the book with reverence and sat it upon the table. After studying the cover he said, "The Book of Levi."

"Is that what it's called?" Alexei asked excitedly.

"Can't you read English?" the Prophet asked casually.

"It's not written in English," Samuel said in reply.

"It's not... ?" he began, then sobered. "Forgive me. This is my first experience with ancient scripture, and I'm afraid I did not recognize the gift when it came. Of course it's not in English; yet to my eyes the words are as legible as if they were, though I can plainly see they are another language."

President Andrews's eyes filled with humble tears, and he silently gave thanks to his beloved Father. "Brothers and sisters, take a seat, and let me read you a page or two."

They found seats as best they could while President Andrews studied the words of the ancient scripture before him. He glanced up, and satisfied that everyone was comfortable, he slowly began. A scribe sat to his left and transcribed every word.

"The record of the People of Omish, children of Levi, sons of Moses, who were taken captive into Babylon during the reign of Nebedkenezer, king of Babylon. Written by the hand of Karush, servant of the prophet of God whose name was Issac ben Jacob, who was born in captivity in

Babylon one-hundred and twelve years following the defeat and fall of Jerusalem by the hand of the Babylonians."

"Praise be unto the God of Israel, and the hope of our salvation. Glory be to him, and to his son, Jesus Christ the Messiah, who according to our faith, and the words of our prophets, must come and be born of a virgin at Jerusalem in the meridian of time."

"We know by these words that in a future day some of our seed will return to Jerusalem and build it up again. But, we also know that our house will not be among those to fulfill this prophecy. For, we know by the word of God that we will be gathered unto a strange land, there to dwindle in quietude and oppression until the fullness of times are fulfilled, and we are called home to Zion, where we will build an holy city, a New Jerusalem, to our Savior, there to meet him at his return in Glory. This because of our continued faith, the former sins of this people, and the will of God in keeping our blood unpolluted that in the last day there may be those of the house of Levi to offer up again a righteous offering unto the Lord . . ."

It was late into the night when President Andrews's voice grew hoarse, and he had to stop. Rather than invite them back for further readings, he promised to work diligently to complete the work of translation of these sacred words scribed to paper where they could be had by all.

As Samuel escorted Alexei and Vladimir and their people back to their tents, the aged Russian walked slowly, his head lowered to his chest. Every now and then he would break his own silence by sighing deeply.

"Tell me what is in your heart," Vladimir asked his uncle.

"It is a glorious thing, what we have just heard. Did you hear that the first words of our scripture proclaim Jesus Christ to be the Son of God?"

"I did. I surely did," he allowed.

"Our people have awaited this glorious day for 2,600 years, and we are alive to see its fulfillment. It is a glorious day!" Alexei proclaimed.

"Praise God!" Vladimir rejoiced as they embraced.

"Praise God!" Samuel agreed, and the unseen keepers of truth seemed to cry in response, "Hallelujah!"

Springtime in Zion was joyful. The breezes were warm, the rains gentle and nourishing. Flowers were profuse and trees and grasses grew lush green. It was April 6th, the day of the special general conference called by President Andrews. A large tent would serve as their meeting place. No room inside the Temple was large enough to house the tens of thousands who wished to attend. A mediocre but competent sound system had been engineered, powered by generators outside the tent. A little ingenuity formed Zion's first television station, and the conference was broadcast in Zion, and in Utah.

Like a new day of Pentecost, the Spirit of the Lord was poured out in profuse abundance. The choir was angelic in its worship and praise, and the conference proceeded with outpourings of truth never before taught in such plainness.

A breathless hush fell across the vast assembly no matter where they were, as their now-aged prophet stood to address them. It was apparent that he had no prepared text, as he gripped the sides of the pulpit and gazed out into the throng.

"Such a righteous assembly of God's Kingdom has never before occurred, my beloved brothers and sisters of Zion," he began, his voice rich with emotion. "Those of you who choose to see with spiritual eyes, will note that the enormous numbers of people here is insignificant to the number of those from the spiritual realm. The heavens are opened, and the union between God's people and His very presence is nearly complete. In a not far-distant day the very Lord of Heaven and Earth will come to His Temple, and we will at last be one!" he proclaimed with fervor. The crowded whispered excitedly, and he waited for a hush to fall over them again.

"This is the era of time that every prophet of every age saw in vision, and yearned to participate in. This is the time. This is the place. This is the dawning of the Millennium. My brothers and sisters, and beloved from the unseen world, as the mouthpiece of God, I declare this day as the beginning of the thousand years of peace the world has awaited since the days of the Garden of Eden. Let all history record this day as the day upon which it began. Let the heavens burst open and rejoice; let the people shout for joy; let all creation witness the glory of God that shall soon cover the world as the waters cover the ocean floor. Rejoice, oh ye people of God, rejoice! I say, for today is that day of days! I proclaim this people Zion, the pure in heart! And I proclaim this land the City of the Living God! This day is the beginning of the Kingdom of God in its fullness upon the earth.

"Let every voice cry Hosanna!" The combined voices of men and angels echoed the words in such jubilation that the very ground beneath their feet trembled, and choirs of angels sang in anthems heard by all.

Then a long silence of nearly a full minute fell upon them, as joy too full to be expressed with words burned in their souls. Finally, his eyes moist and flowing, President Andrews looked across all assembled. "Let me here observe that the millennial reign of peace shall in the beginning rest only upon this blessed valley, and the everlasting hills of our pioneer home.

 Elsewhere wars still rage, and the hearts of men are cold and hateful. They will come with their armies thinking to take away our lives, our homes, and our peace. Yet, as long as we are the pure in heart, the Captain of our souls will fight our battles! We will stand in the robes of the holy priesthood upon the hills and the plains, and call upon the very elements to defend us. If necessary, we will call down pillars of fire to consume them, and send them back into their own lands."

His voice grew strong. "But, my dearly beloved, beloved family, this is not all. Even while they try to destroy us we will send our missionaries forth, armed with the full power of God to call them to repentance. These gloriously-arrayed missionaries shall sweep across the face of the whole earth one last time. Into every land on this globe they shall teach and baptize and invite all of God's children to Zion. For only in Zion, and her Stakes, shall there be peace. Against those who reject or who molest God's chosen messengers, they shall dust off the soles of their feet as a witness against them, and their destruction shall be swift and sure."

The prophet cleared his throat, speaking again with renewed clarity. "From among the Quorum of the Twelve, the finger of God has identified two who will dwell in Jerusalem, there to stand between the armies of Satan, and the children of His ancient covenant, as prophecy has long indicated they would. This very day they arrive there and begin their ministry of mighty works among our long-embattled Jewish brothers in Jerusalem.

The entire congregation sat up with anticipation. "With these words I hereby call twelve thousand high priests and priestesses from every tribe of Israel to assemble as quickly as possible, and to depart into every part of the world to glean the fields. You shall go two by two, without purse or script, without two coats, or two pairs of shoes. You shall go in the power of God, by the power of God, and shall be His instruments to call a world back from the very brink of destruction. The borders of every nation are down, and you shall go unhindered wherever the voice of God sends you."

The President raised his arms in magnificent gesture. "You may well ask, 'How shall we go?' seeing that all transportation has been destroyed by the unholy war still raging upon the face of the land. There are no ships upon the sea, and no airplanes in the air. There are but few automobiles and busses and trains that function. I will tell you how you will go. You will go in the power of God. Each of you shall fast and pray, and fall upon your faces before God until you shall hear His voice assigning to you that part of His vineyard wherein ye shall labor. Thereafter ye shall arise and simply walk in that direction, no matter if a great ocean separates you from your destination; and before many days, and perhaps in the blink of an eye according to your faith, you shall be there. From city to city shall you thus go, and from house to house. We have but a short time to bear this final witness to the children of God."

His voice lowered to a reverent whisper. "Your voice will act as a final testimony against the wicked. You will know when it is right to raise a person from the grasp of the grave, and you will know when it is not. Understand that you shall sorrow for the nations and people you serve. It will tear at your very heartstrings. Yet, you will have brought to the land of Zion and to the valleys of the Everlasting Hills, all those whose names the Lord has written in His Book of Life. When you have found, taught and purified those cut from Celestial cloth, you, my glorious brothers and sisters, shall bring them home. Bring them by the power of God! Take them two from a field, and one from the stall, and three from a family, and ten from a village. Bring them home to receive their blessings in Zion!"

His words rang with intensity. "Yes, we will go in haste! We will not, however, return in haste. It will be a gathering of many years. You will bring the children of God home upon your shoulders and in your arms singing the sacred songs of Zion. After your testimony comes the testimony of unquenchable fire, according to the will of the Great Jehovah."

"You shall not go to the heathen nations until after the Lord comes in Glory. Neither shall you any more than lightly pass over the nations of the Gentiles, as a final witness. But to the house of Israel outside the nation of Israel shall you go, preaching Christ, and Him crucified, and risen again the third day. Those you teach and prepare will largely be the Jews, the members of Christ's true Church who have lived faithful to their covenants, and those of other denominations who have dedicated their lives to Christ. We shall not teach anyone else."

Now his voice rose until it was almost a shout. "Unto those of faith shall you show forth mighty miracles, raising the dead, healing the sick, and causing the blind to see. Unto those with no faith shall you turn away. You shall go to teach, not to be taught. You shall not debate or convince by logic, neither shall you pause to persuade. But, those who can hear, will hear, and all others shall you leave without comment or explanation, for in the few days wherein we may glean the fields, we must hurry before the storms of winter begin."

The congregation was still, listening to one another breathe with pounding hearts at the divine message. "I say unto you this day in the hearing of the eternities, that this is the last time the Gospel of the Kingdom shall be preached on this earth before the Lord comes again in His glory. I declare that the times of the Gentiles are fulfilled, and from this day onward we turn our faces to the lost family of Israel. Thus let it be recorded in heaven.

"This I say in the name of Jesus, the very Christ, the Messiah, the great I AM, Amen!" he cried.

A mighty "Amen!" arose from the collective voices of the righteous of every age. In response, the very hills and valleys of Zion trembled with joy.

President Andrews remained at the pulpit, his hands shaking, his eyes raised toward heaven. After a moment, he looked out across the tens of thousands assembled to hear his words. He smiled lovingly down at them, and spoke again.

"It occurs to me that we have one other task to complete. Before the first missionaries leave to return with the children of God riding upon their shoulders, we must first dedicate the main building of this glorious Temple. It is now almost complete except for many furnishings we must still construct. All systems have been installed and are functioning as designed." He paused and continued with a little irony in his voice. "We don't fully understand what some of those systems are for, but they do seem to be functioning."

The crowd laughed with understanding, since almost all of them had seen or worked on the very systems he was referring to. This technology seemed to have a terrestrial purpose, and its design was remarkable and mysterious. They grew quiet again, and President Andrews continued.

"We will provide the interior furnishings and some trim after it is dedicated, as the Lord instructs. For this reason we will meet in the second floor assembly hall within the Temple at noon this coming Saturday. By that time our faithful technical people, who have in the past blessed our lives with innovative solutions to very demanding problems, will have an even better public address system functioning, or so they tell me." Louder laughter this time.

"In the Temple proper we will request the President of each tribe, and one hundred of their brothers and sisters to be invited by the President, according to instruction by the Spirit. The remainder of your people will meet in the outer temple rim buildings which bear their tribe's name, or upon the spot where that tribe's temple will eventually be built. A representative of the Quorum of the Twelve will be in attendance at each temple wing. This is the pattern for all future meetings. In this way, we will all participate in this and future glorious events. You may believe me when I tell you, this is only the first of many spiritual outpourings such as the world has not known since the city of Enoch was taken to the bosom of God."

His eyes searched the crowd of glowing faces. "Let all who are in favor may manifest it and say Amen!" he called with great fervor.

All arms raised and a single mighty "Amen" again echoed on both sides of the veil.

Several months had passed, and with great fervor and anticipation the Temple had been readied for dedication. The excitement in the air was palpable.

"But Mommy, why can't I go too?" four-year-old Helaman pouted at his mother, who was kneeling to plant a farewell kiss on her son's chubby cheek.

"Because you're not old enough to go to a temple dedication, honey. You have to stay here with your cousins," Melody said matter-of-factly. Then she brightened and ruffled his red hair. "Now don't worry—you're growing like a weed, and soon you'll be as big as Daddy. Then you'll be able to go with us!"

"That's right!" Samuel yelled from the back room. He was laughing as he strode into the living room and snatched little Helaman off the floor, tossing him high into the air. "Hey little Buddy, I think you're getting too big for me to do that much longer!" he said with a wink. He whirled his gleeful son around and around until they were both dizzy, then plunked him safely onto the couch. The boy was giggling so hard that Samuel decided his only recourse was to pull out the big guns.

"Oh no, Buddy," his Daddy warned, his voice low and ominous. "I think I feel some tickles coming on . . ."

"No, Daddy!" Helaman protested in delight.

Samuel's face was deadly serious. "Oh yeah!" Samuel suddenly pulled his hands from his back, tickle fingers flexing menacingly and moving swiftly toward Helaman's round tummy.

"No, Daddy—nooooooo!" Helaman screamed in delight. Finally, Helaman and his Daddy toppled on the couch in one another's arms, laughing hysterically.

Melody was giggling as she watched this exchange. "I sure do love that man of mine," she thought as they were walking together with their older children to the Temple. It would indeed be a day of days.

Samuel, Melody and their family assembled with the others, and could hardly contain themselves in anticipation of what this day of dedication would bring. They had a good view, as they were seated just twenty rows back in the Temple. The room was built after the pattern established in the Kirtland Temple. Both ends of the long hall had a tiered stage with three pulpits on each level. Rows of seats on each level were separated by a breastwork handrail before them. The east end held the presidency of the Melchizedek priesthood, First Presidency and each of the Quorum of the Twelve who had come for this momentous occasion—though the Twelve were presently meeting with the various tribes. The west end was filled with the Presiding Bishopric, and presidency of the Aaronic Priesthood.

On the floor was seating capacity for exactly 2,400 people. These consisted of hand-crafted individual seats which could be lifted and turned around to face either direction. Samuel was quite interested in the fact that the seats were obviously old, and wondered if they had been "borrowed" from some other temple for the occasion. If so, they must have been brought to Zion by the power of God, since no trucking or transportation currently existed anywhere upon the continent.

They sang "Israel, Israel God Is Calling" as the opening hymn, and a choir augmented the singing with a thrilling obligato. There was no piano or organ, and indeed had there been one, it could not have been heard above the voices of the faithful. As they sang, a corridor of light opened on both sides of the eastern pulpits, and a row of men in flowing white robes walked to the seats reserved for the Quorum of the Twelve. These took their places during the song.

As soon as they were in place, another group of twelve men similarly took their places immediately before them. This latter twelve, though also dressed in long white robes, wore a style of clothing noticeably different from the first. Samuel took the occasion, as did many others, to turn and look behind at the Aaronic Priesthood pulpits, which had also been filled with visiting dignitaries from beyond the veil. As they turned again back toward the east, two final beings entered and stepped onto the stage from a corridor of light and took seats to the right and left of the First Presidency. The corridor of light closed and disappeared as they were seated.

Though all these men appeared as tangible as any mortal, they glowed in a way that testified that they were not from this mortal sphere. All assembled saw them. None among them thought it odd or incredible that heavenly beings had appeared. With universal faith, every heart burned with the Holy Spirit in a great outpouring of believing.

President Johnson offered the invocation after which President Andrews again took the highest pulpit.

"Beloved of every age," he began. "Those you see before you may need some introduction. Immediately before me, in the seats normally occupied by the living Quorum of Twelve Apostles, are seated the Twelve chosen by Christ during His earthly ministry. Immediately before them are the Nephite Twelve chosen by the Master shortly after His ministry there in the flesh.

"Seated upon the west podium are various dignitaries from the days of Moses who administered in the offices of the Aaronic Priesthood during their lives. In the highest pulpit are seated Moses, Aaron and Joshua. Before them are dignitaries from various dispensations prior to those times who I shall not introduce by name until they can declare their own dispensation in due time.

"To my right I present a distinguished visitor whom I have had the privilege of laboring with since we arrived in the land of Zion. He was known, and will be known among us, as Brother Joseph, the Prophet of the restoration." Joseph stood, with a smile so broad and genuine that it warmed Samuel's soul.

Brother Joseph was different in appearance than any photos or carvings Samuel had seen. He was, in fact, so much different that without an introduction, Samuel would not have recognized him. What occurred to him at that moment was that Brother Joseph's body was now resurrected, and in the express image of his combined spirit and body, and therefore slightly different in appearance than during his mortality.

After Joseph sat, President Andrews waited for a murmur of excitement to dwindle away.

"To my left, I am pleased to introduce another distinguished guest also instrumental in the establishment of Zion in this dispensation, Brother Brigham Young." A youthful Brother Brigham stood effortlessly and smiled in quiet acknowledgment. He was no longer the rotund man he had been during his mortality, but appeared to be barely old enough for the tightly-clipped beard he wore.

President Andrews continued with vigor. "It is my great pleasure to announce the recent commencement and completion of the great patriarchal council held at Adam-ondi-Ahman." A great murmur of excitement swept across the throng. President Andrews raised a hand for silence. "As the prophet at this time, I was privileged to attend and participate in that great council which took place at the break of day this last April sixth, being one year from our arrival in this valley."

Some actually began to applaud, which quickly died down as President Andrews raised a hand and shook his head.

"It is an understatement to say that the heavens are fully opened once again, and great are our blessings! Behold, my faithful brothers and sisters, behold the men of God seated upon the stands before you. I give you to know that each of these righteous men is a resurrected being. Each of them attended that great council at Adam-ondi-Ahman, and each has been faithful and true, and in time will become gods themselves. Let us give wonder and glory to our God."

The congregation was motionless.

"Let your wonder extend to the profound witness that what they have done, you yourselves are also doing, and in time will inherit alongside those we honor today. Let your wonder extend to praise to our merciful and loving Heavenly Father, and to his beloved Son, our divine Redeemer. All glory to Them! Let us raise a shout of hosanna unto God!

"Hosanna!" President Andrews cried, and the crowd roared back, "Hosanna! Hosanna! Hosanna to God and the Lamb!" they all cried in unison.

It took many minutes for quiet to again fall upon them, for their hearts would not let their tongues be stilled. Many prophesied with voices of joy, many spoke in tongues, and many interpreted what was said. Some among them stared in open awe at visions and heavenly manifestations which only they could see. Samuel thought, "This is truly a Day of Pentecost!"

President Andrews waited until peace settled upon them once again. "Before this day is complete we will see and hear many things. First, Brother Joseph has agreed to address us. This is a glorious and unique opportunity for us!" he said, turning to smile at the Prophet. Then he turned back to the throng.

"Brother Joseph has asked me to instruct you in the new millennial order before he speaks. He also asked me to tell you that he joins us as a guest and by invitation. His dispensation and his stewardship extend beyond the veil, and are in fact never-ending. As much as we honor and love him, he takes no part in the present line of authority as it exists upon the earth today. That authority rests squarely upon my shoulders until I, too, pass beyond the veil."

The congregation nodded in renewed understanding.

"As he speaks to us, every word he says we will receive as counsel and wisdom. But nothing he says will be spoken by way of commandment to our dispensation. Such is true of every other heavenly being here today, and will always be the case. The one exception to this will be when the Lord Jesus Christ Himself appears. He then will govern upon the earth, and we will serve Him, and Him alone."

President looked lovingly upon his waiting friends. "Without further comment, Brother Joseph," he said, and stepped back.

Joseph stood. His was tall, his bearing noble. His hair was a sandy blond and his eyes were piercing blue. He wore a suit of exquisite white, cut in the exact fashion of the days of his mortal experience. He shook President Andrews's hand firmly and stepped to the pulpit. He looked at the microphone suspiciously, then allowed his gaze to sweep across those assembled. A breathless silence fell upon the Saints.

"Greetings, and God's blessings to you all," he said, his voice like an amplified clap of thunder in the large hall. He winced, and then grinned.

"I feel compelled to say, my beloved brothers and sisters, that this is the first time I have spoken using a public address system! It makes me feel like our good Alma over there, whose great wish was to speak with the voice of an angel, like the trump of God unto every people," he said in a voice that echoed loudly through the hall. A ripple of laughter flowed across the room.

Joseph then looked directly at one of the men seated to his left and said, "I believe I will suggest to our friend that he give this a try; it really is quite exhilarating!" This brought louder laughter from the people, and Alma turned in his seat to wave Joseph off with a fond smile.

Joseph grew more serious. "As useful as this technology is which you possess in such abundance, it is nothing, *nothing* I tell you, in comparison to what will shortly come upon you as the blessings of the millennial day quickly unfold before your eyes.

"During its history this nation has blossomed and prospered under the greatest mortal transportation system has ever constructed on this earth. I say to you that in a short time no one will even mention that system, except to hold it in contempt. The days will come when you shall desire to be in a certain place for whatever purpose is in your heart, and you will take one step and be there.

"For many years you have been able to speak and be heard on the other side of the world. As wonderful a missionary tool as this is, the days will shortly come when you shall face an assembly of beings so vast as to fill every square inch of space upon this planet, if they were all present here at once. Every single one of them will be thirsting for the truths you guard in your hearts. You will raise your voices and by the power of God, not by the power of electrons and transformers, you shall address hundreds of thousands—and millions eventually—and they shall clamor for baptism."

The congregation sat in rapt attention, their minds trying to formulate the vision that Brother Joseph was outlining so profoundly.

"The Church of Jesus Christ of Latter-day Saints, before it was torn down and scattered, was adding hundreds of congregations each year. In a short time, you will be adding hundreds of stakes each year. Your biggest challenge will be to teach and train them, and to keep up with the rapid growth of the kingdom. In time, you will cease to build chapels, and will only build Temples, for all will be worthy to enter them and worship there. The Family—a righteous father and a righteous mother who have been sealed under the Holy Spirit of Promise—will be the governing body of the terrestrial world, under Jesus Christ; and you will look to the ecclesiastical Church to receive the priesthood of God and the sacred ordinances."

Melody glanced up at Sam, and he looked at her with a meaningful smile. He squeezed her hand tightly as Brother Joseph continued.

"In a few days the Lord will send 144,000 High Priests and Priestesses into the world to bring the Elect of God to Zion. I say to you that after this great missionary effort, tens of thousands of the Elect of God will come to you, to this very Holy City, every day of the year, seeking the blessings of the House of the Lord."

The excitement at this announcement was palpable, with audible gasps heard from every corner. "You have hitherto built scores of temples. As the Gospel of Christ sweeps the nations of the earth in the not-too-distant future, you will build more Temples than today there are chapels," Joseph said, then fell silent. He gripped both sides of the pulpit and stepped closer to the microphone as if he were about to tell a great secret.

"Why am I telling you this?" he whispered. "Why awaken your minds and hearts to what will shortly come to pass? I will tell you why, it is because President Andrews requested it of me. But, even more importantly, it is because the success of this great work depends entirely upon your faith and obedience in these next few months and years. It has long been the case that God would reveal the fullness of His glorious gospel to worthy people, and those people would slowly drift away and apostatize. It has long been the pattern of mankind that each spiritual blessing is followed by a period of spiritual comfort, then apathy, and then apostasy. It is such a prevailing pattern that you have grown accustomed to it, and even expect it."

He drew a deep breath. "My beloved Saints of the Living God, this must never happen again! Consider the great spiritual height you have achieved by the grace of God. This is the first time such marvelous spiritual manifestations have occurred so ubiquitously since the days of Enoch, and in fact have eclipsed those of that grand era, and my era as well. Consider the fact that scores of resurrected beings are sitting before you now in plain view. This has never happened in the history of the world!"

A thrill went through every soul as they surveyed the glorious models of righteousness seated before them.

"This being so, consider what terrible condemnation would come upon you if you allow yourselves to again fall into apostasy! Consider this, and mark my words—a great warning of God in your ears—know this: that if you ever turn back from these privileges, either in your own lives or as a people, the second coming of Christ will wipe this valley clean of inhabitants, melt this glorious temple to a pile of slag, and erase your names from the Lamb's book of life without a trace."

A few shifted in their seats, but all kept their eyes riveted upon their glowing speaker.

"Then, my friends, when Christ proclaims the work complete, there will be no one left of this great city present to hear His words. He will pass the scepter of His priesthood power to a more worthy people and the days of the Gentiles will truly, ultimately, everlastingly, be ended. Beware! Beware! Beware!" he cried. "I urge you to let nothing call you back into the world. You are now Zion, the pure in heart, and if you falter the whole of creation falters with you!"

He paused for a moment. When he began again his voice was soft.

"As glorious as it was to head the dispensation of the restoration of the Gospel, it was in part a failure. The forces of the evil one nearly succeeded in destroying the work of God before it truly began. What was the weapon the evil one used to nearly destroy us? I will tell you. It was pride. For the pride of our hearts we nearly failed. We came within a breath of losing all God had given us. But for the grace of God, and the labors of faithful Brother Brigham," he said, turning to look Brigham in the eye, "and many others like him, we would have lost our blessings altogether. But, God chose to extend to us mercy that perhaps we did not deserve, and called us out of the jaws of hell, and led us to the Everlasting hills of Deseret where we waited out the days of our divorcement."

A murmur swept across the throng.

"Mark my words, these *have* been days of divorcement. For over two hundred years we have lived under condemnation. This condemnation was nothing more than our own failure to believe what God had promised us. It took these many years for us to awaken our souls to our privilege of building Zion. The timetable of God patiently awaited our awakening to this glory."

His voice shook, and his eyes searched the congregation. "Why were we waiting? Certainly not for God to make up His mind, but for us to become Zion! We, through our pride and apathy, prolonged our days in the wilderness of Deseret that could have, should have been spent in Zion in millennial bliss."

"In some ways our long years in Utah were a refuge—in some ways a blessing, and in some ways a long exile. Had we done what you must now do, we never would have had to made the trek west to Utah. We could have stayed in this very spot, built this very temple, and called in the Millennium upon our heads over two hundred years ago! But the Lord, in His infinite mercy, grace and patience, allowed His people the time they needed to mature into the stature of Zion—all glory to God!"

He stopped short and crouched into the microphone, speaking in a near-whisper.

"I tell you there is one thing that the forces of evil cannot abide, will not tolerate, and upon which they unleash all the unholy power of their fury—and that thing is Zion. You can expect, you *must* expect to become a battle ground. But, this time the Lord will fight your battles, and you will defend your homes and your sacred religion by priesthood power, and Zion will prevail.

"Now, it is your turn to do what we could not," Joseph continued earnestly. "I tell you, I prophesy to you, I warn you in the name of the Living Christ, that the possibility of your failure looms as threatening as it did over us. Choose ye this day that failure shall not occur again. This is the last line of defense. Here we stand firm. Here we set our stakes in the rich soils of righteousness and raise the tents of the tabernacle of God. Here, as never before, do we defy the power of wickedness and for the last time, establish the Kingdom of God! Today is indeed the most glorious day the world has ever known, and we—you and I—are blessed beyond compare to be here."

He let a long silence ensue before continuing. When he spoke again he seemed resigned, and his voice somber.

"There is much more that I wish to tell you which the Holy Spirit directs to postpone until another day. I am sure, now that the veil between the heavens and the Earth is growing thin, that the opportunity to address you again will shortly come."

A new smile played on his lips, and he looked lovingly upon them. "Until then, my dear sisters and brothers, I leave my blessing upon you." He raised his hands high over his head. "I call upon the heavens to open above you. I call down the angels of His presence to guard you and teach you. I pray our Heavenly Father to bless you that your hearts will stand faithful and true in every trial, as I have every confidence and faith they will. In the name of Jesus Christ, Amen!"

A breathless silence answered his "Amen" as Brother Joseph lowered his hands and bowed his head. President Andrews stood and raising a fist into the air, all present cried with him, "Amen! Amen! Hurrah for Zion! Hurrah for Zion!"

The rest of the day was a spiritual ecstasy. When it came time to dismiss, it was nearly six p.m. President Andrews offered the dedicatory prayer. The entire prayer was but a single paragraph, not much more than could be said in several breaths. Yet, it was the most powerful of its kind ever uttered.

"Oh, God, our Heavenly Father. Great and Glorious is Thy Name. Unto Thee do we give all honor and glory, and unto Thee do we dedicate this great house, this holy Temple. Father, for thousands of years have we awaited this profound moment wherein we have built unto Thee a throne upon this earth. We give unto Thee the fruits of our labors, and humbly ask Thee to let Thy glory rest upon it as a pillar of fire by night, and an illuminating cloud by day. Let Thy beloved Son, our Master, take His place upon that throne in His own due time. Henceforth and forever, from this very place let His law go forth to fill the whole world, until His own words are fulfilled wherein he prayed, 'Thy will be done on earth, even as it is in heaven.' In the beloved name of Jesus Christ, Amen."

As the congregation sounded the hosanna shout, a sound like the rushing of a mighty river filled the Temple so that even above the sound of their shouts of praise it was plainly heard. Jesus Christ appeared above the pulpit in His glory, and every soul fell to their knees as they felt His infinite love for them, and His acceptance of the Temple they had worked so hard to build.

Suddenly, across the great throng, the Savior looked directly at Melody as she heard His voice in her mind. "Melody, wait three days, then come to me in my Temple, and bring your righteous Samuel. I will come to you in my glory, and administer the holy gift I promised a lifetime ago I would give you."

Melody was so stunned and delighted that she could only nod. Samuel turned to her and said, "I heard Him too!" He found himself inwardly dancing, for this was the greatest desire of his own heart for Melody, as it was hers as well. They had often spoken of it in reverence.

A moment later, a great ball of light then gathered around the pinnacle of the temple and a beam of light shot from the heavens onto the temple spire, a thousand times more vivid than a shaft of lightning. It reached into the sky as far as the eye of man could behold. So sublimely glorious was this pillar of fire that during the day it affected the air such that a shroud of mist boiled around it, illuminated from inside by the pillar of fire. At night the cloud dispersed, and the fire was visible for a thousand miles. Its brilliance was such that it gave the brightness of midday to the city of God both day and night.

Even though only righteous mortals were at the glorious dedication, not everyone had been given that gift Melody would shortly receive in the Temple. Hence, the Master could not yet walk the streets of His own city in His full glory. Appropriately, a warm blanket of faith-filled desire had laid itself over each soul, so that every member of Zion had turned his or her heart to seeking the greater blessings. It would, in a not far-distant day, become commonplace to meet the Savior of all mankind strolling upon the golden streets of Zion, surrounded in His glory and accompanied by angels, both mortal and otherwise. But that would not occur until every single inhabitant in that great city had received their supernal calling and election, and had been given greater glorious blessings associated with their personal missions.

As they were directed, three days later Samuel escorted his beloved sweetheart to the Temple, where they were thrilled to see Alexei waiting for them in joyful anticipation. After the dear friends embraced and briefly conversed, Alexei solumnly escorted them to the veil of the Temple. After a time, as they emerged through that sacred space Jesus Christ was waiting for them, shining with glory and light. He beamed at her, His blue eyes gleaming with eternal love and delight in her.

Melody gazed into His eyes, and had she not still been clinging to Samuel's arm, she would have fallen to her knees. Instead, she stood looking up at him, for he was nearly a head taller than she, her face glistening with tears.

"Come to me," the Lord said gently, extending his arms to her. In the blink of an eye Melody collapsed into His arms in utter joy. Then she sank to her knees at His feet.

"My God!" she cried out. "My Master! My friend! I remember! I remember you! I have always loved you!"

"And just as wonderfully, I have always loved you!" He replied with equal fervor.

Samuel watched all this with rapture of soul. What was utterly fantastic was that this was a meeting of old friends. There was the inescapable knowledge that Jesus was her Savior, but He was also Melody's oldest and dearest friend. First and foremost, this was a meeting of two people who fiercely loved one another. The Savior's demeanor and words to Melody were of infinite compassion and love.

Whether He held her for seconds or minutes Samuel could not tell. But, when the Savior released her, Melody was different. When she turned to Samuel again, her face full of life, her form was straight and vigorous, her eyes crystal clear and joyful. He caught his breath.

Jesus turned and gently led them toward the Holy of Holies, where His glory suddenly increased and enveloped them. He turned and again gazed deeply into Melody's eyes, and she felt His all-consuming love wash over and through her. Jesus then stretched forth His hand and said, "Look." The room opened to the vastness of creation as Melody was allowed to experience the great vision of all things, and her glorious part in it. Her soul seemed to expand into eternity, and she was enabled to comprehend every detail. She fell to her knees in worship and utter nothingness, now fully knowing for herself that her Heavenly Father, Heavenly Mother, and Jesus Christ are literally in and through all things; that their eternal love permeates every element and creature in the universe.

As she returned to her mortal frame, all she could do was weep, "My Lord, my God. Thank you."

Jesus lovingly raised her to Him and said, "My dearest daughter, what would you desire of me?"

Melody looked intently into His eyes. "Thou knowest what I have desired, Lord."

He smiled at her again, and nodded in acknowledgement of the righteousness of her request. As He placed His eternal hands upon her head, Melody's face became translucent with light as she received the blessing she had most desired in her premortal and mortal life—that of translation. She felt a surge of power and light electrify every cell of her body. The Savior then commissioned Melody in the work of the final gathering Israel and to receive all the powers and authority associated with this divine calling.

Samuel had never felt so much overwhelming joy as he did in that moment, watching his extraordinary companion receive her promised gifts. After the sacred words were spoken, Melody turned to Samuel and with a cry of joy, rushed into his open arms. As he held her, Samuel realized she had transformed into the expression of her glorious premortal self.

Then the Savior's hand reached out and lovingly turned them toward Himself again. They looked up at Him in humility and wonder, questioning what more He might desire. Calling them by name, Jesus Christ spoke these astonishing words:

"My beloved children, I now bind you together, eternally and irrevocably by the Holy Spirit of Promise, and pronounce this blessing upon you and your posterity." Samuel and Melody clung to each other, and wept freely as their merciful Redeemer ordained the fullness of priesthood blessings upon them.

Samuel gazed upon his eternal bride with new eyes, and was astonished to realize he had never truly seen her before this moment.

AND THEY SHALL MAKE WAR AGAINST ZION

The first attack against Zion came one week after the dedication of the Temple. Apparently angered by Zion's refusal to join their nation-state, and the imagined need to control the land upon which the Holy City sat, the Confederate United States, in spite of heavy destructions, gathered an army of thousands just outside the city with heavy weaponry.

There was no warning. Saints were still walking around the Temple rejoicing, when the all-too-familiar scream of an incoming missile rent the air. The computer-guided weapon was targeted upon the great Temple itself. With no warning and no instructions, ten thousand arms came to the square. The shell exploded harmlessly a thousand feet above.

Samuel and Vladimir were the first to see the advancing army. Vladimir had been standing next to Samuel when the shell exploded. The faith-filled Russian turned to his old friend. "Samuel, I could use a lift." So saying, he looped his arm through Samuel's and they started to walk. Except for his beloved wife and Sarah, it was the only time Samuel had taken a mortal with him. It was also the case that he could not transport by the power of God in the view of other people. Yet, there was such an outpouring of pure faith among the people of Zion, that when Samuel turned his mind to the army outside their city, he and Vladimir were instantly standing upon a bluff overlooking a large mechanized army.

"Thank you, my friend," Vladimir said with a smile. "I have been wanting to do that for a very long time," Samuel grinned at him and clapped him good-naturedly on the back. Their faces immediately grew sober as they gazed upon the army. The two men were well within range and bullets began whining past them, kicking up dirt all around. Within a few seconds three other priesthood holders stepped beside them. The approaching army was a dozen miles outside the city, so all who joined them came by the same means. They waited patiently for more to arrive. For some reason, it seemed appropriate to have twelve brethren present before proceeding. Samuel turned around in time to see an old, white-haired man step out of nothingness and stride purposefully toward their group. He immediately recognized him.

"Dad!" Samuel cried out in joy, and leaving his position, ran to meet his father who had stayed in Utah.

After a brief embrace, Jim Mahoy nodded toward the group standing on the rim of the bluff. They joined arms and walked briskly toward them.

"It's fantastic to see you again, Dad! Is this the first time you have traveled by the power of God?" he asked.

Jim nodded. "I guess I took President Andrews's words literally. When the Spirit informed me that I was needed to defend Zion, I started walking that direction as fast as I could, knowing it would take me a month to arrive. I made no preparations, I just started walking as the Spirit directed. I walked only about two blocks and arrived at this bluff with you men facing an army. I presume I have come to Zion?"

"You have!" Samuel exclaimed.

Jim looked stunned, but overjoyed. "Amazing, over 1000 miles in a few blocks! What is the situation here?" he asked, turning his attention to the army arrayed beyond them as they stepped up to the edge.

"We were just waiting for twelve brethren to come," Samuel informed him. "Your arrival makes twelve exactly."

"All right then! Samuel, I'm new at this. Should we destroy them? Who's in charge?" Jim looked out again over the edge. "They have started coming toward us," he said calmly.

"Jesus Christ is in charge," a brother to their right answered, voicing their collective thoughts.

Everyone was silent until a young man in his teens spoke up. "I know you all know a lot more than I do, but I feel we should just send them home," he said without fanfare.

With a collective understanding born of revelation, they all looked at each other, discerning the truth of that inspired statement. Then they unitedly raised their arms to the square. "In the name of Jesus Christ, we command you to return home."

Their words were utterly simple. But what happened next was anything but simple, and in fact, difficult for even the most experienced brethren to understand. It was completely perplexing to the army. They had been advancing steadily toward the bluff, firing as they came. Now they were inexplicably advancing in the opposite direction. In an instant all Samuel could see was the backs of the soldiers. The soldiers blindly continued to fire for a full minute before realizing their former targets had disappeared from their sites.

It took nearly thirty minutes for the soldiers to determine that the bluff, and the few men that were upon it, were behind them. When they finally got turned around and oriented again, they began their advance toward the bluff once more, but instantly found themselves again firing in the wrong direction. Three times they attempted to turn their army around, and three times they found themselves retreating rather than advancing.

At this point they paused as if uncertain what to do. Unable to advance, and fearful to return without even having engaged the enemy, they waited without attempting to move. It soon became apparent to the brethren what the army was waiting for. On the horizon a trail of white appeared, streaking toward them not far above the ground. It had been years since any of the brethren had seen a fighter plane. Yet, there was no question this was what was coming toward them at many times the speed of sound.

"They are determined to defy the will of God, aren't they?" Samuel heard his father say.

"Defiance is a fiery rebellion," someone said from down the line of men.

In exact unison, all twelve arms came to the square. "In the name of Jesus Christ, let the flaming sword of God end the defiance of this enemy of Zion," they said as with one voice, the Spirit dictating the words.

No mortal eyes had ever seen what next occurred. A short distance before them, just beyond the bluff, a wall of fire shot into the sky as the jet screamed toward them. Samuel could see flashes of light as the jet belched rockets and machine gun fire at them. Too late to avoid the wall of fire, the jet attempted to pull up. The plane's roar was nearly deafening as the mighty engines strained to escape the flames. It slammed into the fiery wall and disintegrated in a burst of light, as the entire armament of the plane exploded simultaneously and fell to the ground where the army stood, speechless with fear. The blast was so fierce that it destroyed a dozen vehicles and hundreds of men of the advancing army, yet left the brethren completely unharmed.

Demoralized and disoriented, the soldiers broke into smaller groups and quickly retreated. For nearly an hour the rippling wall of fire continued to reach into the heavens. Every few minutes the retreating troops would look back at it in stark terror. It was nighttime when the last of the troops disappeared into the darkness, never to return. The wall of fire illuminated the land for hundreds of miles. Finally, the brethren turned their faces from the awesome spectacle of their fiery deliverance toward their homes. Instantly the great barrier evaporated. In the ensuing silence they suddenly realized the wall of fire had made a roaring noise not previously noticed. Several brethren observed that the trees and grass that had been directly within the fire were unscorched.

They knelt in a circle and offered profound gratitude to God for their deliverance. As they stood the brethren shook hands, and turned into the darkness. A few steps later they could not be seen.

Samuel, Vladimir and Jim Mahoy were the last to depart. Vladimir took a dozen steps along the ridge to allow some Samuel some privacy with his father, and to wait for his friend to bring him back home.

"Dad, how is Mom?" Samuel asked when they could finally speak.

"Your mother passed away a few weeks ago, Sam," the faithful family patriarch replied soberly.

Samuel gasped, surprised and shocked, and bowed his head in sorrow. He could not have known. Communication between Utah and Zion was limited to the weightiest of matters. "I'm so very, very sorry, Dad," he said finally, his eyes filling with tears. He held his father in a long tearful embrace.

Far to the west, the pillar of fire above the temple continued to lance into the sky, illuminating the ground all around them. Jim looked at his son lovingly, then shook his head, causing his full head of white hair to flash. "She was a righteous and valiant woman, son. But she was ill, and her passing was a great relief to her. There is nothing to mourn. I fully expect to meet her as a resurrected being not many days hence," he said quietly.

Samuel felt the pain of deep grief engulf him, and he missed his precious mother more than he could express. He almost felt cheated, and wished with all his heart that he could have seen her, just spoken with her one last time. His father's words, while hopeful, did not give his son much comfort. "Dad, I know what you're saying, but I really have no concrete feeling about how far off the resurrection might be. It might be years, even decades—who knows?"

He stopped then, realizing he was probably saying something that his grieving father didn't need to hear. "Of course, things in Zion are accelerating quickly," he said more hopefully. "The final scenes are playing out before our very eyes."

Jim turned from his son to look out across the landscape of trees and grass, illuminated entirely by the light from the Temple which was much purer, much whiter than sunlight, and seemed to emphasize every hue beautiful to the eye, bathing the landscape in glowing color. It was an impressive sight. Just standing on the soil of Zion fired his soul.

James Mahoy was eighty-four, and he felt as if his life should have ended long ago but for the pressing need for priesthood holders in Utah. The faithful women of the Church now outnumbered the men nearly ten to one. There was hardly time to get from one crisis to another. He spent all day, every day exercising his faith and his priesthood. He had been ministering in a tent city near Salt Lake City, when his beloved Laura had died. He barely made it home in time for her funeral. How his heart yearned for closure, for a last good-bye, for one more smile from the woman he had loved more than life itself. Without Laura, life did not seem worth living.

Still, it was quite possible he would live until the resurrection, and then what? Would Laura be so different, become so advanced, that she might not want him? Would her resurrected status take her off this earth and onto something else? Must he also await the grave before they could at last be together? He was still in good health, and having been given the power of the priesthood now so markedly manifest, he could reasonably live another twenty years or longer. Twenty years separated from his childhood sweetheart seemed like a prison sentence.

"It is indeed the era long awaited," Jim said with deep emotion, avoiding the subject that seemed more and more upon his mind. "It is an exciting time, a joyful time."

Samuel brushed the tears from his eyes, then spoke with as much energy as he could muster. "Will you come to Zion and live with me and Melody, Dad?" he asked. "You really should see your grandchildren again, and meet your beautiful great-grandchildren. And Dad, the Temple is incredibly magnificent! You've just got to see it from the inside!"

Jim looked kindly at his son. "I would like to, Sam, but I feel compelled to return to Utah. Things are much less settled there. The missionary work is enormous. We don't exclude anyone who comes, so there are many who don't even believe in God, let alone in His restored gospel. Yet, there is great faith among the saints, and marvelous blessings."

Samuel was genuinely disappointed. "Are you sure? We would love for you to be here in Zion with us."

Jim sighed and shook his head. "I would love to be with you, too, Sam. But I have a mission to fulfill that cannot wait." Then he looked at Samuel with a twinkle in his eye. "Besides, I doubt this amazing blessing of traveling by the power of God was meant for sightseeing."

"I suspect that's true," Samuel admitted wryly. "And the work in Utah really does sounds daunting."

"All the work of God is daunting, and all of it is joyous. But at least no one is launching missiles into Utah," Jim said with a tiny smile.

"Why is that? I would have thought Utah would have as many enemies as Zion."

"Not really. The leaders of the nation of New Mexico are very friendly toward us. They see us as the only Americans who cared about them while they were in their poverty. They have actually threatened to attack Texas, or anyone else who molests us," Jim exclaimed.

Samuel was surprised. "That's astonishing!"

"What is astonishing is how the works of God roll forward unhindered." Jim straightened up. "But I must go. I do love you, my son. Do not grieve too much for your mother. The time will pass, and we will all be together again. So, how are Melody and the children?"

"They are all fine. I know they miss you and their grandmother, of course." Samuel reported.

"Of course," Jim said quietly. He put a fatherly arm around Samuel's shoulder. "I am ever and always proud of you, Sam. My precious son—now a servant of the great Jehovah!" His eyes were misty. "You have brought me nothing but joy, you know—all your life." He looked at Samuel with tender eyes, took three steps, then vanished into the night.

Samuel stood for many minutes, his father's sweet words touching his childhood heart, as well as his grown-up one. He silently thanked the Lord for the supernal gift of being a Mahoy.

THE FINAL HARVEST

But, the Prophet said that as one of the 144,000, I should come along as your companion!" Melody proclaimed with undeniable logic. "The Prophet gave me this assignment as well, and I want to go!"

"Melody, I really am excited to be a missionary with you," Sam replied. "You are the Lord's servant, just as I am. But, what about little Helaman?" he asked.

"Helaman will be just fine for a month," Melody assured him. "He adores Sarah, who is the most responsible young woman I know. She can take him to kindergarten and pick him up, and then play with him afterwards. He'll think it's just a big holiday! Besides, with the way travel is these days, we can always pop home for a visit." She stopped and looked at him. "Can't we?" she asked, suddenly unsure.

"I doubt it," Samuel said in complete honesty. "Every mission I've been on for the Lord has pretty much made me stay until it's done."

"Oh," she said. She paused for a long moment, then continued with renewed determination. "Well, then I will just have to learn to get used to it. As your wife, and with this wonderful new gift, I'm committed to doing the Lord's work—whatever that looks like! So let's go get our passports!" she said, then gave him a kiss and hurried into the bedroom to pack.

Samuel laughed softly. "Hey honey, you don't need to pack, you know! The Lord allows us to create anything we need—so no toiletries required!"

She peeked her head out of the bedroom holding her toothbrush, and laughed. "I've got a lot to learn, that's for sure," she said with a grin.

It was late in the evening when Samuel and Melody walked away from the house and their little son, after long hugs and last good-byes. It was many times harder on Sam's tender wife than on himself. There was no doubt in his mind that they would eventually return home, but he did not know exactly when that would be. For Melody, leaving her son even for a few weeks, was much harder than she let on. But no matter the sacrifice or the outcome, she knew that she had personally been called to this mission by God.

When they were about halfway to the Temple and alone on the street, Samuel turned to his beloved companion. "Any thoughts on where we should go?" he asked.

"I just assumed you would decide that," Melody replied with a shaky voice. Her eyes were red. " I have no idea what we are supposed to do."

He reached up and wiped away tears gently with the back of his finger. "This is indeed unusual in that we have no specific assignment from the Brethren. In all such decisions like this it is preferred to make a joint decision with both companions—when we have a companion, that is."

Melody thought about this as she began walking again. About three steps later a look of resolution lit her face. "I know where we should begin," she said, her voice alight with happiness as the Spirit rested upon her.

"Tell me."

"Africa!" she pronounced with a sudden giddy happiness. She had been born in Africa, and the thoughts of returning thrilled her. She still had relatives there she hadn't seen for over twenty years. It had been nearly forty years since Sam himself had been there as a missionary.

"Yes! And more specifically, we are to go to Rhodesia," Samuel said with surety.

"More correctly, Zimbabwe," Melody corrected.

"That's right, they changed the name after the revolution," he said.

Melody sighed with relief. "Okay, I think I'm ready," she said as resolutely as she could.

"Here, take my hand and…"

Melody hesitated, "Wait! What do I do?"

"Just start walking to Africa," Samuel directed. "The three governing principles are first, the commission of God, second, your faith, and third, your destination must be where Jesus Christ wants you to go. Then, pray unto the Father and take a step."

She nodded, and they bowed their heads together. Then, without saying another word, Melody set her face southward and walked with purpose toward Africa. Taking his cue from her, Samuel joyfully strode along with her as they walked side-by-side to a continent on the other side of the globe.

The sky seemed to grow lighter as the road turned to red dirt and the trees became the desert tropical foliage of Africa. Less than a block later they were walking down a row of abandoned homes made of brick and stucco.

"We did it!" Melody cried and turned to give Samuel a big hug.

"Jesus Christ did it, but I must say you did it beautifully. Usually it requires more training."

He held her hand, and they walked in silence for a few minutes, trying to determine where they actually were. "Do you recognize this place?" Samuel asked Melody.

"I don't. None of this looks familiar to me. I know we are in Africa, but exactly where I can't tell," she allowed.

"Wait, what's this?" Samuel said, his attention riveted on something down the road. She quickly saw what he was looking at.

The column of men marching toward them were native Africans. They were waving clubs and machetes over their heads. They had spotted the two missionaries and seemed very excited. They broke into a run toward them.

"Our first teaching opportunity," Melody said with a steady voice.

Samuel was very proud of her for not suggesting they retreat; it spoke of her diamond-hard faith and courage in Christ. "Yeah, even people with clubs need the gospel, perhaps more than any other," he said wryly to her.

The men split and formed a circle around the missionaries, and a few passersby ran in the opposite direction to avoid any involvement. Everyone surrounding them was shouting so that no rational exchange was possible. Clubs and machetes were flashing inches from their bodies. Neither Samuel nor his fearless companion cowered or ducked.

This lack of fear sobered the mob somewhat, and they grew uncertain what to do when their usual methods had not worked. A man with a pistol strapped to his hip stepped forward. Besides being dressed in tattered shirt and knee-length pants, he wore dirty white tennis shoes without laces or socks. But, the most fascinating part of his apparel was the small gold cross hung by a gold chain around his neck. Against his coal-black skin, it shone like the sun.

Samuel stuck out his hand which the leader of the mob grasped reflexively. "We're here to teach you the Gospel," Samuel said with complete confidence. He noticed something miraculous about his own speech; the English coming from his mouth was being changed into a different language. The meaning of every word he spoke was clear to him, yet the sounds were foreign.

The man's grip tightened even as a perplexed look spread across his broad face.

Samuel nodded at his cross. "I see you are a Christian. Do you have any sick who have faith to be healed?"

"How came you to speak the language of my homeland?" the leader asked suspiciously.

"What you hear is the gift of God," Samuel replied. "You are all of different tribes," he said, turning toward the mob. "Which of you hear my words in your native tongue?"

A murmur of acknowledgment came from every man. "Is it possible for a man to speak many languages at the same time? It is only done through the power of God. Now, I ask again, do you have any sick who have faith to be healed? Our time is limited, and we must do our work and pass on," Samuel said without any indication of rudeness. It was simply the case.

The leader surveyed him for a minute before speaking cautiously. "My daughter is sick with a fever, and I fear for her life," he finally said. "Come, she is this way." Though he had said this, he continued to look deeply into Samuel's face for perhaps another ten seconds before turning and striding away. Sam and Melody followed, surrounded by the mob. The men were no longer threatening to kill them for now, but the missionaries knew that this could be a temporary state of affairs.

The group walked nearly a mile to a more prosperous part of town. Samuel was still not sure which city they were in, and chose not to ask. However, during his mission here over forty years ago he had seen the stark disparity between the very rich, and very poor. They were approaching a street lined with large trees, vast lawns and neglected landscaping that had once been beautiful. The homes were actually small mansions. Guards stood before each home. They marched into the gates of the largest home and up a cobblestone drive. There was a jet black Mercedes parked before the front door. The car was covered with dust and looked as if it hadn't been driven in years. Samuel concluded that even the very rich were walking now, as there was no gasoline at any price.

"Stay here," the leader ordered the mob before he took the first of six steps leading to the massive front door. "You," he said, pointing at Samuel, "come with me. The woman stays outside with my men. If you do not heal my daughter, my men will have their games with the white woman. Do you understand?" he threatened menacingly.

"I do. However, you do not," Samuel replied, taking a step closer to the leader and lowering his voice. "We are not here to play games, or to be threatened. Do you love your daughter?" he asked.

"I do," he replied, his eyes narrowing.

"Your action of keeping my wife as a hostage unless God performs to your satisfaction speaks of pitifully weak faith. Do you really expect to be able to threaten God to heal your daughter? Do you expect me, a man of God, to allow you to do this? If you truly desire the power of God in your home, you must quit treating God's servants as enemies. It offends the very

God upon whom you are relying to heal your daughter. Now, I ask you. Do *you* understand?"

There was a moment when the man glared at him; then his concern for his daughter became evidently stronger than his pride. His face softened. "Forgive me," he said, his voice a little choked. He looked at Melody and motioned for her to follow. "Welcome to my home."

They entered the large front doors to find themselves standing on thick, dirty white carpeting. The foyer was spacious, and had a beautiful staircase going up one side. Their host followed a brown trail in the carpet to the left and up the stairs. Samuel followed behind Melody. Only one of the guards followed after them.

They climbed past paintings and delicate statuary to the landing. Turning left they walked down a short hall and into a large, sunny bedroom with bright windows and thin white drapes moving gently in a breeze. The canopy bed had a lacy top and curtains drawn and tied near the front. Melody thought it was like stepping back into a scene from "Gone With The Wind." The only deviation from that image was the fact that the room was filled with stench and smoke.

Near the foot of the bed someone had piled sand on the floor and shaped a fire pit. An African witch doctor sat cross-legged before the smoldering fire, chanting spells in an African language. It was interesting to Samuel that he could not understand the words of the witch doctor, even though he was probably speaking the same language as their host. The witch doctor was nearly naked but for a loin cloth that served almost no useful purpose. His skin was smeared with some liquid he was dipping from a copper pot beside the fire. His head was inside a hideous mask made from a crocodile head.

The most revolting aspect of the African shaman was the incredible stench of death that emanated from his body. Samuel had heard that these so-called holy men never bathed. He was also quite sure the dark liquid he was rubbing on his body was blood, probably human. A feeling of evil emanated from the man, who had stopped chanting to fix steely black eyes on them. Even within the mask, Samuel could feel the hatred that seemed to be emanating from him in waves. Melody swallowed hard, but she did not shrink.

The bed was surrounded by five women who were in a state of mourning. Though they had presently stopped, they had been chanting and mourning when they entered. With a wave of his hand their guide ordered the women back. For the first time they got a look at his daughter. She appeared about sixteen. She was naked from head to toe except for a piece of the sheet laid across her hips. Her skin was glistening with sweat. She slowly turned her head when she perceived the white couple in the room, and blinked as if unable to believe what she was seeing. She reached for the sheet, but was not able to grasp it.

Melody let out a cry and pushed past the women surrounding the bed. She grabbed the sheet and yanked it up to cover the young girl's body. Melody placed a hand on her forehead and spoke in soothing tones. "We are God's servants," she said quietly. "My name is Melody, and we have come to heal you. Do you understand?"

"Yes," the girl said through parched lips, then added, "Thank you."

Melody merely nodded.

"Bring me water!" Melody ordered to no one in particular. In a few seconds someone handed her a glass of brown water. Melody looked at it with distaste. "Bring something that isn't polluted!" she ordered, and set the glass on a nightstand. This time the girl's father demanded angrily that everyone do as Melody had asked. A few minutes later they returned with freshly-squeezed orange juice. Melody helped the girl sip. She meekly allowed Melody to administer to her.

Samuel knelt beside her bed near the girl's head. "Are you a Christian?" he asked. She shifted large black eyes to Samuel.

She tried to speak, and had to try again to make a sound. "I am," she said in a whisper.

"I knew you were. Now I have a favor to ask," Samuel said, leaning near her face. "Will you please ask the witch doctor to leave?"

A look of disgust crossed her sweaty features, and in a voice devoid of strength, yet possessed of an iron will, she said, "Father, order the shaman to go, or I will die from loathing."

Her father seemed electrified by this statement, and ordered the witch doctor to leave. It took several minutes for the grumbling old man to gather up his "holy" possessions and leave the house. Someone stomped out the fire, and in a few minutes the breeze cleared the room.

"Now, please ask everyone but your father to go," Samuel said quietly. This was done with equal grumbling.

Samuel turned to her in earnest, a new feeling of love for her coursing through his soul. "My name is Samuel. I am a man of God."

"I'm Makki. I am a daughter of God," the young girl replied earnestly, though barely above a whisper.

"Do you remember the dream?" Samuel asked, unsure of what his words meant, yet certain they were the right ones.

Her large black eyes rolled up into her sockets slowly, then returned just as slowly. "Yes," she replied. "The two white crows sitting on the fence surrounded by black ones," she said feebly.

"You know the crow is the symbol of your people." Samuel replied.

"I have never seen a white crow," she said.

"What happened in the dream?" Melody asked her gently. The girl slowly turned her eyes toward her kind visitor.

"I was next to the white crows. They pecked me very softly on the head, then flew away. I became white, and flew away, but I came back with the others. Then, I pecked the bird next to me, and it turned white and flew away. Sometimes, when I pecked another bird it stayed black," she said softly. "It was very confusing. The ones who stayed black did not fly away." This explanation took several minutes with long pauses to catch her breath.

"We are the white crows," Melody told her softly.

"I know," Makki replied, her eyes filled with conviction.

Samuel placed his hands upon her head. Melody took her sweaty hand, and bowed her head in prayer.

Samuel spoke with authority. "In the name of Jesus Christ, and by virtue of his holy Priesthood, I command this disease to depart, and for you to arise," he pronounced.

Melody pulled the girl to a sitting position. "Makki, do you have the faith to stand up?" Melody encouraged her gently.

The girl's legs slid to the floor. The pasty look immediately left her face, and her skin grew warm in Melody's hand. With her other hand she held the dirty sheets against her chest. A look of joy crossed her features, and she gazed into Melody's face with calm wonder.

"Bring me clothing," she said to her father, who had watched all this with amazement. He hurriedly found her clothing and brought them. Melody held up the sheet as the girl pulled the dirty dress over her head. She stood and looked around the room. "I thought I was going to depart this world."

Her father cried out in joy, "Thank God!" He rushed to his daughter and held her tightly. Then he left the room, and appeared again with fruit and bread. "Here, you eat, my daughter!" he urged her. She gratefully chewed and swallowed a small portion, then turned toward Melody.

"You must tell me what God expects of me," she implored her. "I want to quickly learn these things and teach them to my people. I have the feeling that the time is very short." She looked at Samuel. "Is this not true?"

"It is true."

Makki smiled. "The Prophet sent you, didn't he," she said confidently.

Samuel nodded. "His name is President Andrews. We are working to gather in the faithful before our Savior returns."

Melody put her arm around the girl. "So, you know about our Prophet?" she questioned her. "Have you heard of the Church of Jesus Christ of Latter-day Saints?

Makki's father stepped forward, his voice strained. "It is true. All my family were baptized into God's true Church years ago. It has been very hard since civil war broke out. I have tried to keep my family safe, but the Church has collapsed here. We have done terrible things. I'm afraid we are not worthy to be gathered," he said with deep sadness.

Melody smiled. "And yet here we are, come to gather you," she said with a happy shrug.

Makki took her father's hand. "My father is a good man. He has done some bad things, yes, but he is still good inside. The evil of these times has been hard."

Samuel placed a hand on her father's shoulder. "I know it is true. What is your name, brother?"

"My name is Mattias Sakka. I am a High Priest, or at least I was once."

Samuel laughed. "You still are. Were you the branch president before the Church collapsed?"

Brother Sakka frowned. "I am ashamed to say that I was the stake president," he replied slowly. "We had wards and a stake here. Many people believed. I did not know how to keep the Church going with so much warfare and bloodshed."

Samuel and Melody suddenly understood. "This is the reason we came to your home first, President Sakka!" Samuel exclaimed. "From this moment you must repent and resume your presidency. End the warfare among your people. Restore everything that you can. Return people's property. Rise up with faith and you will be the means of saving your stake yet."

Sakka's shoulders shook as he hung his head. "My brother, I do want to repent! This is my greatest desire! But can I ever be forgiven?"

Samuel gazed at him with discerning eyes, praying with all his soul for the Lord to confirm what he was about to say. When he received that confirmation, he spoke. "As a servant of the Most High, I declare to you, Brother Sakka, that the Lord will forgive you from this very moment, as you humble yourself before him. Today, at this moment, you can be completely clean through the blood of the Lamb! Repent mightily, my brother, go forward again with unwavering faith in Jesus Christ, and you will receive power to do all things!"

Brother Sakka sank into a chair, praying and weeping for sorrow of his sins. All else in the room was quiet except for the sound of his sobbings, until Makki drew aside to talk with Melody.

"What is your name, my sister?" Makki asked.

"My name is Melody."

"I have a question for you, Sister Melody. I dreamed that all of us will turn white and fly away," she said. "What does this mean, to turn white? Will our skin be white?"

"I believe that this white means purity of the soul," Melody replied.

Makki nodded with understanding, walked back to her weeping father and placed both hands on his bare chest. She gently picked up the cross hanging from his neck. "Father, it is time to stop the war. We must let these white crows peck us. Will you join me, or must I do this alone?"

President Sakka squared his shoulders. "I will go and do as the Lord commands," he said firmly,

Samuel smiled and took Melody's arm. "Very good. We will come back when you are ready," he said. As he and Melody walked downstairs, Samuel turned to his wife. "You have a remarkable gift of charity, my beautiful companion," he said in awe.

They walked out the door and vanished unseen from the street.

The warfare in Zimbabwe had nearly replayed the Nephite tragedy. Outnumbered hundreds to one, the whites in that small nation were systematically hunted down and killed. As the Nephites had done before, they eventually gathered into fortified villages where they could defend themselves as much as possible. Outside Bulawayo their place of refuge was a national park named Matchum Schlopee for the great white rocks scattered about like children's marbles. The rocks were almost perfectly round, some a hundred feet across, most less. The large number of these white boulders made it impossible to attack in a straight line, giving the defenders a considerable advantage. Inside the park a series of lodges and huts had been built years earlier for tourists that were now the inadequate refuge for hundreds of families.

"Hello, the guards!" Samuel called as they approached the first line of boulders. They were alone, and afoot. It was the middle of the day. This was obviously where the defenders had drawn their line of defense because of the obvious signs of savagery everywhere. Melody had to keep her eyes straight forward to keep from being sick. "Hello, the guards!" Samuel called a second time.

"Who goes there?" a voice called back from a short distance.

"We are servants of God, and have come to visit your people!" Samuel called back.

There was a long pause. "Whose side are you on?" the voice called back.

"God's side!" Samuel responded without hesitation.

"I mean, whose bloody side in the war!" the voice returned angrily.

"This is foolishness!" Samuel called back. "We are coming in. Shoot us if you must!" He looked over at Melody, winked, and took her arm as they confidently began to weave their way through the rocks.

"Do you think they'll shoot?" Melody asked with some hesitation.

"Not when they see we are also white, I think."

"You think?" she asked.

"We'll find out shortly," he replied.

Melody shot a glance at him. "I know it doesn't really matter if they shoot us or not," she said, staring nervously up at the menacing rocks above them. "But I have to admit that, even though I know I won't actually die, I do fear the pain of bullets ripping through my body."

Samuel put his arm around her waist, steadying her as they climbed. "My love, let us forget our fears and listen to what the Holy Spirit is saying. Fear is the opposite of faith. We can't have both at the same time."

"I know, and believe me, Sam Mahoy, I have faith! It's just that…"

"Stop where you are!" a man's voice commanded from above them. They both complied. As soon as they had stopped a man stood up atop a bolder to their left. He was aiming a rifle at them. "Go away," he commanded. "If you come another step, I'll shoot you both down!"

"Do you have sick and wounded in camp?" Melody called in reply.

"There are sick and wounded everywhere one looks these days," the man replied disdainfully.

"We have come to help them," she called back.

There was a pause. "Are you doctors?"

"No, servants of God," she replied.

"Got no use for God!" he spit back at them. "He's bloody well left this part of his earth. If you happen to see God, tell him we got no time for 'em! We got no use for you, either, an' we got no food to spare." They heard his gun cock. "I'm going to give you three seconds to turn around or you're both gonna die!"

Melody continued walking toward the narrow passage between the boulders leading into their camp. The guard chambered a round with a loud clunk.

"Stop!" he ordered. Melody continued forward. The man screamed in satanic hatred. "Anybody stupid enough to think they are servants of God needs to die!" From up above her there was a small "click."

"What?" the guard said as he lowered his weapon. He began slapping it to try to make it work.

"Shoot her!" he ordered to someone at his right. Two men stepped into sight atop the boulders. They quickly took aim and pulled their triggers. "Click, click."

"Are you coming, Sam?" Melody asked him without turning toward him. Samuel realized he had stood riveted to his position, fascinated by what was going on. He hurried to catch up. Neither of them said a word to the other as they walked along the single-lane dirt road, but he was thinking about her rebuttal to his instruction about fear and faith. After a minute he had to chuckle to himself. This tremendous faith was vintage Melody Mahoy, but he knew that she was just beginning to comprehend the power to which she had been ordained. Melody looked quizzically at him, but did not ask him why he was smiling.

As they walked past them, Samuel and Melody saw the guards spewing directions into the radio, desperately combing the area to find them. But the men's eyes were blinded, and Sam and Melody calmly walked past them, completely undetected.

The land beyond the boulders was flat, with massive, widely scattered trees. Tall grass and low bushes grew profusely. Before them was a man made lake not more than a hundred yards across and twice that in length. The lake was created by a low concrete dam a short distance away. The water from the lake was flowing over the top of the dam so that no part of the dam was actually visible. It appeared as if the water was going over a waterfall with a very long, straight edge. Because the water atop the dam was only a few inches deep, and moving slowly, it gave anyone walking across the dam the appearance of walking on water. It was a very interesting effect, considering who they were, and how they had gotten to Africa.

The walked across the dam and followed the road to their right. About a hundred feet further it turned left among the trees and brush. A short distance from the lake was a wide clearing surrounded by stone huts with thatched roofs. Several hundred people were going about their business tending to cooking fires and children. There were very few men among them.

Finally, a young woman with a child on her hip noticed them and walked toward them suspiciously.

"Who are you?" she asked, her accent much heavier than Samuel remembered from so many years ago. She almost sounded Australian. But, before they could answer, the same group of men came running into the clearing. In a matter of seconds, the missionaries were surrounded and their hands were quickly tied behind their backs.

"See you soon," Melody said ironically as they roughly dragged her away toward the lake. Samuel was pushed in the same direction by angry hands. He hurried to keep up with Melody who seemed to be receiving the brunt of their anger. A hundred things passed through his mind to say, to explain, accuse, or otherwise interrupt them, but nothing reached his lips. He was left to stumble along trying not to fall each time he was jabbed by the butt of a rifle. Though he felt no pain, he was certain their intent was to bruise or break his ribs.

As they approached the lake Samuel noticed an ominous sign for the first time. It read:

WARNING
MAN EATING CROCODILES
NO FISHING
NO SWIMMING
YOU HAVE BEEN WARNED!

They led Melody beside a small rowboat pulled up on the shore. They paused long enough to pick up a dozen stones and drop them into her pockets.

"Get in," the man whom they had first seen atop the boulder ordered. Then, without waiting for a response, shoved her into the back of the boat. She cried out as she hit her head on the boat's edge. Samuel's protests were answered by several blows to the back of his head. Those guarding him were too busy watching the drama at the lake to wonder why he didn't fall down unconscious from their blows.

"Take her out," the first man ordered. Two others jumped into the boat and in just a few minutes had reached the center of the lake. Samuel watched as a dozen large crocodiles splashed into the lake and swam after the boat. They apparently knew exactly what this meant from previous experience.

"I told you to go back," their leader said as he turned back toward Samuel. His voice was hostile with indignation. Not only did he feel no remorse for what he was about to do, he also felt perfectly justified.

"We came here to help..."

"Shut up!" he screamed.

"If you try to harm my wife, it will damn your soul," Samuel said calmly. For his reward the man slammed the butt of his rifle into his stomach. Samuel was too intent about Melody to remember to double over. He did not even observe the amazed look on his assailant's face.

Samuel watched Melody, who was sitting stiffly in the bow of the boat, facing him. He could plainly see a blue bruise above her right eye. Samuel knew her faith was absolute, as was her power and authority as a translated being. But he could not watch the terrible scene before him. Tears sprang to his eyes, and grief surged through him. He wanted to lash out, to fight them. He had no idea how much resistance he could put up, but knew it would be considerable. Yet, his own will was swallowed up in a greater will. He was not to fight, or even to call comforting words to Melody. He knew that this was Melody's mission, and that no matter how frightened she may be, she would fulfill it with dignity, and would come off conqueror. Samuel silently plead in prayer for his beloved wife.

The man completed his crime with icy hatred. "Throw her in," he ordered. Then turning back to Samuel, added, "Don't worry, you'll be with her in just a few minutes."

Samuel could not take his eyes off of the boat. It was close enough that he could have hit it with a rock. Melody struggled ineffectively for a few seconds before they pushed her out of the boat. She went over the side head-first and hit the water with a big splash. Her thrashing legs hooked the side of the boat. One of the men dived for her leg, but in his haste to throw it into the water, he fell overboard with a cry of surprise and terror.

With her hands tied behind her back and her pockets full of rocks, Melody quickly sank out of sight. The fallen man thrashed about wildly until he caught hold of the side of the boat. The man inside the boat caught his companion's arm just as the first crocodile hit, and he struggled to pull him into the boat. In seconds, the man was carried away, his cries for help a stream of bubbles coming to the surface beside the boat.

Samuel fell to his knees in grief, praying for Melody to be strong. He knew that she was at that moment struggling for breath on the bottom of a lake, and he could do nothing for her, or to allay the fear she was undoubtedly experiencing. Yet, among the many emotions he felt, anger was not one of them. He knew that God would judge them, and this he let carry away what might otherwise have become overwhelming anger.

The survivor in the boat sat looking into the crystal clear water for several minutes before beginning to row back to the dock. Samuel watched the boat slowly return. When it arrived the man stepped out of it and ran into the woods.

"The bloke who died was his brother," the leader told Samuel, his teeth clenched in rage.

"You can't really expect me to feel sorry for the man who just murdered my wife, can you?" Samuel asked in astonishment. In fact, Samuel did feel sorry for the man, but in a way that he could not understand.

"What you feel inside won't be bloody half as bad as what you'll feel on the outside, you blasted fool," his captor hissed, his eyes intense with loathing. "Throw him into the boat," he ordered.

After they loaded his pockets with rocks, Samuel let himself be led into the boat. An argument ensued about who was going to throw him into the lake. Everyone felt as if the lake were now cursed, and loudly refused to do the deed.

Finally, their leader drew his pistol and pointed it at the head of one of his men. "Into the boat," he ordered. The man's face turned red as with lowered head he reluctantly climbed into the boat. Under the threat of death he began slowly rowing toward the middle. When they reached the center of the lake Samuel's back was to the shore. He pondered if he should even resist.

When nothing seemed to be happening, Samuel turned to see a new look of fear on the guard's face. The man's teeth were clenched in stark terror as he stared back at the shore. Samuel turned around in his seat. From underneath the boat dock, a large crocodile was now rising up out of the water, lunging toward the men on the dock. The men were paralyzed with fear, their mouths open in silent screams. Samuel watched their leader aim his pistol at the creature that was coming toward them and fire nine rounds in rapid succession. His hands were shaking so violently that the bullets went whizzing across the water. Samuel wondered why one of them didn't hit the boat. Finally, the leader threw his empty weapon at the crocodile and began running awkwardly backward.

Samuel caught sight of something else moving under the water toward the shore, and his heart leaped.

"Back to the shore!" Samuel ordered. "Row back to the shore!"

"No!" his guard cried, and fumbled with the oars. Samuel easily pulled his hands from his fetters and moved forward in the boat. The man stared at him with huge eyes. Remembering his pistol, the man jerked it from his belt and leveled it at Samuel's head. Samuel swatted at the gun in a movement too swift to actually see. The gun discharged and landed twenty feet from the boat. The guard stared at his bruised hand that had seconds ago held a gun. He began thrashing around trying to get as far away from Samuel as possible.

"Sit still, or you'll fall into the water yourself," Samuel warned him. "We're returning to shore."

"No!" the man cried with insane fear. He then stood, turned and wildly ran off the bow of the boat. His feet were still running when he hit the water. He sank out of sight in a swirl of hungry crocs. Samuel took a seat between the oars, turned the boat quickly, and powered back toward shore with just a few strokes.

Samuel stepped onto the shore just as a moss-covered figure emerged from the lake and stumbled toward him. He caught her in his arms, and began kissing her. Melody's hair was tangled with weeds, and she was muddy from her waist down. She was the most beautiful sight he had ever seen.

"That mud is really thick!" she exclaimed as she drew back from his embrace to catch a breath. "And, it stinks!" she added, wrinkling up her face.

"My brave darling wife!" Samuel cried. "Was it terribly painful?"

Melody shook her head in wonder. "No, it really wasn't," she said, her voice breathless. "Oh yeah, I was scared at first, but then I remembered that the Lord has always kept His promises to me—and suddenly I didn't need air. I didn't need anything."

Samuel's eyes were wet as he gently brushed the mud from her glowing face. "The Lord is so faithful!" he exulted in gratitude.

Melody hugged him tightly. "It's so true! I will never be afraid again!" Her face was shining with absolute faith and trust. "My Redeemer will always deliver me from all sorrow and trouble. Of this I am now certain!"

Then she turned and nodded toward a group of men who had regrouped from their terror and were coming toward them warily. "Let's do what we came here to do!"

Samuel turned and walked toward them. They stopped, and waited for him to arrive. There were about fifteen of them, including a few women who had come from the village.

"Where is your leader?" Samuel asked when he did not see the man who had ordered their execution.

"He ran away. We don't know where he is," one of the men who had not been involved replied. "And we don't agree with what he did. If he returns, we're going to try him for murder. Even though it appears he was not that successful," he added unsteadily as Melody walked up beside Samuel with squishing steps.

"Who are you?" one of the women asked. It was the same one who had first asked them that question when they had originally stepped into the village.

Samuel answered in her tongue. "We are sent by God to assist you. If you have any sick or injured who have faith in Christ, we will heal them. Then, we need to speak to anyone who is, or was a Mormon."

The woman stared at him. "A Mormon? I was," she replied slowly. "I was baptized when I was eight. Why, are you Mormons?"

"We no longer refer to ourselves that way," Samuel informed her. "The Church's new name will soon be The Church of Jesus Christ of Millennial-day Saints."

"Has the millennium begun?" she asked with both excitement and doubt in her voice.

Melody nodded. "In Zion it has! We are here to conduct all true believers to Zion. Are there any true believers here?" she asked.

"I am," a young man said quietly, and stepped forward from the back.

"So am I," a much older woman with gray hair said, "though, I'm not a member of your church." She stepped through the crowd of people until she was directly before Samuel. Her left arm was suspended by a sling. Her left hand was wrapped in a bloody bandage. She was dressed in a ragged dress that appeared to have been worn for months.

"What happened to your arm?" Melody asked her.

"I fell and broke it during the last attack," she replied, looking down at her arm. "It has since become infected."

"Since you are a true believer, in the name of Jesus Christ, and by the holy Priesthood I hold, I rebuke your injury. Take off your sling," Samuel instructed her.

"But I can't. It doesn't feel any better," the woman replied.

"Just take off your sling," Melody said, repeating Samuel's instruction.

"It is intensely painful to remove it," the old woman said, and turned aside. She walked slowly away, her head bowed. This brought a murmur from those assembled.

"Why couldn't you heal her?" the young man asked. "Can you heal anyone?"

"We cannot," Samuel replied. "But Jesus Christ can. She could still be healed. She just did not have the faith to do as I instructed her. It's easy to believe in Christ. It is often something else to believe Christ when He speaks to you. Through my voice, I gave her the words of Christ that would have healed her. It was her choice to not respond."

"That's bloody convenient," someone started to say, but was cut off by another who cried out as she came forward.

"My name is Eleanor Appleby," she said, offering her hand to Samuel, which he shook. She was so thin she almost looked like a young man, but her grip was strong and confident. "I'm not sick, but my oldest son is. He was shot in the last raid. My father was a righteous man. I have great faith in the priesthood. Won't you come heal him? Before it's too late?" she added urgently.

"I will," Samuel replied, and he and Melody began walking briskly with her toward the village, followed by several dozen people. As they walked Samuel hurried to catch up with Eleanor. "Is it possible that your maiden name was Knight?" he asked her.

"It was!" she replied, shocked. "How…"

"And, your mother's name was Elaine, and your father, Thomas?"

"How did you know *that?*" she asked, bewildered.

"Do you remember sitting on an Elder's lap and twisting his tie as he taught your parents the gospel many years ago? You were about seven years old."

"I do!" she cried and stopped walking to face him. "Are you…"

"Yes, I'm Elder Mahoy! I taught your family over thirty years ago. And my companion there is my wife, Sister Mahoy," he said happily.

Eleanor threw her arms around them both, laughing and crying at the same time. "I just don't believe it!" she said over and over.

She started walking again as she excitedly explained, "I have wanted all my life to meet you again." She turned to Melody, who was smiling behind them. "You can't believe how I was in love with your husband, Sister Mahoy. He was my first crush!"

"You were only seven years old," Samuel reminded her.

"Still, that love has endured all these years. It is such a coincidence that you are here!" she said.

"It's no coincidence at all. We are here to finish what I started over thirty years ago," Samuel told her with a smile.

"I believe you," Eleanor said, slowing her walk as her eyes brimmed with tears. "I only wish my parents were here to see you again.".

"What happened to your parents?"

"They were both killed in the battle near the church."

"I'm sorry. They were faithful in the church after I left?"

"Faithful? My father served as the first bishop of the Bulawayo ward. He died defending the church building. He was a great man," Eleanor said with pride.

"Do you have any brothers or sisters?"

"None. I'm the only one. They just had me. I think I was enough," she said with a laugh.

"And what about you? Do you have a husband?"

Eleanor shook her head. "He was also killed, though not defending the church. He died somewhere out in the bush fighting rebels about two years ago."

"I am so sorry. Was he a good man?"

"He truly was. I loved him very much. He was a member, but since the war broke out, he had very little time for the Church."

"Were you married in the temple?" Melody asked her.

Again Eleanor shook her head. "Sadly, no. The war had already begun before we were married. It made travel impossible."

Melody brightened and took her hand. "Then, we will get you to a temple where you can get his work done for him."

"Oh, he would love that. So would I!" Eleanor exclaimed joyfully. Then her voice lowered. "However, there's no chance that will happen in my lifetime," she said with a sigh.

"There is no such thing as 'chance' in the Lord's plans," Melody stated. This brought a questioning glance from Eleanor. She would have said more, but by this time they had reached the makeshift village. Eleanor conducted them to the second stone hut. As they approached, Samuel could see numerous white chips in the stone where bullets had hit.

The village was much larger inside than expected, with concrete floors and an open roof. It had been constructed by the park service during better times. Eleanor led them into the only bedroom and to a cot against the far wall upon which lay a teenage boy. His face was white and beaded with perspiration.

"His name is Moroni Appleby," she said, as she laid a tender hand on his arm. Melody put her arm around Eleanor as Samuel approached him.

"Moroni," Samuel said to the boy. "We are here to heal you. Do you have faith in Jesus Christ?"

"Yes," he replied weakly.

"Are you willing to do as I say?"

The boy looked at him carefully before he spoke. "Yes," he finally said.

"Take my hand," Samuel instructed. Moroni forced his hand to lift from the mattress with great effort. "In the name of Jesus Christ, and according to your faith, and by virtue of the holy Priesthood I hold, I command you to arise from your bed of affliction," he said quietly, yet with deep conviction.

Samuel straightened, still holding onto Moroni's hand. The young man attempted to raise up on an elbow, and failed. "Get up, Moroni," Samuel instructed quietly. Again he tried, and managed to get as far as one elbow, yet his strength was not sufficient to hold his head up. The sheet slid aside, and Samuel caught a glimpse of the bloody bandage on his side. Moroni's wounds were fatal.

"I'm afraid I don't… have enough… faith," Moroni said apologetically, and began to sink back onto his cot.

"No!" Eleanor cried. "Get up, son. Please, get up. Please have the faith. I beg you…" she wailed, her eyes overflowing with tears. Word quickly passed into the outer room of the failure inside, and was followed by angry words from the crowd.

"I … can't," he said and was just about to crumple onto the cot when someone pushed past Eleanor and grabbed Moroni's other hand.

"Yes, you can!" a woman beside him cried. Samuel realized with astonishment that it was the woman he had first attempted to heal that day. Her left arm was no longer in a sling. She pulled Moroni to a sitting position on the cot while he cried out in pain. He stared at her with only partially comprehending eyes.

"Listen to me, Moroni," the woman said, kneeling before him while holding onto his arm to keep him from falling back onto the bed. "Look into my eyes and feel my faith in Christ. I tell you these people are from God. God healed me after I had faith to do what Christ wanted me to do to manifest my faith. It requires enough faith to do what may seem impossible. To me, it seemed impossible to take my arm out of the sling. To you, it seems impossible to stand up. But, you *must* do it. If you want to live, Moroni, you must not only *have* faith, but you must *exercise* your faith." With that she released her grip on his arm and stood.

"She is right, Moroni. It doesn't require strength for you to stand, it requires faith," Melody said to him. "If you want to live, then stand. Let your faith do the impossible, not your body."

A look of determination crossed Moroni's ashen face. Almost immediately that look turned to calm, then peace. With a slow, yet steady movement he levered himself to his feet. He turned toward his mother and crossed the distance between them with two steady steps.

"Mother!" he cried, and embraced her. "I'm healed!"

The room filled with cries of joy and happiness. What was quite odd was that the room beyond had emptied of curious onlookers. They were alone for the moment.

 The older woman turned to Samuel. "By the way, my name is Elizabeth, but I go by Liza. I'm going to go get the others," she announced. Turning toward Melody she asked, "How long can you stay with us?"

"Only a little while. We must hurry."

Liza turned to Moroni's mother. "Eleanor, you know those from your church. You get them. I'll get the others I know have faith. We'll be back shortly," she said happily, and hurried from the room. Eleanor forced herself from her son and followed Liza out the door.

When everyone had arrived there were eleven people in the room besides Samuel and Melody. A tall man dressed in shabby clothing leaned against the wall, nodding kindly to them as they entered the room, and speaking words of encouragement to each.

After Melody had offered an opening prayer, Samuel stood before them.

"My brothers and sisters. Thank you for coming. We have very little time. I apologize for making this meeting brief. The reason we must hurry is because angry men will return soon. By then their anger will be sufficient that they will try to kill you as well as us. If you do not have enough faith to die for our dear Savior, now is the moment when you should leave. It is entirely your choice, but if you wish to live, you should leave quickly."

Samuel said this with as much force as possible without shouting. He let the silence linger into a full two minutes. Finally, a middle-aged man and his wife stood and left the room, slamming the screen door behind them.

"Now we can begin," Samuel said with relief in his voice. "Everyone here has enough faith to die for the Savior. I am going to tell you in great plainness what you need to know. Everything I tell you is the truth. While I tell you these things you will know they are true by a powerful burning in the bosom. When I am done, we will leave your village and begin our journey to the New Jerusalem in America."

He cleared his throat and began. "First, Jesus Christ is the Savior and Redeemer of this world, and of each person here. That means He can save you, here and now.

"Second, Joseph Smith was a great prophet of God who restored the true and everlasting Gospel of Jesus Christ to the earth in 1830.

"Third, the Church of Jesus Christ of Latter-day Saints is that Church, and is the only true and living Church upon the face of the earth, with all the authorized keys and priesthoods of the Lord.

“Fourth, these Saints of the Church of Jesus Christ have returned to middle America, to build the Temple of the New Jerusalem to await the second coming of Christ.

“Fifth, we have come here to your land to find and gather all the faithful to Zion, the New Jerusalem.

“Sixth, those of you who have not yet been baptized in the Church, will have that opportunity as soon as you arrive in Zion.

“Seventh, only the pure in heart can enter Zion. Therefore, you must examine your hearts, repent and prepare your souls, or you will not be allowed to enter there. It is a holy city, and all who dwell within are holy. Already the enemies of Christ have attacked with their armies and have been turned back by pillars of fire.”

“Eighth, in not many days hence Christ will come to His Temple in Zion. We will be there to greet Him, and will walk the streets of Zion by His side. For this reason you can see why only the pure in heart can enter Zion.”

“And, lastly—it is time for us to leave here. Our enemies are organizing their attack as we speak. I must ask you each to answer this question. Do you believe all I have told you?”

A chorus of “Yes!” filled the small stone cabin. Samuel waited until the Holy Spirit bore witness that each had spoken truly.

“We will leave by the back door. Melody, will you take the lead?”

“I will,” Melody replied with a sure voice. “I would like everyone to find a companion and join arms with him or her. Watch the back of the person in front of you, and don’t allow yourself to fall behind, no matter what you might see. Remember how your faith and your willingness to do the impossible healed you? It is the same now.”

Melody looped her arm through Liza’s. “Ready? OK, here we go,” she said, and strode out the door. The tall man in the corner picked up Eleanor’s young daughter and seated her upon his shoulders. Eleanor took her healed teenager’s arm with joy and determination, while Samuel brought up the rear.

A narrow trail wound from the back of the hut and lead straight to the lake. They passed by an outbuilding, and into the trees.

“They’re not here! They’ve escaped!” they heard a familiar voice cry out.

“They must have gone out the back way!” another voice called. A rifle fired to their right, and again off to their left. As the believers walked quickly along they could hear shouts of anger and curses from both sides and behind them. Ahead of them was the lake. There was no way to escape. They walked along as quickly as possible, their minds fixed upon their faith. Ahead of him Samuel heard a voice begin to sing "Come, come ye Saints, no toil or labor fear, but with joy wend your way…" His own voice joined in that holy anthem that seemed even more appropriate now, in the last few moments of their safety, than it ever had for two hundred years.

"There they are!" voices cried. "The lake will stop them. We've got 'em now! Close in! Don't let any of them past!" they heard. "Don't shoot them! We've got better plans for them!" another yelled in rage.

Seconds later the lake came into view, and Melody continued her unbroken stride. None in their small group faltered, even knowing they could not survive more than a few seconds longer. They knew their destination was in God's hands, and they cared not where it might be.

"Here they come!" a voice cried, and a shout of "Hosanna!" followed. The trees quickly grew greener, and dense. The soil beneath their feet changed from red to brown, and the lake before them became a bubbling fountain, with a majestic Temple behind it.

"Go inform the Brethren," the tall man said to a young lad who was standing open-mouthed on the street facing the Temple. The lad obediently hurried away, and the tall man gently gave Eleanor's daughter back to her mother. Then he began shaking the hands of each newcomer, and rejoicing with them.

"Welcome to Zion," he said with joy as he heartily greeted each dusty traveler. They stood wide-eyed with hearts pounding, gazing at the shining city before them. "Welcome to the New Jerusalem—City of the Living God!" he cried.

Samuel left Eleanor weeping for joy in the care of another translated sister of Zion. Then he approached the tall man, and bowed his head. "Thank you for your service, Lord," he whispered so that no one else could hear.

Then Samuel and Melody joined arms and walked toward home.

"Now, that's what I call missionary work!" Melody exclaimed, her face aglow with joy. She knew from that moment that there was no work sweeter.

It had taken them five days to find and bring their little group to Zion. Theirs was the twenty-third group to return. Amazingly enough, the first group had returned a scant six hours after the first missionaries had departed. All over the world people had been prepared by uncountable legions of angels to answer the call to return to Zion. It was simply their duty to find them.

As Isaiah had prophesied, "And they shall bring Thy sons in their arms, and Thy daughters shall be carried upon their shoulders." Truly the 144,000 in all ways fulfilled the scripture, "Kings shall be thy nursing fathers, and their queens thy nursing mothers." In a way marvelous and unexpected, the prophecy of Isaiah that Israel would "come with speed swiftly: none shall be weary nor stumble among them; none shall slumber nor sleep; neither shall the girdle of their loins be loosed, nor the latchet of their shoes be broken" was being fulfilled before their eyes.

Samuel and Melody left on several more missions in the following year, as did thousands of other missionaries. Each of their experiences in gathering the elect from the four quarters of the earth was similar in power as their first together, and every one as miraculous. Very few of them were without incident, and none were without opposition. In every instance Jesus Christ worked anonymously alongside the missionaries, although most did now know it was Him; and those who did, never discussed it.

And this is not all. Whether they came to Zion or not, or were ready to accept the gospel in its fullness, Jesus did not tire of ministering to all His beloved sons and daughters. He met them in their individual needs, wherever they were, and bestowed whatever light they could assimilate. His faithfulness and infinite love were extended to every soul, in every corner of the earth. All of Zion marveled at the grace the Lord poured upon the earth in preparation for His coming.

During the next year, groups of faithful returned almost hourly to Zion. It required every ounce of energy that the City could summon to keep up with the influx of people. Besides housing and feeding them, there was the absolute necessity of teaching, baptizing, and leading them through the process of being ready to receive temple ordinances. All those not ready yet for the Temple were taught outside the City until they were prepared to commit to and live the Millennial Law.

As busy and demanding as all previous years of life in Babylon had been, it was nothing compared to the intensity of what was occurring in Zion. While in Babylon their labors had produced only fatigue and sorrow, the Zion-dwellers were continually empowered with energy, spiritual strength, and seemingly boundless love.

The Final Harvest was indeed the work of angels, and the most joyous to the soul.

28

THE LORD WHOM YE SEEK

This marvelous missionary effort continued day and night for exactly three and one-half years. On the very day the last missionary couple returned home to stay, the Temple was finished. All the interior furnishings were completed and installed. All the many veils, including the one before the throne in the Holy of Holies, were hung. Every piece of artwork was finished, every decoration overlaid with pure gold, gems and other precious materials, and every fingerprint lovingly polished away. It was by far the most perfect building ever built on earth. During those glorious years the pillar of fire continued to blaze above the Temple. Its effect was so marvelous upon the people that they ceased to think of the sun in the heavens as their source of life and light. It was Christ who illuminated their souls, their minds, and their land.

One might have thought such a manifestation of God's divine sanction would have discouraged the enemies of Zion from attacking. For whatever perverse logic those of evil intent use, at first had the opposite effect. Almost every month, some new army brought a force either large or small against them. Without exception they were repulsed by the power of God. Eventually, the tales and terror of Zion spread so wide that none dared to approach her for hundreds of miles.

By the time the great missionary work drew to a close there were over a million inhabitants in Zion. Expanding in all directions, outlying cities had been founded, laid out, and built. Without exception, every structure built prior to the millennium was torn down, its materials salvaged and refurbished to build new and perfectly for the Lord. Since there was no need to accumulate wealth, those things that would have otherwise been considered of immense value became commonplace. Once they became commonplace, they became abundant. The lamp posts, park benches, and statues of Zion were cast of pure gold. For a mile in every direction of the Temple, the streets were made of the same material as the spire of the Temple, thus giving the streets the color of gold, and the appearance of fine crystal. With the holy light of the Temple reflecting upon the streets, walking upon it gave the feeling of walking on water, as if one could look into the pavement and see to the center of the earth, or to the edge of eternity.

As peace spread itself across the lands of Zion, gross desolation of war continued its rapine of the earth. Decimated to near extinction, the armies of the world had no difficulty finding weapons with which to fight, for the face of the whole earth was littered and heaped with them. One had only to stoop to find the means of killing another.

The very evening that the last missionary returned home, the pillar of fire suddenly flashed off as if someone in heaven had turned off a celestial switch. It was nighttime when this occurred, and the sudden darkness was seen and felt by all. With one accord the people rushed into the streets to gaze at the darkened spire of the temple. They each fell to their knees and wept for the loss of His great gift. As powerfully as they prayed, nothing penetrated the heavens, and the Holy Spirit refused to lighten their hearts. Tears ran in rivers upon the golden streets of Zion. For three days the darkness continued unabated, and only silence was heard from the heavens. Though the sun rose and lit the world on its normal course, for those in Zion, it was the blackest of nights. The only explanation they could imagine was that their Savior was no longer in Zion. What it meant, or why He had departed was the subject of intense speculation.

As Samuel and Melody were praying together that night, Samuel heard the voice of the Lord in his mind.

"Come to Jerusalem, my son. You are to assist my two Apostles in their mission."

Samuel immediately turned to Melody with tears in his eyes. "I must go, my darling."

Melody threw her arms around his neck. "I know, Sam. The Lord just told me you are needed in Jerusalem!"

The eyes of the world were now fixed upon Israel. Led by Supreme Commander Aleksander Sarkus, the United World Order considered Jerusalem and its vast resources the key to solidifying its control of the world. Surging from the east, Russia and its conquered Islamic states were also determined to destroy Israel, along with the infidels of the west. The long-prophesied stage had been set.

In the land once familiar with the sandaled feet of the Savior, the war over Jerusalem had now reached its climax. Reduced from a thriving city of over one million to a struggling one hundred-thousand, the survivors of Jerusalem clustered behind hastily-constructed barricades, fighting against the tide of certain extinction. They found themselves surrounded by two vast armies of millions of soldiers and armaments. But unbeknownst to their enemies, the besieged people of Jerusalem were suddenly given a glimmer of guarded hope.

Three years prior to that day, hour, and minute, two strangers in business suits had walked into the walled city. Without introduction, without apology or explanation, they had simply taken up residency within the city. Unknown and unnamed, they had said nothing of their mission, but were quietly preparing the people.

It had been months before that the two strangers first began holding meetings among them. In any time prior they would have been arrested and expelled from their synagogues. Yet, without a formal national, state or local government to intervene, they quietly began teaching belief in Jesus Christ as their true Messiah. At first, very few cared; in fact, it seemed refreshing to speak of God instead of war, even though their doctrine seemed to oppose Judaism. After a year there were a thousand or more Jews who had not only heard the two strangers preach, but who hoped against hope that they spoke truly. The strangers baptized no one, and did not offer to. They simply preached in voices of great conviction concerning Jerusalem, and its preservation, or destruction, according to their own belief in this Jesus whom their fathers had long ago crucified.

By the end of the second year, three thousand or more had heard, and hoped. Yet, all who believed their words did not do so with the intent of rendering obedience. Like their fathers who had crucified Jesus, most of those remaining sought the life of those who now came in His name. This was not because they believed the two strangers to be liars cut from dark cloth; it was because they believed them to be exactly whom they claimed to be: messengers sent by the Christians to turn their hearts, claiming to preserve their lives from annihilation.

As the two strangers now observed a barrage of rockets raining down toward the people, they calmly raised their arms to the square. The missiles suddenly veered sharply, screaming away from their targets and returning to their point of origin, exploding in huge fireballs. As waves of tanks and soldiers tried to penetrate the barricades, a wall of heavenly fire came forth as thousands tried to push through it, perishing instantly in the flames. Most did not know where this heavenly help was coming from.

Commander Sarkus was furious that his attacks had failed, and his assaults grew more vicious. Week after week the Jews were pushed back, but unbeknownst to them, were largely preserved by the godly powers of the two strangers. At the very minute the pillar of fire above the Temple in Zion flashed out, with reckless hate the forces of Commander Sarkus launched a final offensive. U.N. snipers cruelly murdered the two strangers, who were Apostles of the Lamb of God. In that hour the hostile forces of the army overran the barricades and thrashed through the streets of Jerusalem in an orgy of slaughter and rapine not seen since the times of Caesar, as the people fled to the back half of the city.

It was the abomination of desolations spoken of by Daniel, and again by Christ himself. The surging armies systematically sought and murdered every living soul they could find. Theirs was not a mission of conquest; it was a demonic orgy of complete annihilation. For three days it seemed there were no devils in hell—they were all roaming the streets of Jerusalem. Stone by stone, the mostly completed temple at Jerusalem was being dismantled by frenzied hands.

Perhaps the greatest irony of the whole conquest of Jerusalem was the presence of many reporters and television cameras. The whole world, now unitedly under the rule of the seductive Commander Sarkus, watched the destruction of the Christian missionaries and the long-hated Jews with satanic rejoicing. They declared holidays and gave gifts to one another in celebration of the death of the two Christians who had so long kept the brave armies of the world at bay. As was prophesied in scripture, Commander Sarkus, the long-foretold Anti-Christ, in gluttonous pride defiled the very steps of the temple in Jerusalem as he entered the holy sanctuary. Laughing and mocking God, he declared himself to be the god of all the earth. He abated destroying the last of the Jews, savoring this moment so they could despair in his ultimate triumph.

Now that the two Christian strangers were dead, the world watched their bodies lie in the bloodied streets of Jerusalem for three days. They gleefully reasoned that now the war could finally at long last end, because the last enemy had been subdued. They were right, but they were also terribly wrong. It would shortly end, but they were wrong about which enemy would finally be subdued.

On the third day, a light broke through the dense cloud cover over Jerusalem. It was the first of April, and a cold rain had fallen all throughout the night. With the largest mass of the Jews having already been killed, the final order to destroy them was now given. The slaughter began at a diabolical pace.

The city exploded into chaos, and the terrified Jews started fleeing with their families westward out of the city. The soldiers pursued them with heavy gunfire into the Kidron Valley, and soon trapped them against the Mount of Olives, where the Jews faced certain annihilation.

In this moment of the Jews' greatest peril, the sun suddenly burned a hole through the rumbling clouds. A shaft of light fell upon the two disheveled bodies lying in the city. No sooner did it touch them than they were instantly resurrected in a burst of light. The remaining soldiers there shielded their eyes as the two glowing men stood upright, looked directly into the TV cameras, and then were taken up into heaven. The last image the cameras captured was the soles of their feet as the dark clouds of early morning closed around them.

No sooner had this occurred than everyone within miles of the city looked up to see the two glorious strangers rising into the sky. Samuel could plainly see the astonishment on their faces as they saw an even brighter burst of light from which their Messiah emerged in glory. The surrounding army also saw the man descending, and turned their mass of weaponry toward Him.

Samuel could not believe his eyes as dozens of rockets streaked into the sky, all to explode harmlessly far below the Savior's feet. The army in pursuit of the refugees on the ground turned their automatic weapons skyward and emptied their magazines into the air. After that they picked up rocks and bricks and threw them at the sky, their faces twisted in demonic fury. They were actually attempting to make war against the returning Messiah!

The Lord began a steep descent rapidly toward them. In breathless wonder they watched as the Lord drew near and finally settle upon the Mount of Olives. At the exact moment His foot touched the ground, a mighty earthquake shook the earth such that all upon it fell to the ground, decimating the impending army. Beneath the Lord a chasm opened, dividing the mount into two jagged halves nearly a quarter mile apart.

The quaking of the earth ceased suddenly, and those near the wall stood only to find themselves immediately under attack again. A hundred men, women and children fell in death every step they took. Seeing the glorious being standing above the opening in the earth beckoning to them, the survivors surged toward Him and into the cavity that had once been the sacred Mount of Olives.

Their numbers were now very few, and dwindling steadily under the ferocious hail of bullets and rockets. When the last of their numbers finally entered into the canyon below them the Lord held out His left hand exactly as He had His right, and the beam of light which burst from His left hand brought unquenchable fire and destruction upon the pursuing armies. Whereas the light from His right hand had been totally silent, the flame from His left roared above the threshold of hearing. Samuel had never heard the sound of devouring fire, but it was horrendous, as if all the oxygen on the planet were being sucked through a tiny hole.

In utter astonishment, Commander Sarkus fell to the earth, clapping his hands over his ears in writhing pain, and cursed God as he was being consumed by divine flame. Moment by moment the purifying fire thundered across the wastes of Jerusalem, devouring everything as it went: buildings, trees, streets, armies and tanks, rockets, guns, the living and the dead. Nothing escaped—nothing.

As the fires of retribution rolled outward as if in slow motion, the Lord descended into the cavity of the Mount until He stood among those few survivors. Samuel and all those present knew their exact number, and they were fewer than five thousand. At that moment the words and music to a new song entered the minds of those accompanying the Savior, and they lifted their angelic voices in song. In a language unknown, yet so familiar, in voices made perfect by the power of the resurrection, they sang with one heavenly accord. The music was as vast as eternity, yet simple and holy. It both overwhelmed and soothed the soul.

The filthy and bloodied Jews remaining looked around them in wonder, taking in the majesty of what their senses were bringing to them. Then they pressed slowly toward their Messiah who stood in glory before them. They came forward and fell down upon their faces in prayer and solemn gratitude and rejoicing. For they knew, at long last, their conquering Messiah had returned. The long wait that had begun the day their forefathers had departed Egypt was finally over.

An older man, apparently a Jewish leader among them, was the first to arrive at the Savior after crawling to touch their rescuing Messiah's feet with a trembling hand. No sooner did his finger touch divinity than he turned to his people, and in a surge of triumph too grand to be kept inside he cried out:

"He lives!" The cry was taken up like an anthem chant, and every voice joined in. This was not a dream—"He is here, He lives!"

As the old one's eyes fell upon the Messiah's feet, a look of confusion mingled with his expression of joy fell upon him. He straightened upon his knees, and in boldness asked, "Lord, what are these wounds in Thy feet?" Then looking up added, "and in Thy hands?"

This question had the immediate effect of arresting the attention of all present. Everyone turned their faces in wonder toward His hands and feet.

The living Christ tilted his hands so that His palms were toward their faces. "These," the voice of a thousand rushing rivers said in perfect mildness and love, "are the wounds with which I was wounded in the house of my friends. I am Jesus Christ, whom your fathers crucified."

The people fell back in horror.

"Oh, my Lord, my God!" the old man closest to the Lord cried out in anguish. He fell backwards in horror. "My God, forgive us! Forgive us!" he wailed in abject sorrow so deep it seemed as if his soul might depart his body.

"I forgive you," the same kindly voice replied. "Ye are they who were the most believing of my people. Ye are they who did not persecute those whom I had sent among you." A hush of bewildered reverence swept through the crowd, and they all crumpled to the earth in awe.

Jesus gently reached down and lifted the trembling old man to his feet, enfolding him into His bosom of infinite love. Then He spoke to the others. "Arise. Come forth unto me. Feel the wounds in my hands and my feet, and let me heal you. The long separation of my old covenant people is accomplished. The debt is paid and I am come to cleanse you and make you whole and clean again. Come unto me, ye lost sheep of Israel, and I will gather you as a hen gathers her chicks under her wings. Come unto me ye heavy laden, and I will give you that peace which surpasses the understanding of man. The first shall be last, and the last shall be first."

A cry of joy arose from those kneeling before him, yet their joy was burdened with grief. The tears that streaked their filthy faces were partly for having rejected Him for so many generations, the loss of many loved ones, and the relief of deliverance and joy they felt in their glorious Messiah.

Their Messiah knew their pain, and His own face was burdened for their sorrow. "Fear not," he said, his voice so soft that it entered the heart more forcefully than the ears. "They only sleep, and the time of awakening is at hand."

"Mama!" a small voice cried from the entrance to the canyon. "Mama!"

"Natali?" a mother's voice cried out in wonder too impossible to be hope. Samuel watched a ragged mother press her way through the throng as all eyes watched her. She ran to a tiny figure standing alone and scooped her child into her arms. While she cleansed her baby's face with tears and kisses, she literally ran back toward the Savior.

"See, see Natali! It is the Messiah. He has delivered us! He has raised you up!" she cried in a voice that was almost a shriek of elation.

"I remember him," the little one said, and took three bold steps toward her Lord as soon as her mother set her upon her tiny feet.

"Hello, Natali," the voice of infinite love said in perfect mildness. In answer, little Natali rushed into His open arms with a silvery laugh of childlike innocence.

At that moment a man's voice cried in joyous wonder as he embraced his wife who had fallen from his arms in death mere moments ago. She was whole, and together they walked toward their God. Samuel watched, unable to keep tears of wonder, joy and sweet emotion from his eyes as every individual there received the loved ones who had just died in the final assault as the Lord descended to deliver them. Their deliverance was complete, perfect, and immaculately joyful. Samuel had never seen such a tender scene. Then, something happened that was miraculous and healing. Many accompanying the Lord felt His silent invitation to go forth among these struggling souls.

Samuel stepped forward and watched as one of the translated sisters with whom he worked, lifted a corner of her sleeve and gently wipe the face of a teenage girl. The grime of years as well as scars, scabs and bruises of body and soul became clean in a single stroke. She bent forward and dried the girl's tears with her kisses.

Then another angel put her arms around a gray-haired man's shoulders, and when he looked up slowly, she kissed him on the cheek. She joined him in prayer and spoke words of love and consolation.

Samuel lifted a child, all alone and stricken with grief into his lap, and the words of love and healing flowed freely from heart to heart. All this and a thousand other ministrations were done while the Savior walked slowly through the people, blessing, healing, comforting and fulfilling promises made seven millennia earlier. It was a scene of infinite tenderness beyond human understanding.

A cry of joy and praise flowed over those angels standing above this sweet scene, and they burst into song. Long and worshipful, it flowed out across those below. Samuel had never heard such spontaneous purity. For a long time they sang in complete, perfect worship.

Their long-promised Messiah then said to His people, "Lead me to My house that I may cleanse and sanctify it unto the Most High God."

The people shouted with joy, and surged around Him as he walked in the midst of them toward the temple. As they entered the Kidron valley, many graves were opened and scores of the righteous of ages past arose to join the heavenly throng. As they neared the walls of Jerusalem, their Messiah raised His left hand toward the sealed-over Golden Gate and the surrounding bricks turned to dust to form an arched opening. As they entered the holy sanctuary He turned with tears in His eyes, purified and ordained them saying, "The time has fully come that the sons of Levi may offer again an offering unto the Lord in righteousness."

Suddenly, a stream of living water burst forth from under the temple into the valleys below. The water danced and sparkled as it healed everything it touched.

Then, almost as suddenly as it had begun, it was over. Every tear was dried, every pain healed, and every wound closed. With one single accord, Samuel and all with him rose with the Savior into the air, as 5,000 now-glowing Jewish faces strained to catch one last glimpse of their Messiah. Then Christ and His company were gone.

In as little time as it took to ponder what had occurred, Sam found himself with Jehovah coming toward the familiar vistas of Zion, and the Holy Temple of the Most High God.

It was still dark in Zion, and all around the Temple the people of God had kept a constant vigil upon their knees. Melody, her family, and a multitude of the pure in heart had spent many days in fasting and prayer, camping on the Temple grounds, and pleading with the Lord to restore the Temple light. The first hint of morning had begun to show in the Eastern sky when Melody suddenly arose to her feet.

"He's coming," she said as if to herself.

"Who's coming, Melody?" Sarah asked, perplexed.

Melody could not find other words to describe the magnificent feeling that had suddenly burst upon her. "He's coming!" she said more forcefully. Turning to others kneeling nearby on the grounds she repeated, "He's coming to His Temple!"

"Who?" a hundred voices asked her, yet her heart was so filled with rapture that she could not answer. She could only point into the eastern sky at a pinprick of light and exclaim, "Him!"

Every eye turned toward the dot of light moving toward them with perceptible speed.

"It's another missile!" someone proclaimed. "Gather the brethren, quickly!"

"No, it's Him. It's Christ! He's coming to His Temple!" Melody cried with fervency.

Friendly hands patted her back, and a few tried to gently restrain her. Someone mumbled something about Melody being old and weary. She hardly felt their touch as she began jumping from one foot to another.

"Hallelujah!" she cried. "Praise be to God! He comes!"

Then they saw the light. "It's another missile! We are under attack! Let's call upon the power of God to defend us!" some cried.

From other places around them they heard, "Wait, I can see someone in the light!"

Melody's eyes were fixed upon the light as it rapidly approached. In her mind, she could plainly see the personage standing in the light. Her heart soared to the highest joy at the sight.

"Hallelujah!" she cried over and over.

Others began to see. "It *is* He!" they cried. "Look into the light. See! It is the Christ! He is coming to Zion! He is coming to the Temple!" The people cried together, "Hallelujah! Praise be to God!"

By now every eye could see the face of Christ. Though He was in reality still far away, His face and form were plainly visible. His robe was white like the pillar of fire that had once arisen from the Temple. He wore a red sash about His waist which hung to His bare feet. His face was solemn, yet compassionate and infinitely beautiful. He looked at them all, and smiled.

A mere moment later Jehovah was above them, standing in the air just below the clouds. Behind Him were angels and glorified beings in the attitude of rejoicing and praising their God. This was the long-foretold prophecy: Christ was coming to His Temple in the New Jerusalem!

Jesus looked down upon those assembled around the Temple. His countenance softened as he saw them, and His smile warmed every soul. As His hallowed foot touched the first step of the outermost building, the entire structure began to glow. He stepped through the great doors, and an instant later the pillar of fire lanced again from the Temple spire into the heavens. The light from this glorious pillar re-illuminated the landscape for hundreds of miles in every direction.

The Lord was in His temple, never to depart again! The skies rolled back together from opposite horizons, as if a scroll was being rolled into itself, and blue sky and billowing clouds once again drifted above them. The multitude of angels descended, and combined with all present in a spontaneous shout of exaltation:

"Hurrah for Israel, Hurrah for Israel!"

Samuel was walking among the Temple crowd, searching for Melody and his family among the thousands of rejoicing worshippers, when he felt two little arms clasp him tightly around the legs. "Daddy!" his little son Helaman shouted with boyish happiness. Samuel laughed and tossed his son high into the air, while Helaman giggled with delight.

Melody threw her arms around her husband, and affectionately kissed him. "Hey, stranger! I'm thrilled you're finally back! Oh darling, you could not have chosen to come back on a more glorious day!" Samuel's eyes flooded with tears as he held his beloved wife once again, and felt her glorious spirit communicating with his. Their souls were now both complete, whole, and one. They embraced tenderly and long, yearning to never be separated again.

Then Samuel saw the face of someone he had not seen in many years.

"Mother!" he cried as his long-deceased mother stepped forward from the crowd to greet him. He fell into her arms and felt the familiar warmth of her motherly touch. To his eyes she appeared exactly as he remembered her in his childhood—a beautiful young woman in her mid-twenties. He heard Melody laughing to his right, and turned in time to see her clasped in the arms of her own mother, whom she had not seen since her youngest childhood. He knew that Melody had dreamed of this moment all her life.

"Sam," a silvery voice said behind him, and he spun around to find himself face-to-face with someone most dear to him.

"Dawn! Oh Princess!" he cried, new tears springing to his eyes, his voice caught in his throat. She embraced him in joy, repeatedly speaking his name.

"Dawn! Is it really you?" Samuel cried again.

"Oh Sam, I have longed to see you these many years!" she cried. Then unexpectedly, she asked, "Where's Melody?"

For the first time Samuel pondered the improbability of this very situation. Did he love two women? And yet, Melody was the love of his life! At that moment of confusion and hesitancy, he saw Melody moving quickly toward them, her eyes not upon Samuel.

"Dawn!" she cried. "I… I think I remember you! We have been friends for eons of time, haven't we?"

"Yes, Melody! And I still adore you, my friend!" Dawn cried, tenderly embracing her.

"What?" Samuel exclaimed, his mind reeling happily. The odd thing is that even though he didn't remember many of the details, he knew they were right.

Then Dawn turned as a young man approached. She took his arm, beaming at everyone around her. "Sam and Melody, I want you to meet Nathan."

Samuel reached to shake the young man's hand, and a distant premortal memory crystallized in his mind. He started to understand for the first time why Dawn had come into his life and then departed so quickly.

Melody hugged them both, and spoke excitedly. "Don't you remember, Samuel? Before we came to earth, Dawn and Nathan were our dear friends. They had consecrated themselves as eternal companions, and actually gave us the courage to do the same. When we found out that Nathan was required to be born long before Dawn, we wanted to help them. Dawn needed to have the ordinances, and she desired the opportunity to bear children. You and I offered to delay our love to give them those gifts. Father and Mother granted us permission to do so."

Dawn and Nathan nodded happily. "That's right," Dawn said, looking at Nathan with shining eyes.

"You remember all this?" Sam asked Melody incredulously.

"It is an isolated memory with me," Melody assured him. "But what I do remember is bright and pure! The Lord had promised Dawn that He would give you to be her husband on earth who would love and care for her until Nathan and she could be reunited."

"Yes, and I will always be eternally grateful to you, Samuel," Nathan added earnestly.

At that moment, Samuel knew that he had always loved Dawn deeply, but had never planned on spending eternity as her companion. He felt a rush of tremendous peace enter his soul. This was right! This was the only way that eternity could be perfect. He felt Melody slip to his side, and the four friends gathered in a simultaneous embrace.

Then Samuel felt someone approach, and looked up as a familiar young woman ran to Melody, smiling and laughing as she reached to embrace her. He knew immediately this was the precious daughter they had lost so many years before.

"Mother!" Star said with such overwhelming love in her voice that Samuel's heart felt as if it might jump from his chest. He took a step forward, and Star flashed him a brilliant smile. Then she turned back to Melody. "Mother, I have awaited this moment for a long eternity. I love you!" she cried, and after looking at Samuel with loving eyes, she reached out both hands and laid them lightly on her mother's arms. In the blink of an eye she changed, grew smaller and closer to Melody. Samuel could not see exactly what took place, except that a moment later Melody turned toward him, her face alight with joy. She held up a tiny baby girl in her arms.

"Oh, Star, my precious baby girl! I have missed you so long and so terribly! Welcome at last to my arms, my child," Melody cooed softly as she brushed the baby's cheek with her finger and kissed her.

From that day on Zion was different, both in reality, and in the minds of its inhabitants. All knew that Christ was now an inhabitant of Zion. And all knew that the days had come when Christ would finally walk the streets of Zion and greet them with loving words and an embrace.

Zion was at long last, in name and in fact, the City of the Living God. A wondrous thing occurred from that day onward: it became at first gloriously unique, and then commonplace to see Christ walking slowly along the streets of Zion.

One may ponder what such a thing as living with the Lord might be like, yet never in a lifetime really imagine it. For when He now walked among His Zion people, Christ chose to come without His glory. He came as a man, a friend, a loving brother who laid aside His vast and incredible glory to personally minister to His people, answer their fears, and dry their tears. Every part of His being among them was unexpected, and wholly delightful. He called each person by his or her first name, expressing His individual love for them. He invariably thanked them for services rendered in His name. Though with one accord the people fell at His feet to worship Him, feeling completely unworthy, He often raised them up, and asked them to wait until He was in His Glory for such adoration. For now, in this setting, He was a friend among them, not above them.

Almost without exception, each who met Him initially called Him "Jesus." The Lord kindly informed them that "Jesus" was not actually His given name. His mother had called Him "Yeshua"—commonly known as Joshua in English. He informed them that among His friends, He preferred to be called His given name.

No matter who they were, everyone who met Yeshua instantly recognized who He was. Some ran to Him, others lowered their eyes in regret for past deeds long ago abandoned. To these particularly He came, lifting them up, blessing them, filling them with love such as they had never before known. The diseases He healed were now those of the soul, rather than of life or limb. There were none sick in Zion, for illness had long ago been vanquished. But there was sickness and impurity of the soul which had nothing to do with unworthiness, or sins unrepented. The debilitating diseases the living Christ healed were remaining emotional scar tissue upon the soul. With a touch of His hand and a gentle word, He healed them all. None could doubt their worth after experiencing His incalculable love for them—no one.

As intently as they desired to again greet the Lord, Samuel and Melody were in a unique situation wherein they had already been in Christ's presence, and had heard the words of life spoken to them from the Savior's lips. There were many from all nations who had just been gathered into Zion, and who had great need for the healing and gifts of grace that only He could give them. So they did not openly seek opportunity to be with him.

At dusk one evening, Samuel was walking with Melody and little Star when his whole being told him the Master was near. Melody felt it too, took his hand and together they ran toward the lush garden before the Temple. There they saw Him withholding His glory, standing near the edge of a fountain, and holding a young man in His arms. Nearly a dozen small children stood around him, their eyes so fixed upon His face that the young man was nearly unseen by them. Beyond the children stood a small semicircle of adults in various postures of adoration and worship. It was a scene of supernal tenderness and glorious peace.

Samuel and Melody walked quietly to the outer ring of people and watched. Melody held up Star to see Him, who waved her chubby little arms and cooed with delight. Samuel glanced at his wife and saw her face streaked with tears. When he looked back at the Savior, the young man had stepped away. As if time stopped at that moment, the Lord looked directly at Samuel and smiled. In an effortless movement the Savior stood and smoothly walked toward them.

Even though Samuel remembered with vivid detail his glorious previous encounters with the Lord, he would never tire of those piercing eyes that seemed to contain all of eternity in their supernal blue. The people parted as Yeshua came, and He excused Himself with kind politeness as He passed. Many reached out to touch Him as He went by. Samuel felt Melody wrap her arm tightly through his and press her body against him.

"Hello, Samuel!" Yeshua called, still a step away. He extended both arms, and Samuel fell into His embrace. Every sense, every sensation, every emotion was even more poignant than he had recalled. The joy that flooded through him seemed to cause his soul to melt. "I am so grateful," the Savior said as he released Samuel, "for all you have done in my name. You have served me well, my son. Thank you."

"Master, it is I who owe to you all thanks, and honor, and glory!" Samuel replied, as if the burden of his joy could be entirely summed up by these few words.

"You are most welcome," the Lord replied genially, a gentle smile upon His face. The words "Knowest thou the condescension of God?" came strongly into Samuel's mind. His soul cried out with perfect understanding. Here was the mighty Jehovah, the Creator of heaven and earth, the

 Firstborn of the Father, the Savior of mankind, preeminent and most glorious of all Father's children, standing without His glory upon a city street thanking *him*—think of it—thanking *him* for all *he* had done!

With this, Yeshua turned to Melody, who transferred Star to her father's arms.

"My beloved Melody, it is so good to be with you again. You have labored in love as my servant and my friend. You have done all I asked of you—and more. Thank you," Yeshua said earnestly.

Melody fell to her knees. "Oh my dearest Lord! You do not owe me thanks. Anything good I might have done was only through your kind grace and empowerment. It is you who are righteous, Lord—-not me."

Yeshua smiled broadly at her. "You have been obedient to my voice, my daughter. You fully consecrated your life to me and to the Father. This is our greatest joy."

Then He turned to the child in Samuel's arms. "And I see you have your little one again."

Melody smiled radiantly at Samuel as she lifted Star from him and in a single motion, turned and gently pressed the child into the Savior's arms.

"Star! Dear Star!" Yeshua laughed, holding the child first at arm's length, then folding her little body into His bosom. Star giggled happily, her hands reaching for his face. He lowered his face to let her little fingers explore His beard and cheeks. He laughed again and kissed her; then raising His eyes to heaven, He said something most startling. "Father, I thank you for this little one whom you have given unto me. I pray you to bless her, and release her tongue that her parents may hear their baby's joy."

"Hosanna!" Star's little voice cried out. "Hosanna to God, and the Lamb!" she cried. All who stood nearby pressed around to hear this infant whose voice spoke articulately of her adoration for her Savior. Yet, nothing more then came from her voice except the laughing and cooing sounds of her infancy.

At that moment it seemed appropriate to take their child back, and Melody gently received her from Him. As if in explanation, Yeshua said, "Her glorious spirit within her cried out with such joy that the Father wished us to hear. It was a wonderful blessing. Praise be to thee, Father!" He exclaimed happily.

Yeshua then turned back to those surrounding Him, and waved a fond farewell. Their time with the Lord today was now finished, since there could be nothing of greater impact than what had just taken place. So the Zion-dwellers obediently dispersed, often turning backwards that their eyes might linger upon their Savior for as long as possible. Slowly, ever so slowly, they walked homeward. Yet, as they neared their abode, it felt to them as if each step had taken them farther away from Home.

29

FULL CIRCLE

The next evening Dawn came to visit Samuel and Melody. She explained that she had requested this special visit, which had been graciously granted by Father. As she entered their home, Dawn brought with her a spirit of sweet peace and purest love. The three of them spent the evening happily speaking of their former mortal lives, their eternal connection, and rejoicing in Melody and Samuel's beautiful experience with the Savior the day before.

As they spoke of eternal things, Samuel was startled by the advanced truths that Dawn knew and shared with them. Now a resurrected being, she understood mysteries he had never imagined. Her life beyond the grave had given her a thirty-year head start wherein she had absorbed knowledge of the things of God beyond Samuel and Melody's comprehension. Dawn was very careful about what she told them for no other reason than some things could not be explained, but had to be seen, felt and experienced to be understood. Even so, the thoughts she shared with Samuel and Melody were mind-boggling.

The three were still talking excitedly when the sun edged above the horizon of a new day, and Star began to cry for breakfast. Melody stood and stretched, although not a bit tired as she started down the hall to get the baby.

"Melody," Dawn urged, "stay here and let me get Star."

Melody laughed. "No need, my friend. I'll be right back," she assured her. She returned in a minute.

"Here's my little sweetie," Melody said happily as she walked back into the living room. Melody wore a thick white bathrobe, and Samuel marveled at how beautiful she was. Her hair was a vibrant auburn, her face clear and youthful, and her eyes bright. Melody's spirit radiated from her body in a nearly-tangible halo all around her.

She sat beside Samuel and discreetly began nursing Star. She was beaming with happiness and motherly contentment. After a few minutes she called for Sarah, who bounced down the stairs to retrieve Star while the three friends took a walk in the fresh morning air of Zion.

Samuel, Melody and Dawn walked from the house and out into the pale light. The sky was a panorama of pinks and golds spangled across a canvas of rich blue. The streets of crystalline gold glittered richly in the warm light. All around birds were taking up their morning song like a choir of angels singing their prayers. Samuel felt completely, permanently at peace. His heart beat with joy.

"What does it feel like to be a resurrected being?" Samuel finally asked Dawn as they walked slowly down the golden street toward the Temple. It was an odd question, but one that had occurred to him with considerable force. Never before in his life had he been in a position to ask such a question, and the framing of it in his heart sent a thrill of wonder through him.

"It feels like nothing I ever imagined," Dawn replied. "One thing I didn't realize when I was mortal was that the human body is always in pain! You know—a leg hurts, your finger hurts, your tummy hurts, headaches, backaches, side aches, cramps, sprains, cuts, burns. The body is designed to be in continual pain. The first big difference I noticed was the total absence of pain, and yet I still have a physical body."

"I've noticed a lack of pain, too, since being translated," Melody told her. "But I'm told being translated is considerably less powerful than resurrection."

"In many ways, I envy you both, and your mission!" Dawn admitted. "But do you want to see something amazing?" she asked.

"Yes," they both cried.

"It's this," Dawn said, and turned toward them. Stepping closely, she held out a hand between them. She looked in both directions up and down the street, as if concerned that someone might be watching. Satisfied they were alone, she looked back at her hand. It quickly changed to a whiteness rivaling the pillar of fire over the Temple.

Samuel and Melody were astounded. "Wow!" Samuel said in childlike amazement.

Dawn lowered her hand as it quickly changed back to the color of normal flesh. "It's actually an effort to keep it from showing. I have to continually be aware to keep it inside. To be honest, if it were possible to feel discomfort in such a perfect body, I would have to say that keeping the light inside is uncomfortable. I feel like I need to go to some private place and just let myself shine for a while."

"I would like to see that. I can't imagine anything more beautiful!" Melody allowed.

"I can't show my glory on this earth," Dawn said softly. "I don't belong here anymore."

"What do you mean?" Samuel asked.

Dawn sighed and turned to walk again. "It's difficult for me to remain here. I'm no longer a mortal, and must go where people like myself go.

 But before I do, Nathan and I must wait for our sealing, as soon as we can arrange for two mortals to do it."

Samuel looked startled. "You mean, mortals still have to do the temple work for you? I hadn't expected that."

She sighed, then laughed. "Me either, actually. The temple belongs to the mortal world, and to mortal ordinances. I already have my sealing ordinance in place, so my sealing will be transferred to Nathan and me as soon as his ordinances are completed. When we get sealed, we will stand by as mortals perform these sacred ordinances in our behalf."

Dawn stopped to look intently at them. "Nathan and I were hoping you two would do this for us," she asked quietly.

Samuel looked at Melody, and they both nodded.

"Yes, of course!" Melody told her with a grin.

"We would be pleased to do that," Samuel responded happily. "I'll make the arrangements immediately."

Dawn seemed relieved. "Nathan and I have waited thousands of years to be together. Thank you so much," she said with tears in her eyes.

"We are honored," Samuel replied.

Dawn shook her head. "I didn't mean just for the temple work. I meant," she paused to glance shyly at Samuel, "I meant, for taking care of me during my lifetime, and for loving me through everything, and not giving up on me. Even though I know you could have."

Samuel stopped walking to consider his words, while Dawn waited patiently. "It was my honor to love you, and I always did. But shortly before you passed away, there was some part of me that knew our life together was by design a temporary arrangement." He looked at Melody, who gave him an encouraging nod. "After I married Melody, I understood that even more fully. Somewhere deep in my soul, I knew we each had another assignment that would bring us even greater joy."

Samual regarded Dawn with deep gratitude. "I will always love you, too, and remain grateful for our life together."

Dawn nodded and smiled brightly. "Me too, Sam. I feel so grateful to you, and to God!"

"Isn't it crazy?" Samuel replied in earnest. "I don't understand all the reasons that God allows us to go through what we do on earth, and why everything doesn't turn out as we thought it would—but I do praise Him for every experience! I would not have wanted my life to be anything different than what it was—or what it is now."

Melody giggled. "Well, you two, I can honestly say that I would never change a thing in my life, either—as crazy and convoluted as it was at times!" she grinned.

Sam remembered something. "Oh yes, and I never got to thank you for the gift of the diamond that enabled us to bring Alexei's people to Zion!" he exclaimed. "That came just at the right time!"

"It was my fun surprise for you! Little did I know how you would really use it," Dawn laughed.

They walked along in quiet contemplation when Melody suddenly asked, "Dawn, I have a feeling that we have loved one another long before this life. I wonder how long we have actually known each other?"

Dawn shrugged. "I have not yet been given a full memory of the pre-mortal world, either, but I do know it is longer than Sam and I have known one another."

Samuel shook his head, bewildered. "That seems very odd, and very wonderful," he said. "I wonder what forces brought the three of us together?"

"It was love," Dawn told them in a voice colored with wonder. "It was a love so strong that we were willing to make any sacrifice to ensure each other's eternal happiness."

"I believe that," he agreed. "I'm not sure why, but I know it is the truth."

"It will be fun to remember all those things one day," Melody nodded.

The three friends had arrived at the exquisitely-crafted Temple grounds and sat together on a park bench under a sprawling tree, their backs against the outer wall of the Temple. They talked deeply about their profound blessings, the challenges they had faced, and the glorious events that had brought them to this very moment in time.

Then Dawn took Samuel's hand, and said, "My friends, I must go soon. But before I do there is something else of my experience in the world of spirits that I think you might enjoy knowing."

"Please tell us!" Melody urged her.

Dawn drew an excited breath and began. "I received instruction in things you cannot even imagine. I was taught the order of the Gospel as it applies to eternity. See, we have only known the Gospel as it applies to this dispensation, and to this telestial world. The Gospel is actually eternal in its scope, and infinitely vast in the possibilities it affords us!" she said, grasping his hand more tightly.

"The gospel, or the grace and law of Christ, gives us the power to step into any realm or thought process; mere thought becomes reality. Do you understand that? This is the reason that obedience has always been the key to every blessing. We have to learn obedience to God's law, because the time will come that if we were not pure and flawlessly obedient to divine law, we could obliterate portions of existence by our unworthy thoughts."

Sam stared at her. "Wow, I have never contemplated that!" he exclaimed.

"Consider this," she continued. "The time will come when to merely think a thing will be to create it. To desire will be to immediately receive, and to wonder will be to immediately know. I have experienced this in part, and it's so staggering that I can hardly describe the phenomenon."

She took a deep breath, trying to convey her thoughts in a way they could understand. "You see, we have always known that Father lives in a dimension where time does not exist. I was once given the privilege of experiencing that dimension, in a limited way. When a being is in that realm, *all* things are present—you literally see all things at once! I could see yesterday, or a million years ago as easily as I could see my present moment."

Samuel nodded his head, not fully comprehending, only knowing what he had experienced as a translated being. He and Melody nodded for her to go on.

"But here's more truth: Not only do you see, but you comprehend and understand all things frontwards and backwards—infinitely," she exclaimed. "Father is all-powerful because He loves infinitely and knows everything that can be known. He is all-knowing because everything is quite literally before His eyes. He is all-powerful because He understands what he sees, down to the most minute detail. He comprehends, obeys, and lives in accordance with every eternal law."

She smiled at them, perceiving their thoughts. "And yet, because of His infinite capacity, He is able to give his complete focus to every child and every one of his creations at the same time. The human mind cannot understand this, but for God, it is actually very simple for Him to govern His vast domain."

Samuel was hanging onto every word. "Dawn, that is exciting, and most comforting to me," he said. "It's funny—and I've never told anyone this—but I always secretly thought that with the universe that God has to maintain, with children as numerous as the sands of the seashore, and with everything that is required of Him, I thought that perhaps His life could get far too complicated—even for Him!"

Dawn smiled at his confession. "Oh Sam, you are so endearing!" she said warmly, winking at Melody. "God's life the most wonderful existence in the universe. Rest assured on that!"

Sam nodded. "Thank you, Dawn," he said quietly.

She continued, her eyes glowing. "But this is the real truth above all truths," she continued. "God is God not because of His vast power or knowledge, but because of His never-ending, all-encompassing Love. He is God because His love caused Him to take that infinite power and understanding, and turn it into a means of salvation for every one of His children, and for each of His creations. It is this incomprehensible love that is the very substance of our Heavenly Father and Heavenly Mother, and of their Son, Jesus Christ. It is this love that drenches all Their creations—from the greatest to the least. It is this infinite love that makes God, God."

Dawn grew silent as she perceived that, though incomplete, she had said as much as she was able. She stood and turned to face the center spire of the temple as it glowed softly above them. Samuel and Melody stood also.

"By the way, do you know what the pillar of fire is for?" Dawn asked, breaking a long silence between them.

Sam shook his head. "You know, I hadn't really thought there might be an actual purpose to it other than to testify of the glory of God."

"One thing I have learned is that besides being symbolic, everything has a purpose. Nothing is incidental or casual. The pillar of fire is somewhat like an elevator shaft," Dawn told them.

"Really? How is that?" Melody asked.

"All things operate by application of some law. This pillar is an implementation of an eternal law, too. In a symbolic sense it represents the presence of Christ upon the earth. But in an actual sense, it is a physical means by which we come and go upon the earth. It is one of the ways that the heavens and the earth are joined."

Dawn stopped speaking, and they each remained silent for a long time. Then Samuel spoke. "So, is this where we say goodbye?" he asked.

"Only for a short time."

Melody turned to go, then whirled around suddenly. "Sam Mahoy, why don't you play the piano anymore?"

"Probably because I have been way too busy hanging out in Jerusalem," he replied with a chuckle.

Melody burst out laughing, and Dawn smiled, but continued firmly. "Let me make you a promise then. I will return to hear the next song you write," she said. "Is it a deal?"

Sam smiled at her. "Deal." He took Melody's arm and they turned toward the door.

"Please give Nathan our love," Melody called back to her.

"I will! Farewell," Dawn said fondly. She regally walked through the ornate Temple doors and toward the fiery spire which would bring her home.

Then she was gone.

Samuel and Melody strolled together toward the gate of the temple. Then Melody turned and kissed him lightly on the cheek.

"What a wonderful morning this has been! Dawn is a beautiful friend," she told him sincerely. She pulled her jacket around her. "I'd better go home now and take care of Star," she said. "I have the feeling you need a few minutes alone here at the temple. See you in a bit?"

Samuel nodded, knowing she was right. Melody took two steps and disappeared into the morning light. It made Sam smile to watch her use a privilege she had been given as translated priestess.

Sam presently got up and slowly walked into the Temple, his mind surging with new understanding, wonder and delight. There was no sadness in his soul anywhere to be found.

When he passed the open doors to the grand assembly hall his eyes unexpectedly fell upon a large white grand piano sitting in the middle of the hall. All around it the chairs had been moved back so that it appeared to be sitting by itself in a sea of empty chairs. He paused, wanting to touch it, to run his fingers across the silken keys, to hear, even in the briefest way, the long-loved wonder of music as it emerged from his fingers and found its way into the piano and to his soul. However, this was the Temple, and he highly doubted the propriety of doing so. Then he was startled to see someone standing close to him. He looked up to see a familiar face.

Except for the fact that this young man stood several inches above the floor, Samuel would have thought him a mortal temple worker dressed in white suit and tie. The young man smiled, and with his left hand, motioned toward the piano. It was all the invitation Samuel needed.

"Thank you, Helaman," Samuel said, and winked at his dear friend. "You knew I needed to express the music in my soul this morning, didn't you?"

Helaman looked at him with deep adoration and love. "That's what family is for," he said with a smile. "Enjoy this moment, my friend and fellow servant in Christ," he said as embraced Samuel, stepped away, then disappeared into thin air.

Samuel raised the lid of the piano and found himself looking into an instrument of unusual construction. In days long gone by, he had often studied the workmanship of the old grands, but this was unlike anything he had known. Taking a seat upon the upholstered bench, he raised the lid to find himself looking at two rows of keys, rather than one. The nearer row was the familiar black and white piano keys he had always known. Above that, and slanted toward him, was another keyboard unlike any he had yet seen. It was laid out in a pattern similar to the black and white keys, but these keys were all the same level, with no raised keys.

Samuel ran his fingers across the surface and found the keys only separated by slight grooves. As he touched them they did not move downward as expected, but immediately a rich tone emanated from the instrument with striking clarity. He again ran his fingers across the upper keys and listened to the ringing tones it called forth.

As he experimented, Samuel quickly learned that any combination of keys made a beautiful tone. There were no bad chords or notes. He placed both hands on the upper keys, and intuitively played a short rhapsody. He slid his fingers upward on the keys toward the black, and heard the tone go minor. He increased the spacing slightly between his fingers and found rich harmonies of seventh's and ninth's. His musical mind came alive! This was an instrument of instruments! Having spent mere minutes with it he knew it as if he had labored at it for centuries.

But there is a hunger that old memories bring, and his fingers ached for the former tones and keys he had come to love so well. In the few seconds it took to move his hands from the upper keyboard to the lower, he had time to wonder, even fear, if he could still even play the piano at all? He had loved it so well, rejoiced in it, touched people's lives with it, wooed and won his Love with it; the idea of discovering that the gift may have died frightened him.

Samuel cautiously placed his fingers upon the familiar keys and found they were not forgotten. Like the moment one comes to know Christ truly is their everlasting Savior, sweetness flowed through him, his heart burned brightly, and joy swept through him. He threw back his head and let his heart take free command of his fingers. They flew across the keys with boldness and surety. Not only could he still play, but he could play as he had never done before. It suddenly occurred to him that in the almost forty years since his change he had not played the piano simply for the joy of music. This was his first time in all those years, and he found that his fingers were tireless, flawlessly obedient to his mind, and superbly responsive to his will.

But far beyond this, he felt his soul open to that familiar place from where his music sprang, and for the first time in his life he understood.

 This was not so much a connection with the divine, though he knew it was a gift from Heavenly Father. No, this was a connection with who *he* was.

For the first time in his life, Samuel realized that the music which played in a stream of seemingly endless symphonies in his heart, was but a pinprick opening in the veil that had obscured Samuel from himself. This music, whose harmonies thrilled him so, these precious feelings that brought his soul so close to pure worship, these surges of love so powerful they could only find expression in music of surpassing beauty—even the words that upon occasion had startled him with their crystalline clarity—these were all a remnant, a reminder, a small glimpse into his divine soul.

No sooner had these thoughts surged sweetly through his mind than the memory of his life, of Melody, his children, of Helaman, of all those he had ministered to, and all those whom he had loved beyond the power of words to tell, entered his mind. The music then changed; it grew light, joyful and expansive. It began like the sound of a distant bird singing morning vespers, then slowly grew in passion and intensity, dancing upon harmonies of which he had never conceived before. It was alight with melody, and awash with celestial beauty.

Then, the words came as if he were listening to them: words that flowed too quickly for him to speak, too perfectly for him to utter, and too glorious to write down. He gasped, and his fingers came to an immediate stop. Suddenly, as surely as he knew any truth, he knew this: he had known and loved this music long before his mortal birth. This very music was the crowning achievement of his former self, and of someone else eternally important to him. This music was his and Melody's.

As he sat looking at his fingers stilled on the keys, Samuel suddenly understood that this glorious music was the anthem that defined the very essence of who both he was, and who Melody was. It was their shared musical passion which had joined them to one another permortally, and now lit the fire of their eternal future. This music expressed the entire content of their lives—past, present, and forever; it was the symphony of their souls, powerful in content and prophetic in scope. To sing this song was to know all things. It was to love as Christ loves.

In that moment of silence, Samuel realized that he was not yet ready. Like waiting to be given the sealed portion of the Book of Mormon, Samuel knew he must wait for the fullness of that perfect music to manifest itself in him. Sitting in that empty hall of the Temple, surrounded by the swish of silken robes of unseen visitors, he wept. He placed his hands on his head and cried tears of joy. And, with every sob of happiness he knew less and less why he was weeping. Perhaps it was because he had come so close to knowing everything. No, this was not a matter of "perhaps." He wept because he had glimpsed for a moment who he was, and who Melody was; and it was far more than his still-primitive frame could contain.

Samuel slowly closed the lid on the great piano and stood. He bowed his head for a moment and fervently thanked Father for the music in his soul, for this life-changing moment, and for an eternity of music yet to come. He stepped away from the room and walked toward home. He realized that he was not ready to write this music—not for any lack of love, but for lack of eternal perspective.

A finite man cannot write infinite music.

"What's wrong?" Melody asked the instant he walked into the house.

Samuel stepped to the couch, deep in thought. "Nothing, darling." He sank down, then looked at her with longing eyes.. "I just tried to write you a new song. But I couldn't express the overwhelming feelings of my heart—the infinitely precious music that is *you!*"

Melody beamed at him, touched to her core. "Samuel, a song for me? You've never written me a song before!"

Samuel shook his head. "Oh Melody, I wanted it to be so perfect! And for one second, it almost was. But I am so limited, still so limited! I sat at that piano in the temple and realized my nothingness—more today than ever before. And yet, I also know that you and I were and always will be eternal soulmates. My darling, we have been blessed with things few mortals can imagine."

He stopped for a moment, feeling the warmth of the Spirit as he spoke. " I don't know why our lives took such different paths before we were finally allowed to come together—but I do know that everything is exactly as it should be."

Melody sat beside him, and snuggled deeply into his chest. "Yes, my love, everything really *is* as it should be." Then she whispered with deep emotion. "Oh, Sam, I have never been happier in my life than I am right now." She threw her arms around him. "And you, Samuel Mahoy, are the most precious blessing I have received in this mortal existence—except for my Savior!" Her eyes were glowing. "I adore you, my Angel!"

Samuel kissed her tenderly for the millionth time, when something new and unexpected flooded his soul and spirit, taking him by surprise. At that moment he felt more pure love, more exquisite passion, and more reverence for this godly woman than he had ever known in his life—for anyone, at any time.

572 Overwhelmed by the intensity of what he was experiencing, Samuel kissed her neck, her face and her lips over and over, murmuring profound words of love that she hardly understood, but wept to hear.

ANGELS OF FIRE

On the sixth day of April at the break of day, Samuel heard the clarion sound of a trumpet, and he rushed into the street. Still far away, he could see a pinpoint of glory growing brighter as it approached the City. His heart raced wildly, and he shouted, "Hosannah!" as he ran inside to get Melody and his family. The Spirit told him plainly that this was The Day of Days for which they had for so long been waiting: the coming of Christ in His Glory, the Day of Cleansing, the Dawn of the Millennium!

The King of Kings came toward the earth slowly, and all of Zion gathered in the streets to watch His glorious descent. Today His coming was accompanied by magnificent signs in the heavens. A billowing cloud of glory surrounded Him, electrifying the heavens and the earth; a heavenly choir sang resounding hosannas to His name! From the moment of His appearance, upon the horizon they could see infinite shafts of light reaching out from His glorious personage to lift those to Him who were worthy to rise, and worthy of resurrection.

As He came toward the earth the sky convoluted, almost as if it were being rolled up into a scroll. Beyond the blue edges, like a silken curtain had been lifted, one could see into the depths of eternity. To look into the heavens was to behold the glory of God, and to see a vast array of beings, some of whom were praising the holy name of Jesus, and some who were cursing their consequences. What was being rolled back was the veil of mortality which had so long covered the earth. To Samuel's eyes, the sky—one of the elements of the earth's telestial atmosphere—was being superseded. When it was fully gone the earth would no longer be a Telestial world, but a Terrestrial home for the righteous.

This was the Great Day of Days when the Celestial-worthy dead would come forth, one and all. Previous to this only a select faithful few had been resurrected. Today, the long-awaited day of resurrection had fully come!

Christ passed slowly overhead, looking directly into the eyes of those gazing up at Him from the streets of Zion, and communicating His profound love to each one of them. Samuel immediately felt the pull of gravity release him, and he rose up to join his Savior once again. His joy could simply not be contained, nor did he have words to adequately describe this day to future generations of children. If it were possible for any experience to be grander than anything that had happened to him previously, this experience was.

Everyone ever born on the earth with garments now unspotted through the blood of the Lamb and who had been rendered worthy of a Celestial reward, was lifted up to meet Him in the air. The celestial dead were resurrected, their mortal bodies perfected, cleansed, healed of wounds and illnesses of body and spirit, made gloriously beautified, and brought forth triumphantly to join Him. Samuel tearfully joined Melody, their parents, their children, their brothers and sisters, relatives, missionary companions, eternal friends, and fellow-servants in Christ.

It was both a great and a terrible day. Nearly every mortal who rose left loved ones standing upon the ground weeping in deep distress; for those left below knew that the hour of their preparation was past. They had rebelliously procrastinated their repentance one too many days, and had not partaken of the gifts of grace that Christ had so freely offered to them. This knowledge was terrible indeed.

Those who rose had their eyes fixed upon their triumphant Savior, upon loved ones rushing to join Him, and upon the sweet consolation to their mortal suffering. Those who rose all rejoiced in their precious Redeemer, knowing that it was only through His great atonement, through their choosing to obey the Holy Spirit's whisperings, through consecrating all that they were and ever would be—that they were able to rise. They praised God to be clothed in the robes of His righteousness. They each knew they were worthy only through Christ—through His merits and not their own, through His mercy, through His grace. It was a great day of humility for all—both for those who rose, and for those who remained.

Looking behind him, Samuel could see a long, continuous flow of spirits coming from the heavens toward the earth in flowing robes of faithfulness in Christ. Each spirit moved quickly toward the earth, which had willingly given up the elements of their mortal body. Those elements very quickly reassembled into a perfect form, and their joyous spirit stepped into his or her perfected body, emanating with glory and light, never to be separated from it again. Many would throw their heads back, raise both hands high and give a shout of ecstasy as they stood momentarily upon the earth, or reached to embrace a loved one nearby. Immediately thereafter, each would be caught up to join the others in the heavens as they followed Christ in His triumphant return.

Then the Light touched Samuel's body! In that moment, he realized that this was his time to come forth in his long-awaited resurrection! The change that occurred in that fraction-of-a-second was like each cell being electrified by a billion volts of electricity, and each volt bringing a tingle of perfect elation. He watched as light burst from his skin—and in that moment not only his body but his perception of everything changed. His vision now included profound truths previously obscured from his view.

Samuel felt the veil lift from his mind, and though he could not remember everything about his long premortal life, in a flash he saw his own magnificent spirit, which had always been an intimate part of God himself. This knowledge astonished him to the core. Then he comprehended even more profoundly the excruciating and infinite sacrifice that Jesus Christ had wrought for him personally, which at the same time made Samuel more fully realize his own utter nothingness without Christ. He saw who he truly was in the full light of Truth—the nothingness and the magnificent greatness, simultaneously. He wept in humility and joy.

With this new knowledge, Samuel looked in complete adoration toward his Yeshua, by whose power he now stood. New memories then emerged, held back from mortality until this day. What he remembered first and foremost was pure love—unrelenting, infinitely compassionate love which his Brother and Friend had always felt for him. It was like liquid manna to Samuel's soul, the pure essence of life. He comprehended an eternity of their association, their deep friendship, their glorious work together, and their mutual obedience to Father's will.

Heavenly Father! Heavenly Mother! Suddenly his mind was opened to a new and vast panorama of a long and glorious association with his Heavenly Parents. "Oh Father, Mother—how I love you!" he immediately cried out. His heart swelled with unbridled joy and intense longing as he remembered. Yet, today this memory was only a glimpse. The veil still stood largely sentinel to his premortal life. Samuel was apparently not ready yet to know the very beginnings of his own existence, nor the mysteries concerning the origin of all that he called heaven. But for now, this was enough.

Samuel realized with a sudden jolt that Melody was near him. She approached in full glory, and he marveled at her celestial stature, her beauty and her incomprehensible power. She was by every definition a goddess. Her clothing was as bright as the sun. A circle of glory surrounded her head that in every way resembled a crown. As she approached, he found himself alone with her in a vast sea of light. He gazed into her face, and gratefully saw the same tender and familiar smile he had always known. In wonder he contemplated her physical glories, and her enhanced and perfect being, although her features were still recognizable as the Melody he had loved in mortality. But now she was a daughter of pure light, of glorious divine femininity, of infinite capacity and fully-endowed power—and he marveled at the exquisite goddess before him.

"You are a Queen!" Samuel whispered in near worship.

Melody embraced Samuel long and fervently. "All glory to God, who has redeemed me through His grace," she said humbly. Then she released him with a broad smile.

Samuel laughed aloud. There was nothing in his soul but exquisite joy.

Suddenly, Helaman came into view, looking all of twenty-four years old, as he had earlier in the Temple. Samuel cried out for joy and embraced him warmly. "Helaman, my dear friend, this is the glorious dawn of the Millennium for which we have so long prepared! How can I ever thank you for patiently teaching me, and for watching over my family as you did all those years? I will be forever indebted to you—Grandfather!"

Helaman stood tall, and embraced Samuel with joy. "You are indeed a grandson to be proud of, Samuel. It was my honor to serve you and our family!"

Then Bonnie and Lisa joined Sam and Melody, and their entire family excitedly surrounded Helaman, each expressing deep love and profound gratitude for him being the hands of heaven in bringing them all home. These were eternal ties that they knew would never be broken.

"Tham!" a small voice cried out behind him, and he spun around to find his mother Laura leading a small redheaded child by the hand. Samuel fell onto his knees as his baby brother ran into his arms. "Tham! Tham!" he cried repeatedly.

"Jimmy!" Samuel cried. "Oh, Jimmy! I'm so sorry I didn't look down when I drove over the ditch. I just didn't…"

"Tham," the little one interrupted. "It wath not your fault. It wath Heavenly Father'th plan, and we all played our role in it. Let uth rejoith, Tham. Leth's praith God that the time has finally come when we can be together again! Now Mother can raisth me, as she was promisthed!"

Samuel felt his heart healing from years of anguish. "Jimmy, now that you are here, I do rejoice! Oh little brother, you look like a two-year-old, and you're talking the way you used to!" he proclaimed joyfully.

"It may take thome getting used to for both of uth, Tham," Jimmy said, his face next to Samuel. "A few minuteth ago I wath an adult! Now I'm two yearth old, or at leatht my body ith! And I thtill have a lithp!" he said with a grin.

Sam laughed and ruffled his little brother's head like he had so many years ago. With this, Jimmy pulled something out of his pocket, and put his little arms behind his back to keep it a secret.

"I brought you thomething!" Jimmy cried with such happiness that his voice actually squeaked.

"What, Jimmy?" Samuel asked, his eyes sparkling with love.

"Thith!" Jimmy proclaimed and brought from behind his back a long silver flute. He laid it carefully in his big brother's hands. "I thlept with it every night until I could give it back to you," Jimmy said pointedly. He was referring to the nearly 80 years since his burial.

Samuel took the shiny silver flute and turned it over in his hands. It was indeed his flute from so many years ago. Every dent and scratch was very familiar.

"Play my favorite thong," Jimmy said happily. "Play, 'I am a Child of God,'" he said, his voice effervescent with happiness.

Samuel raised the flute to his lips, and played a single note. It was sharp and clear and seemed to reach beyond this world into eternity. Suddenly, a thousand flutes, and a million angelic voices sang the same note as if his had opened some great reservoir holding the music of heaven. Crystalline and beautiful it came. From the depths of his soul he played while kneeling right there on the clouds of heaven. Jimmy laughed, threw back his head and in a voice of a two-year-old, yet with the heart of one infinitely older, sang, "I am a child of God, and He hath thent me here…."

The music had hardly ceased when Jimmy suddenly jumped into his big brother's arms. Samuel stood smiling as Jimmy dangled from his neck, chortling with two-year-old glee. It seemed as if nothing could be more perfect.

At that moment Samuel's eyes shifted across the vast throng of glowing people in the throws of joyful reunion. He saw a beautiful woman walking toward him. Samuel's first thought was to feel amazed she was coming toward him, and secondly, to wonder who this divine creature was. She was so graceful and elegant, so glorious and stunningly beautiful that for a moment he wondered if a goddess had joined the throngs of happy mortals. As she came others saw her glory, and stepped aside, reverently bowing their heads or reaching out to touch her shimmering garments as she passed. These she seemed not to notice, for her eyes were fixed upon Samuel. He had had but a few moment's experience being so near resurrected beings and could not know for certain, but the glory surrounding this soul's resurrection attested to a noble mortal life far superior to most, including his and all whom he loved.

Jimmy slid to the ground just as she stopped directly before Samuel. She placed a hand affectionately on Jimmy's head, which won a beaming smile from him. Samuel couldn't even think of anything to say to this glorious creature. Her eyes were the most perfect blue he had ever seen. Her hair was very light brown, the color of spun gold, her body glorious beyond any mortal definition of perfection.

She smiled at him, and his heart skipped a beat. He almost found himself lapsing into a lad's shyness, which surprised him. Then, gaining control of himself to some extent, he smiled back, then became shy again. She was simply more glorious than anyone he had yet seen, except Christ himself.

"You don't recognize me do you?" she said simply, her smile warm and loving.

"I'm sorry," Samuel replied, his attention and curiosity now completely captured.

"I'm Catherine," she said. Samuel's mind immediately fastened onto a long-ago memory.

"You mean little, blind, deformed Catherine with the angel's voice?" he asked in wonder.

"That's who I was," she beamed. "I've changed a little since then."

"In every way!" Samuel replied. "I'm sorry so many, including myself, couldn't see your beauty then."

"Most, including myself, didn't see it," she answered. "But, more than most, you did. You gave me a chance to glimpse my own inner beauty. You didn't realize it, of course, but singing that song at Christmas, and feeling the outpouring of the Spirit upon everyone there, and suddenly knowing for the first time in my life that there *was* something beautiful inside me, was *the* most important moment of my life. I never stopped singing after that! I have come to thank you for what you did."

"I didn't know…" he began, his mind fumbling for an appropriate response, not wanting to invalidate her feelings, but also not wanting to take credit for something he actually had no idea he had done.

"That is exactly the point," she interrupted him. "You didn't know. You had no reason to know, or to care, or to give me a chance. You did it because you heard the Lord's whisper, and because you were gentle and kind. Your obedience gave me the first real chance I had in my life. I never did go far with my singing. Only a few people could see past my ugly exterior, and it always remained a beauty hidden within. I never married or had children. The only thing I did was to freely forgive, and to love and trust my dear Savior."

Then her face lit up with joy. "But, that one moment you gave me fired my faith, my hope, my love and my happiness for the remainder of my lifetime. Throughout my life I remembered it again and again, and it brought me hope when nothing else could. It was my personal test to be trapped in that body, and though rejected and alone, to remain faithful and return kindness for pain. It was my test—and I passed it, all glory to God! What you gave me, Sam, was a boost enough to see me through all those lonely years."

She stopped and regarded him gratefully. "I know you feel as if it was nothing. But, to me it was everything."

Samuel took a tiny step backward, and bowing slightly from the waist, said, "I am deeply honored to have been a part of your life. It is obvious it was a life of extraordinary righteousness. I am humbled," he said in total honesty, his eyes upon her feet.

At that moment Dawn stepped into their circle of light, holding Nathan's arm. Samuel's mind flooded with clear memories. "Nathan!" he cried and rushed into an embrace with his friend. "Although Dawn introduced us before, until this moment I had not fully remembered you, my beloved friend! It is so marvelous to be with you again!"

Nathan embraced him fiercely. "Samuel, now that you remember, we can speak about these things! I watched everything you did on earth! You were faithful and have done everything you said you would do. Perhaps you don't remember this, but we had several wagers on the outcome of your life. I admit that you won them all—and I owe you everything, buddy!"

"What did we bet?" Samuel chuckled, still clapping Nathan on the back.

"It wasn't so much of a bet, as a hope," Nathan admitted. "You had a difficult life laid before you, and I knew so much of my happiness and hopes with Dawn depended upon you. Do you remember now that we asked you to take care of Dawn for me? You said you would, and you did!"

Samuel's eyes grew larger as new understanding filled his mind. "Yes, I remember that I promised I would wait to be with Melody so that I could take care of Dawn. I knew that Dawn would leave me as soon as her life's mission was completed, and if I was faithful there would still be time for me to marry Melody!"

Dawn stepped forward with a smile. "Sam, I will always love you for what you did for us. You brought me into the covenant, loved me, and allowed me the gift of giving life to two beautiful daughters. We are eternally grateful for you and Melody being sealed for us in the temple." She turned to Melody, bursting with curiosity. "So, Melody—do you remember more clearly now, too?"

Melody stepped forward and threw her arms around Dawn. She began to laugh softly as she clung to Dawn's neck.

"I remember that this was all my idea!" Melody cried joyfully between tears and laughter.

"Yes, it was," Dawn said with a smile. Then she turned and kissed Samuel on both cheeks. "Thank you, Sam."

He grinned happily back at her. "God is so good," he said simply.

Dawn took Melody's hands in her own. "Friends forever," she said fervently.

"Friends forever," Melody rejoined. Then Dawn and Nathan stepped away and were gone in the throngs of people rejoicing all around them.

Melody sank into Samuel's arms. Samuel shook his head as if trying to clear it. "Everything is so different than I ever imagined—and yet it is the perfect outcome," he whispered softly into her ear.

Melody laughed, almost giggling. "I know! Some of it would be a shock if it weren't all such a vast blessing. Oh Sam, I think ours is one of the greatest love stories of all time! What you—what we—did for Dawn and Nathan made our present joys truly possible. It was sacrifice that turned the key. And she and Nathan will now always be our precious friends—forever!"

Samuel laughed in joy. "It all astounds me. And yet, what astounds me most is that you can remember those things much better than I do," he said, still grinning.

"Oh, you will catch up to me one of these days, sweetheart," Melody said with a wry grin as she nestled into his arms. "But for both of us now, these memories will bring us peace. Sweet, sweet peace."

Samuel nodded, and then drew her up gently, one hand on her waist and the other held out to her. "Nothing could be sweeter than this. Come, my darling, and let's dance! I believe that now I can finally keep up with you!" Melody caught her breath, gave him her hand, and they whirled off together in a cloud of eternal bliss.

The Resurrected Lord, all His holy angels and those who had just participated in the Morning of the First Resurrection passed completely around the globe, completing their passage well before midday.

At exactly noon another trumpet sounded as they began circuiting the world a second time. This time there were no choirs singing. As Christ passed over, His glory reached out in a seemingly-solid sphere to touch the earth below. Samuel and Melody watched in wonder as all around them Mother Earth stirred and yielded up her dead. This was the beginning of the Afternoon of the First Resurrection, wherein the Terrestrial spirits of all periods of time came forth. These spirits were resurrected with a lesser degree of glory, so that their glowing countenances might be compared to the brightness of the moon.

In the moment it took for the resurrected spirits to rise from the ground to the heavenly throng, each mind was opened to his or her new resurrected status, much as had occurred to Samuel when he had been resurrected. They began to learn who they were and what their lives might become. From there, a company of angels met each of them, conducting them to family and friends. Because of their enormous numbers—billions upon billions of them—the stream of angels guiding them to their loved ones appeared endless. Samuel had no idea where they were going, or where their new home might be, whether on the earth or somewhere else; but he knew it was glorious beyond description.

Finally, all who were redeemed through the grace of Jesus Christ were caught up into the clouds of heaven to meet Him. Samuel looked upon the earth and saw millions of unclean people still upon it, cowering in terror, and hiding in the ruins of their cities or in caves and forests. He saw them viciously curse God for being unfair and ruthless. He saw them turn upon their neighbors in abject violence. He saw a numberless concourse of evil ones who had been infesting the earth since that day when they were cast out down to it, and he watched in sorrow as they moved to inhabit the mortal bodies remaining there. A thousand evil spirits tried to crowd into one mortal body until the person was thrashing upon the ground.

Jehovah descended quickly with a fierce look of righteous retribution. Again His voice was heard: "Let the devil and his angels be bound!" A wail arose from the earth as in an instant the wicked spirits of the damned were swept from its surface and carried away. Their hatred and evil were at long last gone from the earth, only destined to return for a brief and futile battle a thousand years from hence.

"It is good!" a mighty voice rolled across all the earth. Samuel looked upon the Savior to see a serene look of peace replace the expression of retribution that had been there before. In a voice like the heralding of heavenly trumpets, Christ spoke the words, "Let the earth be cleansed by fire!"

Suddenly, the glory of Christ ignited the ground immediately below them and released a fire of purifying intensity upon the earth. Faster than a fiery flood it spread, devouring everything telestial in its path. People, animals, art, music, technology, buildings and anything telestial simply vanished in the cleansing fire. Gone were the cities, the mighty works of man, the pride and haughtiness of the world—everything meaningless was gone, and all forgotten. All that remained was the exquisite beauty and serenity of the newly-born terrestrial world.

Samuel, Melody, Helaman, Dawn and Nathan, and all the glorious hosts of Christ let forth a mighty cry of triumph, and the Earth opened her mouth with joy: "Hosannah! Blessed be the Name of the Lord!" A trumpet sounded three times, and the voice of God in the hearing of all creation said, "Let the earth rest!"

And for one thousand years of peace, it was so.

THE END

ABOUT JOHN PONTIUS

It was never John's intent to write LDS books or a doctrinal blog or website, but he decided early on to obey the voice of the Lord and discern His will in his life. Hearkening to the Lord's voice was not always easy, but John's difficult journey ended in a far better place than he ever dreamed possible.

After living thirty-three years in Alaska, raising a family there, and building several careers, the Lord sent John and his family to Utah. John and his wife, Terri, who is the love of his life, both grew up in Utah but spent the majority of their lives in "the mission field." Returning to Utah was like coming home and brought them nearer to additional family, children, and grandchildren. Together they have eight children and twenty-one grandchildren.

John had many opportunities to speak at firesides, write books, and begin and maintain his blog, *UnBlogmySoul*. He accomplished many unexpected and amazing things that only the hand of the Lord could have brought to pass. The Lord's hand took John places he did not want to go, but when he actually got there, he recognized them as his "far better land of promise."

John passed away peacefully in his home in 2012, after a lifetime of service to the Lord Jesus Christ.